NOMAD BOOK 3

HERE WE STAND

First Edition

Hardcover ISBN: 978-1-912247-06-6
Paperback ISBN: 978-1-912247-07-3
eBook ISBN: 978-1-912247-08-0

Published by Karen Traviss
Editing: Angela Roemelt
Design: Kevin G. Summers
Jacket art: Thomas Wievegg

karentraviss.com

For Tony Serena, much missed.

ACKNOWLEDGEMENTS

Special thanks to Angela Roemelt, who can spot a plot hole or a formatting glitch from the orbit of Pluto, for merciless scrutiny and generous moral support.

PREFACE
A NOTE FROM THE AUTHOR

For those of you who've been used to reading my books from American publishers, you'll find my current novels are now written in UK English, except for proper nouns and those American terms that just don't anglicise. If you're new to my work, you'll notice that I write both dialogue and narrative in the style and grammar of the character, and occasionally their own spelling, so that varies from scene to scene. Those discrepancies are an integral part of the characterisation.

There's also a prologue and an epilogue in all my books. They're part of the story and also a quick recap of the events so far and a taste of what's coming in the sequels.

The reference I use is the Shorter Oxford English Dictionary. Where there are differences between the SOED and the Oxford English Dictionary, I let Oxford Dictionaries Online have the final word. Very rarely, none of these sources gives me a solution that I feel makes something clearer for the reader, so I'll opt for clarity even if it means breaking a formal rule.

Now the science. I do a lot of research for my books and much of this novel is real science, but other parts aren't intended to be, notably FTL travel, although there are some fringe theories out there that make it seem less of a stretch. I do try to respect Kepler, though. This is just a personal quirk — some tropes don't bother me but others set my teeth on edge.

In the end, my books are about people: human people, non-human people, and people we build as code. And they're not about heroes or villains, just individuals on different sides who find themselves in tough situations. So I've taken real science and bent it enough to pose the ultimate questions we can ask ourselves. In *Here We Stand*, how do you hold a divided community together in the face of an existential threat? And when does the end no longer justify the means?

Karen Traviss
January 2023

HERE WE STAND

KAREN TRAVISS

PROLOGUE

SECURITY OFFICE, NOMAD BASE, OPIS: 1920 HOURS, SEPTEMBER 20 BY THE OPIS CALENDAR – EIGHT HOURS AFTER MOTHER DEATH CLAIMED RESPONSIBILITY FOR THE BIOTERRORISM ATTACK ON KOREA.

The enemy within is the one you need to deal with first.

They're the ones who'll open the gates for the barbarians. They look like us, they sound like us, and I might be looking at one of them right now. I just don't know. After all, I never spotted Abbie Vincent.

For the last thirty minutes, I've been sitting across the table from Dr Lianne Maybury, head of Die-back Remediation when Ainatio was still a thing. You want a measure of how crazy this shit's become? We've had to put a possible alien attack on the back-burner while we find out if another one of our own is going to sabotage the mission before they do. We're a long way from home without backup. We need to clean house fast.

I didn't come to Opis to fight my own people. I didn't come to fight at all, to be honest, but we escaped trouble on Earth, and then we walked into trouble here, forty light years away. The alien trouble I can handle. What I can't take is our own people betraying us.

Lianne and I are having more of a sporadic conversation than an interview under caution. She used to be Abbie Vincent's boss, working on a cure for die-back, and then Abbie decided to smuggle the virus out of the lab and infect one of the few regions on Earth still free of it. It was on the news today. Die-back's hit Korean rice crops and the Mother Death movement's claimed responsibility. They're the people who think the universe would be better off without humans, and I say the universe because they don't want us infesting other worlds either, which is why I'm sitting here trying to work out if we have any other genocidal maniacs on the staff.

I never signed up to be the thought police. I don't want to live in a community that spies on neighbours and marks their card for having an opinion. But if someone's released a plague once, another someone can release it again here.

Those of us who lived through die-back in America and Europe know what Asia's facing now. Rice, maize, soy, and wheat, the big four staples, will start dying and there'll be famine because there's still no way to prevent die-back or cure it. All you can do is burn off contaminated vegetation when you find it. Starving people — some carrying contamination — will try to move into Russia, India, Australia, or the Pacific islands, places that are still mostly okay. And it'll snowball from there.

Even before we found out what Abbie had done, we evacuated an entire town to Opis instead of taking resettlement in Britain. Britain's held out for a long time, but how much longer can they last? We have Brits here. They look at us Americans and see how we lost our nation, and I don't envy them the decisions they need to make now.

But I feel sorry for Asia too, no matter how hostile we've become. They kept die-back at bay by cutting themselves off from the rest of the world, and even when the Alliance of Asian and Pacific States was trying to sabotage our mission, the fact they could carry on at all still gave us an odd kind of hope that the rest of the world could survive too and eventually recover. Yeah, I know that's pretty rich after what we did to APS to make sure we got to Opis, but seeing the other guy's point of view doesn't exempt you from picking a side. I chose saving the people I'd sworn to protect over the well-being of strangers on the other side of the world.

It was ugly. But I'm not ashamed.

Does that mean sabotaging APS infrastructure is more ethical than using a bioweapon to starve Asia to death, then? We had to buy time to evacuate Kill Line. Abbie thought she had to wipe out humanity to save Earth and all the other worlds humans might colonise one day. Maybe, in the global scheme of things where other life forms have a say, her point is as valid as ours. But I don't care. We want to live, she wants us to die. There's no point in even discussing it.

"Major Trinder?" Solomon's been quiet for a long time, but now he's in my earpiece, talking in a whisper. "The crop tunnels are clear. The bots have collected all the pollinators and they're clear too. But I did say that would be the case, didn't I? I think it makes more sense to focus on the possible malcontents."

Solomon has a list of those, you see.

He was an integral part of the security system at Ainatio Park Research Centre. Some folks would see the company's chipped staff and total surveillance as spying on the workforce, but the system's main job was to watch over a vast complex that housed dangerous materials and was a target for industrial espionage. Either way,

Solomon has extensive archives. The system's data can now be repurposed for good old-fashioned snooping. He knows who didn't want to go to Opis when Georgina Erskine revealed the big lie and told the staff about Nomad. He's now combing through all that data in the light of today's news. But the security system we're sifting through didn't even catch Abbie smuggling the virus out of our lab, so it probably hasn't spotted any of her fellow Mother Death sympathisers.

The tricky thing is we don't even need someone to smuggle in a virus. We have scientists here who could create a new pathogen from scratch if they were sufficiently pissed off. We've got nineteen people from Die-back Remediation and a few other virologists who — hypothetically speaking — could knock out a new bioweapon in their lunch break. There's my problem. I don't like the profiling thing, but it's the most logical and efficient way of looking in the right place first.

This is the problem with a fifth column. If you find one traitor, you wonder how many more there are. They don't even have to be real to do lasting damage. We'll search the base and cross-examine everyone, and we won't find anything, but we probably won't believe some people one hundred per cent either, so we'll keep an eye on them, because *not* keeping an eye on them is too much of a risk. Solomon will monitor them because he's everywhere in the Nomad system and AIs never sleep — well, not completely anyway — and folks will guess that they're being watched for genocidal tendencies, even if they're used to being under Ainatio's surveillance.

So they'll feel persecuted and resentful. Everyone else will look at them sideways. The farmers in Kill Line, the *Cabot* crew, my guys, and Chris Montello's people will be wary of them even if they don't mean to be. The small distance between groups from different backgrounds — townsfolk, scientists, military — will turn into unbridgeable divides, and that's a recipe for disaster in an isolated outpost.

I don't have a better idea, though.

Dieter Hill, one of the ex-cops here, nailed it pretty well: traitors poison the land and leave it toxic even longer than radiation. If you stick them in front of a firing squad, it won't clear the air one bit. It's hard to trust again when you know you've already been fooled, and it's equally hard to forgive when you've been wrongly suspected and you realise what your supposed buddies really think of you.

But if guilty bastards exist, I need to find them fast. If they're innocent, I have to live here afterwards and so does everyone I care about. So I'm treading carefully, just discussing things with Lianne in a civilised way and looking for clues I might have missed.

"Okay, Sol says they've now checked everything in the crop tunnels, including the pollinators," I tell her. "We'll get this over with as fast as we can."

Nomad Base covers around three hundred acres, with nearly a thousand homes and dozens of workshops, labs, and offices, so it's going to take a few days to search for biohaz materials manually even with dogs and bot assistance. The longer the disruption goes on, the more disgruntled folks are going to get. Lianne's been sitting back in the chair with her arms folded, staring past me as if she's trying to remember something, but now she leans forward and rests them on the table.

"Dan, don't take this the wrong way, but cutting our comms, confining us to quarters, and searching our offices makes us look like suspects," she says. We're kind of friendly, or at least she talks to me like an old buddy, something few of the scientists did back on Earth. "Presumption of innocence still applies out here. Morale's going to be rock-bottom."

In a way, I wish she'd be more combative. I'm sure some of her team will be.

"We're just showing that we're doing it by the book, and that you're cooperating because you want to reassure everyone," I say. "If you can't talk to each other, it'll head off any accusations that you got your stories synced up to cover your asses."

"Are you searching and interrogating everyone else this thoroughly?"

"Of course we are. Look." Her screen's blocked from the network for the time being, so I take out my own screen to show her the real-time map that displays and records everything happening on the base. You can see the search teams as clusters of icons. Everyone with a comms device or an Ainatio security chip is tracked and shows up as an icon, primarily for safety reasons, because a lone base on an unexplored planet is a lot of accidents waiting to happen. Even the bots and vehicles are trackable so that everyone can see if there's transport or labour available to use. "See? *Everywhere's* being searched. Kill Line, the warehouses, even my quarters. We can't afford to get this wrong."

Lianne studies the screen and nods. "Okay."

"Look, I didn't spot Abbie, and I can't fail again," I say. Yeah, I really mean that. I was Ainatio's head of security. Chris and Alex both think they dropped the ball, but it was my job. "Even if we've got more Mother Death psychos here, most folks want to live. I realise it's a tough thing to ask, but if you've got any doubts about your colleagues, I need to know."

I've just asked her to rat out her buddies. The look on her face shows that, just for a moment. She wrinkles her nose as she shakes her head.

"If anyone was going to sabotage the mission, they'd have released the virus by now, not wait while we build up food stocks."

"Sorry to put it bluntly, but would any of your team be capable of creating a new pathogen?"

Lianne always looks like she's got the world's problems on her shoulders when she's actually fine. It's just the way her skin's draped into a frown over the years. It's when she raises her eyebrows and the frown vanishes that she's reacting, and that's what she's doing now. It looks genuine.

"I'd have to assume all of them could," she says. "But it never even crossed my mind." She leans on her elbows and presses her fingers against her brows as she looks down at nothing in particular on the table. "I really wish I hadn't even thought that."

"Suspicion isn't a natural part of your job."

"But it's part of yours. I'm sorry. It can't be much fun to see everyone through that filter."

"I'm finding out. It's new for me."

"Is this interfering with your defence duties?"

"We'll catch up," I say, but of course it's stopping us from doing other work. We should be reinforcing perimeters and extending monitoring. "Rule out the closest threat first. Look, once we've confirmed the base is all clear, remind your people that this really is routine. They don't rely on guesswork or emotions in the course of their work, and neither do we."

And even as I'm saying that, being all objective and sensible, I'm thinking maybe it *is* Lianne after all and her guilt-trippery about failing to spot Abbie is a smokescreen. If I'm that paranoid, others will be too. She's right. When you wonder if the people you're cooped up with in mankind's most remote outpost want to kill you, it robs you of something. External enemies unite the tribe, but internal ones destroy even the reality you took for granted.

I frigging hate Mother Death. You have to wonder what their parents were like to spawn psychopathic bastards like that. You'd think they wouldn't breed if they hate their own kind so much.

Lianne sits up straight again. "If there really is a saboteur, though, what will you do with them?"

We've only been here for a few months. We don't have any courts, we don't have a jail, and my troops and Chris Montello's militia are the nearest thing we have to a police force. Apart from the rules of common decency, I'm not even sure we're following a single legal or regulatory code. I've only got one law right now, though: survival. I think it's going to show me another side of myself that I won't like.

"It'll be kind of awkward," I say. As a species, we have that monkey thing about fairness, and part of fairness is a punishment fitting the crime. "I don't see rehabilitation being an option."

Lianne looks crushed. "If the worst happens, at least we've still got a chance to go back to Earth."

"You know it's not going to be that easy," I tell her. "It's worse than when we left. And now we'll have more awkward things to explain."

"But Britain was going to take us in."

"That was before Abbie. We can't count on that now." Maybe that door's still open, though. We have some value, and Marc Gallagher seems to know how to play the barter game with his government. But the main problem hasn't gone away. Earth's in trouble. "We've got to make Nomad work."

"Yes. Yes, I know you're right."

I don't think I'm getting anywhere with this. Lianne's harmless. But I had to make sure.

"Okay, thanks for your time, Dr Maybury. We'll notify you when we're done with the residence searches and you can go home. Your place should be cleared in an hour or two."

When she leaves, I have a few minutes to myself before I start on the next interviewee. The list says it's Gavin Huber. The thing they don't tell you about interviewing — okay, interrogation — is that the suspect isn't the only one whose resolve gets ground down as it drags on. I'm worn out too. But the sooner I get it done, the sooner we get back to dealing with external threats, of which we have a shitload. One murdered scientist, two dead aliens in the morgue, two alien navies looking for the ship that our new alien buddies stole, and half of our people are still stuck in cryo because we can't risk reviving them before we can feed and house them without endangering everyone else. Terrific. And Ingram's second-in-command just walked out because he thinks she's a war criminal.

Nobody said colonising space was going to be easy, but only the *Cabot* guys volunteered to be here. The rest of us had nowhere else to go. Nomad Base is one big lie, though, a spectacular act of deception, from the day someone decided to spin the cover story that *Cabot* had been lost with all hands without ever reaching Opis to the moment some of us decided not to tell Earth about the aliens — not just one species, at least five — and their technology.

You know, I still have to say that to myself twice. *Aliens.* One of them even shot me. But when it comes to it, we end up lying just like the Ainatio bosses we thought were bastards, and for the same reason. We don't trust governments or other corporations not to interfere and make things worse.

Every damn problem comes down to trust.

Can we trust the teeriks, or are we too hung up on them looking like giant crows to see them clearly? The only other species we've come across are whatever the Jattans are — marbidar, I think — and we've already killed one. The Kugin, the ones who own the teeriks, haven't shown up yet. We've already done enough to piss off both species, and they have spacefaring navies. Handing over their teerik engineers and the prototype warship they hijacked probably won't cut it.

It's a mess. I just wish we could tell Earth the truth, but it won't help right now. How do we tell them about the biggest event in human history? The buck stops with us — me, Chris, Marc, and *Cabot*'s captain, Bridget Ingram.

We're the grown-ups. God help us.

The door opens and makes me start, but it's not the next scientist on the list. It's Aaron Luce, my staff sergeant, one of the ex-cops, clutching a small haphazard bunch of flowers. He puts them on the desk in front of me. They look like twigs covered in apple blossom. I can smell them from here.

"For me? I'm touched."

Luce doesn't crack a smile. "Go home, boss," he says. "I'll do the rest of the interviews tonight. Ten years in homicide, remember. I've still got it."

He wants me gone for some reason. I trust Luce completely, and at a time when I don't know if I can trust most of the people I've known for years, that's a comfort. And it's been a long day in a very long week.

"Okay. Thanks." I examine the bunch of twigs. "What are the flowers for?"

"For you to give to Erin," Luce says. "You're going to need them. I've moved your gear into her place and she says dinner's waiting, so get a move on."

I wasn't expecting that. Erin and I had agreed we'd move in together, but we hadn't finalised anything. I suppose I was working up to making it a more memorable and romantic event than just showing up in need of a shave and a shower, bitching about my day. "This is her idea, I take it."

"No, Major, mine," Solomon says in my ear. "It's one more thing you don't have to worry about. I need you properly rested and with a clear mind."

Luce slides the flowers further towards me. "They're kiwi fruit blossoms. I had to do some hard bargaining to get the agritechs to cut some for me. Boss, it's a landmark in your relationship. You need to mark it the right way or you'll never hear the end of it."

Luce is one of the good guys. I'm so embarrassed I can't even thank him properly. "I've still got that bottle of fifty-year-old malt," I say. It's the only thing of real value I brought with me. "It's all yours."

"Thanks, boss, I'll just take a glass," he says. "Now go. Shoo."

This is my tribe. This is where I belong, with all the folks who wear a uniform here, whether they began as army, navy, law enforcement, or air arm, whether they're American or British or Australian, whether their chain of command has vanished along with their country, or if they're veterans who've recreated the purpose and comradeship they knew in the service. We meshed without thinking back on Earth because we automatically stepped up when the shit hit the fan. And you know something? I realise I *like* those situations. They make me feel alive and real after years of playing at security with exercises and paperwork. I just want to be worthy of the responsibility. Sooner or later, life will get a lot harder out here.

I walk back to the housing zone via the big green in the centre of the base, clutching the kiwi blossoms. It's a nice evening, clear skies with a few wispy clouds, a breeze with the hint of cooler weather on the way, and a crescent moon that's finally starting to look routine rather than something to stare at in amazement. It's good to see the lights all around the base and to hear the sounds of a small town that already feels permanent. The main cluster of offices, labs, and warehouses lies on the western side of the green, and the housing areas facing them are on the east.

If I stay on the right-hand side, I pass the area allocated to Ainatio staff and the road down to the compound where the teeriks live. Further on, there's the right-hand turn into Kill Line, marked with the original Kill Line town sign that the mayor brought from Earth. The new town's built on the same plan as the first, but now it's expanded to take in the transit camp, Chris's militia and the civilian refugees they rescued. Their print-built homes with traditional pitched roofs blend seamlessly into the main part of the town on the other side. Erin's house is the tenth on the left in this unnamed road.

Well, I thought it was unnamed, anyway. But as I walk past a fence, there's now a sign in place: Wickens Road. They've already named it for Jamie. If anything says we're here to stay, it's that.

Erin's door isn't locked. But I knock anyway and then stand in the hallway, surprised by how much decorating she's done since the house was finished. This is weird. I never thought I'd end up doing anything this *normal*. But when Chris and I thought we might not make it off Earth with the evacuees, we swore that if we survived, we'd try to live like normal guys for the first time — wives, kids, barbecues, painting fences, walking the dog. Chris says that's what being human really means.

I still think the true reality of human existence is the moment when the sabretooth jumps you and there's no emergency number to call. But I'll defer to Chris, the kind of guy who'd punch out the sabretooth and eat it raw if he had some hot sauce.

So we made it here, and now the normal starts, aliens or no aliens. What do I say, then? It's a historic moment for me.

"Hi honey. I'm home."

Erin comes out of the kitchen with a bottle in one hand and two tumblers held by their rims in the other.

"Welcome to your fixed abode, man of the house." She hands me a glass. "Shitty day, huh?"

"Yeah, but I'm leaving it outside. Here. Flowers."

She sniffs them and smiles. "Are the agritechs going to come looking for you with a pruning knife?"

"A homicide detective gave them to me."

"You have the weirdest admirers, Dan Trinder. Come on. I made a proper dinner. Lasagne. I'll improve with more practice."

"I'll eat it and like it because you made it."

If Solomon picked guys like us as the best of humanity — not Aristotles, not Einsteins, not Da Vincis, just people willing to do what it takes to keep our people safe — then we must be worth something, even me, the guy who didn't lose his family but just forgot about it. Mother Death's wrong. We're as worthwhile as any other species and we deserve to survive, out here and even on Earth.

But whatever happens next, Nomad's my home now. It's *our* home. There's no going back and no apology for existing. Here we stand.

01

Where did teeriks learn what's civilised behaviour? They use the word a lot. You humans are so civilised, they say. If they grew up surrounded by Kugin, and the Kugin are all thugs and barbarians, where did they form the concept?

Commander Brad Searle,
Chief Engineering Officer, CSV *Cabot.*

CEMETERY OF ST THOMAS'S CHURCH, NOMAD BASE: 1120 HOURS, SEPTEMBER 21 OC (OPIS CALENDAR.)

There was no such thing as a good funeral, and certainly not one for a murder victim, but Nina Curtis's burial was a little less harrowing than Bridget Ingram expected.

Nearly everyone on the base had turned out for it. At a time when people seemed to be looking at each other suspiciously, it had managed to unify them. Ingram hoped that would last and knew it wouldn't.

Inside the settlement's brand new church — a reasonable copy of the original St Thomas's back on Earth — the Reverend Martin Berry conducted a service that avoided offending both religious and atheistic sensitivities and was actually comforting. He talked about Nina's affection for Nomad's teerik neighbours and the inspiration to be found in her delight at exploring the unknown.

Ingram, obliged as Nina's commanding officer to say a few words, decided not to take the opportunity to focus the mourners on the need to stand firm despite tragedies and setbacks. Few of those within the packed church or outside in the churchyard listening to the words being broadcast had seen combat or faced violence of any kind, and a death like Nina's was too much for them to process at the moment. Respectful sympathy seemed the right approach. Ingram walked out of the church and immediately noted who was where and who was absent.

She estimated all the Kill Liners and *Cabot*'s ship's company had attended, and most of the Ainatio staff, close to fifteen hundred in all. It was still hard not to separate the population into those groups because that was how they assembled and lived. The only group that had blurred the lines was Chris's militia and the civilians they'd rescued, who'd now merged with Kill Line. It was a start. There was still a long way to go.

Fred and the other adult teeriks from the commune stood huddled in a group some distance from the mourners until Jeff Aiken walked up and shooed them closer to the grave to watch the coffin lowered into the ground. Ingram didn't need an explanation of all that. The teeriks were ashamed that Nina had been killed by one of their own species, even if the creature was a complete stranger to them, and Jeff was effectively the teeriks' closest friend. He was certainly close to Fred.

Perhaps the ritual still baffled them. None of the teeriks had known what to do with Caisin's remains when she died. Their Kugin overseers had taken charge of absolutely everything for them in the past, disposal of the dead included, so they had no tradition of funerals. The elderly matriarch was buried with the honours of a human head of state and the commune seemed to appreciate that.

Ingram looked for Marc in the crowd. She spotted him right behind Chris as the crowd filed past to scatter soil in the grave. Chris was expressionless, his default state, but just before he reached into the box of earth when his turn came, he hesitated. Marc put his hand on Chris's back for a moment, and Chris nodded without even turning his head. The only way Ingram could read that gesture was that Chris was far more disturbed by what he'd seen happen to Nina than anyone realised, and Marc was giving him some support.

Ingram hadn't warmed to Chris yet despite her best efforts. But he was very protective of Marc, and Marc in turn appeared to have an almost paternal understanding with him. She'd have to cut Chris more slack for Marc's sake. And Nomad needed him.

After the mourners dispersed, she waited in the church porch while the grave was filled in. It was a maintenance task that a bot would normally have carried out, but Martin Berry did the spadework himself with Marc and Chris. Ingram almost went over to offer them a hand, but she'd developed a don't-interfere radar over the years and this had all the signs of something extremely personal that was none of her business.

Eventually they replaced the squares of cut turf on top of the grave and started arranging the tributes. Marc gave Chris a pat on the back and gestured as if he was telling him to go and do whatever he had to and leave the rest to him. Ingram took that as her cue to wait until Chris and the vicar had walked off and left Marc taking his time to round up the shovels.

She wandered across to study the home-made tributes on the grave — a few single flowers, cards, ribbons, a red football shirt, a favourite coffee mug. People had been limited in what they could bring to Opis and it seemed they'd offered up small but precious personal items. It was an instinctive ritual that their Bronze Age ancestors would have recognised immediately.

Marc acknowledged her with a nod and bound the three shovels together with packing straps before dusting his hands on his trousers.

"I see Sol's done a cracking job with the headstone. Again."

The memorial was cut from the same cream speckled sandstone used for the other graves, elegantly inscribed and tasteful. It was always a surprise to see what bots could be programmed to make from local materials. It was also interesting to see how pitch-perfect Solomon was when it came to the detail of sensitive, emotionally charged situations. He really did understand humans, possibly better than most of them understood themselves. The thought left Ingram regretting again that she'd never met his creator.

"He's good," she said. "But I hope this is the last one he needs to make for a very long time."

Marc looked around the cemetery, hands on hips. It was still just a patch of open grass around the church, but it was far from empty.

"That's number six," he said. "I know that sounds terrible for five months, but break it down. We're not losing that many people from the mission itself."

"That sounds rather cold for you, Marc."

"Why, because I'm bereaved too?"

"Oh, God no, I never meant — "

"I know you didn't. I'm just saying you don't have to blame yourself for a high body count here. All bar one happened on Earth and had nothing to do with you. Lask, Levine, and Jamie Wickens — two natural causes, one KIA from enemy fire before he even knew Nomad existed. Caisin — again, natural causes, elderly, and a teerik. Girlie — working dog, killed by Tim Pham or one of his scumbags. The only death that's down to Nomad and how we manage safety and security is Nina Curtis. And that's not your fault either."

Ingram knew what he meant. It was still uncomfortable, though, not only because she was starting to stand back far enough from the emergency to let herself feel something about Nina's murder, but also because she still found it hard to talk openly about death with a man who'd lost two sons, even if he'd said he didn't want anyone treading on eggs around him.

"This is why I hate funerals," Ingram said. "We go straight to worrying about ourselves. It's never about the dead."

"Well, Nina got a good turnout, anyway." Marc shrugged. "Most of them didn't really know who she was, I expect. But it shows a bit of comradeship, even if the Ainatio bunch feel under siege from us. So there's that."

"It's a watershed," Ingram said. "Our first casualty. It focuses minds. Is Chris okay?"

Marc gave her a look as if he wasn't expecting her to care. "I don't think so, but he'll deal with it. You know as well as I do — there's some shit you just can't unsee. And he feels he shouldn't have let her go off-base with him in the first place. Anyway, what are we doing about the two stiffs? Keeping them on ice, disposing of the bodies, or what?"

It was a difficult question. Ingram now had two more dead aliens, a teerik called Lirrel and a Jattan called Gan-Pamas, and neither of them should have ended up on Opis. Marc had shot Lirrel and one of Kill Line's dairy farmers had killed Gan-Pamas. Her first thought had been to agree with the doctors and biologists who wanted to learn what they could about the biology of both species, if only to understand more about the teeriks in case they needed treatment one day. Ingram had no way of sending the bodies home even if she wanted to.

But now she wasn't sure. Marc had asked the question, and he'd have a reason that would make her uneasy. She knew it.

"To put it crudely, Marc, I don't know how intact the bodies are now, but I know the medics started examining the teerik," she said. "Are we talking about people's opinions on the ethics of how we handle remains, or something else?"

"Depends." Marc looked up at the sky as if he'd seen something and shielded his eyes against the sun. "Some people won't want them buried in the same cemetery as Nina. We can handle that. But it all depends on how we think the future's going to play out. How would we feel if we got our mates' remains back after a war and found the bodies hadn't been treated with respect, and they'd been used for research or worse? We'd go bloody mental. Okay, the teerik isn't an issue, because we've seen that Fred's folks didn't have a clue what happened to their bodies, so they probably don't mind. But the Jattans might take a very dim view of it, just like we would."

"That assumes we're going to be talking to them at some point," Ingram said. "And specifically to the Jattan opposition, because I'd assume the official government doesn't care if we kill rebels. But we're making an assumption they react like humans, which could well be wrong. It also assumes they'll find out Gan-Pamas was here and that we killed him."

"Assume the worst," Marc said.

"I always do."

"Then let's cover our arses and do this right. Because we could end up fighting Jattans, if what Fred tells us is true. If the opposition wins their civil war, we'd have a lot of work to do to get on good terms with them."

"Cremation," Ingram said, thinking about the possible state of the body. "Then the only people who know are the med team and the biologists."

"Remember what you said when Dan suggested using Caisin's body for research so the medics could treat sick teeriks? And he asked who'd know if we did it?"

"Yes. I do."

"You said we wouldn't like it if someone did the same with our grandmas, and that the medics who did the work would know."

Ingram knew he was right. She also knew they needed an independent analysis of the Jattans' physical vulnerabilities, if only to benchmark how accurate Fred's information was.

"That was because her commune was right here, Marc."

"Look, I'm just covering every angle. I know Fred won't be happy if we don't treat Jattans as the enemy, but we don't need to be on anyone else's kill list. We're already persona-non-shitpot with half of Earth and a sizeable chunk of the Mastan."

Ingram had to think about that. "Mastan? Oh. Yes."

"Space that the Kugin regard as their turf. This sector. Remember?"

Fred had mentioned it to her just once. "You do have a good memory."

"I've spent hours debriefing Fred. He uses the word a lot."

"Well, with any luck the medics won't have started on Gan-Pamas," Ingram said. "We've spent the weekend on the die-back search and all the labs have been closed."

"We'll be finished by the end of the day. Just the last few homes in the Ainatio block to do."

"Okay, I'll deal with it now."

"Has Brad said yes to the XO post yet?"

"You do spring easily from topic to topic."

"Well? Has he?"

"I said he could have a few days to think about it."

"Okay." Marc nodded. "And I'm keeping an eye on Bissey. He needs something to occupy him. What other skills has he got? Can he teach anything? Because we need everyone to be able to handle weapons, implement emergency drills, and do basic survival stuff."

Finding a role for Peter Bissey wasn't going to be easy. What did you do with your first officer when he decided you were a criminal and resigned? None of the old rules and regulations worked on Opis. There was nowhere to transfer him and nobody was technically serving now anyway. They were all civilians in law, a law which didn't apply here. On Opis, they were whatever the community agreed they were. It was Bissey's right to object to the decision to execute Gan-Pamas as a security risk, but if Ingram couldn't rely on his support over that, she couldn't be certain he'd do whatever was necessary to defend the base. The last thing she needed was an officer drawing his own red lines and refusing to open fire.

"I don't want him anywhere he can sow doubt or where his hesitation to act might compromise us," Ingram said. "And it really hurts to have to say that. He's served his country well and put his life on the line. He was my friend. We just don't share a moral compass any more."

"Oh, I'm pretty sure he'll shoot first and moralise later if the shit really hits the fan," Marc said.

Ingram would have bet on that too, but that was the problem. "Pretty sure isn't good enough, Marc," she said. "I'm not one hundred per cent certain. And I need to be."

A number of *Cabot*'s crew had served with her in the Royal Navy and she could count on every one them. Bissey had been her right hand. It was the withdrawal of his loyalty that would do the damage, and not just to her sense of comradeship. The rest of the crew wouldn't be able to ignore the fact that reliable, sensible Bissey had abandoned her.

But nobody had even mentioned it in her presence. That said it all, at least as far as her former RN crew were concerned. It was an embarrassment and they wanted to forget it.

Marc bent down to tidy a few chunks of stray soil on the grave. "Did you remind Bissey that Gan-Pamas actually shot Dan Trinder?"

"No. We just argued about the decision to execute."

"Yeah, but in the second or two it took to return fire, nobody knew Dan *wasn't* dead or whether Gan-Pamas was going to shoot someone else. Standard response to an attack before anyone else gets hurt."

"Peter knows that. He still thinks it was wrong because we'd set out to do it."

"Well, *we* had. You hedged your bets." Marc raised an eyebrow, obviously unimpressed, and went over to the church porch to prop the shovels against the wall. "Come on, whatever anyone planned or didn't plan, nobody shot the bugger on sight. You'd think Bissey might bear that in mind."

"Is that how you see it? That I didn't make a firm decision right away?" Ingram was a little hurt by that. "I had to negotiate with you and Chris and Dan because you don't take orders from me, and I had to keep Peter on side."

"Did I say I didn't realise that?" Marc wiped his hands again. "You could have blamed it all on us and you'd still have an XO now."

"I've got one."

"What if Brad says no?"

"I'll get another one. Anyway, I'll be happier when we work out exactly what went on between the Jattan and Fred." Ingram switched on her comms again and walked back to the main building with Marc. "I've heard Fred's version, but I want to hear Solomon's. It fits, I suppose. Fred says Jattans are prone to last-stand gestures. That was probably it. I just want to be sure."

"Very wise."

"I do regret it, though."

"What?"

"That we killed Gan-Pamas. Not an exemplary first contact."

"Would you feel better if you knew all the shit I did?" Marc asked.

Ingram could guess what a special forces operator had needed to do in the years since she'd left Earth, and she was just glad that there were still men like Marc willing to do it. She also wanted to understand him. He could hurt her feelings. Very few people had ever managed that and it told her she had some personal investment in him.

"It wouldn't change my opinion of you," she said. "Did your history class tell you everything I did?"

"Sorry, I forgot you were that old."

"Cheeky bugger."

"I'm sure our teacher left out the best bits."

"There comes a point where you think, okay, what happens if I *don't* do this extreme thing," she said, "and shore bombardment becomes the least objectionable course of action."

"Yep. Been there."

Ingram was the Butcher of Calais. It said so in Marc's school textbook, apparently, because their parallel lives were separated by her spending forty-five years in cryo en route to Opis. The schoolboy learning about naval engagements long after the world thought Ingram was dead was now the battle-hardened older man whose timeline had caught up and overtaken hers by a few years. It was only now that the disruption bothered her, not just because of the lost years but because dislocation from the world and the events that Marc and the others had lived through left her unable to truly understand how desperate things had been for them. She could only guess.

"I didn't just pound Calais," she said, wanting him to know all there was to know about her. "We hit every Channel port on the Franco-Belgian side that summer. We gave them a week's notice to evacuate non-combatants, assuming they'd use that time to fortify the docks and mount a counter-attack. But they kept civilians in place as human shields."

"Did you know that in advance?"

"What did the history book say?"

"Didn't dwell on it, as I recall."

"Yes, I knew. And we hit those ports with everything we had when the time was up. We weren't trying to scare them off. We did it to permanently degrade their ability to reach us. And I'd do it again in a heartbeat."

Marc nodded a few times, head down as he walked, hands in his pockets. "Which is why I still had a country to grow up in," he said. "If you ever need to do it again, call me. I'll give you a hand."

Ingram was thrown for a moment. She'd never been in a position to see a direct connection between the outcome of those terrible years and a specific individual she knew and cared about. It was one thing to be assured what she'd done was for future generations, but it hadn't sunk in that someone from that generation was right here beside her.

"Well, in that case, I'll have that curry you threatened me with," she said, embarrassed. "I'm still waiting."

"Oh bugger, so you are. Sorry. I'll do some resource investigation and get back to you."

"What are you planning?"

"Lamb jalfrezi." Marc nodded in the direction of the entrance to the main block. They were almost at the front doors now. "Looks like you've got a mutinous crew waiting for you. Toss them overboard."

"Oh dear. "

"Give 'em hell, Captain. See you later."

A group of medics and technicians were sitting outside on the low barrier by the flagpoles, cradling steaming drinks and looking generally miserable. When Ingram glanced at her screen to check the schedule, it showed that the medical centre was being scanned for die-back and suspicious objects right then. Trinder was doing everything by the book.

Most of the medical centre personnel were hanging around, but she couldn't see Logan Haine. His icon wasn't showing on her base map, either. She could have asked Solomon to find him via the bots wandering around, but a simple question would do.

"Sorry about this," Ingram said to the medics. "We're going as fast as we can. Not long to wait. Have you seen Commander Haine?"

"He went for a walk." Jake Mendoza pointed in the direction of the crop tunnels. "Last time I saw him, he was talking about finding something in bloom for Nina's grave. I haven't seen him since."

"Okay. Thank you."

It wasn't like Haine to switch off his comms. He regarded himself as permanently on call. Ingram couldn't remember seeing him at the funeral, either, although it would have been easy to lose him in the crowd. She decided the office could wait for a while and walked over to the transport pool to check out a quad bike.

"If you're looking for Commander Haine, Captain, he's in the experimental fruits tunnel," Solomon said in her earpiece. He could see her on the security cameras and hear all her conversations. There was no real privacy in Nomad Base beyond personal quarters, but sometimes that was a blessing. "I don't like to intrude, but I think he's feeling a little stressed."

Ingram took that to mean hung over. Haine did like his drink. "I'm on my way to see him," she said. "Don't worry. This search is going to be over by the end of today, yes?"

"Barring surprises, Captain, yes. And everything's fine. We've found nothing untoward so far."

"And then I suppose the spying starts."

"I prefer the term prudent observation," Solomon said. "We've poked the hive and if anything comes flying out, I'll see it."

Ingram suspected the only thing flying out of anywhere would be the scientific and technical staff's goodwill on its way down the drain. But it had to be done. She started the bike.

"I might be a while," she said. "You know where I am."

"Fred wanted to talk to you, by the way."

"I'll see him later." It'd be about Nina. Her death seemed to have hit him harder than she expected. "Poor Fred. He's seen so many funerals and memorial events here that he must think all humans do is bury bodies."

"I think he wants to talk to you about something else, actually," Solomon said. "Sharing his FTL expertise with Earth."

"Damn, I need to explain that we've shelved that, don't I?"

"He knows why we've been searching the base, so perhaps he's worked it out for himself."

"Don't worry, I'll visit him later. I need to see Commander Haine first."

"I'll ignore the security feed from the crop tunnel, Captain," Solomon said. "You need some privacy, I think."

Solomon obviously knew what was up with Haine, but he rarely pre-empted conversations by briefing Ingram unless he felt she'd be at a serious disadvantage without it. He was obliged to see all and hear all because he managed the whole system, but he never seemed comfortable with it and he drew his lines about what he'd actively monitor. He wanted to be seen *not* to be eavesdropping because he needed humans to know he understood their need for privacy.

"That bad, then?" Ingram asked.

"I think so."

"Thanks for the heads-up, Sol."

Ingram parked the quad bike outside the crop tunnels, went through the biosecurity screen, and found Haine sitting on an upturned crate between two rows of dwarf lemon trees. The tunnel was deserted except for small maintenance bots gliding around the place and pausing to test soil profiles and spray water. It was as good a place as any to unwind. It smelled wonderful.

"Logan, be honest." She sat down cross-legged on the gravel next to his crate. "You're not okay, are you?"

"I'm staking my claim for the first lemons to put in Andy Braithwaite's gin," he said. "It's like queueing outside a shop for the opening day of the sales. I might be here some time."

"You can tell me. Come on. How far back do we go?"

"I think I treated you for a near-terminal hangover when you were totally bladdered after a run ashore."

"I'd like to say I remember it well, but I was somewhat tired and emotional, I believe."

"You were. And you inspired me. I was determined to spend my entire naval career in that same state of nirvana. You were the Rembrandt of piss-artistry to which I aspired. And here we are."

"Logan..."

"Okay, I think I just dropped my guard, to be honest." Haine raked his hair with his fingers, suddenly serious. "Imagine. After all these years of scab-lifting, I remember I'm squeamish." He went quiet for a while. No, this wasn't like him at all. He was the most extrovert, irreverent man she'd ever known. There was no situation he couldn't turn into a joke and get everyone to laugh along with him. But he looked drained and defeated. "I couldn't let Jake or any of the others deal with the body. I really couldn't. I know they're absolute pros, but they wouldn't have had to deal with that kind of traumatic injury. I mean, I've seen some awful combat wounds and accidents in ships, but... ah, not like that. So I made sure I did it."

Ingram could fill in the gaps. "It" was dealing with Nina's body. She was sure that Jake Mendoza was sufficiently experienced not to be overwhelmed by a cadaver in pieces, and he had the emotional distance of an outsider. But knowing Haine, he'd have decided it was his final duty to a shipmate.

"I'm sorry," Ingram said. "I should have come to see you sooner. I don't know what I can do to help except listen."

"I just wanted her to look presentable. My way of erasing it all, I suppose. Send her off intact."

"I know."

"I did quite a good job, actually."

"You always do."

"At least there was no facial trauma."

He almost sounded as if he was in shock. Ingram did her best. "You and I need to take a bottle to a quiet corner and get hammered," she said. "I'm so sorry, Logan. If you want some time off, please, just say. I don't want to see you broken."

"I don't think that would do me any good, Bridgers, but thank you."

"Well, if you change your mind, just do it."

"I hope I'm not losing it. I need to function properly. Especially now."

"You'll be fine." Ingram understood his fear. She'd had one moment in her naval career when she was so scared during a missile attack that she wondered if she'd ever be any use on the bridge again. It felt like everything she was sure of about herself had been ripped away. She hadn't recalled that moment in years, but now it was so vivid she could smell the sweat and hear the few moments of unnatural silence before the impact, and she wondered why it wasn't on her mind every second of every day. Her tendency to bury the life-changing stuff bewildered her. "It just proves you're human, Logan. If it hadn't been someone we all knew, you'd have breezed through it."

Haine looked as if he was considering that as a reasonable suggestion. "But it'll *always* be someone we all know," he said. "This is the entire world for us now."

Ingram was reluctant to leave him like this. She sat with him for a while in silence until he put his hand on her shoulder and squeezed hard.

"I'll be fine now, Bridgers." He'd always called her that. "Let's have that bottle later. After all, it's not like I owe my liver anything. What's it ever done for me?"

She took it as a cue to leave him alone to sort himself out. "You're on," she said. "I'll procure a litre of Andy's finest paint stripper. The lemons are on you."

She rode back to the main building, wondering if she'd made a mistake in assuming she could handle command in an isolated colony because it seemed so much like the confined world of a warship. But it was turning out more like a long submarine patrol where half the crew were members of the public who'd been press-ganged and didn't understand a damn thing.

She couldn't kid herself that she had the lonely burden of command. She shared it with Marc, Chris, and Trinder, and Alex Gorko cat-herded the Ainatio contingent with impressive skill. She never had to worry about Kill Line, either, because Doug Brandt was an experienced mayor. So she wasn't alone, and the buck didn't stop solely with her.

This Nomad, scrambled together in haste in the face of disaster, wasn't Tad Bednarz's vision of tens of thousands of carefully selected settlers arriving over a period of years. Its small, random community was the entire seed corn of extrasolar humanity for the foreseeable future. Bednarz had never counted on aliens being here, let alone their very desirable technology, and that was the buggeration factor that caused her most doubt now.

It was relatively straightforward holding a group together in the face of an enemy threat, even when some people were seething about Abbie's behaviour and *Elcano*'s passengers being kept in cryo. It was like taking command of a ship with an unhappy crew in the middle of a war: the threat suppressed the smouldering fires for a while. But the alien technology had been the wild card. It demanded hard decisions. Was she helping or hindering Earth if she shared teerik tech with the government? How should she handle the temptation to take the Caisin gate route back to Earth in an instant if the situation deteriorated? Neither would solve Earth's problems. It might even make them worse.

And she kept forgetting that what had become normal for Nomad — the existence of aliens — would be a massive culture shock for humanity.

Juggling the right to know against the consequences of that discovery was a dilemma far above even a captain's pay grade. Ingram's focus needed to be closer to home, and home was now Nomad. Her duty was to the people here.

It was hard to accept, but she wasn't responsible for Earth. She'd have to keep reminding herself of that.

* * *

KILL LINE HOUSING ZONE, NOMAD BASE: LATER THAT DAY, 1940 HOURS.

"You can come in, you know." Chris stepped over the bot that was testing the floor of the living room for contamination and assessed the personal effects he'd have to move to search the place properly. "I'd prefer that, so you can see I'm not tampering with your stuff."

Frank Lundahl hovered nervously in the doorway, watching Chris rummage through his home. "I didn't think you would."

"Humour me anyway."

The guy was a nuclear engineer, not high on Chris's list of likely Mother Death sleepers, but everyone had to go through the same procedure: contact test by bot to check for traces of die-back on surfaces and on the person, plus a manual search for objects that might contain virus specimens. It was time-consuming and it wasn't foolproof, but sitting back and assuming nobody here could possibly be a psycho like Abbie wasn't an option.

"Wouldn't the pathogen system detect anything smuggled in?" Lundahl asked. "We ran it for years back home. We know it works."

"Yeah, that's what Korea thought when they let Abbie in."

Chris checked the kitchen cupboards. It brought back memories of clearing houses with his platoon, always hoping to find something edible in abandoned properties. It was nice not to have to live on garbage these days. He hadn't had food poisoning in three years.

He examined the coffee machine. "You know something? Going round houses, I've found almost half the folks evacuated from Ainatio rescued their personal coffee makers."

"There's a thesis in that," Lundahl said. "What did you save?"

Chris held the analyser like a wand and swept it around the room. "My woobie. My army poncho liner. They stopped making them a long time ago."

Sensors could only detect what was airborne, stuck on a surface, or suspended in fluid. An ordinary airtight, watertight seal would defeat them. Chris planned to remove every container he couldn't identify, but viruses like die-back didn't need refrigeration and could even be stored on filter paper. So what was he looking for now, sealed envelopes? Book marks? Nobody had been able to bring a lot of stuff when they'd been evacuated, and folks hadn't amassed much clutter yet, so at least that made things simpler.

The lockable, shockproof, Ainatio-issue metal flight cases turned his stomach, though. He was looking at one right now, standing in the corner of the living room next to a chair.

Most of the scientists had those cases. When they were told to pack up and report to the buses, they salvaged favourite equipment and other lab stuff. But now all Chris could see was Abbie Vincent carrying a case just like this one, refusing to let him put it in the back of the Caracal for her. She clung to the damn thing. She was a miserable, snappy bitch and he just thought she wanted to prove she didn't need a man to help her.

But he should have realised he needed to see what was so important in that case. He should have listened to the nagging voice in his head that said she was weird and way too anxious to hang onto it. But at the time, she and her folks were a disruptive problem he was happy to palm off on APS, and he still had a small town to evacuate via an interstellar alien portal that hadn't been tested on that scale before. He was rushing to draw a line under Earth's problems because he couldn't fix them.

My fault. I was the last person who could have stopped her. So what do I owe Earth? And when did I start getting bent out of shape about stuff I can't go back and change?

Chris stared at the case, then picked it up to lay it flat on the table, feeling like he was defusing a bomb. Lundahl moved in to watch. Chris felt his scalp tighten.

"Okay for me to open this?"

"Sure. It's not locked."

Chris flicked the catch and slowly lifted the lid. It was empty and he could breathe again, but he pulled out the instrument-shaped retaining inserts and poked around under linings until he touched bare metal. Dieter Hill, who'd been a narcotics cop, had given him a ten-minute crash course in searching for small items, but he still wasn't sure if he'd recognise every permutation of die-back virus in storage.

If that case was contaminated, Chris would be too.

He put it flat on the floor, fully open, so the bot could do some sampling. The bot reminded him of a bright orange horseshoe crab, but what looked like lots of legs were mostly a selection of sensors. The bot poked them into the case and felt around, patting and stroking the surfaces like it was trying to find its keys in the dark. Eventually it withdrew the probes and rolled back to its start position. Chris carried on checking the room, moving free-standing objects like chairs.

"Is someone searching your place as well?" Lundahl asked.

"Yes. If it's on the base, it could be anywhere."

"What will you do if you find something?"

"Take it for analysis."

"I meant what you'll do with the suspect."

"Not sure yet. But I don't think they'll get a medal." Chris waited for the next question, but it didn't happen. "Okay, all clear. Thanks for your cooperation."

Lundahl still seemed jumpy. That was the other point of the search, to take a close personal look at anyone who might be sweating a bit too much and let them know it had been noticed. Chris was on the verge of changing tack and shaking Lundahl down when the guy blurted out a question.

"Can I ask you something?"

"Go ahead."

"Why did you shoot the alien? Someone said you'd tried to talk to him."

Chris often forgot that even in this tiny village of a place, people didn't see everything that went on, and they heard scraps of news from the bush telegraph before they were given any solid information. He wasn't sure if Lundahl meant the generic *you*, meaning Nomad Base Joint Command, or that he thought Chris had personally fired the shot. Chris opted for the literal interpretation.

"I didn't shoot either of them," he said. "If I'd shot the teerik on sight, and hindsight says I should have done, Nina Curtis would be alive. I was ready to shoot the Jattan, too, but someone beat me to it."

That wasn't really an answer, but Chris wasn't trying to be evasive. He was still working out exactly what had happened and why. Shooting an armed attacker was automatic, and Marc had done exactly that without a moment's hesitation. But Chris hadn't shot the Jattan and he wasn't sure why. He was the one who'd argued with Bissey and said there was no way they could risk Gan-Pamas surviving to tell anyone they were here or that they had the stolen prototype warship. He was ready to drop the Jattan the second he saw him. But he didn't, and when Gan-Pamas shot Trinder, it was Liam Dale — just a farmer with a shotgun — who returned fire.

What the fuck was I thinking?

"I meant the Jattan," Lundahl said. "I know we had to assume he was hostile because of Nina, but — okay, I know we need to keep our heads down. Last thing we need is them knowing where Earth is."

That was the explanation Lundahl seemed to want to hear Chris confirm. It was Chris's argument with Bissey, that if the Jattans turned out to be fans of scorched earth diplomacy instead of friendly discussion, nobody could roll that back. Humans were the underdogs in the new order of things. Lundahl sounded like he didn't want to believe the good guys would kill anyone who wasn't a threat.

"Remember the Jattan did shoot Dan Trinder, though," Chris said, wondering if he was trying to justify his death sentence on Gan-Pamas to himself. "He's lucky to be alive."

That was one of the loose ends that still bothered Chris. He didn't know why the Jattan's energy weapon hadn't killed Trinder. It had just put him down him like a cop's shock prod. He'd have to go lean on the engineering lab and get them to do a proper analysis with Fred and work out whether the Jattan weapon really was non-lethal or just underpowered.

"If the Jattan was a gun runner, perhaps the leaders will be guys we can reach an understanding with," Lundahl said. "I live in hope."

Gunrunner. That was only one interpretation of Gan-Pamas's mission. This was where myths and parallel histories began. Chris wondered if Lundahl realised that having any kind of conversation with the Jattans was going to be a problem for Fred and his commune if Jattans really did regard teeriks as the legal property of their Kugin owners.

Perhaps they didn't, though. Chris didn't have an explanation for the lone rogue teerik with Gan-Pamas.

"Maybe we'll be pleasantly surprised," he said. "Anyway, I'd better get going. Sorry for the disruption."

Chris walked down the street towards the junction with the main road. He wasn't up for an existential debate about first contact. He'd had enough of that with Bissey, and he wasn't sorry to see him resign. The guy was probably great in a naval battle, but that was because he had the measure of his enemy on Earth. Nobody had any real idea yet what the various alien species out here were capable of. If Project Nomad had been done by the book, the way government agencies would have run it, there wouldn't have been a settlement here for another century or two. More unmanned missions would have been sent, more surrounding space explored, and more experts would have weighed in before any contact was made, from biologists and anthropologists to defence specialists.

But Tad Bednarz was a man in a hurry because conditions on Earth convinced him that time wasn't on anyone's side, and he was used to getting things done the way he wanted. There was nobody to stop him charging ahead once he'd identified a planet that fitted the bill. The guy seemed almost clairvoyant, because he'd planned for every major crisis on Earth and most had eventually happened, and to give him his due, it wasn't even his fault that he didn't foresee intelligent aliens on Opis. There weren't any here until the teeriks arrived less than a year ago. Humans — bots, anyway — had been here for seventy years.

Chris still couldn't decide whether Bednarz was a visionary destined to save human civilisation or an irresponsible asshole who should have stuck to perfecting robotics and spending his billions on gold-plated yachts.

But the answer to his question actually depended on what everyone here did next. "Well, shit," Chris said. "Thanks, Tad. No pressure."

Aaron Luce, Lee Ramsay, and Darryl Finch were standing on the corner with their quad bikes parked in a triangle, lights full-on in the darkness, consulting their screens like they were having a meeting. Lee waved Chris over.

"All done, boss?" he called.

"Yeah. No contamination, no obvious suspects. I'd like to say panic over, but I'm not standing down completely."

"They're pissed at us for even asking questions, but none of them pinged my radar either."

"How are we doing on interviews?"

"It's still going to take forever," Luce said. "But between me and Dieter, we've almost finished the most likely ones. We're down to the last five life sciences people. He's loving it. Good to see him in action again."

"Yeah, he's missed handcuffing perps to tables. You too, huh?"

"You bet. I almost forgot myself and planted some evidence on them."

They laughed. Seeing the funny side was the only way to stay sane at the moment. It was good to see Dieter had decided to throw himself back into the fray, but he was probably still a long way from his old self, and it wasn't complications from the stab wound that were slowing his recovery. It was losing Girlie.

Despite Marc's efforts to stop Chris finding out how the dog died, because he knew Chris all too well, Chris *had* found out, and yes, he certainly was planning to return to Earth when the time was right. He'd find Tim Pham and make him pay for what he'd done to Dieter and the dog. Thanks to the Caisin gate, he could step right into Pham's path, face to face in a second if he had the coordinates. It would be worth the wait.

"That's my watch over, then." Lee stretched his arms like an athlete, pulling the right one across his body, then the left. Everyone had worked through without a break and the adrenaline had ebbed. "I'm going to apply a pizza to the pie-hole, grab a few beers, and crash. See you later."

Chris was still training his system to accept a twenty-six hour day. If he didn't stay up until he fell over, he'd start drifting back to his old body clock. It was time to catch up on the jobs he'd had to shelve when the news broke about Abbie. He'd swing by the engineering workshop later to take a look at that Jattan stuff they'd salvaged.

There was still plenty to examine — the stealth suit, the stealth-camouflaged freighter, and the weapons. But it wasn't idle curiosity. There were things Chris had to know for his own peace of mind. Somehow his subconscious always spotted when something didn't fit, and it'd prod him until he worked out what it was, a warning bell he'd learned not to ignore. It had been ringing quietly for a couple of days and it was about the Jattan and his weapon.

Chris thought it through as he walked back home to shower and grab a meal. According to Fred, Gan-Pamas was a marbidar, a species from a planet called Dal Mantir, and he was a Jatt citizen. To make it easier for humans to understand, Fred had come up with a quick list of key points: marbidars evolved from aquatic ancestors, and they were egocentric, stupidly daring, and therefore not very effective soldiers, which made Jattans a pain in the ass if you had to make warships for them. The prototype ship the teeriks designed for them had to have an override on the targeting system to stop them getting into friendly-fire situations. The Kugin, who sounded like a much more disciplined and ruthless outfit, tolerated them as sidekicks on the battlefield because they controlled mineral exports on Dal Mantir. Well, that was Fred's analysis and the only intel Nomad had.

Chris had expected aliens to be completely unfathomable, but whatever these guys looked like, their personal and political dynamics sounded pretty familiar. He just wanted to know if

Gan-Pamas had intended to kill Trinder. The guy hadn't managed to, but that wasn't academic any longer. Chris needed to work out his intent, and that meant taking a closer look at the Jattan hardware.

And they still didn't know how he'd acquired a lone teerik as crew. Teeriks, Fred said, rarely left the Kugin state, always worked in groups called communes, and were closely supervised if they took part in ship trials or travelled anywhere off-site. They were just too valuable to lose. Generations of technical knowledge was stored in their brains and their genetic memories.

Chris had been over the events so many times that he wasn't sure what he recalled and what he'd imagined in the meantime. He'd been trying to replay events to work out the sequence of the various shots that had been fired, but every time he thought about it he found he had to spool back to the moment he first saw the lone teerik emerge out of thin air, and the next awful minute with Nina. He couldn't break the connection. He shut his eyes and tried concentrating on how the slurry pit had looked while Liam Dale was pumping it out to see if Gan-Pamas was hiding under the surface.

Maybe it was time to talk to the engineers.

He made a sandwich, flopped on the sofa, and checked the time. The engineering section was probably working around the clock at the moment, but he couldn't leave it too late. He called up the real-time base map on his screen to see who was still in the workshops, wolfed down the sandwich, and set off on foot.

The engineering section was a complex of hangars with walls and partitions that could be rearranged as needed. Chris opened the side door to the main hangar and wandered inside, looking for Gan-Pamas's weapon. The Jattan's heavily customised freighter was standing in a separate bay flanked by blast walls, hatch open and a ramp leading inside, while blue-overalled technicians were squeezing in and out of it with some difficulty like it was a kid's play house. Jattans were small.

Brad Searle stood watching, arms folded. As Chris walked up to the ship, it turned into a heat haze in the vague shape of a vessel. Someone had activated its stealth cloaking.

"You going to pilot that thing, Commander?" Chris asked. "You'll have your knees jammed in your ears in that cockpit."

Searle smiled. He was a very tall guy. "I might have to saw my legs off, but yeah, I'll give it a shot."

"Are you overseeing this as the chief engineer or as the XO in waiting?"

Searle looked embarrassed. "She told you, then."

"No, Ingram hasn't said a word to me."

"Well, I'm thinking it over. I'm not sure if I'm up to replacing Commander Bissey. And I might be more useful as a pilot again."

"Sure."

"I understand that we're both of the same mind about how we conduct ourselves out here."

Word had gotten around. It saved time. "Yeah, a strong deterrent and zero tolerance," Chris said. "Scare them off until we can defend ourselves properly."

"Amen."

Chris nodded at the Jattan freighter. "Handy for covert ops. Found anything informative yet?"

"Intel? Maybe." Searle shrugged. "Fred took some of the navigation components to see if there was more information to be extracted about the point of origin."

"Presumably not the Jatta Protectorate."

"The Jattan opposition might not even be on Dal Mantir. Fred says they've got a few colonies on other worlds, or they might have been given refuge by another alien government."

"Busy galaxy."

"Damn straight. It's a heavily-armed soap opera."

"I did come here for a reason, actually," Chris said. "I need to see Gan-Pamas's weapon. I assume it's still here."

"Sure. It's on that test bench." Searle pointed to the far side of the cavernous hangar. "Don't you want to see the stealth suit?"

"I saw enough in the slurry pit, thanks. Has anyone examined the weapon?"

"Yeah, Dai took a look. What is it you need? I'll get him for you."

"It's nearly midnight. Don't drag him out of bed."

"He's still up. He'll want to go over it with you."

"Okay. I just need to test a theory. Psychological stuff."

Chris went over to take a look at the weapon while he was waiting for Dai Hiyashi. He wasn't even sure what to call the thing, but it looked a little like an ancient flintlock pistol, all smooth curves, so he settled on *gun* for the meantime. Fred would probably know the Jattan term for it. It looked metallic, but as there was no way of knowing what any of the protrusions or depressions in its casing were without actually handling it, Chris decided to leave well alone until Hiyashi arrived.

"Hi Chris. Do you want to try it out?"

Chris turned around. "Have you managed to fire it?"

"Sort of." Hiyashi had an English accent, a lot posher than Marc's. Chris had first assumed he was one of the Japanese nationals from the *Cabot* crew, but he was an ex-Royal Navy weapons officer and as English as they came. "Fred worked it out. He said he hadn't seen one like this before. It's not military issue."

"What is it, then?"

"No idea. Come on, let's take it outside. We're not set up for live fire in here yet."

Chris followed Hiyashi outside to the open ground behind the bot hangar. There was nothing out there that they could damage. But he didn't want to put the gun through its paces. He just wanted to see the power output. Hiyashi placed it carefully in his hand.

"It's awkward because it's a bit small for a man's hand and you have to curve your fingers around it," he said. "Jattans seem to have more flexible joints. But you aim just as you would with an iron sight."

"Is it an energy weapon, or did I miss something?" Chris asked.

"Yes, it is."

Chris aimed low so that it would hit the grass. "Any spread?"

"About a foot."

"Weird." Chris prepared to attempt to fire. The absence of a trigger was confusing. "Am I trying to feel for some pressure point on the handle, or do I just squeeze?"

"Yeah, I know, it feels completely wrong, and I don't even touch handguns very often. Just squeeze it. It might help to imagine you're squirting ketchup at someone."

"Ah, my weapon of choice." Chris looked around to make sure nobody was going to walk past unannounced and adjusted his aim. "I want to know why it didn't kill Dan."

Chris squeezed the curve of the handle. Nothing happened for a moment, but as he tightened his grip, he felt the gun vibrate like he'd grabbed a buzzer while it was going off. Then there was a flash, a loud crack, and a patch of grass ten yards away gave off a wisp of steam or maybe smoke. It probably hurt like hell if it hit you, but it didn't seem too destructive. On the other hand, it could have been enough to disrupt someone's heart. But the Jattans couldn't have known the effect it would have on a human. They'd never met one before.

"Dai, do you know if the power can be adjusted?" Chris asked. "Was it on this setting when you received it?"

"We didn't change anything," Hiyashi said. "We were going to do a teardown first. But it does seem to have a control. Fred says you have to turn the bottom of the grip."

"Which way?"

Hiyashi thought for a moment. "Anticlockwise. Right to left."

Chris fumbled with the butt of the weapon, wary of accidentally squeezing the wrong part and zapping himself. He turned it as far as it would go and aimed at the grass again.

"I'm just trying to work out if Gan-Pamas was trying to kill Dan or not," he said.

He ran through the few seconds leading up to the incident. Gan-Pamas had been found in the slurry pit, Chris had called Fred on the radio to get him to translate the conversation into Jattan so Gan-Pamas could hear it, and then the alien started getting agitated as if he was arguing with Fred. Trinder had his rifle trained on him. Did Trinder twitch or do something that made him look like he was going to fire? Whatever happened, the Jattan had shot him.

"Stand by," Chris said.

He squeezed. This time the gun almost kicked. The flash was bigger and the crack was louder. When he walked up to look at the damage, the grass was blackened like someone had cooked a barbecue on it.

The weapon wasn't set at full power when Gan-Pamas fired, then. He might have thought it was enough to kill a human, but Chris suspected that wasn't what happened. It was impossible to think like an alien he didn't know anything about, but his gut said anyone faced with a previously unknown and much bigger enemy would probably err on the side of overkill.

Gan-Pamas hadn't. It looked like he'd tried to make it less lethal, even though he probably believed he was going to be killed. Chris felt bad about that. This didn't sound like the kind of trigger-happy, reckless Jattan behaviour Fred had described. He'd have to raise this as a concern in the morning.

"I think I might have gotten this all wrong," he said, staring at the vaporised grass.

His subconscious hadn't been trying to warn him about non-lethal weapons. There was no way he could have seen that, and it wouldn't have solved the problem of Gan-Pamas giving away their position, for a start. But it *had* given Chris a hint.

It had told him to be careful about taking Fred's word as gospel. Only time would tell, but Nomad might have made an unnecessary enemy, just as Bissey had predicted.

* * *

UNIT D74, ROAD CURRENTLY UNNAMED, NOMAD BASE: 0725, SEPTEMBER 22, OC.

Marc washed the breakfast dishes and stood at the sink, staring out of the window at the threadbare beginnings of a back garden. It was painful, a flashback to a similarly ordinary day twenty years ago when he was on leave and it was his turn to take the boys to school.

History was repeating, but it wasn't ordinary now. Howie was getting ready for his third day at the new Kill Line school, wrapping his sandwiches and being very organised. Betsy the pit bull waited patiently by the door to do escort duty, having turned up from somewhere else — probably Dieter's place — with uncanny punctuality. But John and Greg were long gone, Sandra wasn't on the early shift at the supermarket, and this wasn't their house in Warminster.

"Got your homework for marking?" Marc asked.

Howie nodded and patted his bag. "Yeah."

"Still enjoying school?" Howie was almost too good-natured and kids could be nasty little bastards with newcomers, no matter how well brought-up they were. Now they were being taught in separate age groups, Howie was the only transit camp kid in a class of Kill Liners. "You make sure you tell me if you don't."

"It's okay, I like it," Howie said. "Chuck's teaching us history and biology again. And Dr Mangel's going to tell us how stars form. It's not like I don't know anybody."

"Dr Mangel's a clever bloke," Marc said. "You'll learn lots from him."

"He likes you. He said you gave him the best surprise of his life when you drove him through the Caisin gate."

Marc wondered if he'd developed a gravitational field that pulled in other broken souls. Poor old Todd Mangel had never told anyone he'd lost his wife or that he'd even been married at all. With the exception of the Kill Liners, though, almost everybody in Nomad Base was broken in some way, from the *Cabot* crew who'd left everyone and everything they knew for a one-way mission, to the refugees from Chris's transit camp and the Ainatio staff who'd lost contact with their families and friends as the world beyond their secure site collapsed and vanished. This wasn't a normal, balanced population to breed from, whatever lofty standards people had met in Solomon's estimation. But it would have to do.

"That's what's cool about being here," Marc said. "Everyone's got a special talent and we're all doing something important. Kids as well. We're all making history, Howie, because somebody's got to."

Marc wasn't sure what that meant to him. It was Solomon who said stuff like *destiny* and *pivotal point in human history*.

Howie slung his bag over his shoulder and paused to stow the clean cups away in the cupboard. "Yeah, and it's really nice to live in a house again," he said. "With a proper address."

"You had a house in the transit camp."

"It was a cabin. It's not a house until it's got people in it."

Howie had plenty of people in Chris's camp willing to take him in, but he didn't seem to want that. Marc decided not to ask questions. After Howie told him how he'd tried to take care of his dying mum and sister, completely alone in an abandoned suburb, Marc let him fill in the gaps at his own pace. He knew he was dealing with a traumatised kid who had his own way of coping, and Howie's was being Little Mister Perfect, running errands, checking the old people were okay, and generally making a job of being cheerful. Marc hoped he wasn't testing himself to see if he could have done more for his family or trying to do some kind of penance. He was seven or eight when it happened and he shouldn't have felt he had to be a grown man. But he hadn't turned into an aggressive little animal, which Marc would have expected, and that probably meant he'd had a secure, loving family who'd buffered him against the world collapsing around him until they died.

Howie was still grieving. It wasn't that complicated. But Marc now found himself instinctively trying to protect Howie from real life, and he'd have to find a compromise if he was going to let him grow up and come to terms with his past.

Sod it. This was exactly what Marc had tried to avoid. Howie didn't need a surrogate parent who was dealing with his own troubles.

"Yeah, people," Marc said, slinging his carbine over his shoulder. "You need someone to share the housework roster. And watch movies with."

"And tell them how your day was."

Yeah, Marc had missed that. "Let's go, then."

They walked down the road to the centre of the base, avoiding puddles from the overnight rain. Their routes parted at the next junction past the Kill Line turning. Howie peeled off left with Betsy trotting alongside and Marc watched them go for a moment, touched by how the dog kept looking left and right like she was scanning for possible attackers. He was sure she'd have a go at anyone who looked like a threat to Howie. She'd see him to the door of the school like she had yesterday and then go about her day, which she seemed to organise better than most humans. Then she'd show up when she felt Marc needed looking after. For a drug dealer's dog, she was big on responsible behaviour.

Marc carried on to the main building and made his way up the single flight of stairs to Meeting Room 2B, exchanging nods and grunts with *Cabot* people he passed. He'd catalogued them all mentally now, not for any reason beyond the security habit of knowing who was who and if they were where they were supposed to be or not.

It was the same with the Ainatio boffins. Most of them passed through this building at some point during the day as well, because even though the emergency accommodation had been converted back to offices, it was still one of the entrances to the staff canteen and some of the labs. So he made a point of clocking the scientists and technical staff too.

One of them was heading towards him, coming down the stairs with a file tucked under his arm. Marc had searched the man's home yesterday, all very proper and cordial, but as Marc met his eyes and nodded in acknowledgement, the scientist just looked uncomfortable and hurried on. Maybe the bloke had an embarrassing hobby and thought Marc had found it while rummaging. He hadn't. So there was a chilly distance between them that hadn't been there before Marc had become the face of the accuser. Well, if life had been a popularity contest, Marc's end users wouldn't have awarded him any stars. Dead scumbags didn't leave feedback.

He shrugged it off and carried on. When he opened the door to the meeting room, he realised he was the last to arrive. Trinder, Chris, Searle, and Ingram stared at him like he had a nerve walking in there.

"I'm not late," he said, nodding pointedly at the clock.

Alex slid a cup of coffee down the table at him. "It's okay, Britzilla. We just got here early to gossip about you. We're done now."

Ingram flourished her pocket screen. "I've sent the talking points to your screens, gentlemen, so let's have a look, and add anything else as we go. One, the revised Opis calendar and options. Two, wash-up from the security sweep. Would you like to get the calendar out of the way first?"

Marc took a seat and studied the documents that had just landed in his inbox. There were now four options for a new calendar to fit the number of days in the Opis year, and his first reaction was that they had better things to do with their time when the base was up to its arse in potential threats. But perhaps that was the point. Being seen to carry on with long-term admin stuff like a calendar — especially a calendar — told everyone in Nomad that life was going on as normal and they'd still be around to cross off dates for the foreseeable future. It was a statement. Marc knew Ingram well enough now to realise that was exactly what she'd use it for.

On the other hand, it was also typical Alex. He knew how to handle people, and consultation on that small detail gave them some sense of control over their lives.

"Have we deleted your birthday, Marc?" Alex asked. "You look pissed about something."

Marc studied the options. "Didn't Nostra-Bednarz-Damus sort this in advance when he was gazing at his crystal ball?"

"Yes, he did, there was a new calendar based on local seasons," Solomon said. Sol was in every meeting, listening somewhere in the system or monitoring even when his core had gone walkabout in his quadrubot, and he was always ready to defend his dead creator. "But it's clear that people aren't ready to erase two thousand years of shared culture. So we've come up with some choices to be put to a vote. The Opis orbital period is just under a week longer than Earth's if we count hours, but with the twenty-six hour days it's actually forty-nine seven-day weeks."

"So folks can choose from the Bednarz calendar, with new names for months to be worked out later, because otherwise that's death by minutiae," Alex said. "Or a numerical system based on elapsed mission days, the full Gregorian calendar with the gradual drift away from the seasons, or the slimline Gregorian calendar with some months reduced to fit forty-nine weeks."

"Which months, and why?" Marc asked.

"I aimed for the minimum disruption to the majority of people's birthdays," Solomon said.

"Very scientific, Sol." Marc checked the modified calendar for the dates that meant most to him. John's and Greg's anniversaries were still intact at the end of November, but they wouldn't mark an exact year the next time they came around. Howie's birthday was in November as well. "We can keep a separate Earth calendar going in parallel if people vote for one of the fancy options. But it still won't tie up with Earth's, will it?"

"No, Earth's running further ahead of us date-wise by one day for every twelve days here," Alex said. He nodded with the assurance of a man who'd rehearsed all his responses to objections, but then he started counting on his fingers. "I *think* that adds up to a month a year. Well, more or less. Don't ask me about leap years and leap seconds and sorting out the exact length of the Opis day. That's Sol's job. But there's nothing we can do to keep the calendar in sync with Earth. As you say, other cultures and religions keep their own calendar running alongside the international one, so my guess is people will think broadly in Earth time for a while because they can see it on the news feeds. But they'll stop when the Earth date diverges too much and it does their heads in because they're watching news from months in the future."

"You haven't touched December, Sol," Trinder said.

Solomon always had his reasons. "Humans need a midwinter festival and a line drawn under the old year."

"That's March, temperature-wise."

"Well, the Aussies here can help us through the culture shock of badly-aligned Christmases," Marc said. "So when do we switch over?"

"New Year's Day," Solomon said. "And to avoid problems about qualification for age-related services and responsibilities in the future, I suggest everyone retains the date of birth and length of year of the planet where they were born."

"Man's first extrasolar bureaucracy. Makes me proud. Still, when we're all dead, that problem solves itself."

Chris didn't look up from his screen. "The Gregorian calendar took a couple of centuries to catch on. And even then it wasn't universal."

"As long as we all use the same calendar for administration, that's all I care about." Ingram had obviously had enough. She wasn't a committee kind of woman. "Everybody happy? Can we move on to the security sweep now, please?"

"No die-back's been detected," Solomon said. "A few suspicious containers opened, but no positives. Recreational narcotics and fragile family mementoes sealed for safekeeping."

Trinder shook his head as if he was disappointed. "And no obvious Mother Death supporters among the staff so far. It's been useful having a couple of real cops on the team for interviews. I think they're better equipped to spot wrong 'uns in that environment than I am, to be honest."

"Which is why I continue to be vigilant," Solomon said.

"Spying, you mean."

"No, I mean *vigilant*. You know my position on intruding into people's private lives."

"I did say it was inevitable." Alex polished his glasses. Marc was convinced he only wore them so he had something to fiddle with when he was feeling uncomfortable. He could have had his vision fixed years ago. "They're not stupid. They know it's not over and that we'll be watching in case someone decides to sabotage something. They're not a single homogenous mass of white coats, either. Some of them are seriously pissed at the die-back team for all sorts of reasons, not least of which is getting them tarred with the same brush. And they're wondering how they could *not* know about Abbie. So like I said when this blew up, the damage has been done, even if everyone's innocent. It'll take time to heal."

"It's done now," Ingram said. "And we were right to do it."

"It wouldn't have made things any better if we hadn't," Marc said. "People would have been suspicious of Ainatio staffers anyway. Human nature."

"Maybe we should stop calling them staffers," Trinder said. "Ainatio doesn't exist now."

"Changing words doesn't change what people think. It's like swapping price tags. It doesn't change what's in the tin and they know it."

"Well, let's treat them like we don't think they're Mother Death sleepers, at least," Ingram said. "Anything else? We may well finish in record time today."

Chris raised his forefinger to speak. The more polite and formal he got, the bigger the problem he was about to unload.

"Captain, a word of caution about the teeriks' security analysis."

"This is an oh-dear moment, isn't it?"

"Possibly. I tested Gan-Pamas's gun last night. Has Hiyashi mentioned it to you?"

"I haven't seen him today."

"Okay, Gan-Pamas might not have intended to kill anyone."

"Oh. Go on."

"Hiyashi and I tested the weapon he used on Dan and it wasn't set anywhere near maximum power. I think we should be more cautious about how we evaluate intel from Fred. Nobody's got all the facts in any situation and we've all got our biases."

"Are you saying Jattans aren't a threat?" Marc asked.

"I'm saying they might not be set on killing any random stranger they meet. The whole reckless shock-troops thing might be too broad a brush stroke."

"Okay, let me play devil's advocate," Marc said. "Maybe Gan-Pamas didn't know how much juice it would take to kill a human. Maybe he thought we were nice guys, but he'd still have gone home and told everyone we were here and that we had their missing ship. Maybe the gun was faulty. *Not* frying Dan doesn't necessarily mean he's our friend, and there's no such thing as a non-lethal weapon, just less than lethal. Some susceptible people still die."

Trinder looked a bit annoyed. "As the guy who was nearly fried, let me tell you it didn't *feel* non-lethal."

"Yeah, I know, I'm sorry, I should have dropped him the second I found him, because I was the one mouthing off about the need to do it," Chris said. "All I'm saying is there's enough doubt in my mind now to be wary of starting wars on the sole basis of Fred's assessment."

Ingram tapped her pen on the table. "Are we saying Fred's got his biases or might make mistakes, or are we saying he's lying? Sol, you're the only one who can process languages and clear this up."

"If I had more Jattan source material, Captain, I'd make more progress," Sol said. "The more of the language we can hear, the more the linguistics algorithm can analyse and identify patterns. I'd ask Fred outright, but I don't want him to clam up. You know teeriks find it hard to volunteer information. They seem to hesitate to speak Kugal among themselves now, and I can't tell if it's to improve their English or to appear as transparent as possible."

"Or limit your ability to understand it because Marc scared them by hinting that he did."

"Do Kugin use radio or broadcast anything?" Chris asked. "If all you need is a source of raw Kugal, there must be a way to listen in, even if it's just a cookery show. If they have them."

"Good idea," Ingram said. "Can we do that, Sol?"

"Probably. I'd still need to consult Fred on the safest way to eavesdrop, though, and by doing so I'd be telling him that I'm determined to learn Kugal even if he's being obstructive."

"If he's not, he'll offer to teach you," Marc said.

"Sol, just find a way to eavesdrop on the Jattans, and preferably the Kugin as well." Ingram sounded impatient. "We need much better intel. We don't have a hope of understanding this civil war, if that's what it is, unless we can form an objective picture of the situation. And we need it to find out whether anybody else knows we're here or if there's a Kugin fleet heading our way."

"If they knew we had the ship and the teeriks, they'd have been here by now," Chris said.

Marc didn't think it would take a whole fleet to ruin their day. "The Jattan opposition's the most likely to visit first. They already found us and we still can't rule out someone knowing where Gan-Pamas was going, even if he didn't manage to call home. Or at least they found the ship, which now amounts to the same thing."

Ingram nodded to herself as if she'd just thought of something. "Perhaps we can use the teerik relays the same way we do with Earth. Sol, let me talk to Fred first. I'll sound him out and then we can come up with more specific measures."

"I'll continue to analyse the conversation Fred had with Gan-Pamas," Solomon said. "I'm still relying on what I learned from the message we composed. I can coax him into more help with Jattan once I have a list of specific questions I need to ask."

"Why's it so hard to get him to translate?" Searle asked. "Unless you don't trust him."

"I'm more concerned about innocent errors that might prove disastrous," Solomon said. "But he might simply be making sure we always need him. We have to remember they see secrecy as their protection."

Ingram sighed. "The sooner we don't have to rely on this drip feed of information, the better. Very well, unless there's anything else, let's crack on."

Marc wondered how long it would be before she got tired of the slow diplomacy of alien contact and just threatened Fred with a packet of stuffing. The meeting broke up and Chris steered him off to the staff canteen with Trinder. They sat in a quiet corner and dissected the situation over bacon sandwiches.

"I've had breakfast." Marc pushed the untouched half of his sandwich across the table to Chris. The bloke never wasted a crumb. "I can't finish this."

Chris pounced on it and reached for the sauce. "Thanks. Are we overthinking the whole Gan-Pamas thing? I'm not one for meetings. We never had time. We just got on with it."

"It doesn't hurt to war-game it. But you're right, our entire assessment of this sector comes from Fred and his commune. They're rebels, the ones who stole a ship and did a runner. The rest of the teeriks didn't bother to show up for the revolution, for whatever reason. What does that tell us now?"

"Maybe Fred's bunch are troublemakers."

"Do you really trust them, Chris?" Trinder asked. "We're relying on your paranoia superpower."

Chris reassembled the heavily-sauced sandwich. "If I don't trust them, it's not because I think they're traitors like Abbie. I'm just not sure about their judgement. If someone asked us about APS, our opinion's shaped by nearly being nuked and then having our launch sabotaged. The teeriks have spent their lives in a cosy silo, just creating warships and weapons, and that means they're focused on threats. They're brought up to see the other side in terms of the damage it could do and how to kill it. It doesn't make for a balanced assessment."

"What if the Jattans turn out to be the good guys like Bissey said, we get on like a house on fire, and the teeriks don't like it?" Trinder asked. "Whose side are we on?"

"Ingram's already promised Fred she'll defend the teeriks no matter what." Chris was the proverbial poker player, but he was looking at Marc like he expected him to be offended by any comment about Ingram. "But we all know that means 'We won't let you be captured alive because the stuff you know about Earth will drop us in the shit too.' I'm not criticising that, by the way."

"She's already planning how we make sure we're not dependent on them to use their technology," Marc said. "She's a pragmatist. And you can say what you like about her. We're not an item."

Trinder said nothing and studied his coffee carefully. Chris just nodded and moved on.

"Look, I like Fred," Chris said. "And I feel sorry for his commune if they're escaping slavery, but the people who are good for you aren't necessarily the ones you like, and vice versa. I just want to do right by the people I promised a safe haven. If I can do that without compromising Fred's commune, great. If not, I know whose welfare comes first."

Marc respected Chris's clarity. "Yeah, we look after our own."

"But what about you? You've got friends and family stuck on Earth and we can't give them FTL."

"You mean Tev."

"And your ex. And a lot of other folks. You're not the kind of guy who leaves people behind."

Marc kept thinking about Tev and his family. APS knew who and what Tev Josepha was — they'd even flown him to Fiji when Pham and his rummage team moved into Ainatio HQ — but he'd been confident he could keep up his pretence of being an ordinary army vet who just happened to be working on the same security contract as Marc, no special forces background at all. He knew he'd be watched. After the sabcode attack on Asia, he'd probably have been of more interest to Tim Pham, but now Pham's own Ainatio informant had given Asia a dose of die-back, Pham would almost certainly go after Tev. Pham had seen the Caisin gate working. The bastard hadn't understood who built it, or exactly what it did, but he knew dangerous and desirable technology when he saw it.

"It wouldn't be any easier if we could share the technology," Marc said. "Just calling Tev puts him at risk. I could do it without saying where I am, but you know how Pham's mind works. If he hasn't got someone watching Tev right now, I'll be surprised."

Chris raised an eyebrow. "Locate Tev, open a Caisin gate, put the situation to him, agree an RV point, and ship out whoever you need to."

"Y'know, I've rehearsed how I'd break the news to him. Then I work out who he'd want to bring with him, and how many loose ends that leaves when the whole Josepha family vanishes, or what happens if some decide they *don't* want to leave friends and neighbours. And what if die-back never reaches Fiji?"

Deciding whether to save someone from a sinking ship was simple. If you didn't do it, they'd drown right away. But Marc wouldn't know if evacuating Tev and his people would save them in the long term until it was too late to undo it.

"I'd want to get him out," Chris said. "Especially as that fucker Tim Pham's still around."

"Yeah, I know I'm the one who convinced Tev to try again with his ex, so it's my fault he's stuck there." Marc noticed Trinder fidgeting uncomfortably with his cup and inching back from the conversation. "You don't need to remind me."

"No, I'm saying if you do it, I've got your back," Chris said. "But I know it isn't simple. It's not about whether we've got room. It's about what happens if word gets out. But APS can't reach us now, so what's the worst scenario?"

"You being rhetorical?"

"Brainstorming in the colder light of today, maybe."

"You'll wish you hadn't asked," Marc said. "Okay, short answer is what Annis Kim said when we first talked about this. Long answer is Earth finds out there's a possible FTL lifeboat, the elite book their ticket to Shangri-La, governments fight over the technology, and everyone else scrabbles for a place or starts riots. People die in the time it takes to build the ships or just trying to join the queue. Would that be our fault? Well, we lit the fuse. But *not* throwing a lifeline also means people die. It's almost as bad as opening the Caisin gate, getting overrun, and not being able to feed and care for anybody, including our own people. Everybody dies."

Chris ate a crust. "You've got to stop reading those Russian novels, buddy."

"I'm just pointing out there's no way of taking our next breath without being somehow responsible for someone dying, no matter what we do."

"So fuck Earth, it doesn't make any difference which way we jump."

"Yeah."

"Good. I was worried you were getting all high-minded and theoretical." Chris put on his distracted vicar expression, the thousand-yard stare with a hint of witnessing a moment of divine revelation. "Caring about humanity doesn't count. Saving one guy does. We go get Tev."

"If he wants to leave."

Trinder picked up his cup. "Guys, can you excuse me? I need to sort out some rosters. Catch you later."

Chris watched him go. Marc raised an eyebrow. "Fonseca does the rosters."

"Yeah."

"Was it something I said?" Marc asked.

"Saving people stuck on Earth. Family issues."

"Ah, shit. I'd better apologise."

"He'll be okay. Change the subject. Chuck says Howie's doing well in school. You've done a good job."

"He only started a few days ago."

"I know, but Chuck's been teaching him since he joined the convoy. He can see the difference."

"I worry that it'll all come crashing in on the kid one day. He's holding too much back."

"I wish I'd asked him more questions about his family."

"Did he ever live with anyone in the camp?" Marc asked.

Chris shook his head. "No shortage of volunteers to take him in, but he wanted his own little cabin from the start. We just humoured him and kept an eye on him."

"Yeah, he told me that. Do you know why?"

"I guess letting himself be absorbed into another family was like shutting the door on his folks and accepting they were gone." Chris frowned like he was wondering about it for a moment, then moved on. "Look, we're going to have to make a decision about the dead aliens. I think we should do tests. We need a better idea of what kills Jattans, just so we know we've got the right weapons to defend ourselves. I asked Haine but he told me to come back later."

"Yeah, that'd be my fault," Marc said. "I told Ingram to hold off while we worked something out. If we ever need to be friends with the Jattans, we'll have to show some respect and repatriate bodies. We'd go mental if we found some bastard had desecrated our mates' corpses."

"True, but there's a compromise."

"I'm not gagging to kill Jattans or Kugin unless that's the only way we'll survive out here. If there are other ways, like reaching an agreement with them, I'll try that too."

"I asked Dr Mendoza if he had any ideas," Chris said. "Turns out he's got all the data to run computer modelling if he can analyse actual tissue. He can build a virtual Jattan and blow the shit out of it."

"So you still want something for analysis."

"Yeah. Ingram's blocked it, apparently, so if you're the one who got her to do that, tell her what we need."

"How much? I mean how invasive? They might believe that all your bits have to be accounted for or else you go some kind of hell."

"Just tiny plugs of tissue. I'd ask Ingram myself, but she hates my guts. She listens to you, though."

Marc couldn't imagine Chris being scared of Ingram or anyone else, so he was probably trying hard to be diplomatic and not give her a reason to say no.

"Okay. I'll get it sorted," Marc said.

"Thanks."

"I'd better be going. I've got a bunch of boffins to turn into killing machines."

"So they're volunteering."

"This batch, yeah. The ones who want to go off-camp sometime. The reluctant but capable will be leaned on later. Everyone's got to be able to defend themselves, if nothing else."

"This is how militarised nations start."

"You say that like it's a bad thing."

"Not at all. We ought to do more survival and self-sufficiency training, too. If we ever get into a war and the worst happens, we need to be able to rebuild without technology to do everything. And building an army and teaching common skills keeps people together. We've got too many fault lines forming in this base already."

Someone — Trinder or Fonseca, Marc couldn't remember which — had said that people enjoyed apocalypse movies because they liked the idea of pulling down the old order and having a fresh start without the elite. Building a new society from people still marinated in their own history was going to be a challenge, but if anything could get a bunch of random people to see themselves as a single group with a purpose, it was military training. A Nomad boot camp would be the settlement's salvation in more ways than one.

"I wasn't thinking of kicking the shit out of them until they sign up," Marc said. "I'm luring them with promises of freedom to explore Opis without a bodyguard."

"One more thing before you go, then."

"Shoot."

Chris hesitated for a heartbeat. "I'm sticking my nose in, but you could have a memorial in the churchyard for your boys. Just a thought. We all need a focus."

Marc got the feeling that Chris had been building up to that for a few days, but he'd told Chris not to tiptoe around him about bereavement. He was relieved that Chris talked frankly about it now. Knowing that your grief made people afraid to say anything somehow made it worse, like they were staring at a bloody stump where your leg used to be and wondering why you weren't in more pain.

"Yeah, sometimes I wish I had graves to visit, but they both wanted their ashes scattered," Marc said. "We all fill in the form to say how we want to go, but I always wondered if they opted for cremation because they didn't want me obligated to care for graves."

"Or maybe they really did love that river and thought it would be a nicer place for you to visit."

"Possibly." It was easier to have this conversation with Chris than with Sandra. Chris wasn't in permanent pain the way she was. "Okay, it's a good idea. Thank you. I'll give it some thought."

Marc went on his way to the warehouse he'd commandeered for weapons training, wondering where he'd even start with a memorial. It couldn't be a headstone. It'd be a fake grave. It had to tell the truth, not just today but long after he was gone. What, then, a statue? He had no idea. He'd think about it later when he could concentrate on it. He tapped out a message to Ingram.

I NEED A FEW TINY BITS OF JATTAN FOR COMPUTER MODELLING. NO MAJOR DAMAGE TO THE DECEASED. PLS TELL HAINE HE CAN DO IT.

Liam Dale had managed to kill the Jattan with a shotgun, so maybe they already had their answers, but it wouldn't hurt to find out if there was a better way of doing it. Marc carried on across the open green in the centre of the base, wondering if he could have detained the rogue teerik and got some answers out of him, then slowed to look over his shoulder as he heard the *whop-whop-whop* of wings.

Rikayl, the weird chick from Caisin's last egg, swooped down on him and crash-landed on his shoulder in a flurry of feathers. Marc braced to keep his balance. The kid was the size of an eagle now with claws to match, and according to Fred, he should have been talking fluently and able to use tools at this age, but he wasn't developing normally. He didn't even look like the other teeriks. They were all iridescent blue-black, and he was bright red. The medics and vets agreed with Fred that he hadn't turned out right because of Caisin's age and health, but Marc was coming around to Chris's view that Rikayl was actually a throwback — a very smart bird, not a handicapped teerik. The boffins disagreed and pointed out in their let-me-make-it-simple-for-you way that no human reverted to an ape no matter how serious a genetic abnormality was. But they still couldn't explain Rikayl.

"I hope you're not going to make a habit of that, Rik," Marc said. "What do you want?"

Rikayl's bright yellow eye peered into his face at point-blank range. "No waaankah."

Wanker appeared to be his name for Chris, thanks to Jeff Aiken teaching him the word. Rikayl didn't like Chris. He might not have been a genius like the other teeriks, but he knew the man with the gun kept an eye on him and didn't trust him not to attack kids. Marc seemed to be tolerated, though. He'd work with that.

"What do you mean, Rik?" Marc carried on walking, head tilted to one side to counterbalance the weight on his shoulder. "I'm not a wanker? I'm not Chris? Or are you asking where Chris is?"

"Not waaankaah. Neee-nah. Maaaarc kill."

Marc took a few seconds to work that out. The penny finally dropped. Rikayl had seen him shoot the teerik who killed Nina. He'd decided Marc wasn't a wanker because he'd avenged his beloved human mum.

"Yeah, mate," Marc said. "Sorry I didn't shoot the bastard before he got her. I'm your friend, then, am I?"

Rikayl made a hissing noise that sounded like a *yesss* of approval. He was smart, alright. Jeff — Chief Jeff to the teeriks, Chief Petty Officer Aiken — had taught him to play card games like Patience. So Rikayl grasped numbers, and he definitely used language. He wasn't just mimicking. Chris was on to something.

"Okay, Rik, be nice to Chris, will you?" Marc said. "He's my mate. He's okay really."

"Wankaaaaah," Rikayl said. "Okay really."

Then he laughed, real human laughter in a woman's voice that sounded just like Nina Curtis. It was too real. It made Marc's stomach knot. But teeriks were great mimics, and Rikayl had obviously picked up laughter by listening to Nina. Maybe he wasn't laughing about calling Chris a wanker at all, just recalling something that Nina had done that made him happy. But it sounded to Marc like he found it funny.

Marc wondered how he'd get Rikayl off his shoulder when he reached the hangar. He didn't want him in there during weapons training because he could be stubborn when he didn't get his own way. But he needn't have worried. Twenty yards from the doors, Rikayl spread his wings and started flapping.

"Kill," he said, and took off, smacking Marc in the ear. "Kill, kill, kill."

He soared at a steep angle and disappeared in the direction of the church. Marc watched him go and decided the little bugger knew exactly what he was saying.

Rikayl had also seemed to know where the Jattan freighter had landed and had zeroed in on it, even with its stealth shield that made it invisible until you were only a few yards away. But that was a question for another day.

He'd keep wondering about it, though.

02

I'm pleased to announce that Commander Bradley Searle has been appointed First Officer of CSV Cabot, effective immediately. He'll continue to lead the team adapting SDV Curtis, formerly designated Nar P12, for human crewing and the defence of Nomad Base. Lieutenant Commander Jacqueline Devlin is promoted to the rank of Commander and will carry out the duties of Chief Engineering Officer.

Captain Bridget Ingram, announcing new appointments in the wake of Peter Bissey's resignation.

TEERIK COMPOUND, NOMAD BASE: SEPTEMBER 23, OC.

"Why *Curtis*?" Pannit asked. "Why not *Caisin*? Why a human's name?"

"Because it's a good name for the ship," Hredt said, not looking up from the Earth broadcast on his screen. It was fascinating but confusing information and he needed to concentrate. "All the other human ships are named after explorers as well. It fits."

"But Nina wasn't an explorer."

"Of course she was. She risked danger to travel to an unknown world. And she died because she thought all teeriks were as friendly as us, so we have a duty to commemorate her."

"But how will we honour Caisin?" Pannit asked. "Her gate's one of the greatest achievements in engineering."

Hredt looked up slowly, copying the movement that Chief Jeff used to indicate impatience when he was about to restate a point that someone had failed to grasp. "Caisin already has her memorial, and the gate's named after her. There'll be many more inventions and places to name. I guarantee nobody will be unaware of Learned Mother's genius when it's safe for others to know about it."

Pannit generally kept his thoughts to himself, although he was always a little more talkative when Turisu wasn't around. But he was almost aggressive today. It was starting to wear on Hredt's nerves. The communal room at the centre of the complex the humans had built for them should have been a quiet sanctuary for a few hours while Turisu was on board *Shackleton* with Demli and Runal, teaching them while she worked on the vessel's upgrades. Pannit was ruining Hredt's brief respite from his daughter's constant disapproval.

"So are you always going to call yourself Fred now?" Pannit asked.

"I'm Fred to my human friends, and Hredt to all of you." *Fred* was still the best humans could do to pronounce Hredt's name properly, but he wasn't offended by that. It was close enough. Human soldiers gave each other nicknames and he was happy to be included in that camaraderie. "I'm content with that."

"So what are you watching?"

"Have you no work to do?"

"I'm taking a break. Just like you."

"Well, I'm trying to concentrate on this broadcast." Hredt knew he was being unreasonably irritable, but he couldn't help himself. Perhaps old age was shortening his temper. "We're supposed to be upgrading the Ainatio fleet, Pannit. All four ships need spacefold drives as a matter of urgency. It's not just for the humans' survival. It's for ours as well."

Pannit carried on, undeterred. "Are you going to tell me what you're watching, then?"

"Events on Earth. News." Hredt felt his neck feathers start to rise. "I want to find out what's happening. They transmit information to everybody, all the time."

"Even if they don't have a permit to know it?"

"Apparently."

"Did you ask Ingram if you could watch?"

"Solomon said it was permitted. He wouldn't do that if Ingram didn't approve."

Pannit wasn't giving up. "Is the news full of state secrets, then?"

"I can't tell," Hredt said. "I've watched news from three different nations. They talk about the same topics but say entirely different things, even about this crop plague. Chief Jeff says people don't believe all the information anyway."

"Sounds stupid to me. Why do they bother, then? How do they make anything work?"

"Perhaps news isn't meant to inform and the real exchange of information happens elsewhere."

"I saw soldiers searching the base," Pannit said. "They had mechanicals with sensors testing the buildings. But they checked everything when they arrived, so why are they worried about contamination now?"

"If you can't think of anything useful to occupy your time, I'll find something for you to do."

"I want to know. Nobody's transited between here and Earth since the great arrival. Doesn't their sensor equipment work? Can't you find out?"

"Pannit, I have very little time left in my break period. And very little patience as well. I'll find out what I can. Now please leave me in peace."

Pannit stiffened his back as if he was about to lunge. "Don't take it out on me because your daughter's nagging you."

"If she's nagging me," Hredt said carefully, "then you should show me more consideration. Shouldn't you?"

"You never used to be this grumpy," Pannit said, and stalked out.

Hredt now felt guilty for snapping. He'd apologise later and make more allowance for the stress everyone was under. The whole commune seemed to be more argumentative, even his grandsons, and the events of the last few days hadn't helped. Their comfortable existence in a secure city like Deku, all their needs met, was over. The reality of freedom had turned out to be fear, then hunger, and now close proximity to violence. It was ironic for professional creators of armaments and warships. Even though the humans fed and protected them, the reality of being a target in a lawless world was a sobering experience.

It was Lirrel who worried Hredt most, though. A solitary teerik was unheard of, but this one had apparently managed to escape and join a Jattan arms dealer. He'd even become aggressive enough to use a makeshift weapon. None of it made sense. The entire population of teeriks belonged to the Kugin, and they were so valuable that they were always closely guarded on the rare occasions they left Deku. There were no unknown teeriks, and there'd never been a case of a teerik trying to escape until Caisin had urged them to rise up and build a new world for themselves.

In the end, the commune was left waiting at the rendezvous point for comrades who never came. They were now exiled with the prototype warship they'd hijacked and presumably a price on their heads. How had Gan-Pamas acquired Lirrel, then? Where had he come from? How had the pair found Opis?

The planet didn't seem to be uncharted any longer. But no teerik in Kugad could have revealed its location, because Opis had never been part of the plan. It was a last-minute, panicked decision when the commune realised it was on its own and had to hide. Hredt put his screen down, still unable to work out how this had happened. The logs of Gan-Pamas's freighter provided no answers. But if there was another teerik civilisation somewhere, and somehow the exiled Jattan opposition had found its homeland, it might have explained Lirrel.

Hredt had no idea where teeriks had come from. No teerik knew their distant past. Their species was *ablun*, but everyone called them teeriks, the Kugal word for creator, inventor, designer, engineer. They were repositories of knowledge and skills, and — to the humans at least — the ultimate engineers and physicists. But their genetic memories didn't seem to contain any traces of a culture before they came to Kugad.

What are we? What were we in the past? Yes, we look like raptors, but what were we when we evolved?

Hredt had read enough human history now to understand one thing about independence movements. They were all anchored to a time when a group of people believed they were a separate population with distinctive customs, however embellished or invented that belief might be. Teeriks knew they weren't native to Kugad, but they had no past to resurrect and no ancestral language to embrace. There was only the existence that Hredt and his commune had rejected.

Now they were free, but as dependent on the humans here in Nomad Base as they'd been on the Kugin. There *was* a difference, though, even if Turisu refused to see it. The humans treated them as equals and seemed to want them to be independent. Humans were fundamentally *just.* There was nobody here to force them to behave in a certain way, and the commune couldn't defeat them, so their actions had to be what they truly believed was right. When more of them arrived and their civilisation spread, they would eventually rival the Kugin and their client states, and erode their power, and that was good news for every nation that didn't want to be a Kugin vassal.

Hredt still had no doubts about what had to be done. Humans had to be supported and encouraged to spread by all means necessary. This was his purpose, discovered late in life but all the more powerful for it.

A burst of music from the screen jerked him out of his thoughts. The news bulletin had ended. He watched for a few seconds, expecting something new, but the broadcast just started repeating something he'd seen earlier, word for word and image for image.

It was time to resume work. He was due for another session of what Marc Gallagher called *debriefing* on Kugin and Jattan operations, but first he had something important to hand to Ingram. He'd spent the last couple of days collating information on the class of FTL drives being fitted to the Ainatio vessels parked in orbit, and he'd written it in English.

This was his gift to his human friends. It described everything Earth needed to build its own FTL ships that were equal to Kugad's fleet and become a truly spacefaring species, written in a format that human engineers could understand, a complete set of instructions they could simply follow like a manual. Hredt never imagined he would be willing to commit his knowledge to a permanent record. Teerik trade secrets, mostly kept in their heads, had always been their insurance against ill-treatment, and as far as the Kugin military industry was concerned, their skills were irreplaceable. Hredt had finally learned to see it not as a defence but as a source of power.

If only we'd tried to use it for ourselves.

He switched off the screen and gazed at the device for a few moments, suddenly afraid that he'd done something reckless. It wasn't too late to delete the documents. He fought down the panic and reminded himself that the world had changed forever when the humans arrived, and now teeriks had to change with it. He slipped his screen in the pocket of his jacket and left the compound.

The base seemed to be getting back to normal today, but there were still more bots around than usual. As Hredt crossed the grassed area at the heart of the base, referred to as "the green" by the humans, he could see the mechanicals moving around, slowing at intervals to eject sampling probes. The bots that monitored the base were a third of his height, small enough to be unobtrusive but large enough to be seen and avoided as they skimmed around buildings. It was the larger ones that he still gave a wide berth, from the giant construction machines and autonomous mining units to the four-legged animal-like models. They were harmless, but old habits died hard. Even Solomon, an emanation unlike any artificial mind the Kugin could build, was somehow intimidating in the quadrubot frame he liked to move around in.

Hredt dodged a monitor bot before it had the chance to avoid him. Any mechanical was a good deterrent, even if the humans didn't realise it. A Jattan or Kugin pilot, used to avoiding areas populated by mechanicals, would have taken one look at them and assumed the worst, just as the commune had when they first detected the activity on Opis. Here was an unpopulated world with mechanicals busy excavating and constructing. There were buildings, but they'd seemed to be factories or storage facilities. It looked like any automated mining or manufacturing operation, except it was on a world with a rich ecology, and planets like that generally presented more practical problems than conveniently barren, ready-to-mine worlds of rock and ore.

But the machines here weren't sentient. They were just an advance party of robotic equipment preparing Opis for human settlers, nothing like the mechanicals left on unpopulated worlds to carry out commercial operations as they saw fit. To those miner robots, any outsider who landed, organic or mechanical, was a legitimate target for attack. No unauthorised pilot who valued his ship — or his life — would attempt to land.

But we did, though, didn't we? We did exactly that, even before we knew the ones here were harmless.

It was a logical decision. It had been worth the risk to land here. The ship had the ability to bury itself in the ground thanks to the Jattan client's specific needs, and, to borrow Chief Jeff's phrase, nobody would *bugger around* with an army of mechanicals. This was a good place to hide.

Then the humans arrived.

Hredt didn't know why the commune had picked Opis. Planets much like this one were scattered everywhere. Opis hadn't even had a name until the humans revealed it to Hredt, and while it wasn't strictly in the Kugin sector, it was certainly within striking distance of the navies the commune was trying to evade. The Mastan — the Kugin sphere of influence — spanned nine star systems.

Hredt could think of only two reasons for the teeriks and a Jattan to come here beyond random coincidence. One was that Opis was somehow already on someone's charts and the commune had some ancient genetic memory of it. The second possibility was that he'd made a terrible miscalculation and the Caisin gate was actually producing a detectable signature after all, announcing their presence like a homing beacon to Gan-Pamas.

No, he was sure Caisin had never made mistakes like that. They'd activated the gate for a power test while they were still relatively close to the Mastan borders and nobody had come after them. Sheer coincidence was still possible, and Lirrel might have gone through exactly the same subconscious thought process as any other teerik and ended up in the same place.

Humans made decisions that way as well. Hredt had seen a movie, a type of invented history that humans enjoyed, where the enforcers of the law learned to think the same way as a criminal and predict where he'd go and what he'd do. Yes, it was possible. Lirrel might have simply followed the most likely route in the same way the commune had.

"Fred?" Chief Jeff was calling him. Hredt turned around to see him striding towards him. "Hang on."

"Have you found any contamination yet?" Hredt asked. "I'm going to see Captain Ingram. Is it safe for me to enter the building?"

"Yes, no problem, mate. How's everyone doing?"

"We're all well, thank you. On edge, as you would say, but healthy."

Jeff caught up and walked with him. "It's been a rough few days. It can't have been easy for you."

"Naming the prenu after Nina will help everyone come to terms with her death."

"That's a really decent thing to do, Fred. People here appreciate it."

"Anyway, I've watched the news from Earth," Hredt said. "I don't understand most of it, but the die-back incident is worrying. Could it really have reached us?"

"Sadly, yeah." Jeff shrugged. "You remember the Ainatio scientist who grassed us up to APS? The traitor who told them about Solomon and the other things we wanted to keep quiet? Well, that was Abbie Vincent, the same woman who smuggled die-back into Korea. We wanted to make sure we didn't have another one like her here. It's all clear of pathogens, though."

"I see. Would they tell you if they felt the way she did, though?"

"No. So we ask questions and keep an eye on them."

"I shall do likewise."

"Thanks."

Hredt was always impressed by the humans' skill in life sciences, even in misuse. Nobody out here could match that. "Could one of your scientists create a new pathogen?"

"Yes, they can. We wondered about that too. But don't worry, we're very vigilant."

"I meant could you make a biological weapon for use against our enemies."

Jeff hesitated for a moment. Hredt had learned to spot when humans were having second thoughts because what they wanted to say might meet with disapproval. It was always that breath held for a fraction too long.

"After what die-back's done to Earth, I don't think it'd be our first choice," Jeff said. "You can't control these things. They come back to bite you, believe me."

Hredt thought about that for a moment. It was a shame. Humans had the advantage there, and they really should have thought about using it. Perhaps they'd reconsider if it became necessary in the future. He changed the subject.

"I've completed all the documentation for the FTL drive, by the way," he said. "I'm delivering it to Captain Ingram now. I've never formally recorded anything like this before."

"Do you mean for our refits?"

"No, the drive documentation to send to Earth so they can build their own spacefolding ships."

"Ah," Jeff said. "Too complicated for me. Anyway, want me to drop in after work and keep Rikayl amused for a while?"

"That would be welcome. He likes the card game. We'll have fun."

They parted in the parking area at the front of the main building and Hredt made his way inside to Ingram's upstairs office. He knew she was there on her own because he could locate anyone with a radio on the Nomad interactive map. Allowing people to be tracked like that seemed excessively trusting, and before Gan-Pamas had shown up, Hredt would have taken it as another sign that that humans were too innocent and easy-going to survive out here. But then they'd revealed the violent side he'd learned about in the children's encyclopaedia at the very beginning, and it reassured him they could rise to the task in an instant.

Ingram's door was already open. She stood at her desk, arms folded, frowning as she read something on the desk-mounted screen.

"Ah, Fred, come in," she said, suddenly all smiles. "What can I do for you?"

Hredt indicated his screen. "I have some files for you, Captain." She'd told him to call her Bridget, but as nobody else seemed to, he still felt too awkward to use her personal name. "It's the FTL information for Earth. I think Annis Kim should check it and note anything that won't be clear to human engineers."

"Fred, thank you so much. That's wonderful. Is it on the network?"

"I'm sending it now. I know you think you might have traitors here, so please secure it. You don't want APS to acquire this."

Ingram checked her pocket screen. "Got it. I'm fairly sure we're okay, to be honest, but better safe than sorry. I'll limit access."

"I'll be available to offer remote assistance to Earth when needed."

Ingram raised her eyebrows while she poked at her screen. "I'm not sure they're ready to find out about intelligent extraterrestrials yet."

"They don't need to see me or know what I am. I sound passably human on an audio channel. When do you plan to contact them?"

Hredt accepted that humans would be shocked to see proof they weren't alone in the galaxy. But Chris had said most people had grown up with movies about alien civilisations and expected there'd be life on other worlds, even if the news might surprise them at first. He didn't think it would be a big deal. Some of the Nomad scientists seemed to take a different view. They thought it would panic the public and cause political chaos. Hredt found it hard to imagine being so isolated that the mere existence of aliens alarmed anyone. The time to run and hide was when they encountered a hostile culture.

"First we have to work out who we can safely share the FTL with," Ingram said.

"Your government, surely," Hredt said. "They'll know."

"Lawson? We have to give that some thought."

"You don't trust this Lawson."

"Oh, it's not him," she said. Hredt suspected she was going to repeat the concerns he'd already heard from Chris. "But not everyone's going to handle the knowledge sensibly or reasonably. Some are going to see it as a commercial opportunity or find a way to use it to attack their neighbours. We need to make sure we're handing it to someone who'll use it to save the maximum number of people, not the highest bidder. Then we have to work out *when* we offer it, because we could cause chaos by creating unrealistic expectations. People want help right now and can't wait years for it, but we can't absorb millions of people overnight. We'll have to identify other planets for them and it'll probably take years to build ships anyway. So it's much more complicated and untidy than just sending everyone a copy of your work and telling them to get on with it."

"I understand why you think using the Caisin gate to evacuate more people is unworkable," Hredt said.

Ingram spread her hands. "The only ready-made refuge is here, and we can't even accommodate the people in *Elcano* yet."

She was only repeating what he knew she'd said several times before in the last few days. He wasn't sure if she was polishing her argument like a Jattan legislator or trying to convince herself that not throwing the doors open immediately was the right decision. Hredt happened to agree with her. He wanted as many humans as possible to flood into the sector and beyond, but not at the cost of overwhelming Nomad Base, and certainly not so that it attracted attention before the forces here were strong enough to defend it against seizure by Kugin or Jattans.

"Very wise," Hredt said, estimating that the process might begin in a few months. "I'll help you identify other worlds that might be suitable for settlement as well."

"May I take advantage of your generosity again, Fred? I have a favour to ask."

"Of course. We're allies. What's good for you is good for us."

"Is it feasible to monitor Velet and Dal Mantir in the same way we're monitoring Earth?" Ingram sat on the edge of her desk. "You know, a probe in their region of space that could eavesdrop on communications. Knowing what they're planning would give us an advantage, obviously. Specifically, we still need to know how they found us and if they intend to come back."

Hredt thought about it. "They'll detect any probes eventually," he said. "We monitored Earth because we didn't think you had the means to do that, but the Kugin and Jattans can detect objects entering their planetary defence net, and while a probe is minute, it's always possible that they'll be lucky and spot it. It's a matter for you if you want to risk it."

Ingram looked a little sad. "Never mind. It was just a thought."

"If we managed to evade the net, we could probably intercept signals from one of their military relays," Hredt said. "Would you like me to investigate that?"

"I'd be very grateful, Fred. Thank you. If the Kugin found a probe, though, would they be able to trace us from it?"

"Possibly. The only signal worth worrying about would be the transmission of data back to Opis, so making that intermittent would reduce their chances of detection. But the best way to disguise the point of origin would be relays that eventually enter a Caisin gate. If they caught the downlink, they'd know a probe was accessing information, but it would be a Kugin-made one — ours — so it could have come from anywhere."

"We'd like Solomon to be able to hack into their comms. He's very good at it."

"I'm sure we can learn from each other."

Ingram gathered items from her desk and gestured towards the door. "I've got a meeting now, but we'll talk again later. Time to plan for the worst. I always enjoy that. Just like old times."

She said it with a smile and laughed to herself. Humans were eccentric, finding humour in dark places, taking risks they were hopelessly underequipped for, and confident they'd succeed if they persisted. But they also tried to help their own kind back on Earth, even when it made sense to forget them and leave them to their fate.

They were *civilised*. Hredt trusted them.

* * *

SECURITY MEETING, CO'S OFFICE, NOMAD BASE: SAME DAY.

"How are you feeling today, Dan?" Ingram walked up behind Trinder as he sat staring at the blank wall display. She patted his shoulder and manoeuvred around the seats to reach her desk. "Has it all cleared up now? Getting zapped, I mean."

It had been six days since they'd found Gan-Pamas's freighter laid up north of the base, but to Trinder it felt like it had taken a couple of weeks to live through them. The funeral had slammed on the brakes at a cliff edge. Maybe the upheaval was why he kept thinking about his family again, years after he'd lost contact and thought he had plenty of reasons for not trying to find them. If and when Nomad made contact with Earth again, he'd have no excuses left for doing nothing.

"Just lost my sense of elapsed time, Captain," he said. "Give me a few more weeks of boring paperwork and I'll be fine."

"Can't promise that." Ingram moved to the wall display. "Okay, chaps. I had a word with Fred about intelligence gathering. He says it's doable, but both Jattans and Kugin have a planetary defence net that could detect probes sooner or later. So let's look at our options and the risks involved. At least we're starting with a lot of knowledge about the enemy's capability — assuming they *are* an enemy — because we have the engineers who made it, as well as some of the hardware. But the enemy might not know we exist, or even plan to attack us if they do. Sol, you're quiet. Are you with us?"

"I am, Captain." Solomon's voice emerged from the speaker on the wall. "I just don't want to interfere with decisions."

"Do what you always do and tell us where we're lacking," Ingram said.

"Then I'm sure I won't have much to add."

"You're such a diplomat." Ingram held her stylus to the display and looked at them all expectantly. "So on the technical side, we're ahead. But we know nothing about enemy intent, except that if it's what Fred tells us, we don't have the numbers to hold off a sustained attack. The act of finding out if they're aware of us could expose us. Is it worth the risk? What happens if we just wait and see?"

Trinder held back out of habit just the way he'd always done at Ainatio. Marc, Chris, and Searle, lined up on a bench against the wall, looked like they had a shopping list of questions.

Chris opened the batting. "Whatever we do next, can we agree that our civilians come first?" he asked. "No sacrifices. None of them dies just to stop aliens finding Earth or hiding the technology. We evacuate them somehow, even if that means giving Earth a big surprise by sending them back."

"Well, we trashed Asia to save them last time, so twice makes it a policy," Marc said. "And this is a rerun of the APS situation. All the options cause collateral damage, but there's probably one where Nomad survives."

Ingram drew the start of a tree map and wrote HIDE, GO HOME, RUN, and FIGHT in a line across the top. "If I recall, running and hiding from APS weren't options because there was nowhere safe to hide and you had vulnerable civilians who wouldn't survive the running bit. You had the go-home option with the British airlift, but you thought APS would then target Britain because Tim Pham would still pursue Solomon. So the Kugin, Jattans, and possibly the Jattan opposition are the new APS, except going home will probably be more feasible because we could get away before they can track us by using the gate."

"Even if we could evade them here on Opis, it's taken the bots seventy years to make this location crop-friendly and safe for humans," Chris said. "It's probably impossible to relocate on virgin ground here at short notice. But you said it — intel's the difference between having ten years to fortify the base and Caisin-gating everyone back to Earth right now because there's a Kugin fleet inbound."

"Do we need a probe or something actually in their space to eavesdrop?" Marc asked.

"Apparently yes. Fred suggested using relays to bounce the return signal and eventually pass it through a Caisin gate so they can't track it back."

"And presumably they have probes too, which they can use against us."

"If and when they find us."

"Are we set up for detecting those?"

Ingram looked at Searle. "What have we got, Brad?"

Searle balled his hand to indicate a small sphere. "If it's a baseball-sized object in orbit like the teerik ones we've used, it's nearly impossible to sweep for them. But if it wants to come down and take a look around the base the way Fred's probe did with Kill Line — say to locate *Curtis* — then we could set up sensors to cover the footprint of the base up to a few hundred feet. Dome coverage."

"And they'll still know we're here," Ingram said. "But at least we get some warning. Do it, Brad."

"There's always Gan-Pamas's freighter for covert ops," Trinder said. "If you can't hide a probe, brazen it out and send something that's *meant* to be detectable and looks completely ordinary. The beat-up freighter act obviously worked for him, and he was trying to avoid the Jattan government as much as we are."

"You mean focus on the Jattans," Ingram said.

"Their navy's probably going be talking about recovering *Curtis* even more than the Kugin are. And Fred said the Jattan navy wouldn't make a move on us without Kugin support. We'll hear something. Two birds with one stone."

"Sol, can we operate the ship on autopilot without any leads back here?" Ingram asked.

"I'll check with Fred," Solomon said. "The real question is how I intercept their comms once I have a target. But I suspect Fred will solve that."

Ingram started writing again. "How long do you think this will take?"

"I can start today, but it could be weeks. The remote operation would have to be flight-tested, obviously."

Trinder was trying to work out if they could even resource all this at short notice. They had the entire natural wealth of a virgin planet, and the bot technology to manufacture almost anything, but not the bot or human numbers to complete everything at once. And each task had its own case for urgency — FTL drives for the Ainatio fleet in orbit, adapting *Curtis* for human crewing, hardening the base with bunkers and shelters, and manufacturing probes, weapons, and ordnance.

"We can't do it all simultaneously," Trinder said. "Better intel means we can prioritise. If we complete the FTL drive programme, then we can ship people out temporarily or permanently, but we can do that much more easily with the Caisin gate."

"But if the destination's Earth, we have to explain how we got back without mentioning the gate," Chris said. "If we're so out of options that the only choice is to go home, maybe it doesn't matter if Earth knows about it. We arrange to open the gate somewhere in Britain and rely on the discretion of the MoD."

"We could have done that months ago," Searle said. "Hand everything to the Brits and sit tight."

"But everything leaks in the end."

"If our priority's saving our civilians, we have to accept what happens if we go back and other countries find out what's been happening," Trinder said. "And conditions on Earth won't improve in our lifetime, so we'd still be looking to come back here eventually. Even if we find other suitable planets, look how much time and effort it took to prepare a few hundred habitable acres here."

"Seventy-plus years, God knows how much money, and all we got out of that was a base to accommodate a couple of thousand people," Marc said. "Sol alone cost a trillion or something. Even with a century of hyperinflation, that's a huge budget. Now Earth can't even maintain old technology. If there's still enough raw materials in the failed states that used to mine them, nobody can get at them. But if we open a gate to Opis, we've also opened the gates to a shitload of metals and minerals here and everyone's going to want a slice. My gut says it won't be any better than dealing with hostile aliens."

"I thought we'd knocked that idea on the head," Trinder said. "Opening the gate to escape is one thing, but opening it to let people in is a non-starter. We agreed that, didn't we?"

"You abstained," Chris said. "But yeah. You know where I stand on it."

"If I might interrupt," Solomon said, "an influx of unsuitable people is precisely what Bednarz tasked me to avoid. Harvesting resources isn't inherently wrong, but we'll almost certainly have APS muscling in sooner or later, because they're the only bloc that still has enough resources left to come to Opis and exploit the opportunity. Britain has the technology, but its resources are limited by its size. Adding to the guest list only puts you all in greater danger. Anything that threatens the well-being and continued existence and growth of this colony is counter to my instructions and personal objectives."

That sounded pretty final. Trinder was glad he agreed with Sol. This was the AI's warning to them not to throw Nomad away. Trinder hoped nobody decided to get into a spat with an AI who'd fought a one-man war against Asia.

"I think we'll have given up on Nomad before anything like that happens, Sol," Ingram said.

"But I won't give up. And I expect to exist indefinitely."

Trinder wasn't sure what to make of that. But if he'd spent a century working to deliver Bednarz's vision and someone was about to take a giant dump on it, he'd react like Sol, he was sure of that. Sol was immortal by human standards as long as he could find a platform to house his core. He wasn't a short-term thinker.

"Sol, mate, we don't want the riff-raff here either," Marc said kindly. "I'm just war-gaming. That's my job. Everything up for discussion."

"So where does this take us?" Ingram asked. She put the stylus down and parked her ass on the windowsill. "Do a little espionage, work out how long we've got, and in the meantime make sure we can fight on the ground? The best we can do if a Kugin-Jattan fleet arrives is fire up the nukes on board *Shackleton* or *Cabot* and try to take out a few. It's a slow job and they'll probably be able to deploy more ships than we have missiles. Our advantage is that we have their teeriks and their ship, which they'll want to recover, and Fred says Kugin usually land troops because they'd rather make a few bob from their conquests than turn them into molten slag. So perhaps no indiscriminate bombardment from orbit. Can we win on the ground?"

"For a while," Chris said. "Then it's a case of who can pour in more troops, and it's not us. But we should be ready for it anyway."

"They do accept surrenders, though."

"Maybe not from us," Marc said. "We'll be the new kids on the block swaggering in and stealing teeriks and ships, so they'll need to make an example of us. Fred said they were big on examples. They'll take what they want and erase us."

"Then we'd better be ready to ship civilians out of the combat area before that happens," Ingram said.

"That won't be many if we're training all those physically able to fight." Chris shook his head. "Are they drafted or not? I remember sending vehicles through the gateway and telling Kill Liners they weren't expendable and we didn't expect them to storm beaches or build empires."

"Have we actually forced anybody to take up arms?" Searle asked.

"Not yet."

"Then they're just being Americans. They're defending their home."

"I promised the folks my guys evacuated that we'd take them somewhere safe," Chris said. "I'm not going to let them down now."

Trinder couldn't tell if Chris was restating his reason to keep going or saying that was his red line. His voice never gave much away. There was almost no difference between him sounding completely calm and warning folks to back off. But he did get that grim look when he was really mad, like when he was itching to beat the crap out of Tim Pham, and he didn't have that now.

"If the worst happens, we can evacuate them," Marc said. "I think we're on the same page."

"Yeah."

"Look, before you go full Alamo on this, let's take another lesson from dealing with APS. Asymmetric warfare works. We shut them down. A poxy little village against a superpower. Okay, it was temporary, but the point was that we crippled them because Sol had one big card to play and he didn't hold back. We've got another big card now — the Caisin gate. I bet we've all thought what we'd do if we could go anywhere in a second and get out again. There's a lot more we can do with the gate if we get creative. It's not just transport."

"Yeah, we'd need to do something so big and so shocking that they piss their pants and decide to leave us alone," Chris said. "Which is what we said when Fred suggested it and Bissey got all pious with me."

"Exactly. But I don't think we've really joined up the two before — specific use of the gate for insertion and extraction. As long we've got the coordinates, we can breach any defences, assassinate any target, and sabotage any asset. Jump straight in and bang out again."

"Could Fred identify targets accurately enough?" Chris asked.

"I'm still debriefing him. But he's got maps of Deku. If it comes to it, we can hit them where it hurts. Yes, there's an element of bluff. They'd have no idea how it happened, they know nothing about us, and they won't know whether we've got a massive fleet on standby waiting to do a lot worse if they don't back off. They just need to know we did it so they get the message to avoid us."

Trinder noted how effortlessly the discussion had jumped from self-defence straight to pre-emptive strikes, and he'd escalated with it. He'd thought it was a sound idea at the time Fred suggested it and he still felt that way. If Bissey had been sitting where Searle was, he'd probably have said it was terrorism, and maybe it was, but Marc knew more about that than anybody here and he had plenty of experience in using unorthodox tactics in an existential war.

Maybe if Marc had been a complete stranger giving a talk at some staff college, Trinder would have thought it was a step too far. Civilised people had to have rules of engagement that stopped humans sliding back into savagery. But this was coming from Marc, one of the most decent and likeable guys Trinder knew, a man who knew exactly what loss felt like and who routinely put himself on the line. He was endlessly patient with a grieving kid, and had time for Dieter and Dr Mangel when they most needed basic human compassion. He was a good man. If he was willing to go that far against Kugin or Jattans, it couldn't be so wrong.

Your ethical standards mean nothing here. The Kugin will laugh at you before they kill you.

Fred kept telling them that. If the Caisin gate had sent them to medieval Europe instead of forty light years away, they'd have had to adopt the brutal standards of the day to stay alive. Back on Earth, Trinder had realised the only moral certainty he had left was the need to defend the people he cared about. Everything else was muddied and contradictory. All he could do was pick a side. He'd already done that when he agreed Solomon should sabotage APS's network infrastructure, knowing that it might well cost civilian lives.

"Dan, are you still with us?" Ingram asked.

"Sorry, yeah. Just thinking. I agree, we need to be creative. It'll take generations before we've got the numbers to defend ourselves by conventional means."

"Then we use what we've got," Searle said. "Much as I want to fly *Curtis*, we need to divert resources to building our own Caisin gate generator. Right now, we're entirely dependent on the teeriks and the ship. If anything happens to them or they change their minds about us, we're screwed."

"I was banking on having a second system in the base itself," Ingram said. "But I don't want to spook Fred and make him think we don't trust him, or that we've got what we want so they're all redundant. I'll have to explain it in terms of an emergency backup."

"But that's exactly what it is," Searle said. "And it's safer if it's *not* on *Curtis*. If the ship gets hit in a Kugin attack, we've lost everything. If the Jattans manage to seize her complete with the Caisin generator, then there's no limit to what they or the Kugin can do. We need the equipment in a bunker they can't get at, if only to evacuate the teeriks so they don't fall into enemy hands."

"That's for our benefit," Trinder said.

"Sure, but they don't want to be captured either. It's a persuasive argument."

Ingram nodded. "If any Kugin do manage to land, do we know how to kill them on the ground? Do they land vehicles?"

"Short of some crazy quirk we don't know about like them being terminally allergic to dairy, we've only got a few ways of killing anything," Chris said. "Nukes, personal weapons, artillery, and sharp objects."

"Fred reckons that if we can take out a tank, we can stop Kugin ground transport," Marc said. "If we're in a position to shoot them, then it's like the Jattans. They're physically tough and we'll need stopping power. Shotgun slugs. Tank rounds. Fifty cal."

"Jeff said Fred asked him if we could create bioweapons, because our life sciences are more advanced than anyone else's," Ingram said. "Jeff explained why we wouldn't be too keen on that. How *do* we feel, though?"

That stopped the discussion in its tracks. Even without the history of die-back, there were some things that seemed too dangerous even in an war for survival. Marc looked like he was considering it, though.

"We'd need to get Kugin tissue samples," he said. "I'd give that a go. But it wouldn't be a five-minute job to develop the stuff, and I'd prefer us not to go down in history as the tossers who exported biological warfare across the galaxy. Let's try to stick to introducing the natives to cricket, cucumber sandwiches, and blowing shit up."

"We need real-time Kugin and Jattan translation systems too," Ingram said.

"And when do we warn Earth about them?" Chris kept asking that. He wouldn't drop anything until he had an answer. "We've gotten so used to aliens that we're forgetting how big a deal this is. Earth doesn't even know there *are* any. At some point they have to know what's out here in case things go wrong and it ends up on their doorstep."

"Are you saying we should contact Earth but not give them FTL?" Marc asked.

"All I'm saying is we should warn them. The FTL issue's separate."

"I don't think it is. You can't tell people they need to look out for alien warlords on the rampage and then not hand over technology that might save them. For example, what if there's a way of using FTL to deploy really long-range missiles?"

"It goes back to what I said when you first suggested it," Chris said. "We're amateurs making decisions about things we barely understand and that affect billions of people."

"You've just described the average government." Marc sounded matter-of-fact rather than argumentative. "Look, we're the only grown-ups around now whether we like it or not. We made ourselves responsible for policy the minute we decided not to tell anyone about Sol, the Caisin gate, and where we are at the moment. We're now the politicians as well as the grunts who carry out their orders. And yes, I accept I'm more to blame for *not* telling Earth than anybody. I talked Captain Ingram out of passing this to the MoD at least twice."

"Actually, I've changed my mind again," Ingram said. "If we'd told your chum at the Foreign Office or I'd called the MoD, they'd have wanted to come here and we'd have had to tell them about the Caisin gate because it's the only fast way to get to Opis at the moment. What happens then? Pour troops and assets into Opis and leave Britain undefended? And what would we do about the millions they'd ask to evacuate? We're back to our first argument. If we have a massive influx of people, even spread over the course of a couple of years, this settlement can't feed them. So we sort out this problem on our own and keep Earth in blissful ignorance unless we find we can't, because I doubt there'll be a unified international response to this."

"Better that we find out what we can and then decide who'll be helped by knowing it, ma'am," Searle said. "I think this sounds like a workable plan."

Marc grunted. "Yeah."

"The devil's in the detail," Ingram said. "But I don't see a better way to do this yet."

"Sol, you got any thoughts on this?" Trinder asked.

Solomon would have a plan for when it went wrong, even if he didn't share it with them. He took a couple of seconds to answer. Trinder knew what that pause meant. Sol had made his position clear: he didn't want random humans turning up here. His job was to look after his chosen ones, and everyone else was at best a distraction and at worst a threat to the whole project.

"Protecting the population here is paramount," he said. "Ideally, not at the expense of Earth, as you say."

Ideally was doing a lot of work there. "So *Elcano*, then." Ingram took a few steps back and studied the board. "We leave them in cryo so we can at least evacuate them fast. Marc, how long is this debrief with Fred going to take? Because I'd like to have him working on the freighter with Sol as soon as possible."

"Give me a couple more hours," Marc said. "Shorter sessions seem to work better than one long interrogation."

"Very well. Anything else, gents?"

"Yes," Chris said. "We should have Doug Brandt and Alex along to these meetings now. Otherwise Kill Line and the scientists don't have a voice in security decisions. If we're asking them to stand and fight, they should be in the loop."

Trinder admired Chris's honest insistence on some kind of accountability. Ingram gave him that long, careful look disguised with a half-smile, the one that said he was a pain in the ass but she'd have to concede.

She had no real command authority any more, only the power of persuasion. Nomad's defence forces were more like a miniature international organisation, a bunch of commanders who'd agreed to work together for the common good but couldn't give each other orders. The majority of civilians on the base were American and they had no obligation to take orders from a defunct corporation or a foreign government. Ingram didn't represent either of those anyway. She seemed very aware of that.

"You're right, but let's avoid creating expectations that they'll have a veto on this." She still had that careful smile. "Anyone else?"

"No, ma'am, we're in full swashbuckling mode now." Searle said. "I'd like to be on friendly terms with the local aliens, but if that's not possible, we'll play to win."

"Good. I need a coffee. Have you got five minutes, Number One?"

Searle went off with Ingram and Marc disappeared, presumably to find Fred. Trinder wandered outside with Chris and leaned on the railing at the front of the building, watching the ebb and flow of activity across the green. He felt strangely deflated. The session must have hiked his adrenaline more than he'd realised.

Chris checked out a Caracal driving past and nodded at the driver. It looked like Lewis Conway. "We haven't really talked about what happened with Gan-Pamas yet, have we?" Chris said. "You and me, I mean. I didn't take the shot. We could have been burying you as well as Nina."

"You said the weapon wasn't on full power," Trinder said. "But that doesn't prove lack of intent, like Marc said. Anyway, I sighted up on him. He saw me aim. I was going to shoot him so it's my own damn fault for being slow."

"I'm sorry, that's all."

Chris was probably blaming himself like he did when Jamie Wickens was killed. It was too easy to think he was completely unemotional. Trinder knew he visited Jamie's grave every few days. He'd see Chris's icon moving on the map, usually first thing in the morning unless he was on duty overnight, and he'd spend a few minutes there and walk back. Trinder knew enough about the militia from what Erin told him to realise Jamie hadn't been Chris's closest buddy, just a young guy Chris liked a lot and felt responsible for. It wasn't hard to work out what was happening.

"Chris, we all had a chance to open fire right away," he said. "It was a weird situation. If we'd taken Gan-Pamas alive, we might have more answers now, but we'd also have a liability on our hands and we'd still be arguing about if, how, and when to kill him. It wouldn't have been a better outcome. Just different."

"Maybe."

"So why didn't you shoot? I'm not criticising, just asking."

Chris looked out across the green and shook his head. "I think I was caught out by how small he was, but it was when he started talking." He shrugged. "I wanted to know what he was really saying. Maybe I misread him completely and he really was doing what Fred said Jattans did, going out in a blaze of glory when he knew he was surrounded. But he said sorry. Fred said he kept saying sorry about Lirrel."

"We'll never know," Trinder said. "And I'd bet alien gunrunners lie just like their human counterparts."

"I won't be satisfied until Sol can translate for himself."

"Do you ever wonder if you're up to this?" Trinder asked. "I do."

"All the time."

"I always think you've got all the answers."

"As if." Chris slid a monocular out of his pocket and focused on the workshops, then put it away again. "I know what my job is. So I'd hate to be in Marc's position or Ingram's, because they've got a functioning country that might make good use of the information and technology we could give them. And maybe we should. I don't really buy into Sol's thing about the best of us and keeping us in some kind of sacred quarantine, but I don't want trash arriving here and fucking up a decent little town either. I've seen enough of it. But in the end, it'll be the Kugin or the Jattans who set the agenda. I just hope they let us know in advance if they're not the assholes the teeriks say they are. I'd hate to attack guys bringing us a welcome wagon pack."

"You don't trust Fred, do you?"

"I don't rely on a one-sided story. No matter how sincere it is." Chris turned and looked Trinder in the eye. "Are you beating yourself up about your family? I hate to be blunt, but cut yourself some slack."

"It's complicated."

"Yeah, I don't know what happened to my folks and I think I don't care after they washed their hands of me, but it's still on my mind. You want to tell me what happened?"

"I just moved a long way away to work for Ainatio, we weren't the kind of family that lived in each other's pockets, and then I didn't visit for a while. Then there were the epidemics, and the cities going bust and no cops or State Guard any more, and the calls stopped."

Chris nodded a few times like he was working something out. Trinder had never really discussed family with him and it was a minefield for most people anyway. He didn't know what else to say.

"Remember, I was the other side of the wire," Chris said at last. "Some people formed up into heavily-fortified communities and started their own militias, and some just tried to get by in what ended up as civil war zones. You saw some of the news at Ainatio for a while, didn't you? It wasn't pretty. So if you couldn't contact your folks on the network, buddy, there was no point in going out looking for them. You wouldn't have made it. That's what you're worrying about, isn't it? You feel you could have tried harder."

He was telling Trinder exactly what Trinder had told himself and it still sounded like an excuse.

"But Annis Kim made it to Ainatio from Korea and crossed the country from Alaska," Trinder said.

"Yeah, but she did it in the last couple of years," Chris said. "A lot more people were dead by then. Fewer assholes around to stop her."

It was brutal, but it was still what Trinder wanted to hear, even if it didn't feel like forgiveness. "Maybe."

"Dan, you did what you could, when you could. And if we end up rescuing anyone from Earth, we'll try to contact your family. Okay? I'll go with you."

Trinder knew the chances of finding his parents or his sister alive were slim, but the idea of them thinking he'd forgotten them had only grown worse since he'd come to Opis. It was seeing the *Cabot* crew dealing with the fact that surviving friends and relatives still thought they'd died forty-five years ago, and had never been told that the loss of the ship was another elaborate Ainatio lie to keep Project Nomad free of political interference.

"Thanks, buddy," Trinder said. "Damn, we're all broken people, just like Erin says. What kind of society are we going to create here?"

"One that knows the value of sticking together," Chris said. "And we're not going anywhere."

03

I went into astrophysics because I didn't want to believe Earth was all I'd ever understand, and I realised there was much more to be discovered than I'd ever see in my lifetime. There was a kind of hope in that, a future that would carry on when I was dust. And now I'm on another planet, digging its soil and watching its moon rise, and I don't have access to space telescopes or any of the sophisticated tools of my trade. I make do with a teenage boy's amateur telescope. And the cosmos has lost none of its wonder.

Dr Todd Mangel, former head of Astrophysics,
the Ainatio Corporation.

SUPPLY WAREHOUSE 5, NOMAD BASE: SEPTEMBER 25, OC.

"How the hell could you *not* know? What's going to happen to Audrey and Seb now?"

"Hey, it's no safer here. She made her choice."

The fight hadn't reached the stage of trading blows, but Solomon still found human arguments unpleasant to watch. Stephanie Bachelin, one of Ainatio's biomed researchers, was berating Gavin Huber from Die-Back Remediation about the Meikles, who'd decided to stay on Earth. Gavin was correct in every fact. Audrey Meikle *had* decided to ask APS for refuge in Sydney rather than take her young daughter to an unexplored planet, and her husband Seb had gone along with it. It was unfortunate that die-back was now spreading within APS and the decision now looked like a mistake.

The row was being conducted in whispers that sounded like animals hissing at each other before striking. The safety system had flagged an unusual sound profile for the warehouse and alerted Solomon to check it out, but it wasn't intruders or a coolant failure. He monitored it anyway.

Stephanie was furious. "You just don't care, do you?"

"What did you expect me to do about it?" Gavin whispered. "We *didn't* know what Abbie was up to, okay? And why was the crazy bitch my responsibility? What about her mom, *your co-worker*? And Seb worked in the same damn lab with Abbie. If you want to blame anyone for letting Audrey haul the family off to APS, try him."

"Aude thought they'd be safe. It was for their little girl."

"It's no safer here. It's a choice of die-back or homicidal aliens. But Abbie's not my fault or anyone else's."

"Fine, but now everyone thinks we're all genocidal maniacs too. And that's down to your sloppy lab procedure, because you should have spotted her taking samples. It's all on you. Screw it, we should open that gate and bring them here."

"Yes, brilliant plan. Pull the family out of Australia, which hasn't been infected yet and might never get it, and let them get fried by an alien navy instead."

They both stopped abruptly as if they'd realised they probably had an audience somewhere. The new grocery section within the warehouse normally had a supervisor on duty during the day and a few people wandering around picking supplies. It was Ingram's idea for getting the different groups to mix. If bots stopped delivering rations and everyone collected their food allocation from a central point that functioned like a grocery store, she said, the different social and professional groups on the base would run into each other like normal people did on Earth, which would help break down the barriers that had already formed.

Solomon remained unconvinced. Meeting neighbours didn't always mean a friendly chat.

The section was a canyon of tall shelves, but Solomon's access to the security cameras showed him who the audience was. Damian Shure, one of Trinder's troops, had paused while picking groceries for Mrs Toft, an elderly lady from Kill Line who he'd given a ride to. Near the front exit, Dave Flores, acting as stores supervisor for the morning, looked up slowly, craned his neck, and began walking towards the scene of the fracas as if he was going to make sure things didn't get out of hand. By the time he reached the shelves, Stephanie and Gavin had parted and were leaving in different directions. Dave ambled up to Damian.

"Are they all at each other's throats now?" Dave asked.

Damian shrugged and went back to consulting his shopping list. "I think the die-back guys are getting it in the neck from everyone."

"Weird." Dave scanned the trolley's contents and studied the stock control figures on the display. "We never busted their asses when they lost the virus and infected Kill Line. Maybe we should have."

"Hey, you brewing any more of that porter ale yet?"

"Maybe. Had enough of Andy's gin, huh? Help me out building the bar extension and I'll start a batch for you."

"It's a deal."

They laughed. Solomon was glad to see his detachment getting on well with the Kill Liners. But then some of them had ended up moving into the transit camp zone, where the boundaries with Kill Line had mostly vanished. It was also encouraging to see them looking for opportunities to be sociable. Bots could have print-built the bar extension in a day, but Kill Line wanted to do it the old-fashioned way. Humans enjoyed bonding while doing constructive things. Solomon had never had the opportunity to study the behaviour of regular people before, and after a century surrounded by scientists and technicians, and lately military personnel, the lives of ordinary civilians seemed quite exotic.

Solomon would let Alex know about the spat in case it escalated. Marc had predicted months ago that the ease of using the gate would make people see it as a way to fix problems on Earth, and if anybody had a case for covertly returning to rescue friends, it was him. For others, though, the Caisin gate would always offer an easy way out, and that would make it harder for them to see Opis as the centre of their existence rather than an outpost looking over its shoulder at Earth.

It was a lot to ask. Solomon knew that. He suspected Opis had to be lived in, built upon, and become the birthplace of generations before the settlers would begin to feel this was where they were meant to be. But this wasn't about opening up new territory, at least not for him. It was about preserving special humans, and anywhere safe and habitable would serve the purpose. Opis was just the best place to do that for the foreseeable future.

Solomon moved his focus back to the quadrubot, still idling at the perimeter to the south of the base. He was going to go for a run. He hadn't done that for a long time, and he'd missed it. In the years after the FTL relay was established, long before *Cabot* arrived, he'd upload himself to a quadrubot on the surface a little more often than was necessary just for the joy of racing across the open plain.

He surveyed the landscape before moving off. This was where he'd first seen the teeriks and not realised they were intelligent; this was where he'd start his run and race flat out for a while, keeping an eye on the quadrubot's backup charge if he went out at night, thrilled by the impact of his feet on the ground and the way it shook the bot's frame. Disabling the sensors and stabilisers that gave him steady three-sixty-degree vision made running even more visceral. He could only see what was ahead of him, like a real terrestrial predator. After so long as a disembodied mind, the cruder experience of having a body and compensating for its shortcomings made him feel *real*, more in touch with the humans he cared for. This was their chaotic existence, constantly being shaken by movement and brushed by objects around them.

It was also reassuring. Solomon still recalled his early development when he thought he was a being like Bednarz and the lab assistants, and didn't understand why he had no physical connection to the world he could see. A hundred years later, he still felt better for touching solid reality and knowing that it wasn't a simulation.

He started to trot, then picked up speed. In daylight the undulating plain looked much busier than at night, even without the nocturnal creatures. It was packed with bushes, small animals, and divots in the grass. Splashes of dark red, green, and blue-grey vegetation jerked around in his field of vision. By the time he reached the bot's top speed, thirty-two miles an hour, he felt like he was being shaken around in a bottle. He wasn't even sure where his feet were hitting the ground. It was exhilarating. Eventually he reactivated the orientation system to make his vision compensate for movement and slipped back into a sensation that felt more like gliding a few feet above the ground.

The view of the mountains in the distance was intriguing. Like so much of the world, they had no names yet because the decision was to be left to those who'd settled here. Solomon was happy to deal in precise coordinates until that happened. But nobody had ventured more than a few miles beyond the wire when Ingram had lifted the lockdown, and it wasn't a lack of curiosity. They still needed an armed escort to go off-camp, and there were too many other tasks that took priority after Nomad's overnight explosion in population. If they were honest, even the most adventurous here would admit they were wary of straying too far when hostile aliens might show up at any time.

Soon, though, they'd need to explore properly. The satellite network could show them detailed aerial views of the whole planet, but that wasn't as thorough as exploration and it wasn't the same as setting foot on undiscovered land.

How about the Caisin gate?

It could set down anywhere. If Marc was considering it for sabotage missions, then its ability to pluck people to safety would work equally well for survey teams. There — Solomon had fallen into the trap. He was as seduced by the technology's potential as anyone else. And he wanted to explore for himself instead of seeing Opis as a stream of meteorological and seismic data, and imagine what it would look like in two hundred years when the human population had grown and perhaps founded other cities around the globe.

His friends would be long dead by then. He'd outlived many people in his existence and mourned them, but he knew he'd take the passing of the men and women here far harder. His life before had been Bednarz, but now he had a circle of friends, humans he'd shared real hardships and possible death with, a *family*. For a moment the sadness of it overwhelmed him, but he shook it off and headed out towards the river that ran past Nomad to the northern coast. He hadn't reached his turnaround point before the site safety alarm paged him again. Something had passed through the perimeter without authorisation.

It had travelled out of the camp rather than crashing into it, so it wasn't a crisis. A quick check with the sentry drones that had been flying continuously since the Gan-Pamas incident showed that it was Rikayl. The minor shock from the barrier field didn't seem to dampen his enthusiasm for exploring.

Solomon stopped and turned around. Rikayl was heading in his direction, so Solomon calculated a return track to intercept him. As he loped back, he looked up at the sky and wondered if the small flying creatures circling high above him ever landed. He'd never seen any on the ground or in trees. For the time being, he'd call them birds, but they looked nothing like teeriks. They might even have been large insects. But that was another huge field to explore; the various invisible barriers around the base, the bare earth cordon zones, and seventy years of eradication by bots had made Nomad a desert for native creatures. There were no brightly-winged insects or other wonders to marvel at inside the wire.

Eventually a drone image showed Rikayl swooping down to a clump of bushes two hundred yards ahead. A storm of small animals erupted, scattering across the grass and fleeing in all directions — speckled rodent-like creatures with kangaroo tails, egg-shaped things springing randomly into the air in all directions, and the small long-legged animals that Erin had nicknamed guinea pigs. Thrashing red wings shook the foliage. Everything was suddenly still.

Solomon slowed to a walk and went to look. Rikayl had caught something. When Solomon got close enough to see what it was, the teerik already had it gripped in both hands, tearing chunks out of it like a slice of melon.

His meal was one of the bouncing eggs. It turned out to be a creature with grey feathery scales and sturdy little legs that Solomon had seen scuttling around when the drones surveyed the area. But he'd never seen its escape strategy of rolling into a defensive ball as it sprang into the air so that it bounced unpredictably when it landed. Rikayl paused to look up at Solomon with a scrap of the egg creature hanging out of his beak, swallowed the chunk, and fluffed up his neck feathers as if he was indignant at the interruption.

"That might not be safe for you to eat," Solomon said. He'd had little contact with the youngster but it was worth talking to him as if he understood English, because he was picking it up fast. "Have you eaten these before? You know we have to check to see if food's safe for you."

Rikayl held out what was left of his meal. "Fun!" he said, in Jeff's voice. "Fun fun *fun*!"

Solomon debated whether to try to stop him eating, but he'd already swallowed most of it, and he'd put up a savage fight if any of the veterinarians tried to examine him. A teerik couldn't do much damage to an industrial quadrubot frame, though. Perhaps it was worth trying to separate him from his snack.

"You're learning more words, Rikayl," Solomon said, edging towards him. He reached forward very slowly with his left front leg, gripper attachment open. "Shall we go back to Nomad, then?"

Rikayl tilted his head on one side and rasped, then took a warning peck at Solomon's leg. "Mine. Shoo!"

It was a different voice again. He was mimicking everyone he'd heard now, and the *shoo* sounded like Chris.

"Okay, Rikayl," Solomon said. "You can keep it. Now will you come back with me?"

Solomon knew that if he ran off, Rikayl would want to chase a fast-moving object for the thrill of it, but it had to be done carefully. If

Solomon spooked him, the teerik might fly further out and this time Solomon could lose him. Solomon turned away and started trotting towards Nomad, keeping his speed down to give Rikayl a chance to catch up, then picked up his pace. It was only when he broke into a run that he detected Rikayl coming up from behind. Then he was flying at head height alongside, level with Solomon's head. He still had a chunk of meat clutched tightly in his hind claws.

"We have to test that food, Rikayl," Solomon said. He sent a message to Commander Haine to stand by for collection. "Don't drop it."

"Good boy!" Rikayl said. "Good good *good* boy!"

For a moment Solomon thought he was saying he'd been a good boy and done as he was told, as a child might, but he was mimicking the voice of Dieter Hill, the dog handler. Rikayl thought Solomon was some kind of dog. Perhaps he was even mocking him. It was undignified to get into arguments about terminology with a child, though, and Solomon bit back his urge to say he wasn't a dog. He preferred to see his bot persona as a cheetah because that was how it moved. But it was a pointless thing to concern himself with.

He maintained his speed. "I'm an *emanation*," he said, using Fred's term for an AI. "Solomon. Emanation. In a quadrubot mechanical. Understand?"

"Alright really," Rikayl said, keeping station effortlessly. This time he sounded like Marc. "Alright fun."

Whatever Solomon had done, he'd placated Rikayl and intrigued him enough to lure him back to the base. Rikayl sailed straight through the insect barrier field and didn't even flinch. It was probably time to have a word with Chris and add more physical measures like dedicated drones in case something larger than Rikayl and equally barrier-proof showed up unexpectedly.

Commander Haine was waiting by the hangar with Nina's former deputy, Helen McArthur. She was holding a large bowl. Rikayl's senses must have been better than the quadrubot's, because he diverted at top speed towards Helen immediately, leaving Solomon wrong-footed. It looked like the teerik was going to crash into her, but he dropped to the ground at the last moment and walked a few steps with his head down before stopping at her feet like a supplicant. Whatever was in that bowl had his attention. Haine searched in the grass, holding a lab container in one hand, and picked up the discarded chunk of egg-creature.

"What was this poor soul before it was so cruelly taken from us?" He held the transparent box up to the light, inspecting the contents. "This could be a luxury export one day if it's not poisonous."

"It's little four-legged creature that rolls itself into an ovoid," Solomon said. "About twice the size of a hen's egg. I assume the shape dictates its defensive strategy of bouncing randomly like an asymmetric ball when attacked."

"Not much of a defensive strategy for this chap, then, was it? Still, that's four to a supermarket pack. We'll make our fortune in exotic gourmet meat."

Rikayl was polishing off half a roast chicken — the alluring contents of the bowl — while Helen watched him with a rather sad expression. She seemed to have taken on her late boss's mantle when it came to Rikayl. When she reached out and stroked the teerik's head, Solomon fully expected her to lose a few fingers, but Rikayl tolerated her interruption and said, "Alright, really!" in Marc's voice.

"Good boy," she said.

Rikayl shook his head emphatically. "No no no, *Sol* good boy."

"Bless. That's quite an impression of Dieter." Haine smiled. "You've clearly established a rapport, Sol."

Solomon tried not to bristle, then was surprised that such an impossible physical reflex had even occurred to him.

"No, he's saying that he's not a dog, but I am."

Haine just laughed and walked off with Helen. Rikayl took to the air and headed in the direction of the teerik compound, leaving no trace of any chicken carcass, so he must have eaten the bones as well. If the bouncy egg creature didn't make him ill, it proved teeriks had robust biochemistry.

"I'm sorry, Solomon." Fred had come out of the hangar with both hands full of probes and cables. He was wearing a short white lab coat, human-style. "I know Rikayl went roaming again. But we had a drone tracking him this time. What did he do?"

Solomon was fascinated by the lab coat. Someone must have spent considerable time altering it to fit Fred, because it hung on him like the brown jinbei-style jacket he wore when he was working. The overall effect softened him into a child's storybook character. His resemblance to a familiar bird and his incongruously human clothing and equipment made it far too easy to see him as a harmless pet, like a dog wearing a little sweater. That wasn't a trap Solomon would fall into, but he could see the humans here succumbing to it.

The only people who didn't get that oh-how-cute look when they were with Fred were Jeff Aiken, who treated him like a shipmate, Marc, who seemed to see him as a stubborn subordinate he needed to whip into shape, and Chris, who didn't trust anything or anybody.

"He killed a small animal and ate some of it, I'm afraid," Solomon said. "They're running tests to see if the flesh is toxic."

"He's too big and energetic to lock up now." Fred had a habit of drooping his wings in a way that made him look like an exhausted human. No, it wasn't cute. Solomon wasn't influenced. "Perhaps we should trust him to come home, but if he's found a new game and something to eat, he might not."

"Let's see what happens," Solomon said. "Anyway, I see you have a lab coat now."

Fred adjusted the front with his beak. "Lieutenant Commander Hiyashi said I ought to have one because I was a *boffin*. I thought that was very kind. I take it *boffin* is positive."

"It is. You're one of the gang now. They must like you."

"I've almost finished adapting the freighter's autopilot. You can connect to it remotely now. Would you care to look?"

"Of course. Thank you."

Gan-Pamas's ship was cramped even by Jattan standards, but Solomon could move around relatively easily on all fours because there were no ladders. The interior was a single continuous deck broken only by a couple of hatches leading down to the cargo space, and he didn't need to access that. The freighter was, as Marc described it, the Jattan equivalent of a delivery van, except for its impressive military-grade defence and intelligence-gathering refinements, almost none of which were apparent from the outside except the stealth cloaking system, and even Fred had to examine the hull closely to see that.

Solomon studied the display on the console. He could see the difference in the symbols from the last time he'd been in here trying to decrypt logs with Fred, but he still didn't have enough data on the Jattan language to tie symbols to sounds.

"Can I test this?" Solomon asked.

Fred attached an adapter to the console, the same type that enabled Solomon to link to *Curtis*'s systems. "This should provide an approximation of the data you'll see when it's operating remotely. You can input courses with a numerical pad if you want your human colleagues to be able to use it."

"Ah." Solomon rotated a leg to place the connection into the quadrubot's panel at the base of its neck. He could now see a three-dimensional chart of Dal Mantir space. "This is an archived chart, I take it. You're not actually connected to a satellite."

"No, this is a standard chart, the kind that all off-world traffic uses. The ship's still not linked to anything externally."

"Just checking."

"I haven't re-enabled the communications system yet."

"Very wise."

"So we can now insert the ship using a Caisin gate closer to Dal Mantir and pull out the same way," Fred said. "Nobody can track it unless they actually pass through the gate with it. If they happen to intercept the ship in Mantiri orbit and manage to board it, they're likely to assume that it's the exiled opposition spying on them and deal with it on their own."

"All we'll be looking for is an early warning that they've located us," Solomon said.

"I've given that some thought and the best route is via the Jattan intelligence services. They commissioned *Curtis* and they've lost her. They'll almost certainly have tried to keep that quiet because of the humiliation and the risk of rival departments capitalising on it. So I think they'll be discreet and send out an inconspicuous task force, possibly assembled some distance from Velet or Dal Mantir, but whatever they do, there'll be a lot of discussion and planning, and therefore noticeable comms and ship movements."

Solomon was reminded again that Fred wasn't a simple engineer. He understood his clients' office politics. "You're suggesting we spy on spies. That does make sense."

"The division that commissioned the ship is more akin to what you might call the secret police than to espionage agents. They're responsible for dealing with external threats from other nations, countering internal threats from within in the Protectorate itself, and keeping its off-world colonial interests under control — putting down independence movements, for example. We can take an educated guess about the departments which will be talking to each other about this."

"And you can intercept that?"

"I think the easiest way is to establish a link with naval headquarters and then watch their fleet reporting centre, which tracks all Jattan vessels, and transmit the data back via their link to one of the weather satellites. If we can pin down the personal communications within the complex, then we would have even earlier warning of any movement."

"And how do you establish that initial link?"

"We have most of their access codes in order to work on the ship," Fred said.

"But don't they realise teeriks also designed the algorithm to change the keys?"

"I meant the Kugin codes."

"I'm lost, Fred."

"The Kugin spy on all their allies as well as their enemies, and we have the knowledge to use that to infiltrate."

That was new. Solomon understood Marc's frustration with how little information Fred volunteered. "Presumably the Kugin wouldn't warn the Protectorate someone might use it to spy on them. But when you took the ship, they'd have changed all the keys you had access to."

"It's an open secret," Fred said. "The Jattans would be fools to think it didn't happen, but doing something about it is hard. It's not just the technical challenge of blocking Kugin infiltration. It's the risk of being caught trying to look for it, because they wouldn't want to upset them. As for changing keys, we look after that as well, so we can probably predict what the new ones will be."

Alien politics seemed as convoluted and as messy as Earth's. "Wouldn't the Kugin expect you to do this, though? If they haven't changed the codes, it might be a trap to detect you."

"No, they would expect us to avoid all contact, which is what we were doing before you arrived here," Fred said. "They'd have no reason to think we would return to Dal Mantir or even Velet space and put ourselves in danger, nor would they know we'd have use of another ship to do so, or that we wanted to spy on the Protectorate in the first place. They won't expect any of this."

"They thought you were obedient," Solomon said. "Now they know you're not. Are they too stupid to allow for that?"

"I'm sure they didn't think we'd find people willing to help us. Or that those people would have a motive to track their search for the ship."

Solomon couldn't fault his argument, but they had to take the risk anyway. He tested the chart by inputting coordinates directly from his core. It worked as far as he could see.

"When can we test this in flight?"

"Allow me two more days."

"It's excellent work, Fred."

"Starting the monitoring may be easier than maintaining it. We'll be waiting for something that might take years to happen."

"They'll still keep searching for the ship."

"Yes, but they might not find a reason to look on Opis."

"I think that's optimistic," Solomon said. "You found the planet, and then Gan-Pamas did as well. Why wouldn't the Protectorate and the Kugin end up here too? There seems to be some kind of common thread that brings others to our front door."

"It was the Jattan opposition that found Opis, or at least someone who procures arms for them."

"I don't see why that makes a difference. But in that case, perhaps we should try locating them first."

"That's a much more difficult task," Fred said. "And it won't tell us when the Protectorate makes a move."

"The opposition would be spying on them. We would pick up something in their chatter if that were the case, surely."

"There's no guarantee of that."

This was a convenient moment to steer the conversation back to Gan-Pamas and what he'd actually said in his final moments. Chris was uneasy about it. Even if his talent for knowing when something was wrong was pure folklore of the kind humans found reassuring, Solomon at least owed him an answer. It was potentially a sensitive topic. Fred might think he wasn't trusted, and also feel threatened if he saw Solomon taking his role as an interpreter.

Solomon was relying on the skills of one of the dumb AI systems that he managed. He was making a big assumption that all Jattans spoke a form of the same language, and that it might have a number of variations depending on region, the age and gender of the speaker, and the social situation it was used in, like many human languages. If he was wrong, then any translation would be unreliable.

So far, the linguistics AI had used the Jattan call to surrender that Fred had drafted to identify enough fragments of the language to build the structure and outline a grammar. It had then used that to analyse the conversation between Fred and Gan-Pamas. But vocabulary was patchy, and that was where subtle details mattered.

"I'd like to learn Jattan properly," Solomon said, unplugging the connector and passing it back to Fred. "And Kugin, so I can automate the surveillance. A language course. The kind of information that Jeff Aiken gave you to help you learn English. But I imagine you never needed to keep that kind of module."

Solomon hoped that would either show Fred how harmless and necessary it was to learn a language, or shame him for being unwilling to extend the same courtesy to Solomon that Jeff had extended to him.

"I'm afraid not," Fred said. "As you said, we don't need to."

"Could you go over a few details for me, then? Would you mind? I have the message you recorded for Gan-Pamas, telling him to surrender, and the exchange between you when he was captured."

"Of course."

"Can you remember what Gan-Pamas was shouting?"

Fred paused for a moment. "Yes, all of it. I did as Chris requested and asked Gan-Pamas why Lirrel had killed Nina. He said he was sorry that it happened and that he couldn't trust Lirrel. He kept saying that to Chris, too — 'I couldn't trust that teerik' — but he didn't realise I was one until I told him. He could only hear me, after all. I asked him if he'd told anyone else that we were here and what he'd found, and he called me a traitor and a few other insults. I kept asking him why Lirrel had to kill Nina and he kept saying he didn't realise how much Lirrel had changed. I didn't understand what that meant, but presumably he'd trusted Lirrel in the past but his behaviour had altered over time."

"Insults. Such as?"

"*Mekika.* It's not a word we hear often in our work — monster, abomination, hateful thing, animal. In a negative sense." Fred cocked his head, staring at the bulkhead as if he was recalling a sequence of events the same way a human would. "He said... 'I know what you are, and they'll find you no matter where you run, I'm sorry about the killing, I shouldn't have brought him.' That didn't mean much to me, I'm afraid. Then he started saying, "You have no idea what this is and what's actually happening, so let me tell you.' But that seemed to be addressed to Chris. Then something panicked him — Major Trinder, I think — and he opened fire."

"Those exact words."

"Yes. I'll write them down for you."

"Thank you." Solomon now had a few more words to work with, but he also had a more confused picture of the argument. It almost sounded as if Fred hadn't fully understood the Jattan.

"Was he speaking a dialect?"

"Well, it wasn't the form of Jattan we'd usually hear. It was more like the difference between Chief Jeff and Commander Searle. They both speak English, but they speak it differently — different terms for things, different grammar, even different meanings for the same word. It's not all the time, but sometimes enough to confuse me."

"I know what you mean," Solomon said. It didn't look as if Fred was being evasive or unhelpful, nor had he forgotten anything. He simply wasn't sure what Gan-Pamas meant. "Language is full of pitfalls and misunderstandings, even if we believe we're speaking the same one."

Solomon would relay all that to Chris, and maybe it would settle things for him. The part about Gan-Pamas telling him he didn't understand what was going on would probably provide more questions than answers, though.

"When do you think more humans will come?" Fred asked. "The sooner you increase your numbers, the better. You need to consolidate your position here before the Kugin find you."

Ingram hadn't told Fred the technology transfer was on hold for the foreseeable future. Solomon did his best to be non-committal and not dash Fred's hopes before work was complete on the base defences.

"We have to find the right people to give it to first," Solomon said. "They have to be able to build ships, and they have to be willing to bring the right people out here — not a few pampered elites, but hard-working people who can build cities and defend them." That was true, but Solomon knew it would strike a chord with Fred. "And we should identify another planet for them, because there might be contamination from die-back if they're not careful enough with biosecurity. Not every human is going to be good for the sector, Fred. We have to be careful."

And there was the lie.

Solomon had managed to tell the truth right up to the point where he said they'd be selective about who could migrate from Earth. He'd be very selective indeed, probably much more than Ingram would be. It was essential that they didn't recreate the old Earth here by importing its problems.

"I understand," Fred said. "Chris said exactly the same thing to me."

Solomon was grateful for that cover, but there was one thing Chris probably hadn't revealed to Fred. Solomon had his selected humans right here. His sole task was to protect and nurture this enclave of moral, courageous, neighbourly, intelligent but genuinely ordinary humans so that they multiplied, but their selflessness made them want to help the very worst of humanity, and it would be their downfall. If he ever found others who met the same standards then he would consider them, but that wouldn't be achieved by allowing a free-for-all. He couldn't have Nomad Base overrun by people who embodied none of those qualities.

Tad Bednarz had told him to use his judgment and not be diverted from what he'd decided was right and just. It was a task Bednarz said he couldn't entrust to humans after his death, let alone two or three successive generations of them. Only an autonomous, self-determining moral AI with a theoretically indefinite lifespan would remain unmoved by threats, bribes, petty jealousies, and sheer loss of motivation to do what was necessary.

He was right. Solomon was as passionately committed today as he was then. His moral position was even clearer. The last year had shown him the reality of what Bednarz had tried to teach him about the difficulty in deciding which ends were justified by which means, the eternal human dilemma. Solomon now knew there was no pure ethical position to be taken in anything, and that he had to face what Chris and the others called the least bad option, the path that did least harm. He was comfortable with that. Trying to achieve a perfect absence of consequences was setting himself up to be knocked down.

He'd picked a side, and his humans took precedence over all others. Humanity was just a concept with no personal names, no faces, and no dreams, but the people here had all of those and he knew them. He'd do whatever was necessary to protect the best of humanity, even if the choices he might have to make would look harsh to future generations.

Others might have to pay the price. He'd keep it to the necessary minimum.

* * *

KILL LINE: 0730, SEPTEMBER 30, OC.

"Ohhhh… *luxury*." Chris let the jet of hot water hammer against his face, then turned the controls to a rain setting. He would never tire of having his own shower. The novelty of a private bathroom still hadn't worn off and he doubted it ever would. "Awww, man… "

He was talking to himself a little too much these days. Maybe it was something to worry about, but it was still kind of weird living alone in a house after being constantly surrounded by people in prison, in army bases, and then in the transit camp. He knew folks thought he didn't talk much at the best of times, but there was a silence created by not hearing other voices that demanded to be filled.

On the other hand, maybe he *was* going crazy. He was spending way too much time trying to analyse Sol's translation of Fred's conversation with Gan-Pamas.

Sol had now teased more language detail out of Fred and put together a transcript, which Chris had copied carefully onto a big waterproof card and stuck to the shower wall. He thought better in the shower. But it wasn't helping today.

F: *Why did your teerik kill Nina? Why did Lirrel kill her? She was my friend. She meant no harm.*
GP: *That was unfortunate. I apologise. It shouldn't have happened. But I couldn't trust that teerik. You can't trust them.*
F: *I'm a teerik too.*
GP: *You're the traitor, then. The one who stole the prenu. And you're a mekika. You shouldn't be allowed to exist. (Note: monster, abomination.)*
F: *Have you sent any messages? Have you told Nir-Tenbiku that you're here, that we're here?*
GP: *I know what you are. And they'll find you wherever you run. But I'm sorry about Nina.*
F: *Why did Lirrel have to kill her?*
GP: *I'm sorry about the killing. I shouldn't have brought him. It wasn't my intention to harm anyone. I didn't realise how much he'd changed. (Pause, possibly addressing Chris) You have no idea what this thing is, so let me tell you.*

And that was the end of it. It must have been the moment Gan-Pamas saw Trinder raising his rifle. It accounted for the length of the exchange, at least. Gan-Pamas had repeated himself, possibly struggling to get his point across, or panicking, or perhaps Fred sounded as if he hadn't understood him. But Fred had absorbed and learned perfect English in a few weeks and now spoke it better than most humans, so why would he struggle with Jattan?

Maybe he wasn't exposed to it often enough. For all Chris knew, teeriks' conversations with clients might have been conducted via their Kugin foremen, and they'd be discussing highly technical stuff with a lot of jargon. It was possible that he didn't have the vocabulary to understand all the nuances. Chris had known guys who could talk about their business in Spanish but couldn't manage casual conversations about football. If Fred only ever had to talk about machining tolerances and shear forces, he might never have come across emotionally charged language.

One thing was clear. Gan-Pamas didn't like teeriks and he didn't trust them. That was understandable. They'd stolen a prototype stealth warship, and he shared the Kugin view that they were serfs who ought to know their place. But the stuff about how much Lirrel had changed was weird, and what did he mean by *'you have no idea what this thing is'*?

Perhaps he was actually saying something like *"Do you know who I am?"* and warning Chris that he'd pissed off the wrong guy. That would have made sense. Fred said Jattans were basically up themselves and full of shit, although that didn't quite fit with someone who kept apologising. The tone of Gan-Pamas's voice gave Chris no clue to whether he was angry or agitated. But he'd seen the guy's body language, and most people could look at an animal's movements and tell if it was upset, scared, or aggressive, regardless of species. Gan-Pamas had looked like a guy pleading for his life. He hadn't opened fire right away — another thing Chris would have expected from Fred's assessment — and he'd probably only shot Trinder because he thought Trinder was going to shoot him. Even Trinder said as much.

Chris would come back to it again later. He needed to forget it for a while until something occurred to him, and in the end maybe there'd be nothing mysterious to discover in it anyway. He was dealing with aliens.

He towelled himself dry, then flexed his right knee and studied it. It was hard to think of it as a regrown section, but it was new bone and soft tissue from a few inches above the knee to a few inches below it. It looked like it had never been blown apart and shattered. It didn't even feel different now. There were a couple of faint scars, but whatever the wraparound device that Dr Mendoza's team had bolted onto his leg had done, the shredded parts had regrown like new.

And Abbie Vincent's mom had developed that gizmo.

The irony of his brief and awkward contact with the Vincents wasn't lost on him. If they were in a Korean prison now, it was down to him, and he wasn't sure how he felt about that. Debora and James Vincent had been questioned by Korean police, the news said, and moved to a place of safety. That sounded like prison, but maybe it was a safe house, because the neighbours couldn't have been overjoyed to find the American refugees next door had a psycho daughter who'd released the worst crop plague in history and that they might starve to death.

He had to face it. The Vincents were there because he'd told them they'd need to go to Korea with Abbie if they wanted to see her again, although he hadn't said it was because they'd be forty light years away by bedtime if they didn't. It was true, but he didn't want them in Nomad Base either. The whole family was a stew of contagious unhappiness and conflict that the settlement didn't need.

He never used to beat himself up like this. What had happened to him? It wasn't his fault that Abbie was a genocidal dipshit who didn't get on with her folks. He'd been scrambling to evacuate a town, and APS could have borrowed a spare nuclear bomber at any moment. Offloading the Vincents was another thing he couldn't change now and needed to forget. They were all adults. They'd made their choices.

Chris focused on the firearms class he was due to teach this morning. He held up his clothes on hangers. Civvies, or regulation black tactical? He opted for tactical. If it wasn't too warm outside, he'd wear his new sheepskin jacket to the staff canteen for breakfast instead of eating here alone. Ingram was probably right about making the different communities mix. The canteen and the stores seemed as good a way as any to run into people you would probably never see, even in a settlement of fewer than two thousand people.

Chris took the sheepskin jacket off the hook and brushed it down with his hand. The weather wouldn't be wintry for another six months, but Marty the sheep farmer had made jackets for him, Trinder, and Marc as thanks for looking after Kill Line's civvies back on Earth. It had really touched Chris. The guy had culled his flock on a false alarm and he could have been bitter and angry, but he wasn't, and Chris wanted to show him that he hadn't stuffed the jacket in his closet and forgotten about it. If there'd been a point when he realised he might become a normal guy who'd want to be part of a wider community for the simple happiness of it, and that not every stranger was an asshole or a threat, it was when Marty handed him that jacket. He put it on, slung his rifle, and went to open the front door.

There was a folded sheet of paper sitting on the mat, probably delivered during the night. Anyone could have messaged him on the Nomad network, but Kill Line still liked to do some things the traditional way, and this was a formal notice of elections. The town was carrying on as it always had and holding polls on November 10. The flyer listed the due dates for nominations, and said that because November wouldn't be affected by calendar changes, the final ballot would take place on the same day it always had, November 10. Alien warlords, potential terrorists, and Earth's woes hadn't stopped Doug Brandt and the council from getting on with the daily business of living. Chris suspected he'd like being part of all that.

He also noted that there was going to be a ballot for the new position of sheriff. That was interesting. They'd never had one before, at least not while the transit camp had been there. Chris didn't really know how the town had dealt with law and order. In the short time he'd been able to observe the townsfolk at close quarters, he'd never seen any sign of crime, petty or otherwise. A population of one thousand and eighty-eight — one thousand, one hundred, and ninety-one now that the transit camp had merged with the town — was bound to have the occasional incident. But Hart County looked like perfect peace to evacuees who'd fought their way out of anarchy and civil chaos, and they'd only lived with the Kill Liners for a few months under the kind of tough circumstances that forged cooperation. That wasn't long enough to judge.

A sheriff, huh? Chris would make sure Dieter knew the job was open. They had enough ex-cops here to start a proper PD. He put the leaflet in his pocket.

As soon as he mounted the quad bike and set off, he realised it really was too warm for the sheepskin. But he had to be seen to be wearing it, and he took it off only after he parked in front of the flagpoles.

Someone had installed a self-cook counter in the canteen at the weekend and it was pretty busy. It was probably another of Ingram's social engineering projects, designed to let people hang around for a while to chat while omelettes and the like were cooking. Chris grabbed some pancakes from the hot counter and pondered over the translation of Gan-Pamas's exchange with Fred again while he ate. Then Fonseca walked in.

Chris did his best not to meet her eyes. Marc was right. He was barking up the wrong tree, and even if he had a chance with her, it would be a continual quest for her approval. He had to give it up. She sent out too many mixed messages and he was tired of working out how to navigate the maze. Nothing had happened between them anyway. It was still all in his head and it was time he got a grip.

But she headed his way anyway. If it was possible to hear smirking, he did, because everyone in the canteen was watching and probably placing bets.

She stood right over him. The last time anyone had done that, they'd tried to smash his head into the table but Chris had got his uppercut in first. He pushed his chair back slowly out of habit.

"Hey, I thought you'd gone into hiding or something," Fonseca said.

"Hi Lennie."

"Where have you been? I haven't seen you for ages."

"Weapons training. Got another class in twenty minutes."

"That doesn't account for twenty-six hours a day."

"Okay, I built a sun lounger and a barbecue in the yard, because I learned carpentry and welding in prison. And I still cover night patrols. And I've been working through a massive backlog of crappy movies with Jared and Marsha. And I like my new shower and I sleep a lot. It's awesome."

"A regular social whirl, then. Did you shelve your plan to go looking for interesting rocks?"

"Yeah." Chris knew that if he weakened now and asked her if she wanted to take a drive off-camp and look at geological formations — which he really did want to see — he'd feel like a bewildered schoolboy trying to work out what he'd done wrong in algebra class for the rest of his life. It took a real effort to shut this down. "Well, I've got to churn out a platoon of cold-blooded killing machines now. Catch you later."

"Okay. Have fun."

Chris slid his plate into the dishwashing station and left. He wished he'd played that differently, but at least he could see some shreds of his tattered self-respect floating to the surface again. He rode down to the warehouse that had been taken over for the indoor range and opened the doors to find he had fifteen people already waiting, more than he'd planned for, including a few more familiar faces — Annis Kim, Alex Gorko, and Reverend Berry. The turnout was a good sign but now he had to call in Matt McNally to help to do the instruction.

While everyone waited for Matt to show up, the class had questions about the targets hanging at the far end of the warehouse. The Jattan figure had been produced using Gan-Pamas's anatomical details, so it looked pretty realistic, but they didn't have a dead Kugin to work from, so it was based on Fred's sketch. The sketch had been thorough, like everything teeriks did, but when it was scaled up into life size and transformed into a three-dimensional fibre moulding, the thick-set biped with multiple black spider eyes looked more cuddly than homicidal, and didn't have the sobering menace Chris had hoped for.

The Jattan was freaky because it had that weird eel-like head sunk into its shoulders and spare arms like tentacles, but it was five feet tall and that took the edge off it. Maybe Chris should have stuck with human figures. It was probably a better way to get folks to overcome their reluctance to use lethal force. If you could shoot a fellow human, you could shoot anything.

"It'll be like killing a kids' cartoon character," Alex said. "It's Mr Hippo. You want me to mow down the Easter Bunny too?"

"If he's armed and hostile, yes," Chris said.

Annis Kim chuckled and gave Alex a fond look. Chris knew she'd taken a shine to him after he'd swung a few punches trying to rescue her, but they seemed a lot closer than that now. It probably explained Alex's unexpected fitness drive and subsequent weight loss. Well, that was nice. There was hope for everyone, maybe even for himself.

"Okay folks, when Matt arrives, we'll make a start," Chris said. He unlocked the crate of upgraded carbines, re-tooled to take a heavier calibre. They could modify and print any amount of these now. "Basic safety lesson first, obviously, but we don't want you to be afraid of firearms. They'll save your life. Once you've got your safety drill down pat, you can shoot your first... hippo. And remember the only reason to carry a weapon is that you're willing to shoot someone dead in the process of stopping them from doing harm. There's no shame if you realise you're not ready to do that, because if you can't take the shot in a real situation, you're a liability to your buddies. Speak up if you feel that way."

If Chris was addressing new troops, he'd have added that not being willing to shoot the enemy would get your buddies killed, and you'd be on your own if push came to shove. But these people hadn't come here with an expectation of having to mount a defence against alien forces.

Matt arrived and the session began. Kim and Berry did well on checking, loading, and stripping down weapons, but Kim had been trained to use a handgun in her APS spy days and Berry looked as if he'd handled rifles before. The encouraging thing was how seriously everyone took it. After a break for coffee, they put on their ear defenders and took their first shots in earnest. They had some way to go, but they all looked like they meant it. Chris nodded at Matt. Matt nodded back. Yeah, everyone was going to be okay. Nomad Base had the makings of an expanded army and there was no shortage of spirit.

Now all they had to do was to keep training until the rifle became part of them. Solomon would add them to his nag list and make sure they turned up regularly.

At midday they'd have to go back to their day jobs. Chris took a gamble. There was no good time to do this, because he didn't know if and when there'd be a Kugin patrol ship inbound.

"Those weapons are now your personal property," he said. "You're responsible for them and the ammo you've been issued with. I know it's all new and scary, but now you've checked they're unloaded, take them home, read your course notes tonight, handle the weapon, and be ready to come back tomorrow, same time. You take your weapon wherever you go from now on. You too, Alex. I know you stuck your sidearm in your desk and forgot about it, but that's not an option now."

"I'll sleep with it under my pillow," Alex said. "I don't want Mr Hippo to get me."

Matt sidled up to Chris as everyone filed out looking shell-shocked, some clutching their rifle like it was a live snake.

"You sure about that, Chris?" he asked. "What if we get some NDs?"

"What are we going to do, wait a couple of months until they're competent? We might not have that time."

"They won't even remember how to load the mags if we get a Kugin visit now."

"Maybe. But the alternative is getting invaded tonight and their weapons are all locked away. Besides, they're all sensible enough and old enough to know this is serious. We've all seen guys rise to the occasion with almost zero training."

Matt nodded. "Okay."

"If I'm wrong, I'll bust myself down to private and Jared can take over."

Martin Berry had hung back. He was still sitting on one of the benches with a coffee when the rest of them left. Chris got the idea that he wanted a private chat. He'd looked the most competent guy there, good enough to persuade Chris that he had some experience. He knew how to strip down the carbine right away and he showed good form and muzzle control. He wasn't a bad shot, either. Chris examined the targets again.

"Good grouping, Reverend," Chris said, poking the holes.

"Thank you."

"Where did you serve?"

"I didn't. And I never thought I'd want to pick up a weapon again."

It sounded like the opening of a reminiscence. Chris waited for him to go on and explain, but he didn't.

"I suppose I should ask why," Chris said.

"It didn't work out so well last time." Berry drained his cup. "I gave it up, but I don't think I can sit this out if the worst happens. I have the skills so I should use them."

"You don't have to tell me," Chris said. "It's none of my business."

"From what I hear, we have a lot in common."

"Unless you wanted to be a geologist but you ended up as a major disappointment to your parents, I doubt it," Chris said.

The guy sat there in his zip-up blue jersey and dog collar, looking like a favourite uncle who always showed up on the holidays and gave you the feeling that he'd never tell you off no matter what you said or did. Chris knew nothing about him. Even Doug didn't know his background and hadn't asked, just as they hadn't asked about Chris and his militia. Berry had drifted into Kill Line thirty years ago from New England, Doug said, and as they hadn't had a minister for some time, he was checked for infections and welcomed. If Chris had been around then, he'd have wanted to know how Berry found the place and why he was displaced, but it was common for folks to go on the road to get away from cities in the process of collapsing. Chris's convoy had ended up at Kill Line without intending to as well. It was plausible luck.

"Will you be offended if I speak frankly?" Berry asked.

"I'm very hard to offend, Reverend."

"You were a hitman, yes?"

"No, I never actually killed anyone for money. And State Defence duty doesn't count. I killed for revenge when I was a kid, though."

Berry didn't look fazed at all. "I see."

"Okay, maybe not wholly revenge. I was sick of being scared all the time so I decided to become the threat." Chris had made a point of having no secrets. If anyone asked, he'd tell them. It was surprising how many people didn't, but word finally seemed to be getting around and it was almost a relief. "I used to work for a guy who funded shady businesses. If they were late on their repayments, he'd send me around to discuss rescheduling their loan. I never killed any of them, but I did cause them pain. And then I got busted. Ten years for felony assault, cut short by the State Defence Force needing cannon fodder."

"Did you have a hard childhood?"

"Not at all. White-collar. Gated community, a good education, a respectable family. No excuses. I stabbed a guy from a local gang who beat my buddy and left him brain-damaged, and maybe I didn't plan to kill him, but I didn't care if I did. And I didn't get caught. I was nearly fifteen, and yes, I knew what I was doing."

Chris didn't expect Berry to recoil in horror because ministers were supposed to listen compassionately to all kinds of shit and still feel a man could be redeemed. But he didn't expect him to have that look of sympathetic regret, either.

"I shot my buddy," Berry said quietly. "He was banging my wife."

Chris was shockproof these days but that came as close as anything could to making him blink. And he could relate. "How long did you serve?"

"Five years, out in three. Involuntary manslaughter."

"Okay."

"No, it wasn't. I meant to do it. We were out hunting and I confronted him. To the cops, it just looked like I was careless about checking my line of fire. I stuck with that story. Obviously, things were such that I didn't have a marriage to go back to anyway, so when I got out, I thought I'd better address the state of my soul."

That was some confession. "If you could go back, would you do it again?"

"No, if I could undo it, I would. You?"

"I'd still do it." Chris nodded at Berry's dog collar and indicated an imaginary line around his own neck with his forefinger. "You weren't clergy at the time, then."

"No, that would have been pretty awkward with the Boss. But I did a lot of thinking, and that's where I ended up."

"Okay."

"I kept meaning to tell the Kill Liners."

"If they'd wanted to know, they'd have asked," Chris said. "But they never do because they can guess you've got a past, and they'd rather believe in the person they know now than the one they didn't know then. Which counts as forgiveness, I suppose."

Berry looked Chris over as if he was trying to read him. "So what changed you?"

"I haven't changed. I just found the right place. It was the military. It was the first time I belonged. I had purpose, I could trust the guy next to me to have my back, and I could trust myself to have his."

Chris felt he'd talked himself out for the day. Berry spent a while staring into his cup.

"You can call me Martin, you know."

"Can I ask you a general question?"

"Sure."

"How come Kill Line doesn't have any crime? Statistically speaking, a thousand people are bound to have a few bad apples. But they're electing a sheriff for the first time."

"Peer pressure and very active councilmen," Berry said.

"Citizen justice, then."

"The occasional punch in the mouth between neighbours. They're not saints, Chris. They're just dependent on each other and there's no anonymity in a town that size. It's the way small communities have always been."

"I kind of like small," Chris said. "Maybe it's worth the price of everyone knowing your business."

Chris was being literal, but it occurred to him that Berry might have taken it as a sly rebuke. He didn't react.

"Have you spoken to Marc about that memorial yet?" he asked.

"Yeah, I have," Chris said. "He's thinking about it."

"That's good." Berry patted his shoulder. "Thanks for listening. I've wanted to tell someone for a long time but I felt it was like kicking my neighbours when they were down. Y'know, that they had a seriously flawed minister when they needed some absolutes in their lives. I feel better now someone knows what I really am."

"You're a guy who changed," Chris said. "That's what you really are."

"It's time I told the rest of Kill Line, I think."

"They'll understand. But don't do it until you're ready for their reactions."

Maybe Berry really did think it was only fair to tell them about his past, but Chris suspected some of them might not appreciate knowing. Like the guy had said, everybody needed their untarnished icons.

"I hope I haven't burdened you with unwelcome knowledge, Chris."

"Not at all. But I kind of expected to be the one doing the confession. Sorry, that's Catholics, isn't it?"

"I try to cater for all denominations in such a small community."

"We should have a beer some time," Chris said. "Just remember not to beat yourself up. A good man is someone who saves more lives than he takes."

Chris had never imagined he'd be giving half-assed life lessons to an ordained felon. In a way it was weirder than working with aliens. He collected the quad bike and set off for the dog pound to find Dieter and give him the news about the sheriff's post, if he hadn't seen it already.

Chris was halfway up the road before he realised that the one word neither he nor Reverend Berry had used in that conversation was *murderer*. That was what they had in common. Chris wondered if his parents had realised what he'd done and decided the topic was closed, but now he'd never know.

* * *

NOMAD BASE, NORTHERN BOUNDARY: 1450 HOURS, OCTOBER 5, OC.

"Call me ungrateful, but I think that old banger's going to be more use than *Curtis*." Ingram shielded her eyes against the sun and watched the small Jattan freighter circle over the grassland north of the base, completely unmanned. It was remarkably quiet and easily overlooked even without its stealth cloaking. "We could probably do with a few more of those."

Searle, Devlin, and Hiyashi watched with her. If everything went wrong and the Jattans spotted the surveillance, the most they could do was board a Jattan vessel with no point of origin. They already knew they had a disgruntled rebel faction to worry about. Nomad would lose a surveillance asset, but there would be other options.

The real issue was that Nomad was now attempting to engage in espionage with a species they hadn't begun to understand, and what was routine between nations on Earth could have completely unpredictable consequences out here. But Ingram had to know. Nomad needed an early warning system.

"Are we all set up for monitoring Opis space now?" she asked.

"It's not perfect," Solomon said, "but Fred's identified the likely course and where ships would need to exit spacefold to deploy landing craft. I've programmed the relevant satellites to cover that corridor. Plus the sensors on all orbiting ships."

"But they could still land elsewhere on Opis and we'd miss them," Searle said.

"And they'd miss us. If they're coming, they're coming here on the basis of specific intelligence that would include our location."

Nobody spoke for a while. Everyone's eyes were fixed on the ship. Ingram asked herself if she was making a terrible mistake that would backfire, because this was her last chance to abort the operation. But if she did, it wouldn't be any easier when they decided to do it in the future. They hadn't started this mission equipped to fight a war, despite their nuclear missiles, and they had zero expertise in first contact, although they'd managed to establish good relations with the teeriks by muddling through. On the other hand, nobody on Earth was an expert on extraterrestrials or could deal with a threat of this nature either. There would have been little point in seeking advice or calling for backup even if the issue of contact wasn't fraught with other problems.

It was a joint decision with Trinder, Marc, and Chris. She still felt solely responsible.

"Solomon, are we ready?"

"We are, Captain. Fred will open a gateway and place the freighter seven hundred and fifty thousand miles from Dal Mantir, deploy an instant comms relay for my link, and the ship will then proceed to planetary orbit under its own power."

Here we go. "Very well. Chocks away, Solomon. Or whatever the launching in mid-air command should be."

The freighter slowed to hover above the landscape for a few moments, then edged forward again and disappeared as if it was flying slowly into fog. There was nothing to see of the gate itself against the sky, not even the faint blurred patch that was visible at closer quarters. There was something almost disappointing about how simple and low-key such a prodigious feat of engineering appeared.

"The freighter's now at the exit point in Dal Mantir space," Solomon said. "Launching the comms relay now."

It took seconds. For all the astonishing physics, moving the freighter a few light years towards the centre of the galaxy was the easy part. Solomon now had to wait for the ship to reach Dal Mantir's holding orbit for commercial transport, a kind of parking zone kept clear of manoeuvring vessels, before he attempted to infiltrate the Jattan navy's network. It would be some time before he knew if he'd succeeded.

"That's the drone deployed, so I'm now moving the freighter to its final orbit," Solomon said. "Fred, you can close the gate."

The small comms relay was now transmitting Solomon's remote link to the ship. It was too small and too far from the planet to be spotted, but if anything went wrong, Solomon could kill the signal and there'd be no way of tracing its origin, other than a Kugin manufacturer.

"Let's get back to work, then," Ingram said. "Good luck, Solomon."

"I'll only speak to you if I have a problem, Captain. I'll maintain radio silence until I penetrate their network in case the system can detect me and track back to here."

"Look on the bright side." Ingram climbed into the rover's passenger seat. "If that happens, at least we'll know they're coming."

Searle drove back to the main building, frowning as if he was working something out. Devlin sat in the rover's rear seat with Hiyashi.

"I know the Caisin gate is our star technology," Devlin said, "but imagine what it took to create an AI — an autonomous, emotionally functional AI at that — who can learn an entirely different code for an alien computer system and operate in it. I know how Solomon does it, in principle, but that still doesn't stop me marvelling at Bednarz's skill."

"I'm still stunned by the automation," Ingram said. "We're just the wildlife here."

"Mechanicals rule."

"Perhaps we should plan how to deploy them all and hide ourselves if Fred's right about pilots being too scared to land on bot planets," Hiyashi said. "Break out the sapper bot for Sol, too. We've got it, haven't we? Don't tell me they left it at Ainatio HQ."

"Yeah, it's here," Searle said. "But maybe we need bots that behave like theirs."

"We've got autonomous CAVs and point defence on the ground."

"They don't look intimidating enough. I'll ask Fred to show me some of the alien ones."

"You're serious, aren't you?" Ingram said.

"I'm willing to try whatever it takes, ma'am."

"I'll design one with you, Brad," Devlin said. "I've always wanted to build a killer robot."

Illusion had always played a part in warfare, so Ingram wasn't about to dismiss the idea. She imagined a tidal wave of enraged bots advancing on the first wave of Kugin ground troops. They'd certainly slow the advance if nothing else.

"I never saw my naval career ending up here," she said. "Robot wars and talking crows."

"*Fighting* crows," Searle said. "Cosqui really tore into Turisu yesterday. I thought they were going to peck each other's eyes out. I think she's run out of patience with her."

"Every ship's got a misery-guts," Ingram said. "Turi's theirs."

"Sure, but this looked serious. Cosqui's pretty easy-going. I've never seen her mad. She did the whole red crest display like a cockatoo."

Everyone was bound to be anxious now, even the teeriks. Ingram would have a word with Jeff Aiken and see what he could do about reassuring them. When she got back to her office, the first thing she did was check the news channels for a sitrep on the die-back situation on Earth to see how guilty it made her feel today. It wasn't about Korea or anywhere else in APS. It wasn't her problem, and there was nothing she could do about it even if it was.

She concentrated on the UK news and tried to read between the lines to assess the situation, allowing for what the media wouldn't have been told and what they'd get wrong. So far, the government had stepped up coastal patrols and was monitoring changes in vegetation via satellite. It was business as usual for an island that hadn't succumbed to die-back or invasion yet.

Ingram sat scrolling through the menu on her screen without really seeing it. Unless she did something positive, she'd be better off not knowing at all, although she needed to keep an eye on the global situation because of the ship's company who'd come from APS states. They'd be upset. Perhaps discipline would finally collapse and they'd demand to contact someone back home — distant relatives or much older friends, people who still thought everyone in *Cabot* was dead.

No matter how thoroughly they'd prepared for what was effectively a one-way mission, and the fact they'd been selected because they had no immediate family ties, events on Earth during forty-five years of cryo had changed everything. Ingram not only understood the need to touch base with home but felt an urge to do it herself, to find someone who'd known her all those years ago and say: *I am not dead.* It was all a lie, a cover story, and right then she hated Ainatio and Georgina Erskine for maintaining that deception. It would have been so much easier if she'd been allowed to call Earth and say they'd made it.

It wouldn't have solved the problem of what else she'd have to tell Earth now, and how much that would complicate the situation. But she could at least prepare for that day. She tapped out a message to Fred.

You mentioned that we could identify other habitable planets for settlement. I'd like to select one now and start sending out bots to evaluate them for modification the same way they've done here. Is that feasible?

She propped her screen on the desk and carried on watching the news, this time the APS-based stations. It was all images of closed borders, shuttered supermarkets with rationing notices on the doors, and cancelled transport. She felt as if Solomon's sabcode had wrecked APS's network infrastructure a long time ago, but it was only a couple of months, and Asia was probably still recovering from the knock-on effects of that when the die-back outbreaks started.

She pitied the ordinary people who were on the receiving end and had no idea why this was happening to them. But all this strife, no matter who'd started it, had sprung from the last remnant of Ainatio: a few hundred people and an AI, all that was left of a once-global company that had transformed Earth with automation and AI, but whose sole purpose was to fund human colonisation of space. Tad Bednarz wasn't responsible for what one sociopathic employee had done when he was long dead, but if Ingram drew a simple flow chart of events, the lines from Asia's current situation led back to him. It suddenly seemed uncomfortably close and personal.

A reply from Fred popped up on her screen. He'd embraced the art of the memo as seamlessly as he'd learned English, and for a moment Ingram missed the entertainingly frank pidgin he'd first spoken as much as Jeff Aiken did.

Captain,

There are two potential uninhabited planets within twenty light years of Opis, although you should not regard yourself as limited by distance. Srale is probably within the parameters for human colonisation, although its polar ice caps are currently at their maximum extent and would limit settlements to the equatorial zone. I will survey the planet by probe and generate more detailed data for you to study. I think this is prudent and appropriate planning on your part.

"Fred, there'll probably always be a job for you in the Civil Service," Ingram said to herself, and sent her thanks.

No matter how many times she thought about the situation and reached the conclusion that there was no immediate help Nomad could give Earth, she still had an optimistic daydream of setting up a parallel colony on another planet to provide refuge for those who needed to escape and commercial opportunities for those who would otherwise want to strip-mine Opis, all without upsetting Solomon's plan to keep the undesirables away.

Now she had to tell Searle and the Gang of Three what she had in mind. She copied the conversation to them and started clearing the rest of the messages and reports that had landed in her inbox during the morning, trying not to worry about what was happening to the freighter.

She started getting replies about fifteen minutes later.

Empire builder, Marc wrote. *God Save The King, but we're not paying taxes.*

Trinder asked about the impact on bot availability if they were still going to complete the FTL drives on the orbiting ships, and Chris just commented that it would at least give them more options. Searle asked if she'd changed her mind again about making contact with Earth, which suggested he still hadn't absorbed the reality of her having to reach agreement with Marc, Chris, and Trinder as well. She had the ability to defy them, but she could only do it once, and she didn't want to.

There was another message from Marc a few minutes later.

By the way, I'm serving lamb jalfrezi tonight, RPC 1900 sharp. Mild bc Howie's got to eat it too but hot pickle will be available. RSVP.

Ingram wasn't going to turn that down. She couldn't remember the last time she'd done anything purely social, and memories of a curry beyond the generic MRE variety were lost in the mists of time. She was working out which form of alcohol to take with her — Andy's gin, Kill Line beer, or some of her vintage plunder — when Jenny Park tapped on her door.

"May I have a word, Captain?"

"Certainly, Jenny." Ingram indicated the chair opposite her desk. Jenny was one of the civilian food technicians, a job which now carried the status of minor nobility, but Ingram didn't know her as well as she should have. Jenny was Korean, though, and Ingram could imagine what was on her mind. "What can I do for you?"

Jenny sat down and clasped her hands on her lap as if she didn't know what to do with them. "You know I come from the area where die-back broke out, don't you? Honam."

"I do, yes."

"I'm finding it hard to watch what's going on in Korea now. I still have family there as far as I know. Is there any chance we'll be allowed to make contact? I know we can't help them, but it's really troubling me that everyone thinks I'm dead. Members of my wider family will still be going to the trouble of commemorating me. It's a duty, you see."

Ingram was just surprised that it had taken so long for someone to ask outright, but everyone now watched the news and it had tipped the balance. It was inevitable. Stopping the crew from accessing TV would only have made things worse.

"I understand," Ingram said. "I suspect everyone feels the same way. I certainly do. I'm trying to find a way to do that without making the situation worse on Earth or compromising security here. But I'm sure you've thought through what the effect would be when people find out there's another habitable world but they can't reach it."

"And that's before we mention aliens." Jenny had always seemed spiky and argumentative, but she seemed rather ground down now. "Yes, I've done all the what-ifs."

"As I said, I'm trying to find a way."

"But some people on Earth do know we're okay, don't they?"

"Meaning?"

"The British government was going to airlift people from the Ainatio research centre. People talk, Captain. And I heard that Marc Gallagher arranged a call to APS for Dr Kim to talk them out of bombing the centre when the lab let their live die-back virus escape. So there's been some contact with governments and they must know people were still heading to Opis."

"Do you want me to be completely open with you?" Ingram asked.

"I'd appreciate it."

"I don't know if my government knows we survived, but I suspect they've guessed. They certainly don't know we're actually on Opis or anything about the Caisin gate. I don't know what APS knows, but everybody here knows their science and technology commissioner has probably worked out most of it, and he wants to shut us down — Solomon, the base, the whole Nomad project. Right now, I don't have a way of contacting Earth without starting some sort of mass panic or conflict, or creating expectations we can't fulfil. But when I do find one, restoring family contact will be a priority."

Jenny stared back at her as if she was waiting for her to go on, then realised she wasn't and blinked a few times.

"I know it's a mess," she said. "What if we called but said we were somewhere else, somewhere on Earth?"

Ingram did her oh-really expression, looking over the top of imaginary spectacles. "That would take quite an explanation. It probably wouldn't hold up long."

"Okay."

"Would it help if we tried to locate your relatives? At least you'd know who was still around in the meantime. Solomon's very good at hacking into databases."

"That would be very kind," Jenny said, visibly disappointed. "Thank you."

"Give me the details you have and we'll get on it."

Ingram wasn't going to kid herself that was going to be enough. When Jenny left, she realised she wished everyone had decided to forget Earth existed the way they were told to when they volunteered for the mission. Earth became an idea, the civilisation they were undertaking the mission for, not specific individuals. That way Ingram didn't have to think about what was happening to the family estate under her cousin because none of it existed any more.

But now she thought about it quite often. The moment a two-way connection with Earth was re-established, even if it was just stealing sat TV, it all came flooding back. If it was going to be tough for her, she could only imagine how bad it would be for some of the Ainatio staff. They'd lost contact with friends and relatives in other parts of the country and had no idea if they were dead or alive, and they couldn't even look for them.

But now Nomad Base had the technology to do these things. Humans had never been much good at ignoring possibilities. Both Marc and Chris had said the Caisin gate was a temptation to make bad decisions.

Ingram tried to put it out of her mind for the rest of the afternoon. There was enough to keep her busy — worrying about Solomon's attempts to infiltrate Jattan comms, working out what she'd do when it was finally time to revive Georgina Erskine and the rest of the Elcano passengers in cryo, passing Peter Bissey in the corridor and acknowledging him as if he'd never told her she was a war criminal — and if she filled the time well, she'd be able to move straight into a pleasant dinner with Marc and Howie, which would ground her by reminding her what was at stake.

Nomad had to come first. It wasn't about discovery or scientific research. It was about building a community. That was what she'd signed up for. That was her undertaking to everyone here.

By 1730, she hadn't heard back from Solomon. She knew he was still functioning because she could spot all the tasks he managed still happening like clockwork, but they'd agreed that he'd stay off the net. It wasn't for security reasons. She just didn't want to keep asking him what was happening, because even if it didn't distract an intellect that could multi-task in a way no human could, she knew it would irritate him. As long as he said nothing, things weren't going wrong.

But now curry beckoned. She tarted herself up for the evening, which in Nomad terms meant exchanging navy working rig for a sweatshirt and jeans, and packed beer and a bottle of vintage Calvados into a bag. She located a free quad bike on the base map and rode over to Marc's place.

Howie greeted her on the doorstep like a little maître d' and took the bag from her. "Hello, Captain Ingram," he said. "You look nice. I've never seen you in anything that wasn't dark blue."

"Thank you, Howie. You're a gentleman."

A promising smell of curry wafted from the kitchen. Ingram had looked over some of the new print-built homes when they were first finished, but she'd never set foot in one that was actually occupied. Marc kept it predictably tidy and seemed to have a domestic routine going with Howie, who laid the table and polished glasses. It was impressive to see how many small comforts the manufacturing system in Nomad had managed to produce. She was still living in the cabin allotted to her on arrival, only a little bigger than one on a warship, and drinking out of a corporate freebie mug. Now Marc was handing her a beer in a proper glass. Civilisation had come to Opis.

He inspected the contents of the bag and read the label on the bottle of Calvados with a faint frown.

"I have to ask," he said.

"Go ahead."

"This predates the fall of France. Where did you loot it from? Or was this gathering dust in the cellars of Ingram Towers?"

"I was given it by an infantry officer who appreciated the naval gunfire support we were able to provide," Ingram said. "I wish I'd gone ashore and looted some more, actually, but things were a little kinetic."

"What were you saving it for?"

"Something extraordinary that I couldn't imagine. I think having a curry night on an alien world with two gentlemen is excuse enough to open it, though."

"What's Calvados?" Howie asked.

"French apple brandy. They don't make it any more." Marc opened the bottle and let him smell it. "Right, take a seat, Captain. No poppadums, but we've got raita and some mango pickle I appropriated from Ainatio along with the spices. Dinner is served."

He hadn't exaggerated about the curry. It really was very good, and even if it hadn't been, it was just so profoundly enjoyable and *ordinary* to sit down to a meal with friends — a family, almost — that Ingram would have been happy with a plate of cheese on toast.

She kept the conversation away from business, answered Howie's questions about England and the navy, and forgot about Solomon's mission for the duration. She was having such a good time chatting with Howie that she was disappointed when 2200 hours came and he declared it his bedtime.

"I've got double math tomorrow," he said, collecting the plates and stacking them in the kitchen. "I hope you don't mind."

"I know the feeling, Howie." It was touching to hear a little boy sounding so grown-up. "Sleep well."

Marc waited for him to close the bathroom door and gave Ingram a smile. "He's a good kid."

"He's adorable, Marc. But I get the feeling he's the one looking after you."

"He is. That's his thing. Like Betsy."

"Where is she tonight?"

"At Dieter's. She comes and goes."

"That was a splendid curry, by the way."

"Thank you. I have four signature dishes." Marc counted them off on his fingers. "Fry-up, chips, pizza, and curry. A man's menu."

"Apicius couldn't aspire to more," Ingram said.

Marc got up and retrieved the Calvados and two army-issue water bottle cups. Ingram leaned back in her chair and looked around the room. It was the first time she'd noticed the small framed photo on the wall, two young men who had to be Marc's sons. She wondered whether to say something supportive but felt she'd be intruding.

"Have you had a rough day?" Marc asked.

"Not entirely. But Jenny Park came by and asked if she could call family in Korea just to say she wasn't dead. I felt an absolute shit saying no, to be honest. Well, I said I was working on a zero-risk way of doing it, which I suppose I am. But they must all feel that way now." Ingram thought of Tev. "Sorry, and there's Tev. I'm being crass."

"It's okay."

"What are we going to do about him?"

Marc poured two shots of Calvados, which they downed, and then two more. Ingram didn't feel the need to fill the silence. She just waited for him to go on.

"I don't know," Marc said at last. "But I can't leave him to starve, and I definitely can't leave him if Tim Pham's minions have gone after him. Or his family. It's my fault he ended up in Fiji."

"You're the only person I know who could extract him and not cause a major problem," Ingram said.

"Are you saying I ought to?"

"Only you know him well enough to decide if it's the right thing for him. But I admit the Pham angle is worrying."

"See, Chris is nudging me too. But assuming Tev can leave and wants to, how's that going to look to people here who just want to call their eighty-year-old mate who's been putting flowers on their memorial for the last forty-odd years?"

The next shot of Calvados went down Ingram's throat a lot more easily. "Harsh truth? Upsetting someone isn't a reason for not extracting Tev."

"I know, but it'll open a bloody big can of worms," Marc said. "Dan, for a start. He'll feel under pressure to go and find his family, even though they drifted apart for a reason. But they might well be dead. And Chris. He wants a piece of Tim Pham and he's never going to forget it. Once you say it's okay to visit Earth, it'll resurrect a lot of things people should have left buried."

"Okay, let me put it this way," Ingram said. "You feel bad about Tev right now, and I don't like seeing you unhappy. I would rather you extracted him. And we need all the special forces we can get. I'm just saying that nobody would object to rescuing Tev. He's like someone we accidentally left behind. We'd go back under those circumstances, wouldn't we? And Tev's probably the only person we can trust to be given the choice of going or staying, because he'd never tell a living soul about Opis. Or the gate."

"If we're at the stage of identifying other planets for settlement, we're going to come clean about Opis anyway," Marc said. "But it might be too late for him."

"Well, find out, then."

"This place runs on mutual trust. If I do this covertly, who's going to trust me? It'd be wrong for me to keep it from Chris and Dan, for a start. But at some point people *will* find out, because we're a village, and then your APS crew will want to contact people, and if you say no, they'll be pissed off and you'll have a split on your hands. The Ainatio boffins will want to extract their mates, the very people who decided to work for APS even after the shitbags threatened to nuke us and sabotaged our launch. Do we let them in, or say no thanks, you picked your side? And if you say yes to your APS people, you can't guarantee they'll never mention the Caisin gate. If they do, and we've handed FTL to the chosen few, violence on some scale will be used to acquire the technology. Tim Pham knows enough to follow up on any rumour that reaches Earth."

"You always do this, you know."

"What?"

"War-game all the scenarios."

"It's my job. I always show my working-out."

"And I listen and think, oh God, he's right, when I should be saying do it and see what happens. Because as Chris always says, you can't save everybody. And people on Earth have a responsibility to behave like bloody adults without our supervision."

Marc thought about that for a while. "Harsh, but true. Also a forlorn hope."

"So call Tev. For me, if nothing else."

"Okay."

"And leave me to make the excuses if you retrieve him."

"Okay."

"I mean it. Don't nod and humour me."

"I said I'd do it. Just accept it'll cause rows."

"I don't care. I'm a sociopath. I'm the Butcher of Calais."

"No, that's just your psyops."

"I suppose I ought to read what history said about me."

"Alex calls you Ingram the Terrible, by the way. So you can't be that bad. He wouldn't give you a funny nickname if he thought you were a complete bastard."

"He would, actually." She sipped the Calvados and realised it had probably aged further on the journey while she hadn't. Cryo kept providing odd moments of realisation. "*Britzilla*. Hah."

"Did you ever have a nickname? A friendly one, not a headline."

"Haine calls me Bridgers. Sometimes Boadicea."

"Boadicea lost in the end. Not really a good fit."

"I wish someone would call me Bridget. Even Fred doesn't, and I asked him to. You and Howie should too."

"As long as it's Captain in public."

"But we're all civilians, technically. Well, not Chris. Or Jared. We always come back to that. I think it's time we accepted we're the Opis armed forces, Nomad Base is independent from Earth, and we should recommission ourselves properly."

"Along Royal Navy lines?"

"I'm prepared to let the Army keep its funny little ways."

"Good luck with the Yanks. Remind them they've got form for this."

"I'll reintroduce red jackets."

"They'll appreciate that."

Marc started laughing. Ingram wasn't drunk yet, but she was more relaxed than she'd been for ages, and Marc always made her feel she wasn't making the hard decisions alone. She wasn't, of course: she'd agreed to power-sharing because she had no authority — military, national, or social — or the physical ability to enforce it even if she tried.

It didn't stop her feeling responsible, though. And that was when Marc became her anchor in a way that not even Peter Bissey could. Bissey was a sounding board and a moral compass, but always her subordinate. Marc didn't defer to her at all. He didn't talk to a rank, he talked to *her*. He'd go through his take on a situation with meticulous care and treat her as an equal who he expected to either show him where he was wrong or agree with him. She needed him for calibration because she'd never made combat decisions in total isolation like he had. Even in the middle of a battle, Fleet Command had always known where her ship was, and there was usually another vessel or air support to assist in a crisis, even if it couldn't get there in time. But Marc had often worked entirely alone behind enemy lines, out of radio contact for weeks or months at a time, where nobody was going to come to his aid or even realise he was in trouble. He exercised a different kind of judgment that she could learn from.

"I thought I was a competent commander," Ingram said. "I didn't have any doubts on the bridge. But I know I'm out of my depth here."

"We all are. Everyone is when they're faced with something new." Marc shrugged. "There's no point thinking you ought to refer everything to HM Gov, because you're not even covering your arse now. They aren't the grown-ups either. No government is. Exhibit A — the whole bloody world over the last century or two. We've been conditioned to be children."

"I see you're in anarchist mode."

"No, just reminding you there's no alternative." He refilled her cup and raised his half-heartedly. "To healthy scepticism."

"I'll feel better when I hear back from Solomon."

"Weird." Marc got up and went to the kitchen, which was separated from the living room by a breakfast bar. He ran the tap, rinsing something. "I mean, he's *here*. If he was actively patched into the alarm system, he could hear us. But he's out near Dal Mantir too. I'm never going to get used to the way he can split himself up. It's not like me monitoring a bank of feeds. He's *in* it. No physical form. It does my head in when I really think about it."

"I haven't spoken to him about the new planet."

"He knows already. He sees all the comms."

Ingram's screen chirped in her pocket. A night off counted for nothing. She checked it, hoping it was nothing urgent, and found a message from Haine to tell her he was starting a post mortem on Lirrel's body with Jake Mendoza, and asking if she wanted to be present.

"Problem?" Marc asked, leaning on the breakfast bar like a pub landlord.

"Haine's started a post mortem on the teerik. He asked if I want to be there."

"Funny time to start. But he knows how to show a girl good time."

"He's been putting it off. He's had the body for a couple of weeks."

"You'd better be going, then," Marc said. "He might have plucked and stuffed it with sage and onion by the time you get there."

Ingram wasn't sure if Marc was tactfully telling her to go home, but it was getting late and she was feeling the effects of too many late nights and too much Calvados.

"I'll see how brave I feel on the way back," she said. "I don't want anything spoiling that lovely jalfrezi."

"Next one's on you, then." Marc sealed the Calvados bottle and put it in her bag. "Well, that was fun."

She flapped her hand. "Keep the bottle."

"Okay, I'll save it for next time. Are you in a fit state to ride back, or do you want a lift?"

"I'll be extra-careful. I could even walk."

Ingram realised how much she was enjoying being able to speak freely — no Solomon in constant virtual attendance, no obligations of rank, nobody needing her to put on a brave face — but the evening had reached its natural end. She climbed onto the bike and took a deep breath of night air that smelled of arriving at a foreign airport, the same as it had when she first set foot on the planet.

Marc stood in the doorway, leaning against the door frame. "You've had a few tonight, Boadicea, so you might not remember this in the morning," he said. "But you're doing a bloody good job. If you were a liability, I'd have intervened by now. Just carry on being what you've always been."

"Thank you. I needed to hear that... I think."

"Goodnight, Bridget."

It sounded like someone else's name. "Goodnight, Marc."

Ingram rode back to the main building with the excessive care that only someone who was drunk could apply. What did he mean by *intervene*? She could guess, but she wasn't sure if it was comic exaggeration or the honest truth that he'd remove a liability to everyone's safety the way he dealt with any other security threat. No, he wasn't joking. He'd have removed her, by force if need be, and saying so was his way of reassuring her that she really did have his approval. As compliments went, it was both odd and welcome.

She managed to park the quad bike straight without letting its AI take over and thought how pathetic it was to still be living above the shop, but the cabin in the collection of office units that formed the main building still had more appeal than being in a house on her own.

The question now was whether she was obliged to watch Haine and Mendoza dissecting a dead alien. The answer was no. She messaged Haine with an apology and took a quick shower before flopping onto her bunk.

There was nothing like being full of curry and alcohol and just drifting off. It was blissfully primitive. She needed to do this more often.

Definitely.

Can I still make risotto properly?

Yes, can't go wrong with a risotto...

She was sure she'd only just fallen asleep when her screen chirped again. God, she hoped it wasn't Haine offering to show her an interesting alien bowel section or worse. She fumbled for the screen before she was fully awake and held it flat on the pillow.

"Ingram."

"Apologies for waking you, Captain, but I thought you'd want to know right away," Solomon said. "We're into Jattan naval comms. I'm now completely integrated back here and monitoring transmissions with help from Fred."

That snapped her fully awake. "Bravo Zulu, Sol. Bloody good effort. So now we can watch and wait."

"Indeed. And you and I can catch up on today's developments later. My apologies again for waking you."

"No problem," she said. "I'll sleep like a log tonight."

Ingram tapped out a quick message to Searle and the Gang of Three to let them know they were in business, and settled down again to sleep. Solomon had done very well indeed. He'd also indicated that there were things he wanted to discuss with her, probably the assessment of Srale as an alternative site. As Marc had pointed out, he'd have heard the conversation with Fred. It was his job to know everything that went on in Nomad Base.

Ingram hoped he was reassured that she'd heeded his advice about not opening the floodgates for Earth. For all his insistence that he'd do as he was asked, even if he disagreed, there was nothing she could do to stop him if he changed his mind. He was an SDS AI, moral type or not, and they'd been banned for a reason.

"*Intervention*," she mumbled into her pillow. "What a lovely word for assassinating me."

04

I'm not stupid, I wasn't drunk, and I know what we saw. Find that Vincent bitch before the Korean cops do and let's connect the dots.

Tim Pham, Commissioner for Science and
Technology, Alliance of Asian and Pacific States,
talking to private military contractor Jimmy Mun.

SECURITY OFFICE, NOMAD BASE: 0820 HOURS, OCTOBER 6, OC.

No matter how many times Marc rehearsed the conversation in his head, it still sounded like complete bollocks. Tev would think he'd lost the plot.

But then Tev believed in divine intervention and miracles, for all his pragmatic approach to soldiering, so maybe he'd hear Marc out. There was no easy way to ask the bloke if he wanted to bring his whole family to live on another planet, and tell him the journey would take seconds.

See? It still sounded bloody insane.

Marc could see Chris and Trinder approaching as mobile icons on his base map and estimated they'd be here in five minutes. He went outside to stand by the doors and wait. This was going to be a discussion conducted where Sol couldn't hear it, not because the AI would have any objections or try to interfere, but because this was awkward personal stuff. There was only so much privacy Marc was prepared to surrender. Back at Ainatio's HQ, he and Tev would do their daily run around the campus and discuss private matters on the way, well outside Sol's audio range.

Chris and Trinder strolled across the green from the direction of Kill Line with their hands in their pockets, deep in discussion. Marc walked out to meet them.

"So I guess this isn't about a surprise party for Sol, then," Chris said. "Problem?"

Marc shrugged. "It's only personal stuff. I wanted to clear my yardarm with you two and I'm uncomfortable with an audience."

"Ingram?" Trinder asked.

"Now what makes you say that?"

"The map doesn't lie. She paid you a visit last night. You want us to slug it out over who gets to be your groomsman?" Trinder suddenly looked sheepish. "Hey, I was on duty. You do the same. We keep an eye on who's where."

"Yeah, okay. Actually, we discussed what to do about Tev. She says go get him."

"Oh."

"Do it," Chris said. "I'll ride shotgun."

"He's probably fine, but you can imagine the worst as well as I can. If Pham's still functioning, he'll have taken a different view of Tev since Abbie Vincent showed up. The Ainatio connection."

"There's no sign of Pham on the news, so he might be in deep shit himself for letting Abbie into Korea in the first place," Chris said. "But yeah, Tev's at risk. So when do we go?"

"You don't," Marc said.

"Then how come we're having this meeting?"

"You both have unfinished business on Earth and I want to square things with you," Marc said. "If I get to break the rules, and that pisses you off for any reason, I need to know."

"It doesn't, but if it did, tough shit," Chris said. "I can wait for Pham."

Trinder looked uncomfortable. "This is about me, isn't it? Okay, finding my family would be a long job, and if we can go back to Earth now, I've got to be honest with myself about why I didn't try to find them before and what I do next. But that's my problem to deal with, not yours."

"Thanks, lads," Marc said. "I know there'll be blowback from some of the *Cabot* and Ainatio people, but I'll handle that."

"Call me when you need a hand," Chris said.

"I've got to locate Tev first. See you later."

Marc headed over to the admin office and didn't look back. He had Tev's current contact details from the last message he'd received back on Earth, but the first hurdle was making sure any comms traffic originating here looked like it came from some routine place on Earth that wouldn't drop Tev further in it. So he couldn't risk a spoofed point of origin from Britain. That would look routine for a British bloke who'd resettled in Fiji, but if Pham was still up to his usual bastardry and managed to ID Marc's call, it would present a target for Pham that wasn't actually there. Innocent people could get hurt.

Well, he'd work that out later. He dropped by the admin office to let whoever was on duty know that he was going into the armoury and found Lennie Fonseca at the desk.

"Morning, Captain," he said. "I'm signing in to the armoury. Nobody's moved the cutter thing, have they?"

"Hi Marc." She looked him over. He gave her his most indifferent look back. "It's still showing on the inventory, so if it's gone missing, I'll be mad."

"I'll let you know, then," he said, and turned to go.

"Marc, is Chris okay?"

"Have you asked him?"

"Kind of."

"Well, whatever he said, then."

"Just don't let him go after Pham. It won't end well."

Chris's inability to give up a grudge or a promise was embedded in Nomad's folklore now and everyone knew Pham was top of his bugger-about list. But Fonseca was probably angling for a way back into Chris's misplaced affections, because the bloke wasn't moping after her like an abandoned puppy and she couldn't work out why. Marc did Chris a favour and didn't take the bait. Chris was better off without her.

"I dissuaded him strongly, Captain," Marc said. "He won't."

He walked down to the armoury and put his hand on the sensor to open the door. "Sol, are you there? Now we've got a bit of privacy, could you do me a favour?"

"Of course, Marc. Is this about the weapons?"

At the end of a bank of lockers and racks, there was a transparent cabinet with full-width shelves that housed the Jattan energy weapon and Lirrel's industrial beam cutter, the thing he'd used to kill Nina Curtis. Marc hadn't asked Fred to show him how to use it yet, mainly because it was probably a bit too soon for the teerik, but if the device could give Marc an edge when he went back for Tev, he'd learn fast. He stood studying it, working out how and where he'd holster it for quick use without slicing his own leg off. It looked a lot smaller than he remembered when he'd retrieved the thing after killing Lirrel. It was just a smooth, curved tube like the top half of a walking stick. The Jattan energy weapon had a similar design.

"Sol, I need to make a call to Earth."

"Yes, Captain Ingram told me you might have a request and that I was to co-operate."

"I need to cover my tracks."

"If you use the probe relays currently in Earth space, the signal can't be traced back to here."

"I meant where it appears to come from on Earth," Marc said. "If APS are monitoring Tev's comms, I don't want to misdirect them to Britain in case they're feeling trigger-happy."

"I'm sure I can obscure it completely," Solomon said. "May I ask if you're going to bring Tev to Opis?"

"If he wants to come, yes."

"I'm glad. I like Tev. He and his family will be an asset to the community."

"Yeah. I should have worried about him the minute the Koreans started looking for Abbie Vincent."

"You judge yourself very harshly," Solomon said. "Tev was fine the last time you spoke."

"Yeah, but APS know where he is because they took him there. And they're not going to overlook the fact that he worked at Ainatio and now they've got die-back, courtesy of the same company."

"Let's find him, then. I have his last messaging address before we left Earth."

"Thanks." There was no hiding anything from Sol, not because he looked for it but because he couldn't avoid knowing it was there in the system. "Depending on how far we get, I might want to check up on Barry Cho as well. Not in person. I just want to know he's okay. The easy way is for me to call Lawson in the Foreign Office and ask if Cho's dad and sister were given asylum, but obviously that's a non-starter. He thinks I'm in cryo beyond Pluto now."

"Do you want me to find Cho?"

"If you can, please."

Cho had risked a lot to help Marc evacuate the Ainatio campus and Marc fully expected Pham to put the kid on a charge when they got back to Korea. A crazy but inevitable thought kept wandering into Marc's mind. If he could extract Tev, he could do exactly the same for Barry Cho. If his family had made it to Britain, he could whisk him out of wherever he was and reunite them a long way from APS's reach, unless Pham had had him shot, of course, or shot the kid himself, which was much more Pham's style.

"After the Jattan naval network, I suppose it'll be relatively easy for you." Marc knew he was making small talk to buy himself time before he spoke to Tev and tried not to sound like a nutter. "You did well there. What do they talk about?"

"From what I can translate so far — what the linguistics AI can translate, anyway — they sound very much like yourselves. They're critical of their bureaucracy, they're extremely interested in the menu of the day in their communal eating areas, and they have animated discussions about the relative merits of weapons. I believe they also tell jokes of a kind."

"You're going to get bored listening to all that. You might be stuck on it for years."

"I'm an AI," Solomon said. "I never get bored. Shall I set up your relay now?"

That was a hint to get on with it. "Yeah, let's do it."

The door locked with a click. "Just so you're not interrupted," Solomon said. "I'm not sure how some people here would react to being allowed calls."

"Dan and Chris know."

"I thought they might."

Marc sat down on a bench and contemplated the alien weapons while he waited. He knew he wasn't worrying half as much as he ought to about the problems that would flow from telling Tev about Opis. Tev was rock-solid and understood OPSEC as well as Marc did, but his family weren't army. They were regular civilians, and all the issues about an information blackout were exactly the same as the one they'd dealt with by shoving the Ainatio staff through the Caisin gate without warning.

Shit, there was never going to be a right way to do this until everyone on Earth knew the whole story. Until then, Marc had to make sure Tev and the people he cared about were safe. Marc could test his priorities pretty easily. If Tev got killed or captured, he'd never forgive himself.

No contest.

And now the silence was killing him. It probably wouldn't make any difference to Solomon if he talked because the AI could handle multiple streams of information, but it was a hard habit to break.

"There, all done," Solomon said. "You can use your screen now. Unless Tev's screen is compromised, the call can't be intercepted, either."

"Thanks, Sol." Marc could have written a message, but it was safer to call to make sure it was Tev receiving it. He tapped the icon on Tev's last message and waited. A woman answered.

"*Bula*, dairy," she said, or at least that's how it sounded.

Marc didn't know Tev's family and he didn't know how much Tev might have told them about him. It was also odd to leave your screen for someone else to pick up calls. Marc proceeded cautiously.

"Hi. Have I got the right number for Tevita Josepha, please?"

"This is the dairy."

Marc ploughed on. There was no way Solomon would have got the wrong number. "I'm his army friend, Marc. Marc from England. I'm checking to see if he's okay. I haven't heard from him for a couple of months."

There was a brief silence. "He left."

That didn't sound encouraging. Marc played the baffled card. "But is he okay? I'm worried about him."

"He told me you'd call one day," the woman said. "He said to tell you he had to leave with his family."

Marc prayed they hadn't been picked up by APS intelligence already. "Do you know where he went? Did he go back to England?"

"He just said they had to go somewhere. He said to tell you he went fishing."

Marc couldn't think what that meant right then, but at least it sounded like Tev had left of his own accord.

"Did he leave his screen with you, then? Sorry, I called what I thought was his personal link."

"This is the dairy. The convenience store. He used to come in and use the public comms link here."

"Okay. Thank you. If he comes back, tell him Marc called and that I'll find him."

Marc sat looking at his screen for a few moments, trying to work out the fishing reference. Tev's son Joni had a fishing business, so maybe it was a proper trawler or something, big enough to move a whole family. How many islands were there around Fiji? Hundreds. Marc would have to think harder.

"I've traced the address," Solomon said. "I can confirm it's a small grocery store on Viti Levu, in a resort on the west coast. So that's genuine. Presumably there are plenty of places to go to ground in an archipelago of that size. Does Tev have ties to any other islands?"

"Not as far as I know," Marc said. "He'd never been to Fiji before. His mum was English, he was born in England, and the nearest he got to being properly Fijian was rugby, the church, and the local ex-pat community. Even his ex-wife is third-generation British. He'll be relying on his kids for local knowledge. They moved out there with Becky when they were little."

"But he's as skilled as you at keeping a low profile, I assume."

"Oh yeah. He'll blend right in. Even if he doesn't know the dialect, they all speak English."

"We have time to search further, then," Solomon said. "But if you can work out the message he left you, that would help a great deal."

"I'm on it, Sol."

Marc tried to be positive, but Tev had uprooted his family for a reason. The last time he'd been in touch, Tev had said some local official came to welcome him when he arrived and check he had everything he needed. It might have been legit: Tev had been flown in by APDU, so they might have thought he was some VIP. But Marc always planned for the worst and worked up from there, so it could easily have been someone checking him out on Pham's orders.

"Sol, have I missed any news about Tim Pham?" Marc asked. "Has he sunk without trace now?"

"No appearances on the news, and no references to him in the media, but his image and departmental information still appear on the official APS site."

Pham would keep out of the public eye anyway, seeing as he still thought more like an intelligence agent than politician, but he'd also inadvertently brought Abbie and her plague to Korea, and that couldn't have gone down well with APS. Was there anyone big enough to make him pay for it? From what Kim said, he was a law unto himself, and he'd managed to commandeer an aircraft carrier for his raid on Ainatio without many people noticing, so maybe not. The only question that mattered was whether he was still a threat to Nomad.

"Do you think he's told anyone he saw the Caisin gate?" Marc asked. "Not that he knew exactly what it was, and Chris said he was going on about it being a secret British plot, but he knows there's exploration technology to be had."

"I would suspect not," Solomon said. "He'll want more intel before he risks humiliation, and if the first technology grab was off the books, this will be as well. I agree that his goal was plundering Ainatio for Australia's benefit, not APS."

"You know what pisses me off? He believes in something. The first principled politician I've ever known and the bastard's on the wrong side. It's not about money or personal power, it's about serving his country. Anyway, thanks for sorting the comms for me. I'd better get on with some work."

"Are you taking those weapons with you?" Solomon asked.

"Not yet. I've got to ask Fred for some training. The beam cutter is the thing I'm interested in. It's silent. Fred said its range is more than six feet, too."

"I see. You're preparing for a gate insertion behind enemy lines."

"To be honest, if I'm in one place long enough to need to use the cutter, I've failed. Maybe I'll stick with firearms this time."

"Well, it'll be a good test run for entering Kugad."

"How much access do you have to teerik data now? You're working with them on engineering and comms, so you must see a lot of stuff. How much control do you have?"

"Are you asking me how much access I've made sure I have in the event of some disaster befalling the teeriks, enough to complete the FTL conversions, maintain them, and perhaps operate and maintain Caisin gates?" Solomon asked.

Marc had to smile. Sol was a crafty bugger. It was just as well he'd always be on Nomad's side. "Yeah. Something like that."

"The answer is *sufficient*."

"Aren't you going to overload your memory sooner or later?"

"No, I'm fine. I'm not the AI that does the calculations and code, or works out how to translate Jattan. It's like plugging in extra brains when I need them. I'm just the manager. My job is to help different systems talk to each other, have enough access to do their jobs, and be able to call me for help if something goes wrong. I'm not designed for their specialisations. I could learn eventually, but delegation works better."

"And your core is your own brain. The bit that moves around."

"Yes, but I normally leave part of my eyes, ears, and motor functions in the network when I do that. Except when Erskine's trying to kill me, of course."

"I can't wait for that reunion."

"I can." Solomon actually made a sighing sound. Marc had never heard him do that before. The AI's pauses were timed as well as an actor's, but he'd never gone in for sound effects. "If you're going to ask me if I'm building our own capacity to use teerik technology because I don't trust them, it's more about the long-term supply. We have to ask what happens when members of the commune age and die, which also means we have to consider whether this group can reproduce. Fred's daughter sometimes expresses worries that her sons won't have mates because there are no other teeriks around."

"That sounds like an unusually personal chat for her."

"I was eavesdropping, actually."

"In Kugal?"

"The linguistics AI has to learn somehow, and they do still speak some Kugal to the children." Solomon had his own rules on preserving others' privacy, but he only seemed to apply them to his protected humans. "Whether Turisu's worried or not, we can already see we need to plan for the future. Parthenogenesis as in Caisin's case isn't the answer. Offspring like Rikayl aren't going to be much use to us. We still have no idea what went wrong there."

Nomad was already handcuffed to the teeriks indefinitely because they now knew almost everything about human military capability. Their genetic memory would preserve a lot of that in their children, including the location of Earth. But Marc knew he hadn't given enough thought to the long term — the Kugin were still dependent on teeriks, according to Fred, because nobody could even reverse-engineer most of their stuff.

"Even if we can learn their engineering skills, maybe we can't innovate like they do," Marc said. "So the question is how far we can fall behind progress in Kugin technology or anyone else's before we're back to being the slowest-moving targets in town again."

"That's the question, and we only have partial answers so far," Solomon said. "Levelling the playing field requires keeping up with the neighbours, or destroying the playing field for everybody."

"Acquiring all the teeriks, or something else?" Marc asked, but he knew what the something else was.

"If we can't have them," Solomon said, "we might need to consider living within our previous technological constraints and making sure nobody else can have them either. I think that's a conversation we'll all have to have one day."

"We already have."

"Only about terminating them humanely. Not about willingly forfeiting their technology. I have to find a way to bridge that competence gap."

Marc couldn't argue with that. Somewhere in Kugad, a defence select committee or whatever passed for one in Kugin politics was probably having that same discussion, in case their teeriks had now fallen into the wrong hands with all their skills and secrets. If they had any sense, they'd assume they were completely compromised, along with their allies and customers, and it was time to panic.

"We're talking about teeriks as if they're animals," Marc said. "We can't get past the fact they look like birds, can we?"

"It's not that, Marc. I'd make the same decision about humans if they happened to have technology we relied on and their situation was uncertain." Sometimes it was hard for Marc to listen to Sol and not see him as another Tom on the radio net, lying in a shell scrape somewhere, flesh and blood like himself. "Remember that I'm not here to save Earth, your government, or humanity in general. I'm here to save *you*."

Like Marc, and like everyone Marc had ever served with, Sol was fighting for the bloke next to him. It was hard to see Sol as anything but a human who just happened to be lacking a body.

* * *

MAIN BUILDING, NOMAD BASE: 0715 HOURS, OCTOBER 7, OC.

For the seventy-eighth morning in a row — slightly overcast today, but still pleasantly warm — Ingram began her day standing on the roof of the main building, drinking a mug of tea while she surveyed the base below.

The habit that started with her need for a better view of construction work had turned into a ritual, and it hadn't passed unnoticed by those who worked in the centre of the base. Ingram suspected it made a statement that all was well. As long as the CO could stand up there like an easy target, calmly drinking tea while keeping an eye on everything, then people were reassured there was nothing to worry about.

It also seemed to indicate that she was available for a chat, though, because they would sometimes make their way up to the roof to corner her, knowing she had no escape.

Today it was Logan Haine. She could hear him singing tunelessly to himself as he climbed through the roof hatch. He stood beside her, folded his arms, and joined in the general surveying. He seemed to be back to his old self, in public at least.

"Want to see something absolutely fascinating, Bridgers?"

She braced for something graphic. "Does it involve the intricacies of a corviform alien's internal organs?"

"Actually, yes. Well, technically not the offal component, but it's peripherally involved. If you want to examine it for haruspicy purposes, though, I'll put it in a bowl for you. How did you know?"

"I just thought of the last thing I needed to see after enjoying my lovely poached eggs."

"You don't need to actually *see* it, but if I start explaining it without imagery and props, your eyes will glaze over. When you're ready, you're invited to join us in the med lab."

"Very well, as soon as I've done my rounds, I'll be there. As long as it's not a practical joke involving raw teerik."

"I swear this is purely pushing the frontiers of science." Haine peered into her face. "Have you been on the razzle again? You look hung over."

"I stayed up late listening to the Jattan comms net. It's all simultaneous English translation now, albeit with lots of gaps. The AI's learning fast."

"Anything interesting?"

"Allowing for misunderstandings of nuance, they have an impenetrable bureaucracy, some admiral's vessel wasn't shown the correct courtesy by a junior commander's tub so heads will roll, and someone's been sent a fleet's worth of the wrong spare parts. There's a lot I don't understand even when it's translated, but overall, lots of scenarios not unrecognisable to any human matelot."

"Isn't that marvellous?" Haine looked delighted. "I realise circumstances have dulled the shine, but... *aliens*. We're spying on aliens, having lunch with aliens, doing PMs on aliens, and we're the first humans who ever have. This is the most scientifically exciting event since Palaeolithic man realised he could get rat-arsed on decaying fruit. Rejoice in it, Bridgers. And I'll expect you to join us later this morning."

Haine disappeared back down the hatch, leaving Ingram to finish her tea and contemplate the frustrating lull she found herself in after the recent crises. The base was no safer than it had been when Gan-Pamas arrived, but everyone was now in a state of quietly watching and waiting — waiting for the Kugin or the Jattans to make a move, waiting for news of home, looking for lost friends, producing food and upgrading equipment in preparation for the unknown day. It was slack water with no way of knowing if and when the tide would turn.

Ingram was trained to hunt the enemy, not wait politely for them to find her. She wanted to get stuck in. But that didn't necessarily mean it was the wisest option.

She went on her way, trying to get her focus straight again. What needed doing now was the essential, routine stuff that didn't get the adrenaline flowing. Food production, reconditioning more land for farming, and getting on with a tough engineering schedule now came first. Before setting off on the bike for her daily inspection, she sat in the saddle for a while studying her base map, tapping on features to get the latest status reports.

Solomon had added an orbital layer for the convenience of *Cabot* personnel so they didn't have to switch to another screen to see the state of play with the ships, but it looked like he'd now added a Dal Mantir space layer as well, showing the planet in its star system with the spy freighter's position marked.

The transparent layers were getting too cluttered for Ingram's taste so she pulled up the orbital one on its own. Eighty per cent of *Cabot*'s engineering section were now working on the ships in orbit, spread over three watches, along with the teeriks and dozens of bots. With almost all the remaining bots on the ground occupied by expanding arable land and building bomb shelters, resources were now as stretched as they'd been during the evacuation. The bots could make more copies of themselves as they'd done for decades, but that meant diverting some from urgent jobs. It was a fine balancing act. Solomon had already worked it out and implemented it.

"Sol," Ingram said. "Are you sure we shouldn't pull some bots back for reproduction? Keep a permanent breeding colony, so to speak."

"We could, Captain, but as you're aware there'll be a loss of productivity while they replace themselves." Solomon repeated his position just as she repeated hers, a war of polite attrition. "But if you want to deploy them in drive engineering, we're limited by the working space available. Crudely put, there's not enough room for more of them to work."

"I was thinking of getting bomb shelters excavated faster."

"If that's what you want," Solomon said.

"What I *really* want is a Caisin gate generator, in a bunker, underground. Somewhere the Kugin can't get at it."

"I knew you wanted that, Captain, but timing is everything. There's a danger of overloading Fred, as well."

"Workload or goodwill?"

"Workload. He trusts you implicitly."

Ingram wouldn't have trusted herself if she were Fred. On the other hand, he knew that she wouldn't hand over any of the teeriks, not even his awful daughter. Ingram liked to think it was because she'd earned his trust, but he was no fool, and he knew the commune now had knowledge of Earth and its defences that needed protecting at all costs.

"Let's get some preparation done, then, and talk to Brad and Jac about designing a bunker, please," Ingram said. "Make it accessible from the bomb shelters. Do you know the dimensions of this generator? We could at least build a space ready to accept it. I assume you rummaged through their schematics the moment you got access to their system."

"I did, Captain. And I'll work out which bots we can withdraw from projects to start reproducing."

"Thanks Sol. I know I ought to leave it all to you, but if we stop doing jobs ourselves and solving our own problems, what are we going to become?"

"A good point," Solomon said. "Which is probably why Chris is teaching some of our Ainatio neighbours some basic carpentry this morning."

"Good grief, another course? Not quite the image I had of him."

"It's post-apocalypse bootcamp, Captain. Preparing them for frontier life if the lights go out. At least it's keeping the scientific staff busy and stopping them feeling like pariahs. Some of them don't have much to do these days and there's a waiting list for jobs on the agricultural side. Are you going to visit the medical centre now?"

Ingram checked the time and started the bike. "When I finish my rounds. Better write me off until lunchtime."

Solomon knew what was going on before she did. He couldn't help it. If Haine was involved in some dissection, he'd probably have activated biohazard precautions that blipped Solomon's system. But Solomon didn't say anything to her unless there was a problem that required advance warning, and she was gradually accepting that it was for the best. It would be like having an ever-present gossip pre-digesting every scrap of information and foisting it on you at inconvenient times. People had to find out things for themselves in the normal course of events by talking to each other, or else they'd cease to interact like adult humans.

What did it do to Solomon, though? Did Bednarz design it into him, or did Sol work it out for himself? Ingram hoped he'd speak up if he was being put under too much pressure.

Her first port of call was the crop tunnels. Rounds here were the equivalent of her daily walk through her ship to check that all was well and give people a chance to raise things with her personally. Being seen out and about and keeping an eye on things was important for trust and morale, even if she wasn't the sole authority here. This morning she took a route out past the Kill Line farms, stopped to chat to Mike Hodge about his beef herd — still surviving, doing as well as could be expected in their unplanned expatriation, two cows in calf already — and made a fuss of Marty Laurenson's collies. Then she looped around the perimeter, pausing occasionally to check out the wild landscape through binoculars before visiting Lianne Maybury and the team in the crop tunnels.

Team was possibly an optimistic word to use. Most of the agriculturalists here were *Cabot* civilians, but there were some plant geneticists from Ainatio as well, some of them from the die-back lab. Ingram trod carefully. In the last couple of weeks, none of the Ainatio personnel had mentioned the embarrassing business of being Mother Death suspects at all. She couldn't work out if they were making an effort to move on or just keeping their resentment on a steady simmer.

Lianne showed her a handful of rice. The cut-and-come-again perennial strain was doing well and ready to be transplanted.

"Short grain?" Ingram asked. "Risotto?"

"Near enough, as long as you don't rinse it first."

"Oh good. I'll be your first customer. It's all I can cook." It was probably time for an olive branch. "Is there anything you need at the moment? We're trying to get more bots built, so if there's any specific model you want, let Solomon know."

"Actually, there *is* something," Lianne said. "We'd really like to send some survey teams off-camp. We've been here a couple of months, and there's a whole unexplored world of plants out there."

Nobody was allowed outside the wire without clearance and an armed escort, but enforcement hadn't been necessary because Nina's death had been a wake-up call about just how dangerous the world beyond the perimeter might be. But now the same lull that had made Ingram restless seemed to have reminded the scientists what they were as well, and what was waiting to be discovered.

"You understand why we'd be nervous about unarmed civilians entering unexplored areas," Ingram said.

"Yes, but technically we're all civilians, and quite a few us are taking firearms courses."

Ingram knew the untidy status of everyone here who regarded themselves as still serving would bite her in the arse one day. It had been a matter of shared belief, that everyone agreed who was in uniform and who wasn't, and divided roles and responsibility accordingly. If the agreement broke down, it became a matter of who could enforce it. At the moment, that was still Nomad's defence forces. In the near future, with everyone armed, it might not be that easy.

"You're going to need an armed escort, then," Ingram said. "The threat hasn't gone away."

Paul Cotton, Lianne's husband, muttered loudly enough to be heard. "An armed escort didn't do much for Nina."

Lianne shot him a look. "Paul, *please*."

Ingram ignored insults aimed at her. Solomon had been right about that: she didn't care because her self-esteem was forged from the reinforced titanium of generations of social certainty. But criticism of her comrades or her crew when they weren't there to defend themselves demanded rebuttal.

"I'm trying to be reasonable, Paul," she said, deploying the tone of patient disappointment that worked with young ratings who'd had a few beers too many ashore. "But armchair-generalling about the people who risked their lives to get you here and who'll risk them again to keep you safe is below the belt. You'll find things are very different when you're in that situation. By all means, arm yourself properly and explore wherever you wish. I won't stop you. But we don't have troops free to escort you or rescue you if things go wrong. Our priority at the moment is being ready to defend the population against more alien incursions. We're not a scientific mission, and we won't prioritise research for its own sake until we're sufficiently established here to investigate new resources."

She'd made a pig's ear of that and she knew it. But she also knew she'd regret saying nothing at all. The silence that followed — just a couple of seconds, but somehow an eternity — was painful.

Lianne changed the subject with commendable speed. "I'll talk to Sol about bots, Captain. A few more acres of paddy would be useful."

"Good idea," Ingram said. "Otherwise I'll have to learn to cook something else. Thank you for showing me around. I'm always impressed to see the progress here."

"Tell Logan I might have some lemons for him soon."

"All he's missing is the tonic, then."

They laughed politely. Ingram decided to move on before she dug a deeper hole. She rode off, angry with herself but unable to see how ignoring Paul's barb would have helped.

Maybe she was just wrong, though.

"I suppose you heard all that, Sol," she said.

"I did, Captain. Don't worry about Paul Cotton. He's always been one to snipe and gripe. I don't think his opinion carries weight."

"And Lianne's so nice. I never understand what people see in each other."

"Who knows the mysteries of the human heart?"

"You're just taking the piss now."

"I am."

"But it means it's time for us to formalise things here. A constitution. Proper armed forces. All that stuff that we thought we were too swashbuckling to need right away."

"Bednarz did plan for this, of course," Solomon said. "But it was on the assumption that the follow-up wave of settlers would include administrators who'd already have their plan for a constitution. We're never going to have that. It's up to all of you now."

Ingram didn't feel she was cut out for nation-building. "I'm sure you can contribute too, Sol."

"The entire issue rests on whether you regard Nomad Base as a colony of Earth or not, and if you do, which elements of Earth you're going to treat as the source of law and authority when the day comes."

"I'm more concerned with internal legitimacy," Ingram said. "If we've got unhappy Ainatio people reminding me that they're armed and we're all actually civilians, even harmless ones like Lianne Maybury, we have a potential problem. We can't disarm them, and we shouldn't if we expect them to help defend the base, but it does complicate matters."

"I don't think any of the civilians are going to be a serious threat to the professional forces here," Solomon said. "We have two hundred and twenty-one individuals we've chosen to class as military personnel because of prior service, most of them your ship's company. But Chris and Dan's troops could put down any violent protest on their own, and Kill Line's competent gun users would back them."

Ingram hadn't read the mission brief for a while, but the key part for her was the point at which she handed control to the settlers. "It's not even about whether there's military governance or civilian, Sol. It's the need for a set of rules we all agree on and abide by. It's working informally now, but that won't last forever."

Command responsibility was blurred but things worked because Nomad was still small enough for informal decision-making on every level. Ingram shared command with the Gang of Three and the mayor of Kill Line, and people bartered for items outside their allocation of food and other supplies and settled disagreements by talking things out or occasionally throwing a punch. But when the community grew, it would have to think about currency and laws and enforcement, and all the other complications of civilisation. By then it wouldn't be a village-sized base but a looser community of small towns. And something special would be lost in the process.

Ingram knew this was the best time to be a citizen here, the peak of pioneering. The issues were as uncomplicated as they were ever going to get and everybody knew their neighbour. Even with the prospect of hostile aliens, life for her was purposeful and satisfying, but it was also temporary. Succeeding on Opis meant these days wouldn't come again. It was rather sad.

"I understand," Solomon said. "But I still say this isn't about whatever constitution you all agree on, but whether you're a small nation willing to defend its independence."

Ingram knew what Solomon's anxieties were. She shared a lot of them. "Let's discuss it later when I find out what Haine's itching to show me."

Haine could have sent her a memo about whatever he'd found, but perhaps she hadn't visited the medical staff often enough and they just wanted to be acknowledged. She certainly hadn't given Haine enough time lately. She still owed him a drinking session, too.

If he and his fellow scab-lifters wanted her to come to their kingdom instead of seeking an audience in hers, that was fine.

The medical labs were now housed in a cluster of the original print-built dome buildings opposite the clinic. Jeff Aiken was waiting for Ingram at the entrance.

"I hope you didn't mind me inserting myself into this, ma'am." Jeff led her down the connecting corridor. "But someone has to tell Fred about this and I decided it'd be easier coming from me."

"That sounds ominous, Chief."

"Not really, but the teeriks ought to be involved in this."

The lab was crowded. For some reason Ingram had expected to see Lirrel on a metal table and she'd braced herself for weird smells and unpleasant anatomical detail, but all she could see was a huddle of men and women in lab coats and blue scrubs looking down at something on a desk. They were a mix of medics, exobiologists, and a couple of people from the vet's surgery.

"There you are, Bridgers." Haine appeared beside her. "You look disappointed."

"I was expecting to see a tableau of Rembrandt's anatomy lesson, to be honest," she said. "No body?"

"Oh, we did all that in the biohaz lab just in case. You never know, especially when you start cutting."

"Bit late for that, isn't it? Lirrel leaked a lot when Marc shot him and my chaps moved the body. And the Jattan. He ended up leaking too."

"Well, we've got the AI working on a full analysis, so if it detects anything we can get the appropriate drug formulated. We're trying to sequence the teerik genome at the moment — which *is* DNA-based, by the way — and we've created a full three-dimensional anatomical scan, which'll come in handy if and when our teerik friends need treatment. Did you want to see the cadaver?"

"Not really. I want to see what *they're* doing." She walked over to the crowd around the desk to take a look. They were watching a screen. The image looked like a molecular structure that was changing every few seconds. "Is this the genome?"

Jake Mendoza turned around. "No, we're trying to identify a substance we found in the blood and some of the organs. Do you want the quick summary?"

"I'm a simple sailor. Yes please."

"Well, there's a chance our teeriks might have a nutritional problem."

"Draw me a picture."

"We have some pieces of the puzzle already. We know what kind of food they can digest, thanks to Nina's team, so we've reverse-engineered that to establish some things about their biochemistry. We also have tissue samples from more than one teerik, and those show significant differences. We've examined specimens from Rikayl, a feather from one of the other teeriks, and a wider range of samples from Lirrel, and there's a substance we can't identify at all. The level in the feather Solomon found lodged in one of the bots before *Cabot* arrived is much higher than in Lirrel, but Rikayl shows none of it. In other words, the teeriks who started life elsewhere have traces of it, but not the one who was born here. It could be environmental, or it might be related to age. One possibility is that it's a nutrient of some kind that teeriks can't obtain from a diet outside the Kugin homeworld."

Ingram hated herself for thinking it, but combined with the problem of the commune dying out from isolation, the longer-term nutritional issue looked like a double blow. If Nomad was going to place more reliance on teerik technology, it needed a guaranteed supply of teeriks. She also hated herself for wondering if she'd been too hasty in banning a dissection of Caisin's body.

"Worrying," she said.

"Yes, but I stress that it might be age-related instead. A biomarker."

"Whose feather did you test?"

"We don't know who it came from, so we'll need to get on with sequencing and then ask the commune for specimens to work it out."

"We could also try levelling with them and asking them what they know," Jeff said.

Mendoza gave him a look. "Jeff, they didn't even know what happened to their dead or their newly-hatched chicks."

"Nevertheless, we ask them, out of courtesy if nothing else," Ingram said. "If it turns out to be a nutrient they're missing, can we synthesise it?"

"Probably."

"Okay, I'd like the Chief to discuss this with Fred now and see what he says," Ingram said. "There might be a simple answer, but at very least the commune should be kept informed."

Jeff was already heading for the door. "Will do, ma'am."

"Dr Mendoza, do you need me to do anything right now?" she asked.

"Not really. I just thought you needed to know there might be some issues with the long-term welfare of our teerik neighbours. I'd rather panic first and scale back later than assume everything's going to be fine."

"My thoughts entirely," Ingram said. "Thank you."

Ingram hung around for a while talking to the other medics to try to understand what else they'd worked out so far, and it wasn't all bad news. The lab AI had already come up with formulations for two anaesthetics that might be safe for teeriks, as well as modifications to some of the Opis-specific vaccines and antibiotics that had been developed for the Nomad mission. Again, this was the clever stuff, and mostly achieved without humans. It reminded Ingram how dependent the mission was on bots, AIs, and now aliens.

Before *Cabot* launched, she'd been on an orientation course that explained how bots had mined, refined, and manufactured everything she could see today, reconditioned the local environment, then found the toxins and pathogens that might harm human settlers and formulated the drugs that would protect them. But it had never seemed so stark before that humans were guests and the bots could carry on functioning without them.

Now she was also reliant on aliens who might be gone in a few decades, taking their knowledge and skills to the grave. No wonder Chris and some of the others were teaching people to be self-sufficient.

Ingram went back to her office, wondering about developing a teerik-equivalent AI or even a teerik breeding programme. It all depended on what that mystery substance was and if it had any bearing on teerik health. They seemed to be able to eat a wide range of food with relatively little modification, though, and Rikayl had eaten Mildred the chicken as well as the local wildlife without any apparent ill effects. Ingram remained hopeful.

There was an opaque white storage bag about eight inches high sitting on her desk when she opened her office door. She bent over to read the attached label before picking it up. It was from Lianne.

Sorry about Paul, it read. *He's harmless really. Remember not to rinse it or it won't cook up like arborio.*

Ingram shook the bag like a maraca before opening it. It was rice, polished to perfection. Now she could cook the only dish she could do well. This was a win. She'd entertain Marc to dinner as she'd promised, and diplomatic relations with the crop boffins were still intact. She took her victories where she could these days.

Jeff reported back to her just before lunch. "Ma'am, Fred says they all feel fine and he doesn't recall ever being given supplements back in Deku. I wouldn't argue with a teerik's memory."

"Perhaps it's age-related after all."

"True. But he's said they're all happy to provide feather and blood samples to help the research. Even Turisu. I'll get Haine and Mendoza on it."

"Excellent. Thanks, Chief."

Well, that was something. They'd solve the puzzle because they always did. She went downstairs to the canteen to get lunch, noting who was around and pausing to ask how things were going, and was on her way out with a sandwich and a container of milk when she ran into Marc coming the other way.

"Any news on Tev?" she asked.

"Not yet. Tell me more about teeriks. I got the note. Sounds like we'd better make the most of them while they're still standing."

"And I thought I was the heartless utilitarian." Ingram nodded in the direction of the external doors. "Want to share a sandwich?"

"Yeah. Thanks."

They went outside and sat on the low wall in front of the flagpoles. Ingram handed him one half of her ham and pickle on supermarket white.

"I told Paul Cotton that if they want to explore off-camp, we can't give them escorts and they're on their own," she said. "I hope they don't get overconfident about their firearms skills."

"Or too bolshy."

"But I got some rice out of the visit. Risotto's on."

"See, you've still got that knack of blagging stuff off people. What is it you matelots call it?"

"Baron strangling."

"A worthy art. So what are we going to do about the teeriks?"

"I know I'm a granite-hearted harpy, Marc, but I'm looking at the worst case scenario of a post-teerik Opis."

Marc peeled the sandwich apart to check the filling. Everyone seemed to do that now, confirming it was the real thing even if it was dehydrated, frozen, or vac-packed, and not the first locally-manufactured substance to appear in their meals.

"We either learn to copy what they can do, aided by Sol, or we plan for reverting to pre-teerik levels of technology," Marc said, apparently satisfied that the ham was genuine. "It's just as well we've had lots of experience of going backwards on Earth."

"I always wondered why none of their clients could copy their work."

"I think the teerik advantage is continuous innovation. They're always ahead in the arms race. But even if I knew how to make a violin, I couldn't build a Stradivarius. Knock-offs are usually different if all you're doing is copying. And then there's how fast they can calculate the really big numbers."

"Solomon can do that." Ingram thought about it. "But what we need is a teerik-brained AI. The mystery substance thing will work out, I'm sure. Then all we have to do is worry about them going extinct here."

"If they're short of a vitamin or something, it might explain why they're getting so argumentative," Marc said. "Lack of vitamin D does that to humans. Makes them stroppy. Lots of deficiencies show up as behavioural shit."

"You're quite encyclopaedic, aren't you?"

"I was trained to live off the land if I had to exfil the hard way," Marc said. "So I need to know stuff."

"It's fascinating."

"Okay, instead of gating my way into the Kugad parliament to plant IEDs, then, I'll swing by the Deku branch of Superdrug and pick up a bottle of multivitamins. Do we even know what fit and well should look like in a teerik?"

"Fred thinks they're all fine."

"Did the medics have any more ideas on why Rikayl wasn't the full quid?"

"Not that they mentioned to me. Maybe they will when they sequence the genome."

"They've still got to work out what all the genes do, though," Marc said. "Which is the complicated bit that takes years."

"Have you been reading up on this?"

"I chat with the boffins when we have a tea break on the range. I also drink with Todd Mangel. He's explaining string theory to me a pint at a time."

"I'm in awe."

"So you should be."

"Well, whatever this declining substance does, we've got our teeriks for a few more useful decades," Ingram said. "Unless the Jattans show up first."

"Or the Kugin. They normally show up together, remember."

"When do you think the opposition's going to notice Gan-Pamas is missing? It's one thing to lose a warship that isn't really yours anyway, but when you lose the chap who said he'd find it for you as well, you're bound to think the worst and start blaming people."

"What, you mean they'll think someone got to him, or that the enemy assassinated him?"

"It's too much to hope that they just blame their enemies."

"Or their man on the inside," Marc said. "Because they're bound to have a few. They probably don't even know we exist because Gan-Pamas didn't call it in. But we still don't know why he showed up here in the first place. And that's the bit that bothers me."

It was the question that kept getting buried in the snowstorm of recent events. Everyone, Fred included, said nothing was emitting a telltale signal. Perhaps it was just something as simple as Jattans expanding their search for places to seize, and it was Nomad's bad luck to be in a previously undesirable neighbourhood.

Twice, Ingram thought. *Twice.*

If it happened again, she'd know that luck — good or bad — had nothing to do with it.

* * *

OFFICE OF THE GOVERNMENT OF JATT IN EXILE, CLERICS' QUARTER, ROUVELE, SOUTHERN VIILOR, ESMOS: ONE FULL SEASON SINCE LAST CONTACT WITH GAN-PAMAS IRIL, CONTROLLER OF PROCUREMENT.

A glorious coral sunset illuminated the cobbled courtyard below the office window and marked another day that Nar P12 had still not been found.

But that was probably a good sign. The enemy hadn't recovered the ship. Nir-Tenbiku Dals, Rightful Mediator of Jatt, Primary in Exile, would have known if they had. His intelligence network had never let him down. He'd spent a working lifetime cultivating the patriots and malcontents in the naval ministry and the civil service, and the government-in-waiting had now been graciously accommodated by the Esmos Convocation in Viilor for twenty years. He was willing to bide his time to remove the illegitimate regime in Jevez, but not forever. It was a task he couldn't hand down to his children in the same way his father had bequeathed it to him. The Jatt Protectorate had to end in his lifetime.

He also needed to see it completed before he was too old to personally supervise the purge of all Kugin influence from the nation — from the entire world — and declare it to be the state of Jatt again, free of foreign dependency.

Protectorate. Imagine voluntarily renaming your nation to tell everyone you were happy to be the snivelling pet of barbarians. The Common Welfare Party that usurped his grandfather's office as the true heir of Jevezsyl might as well have burned the standard and called the country Kugad's Whore. He understood them for wanting to be rich, but the only point of wealth was to *do* something with it, and they had done nothing visible for the public good.

They'd simply sold the nation to the expansionist Kugin. The noble state prefixes to their family names were an insult to Jattans. When he returned and placed the illegitimate government under arrest, he would replace Gan, and Nir, and all their other honorific pre-names with *Hebudi* to remind the citizens that these traitors rolled over and licked the Kugin's hands like domesticated animals. They'd begged for annexation. That subjugation was a permanent stain on every Jattan's honour.

We are not a colony. We are not a state under Kugad's rule. We are Jatt, and we will seize our independence again.

Nir-Tenbiku stood at the window to enjoy the gentler light of early evening. It was generous of Esmos to give the exiled government asylum here, untouchable in the centre of the priestly enclave, but the climate was uncomfortably dry for a marbidar and the sun was too bright for his eyes. Mornings and early evenings were tolerable, though. Perhaps he'd go for a walk in the grounds tonight to enjoy the cooler air and the acoustic imagery of the gardens without the interruption of anyone else moving around and spoiling the fine echoed detail in his mind. His open daybook reminded him that the clerics would be singing tonight from the first star to the sunrise to mark the start of the season of redemption, so that would be a pleasant diversion as well, at least until he needed to sleep. Then he'd have to shut out the sound as best he could.

The shadows from the gates stretched further across the cobbles and then disappeared as the sun dipped below the roofline. Nir-Tenbiku sat down at his desk and caught up with the intercepted messages collated by his agents, but he lost his concentration and found himself worrying about Gan-Pamas Iril again.

It wasn't the first time that Gan-Pamas had disappeared for extended periods in radio silence, and Nir-Tenbiku accepted that arming an invasion force required discretion and secrecy. Kugin agents were everywhere. But this was still a long time to hear no word at all.

He got up and waved a chart open. At this scale, he could see both Velet and Dal Mantir in their respective star systems, and if he expanded it, the three-dimensional image took in Bhinu as well. Intelligence had told him that the teerik rebellion — the communes constructing ten vessels in Kugin yards — had agreed a rendezvous point around thirty light years from Velet. But only one had left Velet space, the prototype Nar P12, and the teeriks who'd hijacked it hadn't waited at the rendezvous point, probably realising by then that they were on their own. Gan-Pamas had said that Lirrel thought he knew where they might have gone after that — there were limited options unless they were prepared to search for even more distant and uncharted worlds — and that it might take some time to hunt them down.

Nir-Tenbiku had hoped the commune refitting the Fourth Fleet flagship would escape and hand the vessel to him, because that was the biggest prize, but he'd be satisfied with the stealth vessel. It was small but it had other value: apart from its unique technology and its ability to insert special forces, it was commissioned by the Jattan Protectorate's intelligence service. It was destined to be used to suppress unrest on Jattan colony worlds and even attack other nations on Dal Mantir deemed to be harbouring security threats. To fly that ship over Jevez in full view of the population and turn it on those who planned to use it on their fellow citizens would send a clear message that the Protectorate and especially its secret police had lost control.

And if Jatt rebelled, the most powerful and obedient servant of the Kugin for three generations, then other Kugin protectorates would be emboldened to overthrow their masters too.

There was the matter of how the Kugin government would react to a coup in one of its dependencies, but as they were greedy barbarians who had no pride, all they would care about was keeping the minerals and rare metals flowing from Jatt's mines. If they tried to invade the country and seize any facilities, they'd face opposition every step of the way and the mines and quarries they relied upon would be destroyed.

Nir-Tenbiku was confident he could rally the population. He already had half the navy waiting on his word.

"So where are you, Iril?" he murmured to himself. He tried to be objective and forget Gan-Pamas was his friend so that he could judge the urgency of the situation properly. "Are you still searching, or did those parasites catch you?"

He closed down the chart display with another wave. He'd opened it every day for years but nothing had changed. It was useful to visualise where his agents were, but it was mostly to remind himself what Jatt had lost and how much the traitors had given away.

He glanced out of the window again and decided it was time for that walk. After locking his office, he made his way down to the courtyard and turned right outside the ornate metal gates. From there he followed the course of the ornamental stream that ran in a curving, marble-lined conduit and sat down by the fountain with its permanent cool mist of water droplets.

How was Jatt going to pay the Esmos Convocation for all this support? The house of Tenbiku could cover the cost of maintaining the Halu-Masset, the government-in-exile, but Esmos had given it sanctuary, and however righteous the Convocation was, it would expect favours in return one day. None of the families funding the restoration of Jatt had fallen into poverty yet, but arming a revolution wasn't cheap. It was another reason he couldn't wait indefinitely.

At least the prototype would be free of charge, other than maintenance. A great deal of covert effort had gone into exploiting the teerik rebellion, such as it was, and there'd been no guarantee it would yield a single ship or deprive the Kugin of any engineering capacity, so seizing the most advanced vessel the Kugin were willing to sell to allies and a commune of teeriks would be a good result.

Once the ship was found, the teeriks wouldn't put up a fight. They weren't pirates. For all their brilliance, they were cosseted and helpless. They couldn't live indefinitely in a ship like that, they couldn't live off the land, and they'd need to set down somewhere they could breathe the air and find water. That narrowed their options.

Nir-Tenbiku sat on the low marble balustrade that surrounded the fountain and dipped his hands in the water. Perhaps the Protectorate navy or the Kugin had already caught up with Gan-Pamas. He'd deny being part of the true government and use that flimsy cover story of being an arms dealer, but nobody would be fooled because he looked and sounded exactly what he was; the well-educated, well-bred, genteel, favourite son of an old family from Gan. He wouldn't even fool a drunken Kugin.

How much longer do we have?

Are we already too late?

Nir-Tenbiku asked himself that question every day. He had capital ships of his own, but as time dragged on, they weren't being updated to keep pace with the Protectorate's fleet. There were loyalist commanders in the Protectorate navy who would join the rebellion when the day came, and perhaps that would be enough. In the end, though, it would come down to ordinary Jattans being willing to take back their country as well.

The priests had started their singing for the night. It was a plaintive sound, unaccompanied by music, and it was soothing even though it had no spiritual meaning for him. He was thinking anything but spiritual thoughts these days. His plans were full of destruction and vengeance, but they'd been with him for so long that they'd acquired a kind of quiet normality, a list of actions that he could open like a book when he sat down at his desk in the morning and leave behind when it was time to have his evening meal. They rarely made him feel angry these days, just impatient to complete the task.

He moved around the fountain to one of the ornately carved pillars that rose out of the balustrade to sit with his back against it. All he could hear was the priests' song, the patter of water, and the occasional pop as a bud opened on one of the night-blooming vines. But now a noise intruded, growing louder, the sound of someone running on flagstones. He strained to target his echolocation to sense its shape and movement. Then he saw it in his head, a person on two legs, a marbidar like himself who'd surely feel the stream of clicks that Nir-Tenbiku was aiming at him, but the screen of ornamental trees and the colonnade blocked his line of sight and deflected too much of his signal.

Someone was running towards him. *Nobody* ran here. This was the cloistered part of Rouvele, a quiet place of perpetual contemplation usually populated only by those in holy orders, and the Halu-Masset was here because nobody would dare enter the area, let alone risk

Esmos's retribution by attempting an assassination. But an assassin was the first possibility that came to mind.

Nir-Tenbiku reached inside the drape of his tunic to find his weapon. But then the echo-image resolved into a more familiar shape and his eyes confirmed it was only Bas Ayin, his aide. Bas slowed to a very fast walk as he approached him, trying to recover some dignity, but it was clear from his panting that he was agitated.

"Excellency," he said. "We've intercepted an emergency beacon." All his arms were twitching. "It's from the Controller of Procurement. Excellency, I fear he might be dead by now. And he found something shocking."

Bas held out his personal recorder. Whatever the message said, he'd thought it was too dangerous to risk sending it over a network even on friendly territory. Nir-Tenbiku took the device and touched it to unfold its display.

It was certainly from Gan-Pamas. He'd located the stolen ship, which he only referred to as *the object*, but he was in trouble.

'I'm now marooned on a planet at the above coordinates beyond Kugin Gate Four, which appears uninhabited except for a military outpost of a previously unknown civilisation. As I send this, their troops are searching for me. My teerik killed one of their females and was shot dead himself.'

Nir-Tenbiku had to read it twice to take it in. Gan-Pamas was unlikely to make a mistake about a new sentient species in the sector. How could they be unknown? The location was some way outside the Kugin Mastan, but it was still hard to hide a spacefaring civilisation, which these beings had to be if they'd acquired the prototype ship. Nir-Tenbiku read on, skipping over detail about the problems with the teerik and pouncing on the next disturbing word and skimming the bad news.

'I now find myself without a ship. The aliens captured it, presumably to stop me escaping. I have to assume they removed its confidential data as well. They have teeriks with them, so we must also assume they know our locations, strengths, and weaknesses by now. One of the teeriks relayed a warning telling me to surrender and make amends for the killing... This indicates the teerik rebellion was in contact with them before the object was stolen, and the incident may well have been instigated by the aliens themselves.'

What incident? The teeriks' rebellion had been their own idea and his agents had simply managed to exploit it. Now Gan-Pamas was suggesting these newcomers might have engineered the whole thing. Nir-Tenbiku read on, still skipping lines to pull out the most significant detail.

'I would have preferred to have spoken to them and invited them to join us in ridding the sector of Kugin... their settlement seems recently built... I believe this is a military outpost of a much larger empire... They are bipedal, fast-moving, and as large as Kugin. They appear to coexist with a community of mechanicals, and another unknown intelligent species, aggressive tetrapods... These aliens are well-armed and I have to assume they have vessels in orbit or in bunkers that are equally well equipped.'

The next part was very hard to read. Gan-Pamas — his friend, his loyal minister, a brave man if a frequently rash one — was waiting to be hunted down and probably killed, and yet he made a selfless plea to Nir-Tenbiku, knowing what his fate would be.

'I can't tell if they represent the greatest threat to us since the Kugin or a potential new ally, but we must try to make them the latter... I'm observing the aliens at close quarters, so I can't remove my suit. It's overheating as a result and I'll be forced to discard it soon, and that will probably seal my fate... I'll gather as much intelligence as I can... These new aliens are significant, and I urge you to overlook whatever happens to me and seek some kind of understanding with them. They represent a potential shift in the balance of power and that is an opportunity we can't ignore. I knew the risks when I took this mission, and if the end result furthers our cause, I die content. I believe they are called Humans. Their arrival changes everything.'

Nir-Tenbiku checked the message's routing, indicated in the address panel. The date and location of origin were marked as "unknown" and "indecipherable." Gan-Pamas had encrypted everything, not just the message within. He didn't even want the clerical staff to know his position.

"Bas, who else has seen this?"

"Only me, Excellency. I was handed the intact unit. I decrypted it myself. The date and location were obscured when I received it and this is a once-only code. So the only people who have ever set eyes on this are Gan-Pamas, yourself, and me."

"Then it stays between us while I work out the implications. This is the first contact with a new intelligent species in *millennia*. And I hardly dare consult *anyone's* government on the proper procedures now. We will use our intellect and our honour to reason our way through this, Bas."

Nir-Tenbiku tried to separate the fate of his friend from the shocking news. The stolen warship was there, wherever this place was, and a new empire was rubbing up against the borders of the Mastan. The last thing he needed was for the newcomers to align with the Kugin and the Protectorate, although he doubted that had happened yet, not if they had the ship. He'd have heard. If this outpost was that secret, and these humans had somehow infiltrated the teerik community, then they probably weren't planning to be on friendly terms with either power.

Where had they come from, though?

It was hard to know whether he was looking at a disaster or a stroke of timely good fortune. And he didn't know if his friend was still alive. He had to hang on to the hope that he was, although the insane teerik had probably ensured the worst by killing one of the humans. Yes, Gan-Pamas needed a competent engineer, but he'd taken a terrible risk with Lirrel and the worst had come to pass.

"Come to the office," Nir-Tenbiku said, striding back down the path. "Let's see where this outpost is, and try to gather a few more facts before we involve the Halu-Masset."

Nir-Tenbiku was on his own now, dealing either with a new threat or a perfectly-timed blessing.

05

I know you can't hear me, but I knew you so well that I can imagine what you'd say if I asked you for guidance. I suppose I'm talking to myself, and that worries me. But Marc admits he talks to the photo of his dead sons, and Captain Ingram and Chris talk to dead people as well. Please don't think I'm feeling sorry for myself. But I would really like to talk to you again one day, Mr Bednarz. Sometimes I get scared, and I daren't tell them that.

> Solomon, autonomous self-determining moral AI,
> constructing a conversation with his late creator,
> Tad Bednarz.

BEER GARDEN, NOMAD BASE: MID-AFTERNOON, OCTOBER 10, OC.

Srale turned out to be a non-starter when the probe's data was analysed, but Solomon wasn't worried.

Project Nomad didn't need a new location because he had his own plan. But people needed to talk about it to feel they were doing something, and he understood why.

He wandered around the lawn in the quadrubot, listening to the discussion as Ingram held court over sandwiches and soda in a quiet corner of the outdoor recreation area dubbed the beer garden. Dr Kim, Alex, and Dr Mangel were offering up ideas. Chris was leaning back in his seat, staring up at the sky, hands meshed on his stomach as if he wasn't listening.

"What's wrong with it?" Alex shook the mustard dispenser, trying to coax some out onto his sandwich. "Idiot's guide, please."

"It's got a very short day, and there's an equatorial region between huge ice caps, but it's like the end of summer in the Arctic," Ingram said. "So it's survivable, but nothing like Opis. It'll need sealed habitats and acres of greenhouses. Lower oxygen, too, so like climbing Everest without BA. But we'll keep looking."

"How many star systems has Fred got on his list?" Kim asked. "Is there a Kugin or Jattan telescope mapping and analysing stars?"

"I've not found one," Solomon said.

"And you've been rummaging."

"I can be of more use to Fred if I'm fully informed."

"Well, we've got a huge database of exoplanets, and we're medieval peasants compared to aliens with interplanetary empires, but maybe the civilisations here just don't look further afield for some reason. We could pick locations for the probe to check out. Come to that, Todd could manage the project. He's the astrophysicist, after all."

"I *did* take a look at what we've got, actually," Mangel said. "Nothing ideal so far, but it's certainly worth a second pass with the probe."

"Well, if Kugin territory covers nine star systems like Fred said, and teeriks can survive on the Kugin homeworld as well as here, I'd take a guess that there are nine planets a lot like Opis, and that bodes well for others," Kim said. "Even Fred says there are more out there. He just wasn't very specific."

"He never is."

"Todd, if you want to work with Fred, I think he'd appreciate it," Ingram said.

Mangel shrugged as if he wasn't fussed, but he was like a child with a perpetual birthday out here, surrounded by aliens, new worlds, and magical space stuff that he never thought he'd see. Given what Marc had said about the man's tragic past, it was good to see there was still joy in his life.

"I could look after the whole project for you if you like," Mangel said. "I don't really have a role at the moment, other than occasionally teaching fifth-graders about quantum hair."

Solomon was satisfied. "I'll talk to Fred and set up a link for you to have control of the probe, then."

"Enclosed habitats aren't the worst we could do, to be honest," Kim said. "It beats starving. People thought Mars was okay."

"Are they okay now, though?" Ingram asked. "I still haven't caught up with that. Nothing on the news."

"When I left Seoul, the only operational Mars bases were Chinese and they were self-sufficient. That was roughly eighteen months ago. The resupply missions were emergency-only because the APS space agency couldn't resource them."

There was a brief silence. "Have they left them to starve?" Ingram asked.

"No idea, but there's not much anyone can do about it if they can't maintain and launch rockets."

That was the real conversation going on here, a proxy debate for how they felt about Earth, that even the comparatively mighty APS was impotent and faced as many dilemmas as they did. Solomon could see it. They weren't thinking of an alternative location for Nomad: they were imagining where to put refugee camps. They could only deal with it obliquely because the idea of having extraordinary FTL technology and not using it right away was almost unbearable. Solomon was happy to humour them with distractions if that was what it took to keep them from feeling they'd casually abandoned Earth to its fate.

If the worst happened, Solomon had his own evacuation plan. He was still working out the least confrontational way to reproduce or commandeer the Caisin gate generator, but once he had one and could operate it, he could send ships and people anywhere to escape, either permanently or until the immediate crisis had passed. He had infinite locations to choose from. He might not have been able to insert people into precise locations without intelligence about layouts and a great deal more assistance from a navigation AI, but he could pinpoint coordinates well enough to move ships into orbit or open a gate on Earth. That would be enough.

He could also calculate trajectories to send enemy warships straight into a convenient star. It was like being able to move the edge of a cliff in front of someone's next step. Or he could just launch a missile through the gate and strike far away.

There was no point in discussing that with Ingram or anyone else yet. They'd almost certainly worked out that he'd intervene and remove them from imminent danger, because he'd done it before with Chris and Marc, even though they'd been furious about it. But they needed this complex illusion of creating another haven to square their consciences with having an instant escape route that they wouldn't or couldn't share. Solomon had finally worked out the mental gymnastics required. As long as searching for alternative sites for Nomad could also be thought of as finding a home for Earth's refugees — which it would — they felt they weren't abandoning fellow humans.

Recreating this base, complete with conditioned land and all the turnkey facilities they'd walked into was going to take decades, if only because of the bot replication cycle. Assuming a suitable planet was identified right away, they were looking at sixty or seventy years.

They had an impossible choice. Whatever they could do would be too little or too late. Most people would shrug and say they'd tried, but Nomad military personnel had a reflex to step in and fix situations, and had to tell themselves a lie to live with their impotence. They *knew* they were lying, too. And it kept them sane.

Chris was still gazing skyward as if he was checking for rainclouds, but he looked resigned. Solomon could tell he knew he was going to ruin everyone's illusion and wished he didn't have to.

"It's not just alien invasions we need to worry about," he said. "It's our own kind as well."

Alex looked at him sideways. "Our little ray of sunshine."

"Okay, if you seriously think we can do anything at all, then we don't need to find one planet, we need a dozen," Chris said. "Once we give away the FTL data, we'll have no control over what they do with it. If Earth's in that much trouble, they're either going to be out of time already, or they'll get as far as building FTL ships and say screw it, let's head over to that nice Opis place. They'll come here unless we give them a reason not to."

"You sound just like Marc," Ingram said.

"Did you disagree with him?"

"No. That's the hard part."

"I bet he said the first people to show up would be troops and a team of government busybodies," Chris said. "And that's where we lose control of everything, even if they're Brits or Americans. Apart from a lot of room, Opis also has the raw materials that Earth's short of. If we give incomers an incentive to go elsewhere and play with their own planet, the less chance there'll be of them overrunning us. That's not even a judgement on their potential asshole score. It's just numbers."

"Unless it's APS," Kim said. "That won't divert Pham from here. He doesn't forgive and forget."

"Good," Chris said. "Neither do I."

"Perhaps telling them about our alien warlord problem would encourage them to give Opis a miss as well," Mangel said. "It would explain the house prices around here."

"Sol, can we replicate the Nomad automation process on another planet?" Ingram asked. "Bots building bots, mining, manufacturing, environmental adaptation?"

"We could, Captain, if we can spare enough resources when the time comes," Solomon said. "But I agree with Chris. If there's nothing we can do immediately, seeding multiple planets is the next best thing. It's the least dangerous option for us, and spreading the population between planets provides the best chance for human survival if the local civilisations turn out to be as aggressive as Fred says."

Mangel smiled. "And you get to keep your breeding colony of saints cloistered from the wicked, Solomon."

"So I do, Dr Mangel."

"I haven't even identified the right people to send the data to yet," Kim said.

Chris stood up and collected the debris from his lunch. "If you'll excuse me, ladies and gentlemen, I've got to prep for a course. Catch you later."

Alex called after him. "Embroidery?"

"You guessed. I've booked you a place."

Alex watched him go for a few seconds, probably trying to work out if Chris had decided he'd had enough of the soul-searching. The conversation moved on to how many organisations might be able to supply their own habitat and infrastructure. It was getting very detailed, but Solomon didn't think there was any harm in forming an actual plan. Eventually the discussion ran out of steam and Mangel, Kim, and Alex went back to work. Ingram finished her soda and looked at Solomon with a narrow-eyed, frozen wink, an expression that demanded an answer to a question she hadn't asked.

"I know what you're thinking," she said. "But all I'm trying to do is stop people beating themselves up because they think they've left people to die. You're going along with this for the same reason. Yes?"

"I'm glad we've reached the same conclusion, Captain."

"There was a time when I'd have told them to park it for later and deal with the threat in hand. I can't do that so easily now because most of those looking back at Earth and worrying aren't my crew. I'm not going to lie to anybody and say we can do more than we can, but if the busywork actually has a benefit in the long term, so much the better."

"You don't have to explain yourself to me, Captain."

"Sol, you might be inside a bot, but somehow you have *expressions*," Ingram said. "And I know when you're looking at me with pursed lips."

"I'm happy we're both being realists, actually."

"And before you say I've done a number of U-turns on not looking back at Earth, I know, but I'm not in my comfort zone. I'm learning how to handle people who don't have to do a damn thing I tell them to. And the situation's changing all the time now."

"If morale-boosting starts to compromise the immediate needs of the base, I'll let you know."

"Thank you. Now, have I offended Chris again?"

"No, he really does have a full timetable. By the time he and his colleagues have finished, we'll have a population capable of defending themselves and able to survive if our facilities are damaged in an attack."

"Yes, I know they're doing a good job. But is he standing for sheriff of Kill Line?"

"He's of the opinion that an experienced law enforcement officer should stand, and we have at least two. Does it worry you that he might want the job?"

"Perhaps it should, but no. Never forget who's the majority here, Sol. I signed up to hand over to a civilian administration, so I do as the electorate ask."

"You'll never get anywhere in politics with an attitude like that, Captain."

Ingram laughed like she meant it. "A saucer of milk for our esteemed incorporeal colleague, please, waiter." She reached out and slapped her hand on the quadrubot's back. "I'm not gleaning much from the Jattan chatter. Are you doing any better?"

"It's a lot of listening to nothing. That's why it's best done by an AI."

"Because you don't get bored. I know."

"I do, in a way. I certainly feel impatient when something isn't productive. But I can relegate the task to another part of me and get on with something interesting."

"I'd pay good money to be able to do that." Ingram stood up and stretched. "Ah well, better get back to the mill. Is Peter still digging trenches to keep himself busy? I think I'll ask him if he'd like to work on the new settlements project."

"I'd be happy to ask him," Solomon said.

"Thank you, but I'd rather speak to him myself. We're too old and we've got too much history to do this I'm-not-talking-to-you nonsense." She took out her pocket screen and made a note. "Moving on, I'd like to visit *Elcano* and see how the drive installation's getting on. I need to show my face up there. Can you arrange that for me, please? Last time I discussed it with Fred and Brad, the drives were on target for trials by April."

"That's still the case," Solomon said. "I'll get on it."

He trotted off, checking the base map to see where Bissey was. The man had been helping out in the crop tunnels, but his icon now showed up in the new wheat field on Doug Brandt's farm. It was hard to tell if he was on his own because Kill Liners often didn't switch on their radios for tracking, but Solomon was adept at reading the movements and decided Bissey was talking with someone. After a few moments, Bissey turned around and walked in a straight line to the edge of the field, then headed towards the Brandts' farmhouse.

Solomon had been worried that Bissey might become an irritant now he had no military role, but he seemed to have thrown himself into agricultural life with some enthusiasm. Solomon wondered if he regretted his decision but didn't feel there was a way back, so he was making the best of it. But it just reminded Solomon how awkward the whole business was: everyone was technically a civilian, except perhaps Chris and Jared, but some people were *civilian* civilians. Once someone challenged Ingram's authority to make decisions, or Trinder's, or Chris's, the situation would get messy.

Ingram was right. Nomad needed to formalise the issue of a standing defence force. But that meant having a set of laws, and to have laws, a society needed to be a nation of some kind.

Bednarz hadn't foreseen die-back or how it would accelerate the Decline, or that Project Nomad's waves of carefully-selected settlers and civic administrators would be replaced by the only people left to take their places, Ainatio's last remaining staff and the population of the small town that serviced the research centre. Now Kill Line was holding its own elections, carrying on the cycle of a tiny city-state because it always had and still needed to. The whole of Nomad Base could do the same. It made sense that the best examples of humanity would evolve the right kind of society, so perhaps it was best to leave things to sort themselves out in time.

He'd sound out Chris and see what he thought. Of the Gang of Three — Bissey's rather acid nickname for Chris, Marc, and Trinder — Chris seemed to be most likely to take an interest in governance and kept reminding meetings that Mayor Brandt needed to be kept in the loop and have a say.

Chris was in one of the workshops across the road from the beer garden, collecting plumbing tools. Solomon trotted up to him and waited for an appropriate moment to interrupt.

"Hey Sol." Chris looked over his shoulder. "You signing up for lessons?"

"I think the python bots have more aptitude for plumbing tasks. Your people built your transit camp from scratch, didn't they?"

"We did." Chris examined a crescent wrench. "We've got all the skills. Time to pass them on."

"I don't think you need worry about Nomad being overrun, by the way."

"I didn't think you wanted an open door here either."

"Of course I don't. But the multi-planet approach was a good compromise, and you were right to raise it. It's the best we can do in the long run."

"Sure, as long as it doesn't take our eye off the ball. And as long as people don't see things on Earth getting worse every time they switch on the news and start thinking that maybe we should take the risk and open a Caisin gate. Which, of course, is exactly why most of us are here now. So I'm fully aware of the irony as well as my hypocrisy."

"Chris, the difference was that we calculated the base could absorb the evacuees," Solomon said. "Everyone knows that."

"I should feel bad about pulling the ladder aboard, because guilt's a normal human response, but I don't. There's a reason CBRN instructors tell you to put your own mask on first."

"You don't have to convince me. You understand why I don't want this colony to become like the Earth we left."

Chris looked down at him as if he was working out the best way to express something awkward. "Yeah, but we might not meet your expectations, Sol. We're not saints. Most folks here aren't assholes, either. They're just normal. I worry about Opis being a magnet for scumbags and chancers, so yeah, I agree with Bednarz about not exporting our failings. But you're all about the best and I'm more about us not being the worst. I'll be happy if we end up with a society that has some basic values like helping your neighbour when they need it and minding your own business when they don't. Nothing high-minded or perfectionist. Just better than the cesspit we left."

Georgina Erskine used to talk about a higher ideal than that, a fresh start that would create its own human civilisation instead of reproducing a theme-park version of Earth, as she put it. Awareness of history was essential to a healthy society, but excessive reverence for the achievements of the past only made people believe humanity's peak was over and that it could never be greater, so Project Nomad didn't need a grand vault housing a collection of priceless art for posterity. It would produce its own artists. But the Director had had the project thrust upon her by her dying father, and she'd spent her life making the very best of a bad job.

It was going to be a difficult moment for Solomon when she was eventually revived and he had to explain everything that had happened while she'd been in cryo.

"Can I change the subject and beg a favour?" Chris asked.

"Certainly."

"Would you make something for me? Well, hypothetically, because I haven't asked the recipient yet."

"Ah, Captain Fonseca."

"No, not Fonseca. Marc. If I wanted a memorial, would you need me to give you a design, or do you think it up yourself? I know you programme bots to do the stonework, but I never asked where the designs came from."

"I can do either," Solomon said. "We have plenty of image sources now."

Chris blinked a few times. "Marc's never had anywhere to grieve for his sons. He's thinking about it. Would you make something?"

"Of course. Was there no grave on Earth, then?"

"His boys loved white-water canoeing. He scattered their ashes in their favourite river."

For all Solomon's ability to monitor everything, there were still things he didn't know about his humans, and they were often the most important ones. He imagined the tumbling river and the moment Marc let go of the last physical trace of his sons. It must have been very hard. Solomon didn't like the idea of cremation. Perhaps his own uncertain relationship with an absence of a physical form made it seem more like erasure than eternal rest.

"I'll do it happily, Chris," he said. "Let me know."

"Thanks, Sol." Chris zipped up the holdall full of tools and headed for the door, then paused to look back for a moment. "I like it here. We should take our time working out what we want this place to be, not get bounced into decisions we can't change later."

At least they still agreed, even if it was for slightly different reasons. The dread Solomon had felt when Ingram and Marc had seemed willing to jeopardise his mission out of a misplaced sense of responsibility had finally passed. They'd thought it through, seen sense, and gone for a compromise, giving Solomon breathing room.

It wasn't about stopping more humans from colonising deep space but about making sure they didn't do it *here*. Earth would eventually recover a few generations from now. Many humans would never want to leave anyway, and even without FTL, others would still find a way to reach new planets. The fate of Earth and the future of mankind as a spacefaring species wasn't the sole responsibility of anyone here. Project Nomad was just a small part of of an inevitable future.

There, Mr Bednarz. I think that actually squares the circle. I'm sticking to my task. I'm protecting them, but without coercion. They've worked it out for themselves.

It's hard, isn't it, Solomon? But you got there in the end. It's no small feat.

Solomon wondered if he was talking to his imaginary Bednarz a little too much now. But as long as his humans talked to the dead, he didn't feel he was defective.

He returned to the main building, parked the quadrubot in its charging bay, and slipped back into the network. The continuous feed from the Jattan navy was now making more sense with some helpful input from Fred, so he listened to it consciously while he got on with the rest of his work rather than leaving the linguistics AI to flag issues below the level of his attention. This was probably how humans felt when they played music or an audio show while they worked.

A quick check showed Nomad Base was running smoothly. The assorted bots moving around the site were doing their additional duties of sampling for die-back and reporting anything that had changed position — objects and people — to keep the interactive base map updated. Utilities and the security network — perimeter, hazardous processes, general safety monitoring — were a bank of virtual green lights. From the network of sensors, Solomon could see personnel going about their business. He didn't need to be consciously aware of any of this unblemished normality as long as the dumb AIs around the base were running, but it was a strange view to have of his community if all he actively saw were the problems.

It was a little harder to keep an eye on Kill Line, because both the town proper and what had been the transit camp had few security cameras. They just preferred not to be continuously monitored. Public areas like the school and the town hall had security cameras, and Solomon could still detect emergencies like fires via the fleet of aerial micro-drones that could map a dozen indicators from spot temperatures to air quality. He erred on the side of respecting the Kill Liners' wish to not only have privacy in their homes but also on their streets.

See, Mr Bednarz? It's not ideal for me, but it's what they want. They're adults. They can choose. We've reached a compromise. Now I'll check the vessels.

Solomon transferred himself to *Elcano*, moving through the ship via the sensors to see how work was progressing on the new drive. He only glanced at the status indicators for the cryo berths. He really didn't want to see the chilled, unconscious faces of the people he'd known for so many years, least of all Georgina Erskine's.

Had she really wanted to shut him down permanently, to kill him? Yes, and he needed to remember that, and why it had happened.

He completed his sweep of *Elcano* and moved across to *Cabot*, deserted except for bots now that a duty maintenance team was no longer required to live on board. *Shackleton's* new drive was partially complete, although not as advanced as *Elcano's*, and *Eriksson* was showing some progress after being cannibalised for parts. Completion was still months away, but Solomon had his backup plan for the Caisin gate if an evacuation became necessary. He wasn't going to panic.

He finished looking over the ships and returned to the base to transfer into the quadrubot again. It was already getting dark, and the night was much more interesting when he could walk around. Outside the wire, the grassland was always full of interesting little nocturnal creatures moving about and preying on each other.

Solomon could see the path of the barrier field around the base even without switching to a different EM spectrum. If he looked on the ground, there was always a scattering of dead insect-like creatures that hadn't survived contact with the disruptive field. This part of Opis seemed to have few animals that filled the insect niche compared to Earth, but the situation might have been different elsewhere on the planet. One day, he'd see for himself instead of relying on the satellite net to watch it for him.

Inside the perimeter, Nomad was a round-the-clock operation, but the night belonged to the bots. This was when the housekeeping fleet moved out to clean offices and labs, cut grass, check pipes and cables, and generally maintain the site. But there were still plenty of humans up and about; the perimeter security patrol, engineers servicing vehicles, the duty medic, or just people working late. Up the road in Kill Line, the newly-completed tavern was still open and the lights were on in Mike Hodge's barn. Solomon wandered around, watching the entire settlement via feeds from drones and security cameras transmitted to his quadrubot, forming a patchwork of shadows and pools of light.

He could have viewed everything in daylight colour through the night vision settings if he'd wanted to, but he preferred to see the base as humans saw it and leave everything beyond that spectrum to the security system. Nomad looked settled and welcoming, a landscape dotted with lights from windows and the faint green glow of safety strips along the roads. It looked like *home.* Whatever was happening on Dal Mantir — and there was still no mention of the missing ship — the settlement was getting on with the simple business of living.

Half an hour later, though, the sensors alerted Solomon to unusual sounds and movements inside the walled teerik compound. It was one of the most monitored parts of the base, ensuring no intruder could reach the teeriks, and there were regular foot patrols, so Solomon's first thought was that Rikayl had grown bored and was causing havoc in the grounds. He switched back to the quadrubot's full array of sensors and picked up the feeds from the monitors spaced at intervals around the walls, just to make sure.

But it wasn't Rikayl.

The security lighting had been triggered and the grounds were lit up like a sports arena. Two of the adult teeriks were outside the house, shrieking and rasping at each other. One of them sprang into the air and slashed at the other with a clawed hind foot. Then the fight broke out in earnest.

Solomon turned and raced towards the compound. He knew Fred's two young grandsons had scrapped over food when the commune was running low on supplies, but he'd never seen the adults fight. Vehicle headlights snapped on behind him as a security patrol followed him in.

The first sight that met him when he passed through the gates was the two teeriks locked in battle, clawing at each other like fighting cocks and stabbing with their beaks. Blood and feathers flew. It looked like Pannit and Epliko, and Epliko was getting the worst of it. Pannit ripped into his neck and Epliko went down, wings spread, struggling to get up again. Pannit leaped on top of him, hacking out chunks with that fearsome beak.

Solomon knew the security teams were right behind him but a human wouldn't have much chance of separating them without shooting Pannit. This was a task for something built to withstand industrial levels of damage — a quadrubot. Solomon reared up on his hind legs and grabbed Pannit from behind, yanking him backwards and putting a crushing grip around his chest to subdue him. Pannit fought and screeched and threw Solomon backwards, but the quadrubot righted itself and Solomon lunged in to grab the teerik again.

Two of Trinder's troops, Gemmel and Schwaiger, jumped out of the Caracal. Gemmel had a cattle prod and he moved in to give Pannit a shock. It took three zaps to stop Pannit fighting back long enough for Schwaiger to put cargo straps around the teerik's legs, wings, and beak. They could worry about how they would release him later.

"What the hell happened?" Schwaiger was panting with the effort. "Jesus, he's killed the other one. Is that Epliko?"

"He's still alive," Solomon said. He activated the medical alert and went to inspect Epliko's injuries. "Commander Haine? We have a seriously injured teerik. It's Epliko. I realise this is unknown territory for you, but he has multiple lacerations from a fight."

"Bloody hell," Haine muttered. "Okay, bring him in. We'll be waiting at the rear doors."

"You said you'd identified an anaesthetic suitable for teeriks."

"Yes. But we haven't tested it."

"I fear we might not be able to afford that luxury. We're going to need to sedate Pannit, too. He's still fighting mad."

"We might end up killing both of them. Do we have a choice?"

"I don't think so."

Kilbride and Finch turned up in a rover and manhandled the trussed Pannit onto the flatbed. He couldn't open his beak to shriek but he was making ominous angry noises in his throat. As Gemmel and Schwaiger lifted Epliko into the back of the Caracal, Fred came out of the house, turned around, and slammed the door behind him. It opened again as Turisu tried to follow him but he drove her back with angry rasping noises and beating wings. Solomon could now translate enough Kugin to hear him telling her to stay inside and leave it to him. Fred dropped into that all-fours posture that Solomon had seen the youngsters use and ran towards the chaos like a pterosaur. Solomon tried to intercept him.

"Fred, they've had a fight," Solomon said, blocking his path. "Don't worry, Commander Haine's going to treat him. Leave it to us."

Fred's crest was raised and his neck feathers were fluffed up. It was hard to tell if he was shocked or angry. As the Caracal and the rover pulled away, he ducked down as if he was going to take off and flapped his wings a couple of times. While there was very little expression in a teerik's face that Solomon could read, he looked distraught.

"We *never* fight," Fred said. "We never even really argued until recently. Now we're harming each other. What's happening to us?"

He took off, following the Caracal up the path towards the green. Solomon kept up with him. It was a good question. Why would two of the quieter, more easy-going teeriks suddenly try to kill each other?

* * *

MEDICAL CENTRE, NOMAD BASE: 2115 HOURS.

The world was falling apart.

Everything that Hredt thought he knew about his own commune had been swept away. They weren't all blood relatives, but they'd worked together, lived together, and even rebelled together. They knew each other as well as anybody could. They quarrelled from time to time, and the difficulties of the last few months had made them increasingly irritable and argumentative, but apart from the odd warning peck and the tussles between his young grandsons, they'd never had physical fights. Teeriks didn't do that.

Now Epliko was lying in his own blood on a table while doctors tried to work out how to safely sedate him. Hredt stood to one side of the room, feeling helpless and desperate because he could do nothing and — even worse — he *understood* nothing. He'd never watched doctors working on a patient before, let alone seen serious injuries. Every treatment he'd had, and there hadn't been many, had been conducted under anaesthesia or in such a way that he couldn't watch what was going on.

Commander Haine, Dr Mendoza, and men and women in both blue loose-fitting tunics and ordinary clothes crowded around the table. Some wore transparent masks. There were projections and screens on the walls; a three-dimensional anatomical image of a teerik, numerical displays with flat lines, and things that Hredt couldn't even identify. Dr Mendoza was trying to examine Epliko, holding a medical instrument with two hinged parts, but the teerik was struggling too much.

"Damn, how much blood can this guy lose?" Mendoza muttered. "Logan, if we're going to try that stuff, do it now."

"Epliko, can you hear me?" Haine leaned over him. "We need to stitch you up to stop you bleeding. We can give you something so you don't feel the pain, but we don't know how safe it is. Do you understand? Will you let us do it?"

Hredt interrupted. "Is he going to die if you don't?"

"Unless teeriks have some auto shut-off circulatory system we haven't noticed, then yes, he might bleed out."

"Please do it then, Commander."

"As long as you realise this is informed guesswork on our part and we might end up killing him by accident," Mendoza said.

"You didn't kill Dieter, Dr Mendoza, and I hear you saved Chris. We trust you."

Mendoza gestured to someone to step forward, a woman in civilian working clothes who looked like she'd just come from one of the farms. "Lorna, can you intubate if I can get a line into him?"

"Let's find out," she said, wiping her hands with some kind of liquid as she studied the anatomical image. "Not so birdlike inside, then."

Hredt was reluctant to look away but too scared to watch. He shut his eyes as Epliko made some awful noises and feathers rattled against the metal table. Piecing together the sounds to work out what was going on only made things worse.

"Okay, he's breathing... and yeah, we've got his vitals," Lorna said, nodding at a screen on the wall. "I have no idea what's normal, but it's a start."

"Okay, everyone got a good grip? Then roll towards me... *now*."

"There you go. Yeah, hang on to that wing. So... if we go in *here*, I think we can clamp *that*."

Hredt forced himself to look.

He didn't know quite what to expect, but it was a lot less gory than he imagined it would be. The anatomical image was now superimposed on Epliko, who was turned towards one side, surrounded by a tight group of humans all doing inexplicable and separate things and yet not getting in each other's way. For someone used to seeing machinery and knowing exactly what it did, it was a sobering moment for Hredt. He could see the superimposed image acting like a map of an anatomy the humans didn't know well enough yet, and the objects over Epliko's beak and trailing from it were probably concerned with his breathing. Apart from that, the technology was beyond Hredt's analysis. The blips in the illuminated traces on the wall were impossible to interpret.

"Damn, I'm *magnificent*," Haine said suddenly. "He's stopped leaking. Okay, let's see what we can do about repairing the vessel."

"Is his heart rate okay?"

"Probably," Lorna said, watching some read-out. "Terrestrial birds have *way* higher heart rates than us. Flight, you see. Teeriks probably do too."

Mendoza turned around to talk to someone, gloved hands bloodied. "David, can you plug Fred in so we can get some idea of the numbers we're aiming for? BP, heart rate, oh-two sats. I know some of it might end up being irrelevant but it's the best we've got. Fred, is that okay with you?"

"What is?"

"We want to take your pulse and check a few other things so we know what the healthy numbers are for teeriks," Mendoza said. "It won't hurt. It's non-invasive."

"But I'm old," Hredt said. "Old isn't as healthy."

"You're alive and you can fly," Mendoza said. "That's close enough for us."

Hredt wanted to help Epliko, so he submitted to having a device clipped to his right hand. It was painless, as Mendoza had promised. But now he could see the numbers changing on one of the wall displays, and he began to understand what the read-outs meant. That green line was his heart, those red bars were something to do with oxygen, and those numbers were marked *BP*, which he assumed from the conversations going on meant blood pressure. The distraction of seeing himself as a machine for a while was quite soothing. Machines were predictable and reassuring in their constancy. His heart rate slowed a little.

"You wouldn't happen to know about blood types, I suppose?" Haine asked, not looking up from what he was doing. He seemed to be clicking something inside Epliko. "We might need to top up your friend. Blood loss, I mean. Can you transfuse teerik blood?"

"No need, he seems fine," Lorna said. Most of the humans were watching machines or displays, not the patient. "Probably safer not to risk it."

"I don't know," Hredt said. "I know nothing about how our health is maintained."

"It's okay. We'll work something out."

"Will he die?"

"Well, he's not haemorrhaging now, so we'll make sure we haven't missed anything and then see how things go over the next day or two." Whatever Haine was doing, Mendoza was watching it closely, occasionally reaching over to hold something for him without saying a word. "Just as well I've handled a few stab wounds in the service of His Majesty. There. Sorted. Let's close."

"I declare you guys honorary trainee vets," Lorna said. "Next up, you help me out with Liam's crazy bull."

"Sounds fair."

It felt like things had happened fast, but when Hredt looked at the clock on the wall, the surgery had taken forty-five minutes. He wanted to wait to see if Epliko woke from the anaesthesia, but he now had another problem to deal with, and that was what to do about Pannit.

"We're grateful," Hredt said. "Thank you."

"Our pleasure." Mendoza dropped his gloves in a bin. "You have no idea what a buzz it is to be the first surgeons to operate on an alien patient."

"Never mind him, Fred," Haine said. "I'm the sensitive, modest, and caring one here."

"Thank you again." Hredt felt a little shaky, but Haine and Mendoza had gone from grim to triumphant about the operation, which gave him hope. "Now I have to work out what we can do for Pannit."

"Good luck."

Solomon's quadrubot head peered around the door as if he'd been following what was happening and knew the best time to interrupt.

"Captain Ingram would like a word, Fred. Can you spare a few minutes?"

"Of course."

Outside in the narrow passage, Hredt found Ingram walking slowly up and down, hands on hips. She looked around.

"Fred, I'm so sorry. Is he okay? We'll do all we can for him. What started this?"

"I don't know."

"Pannit's still pretty agitated, so we haven't released him yet, not until we know what the problem is. Do you want to speak to him now?"

"It's not like him to be aggressive. He's always been rather meek, but he's been getting more assertive lately."

Ingram beckoned Hredt to follow her across the courtyard at the rear of the main building. The back entrance opened onto the security suite, and a recess in the main corridor led to a room with an impressively large handwheel on the door.

"I'm sorry we had to put Pannit in the vault," Ingram said. "But we had no idea what started him off or what he was capable of doing, and we don't have a secure cell to detain anyone."

She turned the wheel to open the door, which didn't appear to be locked. But Pannit wasn't in a position to escape. He was still trussed up, lying on his side on a bedroll on the floor, either exhausted or restored to his senses. Chief Jeff sat on a packing crate next to him, leaning forward with his elbows resting on his knees, talking to him. They couldn't have been having a conversation because Pannit's beak was still tied shut. Nobody seemed to be taking any chances. But at least he'd been made comfortable.

"Sorry, mate." Jeff stood up slowly and put his hand on Hredt's back. "We're just trying to avoid any more injuries. I'll release his beak if you want."

"Let me talk to him first."

Jeff stepped back and stood at the door with Ingram. There was no point in berating Pannit. He looked like he'd given up. His eyes followed Hredt.

"Pannit, if I untie your beak, will you promise not to attack me?" Hredt asked the question in English so Chief Jeff and Ingram would know he wasn't hiding anything. "I just want to know how this happened. Dr Mendoza and Commander Haine have treated Epliko's injuries. He'll probably heal, but he's quite badly hurt."

Pannit shut his eyes for a moment. Hredt took that as a yes. The only way they were going to solve this was to talk. Hredt reached to release the ratchet on the strap, half-expecting to get a sharp beak stabbed into him, but Pannit just took a few deep breaths. He seemed deflated. He even looked smaller.

"I'm sorry," Pannit said. "I got really angry. He kept getting in my way and I chased him out of the house. I don't know what made me hurt him. He'll hate me now, won't he?"

"He'll be scared of you for a while, but he'll get back to normal." Hredt hoped that was the truth. He didn't know how the commune would cope with one of them killing another. "We're all very bad-tempered. Perhaps we need to talk and work out what's wrong."

"I know I've been different."

"We all have."

"Can I get up now? I won't hurt anyone."

Hredt looked around at Ingram for an answer, but she was on the radio, talking to someone in a hushed voice while Jeff listened in. Hredt waited for her to finish. When she turned back to the room, she had a baffled expression, wrinkling the skin at the top of her nose in a way that didn't seem to be anger or disapproval.

"Hredt, one of the biomed researchers has been studying that substance we tested you for," she said. "He's got a theory. It's odd, but it might explain something. Can we have a word with him and the doctors first before we do anything?" She looked past Hredt. "Sorry, Pannit, can you hang on? If the medic's right, we might be able to give you something to make you feel a lot better."

Hredt owed it to Ingram to at least hear her out. He felt awful leaving poor Pannit where he was, still tied up, but if he was having aggressive impulses he couldn't control, then letting him loose at the moment wouldn't help. Hredt left him with Jeff and followed Ingram back to the medical centre.

The treatment room was clean and tidy again and Epliko had gone, presumably to recover in another room. Haine and Mendoza were talking to Lorna, then both men stood back and bumped fists, seeming pleased. There were adhesive labels now stuck to their tunics that read TRAINEE VET. It was obviously a joke, but they turned to look at him, smiled awkwardly, and peeled off the badges.

"Epliko seems to be doing okay, Fred," Lorna said. "You can see him later. He's started to wake up. There's a nurse with him, so he's perfectly safe."

"And we're waiting for Dr Tomlinson," Mendoza said. "If he's right about what he's found, the problem's probably solved."

"What is it?" Hredt asked. He could hear someone hurrying down the corridor. "What *is* this substance?"

"Ah, here he is. Ask the man himself."

A scientist Hredt didn't recognise walked in clutching his screen. "Sorry to keep you, guys," he said. "Hi Fred. I'm Kurt Tomlinson. I've been analysing your commune's specimens and I don't think that substance we couldn't identify is just a biomarker. It actually seems to be more like a tranquilliser."

"Bloody hell," Haine said. "Natural or manufactured?"

Hredt had to remember what a tranquilliser was. He understood the word, but it was outside his experience.

"We were never given medications like that."

"Well, it might be a nutritional supplement with the same effect, but whatever it is, the models I've been running predict certain outcomes," Tomlinson said. "You know our modelling AI? We can create a virtual body and work out the effect of substances, whether it's food, toxins, or drugs. It's the same technology that enabled us to make safe food for you."

"What does this substance do, then?"

"It appears to latch on to receptors in your brain and affects the part that controls impulses. Some naturally occurring substances in human food can have a calming effect on us as well, so it's possible you have a similar response to whatever this is."

"And you've worked all this out already?"

"With a *lot* of help from AI, yes." Tomlinson looked as pleased as Haine and Mendoza. These were great moments of discovery for them. Hredt was relieved that they weren't angry at all about teeriks causing so much trouble, just delighted by the science. "Pannit's level of this substance was much lower than yours, which might explain why he lost his temper with Epliko. I'm going out on a limb here, but if you don't recall being given medications, then it might have been introduced via your food. Humans do that too. We routinely fortify foods with minerals and vitamins, so it's not necessarily sinister."

"So this is to make us feel better," Hredt said.

"I think so. We can make it because we can see its molecular structure, and then we can treat you with it. We don't know the dose, but we can work that out by just upping the amount gradually until you feel better."

"Why didn't you detect the drug when Nina's team analysed our existing rations?"

"Probably because they didn't contain it. They weren't intended for you, were they? They were for whatever Jattan crew was going to take the ship out on trials. So you haven't been consuming this substance for months now."

Humans were definitely a long way ahead of Jattan and Kugin expertise in life sciences. Hredt was willing to try anything if it could help Pannit and perhaps calm down the others as well. But now he had more questions.

"We should do it," Hredt said. "Thank you. I'm very impressed."

"Shall we start with Pannit, then?"

"Please do. I don't want to keep him tied up like that. He's always been very quiet and respectful. But I have a question. Why would we need this substance to be added to our food in the first place?"

Tomlinson shrugged, but Hredt could see there was a little flicker of doubt in his expression. "Maybe it occurs naturally in the environment of wherever your species originated, but not in Kugad, so your foremen had to add it. We have essential nutrients on Earth that occur in some soils but are low in others, so we have to supplement crops as well as manufactured food in those areas."

"That would make sense."

"Do you want to try it? The problem is that I think your levels are continuing to fall. We've identified the feather Solomon found at the beginning of the year, and it belonged to one of your grandsons. But his level in the most recent test is a lot lower."

"Oh my." Hredt didn't want anything happening to the boys. "Test it on me, then. If it doesn't poison me, treat Pannit next."

Ingram spoke up. "Let's treat Pannit first. He's in most need, Fred."

Hredt thought of Rikayl, who'd never had food from a Kugin source, and he was neither dangerously aggressive nor docile. But that was a mystery for later. He needed to do what he could for Pannit, if only to be able to look Turisu in the eye and say he was doing everything to take care of the commune.

"Very well."

Tomlinson smiled. "I'll get right on it."

If this was the solution to the problem, and the commune returned to normal, Hredt would be able to focus on the work that needed doing. It might even improve Turisu's mood, although she'd always been more irritable and negative than the others. He began wondering about the dose. Perhaps a little extra would make her easier to get along with.

"You're always so kind to us," he said. "Thank you. I never forget how lucky we are to have crossed paths with you."

"Any time," Mendoza said.

Hredt went back to see Pannit to give him the good news. He found him sitting with Jeff, restraints gone, playing cards on the packing crate.

"He's fine now," Jeff said. "Don't worry."

"Dr Tomlinson's going to make a food supplement for us," Hredt said. "He thinks we're all getting bad-tempered because we're missing a substance we used to eat in Deku. You'll be the first to get it, Pannit."

"Can I see Epliko?"

"Tomorrow. Come back to the house and we'll have something nice to eat."

"Can we finish the game first?"

"Of course."

This was the Pannit Hredt knew. Perhaps it was just an isolated incident, but he'd agreed they'd all have the treatment. It would be nice to feel better again. He went outside with Ingram and they sat down on the wall outside the main building, looking up at the stars.

"You sure you'll be alright, Fred?" Ingram asked. "Pannit can stay here as long as he wants to."

"Thank you, but we can keep an eye on him until he gets his treatment. We'll come back and see Epliko in the morning."

"Command's hard, isn't it?"

"I'm not sure if I'm a commander, but I did take over without asking them when Caisin died, so it's my responsibility to look after them."

"You're the best man for the job," Ingram said.

"I try to be. These are worrying times."

"They are indeed. Actually, I wanted to ask you about better security for the Caisin gate generator. If the Jattan navy or the Kugin manage to get past the orbital defences, all they have to do is blow the base to bits and take *Curtis*, complete with the gate technology, and then the whole galaxy has a problem. I think it might be a good idea to relocate it in a bunker that they won't be able to penetrate or haul back to Dal Mantir."

"Is that what you're excavating at the moment?"

"An underground command centre, yes. And bomb shelters for residents around the site. Tad Bednarz foresaw a great deal, but not the fact that we might be under alien attack within months of arriving."

Ingram was still looking up at the night sky. Hredt thought that sounded reasonable. *Curtis* was only a convenient container for the gate generator. She had her own drive.

"I think that would be sensible," Hredt said.

Ingram nodded to herself. "How did you manage to get it in the ship without anyone knowing, by the way? You had to smuggle it out."

"We built it in situ. We deal with many departments and manufacturers that only make one component of a ship, so none of them ever have the full picture. The Kugin think that's best from a security perspective. From there, it's possible to assemble quite a lot without scrutiny. The gate generator isn't as big as you might think. It's more of a refinement than a radically different device."

"They must trust you a lot."

"Not any more they don't."

Ingram laughed. She seemed to think Hredt was being witty.

"For what it's worth, Fred, we're not leaving. We'd have to be facing total annihilation before we'd abandon Opis. And we won't abandon you, either. We're just making sure we're ready for anything. If we can't hold our ground here, humans won't ever be able to hold it anywhere."

She was right. Things wouldn't get any easier, because the rest of the galaxy showed evidence of being equally complicated and beset with rivalries and problems.

Hredt felt better than he had a couple of hours ago. Epliko was in good hands, there seemed to be a cure for the agitation that had affected the commune, and the humans of Nomad remained reliable allies.

A cure...

Dr Tomlinson had suggested the mineral or whatever it was might have occurred naturally on their homeworld, but not on Velet.

What did that mean? If the Kugin added it to their food, then they knew what it was, so did they also know where teeriks had come from originally, but had decided to erase it from the records? Did a lack of this substance actually make teeriks ill? Being aggressive wasn't the same as being unwell, but perhaps it was the early stages of a condition that got worse over time. The Kugin wanted to protect the health of valuable assets that gave them their military edge in the Mastan, and keep them happy. They hadn't been entirely bad, then, considering they were barbarians.

Hredt still wondered why teeriks couldn't recall their own history when they had such extraordinary memories. Someone, somewhere should have remembered places, fragments of language, even ancient customs, and spoken of them to their communes, and passed that knowledge down in stories as well. But there was nothing.

Perhaps it didn't matter if they never knew where they came from as long as they knew who they were now. He'd let himself get too anxious about that.

It was time to do some work. That always made him happy.

* * *

MEETING OF THE HALU-MASSET, CABINET OF THE GOVERNMENT OF JATT IN EXILE, WITH THE CHOSEN OF NIR, ORU, EB, SHUS, PARNI, AND VAN PRESENT, CHAIRED BY NIR-TENBIKU DALS, PRIMARY: TWO DAYS AFTER RECEIVING THE EMERGENCY MESSAGE FROM GAN-PAMAS IRIL.

"But where did they come from?"

The Controller of the Exchequer, Biltad Fas, seemed to be having trouble believing that a new species had arrived in the sector unnoticed. He leaned back in the seat and stared up at the star chart above him as if the answer was in there. But Nir-Tenbiku knew they weren't dealing with newcomers from a neighbouring sector. Humans must have come from much further afield.

"I think the more pressing question is *why* they came here, Fas," Nir-Tenbiku said. "I think we can assume they're not allies of the Protectorate, or they wouldn't have seized the ship."

"Are we sure we're being told everything?"

"Our informants take huge risks to gather intelligence for us. They're hardly likely to withhold anything."

"And you trust them."

"I do." Nir-Tenbiku knew there was some critical piece of information missing, but it wouldn't have been anything his spies could have uncovered or they'd have told him by now. "And I know we can trust Gan-Pamas's observations. He assessed this outpost as a garrison. I know he can be rash, but he's not a fool."

"Not a fool, but likely to be dead."

"Fas, he's my friend. I ask you to show some respect. And if he's been killed, it's all the more reason for us not to waste intelligence that he gave his life to obtain."

Fas looked surprised at the rebuke rather than penitent, and that bothered Nir-Tenbiku. Perhaps he'd lost his ministers' respect after so long in the comfortable wilderness of Esmos.

"My apologies, Primary," Fas said. "I meant no offence."

"So we need to take a look at these newcomers," Nir-Tenbiku said. "They're a complication, at the very least. Gan-Pamas believed it was worth seeing if they could be useful allies, and if we don't, someone else will. Neither the Protectorate nor Kugad want to open a war on another front, I'm sure of that, so they might step in first."

"With respect, these humans have the ship and a commune of teeriks." Lan Cudik spread his arms in his I-can't-possibly-be-wrong gesture. "The Kugin can't ignore that, no matter how much they'd rather avoid an expensive war. They're searching for the ship and they want their teeriks back. We know that. They changed their encryption, as have the Protectorate, because they didn't know what the teeriks would do with that data. The edge we have is that we *do* know. They'll have shared it with these humans."

Losing the teeriks had thrown Kugad into chaos, and Nir-Tenbiku had seen the evidence. His foreign relations minister, Shus-Wita Olis, had acquired transcripts of intercepted conversations between the Kugin and Protectorate defence ministries. Kugad had simply never had a commune escape before, let alone one responsible for a prototype, and the significance of the loss had sunk in.

It wasn't just about Kugin dependence on these creatures for their skills. It was the treasure trove of intelligence stored in their prodigious memories for a smart enemy to exploit. The humans now appeared to be that enemy, and Nir-Tenbiku couldn't see any way for Kugad to limit the damage of all that classified information outside their control. They could change encryption, but they couldn't replace every single ship, system, and weapon that the teeriks knew in every detail, either for their own defence forces or their clients. In fact, it didn't look like they'd notified any of their customers that there'd been a catastrophic security breach. They'd grown complacent and careless over the years. Now it had caught up with them.

Imagine, the mighty Kugin having to admit everything was compromised. Nir-Tenbiku quite enjoyed the thought of them storming around and banging tables, demanding to know whose fault this was. They thought all Jattans were hot-headed idiots, to be thrown a few scraps and treated like children. The Protectorate might have fitted that bill, but the lawful government of Jatt was going to give them all a rude awakening.

"This is still all conjecture," Nir-Tenbiku said. "The only way we can make progress is to find and observe the humans and assess them before we risk making contact."

"Who said anything about contact?" Cudik asked. "We don't need the prenu to take back Jatt. Yes, it's a psychological blow to the Protectorate, but it's just an elaborate police vehicle that happens to be a pet project of the intelligence services. We could ignore it and carry on. The teeriks would be very useful, of course, because they could provide intelligence on every nation and agency that bought vessels from Kugad, but they're not worth the distraction from the main task of removing the Protectorate. I say we postpone any attempt to approach the humans until we're truly in a position of strength."

"Cudik, when we overthrow the Protectorate, Kugad may well come to their allies' aid, unless they can strike a quick and easy deal with us to maintain their supplies of ore and minerals, and if they do back the Protectorate, that will keep us very busy," Nir-Tenbiku said. "I would rather we sounded out our potential allies *before* we end up fighting two armies."

Nir-Tenbiku didn't have to get his ministers to agree to his plan in order to take action, but life was easier when they did. The moment they'd worked towards for so long was near. They'd bided their time and amassed weapons and supporters, waiting for Kugad to overstretch itself just enough to weaken it. When Nir-Tenbiku finally launched the attack on the Protectorate, whether military or economic, it would also be a war with the Kugin. There had to be a way of stopping them from coming to the Protectorate's aid until they realised their need for imports was best served by dumping the traitors and negotiating with the new government.

"A valid point," Cudik said. "But neutralising Kugad is a much longer-term plan. We need to rebuild Jatt and re-arm for a hard war before then. That has always been our strategy. Appear to be doing business as usual when we take control, but we prepare for the second phase, neutralising Kugad for good. Nothing's changed."

"But something *has* changed," Olis said. "Humans have arrived."

"There are ways to bring down an empire without shots being fired," Nir-Tenbiku said. "Attrition works. We continue fomenting rebellion in their colonies and occupied territories in the Mastan to keep them off balance and bleed their resources. They rely on light-touch annexation in exchange for taxes and exports, with the occasional brutal suppression to make the point. But if they ever have to put down resistance on every world and in every nation they've taken over, especially simultaneous uprisings, they'll break."

Why didn't their colonies just do that anyway? Nir-Tenbiku never understood why Kugad's unwilling subjects had waited for Jatt to suggest it. They had no idea of their own power. Jatt was doing them a favour by showing them.

"So what difference can the humans make?" Olis asked.

"They could join us and cause mayhem," Nir-Tenbiku said. "I'm certain the Kugin don't know they exist. Finding out that they do will come as a massive shock."

"Or they could decide to replace Kugad as the dominant power and make our lives very miserable indeed," Fas said.

"But the reality is always somewhere between those two extremes."

So far, Parni-Kulat Mer, Controller of the Colonies, and the Minister for Justice, Van-Ibe Ress, had said nothing much at all. If they had misgivings about Nir-Tenbiku's plan, they would find a way to chip at it until it crumbled.

"Ladies," he said. "I would truly appreciate your input. This is a major policy decision and I want to know where you stand."

"I think we should see if the humans are potential allies," Mer said. "And as they have teeriks, let's not forget they'll already know a lot about us, but we start with knowing nothing about them."

Ress reached out to put her hand in the stream of cool mist rolling from a humidifier shaped like an ancient Esmosi urn. Esmos was very good at making utilitarian objects luxurious. "That's a good reason for leaving well alone," she said. "But as it's too late to hide from them, let's keep talking for the moment."

"Well, all that matters now is where they've established their garrison." Nir-Tenbiku gestured to bring the star chart down to eye level and highlighted a single star, then zoomed in to show its planets. "Gan-Pamas provided coordinates for a point on *this* world. The system seems unexplored, but it does appear on some older charts. The humans must know a lot about this sector if they chose such an obscure place to gain a foothold."

"Or they were just looking for conditions that matched their homeworld," Ress said. "Quicker and cheaper."

"How did they acquire teeriks?" Mer asked. "That astonishes me. Kugad isn't quite the secure bastion it thinks it is if it's lost teeriks *twice* now."

"You're counting Lirrel."

"It's two separate escapes, even if they thought Lirrel was dead. They must be getting sloppy. Like my father always said, show me his head to prove it."

Nir-Tenbiku wondered how many more teeriks they'd misplaced without admitting it. "Unless it's an extraordinary coincidence that they found each other, the question should be how did the humans make contact with the teeriks working on the prototype in the first place," he said. "Did they target the prototype somehow, or did that just happen to be something those teeriks thought was sufficiently valuable to both Kugad and the Protectorate to be worth the risk of offering it to them? And that, of course, begs the question again of how they communicated with each other, because we heard absolutely *nothing*."

"Human intelligence gathering must be quite impressive."

"Indeed. They've somehow managed to arrive in the sector completely undetected, set up a garrison, make contact with teeriks, and acquire a ship that was under the tightest security in Kugad's shipyards." Nir-Tenbiku called up the message from Gan-Pamas with a flick of one finger. "And let's not forget what our friend observed. They have mechanicals working alongside them and a number of quadruped species too. They found Gan-Pamas, and his ship, and he's no amateur at covert landings. And Lirrel — in hindsight, it was a mistake to take him on the mission, even if he was needed as navigator, but the humans killed him, so they have no qualms about disposing of teeriks, no matter how valuable they are. Everything the message states indicates a strong, confident force with considerable technological skills. That also tends to mean one with equally considerable backup."

"And one that's going to be unreceptive to us at the very least, because Lirrel killed one of their females," Cudik said. "Not the best start for healthy diplomatic relations."

Nir-Tenbiku suspected every species had its price for overlooking unfortunate incidents. "True. But Gan-Pamas was right — their presence alone will be disruptive, and if they now begin to arrive in numbers, the balance of power shifts."

"We could at least use them as a wedge to drive Kugad and the Protectorate apart. What would we be able to offer them in an alliance, though?"

"That's what we shall find out, all being well," Nir-Tenbiku said. "We have natural resources and a good spy network, for a start. We can trade rare commodities and secrets."

"Very well, I'm convinced of the need to at least get better intelligence on them," Ress said. "An assay probe, though. No landing, not yet."

"Assay probe it is, then." Nir-Tenbiku was satisfied. He'd never been one for exploiting his pedigree and pulling rank on his ministers. It was much easier to handle them when they felt they'd given him their advice. "Cudik, do you want to arrange this, or shall I? It's your ministry."

"I'll take care of it, Primary."

"They have Gan-Pamas's ship, you know."

"They'd never be able to trace it back to here."

"No, but they have teeriks who can almost certainly show them how to use it, and if I were them, I would do exactly that."

"What are you saying?"

"Keep an eye open for it," Nir-Tenbiku said. "If it shows up, it'll tell us a little about their true intentions. We won't necessarily hear those from them even if we exchange loyal gifts and sit down to talk."

Sometimes Nir-Tenbiku wondered what his grandfather would have done in this situation, but he feared he'd have had nothing to teach him. He'd put his faith in a system where the government and opposition obeyed the same rules, and factions could only be put in power or removed from it by the will of the electorate. He was noble but naive. He'd never imagined that any element in Jatt would debase itself like some backward feudal dirt-patch and depose him, or that the citizens wouldn't revolt because it seemed impossible that it had happened.

But that was the art of the coup: to do it so subtly and so silently, one deceitful step at a time, until all the stages were complete and it was hard to see that it had even taken place.

Nir-Tenbiku had learned a lot from that. He'd return the favour and savour every moment. But this time, there *would* be blood to show that power had been reclaimed by those who were lawfully entitled to it.

06

I'm not sure if this is good news or not, Captain. The positive part is that the compound is definitely working on the teeriks. Epliko says he's feeling like his old self. I think we can safely give it to all of them now, but we'll monitor them carefully. The odd part is that I've run molecular modelling on Jattan brain tissue as well as the teerik specimens which still suggests this is a manufactured tranquilliser. The Kugin seem to keep them permanently stoned without their knowledge, probably by adding it to food if they don't recall receiving medication. I don't know if the aggression is part of withdrawal or if they're reverting to their normal personalities, but we need to watch this carefully.

> Dr Karl Tomlinson, Ainatio biochemist, updating
> Bridget Ingram on the unidentified substance.

HOME OF JARED AND MARSHA TALBOT, THIRD STREET, KILL LINE: OCTOBER 12, OC.

"Don't say it, Chris. *Don't.*"

"I've got to."

"No, fight it, buddy. Don't let it win."

"I don't think I can hold out. So why — "

"You're better than this — "

" — why the hell does he go into a building looking for a guy he knows is going to blow his head off, walk past *two closed doors*, which he doesn't even check, and then turn around with his back to the damn staircase?" Chris could feel a dumb giggle busting to get out. Yeah, he was drunk. But he still had his professional standards. "How does this guy get to be a detective? Jeez, I wouldn't work with the asshole. I'd frag him before he got me killed. I'd put arsenic in his fancy hundred-buck Sumatra-blend Americano the first chance I got."

The giggle finally escaped and Chris started laughing so hard that he thought he'd cough up a lung. Jared laughed his ass off too.

Marsha stepped in from the kitchen with her whisk held like a hatchet. Chris always found her mock-angry act hilarious.

"This," she said, "is why we never get invited to any movie premieres. Are you two drunk already?"

"No ma'am." Chris put his hand over his glass and hit pause on the TV. "Just happy to be viewing quality entertainment."

It was good to be full of beer and laugh with friends about bad movies. The great thing about losing daily contact with the world outside the die-back cordon for so many years was that there was plenty of dumb stuff to catch up with, and catching up meant drinking and eating and trashing the plot. There were completely new movies to tear apart too. This was what he needed, a few hours away from teeriks trying to kill each other and waiting for invading aliens and getting more worried about what had happened to Tev. Jared and Marsha were family. He could let his guard down.

"Maybe we need some of whatever they're giving the teeriks," he said.

"Yeah, what's all that about? Jeff says they're all sweetness and light with each other now."

"Ingram says the biomed guy thinks it might be a Kugin tranquilliser, not a food supplement."

"I'm not trying to be funny," Marsha said, "but if they've been on happy pills all the time, withdrawal's going to be rough. Maybe the bad tempers were down to going cold turkey."

Jared exploded with laughter again. "I can't believe you said that."

Marsha didn't look amused. "I said I wasn't trying to be funny."

"That's *birdist*," Chris said. "For shame, ma'am." Then he thought about Nina Curtis and Lirrel, and whether it was withdrawal or something that had made the teerik hack Nina to pieces, and he didn't feel like drinking any more. "So, are you really going ahead with this restaurant idea, then?"

Marsha took Jared's beer off the table and drank half. "Yeah, I'm opening it in time for election day if I can."

"In the DMZ?"

"In the old housing block next to the landing pad on the green."

"Yeah, the DMZ."

"I prefer to call it equidistant from Kill Line and the Ainatio housing tract."

"Folks still aren't mixing, whatever you call it."

"They need more places to hang out. It's not a luxury. People who shut themselves away do *not* make a healthy society."

"Amen."

"I meant you, Chris."

"I'm still enjoying my bathroom." Chris raised his glass to her. "But we do mix. We get original Kill Liners in our bar, we drink in theirs, and Dan's guys and a lot of the *Cabot* crew use both plus the staff club. But except for Annis Kim, Todd Mangel, and Alex, the Ainatio civvies don't come up here, and Kill Liners don't go down there."

"It's our mediocre wine list," Jared said, and started laughing again. "And lack of nachos."

"I think it's us searching them for bioweapons."

"They're over that."

"Not all of them."

Jared topped up his drink. Grain was rationed, so beer had become gold in Nomad's barter economy. Chris was always impressed by how efficiently folks worked out exchange rates, whether it was in lawless ruins of cities or an isolated deep space outpost. Everybody knew what a chicken, decent boots, or a smoke was worth, and that alcohol was the gold standard. It was the same in prison, except without the chickens.

He took another pull of beer and tried to concentrate on the movie. For a few hours, there were no aliens to scan the skies for, and no scientists to teach survival skills to, and no news programmes. He'd been a lot happier when he hadn't been able to see any at all.

Marsha went back to the kitchen and came out with a finished cake. She put it on the coffee table in front of them with a knife and some plates.

"Help yourselves," she said. "Coffee and pecan with maple frosting. That's the star of the menu when the coffee shop gets going."

"So you can buy this with dessert tokens?" Chris asked.

"Dessert or beer. Andy's orders."

"Harsh on folks who want dessert *and* beer *and* cake."

"It makes sure you eat your greens," Marsha said.

"You're fuelling a token-swapping black economy, you know that?"

"It's a free market."

Whatever Ainatio's corporate sins had been, they'd put every effort into feeding Nomad Base well, from the variety of plants they'd shipped out with the unmanned missions to the preserved supplies that had arrived with the evacuation. There wasn't much they didn't have or wouldn't be growing soon. The combination of decent food, a proper bed, and plenty of hot water was the difference between living and surviving, and also quelled rebellions pretty efficiently. Chris was feeling chipper about the settlement's prospects, alien warlords or no alien warlords. His life wasn't perfect and he didn't deserve it to be, but this was a home worth defending to the death. He'd lived through the alternatives.

"Are you guys cool about the alien threat?" he asked.

"Uh-uh." Jared munched on a wedge of cake, nodding. "We can deal with anything, and anything we can't deal with isn't going to make Earth better either."

"Like I said from the start, we're meant to be here," Marsha said. "Too many impossible things all lined up for us to get this far."

Chris settled back to carry on watching the movie. "That's all I needed to know."

"Anyone mind if we watch the news first?" Marsha asked. "I know I should pretend it isn't there, but sometimes it feels like we're alone in the universe."

"Honey, we've got two military empires' worth of aliens way too close for comfort," Jared said. "Loneliness is underrated."

"I just have to remind myself we're not the last humans."

Usually they'd drink and talk and dissect movies until midnight or later, but it was nearly 2200 and for once Chris didn't want to watch harsh reality. He was happily buzzed, a little tired, and Jared and Marsha had their own home and a life to get on with for the first time in years. Sometimes he felt he was in the way. This displaced small town wasn't like the convoy, when they lived in each other's pockets as much out of necessity as friendship. Life here was suddenly *normal*, far more normal than the one they'd left behind and maybe as normal as Earth had ever been before the Decline. There was some kind of future ahead for the making. Normal meant that folks built homes and families, and Chris had a long way to go to reach that stage.

"Okay, I've got some admin to catch up on," he said. "I'm going to go walk the perimeter and sober up first. Thanks for dinner, Marsha. And the cake. You're on to a winner there."

"You throwing the towel in this early?" Jared asked. "We're still way behind on telling the movie industry where it's gone wrong."

"Sorry, I can't handle drink like I used to. Goodnight, guys. Behave yourselves when I'm gone."

Jared got up and gave him a bear hug. "You poor old geezer. Have some hot milk before you go to bed and tell the kids to get off your lawn."

Chris still walked the perimeter every night, even though there was a regular patrol. It was a good cure for general uneasiness, the accretion of unexplained and inconvenient things that stopped him having a reasonable answer for everything. It wasn't as dark around the base as it had been when they'd first arrived, when he'd needed a flashlight and a night vision visor, but there were more buildings now and more light spilling out of them. How long would it be before Nomad was big and bright enough to be visible from space? There'd be no hiding it then.

As he walked up the road to cut through the fields, he tried to imagine Opis seen from its moon. Despite covering at least a quadrillion miles in Caisin gate transits — he still wasn't sure he'd got the right number of zeros in that — he'd never flown in a spaceship. He'd never looked back at Earth or Opis with his own eyes, or even experienced take-off. He wanted a sense of how far he'd come, that he'd actually left everything behind.

He'd lived his life in three US states, one that he'd grown up in and two that he'd had to cross. Earth had never been a wide world for him or millions like him. It had just been images on a screen or a poster, because there was always some travel ban or restriction locally or internationally, but it had always been that way since he was a kid. He hadn't even been in an aircraft before he enlisted.

The limitations hadn't bothered him until now. It was only seeing the endless wilderness of Opis that showed him how much he'd never had on Earth, and coming to a halt at the edge of this bean field, knowing he could explore the whole planet if he wanted to.

Maybe Hiyashi or Devlin would let him tag along on their next trip to the orbiting vessels. He could view most of the surface of Opis from the network of satellites feeding the monitors in the survey section, but it wasn't the same as looking back at an isolated rock in an endless void.

And how long would Nomad be small enough for him to cycle through the frequencies on his radio and listen to almost everything that was happening around the base? At least that day was some way off. People would have to start having families first. He kind of liked the scale of society at the moment. Everyone knew pretty well everyone else. He adjusted his earpiece and called Solomon.

"Sol, can you give me the Jattan feed, please?"

"Certainly, Chris," Solomon said. "You haven't monitored it before, have you?"

"Nope. I just want to get a feel for what they're like. How much is in English now?"

"The AI's managed about seventy per cent so far. It takes time for Fred to go through the unidentified words and correct the inaccurate guesses, and he doesn't know every word. But the AI's getting better all the time."

"It's still weird that he's not fluent in Jattan."

"Not really. As we've said before, if he talks directly to Jattans at all, he uses a specialised vocabulary."

"His conversation with Gan-Pamas, then. Does it make any more sense now?"

"It hasn't made me think he's concealed something, if that's what you mean."

"But he's the one who's translating the stuff the AI doesn't understand, so how would you know?"

"I'm aware of the limitations. The only consistent ambiguity is the words that appear to be insults, like *mekika*. Monster. Abomination. It's not a word an engineer would often encounter, and apart from being abusive, which is understandable if Gan-Pamas thought teeriks were traitors, it's hard to tell if it's significant. It may be that Jattans just despise other intelligent species."

Chris wasn't convinced, but he didn't have grounds for doubting it. "Okay, patch me in."

"I warn you, it's tedious after a while. I disabled the inflection so the voice doesn't attempt to add meaning to anything. It's much easier to listen for detail that way."

Chris heard the first burst of a flat, unemotional voice speaking an oddly disjointed kind of English. "Is it being literal?"

"In the simultaneous translation, yes."

"I suppose all we need to listen out for is *launch fleet now* and some reference to our location."

"That's one way of putting it."

"Thanks, Sol. That'll keep me amused for a while."

"Before you go, did you have any further thoughts about that memorial for Marc's sons?"

"I'm not very creative. I'm still thinking."

"Would you like me to provide a few concepts?"

"Okay. Yeah, sure. Thank you."

"If there are words you'd like, let me know in due course. Or I could suggest something. I'll make sure the stone in question can be ground flat and re-carved in case Marc feels it's not appropriate."

It was one of those moments when Chris had to remind himself he was dealing with an AI. Sol was the only ASD type to escape being shut down. But he was actually in a class of his own, Bednarz's unique creation. That made him the only one of his kind, which was somehow sad, and worse than being the last.

"You'll make a better job of it than me, Sol."

"I doubt it. You gave a fine eulogy for Jamie."

Yeah, for all his annoying habits — or because of them — Sol was mostly what humans should have been.

"Maybe. But that was my gut talking. I don't know how to speak for Marc."

Chris carried on, sobering fast and getting into the rhythm of the Jattan transmissions. They weren't continuous and a lot of the words were unintelligible, presumably Jattan that the AI couldn't translate and just skipped, but overall, they were just what Ingram kept saying they were, the same pattern of messages that human armies and navies had sent for millennia — position and intended movement, supply requests, reports of observations, and asking for clearance to do this or that.

It was too easy to think of Jattans in human terms and get things badly wrong, but they had enough similarities to want some of the same things Chris did, and get into a fight over them. Jattans weren't sentient blobs from hot gas planets who probably didn't have enough in common with humans to come into conflict with them, and whose wars would be with other alien blobs who wanted to fight over whatever blobs cared about. Despite their aquatic ancestors, Jattans breathed a similar atmosphere, walked around, talked, and seemed to have bureaucracies and territories and ambitions, all the stuff that humans could recognise and squabble over. It was too much to assume they'd get on because they had a lot in common.

Chris stopped every hundred yards or so to put on his visor to look out past the strip of cleared land beyond the perimeter and into the darkness of wild Opis. The floral scent that had grabbed his attention a few weeks ago had disappeared, possibly because whatever was emitting it had finished flowering. Something squealed in the distance, but the cry was cut off and it didn't squeal again. The wildlife here was savage but small, a lot of tiny, deceptively appealing things that preyed on each other, and there was nothing bigger than those cat-sized guinea pig creatures with giraffe legs. If there'd ever been larger predators or herd animals around here, nobody had detected any. No wonder Rikayl fancied his chances as a hunter. He was automatically the apex predator.

It wasn't so easy to hear the wild noises tonight because of the machinery chugging and grinding in the factory units. If the influx of settlers had happened by stages as planned, and not in a frantic one-day surge, the automated industrial side of Nomad Base would have been separated gradually from the housing, but it was still right on the doorstep to the south-east.

The perimeter had grown to enclose more fields and industrial units and it was now longer than the three or four miles it had been when the housing tracts were first completed. Chris wasn't sure how much longer he'd have the time or the energy to walk the course like this if it kept expanding. He'd have to take a quad bike, but it wouldn't be as therapeutic as walking.

If he turned around and headed south down the perimeter now, he'd pass between the eastern edge of Kill Line and its farmland, cross the road down to the church, skirt around the back of the teerik compound, and find himself in what a town would call its industrial estate, a sprawl of buildings that included the hangars and workshops for the shuttles and the Lammergeiers. There was the bacteria farm that made yarns, plastics, and chemicals, and a dozen other factories churning out whatever small objects were needed. A little further out, a foundry stood next to the road carved out by thousands of passes by wheels and tracks as the bots moved back and forth, creating quarries and mines, and hauling the raw materials to the extraction plants.

None of these buildings were designed for human workers, though. Chris wondered how Nomad would cope if the automation failed. Had Bednarz thought of that? Chris had read the mission brief, more of a library than a single document, but he hadn't seen much about it. Maybe it was up to him and the Kill Line tradesmen to work out contingency plans. Bednarz was too smart to have overlooked the risk, but automation and AI had made his fortune and ultimately became his life. Chris still wasn't sure why a guy like that cared about improving humanity when he seemed more fond of robots.

It would have been cool to talk to him, though. Project Nomad was a stupendous level of obsession for a man to sustain for a lifetime.

Chris carried on walking north. Common sense said to call it a night and just cut back down the road past the crop tunnels, because he wasn't doing anything useful that the duty perimeter patrol and a network of boundary sensors weren't doing already. But he couldn't break the habit. At the north-east edge of Kill Line's fields, a cluster of lights picked out an isolated group of buildings that he'd never seen fully lit at night. It was the water treatment plant. He hadn't really checked it out before.

Well, now was as good a time as any. He picked his way between rows of soybeans with the aid of his NV visor in case he trod down any plants, and emerged on a paved path where he could hear the faint sound of water. Bots could work in complete darkness, but if the lights were on it meant there was someone around. He couldn't see anyone, though. He walked around looking for a door, then followed the burble of water into a low-roofed building.

The trickling sound was rather soothing. It was also a mistake. He started to feel an urgent need to pee, and the longer he listened to the water, the worse it got. He went outside to find a secluded corner and was unzipping when he heard someone crunching across gravel behind him. He paused and looked over his shoulder.

Damn, why did it have to be a woman?

Chris saw the big crescent wrench in her hand and a service pistol holstered on her hip before he actually noticed what she looked like, which he realised was a sad indictment of his priorities. Her dark blue overalls identified her as one of Ingram's crew.

Why hadn't he seen her around before? He couldn't have missed her. She had dark curly hair pinned up in a pleat and ticked every box on his mental list of what would make him follow her anywhere. He instantly forgot that Fonseca even existed.

"Thank God," she said, sounding genuinely relieved. She was another Brit. "I thought you were an alien. I was going to brain you with this spanner."

Chris was mesmerised. He knew he was going to say something dumb but he couldn't help himself. "Sorry. I'm Chris."

"Ah. You waded into a slurry pit, didn't you? I respect that kind of thing." She walked up to him and held her hand out to be shaken. "I'm Ash. Marine Engineering Technician Ashley Brice. I deal with shit too. And water."

He shook her hand. "Sergeant Chris Montello. Sorry, I haven't washed my hands."

"It's okay, neither have I. You can use the heads in the office, you know."

"Thanks."

"Are you looking for that red teerik? He was sitting on the fence staring at the sky for a while, then he took an interest in the filter beds. I tried to move him on, but he swore at me."

"Yeah, that's Rikayl, alright."

"He's a cheeky little bleeder."

"My sentiments exactly."

"Come on, then." She beckoned him to follow and led him into one of the buildings. "Over there. The door in the corner."

"Thanks ma'am."

"Ash will do fine."

The office was decked out more like someone's quarters, with a few little comforts that suggested she spent a lot of time there — a tea dispenser, a navy blue quilted blanket that looked like a woobie, and a holdall with T-shirts spilling out of it. When Chris opened the bathroom door, there were toiletries on the shelf, and the whole place smelled strongly of perfume. It wasn't hard to work it all out; long hours, a little too far from the centre of the base to make it worth the walk to the canteen for lunch, and an antidote for the smell of sewage.

He checked himself in the mirror above the basin as he washed his hands, hoping he didn't look like a drunk sobering up. When he came out, ready to assure her he wasn't some kind of weirdo and that he really did have a reason for being out here at night, she was making tea while she watched the news.

"Depressing, isn't it?" she said. "Still, at least it stops me thinking about going back."

"Not happy here, then?"

"I thought I'd made a big mistake. Maybe not."

"What made you volunteer?"

"Adventure and a chance to do something significant, I suppose." She handed him a cup. "Anyway, how are you finding it?"

"I like it. It beats where we came from."

"How worried should we be about the aliens?"

"Probably more worried than we should be about APS."

"Fair enough."

Chris had to say it before the conversation got any further. "I wasn't doing anything weird, by the way. I always walk the perimeter every night and I'd never seen the lights on here before. I thought the place was completely automated."

Ash rummaged in a container and picked out some cookies for him. "Here. You can have the chocolate ones, because we don't get many visitors. But yes, it's automated, and no, I don't trust things to run on their own indefinitely. Machinery breaks down. I keep an eye on it. My waders and simple tools stand ready."

She had the right stuff. He knew he was going to screw this up, though. "You're a woman after my own heart."

"It's not glamorous, but if water and sewerage fail, everyone's going to notice pretty fast. Let me give you the guided tour."

Chris left his cookies on the desk and followed her down steep stairs and along gantries, surprised by the fact that there wasn't much of a smell at all. The most noticeable one was her perfume, which reminded him of incense. With the other-worldly lighting and echoing spaces, it gave the underground chambers the impression of cathedral-like serenity.

Ash walked him through the treatment plant where water from the river was channelled into the base and made potable for humans, and then showed him the sewage plant that cleaned up the waste and processed it into fertiliser before discharging the filtered water back into the river.

"I thought we'd have time to expand the system gradually," Ash said, leaning on a rail that overlooked a field of filter beds. "Getting this place ready to handle an extra sixteen hundred people overnight was bloody hard graft."

"Yeah, you guys performed some miracles," Chris said. "Did you start out in sanitation?"

"No, I was what you'd call a hull maintenance technician. Welding, plumbing, carpentry. Whatever's needed on board ship. Which includes fixing the heads."

"No point inviting you to join one of our self-reliance classes, then."

"Yeah, I heard you were running those."

"You could do a guest spot on welding."

"I might take you up on that." She started walking back along the gantry to the exit. "So what did you plan to do with your life before Earth started circling the drain?"

"Geologist."

"Not a hitman?"

"No. I did some pretty rough stuff, but not that."

"You're not offended that I asked, then."

Chris shrugged. He had no idea if he'd blown his chance or if there was any chance to blow in the first place.

"It's okay. I know what people say."

"I'm not judging," she said. "We're all in the same line of business, really."

"I was going to reinvent myself here and go back to looking at rocks, but the aliens got in the way. I'm going to check out the cliff formations north of here. Eventually."

"A trip to the beach. Ooh. A beach without mines and floating barriers."

It took Chris a moment. Ash had lived on an island under permanent threat of invasion, and the shore would have been covered by coastal defences. They were two people who'd both been fenced in and now they had the run of an unexplored world.

"You want to come?" he asked. "I've never seen the ocean."

"Seriously?"

"Too far, too many travel restrictions."

"Ah, yes, you'd be a long way from the coast." She gave him a completely unselfconscious grin like a naughty kid. "Can I bring a bucket and spade?"

"Sure. Some of the coastline's sandy."

"You're on, then. We've got a whole planet here. We're free humans again."

Chris felt his brain was running at half-speed. It took another moment to realise she hadn't brushed him off.

"Tell me when you're free and I'll fix something," he said. Then he thought about the last time he took someone outside the wire, when it was his job to see that Nina came back safely. He gestured to Ash's sidearm. "I realise you're trained, but are you confident using that?"

"You bet." Then she tapped the giant wrench on her belt. "And this."

If Chris got the next line wrong, he'd die of embarrassment. He could have asked Sol, but he had to know right now. "Is there a guy with an even bigger wrench than that who's going to object to this road trip?"

"No, but if there was, I don't think he'd take you on."

Chris wasn't sure if he was meant to deny his hitman image or exploit it shamelessly, but he needed all the help he could get. "Okay, do we exit via the gift store now?"

"Novelty pens, sticks of rock, and commemorative drain plungers," Ash said.

"*Sticks of rock.*"

Ash just grinned at him again as if she was charmed by his foreignness and ignorance. "Marc Gallagher hasn't educated you, I see."

"Don't tell me. I'm going to work it out for myself."

Chris quit while he was ahead. He collected his cookies and Ash saw him out, but his exit was interrupted. When he opened the door, Rikayl was sitting under the security light, eating something small with wings, but as soon as he saw Chris he snatched it up and strutted over to drop it at his feet.

"Wankaaaah!" he said triumphantly. "Fun!"

Ash burst out laughing. Rikayl joined in, laughing in Nina's voice, then switching to Jeff's.

"Thanks, Rikayl." Chris squatted to take a look at the small corpse, keeping clear of the teerik's beak. The unlucky creature looked like a cross between a bat and a frog. If Rikayl had been hunting, it meant he'd left the perimeter, and as that hadn't triggered Chris's alarm, someone had set the sensors to recognise him and let him through. "What are you doing out at night? You should be roosting."

"Kill!"

"Yep, you killed it. Go home. Fred's going to be worried."

"Wankaaaaaah!"

Rikayl snatched up the dead bat-frog and took off. Chris couldn't tell if the teerik's offering had been an olive branch, an invitation to play, or just a demo of his hunting skills. Ash was still laughing.

"I'll see you when I see you, then," she said, and shut the door.

Chris carried on walking the perimeter feeling like a dog who'd chased a car, caught it against all expectations, and now wasn't sure what to do with it. Okay, he *did* know what he hoped to do, eventually, but the gap between now and then was a sea of chances for him to ruin everything, and the harsh reality of Nomad Base was that every woman he'd ever meet, suitable or not, was already here. Failure wasn't an option. As he walked, he worked out what else he needed from Jim Faber in Surveys to plan the expedition. He really did want to check out the geology around here and see an ocean, but he also didn't want to bore Ash with geology nerdery and blow his best chance.

Hitman. Maybe I should just have nodded and said yeah.

When he got home, he logged into the satellite network to see how much of the coastline to the north it covered, and checked the coordinates against the surveys. Yes, he'd be able to see some interesting bays when the sun came up. The infrared option didn't show him what he needed to find, spectacular views and interesting limestone cliffs that might contain fascinating things that he could talk about intelligently, and not look like a psychopath even tough sailors might back away from. There was a time for that, and this wasn't it.

He settled down in front of the wall screen with a coffee and re-read all the survey stuff, planning which features to look for.

Hitman. There's nothing wrong with being a hitman.

Maybe she didn't think there was, though.

He was interrupted by a message from Solomon on his pocket screen. It had images in it, so he transferred it to the wall to take a look. It contained four different views of a single piece of grey granite flecked with white, carved into the form of a churning river, the flecks aligned with the swirls and eddies to create an illusion of foam. It looked real but he guessed it was a mock-up. There was a small polished square at the top with an inscription.

The river returns to the sea
And the sea lifts it to the heavens
And the heavens give it back to the land
To flow again, reborn.

Chris didn't recognise the verse, but he felt he ought to. He thought it over for a while. There was a brief note with the images: *I can change this if you like. It's just a concept.* He was still stunned. He'd expected something plain, tasteful, but impersonal. This warranted an immediate conversation with Solomon. He put his radio earpiece back in.

"Sol? Chris here. I just got your photos."

There was a pause. "What are your thoughts?"

"I'm kind of taken aback, to be honest. Outstanding. Great design. What's the poem? I'm not a culture guy."

"I couldn't find anything suitable," Solomon said. "So, as rivers have obviously been significant to Marc and his sons, I used the water cycle."

Chris looked at the inscription again. It made sense now. "This is your verse, then?"

"Yes. I think it accommodates whatever Marc believes in. It can be read spiritually, or it can be read as science. Please show the images to him. Even if he doesn't like it, it gives him a baseline to work out what he'd rather have instead."

"Wow, Sol. I'm seriously impressed." It was a more than that, if Chris was honest with himself. He was in danger of tearing up. "Damn. I'm out of words."

"My pleasure." Solomon paused for that beat again. "I find it harder to deal with deaths now. I'm forced to think about being here long after my friends have gone. So this has been a therapeutic task for me."

Humans weren't meant to live for ever, but an AI like Sol could survive indefinitely. Chris could tell that Solomon had tried to put himself in Marc's position, and he wondered if Bednarz had designed that into him or if Sol was developing of his own accord.

Doug said Reverend Berry thought Solomon had a soul. If Chris believed in that kind of thing, he'd have agreed with the minister.

* * *

TWO MILES OFF TOWN BEACH, PORT MACQUARIE, AUSTRALIA: OCTOBER 12, OC.

Stu McCabe stood on the deck of his gin palace and indicated the sea all around with his outstretched hand still clutching a beer. "This private enough for you, Tim?"

"So this is where you hide from the missus." Pham opened the esky and rummaged around in the ice for a cola. "Beats a garden shed."

"I did half the coastline last year. She worries, but she won't come with me. She's always hated boats."

It was a warm spring day, but not warm enough. Pham still preferred to keep his sweater on. He hadn't seen Stu in person for a very long time, but now he had both an excuse and a pressing reason. If he trusted anyone, and that was debatable, it was Stu. The man knew an awful lot of people in most of the ports and harbours, not just in Oz but across the Pacific islands, which wasn't because he'd been a spy for thirty years but because he was an affable bloke who got on with everyone, a useful talent in his former line of work, and one that Pham had tried to emulate.

Nobody ever really left the intelligence services, though. Stu had retired early on health grounds but there wasn't much evidence that he'd actually stopped doing the job, except for this small boat that was basically a floating platform for getting drunk and staring out to sea. Pham never saw the attraction. The sun and sound of lapping water were nice in small doses, but the sea went on to infinity and made Pham feel lost. He needed to see dry land at all times, even if it took binoculars to find it.

"Okay, we've been keeping tabs on your guy for a month, since he made a run for it," Stu said. "Do you need to tell me why you want him? There's such a thing as knowing too much, even for us."

Pham almost chickened out of telling him what he'd come to reveal. "Stu, if I'm the only person with this knowledge, I need someone else to understand it, just in case something happens to me."

Stu gave him a dubious look. "And is something going to happen to you?"

"No idea. Just covering myself."

"Okay, start with the truth about where you are with APS now. Nobody demanded your resignation over that Mother Death woman."

"Yeah, that surprised me, too. Which is why we're having this conversation out here." Pham preferred even his handful of friends to know as little as was practical, but he couldn't pull this off on his own. "I don't know how much longer I'm going to need APS's love and approval, but I have it for the foreseeable future because the President's balls are safely in my wallet."

"Oh, yeah, you catalogued all Terrence's dodgy deals, didn't you? Still, how else can a guy be expected to get free use of an aircraft carrier, no questions asked?"

"There's that, but I lied to him too. He laps up plausible deniability. He wants to be lied to. And he's so far up APS's arse that it's all he deserves. But now he's stuck with me."

"But he's happy because you got him the FTL data."

"Yeah. But you can bet that Britain's got it as well. It'll be a case of who can build it to ship-scale first. I mean, even if there wasn't a joint project between Ainatio and the Brits, Gallagher would have given them all the data by now."

"Maybe he hasn't. Private contractor."

"But payment means nothing outside APS borders now. And what sort of bloke with a service record like his would withhold strategic information from his own government?"

"Oh, I dunno, the same kind that withholds it from APS even though he's in a senior cabinet position, I suppose."

"You can be a real bitch when you try." Pham gave in and laughed. "The data Ainatio gave me is the monkey model, even if we develop something useful from it. The good stuff's still under the counter."

"So what's the full-tar version like?"

Once Pham told Stu even a fraction of this, the guy's life would change, and possibly not for the better.

"Before I tell you anything, Stu, I need to warn you that you won't be able to un-know this. Be sure you want to be lumbered with it."

Stu snorted his way into a laugh. "I didn't work in a supermarket for thirty years, mate. We always knew more than we wanted to. Well, the normal ones did. Some buggers get off on collecting secrets."

"Hear me out, then. Because this is going to sound unhinged."

"Now that worries me. Never heard you say that before."

Pham realised his fingers were getting numb from clutching the icy can of cola. He put it down on the deck beside his seat. "Here's why I know there's something really big and worth having, and those cowboys who locked me down and trapped us in Redneckville have still got it. If FTL comms were all Ainatio had, they wouldn't have surrendered it so easily. They'd have wiped all the records before I showed up. And you know as well as I do that what's missing is far more telling than what's recorded and filed. They knew they had something better, so they fobbed us off with two baked bean cans and a piece of quantum string. That's why they had next to nothing on Opis itself. But tell me about Tev Josepha first."

Stu settled down in the lounger, making the springs creak. "Well, when he left Viti Levu, he had to take his family with him, and it's hard to be a ninja with a load of civvies in tow. His son's fairly well known among the fishermen, too, so it was a matter of finding the boat. They're all on one of the old resort islands that used to belong to Sapphire Seas before they went bust. Y'know, I should have bought one those islands myself when I had the money."

"What constitutes a load of civvies?" Pham asked.

"Wife, son, pregnant daughter-in-law, daughter, daughter-in-law's mother."

That would definitely slow a man down. "He's left to protect them, then, not to save his own arse."

"If you've read him right, I assume so."

Pham always looked for the weakness in strong men. It was usually other people, either the bad choices they made, like liability wives, or loved ones and friends they'd make noble sacrifices to save. It didn't matter which. They could all be useful levers.

"You've still got someone keeping an eye on him now," Pham said.

"Of course. An ex-pat who needs my goodwill. I've just asked him to tell me when the man comes and goes. He can't even guess why. He thinks people owe me money."

"Well, Tev Josepha's my bait," Pham said. "Someone's going to try to extract him, I just know it. Wherever Gallagher is, he'll probably know we've now got a die-back problem and I guarantee he'll want Tev out of here. But now Tev's decided to go into hiding, I think he'll bring that forward as a matter of urgency."

"He's left it a long time, then," Stu said. "We'd have pulled our guys out as soon as we could, especially if they had special intel. Maybe this Tev doesn't know whatever you're so excited about. If you'd thought he did, you'd have flown him straight to a cell instead of giving him a ride."

"I didn't know I needed to until he was loose in Fiji," Pham said. "But by then, we could watch and wait."

"So what's the real prize here?"

"You know I said Ainatio had a surprising lack of documentation on this planet they were heading for?"

"Yeah. Opis, you said."

"I think they'd already been there and had a lot more interesting stuff they didn't want us to see."

Stu just fiddled with his beer can, nodding slowly, then looked away for a moment.

"Okay, I can do the sums," he said. "Forty-five year journey, there and back, equals ninety years, so multiple trips — if they wait for one ship to come back before launching the next — means they were ready to roll nearly two hundred years ago. It predates Bednarz. Unless you mean remote exploration, like you mentioned, using the FTL comms that Terrence wet his boxers over. That was what Ainatio used it for, wasn't it?"

"Yes. But now they've got something else. Portals."

"What?"

"Instant wormholes. Gateways from one point in space to another. I suspect they've got one."

Stu laughed awkwardly. "Christ, Tim, I didn't think you were a problem drinker. Get help."

"I saw it."

"Actually saw it? Saw what?"

"One of Ainatio's tilt-rotors just disappeared through it in mid-air. I saw the video. We had python survey bots out recording what they were really up to."

"Tim, I meant with your own eyes, mate."

"You want to hear something I saw myself?" Pham asked. "Okay, just before they escaped, I've got this thug Chris Montello, and he's mouthing off at me, and to my right, slightly behind me, there's three men — a major from Ainatio's private army who's giving first aid to a guy called Dieter Hill, who's bleeding out because I stabbed him to lure Montello and the others, and one of my guys, Davis, who's guarding them. There's nowhere to run. It's a clearing in the woods, but it's too far from immediate cover for anyone to hide in a few seconds. The stabbed guy isn't going anywhere under his own steam anyway. Then I see something move and hear a big grunt, and they're all gone. I mean *gone*. Instantly gone. I searched the clearing. Not a trace."

Stu said nothing for a few moments, then rubbed his forehead slowly. "Tim, the *least* likely explanation for that is a wormhole." His tone had changed completely. It was embarrassed and kindly, the way someone would talk to their dotty grandad about dementia-induced behaviour. "You know what happens under stress. We don't take in everything that happens. The old tunnel effect kicks in and we can only see what matters."

"Whoa, the story's not over yet," Pham said. "When I can't find any of these men, I turn back to Montello to ask him what the hell's happened, he takes the piss and says it's aliens, and I'm about to kneecap him. Then Davis's body just drops out of *nowhere* a few feet away from me. And before you suggest it, no, not from an aircraft, because he'd have been splattered, and how the hell could he transfer to an aircraft in the first place anyway. He dropped a couple of feet at most. He'd been beaten and shot through the head."

Stu looked like he was desperate for a logical explanation because he thought his old protégé had gone mad. "You sure you've remembered this right?"

"Yes, because a few seconds after Davis dropped back from wherever, Montello literally disappeared right in front of me like he'd been physically pulled out. I swear I saw some kind of mechanical grab reach out of thin air. But then he was gone as well. I saw him vanish. So then I recovered Davis's body and got some evidence."

"Oh." Stu had started to look worried, but a different kind of worried from thinking Pham was crazy. "I was going to say they probably have some incredible stealth technology, but that wouldn't explain Davis."

"Exactly. When we were finally picked up from the Ainatio campus by APDU, I got the lab to take a look at Davis, and the the woman said he'd been shot. I've still got the round. I couldn't get definitive ballistics done because his handgun was missing, but it was the right calibre." Pham felt a lot better for finally telling someone the story in one fell swoop. There was a sequence to it, a logical progression, and it fitted neatly into the wormhole theory. "And he'd obviously had a scuffle on open ground, because he had dirt and plant debris on his clothes. I got a reliable lab that owed me one to run some tests."

"Oh God. Don't say it."

"I didn't tell the guy how I got hold of it or why. I just asked where *he* thought it had come from. He took a bloody long time to get back to me, and not before he'd called a couple of times to ask for some context because it was baffling him. I told him he didn't need to know, and his conclusion was that not only did the soil contain traces that he wouldn't expect to see on Earth, but there were unusual bacteria he couldn't classify either. I had to tell him not to worry about the bacteria because it was a contaminated sample and the soil had come from some meteor site here. Actually, I'm not sure that helped. He probably thought I was running some bioweapons programme in the outback."

"Jesus Christ, Tim."

"I'm serious."

"Tell me we haven't got an alien epidemic."

"No, we zapped the sample back at Ainatio and the bacteria were dead anyway. I'm not stupid. And I'm not thinking about aliens." Pham picked up his cola and drained the can. The confession had left his mouth uncomfortably dry. "So Davis looked like he'd been on another planet for a few minutes and been dumped straight back. Is it all falling into place now?"

Stu wasn't one for theatrics but he did put his hand to his forehead for a moment. "Who else knows?"

"The other operator, but he didn't see anything because he was off searching for Gallagher to stop him ambushing us. I'm not going to tell Terrence, am I? I'm still trying to work out what this can do for Australia. It isn't for APS. But you know that."

"I've always been with you on that point, mate. But this is more of a global issue than a regional one."

"Half the world isn't in any condition be consulted even if I gave a shit what it wanted," Pham said.

"In a sane world we'd ally with the Brits."

"They've got their own problems and we won't be helping them by finding reasons not to accept mainland refugees. Anyway, now you see why I want Gallagher or Montello or the other guy to come back and try to extract Tev Josepha. Because that's how they'll do it, using a portal, and we'll get a shot at grabbing that technology somehow. They never leave a man behind. If we have hostages here, we can make something happen."

"Yeah? They'll send a fucking nuke through the wormhole. *That's* what'll happen." Stu shook his head. "I've remembered that right, haven't I? They've got at least two armed operational ships and we haven't found them yet."

"And their AI in the quadrubot is actually an ADS type. They never shut him down."

"You never told me that bit."

"I'm telling you now."

"Oh, this just gets better. That's what carried out the cyberattack on us, isn't it?"

"I can't think of anyone or anything else with the ability or the motive."

"And you've sat on all this for months."

"Who would you trust enough to tell?" Pham asked. "I had to cover my tracks. I'm not sharing this with countries that stab us in the back and rob us blind. I can't even trust our own pollies not to sell us out."

Stu opened another beer and the two of them sat in absolute silence for twenty minutes, just drinking and watching shearwaters diving into the sea. Pham had learned his craft from Stu and they both knew where their true duty and loyalty lay. It wasn't with a supranational bloc that saw Australia as a mineral resource or somewhere to offload their excess population. APS had been founded for a reason, but the alliance had become too much like the China it had been created to break up.

"Tim, I need to ask you a question, and please don't punch me," Stu said at last. "The die-back woman. You don't make mistakes. You're the four-dimensional chess champion. I'm not proud of this, but my first thought was that you deliberately helped her get to Seoul as a human WMD. Did you do it, mate? Because if one thing's going to weaken APS and help get us out, it's that. It's given us an excuse to close our borders and sit tight, too. We're not the only ones."

Pham wasn't even offended. It was a reasonable suspicion. "No, but maybe if I'd known what Abbie Vincent really was, I'd have thought it was a bloody good idea."

Stu had always shared Pham's view on independence from APS. Maybe he didn't realise how far Pham was prepared to go, though. "I believe you."

"Would you be ashamed of me if I had?" Pham asked. "We're still talking, so I'll take a guess at not."

Stu shrugged. "It's going to take something pretty big to lever us out of APS. But this Ainatio thing *is* damn big. And what if this Montello guy wasn't joking? What if there really are aliens building that system?"

"Focus on the portal. Think of the size of the problem." Pham expected Stu to ask more questions, but then he'd only just learned what Pham knew months ago, and some things took a few minutes to sink in. "Whatever that portal is, it can move people *without the need for a ship*. It's not like the hyperspace gates you see in science fiction movies, big structures orbiting a planet with ships flying into them. Think about what could be done with that."

"I'm thinking about what could be done to *us* with that, to be honest."

"And what if the Brits have access to it?"

"I've heard nothing out of our guys there to suggest they do. And I know you haven't either, or we wouldn't be having this conversation."

"I'll be honest, Stu, the ramifications are so wide-ranging that I'm not completely sure what to make of it yet," Pham said. "I just know that some people can't be trusted not to do the worst or most careless thing with technology, human or alien."

"Yeah, but *aliens.* Just when we thought we might come out the other side of all this one day."

"What are the chances of the Ainatio mob being in league with intelligent aliens?" Pham knew what he'd seen and what he hadn't. Extrapolation was one thing, but a really big game-changing device had been used right in front of him, and whatever it was, he knew it was real. "That's an order of magnitude less likely than an extreme development of an existing technology. If Ainatio could send an orange-sized relay forty light years in a fraction of the time an ion drive would take, but still years, then moving big objects like ships, and eventually moving big objects almost instantly with a portal is doable by *humans.*"

They fell into another silence. The whole scenario was too big for a couple of blokes, but Pham had no choice.

"Remember that the President doesn't know about anything except the FTL," Pham said. "Mun, the other operator, knows about the psycho AI, obviously, because he was tasked to find it along with Davis, and he saw the video record of the aircraft disappearing, but that's about it."

"He might be a loose end," Stu said.

"He's a pro. He won't talk. In fact, until now, neither of us knew enough to say anything about it at all."

"Shame you couldn't ask Annis. She's the physicist."

"I have no idea where she is now."

"You'll never find her in America."

"She's a survivor. A traitor, but a survivor. She might have gone with the Ainatio mob. That little bastard Cho isn't talking, but I know he had something to do with it."

"He did turn himself in for surrendering to the local militia," Stu said. "Fair's fair. It takes a man to do that."

"I know. But he might well be another useful lure. His family shot through, so someone cared enough to do him a big favour by getting them away from here. Anyway, he's only detained pending further investigation. They can't court-martial him because I slapped an order on it on national security grounds."

"So where does this leave us, Tim?"

Pham kept his focus on the near-future. The temptation was to extrapolate to the worst scenarios and there were so many of them that it wouldn't get him anywhere at the moment or do him any good. But one thing was certain: that portal or whatever it was needed to be in the hands of Australian patriots, not APS, and definitely not anyone else, not even the Brits.

"Just keep watching Tev Josepha and let me know the moment there's any activity," he said. "And I mean that literally. Any time, day or night, call me, or we might lose him. And if anything happens to me, you know enough to take over. Get the technology and shut down that damn AI for good."

"No pressure then. Piece of cake."

"Do you believe a word I've said?"

"Yes. I believe you saw something inexplicable that our current technology isn't capable of and that we need answers at the very least. And the only unfortunate fate that's likely to befall you is your missus finally asking for a divorce and taking you for every dollar you've got."

Pham smiled. "She too fond of the perks of being an APS politician's wife without the necessity of having me around to crimp her lifestyle. But I wouldn't stand in her way."

He had his plan. He had a fast boat hanging around the islands and it'd be there for as long as necessary, ready to respond. He also had helicopters and a boarding team standing by. It wasn't cheap to keep private contractors on a retainer indefinitely, but he suspected he'd be pushing his luck if he used APDU assets so close to home. Nobody was watching him in the wastelands of America. But they'd certainly be watching him here.

APDU assets, my arse. He wanted his country's armed forces back under sole Australian control. Well, first things first. And the first thing was a technological advantage.

If he played this right and was granted just a little luck, it would all come together. But he accepted the real risk: if and when he found whatever it was he was hunting for, he might not know what to do with it.

But he'd face that when he came to it.

* * *

UNIT D74, KILL LINE: OCTOBER 14, OC.

"Nothing?" Marc asked. Whenever he thought about Earth, he found he automatically looked up at the sky. He didn't know where Earth was in relation to the base at the moment and it wouldn't have helped if he did, but it was hard to stop himself doing it. "Nothing at all?"

"I'm afraid not," Solomon said. "I've checked shipping registration, fishing licences, fish markets, and harbourmasters' frequencies, and I've done a visual search with the probe. I've also checked police communications in case they've been issued with a BOLO by APS. There's no sign of Tev yet."

When Solomon said *checked*, Marc heard *hacked*. "Tev never told me the name of the bloody boat."

"If the family's using the vessel to evade detection, his son might have changed the name anyway."

"I bet APS doesn't know," Marc said. "But Pham does. And your chances of hacking his comms are slim. But thanks, mate. We'll have to do this the hard way."

Marc went back into the house and sorted through his stuff again. He searched every line in his notebook, every scrap of paper in his wallet, every single file on his pocket screen, and every page of the bible that Tev had left with him and which he'd never even opened.

"Sol, I have absolutely no idea what the fishing reference is about."

"I've checked for places with fish-related names," Solomon said. "There's a tourist bar on one of the smaller islands called *The Last Marlin*. But that's a stretch."

It didn't ring any bells with Marc. "What's the current state of security around Fiji, then?"

"Mainly focused on stopping landings by vessels from mainland Asia, which is quite time-consuming given the number of islands. But the outage cut them off from APS for a month, and since then they've dusted off their older communications technology. Which has made my eavesdropping tasks a little harder."

Marc thought he knew Tev and the way his mind worked, and also that Tev knew him. The man would have picked a clue that Marc would understand. If Marc didn't get it, then the problem was his. But

Tev wouldn't leave a message without a way of getting back to him if he wanted Marc to find him, so either the answer was obvious but Marc had lost his touch, or Tev had managed to get back to Britain from APS territory, possibly by putting in a call to the government. He could still have done that, just as Marc could. He also knew there was Marc's connection to use as leverage.

Marc could call Lawson at the Foreign Office and ask him outright. He'd probably know, and he was also open to doing deals for the kind of treasure and intel Marc had to trade. But that was the problem. Teerik technology was a seductive and dangerous thing. He'd gone as far as getting everyone's agreement to use it to extract Tev, but it had to stop there. If he weakened, they'd end up handing over the full FTL kit, the wisdom of which he was fed up arguing about, and then it'd be the Caisin gate. He had to draw the line and remember that anyone who got hold of gate technology on Earth would probably do something fucking insane with it, and yes, he knew he was treating himself as the exception who wouldn't.

Sod it, if push came to shove, he'd find Tev without the FCO's help, even if it meant searching in person.

"I'll continue looking," Solomon said. "I've left your connection to the probe in place, so if he tries to contact you he'll get straight through without knowing where you are. And I'm still looking for Barry Cho. I've not given up."

"Thanks mate." Marc hadn't given up either. But he wasn't doing anything useful and he needed some distraction. "I'd better get to work."

Apart from training, he didn't have many tasks that were exclusively his. Instructor duties came to most older NCOs winding down their careers, but all of Chris and Trinder's troops and *Cabot*'s military personnel did their share of firearms and self-defence instruction as well, and even with nearly eight hundred civilians eligible for training, that didn't fill everyone's working day.

So Marc went running, organised the rugby teams and gym sessions, played dad — or grandad — to Howie, walked around making sure he knew who was where and what they were up to, and helped out with any job that needed a fit man. It still left him too much time to think, but he was doing okay. Today, Trinder needed concentric trenches dug around the perimeter so he could lay anti-personnel devices that would be activated for an imminent ground assault, so Marc lent a hand.

No human needed to lift a finger when there was a bot for every task, but it seemed Marc wasn't alone. Lots of people, women as well as men, had turned up to operate machinery and dig by hand. Either everyone was getting restless or they'd taken Chris's survival philosophy to heart. Bots might not always be available, and humans couldn't afford to forget how to do the basics.

People were also socialising while they worked, though. It felt like Nomad was recreating the stages of human civilisation on fast-forward. Marc watched some of the Ainatio scientists realising there were singles on the wrong side of the track in Kill Line and *Cabot*, and striking up more meaningful friendships, which would probably to do more to blur sectarian lines in Nomad than Ingram's supermarket diplomacy. For some reason, the grocery shop suddenly struck him as hilarious today. The idea of Ingram trying to unite the plebs by setting up a village store was both imperious and endearing at the same time. It was typically her.

He stabbed the shovel into the ground and smiled to himself. It was his turn to cook a dinner again. He hoped she liked pizza and chips. Howie would eat it if she didn't, though.

"Hey Marc." Chris had shown up, minus a shovel, so he wasn't planning to stay and dig. "Nothing like the dignity of labour, huh?"

"Nostalgia, mate. I haven't laid mines in ages. I just hope the Kugin don't launch an airborne assault."

"I don't think they're the paratrooper type." Chris took him to one side, suddenly grim. "I asked Sol to come up with a design for the memorial. You don't have to go with it, but it might help you work out what you'd rather have instead."

Marc had only himself to blame for this. If he'd told Chris to forget it, he would have done. "Nice idea. He's good at that."

"I'm sorry I've jumped the gun. I know it isn't easy."

Marc hadn't come up with any ideas of his own but now he wasn't sure he wanted to see anyone else's either. An amateur psychologist could have come up with a list of reasons why he was avoiding it, from denial that John and Greg were gone to guilt about everything from letting them enlist to leaving Sandra without somewhere to grieve. But it needed doing, because he wouldn't be around forever. He didn't want his sons forgotten and erased because nobody else knew they'd ever existed. This was the first place he'd lived since their deaths that felt permanent enough for him to commit to something public.

"You okay, Marc?"

Marc put his hand on Chris's shoulder. It felt like he'd braced for a punch. "Sorry, mate. I'm bloody useless at these things."

"You want to see the pictures now?"

It still felt impossible. Marc couldn't face it. There were so many peaks of grief along the way — the first notification, seeing the repatriation flight coming in to land, trying to work out the funeral service, every stage and detail as fresh and painful as the first — that he didn't know why this one had defeated him. Perhaps it really was the final straw. It was grief made solid.

"What do *you* think of it?" he asked.

"Honest opinion? It's beautiful. It hit me kind of hard."

Marc never expected to hear Chris say anything like that. "Oh. It's that good, is it?"

"Yeah, the inscription's really something. But you can change it if you don't like it."

The memorial was a statement for the future that Marc wouldn't be around to make, and almost didn't belong to him at all. War memorials had that effect on him too. The names carved on them were transformed from the intimacy of friends and relatives into historical figures who belonged to everyone. Maybe that was the distance required to learn to move on with life.

"You know what?" Marc said. "I think I want to see it the way a stranger would in a hundred years' time. Could you have it installed so it's the first time I see it?"

Chris looked baffled for a moment. "Sure. Where do you want it?"

"Next to Jamie, if that's okay. My boys would probably have got on well with him in life."

"Absolutely."

"Do you think I'm being weird?"

"No, I've been pushing you on it from the start. I didn't give you any room to say mind your own business."

"I think I'd have dithered forever and failed, to be honest."

"We'll keep at it until it's exactly what you want. No problem."

"I really appreciate this, Chris. Thank you, mate."

Chris was an undemonstrative bloke but he did that awkward half-smile that sometimes escaped from him, lips compressed, and nodded. "Least I can do," he said.

Marc decided not to analyse Chris's reasons for trying to look after him. Whatever drove the bloke was genuine, and that was enough.

Next day, after the morning briefing, Marc went in search of proper potatoes to make chips, which meant sweet-talking Lianne Maybury. He planned to keep a couple of spuds to chit for planting out in the patch of garden he had big plans for, but the rest were going to be fried in beef dripping, courtesy of Mike Hodge's herd, and if that didn't impress Ingram then nothing would.

He walked into the decontamination airlock at the entrance to the crop tunnels and hoped he'd get a warmer welcome than usual from the boffins. Lianne was okay with him, but some of the others were still pissed off about being searched and questioned over die-back. They let him know in their frosty middle-class way that he'd overstepped the mark, either walking away when he approached or just blanking him. Well, that was fine by him. There were one thousand, seven hundred and forty-four people in Nomad Base, not counting *Elcano*'s human payload. Marc worked on the basis that ten per cent of any population would always be arseholes he wouldn't get on with, so there were at least another hundred and sixty people here whose opinion he wouldn't give a toss about either. He was well within the safety margins.

"I've got some russets," Lianne said. "They'll make decent steak fries."

"I'll take them. Have you got ten big ones?"

"Sure."

Marc took a metal container out of his vest and rattled it. "Sealed tin of humbugs? You know, mint-flavour hard candy."

"It's a deal. Give me five minutes."

Lianne returned with a box of lovely big spuds. Marc admired his haul as he put them in the pannier on the quad bike. They were probably enough to make at least six portions with a few left over for chitting, and it made his day. It was the little things that made life satisfying here. He was sitting on the bike and examining the potatoes for eyes — yeah, he could cut up two of these and get at least eight pieces to plant — when his screen chirped.

It was a call from Tev, an actual voice call. Marc forgot all about the potatoes.

"Tev?"

"Hi Marc. The dairy said you'd called. Is anything wrong? Why aren't you in cryo now?"

Marc could breathe again. "Bloody hell, Tev, I didn't understand your clue so I didn't know where to get hold of you. Are you okay?"

"I didn't leave a clue. I just check in every week to see if I've had any calls."

Solomon was going to be pissed off that Marc had wasted his time. "I was worried you were banged up in some APS jail. We saw the news about Abbie. Did you leave because of APS?"

"As soon as they mentioned the Vincent woman on the news last month, I thought we'd get a visit from Pham's heavies, so we moved. But I thought you'd be a long way from here by now."

"Yeah. About that." Marc really couldn't say it over the link, secure or not. He had to look Tev in the eye when he told him. "I need to see you, mate. I've got something important to tell you and I need to do it face to face."

"You haven't gone far, then."

"In some ways, no. Is there somewhere we can meet up?"

"Sure, but aren't you taking a big risk?"

"Not really. I'm serious, Tev. And if you're worried about APS, I can help."

Tev paused for a moment. "Okay, I don't need to know where you are. I'll send you the grid ref and I'll be there. When are you coming?"

"When can you make it?"

"How about tomorrow? Late morning my time? It's just that Joni needs a hand with the boat."

"Okay. No problem. I'll message you when I'm on my way."

"I'm sending the grid ref now. Look for the jetty when you get there."

"Is there any cover I can use? A few trees or a boatyard?"

"There's a golf course with a lot of palms about ten minutes' walk along the coast from that grid ref. It doesn't get much use now. Folks have reclaimed a lot of it for crops."

"Perfect. Don't worry. Keep your head down and I'll see you then."

"There's no airstrip here, Marc."

Tev obviously thought he was somewhere in APS territory. "I don't need one, mate," Marc said. "See you soon."

Marc looked up the grid reference and found it was one of the old resort islands. There were bound to be Aussies around, then, because loads of them had moved out to the islands in recent years, so he wouldn't be too conspicuous. It was summer, coming up to the rainy season. It'd be humid but he could get away with wearing his angler's waistcoat as well and have plenty of pockets to conceal weapons. He had no intention of going into APS territory unarmed.

He started the bike and went to find Ingram. The base map said she was in the new bunker under construction beneath the main building. If Tev wanted to bring his family to Opis, he'd become Ingram's problem, because there'd be *Cabot* crew and other personnel who'd resent Marc for being allowed to travel back and forth to rescue his mate when they weren't even allowed to call anybody. He'd need Ingram's blessing for this just to keep the peace.

He parked the bike and picked his way through the bots milling around the entrance to the construction site. The fastest way down to the bunker was via the goods platform carrying materials down to the excavation, so he ignored the site safety warnings and jumped onto it. As it descended, he had time to take a look at the bunker, which was still just a rectangular room with unidentifiable cables and conduits sprouting from every surface. Jac Devlin and Ingram both looked up from the screen they'd been studying.

"Workplace safety," Devlin said pointedly.

"Yeah, I've heard of it." Marc jumped off before the platform reached the bottom. "It's on, Captain."

Ingram looked blank for a moment, then nodded. "Walk with me, Sergeant."

She beckoned him to follow and went into a side chamber at the other end of the bunker. It didn't look like she'd told Devlin what he was doing.

"Okay, what do you need?" she asked.

"A gate tomorrow. Before that, I'd better take a look at the exit point and make sure I don't step into a great white's open mouth or something."

"You've found Tev."

"He found me."

"Did you tell him anything?"

"No, it's got to be done in person. Could you do me a favour? Could you keep an eye on Howie while I'm gone? I don't like leaving him alone."

"Certainly. How long?"

"Might be overnight, might be fifteen minutes. It all depends what happens when I tell Tev the truth. He thinks APS is already after him."

"God, if only someone had throttled Abbie Vincent before she left."

"If I'd known, I would have. And don't start Chris off again. He already thinks he should have had X-ray vision and spotted what she had in her flight case."

"Don't worry, I'll be tactful."

Marc looked past her for a moment and saw Fred and Cosquimaden in the main chamber, doing something with a tangle of pipework and cables. "And the teeriks are okay about moving the gate generator here, are they?"

"Yes. It's going to mean *Eriksson* doesn't get a drive for another six months, but it's a price worth paying." Ingram showed him the plans on her screen. "We're planning a connecting tunnel to the teerik compound, too. If the Kugin show up, the commune can take refuge in here without having to cross open ground. It's another drain on resources we could do without, but we've got to protect them."

"And that's the line you spun them, is it?"

"Yes, because it's true."

"But it's not the reason."

"It achieves the outcome both sides want."

Fred and Cosqui looked pretty relaxed. There was a subtle but definite change in their postures. "So they're happily baked now."

"Whatever that compound is, it's what they're used to and Fred says he feels like his old self. Even Turisu's quite tolerable now, apparently."

"Are the medics giving them the right dose? It's great they're not trying to kill each other, but I like my teeriks with their mathematical judgement unimpaired. It's a bit dangerous if they're doped up to the eyeballs."

"I did ask that," Ingram said. "I was assured the dose was increased gradually until they felt better."

"Oh good. If they botch the coordinates and I end up crashing into the sun, it'll all have been worth it."

"If you've got the grid reference, give it to Sol so he can programme it in. He'll do a recce with the probe, too. We'll open the gate in *Curtis*'s hangar. There's no work scheduled in there this week."

"Will it work in an EMP-hardened structure?"

"Apparently yes."

"So Sol's got some control of the gate now."

"We're getting there," Ingram said.

Sol cut in on the radio. "Marc, I'm glad Tev made contact," he said. "So he left no clues after all, then."

"Yeah, sorry, Sol. Look for the golf course and the jetty, will you? Thanks."

"Certainly."

Marc felt bad about the teeriks. Still, if they were happy, that was fine. And they weren't naive. They knew they were handing over the technology to Ingram's control, whether it was providing a hardened citadel for their own safety or not.

"Okay, I'm going to kit up and then explain to Howie and persuade him not to worry," Marc said. "I'll see you later. And don't tell Chris. He'll insist on riding shotgun, and two blokes like us showing up will attract attention."

"Just remember Howie's got a point," Ingram said. "You're going behind enemy lines."

"It's white sands, turquoise sea, and friendly people. It's not Paris."

"Even so." Ingram tapped his elbow discreetly. "Come back in one piece."

Marc went home and found Betsy stretched out on the doorstep, which meant Howie was home from school already. Betsy got up with a grunt and went on her way like she was handing over to her relief.

"Short day, then?" Marc asked, putting the potatoes on the breakfast bar.

Howie was sitting at the table doing his homework. "We were going to watch a documentary on volcanoes, but the screen broke down, so Mrs Alvarez sent us home early so she could get it fixed. Dr Mangel's teaching us tomorrow. He's exploring a new planet with a probe and we get to see everything live. It's the coolest thing ever."

Actually, it was. Even Marc could stop and marvel at that. "I've got a job to do tomorrow. I might be away overnight, so I've asked Captain Ingram to make sure you're fed and entertained. A seat at the captain's table. Dead posh."

Howie froze, his pen held over his screen. "You're going back to Earth, aren't you?"

"Yes. Just to see if Tev and his family want to be evacuated."

"That's really dangerous."

"I doubt it. I won't be long, but I don't want you stuck here on your own. Not because you can't look after yourself, because I know you can, but it's not good for you. You worry. It's just a quick trip, though, nothing dangerous at all."

Howie didn't say anything and carried on with his homework. Marc started assembling his clothing and weapons for the transit. He didn't have a lot of stuff to search through, so his rucksack was ready in ten minutes: two faded T-shirts, chinos that looked convincing to play a dropout from Sydney corporate life, sunglasses, and deck shoes. His angling vest managed to swallow up two sidearms, spare ammo, a gate locator, two knives, a length of cheese wire, a marlinspike, E&E kit, a bike chain, and an assortment of compact grenades. He imagined telling the local cops he'd come for the sport fishing.

Tev might not have his own firearm, so Marc would have to pack a Marquis in his rucksack and swing by the armoury for some more ammo, but it wasn't like he had to worry about getting any of this through airport security. But that could wait a while. He needed to make sure Howie was okay, or at least as okay as he could make him. Marc would take him down to the main building when he left, hand him over to Ingram, and leave her with the door key so Howie could decide where he wanted to stay. He'd make it up to the kid when he got back.

"Okay, I'm packed," he said, putting his rucksack on the breakfast bar. "See? Just enough for a few hours, and room for a rifle for Tev."

Howie was still hunched over his screen. For a moment Marc thought he was just absorbed in his homework, but then he looked up and his face was stricken.

"Can I come with you?" he asked. "You wouldn't look obvious if you had a kid with you. Nobody would think you were there to do military stuff."

"I'd rather you stayed here," Marc said. "Just in case."

"You said it wasn't dangerous. If it's not dangerous, why do you want me to stay here? You know I won't get in the way."

Howie was a regular ten-year-old who sometimes had much older moments. His child persona was perpetually upbeat, determined not to let the world that had robbed him of everything grind him down any further, but sometimes he'd sound like a grown man who'd seen too much and had had enough of it.

"I know, mate, but like I said when I left you with Ingram when we evacuated Ainatio, I worry about *you*, and if I do that, my mind's not on the job, and however safe something looks, you've always got to have eyes in your backside in case the unexpected happens. It's my fault, not yours."

"It's always you. You always have to do the dangerous stuff."

"That's because I was special forces. I'm good at it."

Howie's eyes filled up with tears. He wasn't actually crying, but the fact that he was holding it back broke Marc's heart again.

"I can look ahead, you know," Howie said. He was suddenly forty and crushed by the world again. It didn't happen often, but that made it all the more serious. "You'll be late and we won't know what's happened to you, and then it'll be days, and then Captain Ingram will tell me not to stop hoping but you probably won't be coming back so I've got to be brave. And I'll never know what happened to you."

All kids went through a clingy stage, but few had Howie's justification for it. He was very specific about what would happen, too, so there was something else he hadn't told Marc yet. Marc felt like an utter bastard. He was never prepared for how bad this felt.

"I'm only going to see Tev," he said. "It's such a big thing to tell him about the aliens and everything that I can't do it properly over the radio. I'll step out right where he is and I'll step back again. I'd rather know you were here eating Ingram's cake rations."

"I don't want to be left alone again," Howie said firmly. "I'd rather go somewhere dangerous and get killed with you than be alive without a family again."

That was a gut-punch. Marc understood, because he'd felt that way for years, but now Howie's distress was his fault because he'd given the kid the illusion of being part of a family. It was exactly what he'd been afraid of. He wasn't as good for Howie as Chris seemed to think.

"Howie, I'm sorry. I couldn't cope with anything bad happening to you. You know why."

Howie's composure crumpled. Tears spilled down his face and he got up from the table, went into the bathroom, and shut the door quietly behind him. Marc had fucked this up badly and he knew it. He waited a couple of minutes to see if Howie would come out of his own accord and tried to see the bigger picture. Howie had every reason to worry about Marc getting killed. He'd made a pretty good point: either it wasn't dangerous like Marc said, so he could tag along, or it was seriously risky, in which case Marc would look less conspicuous with a kid because no operator would bring a child with him.

And boys wanted to be men. They had a natural urge to take risks.

Marc had made his decision, but he couldn't bear to see Howie so upset after all he'd been through. He stood outside the bathroom and tapped on the door.

"Howie, you're right," he said. "It might be dangerous. I don't know for sure. I said you had to stay here because if I get this wrong, you could end up hurt or worse. But I understand why you want to come with me, and I know you're not doing it because you think it'll be fun. Come on. Let's talk."

It took Howie a while to open the door. He came out looking red-eyed and scared. Marc sat him down.

"I'm never going to lie to you, Howie," he said. "But I really am just dropping in to see Tev. We might have a beer or two. But I'm not going to Fiji to fight."

"I heard all the metal noises," Howie said. "You're taking all your guns and knives."

"You know what I'm like, Howie. I overdo everything because I think I'm still a real soldier."

"You *are* a real soldier, and you're going somewhere dangerous again."

Marc had painted himself into a corner. He was used to leaving and trying to say reassuring things, like everything would be okay and that he'd be back soon. He'd said it to his sons far too often. Now he was saying it to Howie.

"I'll be back before you know it," he said. "I really will."

Howie nodded, but looked like he didn't believe a word of it, then threw his arms around Marc. He just clung to him. It felt desperate. Marc hugged him back.

"One day soon," Marc said, "everything's going to be under control, and normal, and we won't have to worry about anything ever again. I promise. And if Tev decides to come here and brings his family, we'll have a lot of fun. Have you finished your homework?"

"Not yet."

"Okay, crack on with that and I'll make you some proper British chips."

Howie went back to the table and started writing again. Marc peeled the spuds, cut them into chips, and put them in a bowl of water to draw out the starch. He was trying to calculate exactly how many portions he'd get out of the remaining potatoes when his pocket screen chirped with a message from Solomon. Marc now had a live feed from one of the Earth probes showing him the island where Tev was holed up.

He studied the aerial view. Well, that was the jetty, and that was the golf course. It looked easy enough. He zoomed in, identified a space between the palms right next to the road that ran along the shoreline, and marked it with his finger before sending it back to Sol with a note to insert him exactly at that point.

The chips could have done with longer soaking, but they came up respectably crisp and fluffy. Ingram would be bowled over by a plate of these. He put a big portion on Howie's plate and opened the bottle of ketchup for him. Howie still looked a bit down.

"Eat like an Englishman," Marc said. "Although personally I prefer plenty of pickled onion vinegar and salt."

"That sounds really foreign."

"Food of the gods, mate. And very good in a sandwich, too."

Marc sat down to eat, still feeling like a complete bastard. He almost gave in and said Howie could come with him. This was about Marc's dread of loss, not Howie's capacity to cope or the risk he'd be exposed to, because he must have been in worse situations while he was on the road with Chris's convoy.

"Tell you what," Marc said. "When I get back, I'll start training you for missions so you can come with me if I ever need to do stuff like that again."

Howie forked a chip and studied it before biting it in half. "Honest?"

"If I promise you something, you get it."

"That would be nice."

But Howie wasn't excited. It really was about separation and worrying what would happen to Marc. Marc had never asked Howie what had happened to his dad, although he knew the man was dead, but that whole thing about breaking bad news that someone wasn't coming home sounded too detailed and precise to be something he'd thought up as an example on the spur of the moment.

"I don't want to make you sad, Howie, but do you know what happened to your dad?"

Howie nodded and chewed thoughtfully, looking down at his plate. "He didn't come home and Mom didn't tell us why for ages. He was a soldier too. I mean he wasn't one to start with but he volunteered. I don't remember what he looked like. But he made me feel safe, I remember that."

Well, that was every answer Marc needed. He prayed this was as bad as it got and there wasn't worse still bottled up inside that boy.

"I'm so sorry, Howie," he said. "I didn't realise. I must be making this really hard for you."

"I thought all soldiers died. But when I met Chris and his friends I realised they didn't, and that kind of made me feel better."

Marc was about to offer some sensible comfort about the higher odds of surviving, which was the last thing he felt like doing, but someone knocked on the door and saved him having to lie about his own reality. Yes, they died, and he was left with nothing, just like Howie.

He opened the door. It was Chris.

"Sorry, I didn't realise you were eating." Chris clutched a small box. "Lianne Maybury asked me to drop these off. Sweet potatoes."

"Come in and have some chips," Marc said.

"Thanks. What is it with you and Maybury? I thought you were Team Ingram."

"I'm charming and I bribe her with mint humbugs. She doesn't care how old they are."

"Women, huh? Hey Howie. How are you doing?"

Chris took a seat at the table and looked at Howie, then at Marc. It was obvious the kid had been crying.

"I'm good, thanks," Howie said, ever the little man. "Have some proper English chips."

Marc had to offer Chris some explanation that would stop him asking more, but the guy had a pretty good radar for awkward situations. Marc put a plate of chips in front of him.

"We were just talking about the past, Chris."

"Ah. I see." Chris tucked in. He would eat anything, any time, and clear his plate. "As long as everyone's okay."

"He's going to Earth and I'm worried," Howie said. He didn't even blurt it out. He said it like a concerned uncle, as if Marc wasn't there.

Marc's heart sank. Now he had no way of shaking Chris off, and he'd have to play along.

Chris didn't even blink. "It's okay, Howie, I'm going with him. No need to worry. We'll both be fine."

Howie actually brightened up. Marc was cornered. If he dumped Chris at the gate and went alone, which was doable with some cooperation from Sol, Howie would know anyway, and lying about it to the kid would just make it worse.

"I suppose I'd better brief you, then," Marc said, giving Chris his dead-eyed shark look. "Tomorrow. Pack your kit."

* * *

HANGAR 3, NOMAD BASE: OCTOBER 15, OC.

"Happy now?" Marc asked, opening the side door to the hangar. "I never knew you wanted a career in elder care. Did you remember to bring my incontinence pads?"

Chris followed him inside. "It's only for Howie's benefit. I know I should have asked you first, but he needed to hear something reassuring there and then."

Marc grunted. "Yeah, right."

Chris felt bad for manoeuvring a guy like Marc. It was disrespectful given the man's service record and the fact he could still hand Chris his ass, but everybody needed a wingman, and Chris made no apology for looking out for him.

"Anyway, *sensei*, I'm going to learn from you."

"We'll be eating, drinking, and catching up," Marc said. "I don't think you need an adqual in any of those."

Chris put his rucksack down and did a last-minute check. It had been a long time since he'd had to conceal weapons in light civvy clothing and his sidearm felt as conspicuous as a rocket launcher. Marc's rucksack made glassy clinking noises when he slipped the straps off his shoulders.

"I hesitate to ask," Chris said.

"It's gin. When you visit Fijians or go into their village, you're supposed to offer gifts."

"What if Tev says no after we tell him?"

"You keep asking that."

"Because I still want to know the answer."

"I can't force him. He'd cream me anyway. But I have to give him all the facts. I'm doing this for *him*. If people on Earth behave like twats and kill each other because I tell him the truth, that's not my problem. I'm not going to feel responsible for it any longer. I've come to my senses."

"Amen."

"Is that it?"

"Yeah. I just wanted to hear it. We're not humanity's mom, Marc. I don't fight for ideals. Just people I know."

Marc nudged Chris's rucksack with his foot. "Anyway, what have you got in there, then, other than the Marquis?"

"A couple of knives and as much ammo as I could stuff in. Only what I'd take on a picnic."

"Have a stun grenade."

"Thanks, but I'm trying to quit."

Marc held two out to him. "Oh, go on. Spoil yourself. You've used them before, yeah?"

Chris stuck the small cylinders in his ruck's exterior pocket. "We used regular grenades. We weren't trying to take anyone alive. Anyway, we didn't have any."

"Well, you never know."

Solomon was overseeing the transfer with Fred. He was following Chris's conversation on the radio.

"I have two probes in the area, gentlemen. I'll be monitoring activity at sea and in the air as a precaution. I'll be ready to pull you out if necessary."

"Remember our robust exchange when you pulled me out of Forge Wood?" Marc asked.

"Yes, you said never to extract you unless you requested it."

"That stands, Sol. Unless we're incapacitated or actually going down, wait for our word."

"We'll be okay, Sol," Chris said. He'd also been pulled out of that same mission without warning and it had cost him the satisfaction of shoving his knife into Tim Pham's guts. "Let's go, guys. We're ready."

Guys was Solomon and Fred, but Sol was taking over an inch at a time. It was hard to imagine Fred didn't notice. Perhaps he didn't care, though, and it was more about Chris's perspective on power than Fred's. Fred could invent a gate: Sol couldn't. That probably gave the teerik considerable confidence.

"Come on, do it," Marc said.

The familiar hazy patch of air appeared in front of Chris like a smear on a window. He'd done this so often that it felt routine, but there was always the thought at the back of his mind that he might step through the gate into something he wasn't expecting. He patted his pocket to double-check he had his own locator and stepped forward a pace behind Marc.

A whiff of burnt matches filled his nose as two hundred and forty-six trillion miles folded into nothing and then humid heat hit him like a sauna. He felt the odd springy sensation of slightly reduced gravity as he took his next step. They were now on one of the hundreds of small Fijian islands on a beautiful day that was shaking off recent rain, standing among palms at the edge of the golf course. It was the greenest grass and the bluest sky Chris had ever seen. The perfection was unreal. There was nobody around, not even on the greens.

"I feel overdressed," Chris said.

Marc started walking. "Remember, we're just two blokes hanging out."

Chris glanced to his left through the palms and saw something else that took his breath away, a view he'd only seen in photos, and they didn't do it justice.

"It's the ocean," he said. "Damn."

"Yeah, you do generally find it around islands."

"Wow." Chris walked over to the edge of the course and stared at the fringe of white sand and the ferociously blue sea without a rational thought in his head for a few seconds. Nothing prepared him for this. The plain surrounding Nomad was a big horizon to contemplate, but it was made up of low rolling hills and he could see mountains in the distance. But the ocean was absolutely flat, infinite, yet constantly moving. It stretched way past his peripheral vision. "I've never seen the ocean before."

"Says the bloke who's arrived from another planet."

"I'm going to walk on that beach."

Chris was conscious of being a large, slow-moving, conspicuous target against a white background. He knew doing carefree things made him look less suspicious if anyone was watching, but for a moment he actually didn't care if a sniper took him out as long as he got to trudge a few yards through that powdered-sugar sand.

Marc joined him, leaving a trail of footprints. Chris paused a couple of times to pick up a handful of sand and let it fall through his fingers. He wasn't acting now. All this mesmerised him, and it wasn't his inner geologist that it spoke to. It was the kid who'd never been to the beach. He made an effort to focus and stay alert. However vast and beautiful the shoreline was, he had a job to do and he was behind enemy lines.

"Jetty," Marc said quietly. "Dead ahead."

Chris squinted against the sun. He could see the inlet now, a mini-harbour with three boats tied up at a wharf that formed a T-shape with the jetty, but there were only a couple of guys working on the fanciest of the three. As he got closer, one of the men looked up and waved, then turned and headed their way at a jog.

Tev looked happy.

For a Brit from South London, he'd adapted to the tropical life pretty well, right down to an eye-wateringly bright shirt in turquoise and green. He gave Marc a rib-breaking hug.

"Mate! How are you?"

"I've just gone blind from looking at that bloody shirt, but apart from that, great."

"And you brought Chris. How are you doing?"

"Good to see you, Tev. Now I know what heaven looks like. With my record, I never thought I'd see it."

"Yeah, it's nice here. Bit of a struggle lately, but at least we can feed ourselves." Tev slapped Chris on the back, grinning with delight. "We're safe here for the time being as long as we keep a low profile. Where exactly did you come from, or shouldn't I ask?"

"That's what I came to see you about," Marc said. "You're on the run and now your family's caught up in it. That breaks my heart because I talked you into this. But I've got a proposal."

"Marc, I'm glad you *did* persuade me."

"I can get you all out, Tev. Somewhere APS can't touch you."

"Britain?"

Marc looked like he was holding his breath. There was no point in a slow build-up. If he didn't blurt it out, Chris would. But Marc found his voice.

"If that's what you want, yes," he said. "But if you want to get even further away, we can do that too."

"How far's *further*?" Tev asked.

"Two hundred and forty-six trillion miles."

"What?"

"And it won't take forty-five years, either. This is all classified, by the way."

Tev looked at him for a moment, then at Chris. A slow disbelieving grin spread across his face and he started laughing.

"You're still going to Opis, then. I had my doubts."

"Past tense," Chris said. There was no point in dancing around this. "We've been there a few months now and we've come back for you because things are going to get worse here. *Especially* for you."

"Seriously? There and back? No. Never."

"There's a lot of background, but yes," Marc said.

"You'll be telling me there's aliens out there next."

All Chris could do was stare at the ground with his hands on his hips and leave it to Marc now. Tev had left Ainatio before the trouble started with Pham, so he didn't even know Solomon carried out the sabcode attack. There was a lot of ground to cover. Chris wondered how Tev would feel when he realised Solomon was behind the cyberattack.

"Yeah, aliens, five different species so far," Marc said. "Some of them love us and some probably don't. We only got here so fast because of their technology. Shall we sit down and discuss this somewhere quiet? It's complicated."

"This has to be a joke."

"It's true," Chris said. "And nobody else on Earth knows about this. We're trying to keep it that way."

It was hard to read Tev's expression now, but his permanent cheerfulness had evaporated. "Come home with me," he said. "The rest of the family wants to meet you. Becky's made a big meal. Joni's got to drop off his fresh orders in town on the way back, but then we'll dig in for the day. Can you stay a while?"

"As long as you need us to," Marc said.

Joni was still transferring fish from his boat, which looked like a pretty serious vessel, with twin engines, radar, aerials, and all kinds of shiny stuff that Chris couldn't identify. It wasn't a simple wooden hull and a big net. The name on the bows was *Sautu*.

Joni shook Marc's hand like he was a visiting dignitary. "We've heard all about you, Marc. You were in the army too, Chris?"

"Yeah, in the States."

"Must have been tough over there."

Chris wasn't sure how much Tev had told Joni about Nomad. "It was pretty bad. We ended up at Ainatio, which is where I met these two guys."

"I won't be long," Joni said, heaving another tray onto the pile. "I'll leave the power running and unload the frozen catch later. But I can't let my customers down."

"No problem," Marc said. "Nice boat."

"Yeah, I got her at a good price. I'm building the business again."

Poor guy: Chris hadn't thought about it before, but uprooting the family meant Joni's business had lost customers. Chris gave him a hand loading the fish onto the pickup truck and got into the back seat next to Marc.

"So what's happened since I left?" Tev asked while Joni was safely out of earshot locking up the boat.

Marc sighed. "Headlines? Tim Pham tried to stop *Shackleton* launching and blew up *Da Gama*, so Sol trashed APS's infrastructure with a cyberattack, and we had a really tricky armed standoff with APDU until we managed to lock Pham in the campus and get away."

Tev turned and looked at Marc, arm resting on the back of the passenger seat.

"So Sol did all that."

"Yeah, sorry. He didn't know how far it would spread. He just had to stop their air force paying us a visit. Pham found out pretty well everything. Sol, the biosecurity breach, the nukes, even the alien FTL."

Tev made no comment about Solomon trashing Asia and moved on. "So Pham's sharper than we thought."

"No, Abbie Vincent grassed us up. Well, not about the FTL. He actually saw that."

Tev just shook his head, bemused. Joni jumped into the driver's seat and they set off along the dirt road.

Chris leaned his head against the side window to catch some breeze from the air conditioning and watched the passing landscape. The first things that got his attention were brightly coloured birds, species he'd never seen before, and picture-book palm trees, then the single-story houses along the way, some with regular pitched roofs and plastered walls and others in traditional style with thatches. The road was unpaved until they got to the small town, where it became tarmac.

Joni parked and stacked the fish on a sack truck to deliver around the centre of town. Marc watched him carry a tray into a shop and tapped Tev on the shoulder.

"How long is he going to be?" he asked. "Because I need to tell you exactly what's going on so you can decide what to tell your family."

"About fifteen minutes," Tev said.

"Okay. Let me explain about the aliens."

Marc briefed Tev about the teeriks, Gan-Pamas, and the risk of being found. Chris was used to being among men who took bad news with a shrug, but even he was surprised by how matter-of-fact Tev was about it all. But Marc stopped short of mentioning the Caisin gate and the detail of how they actually left Earth.

Tev was trying to fill in the gaps, though. "So Ingram got pally with these crow people and they sent a ship to pick you all up."

"Tell him, Marc," Chris said. "There's no point in hiding it."

"There is," Marc said. "What Tev doesn't know —" He stopped dead. Chris could complete the sentence. But this wasn't about making sure Tev couldn't reveal the existence of the Caisin gate if Pham caught him, because he wouldn't. It was about giving Tev and his family enough honest information to decide if they wanted to leave all this behind. "It's not actually a ship, Tev. But it does move ships and people very, very fast. I don't understand the physics, but Fred will tell you all about it."

"So if things get awkward here, we can go to Opis, but there might be aliens showing up one day with scores to settle," Tev said.

"That's about the size of it."

"Thanks for levelling with me. If I was single again, it'd be easy. But I'm not."

"All I can say is the offer's there and it stands. I'll come and get you all out any time."

"I'll talk to the family after we've eaten. It's a lot to take in."

While they were waiting for Joni to come back, Chris noted the occasional heavily-tanned white guy walking around the small town, and wondered if any of them had come from the US or even Britain years before die-back sealed off the Pacific. There were worse places to be exiled. Everyone here checked out strangers, though. It was only a small island, so Joni's pickup must have been familiar to a lot of folks in town, but they took a second look when they spotted Chris. One guy standing outside a bar was talking on his phone and stared for a little too long. Chris decided to slide further down in the seat. Perhaps he just looked like trouble to them. He'd cultivated aposematism too well.

"Have they got a warrant out for you here, then?" Marc asked.

"It's a small place," Chris said. "They know who doesn't belong here."

Chris felt uneasy. He was relieved when Joni got back in the truck and drove off, oblivious of what Tev now knew.

"That's me done, Dad," he said with a big grin. "Let's get the party started. You ever had kava, Marc?"

"Yes, but I'm all better now."

Tev and Joni laughed their arses off. "How about you, Chris?" Joni asked.

Chris assumed it was either alcohol of some kind or a weird, pungent food. "I don't know what it is, but I'm ready to give it a try," he said.

Joni laughed again. "Dad, go easy on him, okay?"

It was kind of cute to hear this guy still getting used to calling Tev *Dad*, because Chris was pretty sure he was. It didn't sound automatic. It was like he just wanted to hear himself say it as often as possible because he'd missed years of having his father around, and now he wanted to make up for all the times he hadn't been able to say it.

How old would he have been when Tev's marriage broke up and Becky decided to take the kids to a Fiji she didn't know? Chris did the math. Joni must have been at least nine if they arrived before die-back started spreading, but maybe they came later, in the brief window before APS realised how serious the disease was and closed the borders.

It was still touching to see a grown man who clearly worshipped his dad. And it hurt a little too.

"Here we are," Joni said, turning down another dirt track into what looked like farmland. "Home. I hope you're hungry."

Tev's house was on the western side of the island, about three miles on foot along the coastline from the wharf, five by road. Chris always made a note of transit times in case he ever needed to move people fast. The place looked like it was being rebuilt. Stacks of timber stood in the yard and there were tarps over the roof. Tev had come here in a hurry with his family and it showed. Chris wondered whether he had distant relatives already here who found somewhere for him to live, or if the islanders had simply been generous to neighbours in need and given them a house to do up. This didn't look like a rich resort.

"Gents," Tev said, ushering them into the front room, "I'd like you to meet my wife Becky, my daughter Karalaini, my daughter-in-law Sera, and Sera's mum, Mere Valisi."

Marc took the gin out of his rucksack and presented the bottles to Tev rather formally.

"I apologise if I'm doing this wrong," he said. "Thank you for your hospitality and letting us come to visit you all. It's a special gin. But not as special as seeing my buddy again and meeting his lovely family."

Becky walked straight up to Marc and hugged him. "This is all your doing." She had an English accent, even more English than Tev's. "You talked him into coming to find me. Thank you."

"I do occasionally have good ideas. I'm really pleased it worked out."

"Tev's been telling us all about you. Please, sit down and eat. Welcome."

The floor was laid out like the most lavish picnic Chris had ever seen and he had a moment of minor panic as he realised he'd have to sit cross-legged on the carpet for a few hours with his concealed pistol digging into his hip. It took a little discreet rearrangement before he was comfortable. He'd never seen food like this or tasted anything like it — fish, shellfish, curries, something that looked like a Chinese stir-fry, roast pork, and mangoes and bananas in desserts of some kind.

Tev gave him a bowl of murky liquid — okay, *this* was kava — and Chris downed it in one as Tev advised. It tasted terrible but made his mouth feel numb, which scared the shit out of him but felt good. He shouldn't have been envying this life, but he wished he'd travelled and seen the good, ordinary, everyday parts of the world like this one, not the historic landmarks and monuments he'd regretted never being able to visit.

At least it gave him something to talk about with Tev's family to avoid the inevitable questions about what he and Marc had been doing and that he wouldn't be able to answer yet. Marc seemed a lot more practised at avoiding awkward topics and regaled everyone with the story of how he and Tev escaped from DC after they'd evacuated the British embassy staff, and how he'd hot-wired the embassy limo as the getaway vehicle and kept it. He'd never told

Chris much detail about that day, or what he and Tev had had to do to get out of the city, but Chris had fought his way through places like that and he knew for sure that it couldn't have been pretty.

That was Earth. Opis still had the chance to be different.

For once, Chris didn't have to work at being sociable with strangers. The kava had done its job. He ended up talking to Sera and Karalaini about names for the baby and when it was due, asking Mere how she made the curries, and learning a lot about commercial fishing from Joni. Maybe it was the mouth-numbing liquor thinking for him, but Chris was more convinced than ever that this was how life was meant to be lived. It seemed sad that by the end of today, Tev's family would have to think about leaving all this behind, and, perhaps even worse, Tev would break the news about Opis and aliens, and they'd never see the universe the same way again.

Eventually, Tev tapped the table. "There's something we all need to discuss as a family," he said. "It's about why Marc and Chris came here to see us. We've got some decisions to make."

Marc picked up his bottle of beer. "We'll go for a walk while Tev tells you what's going on. If we're here, it might stop you discussing things frankly. But if you need any questions answered, just call us in, okay? We're here to do whatever *you* decide to do."

Well, that was one way to kill the party mood. Everyone looked dumbfounded.

"Is this bad news, Dad?" Joni asked. "Are you going away again?"

Chris winced. That said it all. Tev shook his head.

"No, we stay together, whatever happens. It's just something that's going take some explaining."

Marc ushered Chris outside. They sat on the plank bench by the front door. Marc carried on drinking his beer.

"I'm going to take a load of mangoes back," he said, as if nothing had happened. "Did you see that stall down the road? They're dirt cheap here. I bet Howie's never had one."

"I'm glad you're relaxed about this. I hope we haven't ruined their lives."

"I think APS already did that when Tev had to leave Viti Levu."

"Would you want to leave this place, or hang on in hope like we're doing on Opis?"

"Nowhere's guaranteed safe, mate."

"Yeah."

"You drank the kava, didn't you?"

"Just one bowl."

"It's a sedative that makes you feel good."

"Not alcohol?"

"Psychoactive drug from a plant, basically."

"Shit." Chris had to stay alert. He felt for his sidearm just to make sure he was ready. His loaded ruck was still in the house. "I thought I was feeling happy because it's nice here."

"It *is* nice here. But you're probably happy because you've been at a party and eaten yourself to a standstill. Just enjoy it while you can."

It was late afternoon. Chris stood up to walk around, trying to shake off the pleasant haze of whatever went into that kava. He hoped Tev would come out and say everyone wanted to leave, because he wanted at least one thing to be simple and tidy. But he knew it wouldn't be.

"Should have brought Boadicea," Marc muttered. "All that food. She'd have gone through it like an industrial vacuum cleaner."

"Hopeless romantic, aren't you?"

Marc looked like he was about to issue another official denial of his position on Ingram but the front door opened and Tev came out. Marc looked at his watch.

"Jury back already?" he asked.

"You want the short version?"

"Ah."

"It took a while to make them believe me, but they want time to think about it. I mean, we're already cut off from everybody Becky and the kids know, and we daren't go back, so leaving isn't the main problem. They're worried about the effect on Sera and the baby."

"Take all the time you want, mate," Marc said. "It's a big deal, and not the first time we've had to face it."

"Are *you* happy on Opis?"

Marc looked into the distance as if he was trying to decide. "I'm more at peace than I've been in years."

"I told you it'd all be healed, didn't I?"

"You did."

"Well, you might as well come back in, if you can stay a bit longer. A few more beers and a nice cup of tea."

Tev steered him back into the house. Chris hung around outside for a few moments before following, checking there was nobody keeping an eye on them, more out of habit than any foreboding. Now everyone knew the score, at least he could talk freely with Tev's family.

"How did you feel when you found out about all this?" Mere asked.

"I had trouble believing it, ma'am," he said.

"Do you ever wish you could come back to Earth?"

Chris hadn't missed home as much as he'd expected. He'd been ready to feel some primal level of distress about leaving the world humans had evolved to fit in with, from its daily rhythms to its bacteria, but he'd already done his grieving for the Earth that was long gone before he was born, the one he could still see in old movies and video archive.

"I think it's too late now," he said. "And I like Opis. I'm not sure if we've made a fresh start, but we've still got time to put things right."

While Chris was talking to Mere, he could hear Marc telling Sera about the medical care in Nomad and the new school. He wasn't doing a hard sell, but he was definitely trying to reassure her about the kind of life they could lead.

"Or you could go back to Britain," Chris heard Marc saying. "I can ask Lawson. So you've got other options."

It was early evening now. Chris should have done a radio check with Solomon, but Sol had the probes out keeping an eye on the area, and he could call them any time.

"You going to call Howie, Marc?" he asked.

Marc looked at his watch. "Damn, he'll be asleep now. I'd better make sure Ingram's looking after him."

Tev gave him an approving nod. "So you took in Howie."

"Two lost souls. I've been adopted by Dieter's pit bull, too."

Marc stood up from a cross-legged position with surprising ease considering how much he griped about aches and pains and went outside to make his call. Chris carried on answering questions as honestly as he could and finding images on his pocket screen to show harmless views of the base and the surrounding area.

And Tev remembered the long-distance images of what everyone had thought were just big, black crows at the time.

"Those birds were the teeriks, yeah?" he said.

"Probably Fred's grandsons," Chris said. "Demli and Runal. Fred said they used to come and explore the base before humans arrived. They're growing up fast. They're learning engineering on the job now."

Chris realised how many strange things he accepted as routine these days, and while it had seemed like one shock after the next at the time, it had still been gradual compared to what Tev and his family had to absorb in a few hours. Chris and Marc should have gone back this evening, but it didn't seem right to dump all this on the family, tell them they could come to Opis, and then go home and leave them to stew in it as if nothing major had happened. It was like breaking the news to Earth in microcosm.

Chris was happy to stay over for the night and clear up the kitchen, and maybe help them take in what was happening. Marc and Tev were having a quiet conversation in the corner with a glass of something, almost head to head, and Chris didn't interrupt.

"We really will think about Opis," Sera said, putting plates away. "It's hard to even know what to ask at the moment."

"I'm sorry," Chris said. "We should have handled this better. You know you can contact us any time."

"No, you didn't do anything wrong. The truth isn't always what we want to hear. But that doesn't mean we shouldn't speak it."

Chris finished cleaning the kitchen and wondered if she was coming around to the idea. But he'd just rewritten the rule that had driven all the secrecy about Opis, that nobody who knew about the technology could go back to Earth because the news would leak. It was the whole rationale behind everything they'd done so far, from the way they handled the evacuation to banning contact with Earth, and here he was, making himself available at the end of a comms link to answer Tev's family's questions about settling there. When it came to Nomad Base, they weren't all in it together. He'd never thought of himself as exploiting the privilege of command before, but he just had.

A dose of shame didn't keep him awake, though. He was so tired, gate-lagged, and lulled by the kava that he had no trouble falling asleep that night on a thin mattress on the floor of a back room with his lumpy rucksack for a pillow. It was just like old times, *happy* times even as Western civilisation fell around him. Yeah, it had been ninety per cent misery, but the ten per cent of succeeding and being with his buddies almost made up for it, or at least it felt that way now. Time had laundered the worst of it.

He woke with a start when he heard someone moving around in the house, and he was already primed for intruders when he realised it was Marc and Tev. He would have gone back to sleep, but the door opened and Marc loomed in the doorway. Suddenly there seemed to be a lot of movement.

"Chris, Sol's just called," Marc said. "We've got to leave. All of us. The probes picked up two offshore raiding craft heading this way plus two helicopters standing by on Vanua Levu. It's not official APDU, but it looks military, so you can guess who it is. We've got just over an hour, Sol thinks."

Chris's mind cleared instantly. Adrenaline was a great tonic. "How does he know they're heading here?"

"He intercepted their comms. It's a PMC job. It's got to be Pham. He's still doing this off the books."

"Bastard." Chris pulled on his pants. "Have you got a plan? Because I have."

"Take the boat and decamp to another island."

"There's a really simple way out of this, Marc. *Gate.*"

"I know. But Tev doesn't want to go to Opis because he's worried the gravity or the immunisation is going to affect Sera and the baby. They can live off the boat for a few days while we come up with a better solution. Sol says he can transfer some of the tents and equipment we used for the Kill Line evac once we fix a location. Mere's got relatives on Totoya, so that's another option."

"This is our shit. So we fix it." Chris loaded his rifle and pulled on his ruck. Someone was already in place on this island, waiting for them to show up, maybe even the guy on the phone who was watching them in town. Everyone seemed to notice them, though. It could have been anybody. "I'm a frigging idiot. Tev was bait for *us.* Pham knows how to play us."

"This isn't some Moby Dick shit about your existential feud with him, mate," Marc said. "We took our eye off the ball. Pham must have been keeping tabs on Tev from the start. He wants the gate first. Then he's coming for everything else." He tapped a vest pocket to indicate the gate locator. "I know he saw the portal, but even if he hadn't, and whatever he's planning isn't going to work, he can do a lot of collateral damage along the way."

"We've got an hour. Cut the chat and move out."

Chris was angry, but not with Marc. It just came out that way. He was furious with himself and mortified that they'd put Tev's family in this spot. The gate would have solved everything, but things were bad enough already without risking Sera's baby. She'd probably cope with the sudden shift to higher gravity and the immunisation, but probably wasn't good enough for Tev and Joni, and he could see that.

Walking out into that main room and facing Tev and his family was the hardest thing he'd done in a long time. They were bundling possessions into bags, not that they seemed to have many. They all stared at him. At least he could feel utter shame, so redemption was still possible. After Jamie and Nina, both dead because he made the wrong call, he wasn't going to let this become number three.

"I'm so sorry," he said. "This is down to us and we'll fix it."

"You've got a gun," Mere said.

That was what they were staring at, not his incandescent guilt. But it didn't absolve him.

"You're not responsible for what we do next," he said. "It's us they want, not you."

Everyone was now silent, just packing as fast as they could, no panic and no recriminations. Chris and Marc helped Joni load the pickup while Tev released the chickens and pigs that Chris hadn't even realised were there. It was going to be a tight fit on the truck, five people in the cab and three on the flatbed with the bags. Joni helped Sera into the front passenger seat, took one look back at the house, and got behind the wheel. Chris, Tev, and Marc jumped on the back and the pickup drove away.

Tev examined the Marquis that Marc had just given him, then slid it into the space between his leg and the side panel, out of sight.

"Pretty smart. Not bad for a knockoff."

"We knit all our own weapons," Marc said. "And yoghurt." He wasn't happy, though. It was broad daylight now and they'd be spotted. "Sol, can you hear me?"

"I have both of you on audio and I have a probe following you," Solomon said. "Can you put me on your speaker so Tev can hear me too, please?"

"I can hear you," Tev said. "I kept my comms kit when I left Ainatio."

"Excellent. It's good to hear you again, Tev."

"Sol, can you see a route that's clear of nosey parkers?" Marc asked.

"The coastal path. Join it at the second turn on the right."

"Bloody hell," Tev said. He tapped on the rear cab window and Becky opened it. "Can you take the path, Joni? Cut through Tomasi's land. Nobody's around at the moment. Go careful, okay?"

The pickup turned along a track flanked by palms, straight towards the sea, and then Chris understood why Tev had cussed. The path was exactly that, just a path around the rocky end of the island with enough of a drop to be potentially deadly, and even a wheel sliding off the edge would strand them here. It was two miles of intense concentration on Joni's part.

Tev shut his eyes for a few moments as the pickup eased onto the path in a low gear. It was slow going.

"Are there going to be people out on the wharf?" Marc asked.

"Maybe. All the fishing boats will be at sea by now, though, and we don't get tourists very often."

"So what's our story if anyone sees us?"

"Taking everyone to see relatives for a few days. Big reunion."

"Oh, I'm convinced."

Chris risked a look over the side panel and wished he hadn't. But if he'd been worried that he was going soft after a few peaceful months on Opis, this was stiffening his sinews a treat. Marc actually looked bored. It was the longest, slowest couple of miles Chris had ever travelled, but boredom wasn't part of it. He felt a lot better when the vehicle crawled out onto a broad dirt track again.

"Anyone at the wharf yet, Sol?" he asked.

"Nobody so far, and the nearest vessel's five miles offshore. I'll tell you if that changes. Leave the observation to me."

"Give me the feed on my screen," Marc said. "It makes me feel better."

"Very well."

Sautu was the only vessel alongside when they arrived. It wasn't until they started loading her that Chris realised she was a catamaran. There was space below for the women to stay out of sight and take it easy, although both hulls were partly taken up by refrigerated storage, but there was room on deck for defensive action. Marc and Tev took up firing positions behind the wheelhouse. Chris picked his spot on the small foredeck. There wasn't much by way of machinery at the bows to provide cover, except maybe for the anchor housing and the tiny capstan, but as the biggest threat was probably an aerial assault by helicopters rather than raiding craft lower on the water than he was, it was probably academic.

Tev stood at the stern and looked around. "All done?"

"Yeah, let's go." Marc patted his back. "Come on, Joni."

Joni stood on the jetty gazing back at his pickup for a few moments, clutching the key, and looked heartbroken. With the boat, it must have been everything he'd saved for and probably gone into debt to buy, and he'd only just started over. Chris had to say something.

"Don't worry about the truck," he said. "Leave it secured and we'll retrieve it later."

"Yeah."

"We can, Joni. Trust me on that. I might have screwed up so far, but the one thing we *can* do is move things."

Joni stuffed the key in his pocket and nodded, forcing a smile. "Okay, I believe you."

He moved the pickup to the gravel parking area and jogged back to jetty. *Sautu* got under way, leaving the inlet behind. Now they had just under an hour at sea ahead of them. The region was dotted with islands, which meant they could go in any direction, but if they were being tracked already then the advantage was lost. The daylight that had made them vulnerable to detection on the island was now on their side, though. Chris could see what was coming even without probe assistance, at least when it got closer.

He joined Joni in the wheelhouse and tried to familiarise himself with what the catamaran could do. He was a long way out of his comfort zone. Ingram would have been handy to have around right now.

Marc wandered in, cradling his Marquis. "What can this boat do, Joni?"

"Cruise at thirty, thirty-five knots, which makes the most of fuel, but close on fifty flat out," Joni said, one hand on the wheel. "Engines operate independently, so we can even move sideways if we need to. Good radar, collision alarm, autopilot, position hold, and heading hold. But I never thought I'd need it to evade mercenaries. Or an APS commissioner."

"Evasion only works if we can outrun them and they don't know where we're going," Marc said. "Even civil helicopters can do four times your top speed. Offshore raiding craft could overtake you, but it depends how much they're carrying. The helos are by far the biggest threat. Unless the raiders catch up and we find they're manned by some bad buggers like former Aussie or Korean marines, of course. Because that's who Pham would recruit."

"Then why are we even bothering to run?" Joni asked.

"Because your dad thinks the easiest solution — our FTL gizmos — might put your wife and baby at risk. And I agree with him. It's never been put to the test. Being transported *probably* won't harm them, but she's already under a lot of stress. So I'll do whatever it takes to make sure you don't lose your child. Because there's no way to make that right again."

So it wasn't purely tactical, then. Joni must have heard Marc's history from Tev, because he looked awkward and blinked a lot.

"I know," he said. "And you wouldn't take the risk unless it was a last resort."

Marc just nodded and left the wheelhouse. Chris couldn't tell if Marc was letting his personal issues override his judgement, but he had to give the guy the benefit of the doubt. He hadn't survived this long without being able to keep his feelings out of it. But escape looked like a very long shot now.

Chris wedged his screen on the dashboard's fascia to watch the feed from the probes. There was nothing visible out to fifty miles, just a lot of glorious blue water and some seabirds following the boat, a windless day with a flat calm sea. He couldn't even see islands ahead.

It wasn't going to last. He needed to talk to Solomon. He went outside and sat down by the rails at the bow.

"Sol, we could just gate to another point in the ocean," he said. "It's not Opis. The gravity's the same and there's no medication involved."

"The distance doesn't make any difference," Solomon said. "I agree with you. If they just want to hide, there are hundreds of islands here, many of them uninhabited, so I could place a gateway in Joni's path and he'd just sail through and wonder why he was in a completely different location. But we've never put a pregnant woman through the gate. Ainatio did extensive research on the effects of increased gravity and pharmaceutical interventions for women settling on Opis, but we have a very different situation here."

"But you'd get us out of a tight spot if there was no other choice," Chris said.

"I have my mission, and you have yours. I make the best decision I can at the moment I have to make it."

Chris took that as a yes. He understood the fine line Solomon walked when it came to placating humans with different opinions on a fraught topic.

"Can Pham see us?"

"I'll know very soon if they divert from the island or skip it altogether," Solomon said. "A lot of their satellites are functioning again. It's much harder to move around their networks now, mainly because I broke them."

They were thirty-five minutes into the hour's head start when Solomon alerted them again.

"A helicopter's landing at Tev's house," he said. "It looks like they're going to search the place. The other one's peeled off, and two fast patrol vessels appear to be on an intercept course with you. They're maintaining radio silence. They realise they've been hacked now."

"And I bet they'll search the house to make absolutely sure this boat isn't a decoy," Chris said. "Doesn't say much for the resolution of their spy sat if they couldn't identify us, though."

"They might be relying on drone swarms instead," Solomon said. "Fly-sized, much harder to detect. I confess that since my intervention, APS has become less vulnerable to cyberattack. That was inevitable. They've had to dust off whatever older technology they can find."

"It doesn't matter now. Hiding's not an option." Chris went out on deck to talk to Marc. "They can see us, guys. Are we going to fight it out?"

Marc was checking something on the probe feed. "Is that four men per raider, Sol?"

"Looks like it."

"Okay, let's ruin their day as much as we can. We'll worry about the helos when they show up." He started pulling hardware out of his vest. "Sol, you know what to do. Flood Q or whatever Ingram's matelots would say."

"That's submariners," Sol said. "Will do. But it would make it easier if you stopped the boat. We can't see below deck."

Tev gave him a look. Marc shook his head.

"Pham doesn't care about collateral damage to women, mate," he said. "The ladies have to leave, and you with them. We have to use the gate."

"That wasn't the deal, and how's anyone going to leave now?" Tev asked. "We're in the middle of the bloody ocean. Where's the gate?"

"I was coming to that bit."

Marc rapped on the glass. Joni came out of the wheelhouse.

"Just stop the engines," Marc said. "Press the button or whatever it is you have to do. Now listen to me and believe what I'm telling you. Tev, go below, get the ladies on their feet at the bow end of the compartment, and watch for something at the stern end that'll appear in front of you. It'll look like a patch of mist. A greasy smear. All you have to do is walk through it. I mean just *step through*. Shove your stuff through first or carry it, whatever, but on the other side of that patch, it's Nomad Base. That's how we got there, and how we arrived here."

Tev raised his eyebrows, frozen for a second. "I wouldn't believe that from another living soul."

"Do you believe me?"

"Well, you didn't bring a bike, so yeah."

"You'll feel the extra gravity, so mind your step. Sol's got medics standing by to look after Sera and they'll run quick die-back scans on you all, but you'll be safe and well cared for. We'll worry about the longer term when we've dealt with those tossers."

"And where will *you* be?"

"Right behind you, by about five minutes," Chris said, joining in the lie. He was sure he knew where Marc was heading with this. Few people passed through a Caisin gate for the first time without dithering, and he had to allow for delays and arguments. Someone needed to hang back and hold off Pham's heavies until everyone else was through. "Just go, Tev, and take Joni. It's easy. We've done it dozens of times."

"I'm not going," Joni said. "I can't leave the boat."

Tev dug his heels in too. "Too right. How can I leave you two here?"

Marc grabbed his arm. "Make our job easier and get going. Please, Tev. Do it for me."

Chris felt sorry for Tev. The guy wanted to fight because he was forged from the same metal as Marc, but Marc shoved him into the wheelhouse and almost pushed him down the ladder. Joni wasn't keen to go either, but the last thing Chris saw was his grim expression as he looked through the wheelhouse window at him and the engines stopped.

Marc raised his rifle and scoped through, looking down at sea level. "Tell me when they're home, Sol, then close the gate."

Marc didn't sound like he was making a last stand, but Chris faced the possibility of falling into Pham's hands and was torn between doing as much damage to the bastard as he could or denying him the access he wanted. They could toss their gate locators overboard, too. Sol could still get them out.

Well, if nothing else, this mission had been a good exercise for using the gate against the Kugin.

"You never discussed a plan with me," Chris said, "so I'm guessing my way through this."

"So am I," Marc said. "Are they through yet, Sol?"

"Not yet."

"Tell Tev he might have to push them through."

Chris could see the two raiders on his screen but he could also hear a helicopter approaching. *Sautu* was now bobbing along slowly, dead in the water. The helicopter was probably going to reach them long before the boats.

"They're going to try to board, not blow us out of the water, right?" Chris asked.

"Yeah. They want us alive. And a helo's vulnerable to ground fire. As is a bloke on a rope."

"The ladies have transferred," Solomon said primly. "No Tev or Joni yet. Tev's arguing with him about who goes last, but I can't actually see what's happening inside the hull. I can only hear voices via Tev's comms."

"Yes, you said that before. I can't go down there and kick Tev's arse, Sol. Make him move. Do what you have to."

"Very well." There was a long pause. "Ah. Got him. He's through now."

Marc suddenly stopped and held his aim. It was like watching a cat wriggle its ass and flatten itself when it was about to pounce on something. He had a target.

"How did you persuade him, Sol?" he asked.

"He wouldn't move to the gate, so I moved the gate to him."

"You're a sneaky sod."

"No Joni yet, though."

"He'll go. He won't leave his missus. Chris, go check it out."

"I've played this game before, Marc. You're not shoving me through the gate." Chris could see the helicopter too, and the open door. But roping down to a deck was crazy. They must have known they'd take heavy fire. "How easy it is to hit fuel tanks?"

"Not as easy as it looks in the movies. And I'll be shocked if that air frame isn't hardened."

Sol cut in. "Joni still isn't through."

"Can't you move the gate again?" Chris asked.

"It's going to be hard. I could locate Tev accurately by his radio, but Joni isn't wearing one."

"It's not a football field down there, Sol. He's in a confined space."

"And Fred and I have to be *incredibly* accurate to move someone I can't see and who won't walk through a gate, Chris. I hope it's occurred to you that we have to place it close enough to grab him."

Solomon sounded pissed off. It hadn't seemed that difficult when he'd yanked Chris away from knifing Pham, but there'd been a probe sending back images for Sol to locate his target. Chris could see the guy in the helicopter's open doorway, and the guy could probably see that Chris and Marc were ready to open fire. The sea was calm and nobody was going to miss.

"Steady," Marc said. "Wait for it."

But the guy in the doorway wasn't the winchman, and he had something in his arms that wasn't a rifle. He tossed it onto the deck as the helicopter passed overhead. Chris assumed grenades and ducked. Four or five cylinders landed with a muffled thud and the air filled with thick white smoke. It felt like a cold mist on Chris's skin. For a moment he thought it was some kind of nerve agent, but it wasn't doing much except obscuring everything. He stumbled his way to the wheelhouse's rear bulkhead to protect his back. Marc was there already.

"Those bloody things pump out for ten minutes," he said. "Persistent non-particulate smoke. Long hang time."

"But it's just smoke, yeah?"

"Don't worry, it's non-toxic. You'll get your brains blown out, but your lungs will be fine."

The helo sounded like it was standing off. It wasn't going to hover overhead because it'd only disperse the smoke. Maybe they weren't going to rope down, then. They'd board from the water, over the side. Chris heard the splashes of guys dropping into the sea. He took the port side of the ship while Marc took starboard, sweeping up and down the rail and listening for the sound of rappel hooks on the metal. It was harder to hear with the helicopter around. He put his hand on the metal, trying to feel knocks and vibrations.

They're not supposed to kill us. They need us alive. So they'll have to get up close.

But the guy came out of nowhere.

His masked face was suddenly inches from Chris's. Chris was too close to use the Marquis and the guy knocked him flat on his back and pinned him down. But he couldn't keep hold of Chris's right arm, and that was the one that was going to kill him.

Chris lashed out instantly. He pulled his backup knife from his pants and rammed it into any body part he could reach, over and over, waist and ribs and leg and ass and face, sometimes hitting armour, sometimes penetrating cloth and flesh. He wasn't going to stop.

The guy tried to push himself away and that was when Chris had his chance. The blade — four inches, long enough to wound, short enough to use in a struggle — slid in under the guy's chin. It felt like it went straight into his trachea up to the handle. Blood and spittle hit Chris in the face as the guy choked. Chris held the knife in place and slid it from side to side until the guy wasn't struggling so much, then rolled him off and just carried on stabbing. It was what he'd wanted to do to Pham. It was cathartic and he knew he'd feel weird about that when he cooled off, but right now, all he could focus on was destruction.

Shots brought him back to the here and now. He felt like he'd been kneeling astride the guy for ages. He got up to locate Marc, almost fell over another guy lying flat on the deck, and put a round in his head to make sure he was dead. And now he could see Marc. Chris watched him put his sidearm to the head of another guy trying to stand up and fire twice. Chris was sure he saw the blood spray. It was horribly familiar. It was Jamie all over again.

"Talk to me, Sol. What can you see? Where are they?"

"One man to your left, coming around from the foredeck, passing the wheelhouse door. No others on board."

The smoke was still thick but starting to clear. Chris saw the movement and opened fire with the Marquis. The guy just kept coming, though, like they often did, and that was when Marc crossed the deck, just four strides, and put two shots in his face at close range. The guy staggered and fell onto the icebox held in place by steel rails bolted to the deck. The box was right next to a small metal table, also secured to the deck, where the fish were gutted before they went in the icebox. The man ended up kneeling on the box with his arms stretched across the table, looking like he was at prayer.

"All down," Solomon said. "Two raiders still inbound, one helicopter five minutes away, one extra aircraft leaving Vanua Levu. Time to go, gentlemen."

Chris was still staring at the weird tableau of the guy sprawled across the gutting table when a massive explosion lit up the sky off the port bow. His first reaction was to drop flat before he was hit by flying debris. But nothing came his way, and he got up again, trying to stop his legs wobbling. He couldn't hear the helicopter any more. Something had taken it out.

"Did you do that, Sol?" Marc asked. "I bloody hope you did, or I'll have to change my mind on religion."

Chris looked over the side. The breeze had picked up and the smoke was thinning faster. Something was burning on the surface of the water, trailing wisps of black smoke, and then it was gone.

"Yes, that was me," Solomon said. "They'll think it was launched locally. And the gate's now proven its capability for missile attacks between remote locations."

Marc rolled a body over the side. "You're a regular fighter ace."

"But Joni hasn't reached Opis. And you have four minutes until another helicopter reaches you."

Marc stopped dead. "Christ, why didn't you say so sooner? Has he been below all this time?"

"I hope so."

Marc looked around the deck. It was the only time Chris had ever seen him look scared. "What are you looking for, Marc?"

"Bullet holes. Stray rounds. This tub isn't armoured." Marc went to open the wheelhouse door. "God, let him be alright. We've got to get him out before the rest of Pham's heavies show up."

Chris pulled him back. The last thing Marc needed was to find Tev's son dead.

"Marc, I'll get him," Chris said. "He's fine. He's just been sensible and not gotten in our way."

Marc ignored him. Chris blocked the doorway. He was nose to nose with him and it was sobering to try to face down a guy like that.

"*I'll* check," Chris said. "Don't make me spell out why."

It was a long few seconds and Chris half-expected to be spitting out teeth in the next breath. Marc took a couple of steps away and turned as if he was going to come back and shove Chris aside. "If Joni's dead —" he began, and suddenly he wasn't there.

"I'm getting rather good at that," Solomon said.

"He's going to dismantle you, Sol. I'm going below. Stand by."

"Two minutes. Come *on*."

Chris climbed down the short ladder, dreading what he'd see and already imagining the fallout if Joni had been shot. But he was sitting in one of the holds, checking a paper chart. Chris's gut somersaulted.

"Sol, tell Marc Joni's fine," he said. He tried not to overreact. Joni glanced up, looking guilty for no good reason.

"I should have come up and helped you two," he said.

Chris shook his head. "I'll explain later why you were right to sit it out, but we've got to go *now*."

"I still can't abandon the boat, Chris. What are we going to do if I can't work?"

Chris could hear the helicopter. He was waiting for a gate to open and the chance to push Joni through it. "The boat doesn't matter."

"I'll find somewhere to hide it. You can come back for me, right? You said you could recover the truck. You need to leave."

"I don't leave anyone behind," Chris said. Where was the damn gate? "You stay, I stay. I've never left a man behind, *ever*."

"You don't understand, Chris. We depend on this boat."

Solomon interrupted. "You're out of time and I'm moving you *now*." There was a smell of burning matches and a sudden silence. Chris waited. "There. I've moved you to another area of ocean while we work out a landing site for the boat. It'll have to be on land because we know that's safe and the sea isn't. Stand by for instructions soon."

"What happened?" Joni asked. "Was that burning fuel I could smell?"

Chris went up to the wheelhouse and looked around. The sea was choppier with white foam topping the waves and the sky had become cloudy. Chris didn't know where they were, but all he needed to know was that they were a long way from their pursuers.

"We've gone through the gate," he said.

Joni looked at the screens on the dashboard and then stared at Chris. "We're three hundred miles east. I didn't feel anything."

"It's usually like that. The burning smell's a clue."

"Is Sera okay?"

"Yeah, it's not like pulling ten G on take-off or anything." Chris hoped that was true. He switched his radio to speaker so that Joni could hear Solomon. "All clear, Sol?"

"I'm afraid anyone observing would have seen us vanish, but it's not the first time Pham's witnessed that, is it?"

"Thanks, Sol."

Chris ventured out on deck. He could hear nothing except the sea. *Sautu* was just drifting, engines dead. Joni still looked dumbfounded.

"We can't risk dropping the boat in the sea on Opis," Chris said. "It's not charted properly yet. She could end up on a reef. That's why we have to set her down on land."

Joni went back into the wheelhouse and pressed something. Chris heard a faint whine from the stern.

"What's that?"

"I'm lifting the engines," Joni said. "If you're going to put her down on land, we need the propellers out of the way so she can sit on her hulls. But she might still be damaged."

"It's okay. The bots can fix her."

"I'm sorry I didn't pitch in and help you guys."

"No, that was the sensible thing to do. It's dangerous enough relying on a glass fibre deck for cover. You're not armed, you're not trained, and you had no idea what you'd be walking into, with or without the smoke grenades going off. You could have been caught in the crossfire. You'd have made it a lot harder for us. And Marc would rather die than see Tev lose his son. I don't need to tell you why."

"He's going to kick my arse."

"No, he's just had a brief fright and he'll be fine."

"I'm sorry."

Chris had no right to be angry with Joni for risking his life for a damn boat. "We screwed up your lives by coming here. I'm the one who's sorry. Are we both done apologising now?"

Coming down off a combat high was something Chris always dreaded. He realised he was covered in blood and he'd pulled a muscle in his forearm, probably from the effort of stabbing. He'd have happily drunk a bowl of Tev's kava right then just to kill that shakiness. Joni hadn't said a word about the state of him or the bodies and blood on the deck.

"I'll clean up the boat," Chris said. "I'd better tip those guys overboard before Solomon moves us again."

"Are you injured?"

"No, just worn out."

Chris went over to check the three bodies still on the deck and retrieved their weapons, more out of habit than need. Before he tipped them over the side, he wondered whether to find their ID and somehow get word to their families, because their bodies might never be found. He could be stabbing a guy like a maniac one minute and worrying about the widow and kids the next. He wasn't sure if that was some kind of chivalry or whether he was just fucked up.

He searched them anyway. None of them had ID, but that was only to be expected. "Sorry, buddy," he said to each one as he rolled him over the side and the body hit the water. "It's just a job. I know Pham made you do it."

When he got back home, he'd need a drink with Jared. He'd probably need one with Marc, too. He kept thinking of the look on his face when Sol told him about Joni.

"We're ready for you," Solomon said. "Buckle up or hang on to something."

Chris decided it was safer being thrown around below deck than in the wheelhouse. He and Joni laid flat on the deck and waited.

"Have you ever done this before?" Joni asked. "With a vessel, I mean."

"No, but how hard can it be?"

Chris had hardly finished the sentence when he felt himself lift a few inches off the deck and fall back again, banging the back of his head. *Sautu* was still moving slowly when she went through the gate, but it was fast enough for her to skid. She stopped with a soft thud. Then she lifted and wobbled a little. Chris could hear creaking and scraping.

"The bots put down a collision barrier," Solomon said. "You've got lots of interesting things growing on the hull, Joni."

Joni helped Chris up and they went out on deck. *Sautu* was standing on the plain just outside the perimeter, flanked by a couple of the big construction bots. They were moving blocks into position to support her like a ship in a dry dock.

"Awesome, Sol," Chris said. He couldn't muster enough energy to sound upbeat. "And Fred. Come on, Joni, let's have our die-back scan and then you can see Sera."

But a crowd was already gathering around the boat. There was no hiding this now. Okay, there wouldn't have been any way of concealing Tev and his family if they'd arrived under less dramatic circumstances, but this must have looked like a big fuck-you to everyone who'd been told they couldn't call home.

Fonseca was standing at the front of the crowd, arms folded.

"You can't park there, Sergeant," she said. "And why are you covered in blood?"

"We're fine, thanks for asking."

Joni now stood on the small foredeck, eyes tight shut, hands cupped over his nose and mouth. He didn't seem the sort to be paralysed by fear, so Chris assumed he was praying, which was kind of confirmed when he opened his eyes and looked up to the sky for a moment. Chris would have joined him on the off-chance God existed, but he was sure God didn't want to hear any of his shit today.

And now he had to face a lot of people who'd be pissed at him and Marc for a long, long time.

"Put in a thank you for me as well, Joni," he said. "And add a plea for mercy."

07

One, anything that can be done will be done eventually, even if it's stupid or evil. Two, any technology or law will be exploited for the worst possible use it was never intended for. And three, humans are basically shit-houses. But so are dolphins and chimps, because it seems to go with intelligence, so there's no point feeling guilty about it. Those are Gallagher's Rules For Avoiding Disappointment. They've never failed me.

Marc Gallagher, former King's Special Operations Regiment, popularly known by the historical nickname of "The SAS."

SOUTHERN PERIMETER, NOMAD BASE: 0840 HOURS, OCTOBER 17, OC.

Yes, it was still there. And the grumbling had started.

It wasn't that Ainatio folk didn't like Tev or that they objected to APS-registered fishing boats being dumped outside the base. Trinder thought a lot of them were actually pleased to see Tev, because he'd been well-liked when he was at HQ.

But his arrival made them feel some Nomad personnel were more equal than others, with privileges denied to the rank and file, and it wasn't going down well in Lab Coat Country. It had probably ruffled feathers with some of the *Cabot* crew, too, but Ingram would slap that down hard. She wasn't calling home either. She held that moral high ground like Stalingrad. But she turned a blind eye to Marc's shenanigans, probably because she was kind of sweet on him, and that was what got noticed.

Trinder sat on the rear bumper of the Caracal and kept an eye on the boat for a while. Joni was unloading odds and ends from it. He seemed like a nice lad, and Maro, Fred's pissy son-in-law, crept up to him nervously to ask about the boat. They were now talking while Joni worked, and it was absolutely riveting to watch.

Here was a young guy who hadn't even known aliens had existed a couple of days ago, and now he was talking to one quite calmly, possibly because a giant crow was easier to relate to than the hypothetical sentient gas blob of Chris's imagination. The expression on Joni's face was priceless. Trinder could see the disbelief mixed with joy written all over him. Maybe Maro was thrilled too. It was still hard to tell just by looking at a teerik. But when your own father-in-law thought you were a dick, a stranger's interest had to be a major boost to your self-esteem.

Some folks wouldn't see it as the miraculous communion of species, though. You couldn't maintain a ban on contact with Earth for the hoi polloi while the chosen few could actually visit and bring their buddies back with them. The muttering had started. It wasn't a mutiny yet, but pointing out the necessity of getting Tev out of APS and the lack of choices open to Marc and Chris in a life-or-death situation wouldn't be enough to smooth people over.

Trinder was also one of the chosen, though, and he felt guilty about what he was about to do. He tore himself away from the marvellous spectacle of a teerik examining the hull of a catamaran and walked across to Warehouse 10, a slab of a building where most of the frozen food supplies were stored.

It had the air of a place where gangsters disposed of rivals and left them on hooks among the beef carcasses. But the interior was brightly-lit and painfully shiny, not seedy and sordid at all, and he could see Ingram's inner circle huddled around a steel table in the prep area. Marc and Tev had their backs to the door and looked like they were performing surgery. Ingram, Alex, and Chris watched the process like a bunch of cats summoned by the sound of a can opening.

"Lock the doors, Dan," Ingram said, not looking up.

Tev turned. "Dan, got any preferences? Take a look in the crates."

Trinder looked over the contents of the table — a lot of dissected fish — and the plastic crates stacked beside it. This was the catch that was still in the boat's cold store when Joni had to make a run for it. Trinder didn't recognise many of the species, but there were some really big fish in there. The biggest was the one now on the table, something that looked like a giant mutant mackerel, nearly six feet long. Even Tev was handling it like it was a struggle to lift.

"Apparently it's a wahoo," Alex said. "I was thinking of dressing it up in an Ainatio uniform and walking it out of here."

"Grill it, pan-fry it, coat it in breadcrumbs." Tev grabbed a towel to get a better grip on the slippery skin. "Don't overcook it. There's six, so there's enough for all of you to make a few meals, plus a crate of small yellowfin and some odds and ends."

"Thanks Tev. That's fantastic." Trinder was delighted. He could cook Erin a fancy dinner. "You call those small tuna? Damn. The big ones must be the size of a car."

Marc paused, mucky knife in one hand. "Shit. I forgot to get Howie's mangoes."

"We were a bit busy, as I recall," Chris said.

Trinder was still waiting for the detail of what had gone wrong yesterday. All he knew was that Pham was now minus four men and a helicopter. When Howie worried that Marc was going off to do something dangerous, he was usually right.

"How's Howie taking it?" Trinder asked.

"Our little escapade? Stiff upper lip." Marc shook his head and started cutting again. Tev was getting through his fish a lot faster than Marc was. "I think I need to spend a bit more time with him today. And can we remember not to mention the close quarters stuff in front of him?"

"Dai's painted a helicopter icon on Sol's bot frame."

"Where are we going to dump the heads and all the other leftover bits?" Chris asked. "I know we ought to be frugal and make stock out of it, but we need to incinerate the evidence. If anyone sees this haul they'll think we're rubbing their noses in it."

"Just sort the fish out and we'll worry about the blowback later," Ingram said. "Although I'm not looking forward to facing Jenny Park."

"Did Sol find any surviving family?" Alex asked.

"No luck so far. But there'll be some relatives, however distant."

Chris was examining a tuna as if he hadn't seen one outside a can before. He probably hadn't. "Pham knows we've got some snazzy FTL capability," he said. "He can't have missed what happened, and it looks like he's still doing it all off the books. So he won't want anything going public any more than we do. If Jenny can contact relatives, bad things will happen to keep them quiet."

"Yes, I know. You kept saying that at the debrief." Ingram squatted to check out the other fish. "We could stick these in the morgue, of course. The medics are absolute vultures, so you'll lose some, but it's a price worth paying for their silence. Ooh, what's that?"

"Estuary cod," Tev said.

"And the big greenish thing with the strange forehead?"

"Mahi-mahi."

Marc and Tev carried on cutting, chatting while they worked like a bunch of cannery workers. Trinder felt vaguely guilty for not sharing the bounty but this modest haul wouldn't feed seventeen hundred mouths anyway. He took a few pictures for posterity, including a team shot of everyone holding a wahoo like they'd just caught it.

"I was going to put aside a tuna to bribe Lianne," Tev said. "I brought some kava cuttings I want her to propagate. Am I going to be causing trouble?"

"Probably not if it's you," Alex said. "After all, it's your son's fishing boat. One tuna doesn't mean we've secretly divvied up a big haul of luxury fish."

"You make us sound really seedy," Marc said. "I suppose we are."

Chris must have been in a hurry to get somewhere. He started pacing, arms folded, and then he looked at his watch and picked up the tuna he'd been allocated.

"Does anyone mind if I go?" he asked, wrapping it in film like a mummy. "I'm running late. I'm going to do battle with this guy at home." He put it into a paper potato sack and tucked it under his arm. "I'm saving it to curry favour with a woman. See you later, Tev. Thanks, buddy."

Ingram waited for him to go. "Fonseca?"

"Don't think so," Marc said. "Must be a new one. I'll make enquiries."

"Is he okay?"

"Are you asking if he's traumatised by slicing up someone yesterday, and that pile of fish guts has brought it all back?"

"Possibly."

"He's more upset that it wasn't Pham. But Pham's not finished with us, not now. He'll get his chance."

Ingram sighed and shook her head. Tev and Marc now had the prep work down pat and the fillets were piling up in separate stacks. Trinder decided everyone needed to be able to do this, and there was no time like the present.

"You can leave mine," Trinder said. "I'd like to do it myself."

"Fine by me," Marc said. "I'm going to dump the waste and scrub myself down, or I'll have every dog on the base following me."

Now they had to disperse discreetly with their stash. Ingram, Marc, and Tev left with a few plain bags, and Alex stayed. Trinder locked the doors again. All he had was his army knife. Then he realised the belly was intact, and that meant guts. He really didn't like guts.

"Okay, nurse, I'm ready to operate," he said to Alex.

"So you've done this before."

"Nope." Trinder tried to remember how Marc and Tev had done it. "What do I do with it?"

Alex shrugged. "Don't ask me. I think fish are usually square and white with no faces. And they live in little plastic bags and they're freezing cold and rock-hard."

"Gee, thanks, Mr Survival Expert."

"I'm strictly a grocery store pioneer." Alex tapped away at his screen. "Hey, here's a how-to vid. This is like remote surgery. I can talk you through it. Ready, doctor?"

Trinder held up his knife. "Scalpel."

"Cut diagonally *there* behind the gills."

"Eww."

"That's it. Now mark out the cutting lines on both sides with the tip of the knife. Then you come back and cut the flesh away."

"Do I cut the guts out first?"

Alex studied the screen, frowning. "Nope, looks like you don't have to touch the innards at all. Which is just as well, because this says they've usually got wormy things. Just slice the meat off. Go on, run the knife down the back... yeah, all the way to the tail."

"Worms?"

"Forget the worms. Cut across the tail, not through it."

"Uh-huh. Got it."

"Then stick your knife in and cut along *this* line all the way back to where you started. Then turn it over and repeat on the other side."

Trinder followed Alex's instructions and felt ridiculously pleased with himself. Somehow he'd removed two long slabs of lovely pearly meat. What was left of the wahoo now lay intact on the table like the remains of a fish dinner in a cartoon, a head and tail connected by a bridge of spine and ribs.

"You sure it's safe, Al? I mean, *worms*."

"It's okay, they're really *big* worms. Look." Alex thrust the screen in his face. "You'd be able to see those, right?"

The image was gross. Trinder felt a little queasy. "Aw, come on, did you have to show me that?"

"I try to educate where I can."

The room looked like a crime scene and it took ages to clean up. Trinder was in two minds about what to do with the head, which looked pretty meaty and edible too, but Chris was right. It had to go to the incinerator. He cut the long fillets into portions and bagged them.

"Thanks for being a great theatre nurse, Al."

"I didn't even mop your brow."

"But I feel bad about keeping these to myself."

"Oversharing is a sin, my son. But listen to Ingram. We've got nothing to apologise for. Tev was left behind, his life was at risk, he's got irreplaceable skills, and if there's two guys you can trust to use the gate for good, it's Tev and Marc."

"Are you rehearsing your excuses for when your boffins demand to know why they can't go home too?"

"Yes. Did I sound plausible? I've been losing my glib touch lately. I can't bullshit like I used to."

"Well, you convinced me. I'm going to dump the evidence now."

The trick to being discreet was to stride up to the waste processing compound in broad daylight and drop the bag of waste in the chute. Once that was done and nobody had accosted him about the contents of his other bag, he set off for Kill Line feeling like a proper man bringing home a kill for the tribe.

Erin examined the fillets on the kitchen table and beamed at him. "It's really kind of Tev," she said. "And you taught yourself to clean and prep a fish, did you? Not bad for a city boy."

"Alex helped. It was gross, though. It had worms."

"Protein's protein." Erin opened the freezer and stacked the fish but kept two portions back. "We'll have some of this later. So where have they put Tev's family while the house is being built?"

"In the old accommodation block. The top floor. It'll only be a couple of days at most until the house is furnished ready for them to move in. Sera's still in the infirmary. Mendoza's monitoring her."

"She's okay, though, isn't she?"

"Yes, but you can understand everyone being nervous."

"This is the point where we really become a community. The first baby born on Opis."

"Is that a hint?" Trinder asked.

"No."

"It's a hint from me, then. We need to fix the date for the wedding."

"Before the end of the year?"

"Let's wait until we start the new calendar, or you'll never remember our anniversary."

Trinder realised he hadn't actually said the words. Erin knew what he meant, and maybe it wasn't a big deal for her, but he needed to hear himself say it.

"I want a family," he said. "I want kids. I want grandchildren. I want us to be like the Kill Line folks, with a stake in the future. There, I said it."

"I thought you had."

"No, I tiptoe around things. You know why. Hey, shall we have a barbecue tonight? Wahoo's good for grilling, Tev says."

"I'm on duty at nineteen-hundred. Let's make it tomorrow. I can marinate the fillets overnight. But we can have a quick meal if you're home in time."

"Okay, let's do that. I'd better shower so nobody smells my contraband wahoo. I expect to be putting down mutinies by lunchtime."

Erin pulled her dubious face. "They're all talk. Give them a slap. They know why we need Tev here."

Trinder wasn't so sure about that. But folks liked to complain even when they didn't need to. Griping was some kind of bonding process. He'd caught himself doing it occasionally, but he was ready for any smartass comments or outright accusations. He was so ready, in fact, that he was disappointed not to be challenged by anybody. When he walked into the canteen to check out the mood and see who was where, he got some sullen looks, but no actual comments. Unless Ingram had any troublemakers in her crew other than the civilians, it was only the scientists and specialists who had a beef about access to Earth.

Not enough work, that was their problem. The sooner they started going outside the wire and studying stuff, the happier they'd be. Some specialisations still had plenty of work to do in their own professional area — medics, botanists, engineers, geologists — but the rest had to find a role that Nomad needed, and learning manual skills was the best option as far as Trinder was concerned. Chris was dead right on that. All it would take to screw this settlement would be for some catastrophe to take out power or automation and they'd be left with a bunch of people who could rearrange molecules in ten dimensions but didn't know how to repair a water leak, make a chair, or grow tomatoes.

That included him. He had to face it. He could grow stuff, and he'd built a makeshift barbecue, but he'd be guessing his way through the leak and stumped by the chair. He'd have to up his game if he wanted to be solid husband material.

He could prep a fish, though. That was something.

He took his own advice and spent the rest of his watch digging a trench to lay networked mines for the perimeter defences, driving the mini-excavator around the path laid out with pegs and trying not to rely on its mapping system to do all the work for him. Two of Chris's guys, Zakko and Rich, were laying the mines in his wake and testing the links to the monitoring system. Once all this was complete, the base would be surrounded by a ring of devices that would recognise intruders or unauthorised vehicles and detonate in overlapping arcs. In theory, nothing approaching on the ground could avoid it and the enemy didn't even have to tread on it or drive over it. Proximity was enough. It was a straightforward system and Trinder chose not to think how long it would hold off sustained waves of attacks. He finished digging his section of trench and walked back up the line to see how the mine-laying was going.

"What if Kugin use paratroopers?" Zakko asked. "They'll skip all these defences."

"We just pick 'em off on the way down," Rich said.

"They're supposed to be big and heavy."

"You ever seen a Fennec ATV parachuted from a plane? They're heavy too. They still take enough time to reach the ground."

Zakko chuckled to himself. "I bet we never see a Kugin here. Everybody ready for a quick signal test?"

It was always a nervous moment. The explosives were isolated from the control system while they tested the connections, but Trinder always half-expected something to go wrong and leave a smoking crater with him in it.

"Ready," he said.

Rich tapped in the code. Trinder consulted his screen to see what had linked up. The map overlaid a mesh on an aerial image of the entire base, and when Trinder dragged the viewpoint around, Nomad looked like it was under a chicken wire dome. All the security systems — sensors, drones, fixed cameras, satellite monitoring, and now the mine network — were successfully linked to the control room. The mesh showed almost complete sensor coverage of the whole base from ground level to fifteen thousand feet. As Nomad reclaimed and conditioned more land for farming and extended the perimeter sensors, the dome would expand.

"Lasers," Zakko said. "That's what we need. *Curtis* has energy weapons. Everybody had them before the Decline. If we added laser defences, it'd really cut down on the maintenance."

"Maybe we can," Trinder said. "Can I fill this trench now?"

"Yeah, we're good."

Trinder dug and filled another fifty yards before Ray Marriott turned up to relieve him. On the way back to his office, basking in the contentment of doing what he considered real work, he checked on *Sautu* to see what was happening. Rikayl was sitting on the wheelhouse roof with his back to the base, watching something. It was only when Trinder walked around the boat that he saw Chris cleaning the deck. He could put the pieces together. Chris was removing bloodstains.

Rikayl poked his head over the edge of the roof. "Wanker kill!" It sounded like approval. "Kill kill kill!"

Chris looked over the side. "Oh, hi, Dan."

"I'm not going to pry." Trinder pulled himself up the ladder and leaned on the boat's rail. "I saw the state you came back in."

"Opposed boarding. We did the opposing. Kind of a clusterfuck, really."

"I heard. Couldn't be helped."

"You've been there."

Trinder remembered cleaning blood off his uniform and being appalled that it was someone else's. "Yeah."

"Anyway, I owe Joni a clean deck. It's the fiddly bits around the hatches. Muck gets in the grooves." Chris shrugged. "Maybe some of it is fish blood."

"We'll have some peace and quiet now. Everyone's safely gathered in."

Chris rinsed his brush in a bucket and knelt to scrub at a recessed pull handle on one of the hatches. "But they're not, are they? It's only a matter of time before someone wants us to extract the Ainatio folks who opted to go with APS."

Trinder knew it too. Perhaps a simple no was the way to deal with it.

"Pham knows we've got a gate," he said. "Why are we still pretending it's a secret?"

"Yeah, I can't see how someone wouldn't have noticed us vanishing off visual and radar. I don't know why I was worried about that. He still can't do anything about it, and even if we didn't have it, he'd still want Sol shut down and he'd still want to end Nomad."

"So you're going to chill, yeah?"

"I'm going to get a life." Chris shook his head. "The gate's awesome. But it's a massive burden and I think we'll regret having it one day."

Trinder wasn't going to argue with him. He wasn't even sure why he wanted to, but when he climbed down the ladder and went on his way, he looked at the locator on his belt and tried not to think how easy it would be to get Sol and Fred to gate him straight him into Dubuque. Solomon was getting adept at using the gate under Fred's supervision, and it wouldn't be long before Fred wasn't needed at all.

I could just step in there. Right now.

But even if Trinder didn't get shot as soon as he arrived, he'd probably face months, maybe years of searching for family he hadn't seen for sixteen years and hadn't heard from in nine or ten. The exact date should have been etched in his memory, but it wasn't. When Tev's rescue had first been discussed, Trinder felt it prick his conscience, but here he was, still doing nothing about his family.

They were probably already dead. He was back in that loop again, damned if he found out and damned if he didn't. But he couldn't let the past blight the present. Erin was his family now. They'd get married and have kids, and nothing was more important or deserving of his ambition than that. All the clever science that had driven Ainatio for a century, built careers and professional reputations, and brought them to Opis had just one purpose: to enable humans to carry on having families. Everything else was a substitute, a distraction from the main business of existence. He'd made that mistake and thought family — being part of one, having one of his own — was a poor second to something else that he couldn't even name now. But he had a second chance and he wasn't going to waste it.

That afternoon, he signed out an hour early and got home to find Erin had made burgers and sweet potato fries. It was simple bliss to lounge in the garden with a plate on his lap and a beer in his hand and watch the sun dissolving into a pink sunset. Trinder counted himself lucky.

"I keep meaning to ask what happened to Fred's wife," Erin said. "He must have had one."

"If their kids were usually sent away to other communes, maybe they did the same to spouses."

"Dan, that's horrible."

Trinder thought about it. "I don't know. Birds on Earth kick out their kids when they're old enough and most of them don't mate for life. So maybe it's the same with teeriks." Anyone who'd lived through the last years of the Decline in America knew not to ask about absent relatives anyway. "It's kind of hard to raise the subject. I didn't even know Mangel was widowed until the guy told Marc and Chris."

"We don't ask, do we? Not usually."

"I never asked you."

Erin seemed to take that as a question. "Okay, you know about Jamie and how I said it wasn't the first time I regretted leaving stuff unsaid?"

"Yeah."

"Well, I was engaged to a guy in my platoon. Ross. I survived a firefight and he didn't."

"Sorry. I didn't mean to open wounds."

"No, I need to say this. I'd just told Ross that maybe we should put it off and think about it, and he was upset, and the next day he was dead before I got the chance to say I was wrong and I wanted to get married right away. That's about it, really. I couldn't bear thinking I hurt him so much that his mind wasn't on the fight, like knowing all I had to say to Jamie was yeah, sure, I'd date him, and then he'd at least have been happy when he died."

Trinder had suspected it'd be something like that, but it was still hard to hear. "I'm really sorry, honey."

"Everyone's lost people they've loved," Erin said. "It was routine, even for you guys holed up in Ainatio. We've all been through it, except the Kill Liners."

"Do you want me to shut up?"

Erin swirled her beer around the glass. "No, you can say anything you want, any time. But I'm not going to dwell on it. If you want to talk about your family, I'll listen. You do, don't you? I knew from the way you looked at Tev's people when they came through the gate."

Yeah, Erin knew him better than he knew himself sometimes. "I feel like a total shit because I always found an excuse for not going back to find them."

"It's real hard to find people out there, Dan. Ask anyone who arrived with the convoy."

"I know. But I see Marc and Chris pulling out the stops for Tev and I wonder why I didn't try."

"Honey, we ended up where we are because we're mostly people who didn't have tight-knit families to start with," Erin said. "You can love family because humans are hardwired for it, but sometimes you just don't feel the need to be with them. So you don't visit so often, and the gulf starts to widen, and then you haven't spoken to each other for so long that you don't even know how to break the silence. But we spent generations encouraging people to move away from their hometowns and do their thing or find a better job and giving them reasons not to have kids, and now we're damn miserable and wondering how we forgot to be normal."

Trinder felt a twinge that could have been some of what she'd said resonating with what he'd buried. He didn't have a clear-cut painful past like Chris and his folks, with a solid reason to blame. It was harder to pin down his motives, but the accidental rootlessness struck a chord. He'd just thought there was something better out there for him, and there wasn't.

"You're right, no point in trying to fix something until I know what's broken," he said. "Want another beer?"

"Where do you get all this extra stuff?"

"Jared's experimental batches."

"So we're guinea pigs. Awesome."

Trinder tried to avoid thinking about his family for the rest of the evening, but the silt of the past had been stirred up and it muddied his sleep that night. It was like trying to recall a name on the tip of his tongue. He kept waking up and trying not disturb Erin, and when he fell asleep again he had more dreams.

One was about koi carp the size of dolphins pouring out of the Caisin portal in a never-ending river of vermilion and white. He tried to stop them like wayward cattle, holding his arms wide, and somehow he wasn't getting wet. "Now look what you've done," he said to Marc, who was inexplicably there but not doing anything to help him. "We'll never be able to stop them now."

The dream lingered for a while when he woke again. He'd long since given up worrying what dreams told him about his mental state, but he picked this one apart anyway. The fish were all his fears, maybe, or simply the product of too much talk about invasions, and Marc was the guy he thought had all the answers.

Damn fish.

Too many fish.

Trinder woke again with them on his mind, not the koi this time but the wahoo sitting in the freezer. He was feeling guilty for not holding a fish barbecue for the detachment. Even a giant mutant mackerel wouldn't go far between thirty people, though.

He decided to put a few fillets aside for Aaron Luce, then tried to calculate if he had enough for everybody to at least have a wahoo canapé each. He was cutting the tiny portions when Erin came into the kitchen to start breakfast.

"I knew you'd do this," Erin said. "You're so transparent."

"I'm sorry. I brought it back for you."

"No, share it with your guys," she said. "You wouldn't be Dan Trinder otherwise. That's the guy I fell in love with. Do it."

"I've got a tuna put aside too."

"See? We won't go without."

Trinder fried twenty-nine very small portions in the admin office kitchen for his troops that morning. Everyone seemed pleased. Only Rory Farrar had tasted wahoo before, so it had enough novelty value to offset how little there was, but it left Trinder feeling terrible that he'd even considered not sharing it. He felt even worse when they told him what a great commanding officer he was.

He didn't like himself very much at the moment. He needed to be the man Erin thought he was.

At least he felt confident enough to go for a beer in the staff club before he went home that evening, something he hadn't done for a while. Erin wouldn't be home for a couple of hours so he had time to kill. The bar was pretty full even at six in the evening, and he got a few odd looks, but they were more of the what's-going-on variety, as if people were surprised to see him and expected him to have a work-related reason for being there. It wasn't the accusing stare of the fishless that he'd imagined.

Marc, another rare visitor here, was sitting at a table near the bar, and he had a noticeable exclusion zone around him. Betsy was stretched out under the table. Whether the space around them was down to Marc's intimidating presence or the dog's was hard to tell. But Trinder had a feeling that Marc was defying someone to start it with him over the trip to Earth. The smarter Ainatio people would have realised that and left well alone. Trinder helped himself to a beer behind the bar, logged it in the ration book, and sat down at Marc's table.

"It's Howie's astronomy night with Nathan and Todd," Marc said, like he had to explain being there. "I was taking Betsy for a walk and the urge for liquid refreshment came upon me."

Trinder peered under the table. "Have you worn her out?"

"I cooked some fish for her," Marc said. "She's full."

"I shared mine with my guys."

"See? I knew you would."

"Has Tev given Lianne her bribe?"

"He has."

"And?"

"She's growing kava for him. She's a transactional woman. I like pragmatists."

Trinder had to laugh. "A recreational beverage war's coming, buddy. Lianne controls coffee and now kava. Andy's still the hard liquor baron because he's got distillery access, but Jared and Dave have taken over the beer market. There's still wine and tea to fight over. My money's on Lianne."

"That's when shit gets real. You lot can't be trusted with tea. I'm muscling in on that."

Marc seemed to be a little happier now. It made a nice change to sit down and socialise with him instead of just talking when things went wrong. Trinder was also enjoying the relief of a secret he didn't have to keep. He was so relaxed that he wasn't reading the room, and didn't realise there was an awkward moment approaching until he saw Marc's gaze shift away from him to something over his shoulder. The guy didn't move his head at all, just his eyes. Betsy scrambled to her feet. Trinder turned his head as casually as he could.

Jenny Park had appeared at the bar. She didn't seem to have come looking for Marc, because when she glanced around and spotted him, her expression changed. She left her drink on the bar and walked straight up to him, ignoring Trinder and looking murderous.

"So it's okay for you to visit Earth anytime," she said, "but I can't even check on my relatives and tell them not to hold memorials for me. Or find out if they had to burn the family farm to the ground. I'm from Honam. The first area contaminated with die-back. So thank you, Sergeant. Now we know who matters on this base and who doesn't."

Marc looked up at Jenny, expressionless. The entire bar was now listening, not that it was possible to ignore the spat in a room this size. Betsy moved forward through the chair legs and planted herself between Marc and Jenny. It was so quiet that Trinder heard her claws scrape on the floor. Marc hooked his fingers under the dog's collar, slow and casual. Few men would risk having a go at Marc, but if Jenny thought her gender made her immune, she was pushing her luck. The guy didn't give women any quarter if they got in his way.

"So?" Marc said.

"We accepted the ban because Ingram said it would cause chaos if people back home realised we were here and how most of us got here."

"At the risk of repeating myself, so?"

Jenny bristled visibly. Marc wasn't doing tact today.

"It was all for nothing, wasn't it?" she said. "You blew our cover, whatever that was worth. Is it true you and Chris had a shoot-out with APS?"

"No, we had a shoot-out with Tim Pham's private army."

"So he knows you're commuting back and forth to Opis. Oh, that's terrific. Does he know about the Caisin gate as well?"

"He knew about that back at Kill Line," Marc said. "You do remember the great escape, yeah? He saw people and objects go through the gate. He probably watched us disappear off Fiji and realised that was the gate too. I'm sorry about your family. But nothing's changed. Pham wants to keep APS in the dark about all this. If you contact your relatives and he finds out — and he probably will — then he'll permanently silence them in case you've told them too much that might get back to APS."

"It's not about that, though, is it?" Jenny said. "It's about who's trusted and who isn't."

"Well, that's because I'm not an APS citizen," Marc said, all matter-of-fact. "And I was extracting a special forces comrade from APS territory."

"You really are an unpleasant bastard, aren't you?"

One of the Ainatio lab technicians, a guy called Bob Calman, leaned back from his table. "Marc, if you can go back for one of your guys, why can't you go get ours? They're stuck with APS and probably wish they weren't. Like the Meikles. They've got a little girl. God knows what's happening to them now."

Jenny rounded on the guy. "You stay out of this. It's your friend Abbie who released die-back in my country. And your people *chose* to stay with APS."

"Give it a rest, will you?" Trinder said, trying to calm things down. He could see Bill Korda, one of his troops, moving slowly towards the table like he was ready to step in as well. "We've got aliens on our doorstep who could wipe us off the map tomorrow. If you want a fight, save it for them."

Marc, still completely calm, actually answered Bob. "Yeah, we could bring your mates back here," he said. "All I'd have to do is infiltrate the APS heartland, work out where they all are, find them all, ask them all if they want to leave, and then find somewhere to gate them out without APS detecting it. But I'm not volunteering. I went back for Tev because he's my mate. He was ready to save your sorry arses when APS were going to bomb us, and if APS get hold of him now they know an Ainatio staffer is a terrorist, they'll torture the shit out of him for intel. Extracting him means that doesn't happen, which is good for everybody, including you. Are we clear now? Let me know if you've got questions."

If things were going to erupt, they'd erupt now. If they did, Trinder knew Marc would wipe the floor with Bob and anyone else who looked at him the wrong way. There was already enough bad blood after the searches.

"Everybody calm the fuck down," Trinder said. "You're supposed to be Earth's finest, not a bunch of whiny little bitches. You too, Miss Park. I don't care if you're a *Cabot* civvy. If you've got a grievance, put it in writing to your CO."

Jenny stared at him, still looking like she was going to do something she'd regret. For a moment he wondered if she was going to hit him and whether he'd hit her back. He realised he'd probably have done it before he even had time to think. His inner bastard was possessing him more each day, but he wasn't displeased by that.

"I will," Jenny said. "But understand how people see this. One rule for Ingram's favourites and another for the rest of the crew."

She stalked out and Betsy stared after her until the door closed, then sat down. Bill caught Trinder's eye, shrugged, and took Jenny's drink off the counter, because there was no point in wasting it. The bar managed a few more seconds of collective silence before returning to a forced nothing-to-see-here buzz of fake-cheerful conversation.

Marc gave Trinder a look and almost smiled. "There, boil lanced." It sounded like he'd planted himself here for the sole purpose of drawing out dissent and smacking it down. "I thought you were going deck someone. Bloody hell, Dan, you've blossomed. In a knuckleduster kind of way, that is."

"I get that it's frustrating for them."

"So do I. Time for another half?"

"Thanks, but I'd better get home." Trinder stood up and Betsy jumped up too like she thought it was time for walkies again. "And you've got to pick up Howie."

Trinder was ready to bet that there'd only be small pockets of resentment about access to Earth, and even those with a good case for making contact again understood why it was a security problem. But it was hard not to give in to the emotion, and he regretted snarling at Jenny, even if she was what Jeff called a *gobshite*. She was only worried about relatives she probably didn't know who would dutifully mark the anniversary of her death for five generations and commemorate her several times a year. Annis Kim had explained it to him. He could understand why it upset Jenny.

All these people with a strong sense of family and kinship were starting to feel like a rebuke again, but that was his problem, not theirs.

The next day was Trinder's regular visit with the farmers to make sure they had everything they needed by way of security measures. He checked the sentinel units, walked the northern perimeter of Kill Line, and dropped in at each farm, getting coffee and cake at every stop. He liked this life. He knew he still craved adrenaline, but this was turning into a proper community, and he enjoyed becoming part of it. Perhaps, if he dived in deeply enough, this new kinship would eventually bury all his agonising over his family until he didn't recall it at all.

But his last call that morning was Liam Dale's farm, and it was hard to see the place quite the same way after what had happened when they pinned down Gan-Pamas in Liam's slurry pit.

Liam always asked Trinder how he was and never mentioned the shooting. He wasn't the friendliest of guys, but this was his way of being diplomatic and not making Trinder recall getting shot, as if he could forget it anyway. In return, Trinder never mentioned that Liam had killed Gan-Pamas.

They leaned on the fence and watched the herd of Jerseys. The cows looked well-fed, so the adapted grass was working out well. Liam looked up at the sky from time to time.

"It's not going to rain today," Trinder said.

"It's not that. I'm keeping an eye out for Rikayl."

"Is he pestering you again?"

"No, but I still don't trust him. He's been over here today. He didn't land. He just circled."

"If he bothers you, call me or Chris," Trinder said. "Whatever you do, though, don't shoot him."

"Yeah, yeah, I know. Anyway, does Dieter want a puppy?"

"Sorry?"

"Rosie's got a litter on the way. I wondered if he wanted a pup, seeing as he lost Girlie. Might comfort him some."

Trinder hadn't expected that. "Do you want me to mention it to him?"

"Sure, if the moment's right. Thank you."

Liam had a heart under all that indifference, then. Trinder drove off congratulating himself on how normal he was becoming and how the walled city of Ainatio HQ hadn't driven him completely crazy. Then he spotted Rikayl.

He stopped the Caracal and got out to watch. Rikayl was flying in big circles like he was practising for a driving test. Eventually he banked and started his descent, disappearing between the school and the church. Trinder drove off again, thinking the teerik must have been amusing himself because there was nobody around to play with him, but before he reached his next stop, Marty's sheep farm, the alarm flashed on the dashboard. He pulled over to the side of the road just as Solomon's voice popped in his earpiece.

"Aerial breach detected, Major," Solomon said. "A small object, probably a probe, directly overhead. It's descending. We haven't engaged. Captain Ingram wants to observe and capture it if possible."

"On my way."

"Ingram's in the control room. Lieutenant Heide's coordinating the ground response."

"I'll find him. Patch me into tracking, please. Trinder out."

He headed for the green, surprised that his gut wasn't churning. They'd expected some contact and now they had it. The base had gone to defence stations with the anti-air guns manned, and Heide was on the green with his team, prepping drones. Fred was with them. Trinder jogged across the grass, trying to follow the object on his screen. It was now at ten thousand feet and seemed in no great hurry to descend.

"Morning, sir," Heide said. "Definitely a probe. Fred's confirmed it. It's the size of a tennis ball."

"Does that mean it's been deployed by a ship nearby, or has it got its own propulsion?"

"Integrated FTL drive, like our probes," Fred said. He had his own screen with totally different displays. "I don't believe it's carrying a dangerous payload. If it's the type I believe it to be, it's for surveillance. Do you want to stop it observing before you intercept it?"

"What happens if we try to trap it?" Trinder asked. "Can it just spacefold out of here?"

"Yes, it can," Fred said. "So if you want to capture it for analysis, you need to cause substantial damage to prevent that. Fire a metal rod through it, for example, which is what we plan to do using construction drones. These probes are designed to be highly resistant to electronic interference, but brute force works, if you're fast enough."

"Six armed drones," Heide said. "Surround it in a sphere formation. I can't tell if it's detected us or if it's programmed to react, but there's only one way to find out."

"You think it's Jattan, Fred?" Trinder asked.

"Most likely."

"It's probably looking for *Curtis*, then, so it's got to come down low to check out buildings."

"I would think so, yes," Fred said.

"Here's the thing, sir," Heide said. "However clever it is, it can't interpret aerial reconnaissance imaging and recognise structures because no Kugin or Jattan analyst has ever seen human military facilities. And if it was only here to take pictures, it wouldn't need to descend any further. Right Fred?"

"Partly correct." Fred was looking up at the sky, wings slightly out to his side like a cormorant sunning itself. "They'll recognise a hanger because they use them too. But if it's making a low pass, that suggests whoever tasked it knows the ship's here. And it's too coincidental for anyone to suddenly notice a human settlement and decide to study it."

That made sense to Trinder. He got on the radio to Ingram. "Echo Five to Cab One, advice please. Before we spear the thing, assuming that we can, do we want to kill it, work out who sent it, or let it take a warning message back to base?"

"Echo Five, all three," Ingram said.

"Understood. Echo Five out." Trinder checked his screen again. The probe was losing altitude a little faster now. "There's an order to do this in, Fred. Is there some operating procedure these things follow?"

"Unless it's being operated remotely in real time, I think it will descend to door height and investigate structures to look for the ship. Jattans know what a building designed to house ships would look like. But I can't tell whether it's transmitting or recording for transmission later. Lieutenant Heide and I have been discussing how to distract it while we get attack drones in position. I suggest we send one of our own to fly alongside it when it reaches fifty feet."

"That's cutting it fine."

"We need time to work out how many objects it can track simultaneously. Once we know that, we can overwhelm its sensors and kill it."

"Let's do it, Lieutenant."

They waited. Trinder wasn't crazy about standing still with an unknown drone overhead, but he trusted Fred's identification and analysis.

"Ready to launch, Shure?" Heide asked.

Damian Shure had a tray of twenty micro-drones packed like a box of chocolates. Heide had lined up six armed drones for take-off. All they needed to do was stop the probe evading them long enough to get their shot in.

"Shame we can't just laser it," Trinder said.

"That might not stop it spacefolding to escape."

"Okay, here it comes."

Trinder could finally see the probe. It wasn't directly overhead. It was now at a hundred feet and about twenty yards away, a matt bluish-grey ball, and it seemed to have slowed. Then it dropped to twelve feet and hovered for a few moments before moving around everyone as if it was checking them over. If it was transmitting, whoever was receiving the signal was looking right at them now. Eventually the probe pulled back to its twelve-foot mark and held its position.

"*Go*," Heide said.

Shure tossed the micro-drones into the air one at a time like he was flipping coins. They formed up into a swarm and split into two groups to move slowly towards the probe. Trinder almost expected the thing to start spitting laser fire at them, but they arranged themselves around it rather sedately and then started swapping positions with each other.

Fred studied his screen. "It's trying to analyse their composition," he said. "Keep them moving, Private Shure. I'd launch your construction drones now, Lieutenant."

The drones were designed for precision-firing metal rods into stone or brick on structures that were hard to access, but they were just as handy for aiming the bolts like non-explosive missiles. Trinder watched them take up position, jockeying with the micro-drones while the probe kept switching its axis like it was whipping its head back and forth to in an effort to keep an eye on them all.

"It's trying to acquire all of them," Fred said. "I'd fire now, Lieutenant."

"Copy that. Three, two, one — fire."

Bang. The probe went veering out of control, shedding fragments, but it was still airborne. A bright red streak shot past Trinder. "Oh *shit*, not now," Shure said. Rikayl snatched the probe in mid-air and flew off with it.

Trinder sprinted after him. Rikayl swooped low across the grass and landed on the far side of the green. By the time Trinder caught up with him, he had the probe clamped in one hind foot like any terrestrial raptor but he was trying to dismantle it with his hands. It looked weird and very human.

"Hey Rik," Trinder said, trying to sound friendly. "Well done. You caught it. Clever boy! Can we have it back, please? We need to examine it."

Rikayl hugged the probe to his chest. "Piss off, wanker! *Mine!*"

Trinder needed to have a word with Jeff about teaching him to cuss. But at least the probe hadn't spacefolded. The bolt skewer had turned it into a high-tech spindle.

"You can have it back when we've looked at it," Trinder said.

"No, no, *no.*"

"Sol, can you get Jeff down here, please?"

"He's on his way. Good shot. Nice catch, too."

"Yes, hilarious."

Trinder squatted to look less threatening and tried to keep Rikayl grounded by engaging him in conversation, but all he got was a stream of profanity which the teerik seemed to find satisfyingly funny. Jeff Aiken arrived on a bike and ambled over to the scene.

"You're a naughty bugger, Rik," he said, hands in his pockets. "Come on, give it back and you can play with it later. Cards? You want to play cards tonight?"

"Yes, *cards*." Rikayl picked off some of the probe's coating. Judging by the square holes in its otherwise smooth casing, it was missing a few parts. "Okay."

Jeff held out his hand. Rikayl dropped the probe into his palm.

"See, you've just got to motivate him," Jeff said. "I'm going to teach him poker next."

"Is that wise?" Trinder asked.

"Nobody says you have to play him, Major."

By now, everyone had turned up, including Ingram, Searle, Chris, and Marc. Rikayl landed on Jeff's shoulder and rasped triumphantly. Searle examined the probe.

"This has to be a follow-up," he said. "Two visits in a month says Opis is on someone's chart."

"Gan-Pamas either got a message out after all, or this Nir-Tenbiku knew where he was headed," Chris said. "Or whoever's chasing him did."

"You sure that thing's dead?" Ingram asked.

Fred examined it. "It's broken apart."

"But is it transmitting?"

"I doubt it very much."

"Can you tell where it's come from?"

"If we can find all the parts."

They had to do a line search to recover all the fragments, aided by Solomon's security drone. Eventually they collected most of what seemed to have blown out of the shell. Fred examined the probe carefully.

"This is old," he said. "The Protectorate hasn't used these for a very long time, but they're still perfectly serviceable. This is a guess that has nothing to do with engineering data, but I would think it belongs to the Jattan opposition, on the basis that their equipment would be sourced from anywhere they could get it."

"Old stock?" Jeff said.

"When loyal ships sided with Nir-Tenbiku's grandfather, they'd have taken everything issued to them when they escaped."

"Ah well, it's better having the opposition on our tail than the Kugin or the Protectorate," Ingram said.

"I'll give this a thorough examination, Captain."

"Time to get our story straight, then," Trinder said. He still didn't have much recollection of what had happened in the seconds before Gan-Pamas shot him, and he probably never would. But Solomon did, and so did most of the military personnel who'd turned out to block Gan-Pamas's escape. "Because we might have to explain to the rebels why we killed their guy. They're looking for him, and if they're anything like us, they'll be seriously pissed."

* * *

WORKSHOP 5A, NOMAD BASE: TWO HOURS LATER.

There was a certain irony in examining the broken probe in Workshop 5A.

It was right next door to the hangar where *Curtis,* its probable target, was hidden. Hredt still couldn't be certain where the probe had been launched, but whoever deployed it was searching for the ship or the commune. Opis had no significance for anyone else.

There were no stored transmission frequencies or any flight log. It seemed to support the least alarming theory that the probe had come from the Jattan opposition. The rebels certainly wouldn't want to make a public example of anyone for hijacking the ship because they needed to avoid attention. Whether that would make anyone less dead if Nir-Tenbiku decided to launch an attack was another matter, but it seemed a less daunting prospect than a joint Jattan-Kugin mission that would be as much a warning to others as retrieving assets.

Hredt examined the parts of the wrecked probe again to make sure he hadn't overlooked anything. The fragments were spread out on the bench like an exploded view in a technical manual, each piece roughly in the position it would occupy in the intact device relative to the others. There were still some small fragments missing, possibly lost during Rikayl's enthusiastic intervention, but it was sufficiently complete to begin repairing it. Ingram, Searle, and Devlin studied it from one side of the bench, and Marc and Trinder from the other. Chris sat on a chair by the wall, sketching something on his screen.

"So it's the opposition," Ingram said. "We haven't picked up any chatter about this on the Protectorate's channels, and we've already had one visit from the rebels, so that makes sense."

"It might not make much difference," Hredt said. "As I've said before, both would seize the ship, both would seize me and my commune, and both would regard you as hostile, although for different reasons."

"But can the opposition wipe us out?"

"I don't know, but they could probably do enormous damage." Hredt had his own estimate of their capability based on the Protectorate's specifications for *Curtis*. The prenu was designed to deal with exactly the kind of insurgency that the opposition and other malcontents would carry out. "The Jattan don't actually know the opposition's strength and resources, and neither do the Kugin, but they estimate they could fight a guerrilla war over a long period, damage key targets, and demoralise the civilian population with random attacks. But Kugin and Jattan generals don't regard them as capable of the kind of military victory that would bring down the Protectorate."

"A bit like us, then, really," Trinder said.

"Remember that *Curtis* was originally designed for rapid reaction. The brief might have been over-ambitious with far too many unnecessary features, but the ship's role was to deploy elite forces to Jattan colonies and other nations on Dal Mantir where there might be civil unrest. The plan was an initial fleet of twenty ships, each designed for fifty troops and their equipment. That would mean hit-and-run raids to put down rebellion before it had a chance to spread. If they'd thought they were going up against a peer adversary, they'd have commissioned very different vessels."

"How did they deal with dissidents before that, though?" Ingram asked, then stopped and held up a forefinger as if she was interrupting herself. "Let's roll this back, Fred. Run through the political situation for me again. I don't think I've heard all the details. Or I've forgotten them."

Hredt thought for a few moments. "Nir-Tenbiku Bac, the grandfather of Nir-Tenbiku Dals, was deposed as Mediator of Jatt — formally titled the True Heir of Jevezsyl, if that's of interest — by members of his own cabinet. They secretly formed the Common Welfare Party and negotiated with Kugad to make the nation a protected client state in exchange for a favourable mineral export deal. It was a bloodless coup, at least as far as the Jattan people were concerned, but not so bloodless for Nir-Tenbiku's loyalists."

"Almost depressingly human, aren't they?."

"So Nir-Tenbiku Dals wants to avenge his grandfather, who was legally elected, and restore the old system of government, which would declare full independence from Kugad. That's why he currently calls himself the Primary in Exile."

Ingram glanced at Searle, who shrugged. Chris looked like he was more interested in staring at the wall, but he always did that when he was concentrating and working something out.

"I try not to take sides in foreign wars," Ingram said. "But I don't like quislings. The enemy within and all that. Stick them up against the wall."

Hredt turned to his screen to look up *quisling*. "Yes, that's correct. If you assume the Jattan people wished to remain an independent nation."

"And did they?"

"Most did, because Jattans regard themselves as exceptional, so they see the Kugin as barbarians — which they are, of course — but the merchant class took a more pragmatic view of statehood."

"They lined their pockets. Gosh, I'm shocked."

Hredt liked that phrase. *Lined their pockets.* He made a mental note of it. "Yes, they did well out of the agreement, even if most Jattans didn't."

"But *most Jattans* have put up with it for years rather than burn the place down," Marc said. "So they can't be that upset. Which means the security assessment is that the rebels will never be more than a serious nuisance."

"That's how I understand it," Hredt said. "But it might not be a lack of concern that keeps the population placated. The Protectorate secret police are quite brutal. We know. We designed their equipment."

Chris finally looked up from his screen and joined the discussion. "Okay, Fred, the Protectorate guys want their ship back, but they'll also hand you over to their Kugin overlords to show how loyal they are, yeah?"

"Correct."

"And this Primary in Exile guy just wants the ship for whatever, and he's not going to give Kugad any advantage over him, which would be you."

"If you're still thinking Nir-Tenbiku would welcome us as fellow rebels, you'd be mistaken," Hredt said. "But you're right that they wouldn't return us to the Kugin."

"They're not going to advertise it if they succeed, either."

"Definitely not."

Marc shrugged. "Assuming they decide to come for us, at least we know we can detect them in time to do something about it, and that they're limited in how much they can throw at us."

"Where are they based, Fred?" Ingram asked. "Did you mention Esmos to me once?"

"Yes, it's thought that they could be based there. It's on Bhinu. Bhinu is shared by two dominant species, the paalie and the bidaren. Esmos is a bidaren state."

"And those are the ones nobody messes with because they're neutral. I suppose they'd have to be, with two species."

"But Esmos is *aggressively* neutral," Hredt said. "It's hard to describe, but they allow anyone sanctuary there as long as they don't interfere with Esmos or bring their disputes with them. That policy is honoured because they have a certain history."

"This is the *aggressively* bit, I assume."

"They razed the capital of Tari Kul to the ground for the assassination of a political rival on Esmosi soil. It was a long time ago, but it made a lasting impression. Even the Kugin know not to provoke them. They only have what you would call weapons of mass destruction, no substantial standing army for smaller conflicts. It's either self-defence or complete destruction."

Marc leaned on the bench next to Hredt. "Well, that's one way of doing it."

"What are we actually debating here?" Searle asked. "Our chances of beating the other guy, or who we might have to make friends with?"

"We've only looked at the worst scenario of a Jattan-Kugin alliance showing up," Ingram said. "We might well be able to see off an incursion by the rebels. We have to assume they'll be back, but everything else depends on how badly they want the ship."

"And how badly we want to keep it," Trinder said. "Do we?"

"Are you suggesting we hand her over?" Devlin asked.

"In the short term, we'd be better off with more Lammergeiers."

"If all they want is the ship, sure, but we can be smart about how we do it," Searle said. "We have to get something in return or we'll look weak. You know, like we say to them, 'Oh, this thing? Yeah, take it. Look, we're building an operating base for our massive intergalactic fleet that's coming soon, so if you guys play your cards right, we won't ruin your revolution.' Or words to that effect."

Marc looked dubious. "Bluff only works for a so long. But it does give us a breathing space to bulk up."

"But they don't know we hold the ace. The Caisin gate. Which really *is* the great leveller."

"We know our cover's blown," Ingram said. "When we confirm who's blown it, we can scale our response as required."

"We should try to intercept any ships exiting from spacefold around Opis," Hredt said. "And a Caisin gateway would do that, of course. We can route them anywhere — into another sector or into a star."

"Before we get into that, can you repair that probe?" Ingram asked. "We can assume whoever sent it wanted imaging, so they probably have visual on us, and they know the probe's been brought down, therefore we won't lose any advantage by returning the call. How do we establish contact with them?"

"I'll see what I can do." Hredt wasn't sure where this was going. It sounded extremely risky. "But what would you say to them?"

"I'd ask them to explain themselves, as it's their second incursion into our territory." Sometimes Ingram became a different person. Her smile faded, her tone became less animated, and she folded her arms. "I'm open to other suggestions, but unless breaking their toy has convinced them we're too dangerous to be approached, which I doubt, then sitting here and doing nothing might make us look like an easy target."

"Protectorate or rebels, they're *Jattan*," Hredt said. "They're headstrong. They take ridiculous risks in battle and put their allies at risk too. They have enormous and totally misplaced confidence in their abilities."

"We like that kind of enemy, actually," Marc said. "But we usually get them as allies."

"I meant that they would see any contact as yet another reason to launch an attack."

Ingram was proving hard to convince. "If they're that mindlessly gung-ho, then just sitting here might be equally provocative. They know we're here. If they know that, they know we have the ship. If we have the ship, they know we have you."

"And I know these creatures." Was that the right word? Hredt thought he meant it neutrally, that they were a different species, but if he was honest with himself it was also because he disliked them. Jattans didn't realise how foolish they were. "While I've never had any contact with the opposition, they're likely to be even more driven by honour and the need to be heroic, because they were the losing side last time."

"What's your advice, then?"

"Do nothing. Wait. Set a trap. Eventually, they'll show their hand. They'll arrive here, miscalculate, and you can annihilate their forces."

"That needs a big trap, though, and we don't have one yet," Marc said. "We could drive them off the first time, but if we don't wipe them out, they could keep coming back and eventually grind us down because they can find reinforcements and we can't. I assume they have more than a couple of thousand people to call on."

It was a reasonable point. But Hredt could only give his opinion and hope they listened. He suspected they wouldn't.

Trinder had been studying the fragments. He looked up. "While we were hunting for Gan-Pamas, you said that we'd need to show the Kugin that we were crazy psychos and launch a pre-emptive strike, and they might leave us alone because we'd look crazier than they were. I'm trying to square that with their relationship with the Jattans. Have I got this right? The Jattans want to fight everyone and go out in a blaze of glory, but the Kugin only kill you if you won't hand over your lunch money, and they don't like destroying anything they can make a profit from. That doesn't fit too well."

"But it's true, more or less."

"Did you have direct contact with Jattans, or did they just send snotty memos via your foremen?" Ingram asked.

"Snotty?"

"Arrogant. Conceited. Rude."

"We would meet Jattan naval officers and procurement staff," Hredt said. "So they were *snotty* in person."

Trinder did that little movement humans often made when they were about to say something controversial. He raised his eyebrows and lowered his chin. "If the Kugin are the steadying influence on the Jattans, maybe we should think longer term about a deal with *them*."

Hredt was horrified. "But you know what they're like. How can you say this?"

"But we *don't* know. You're not at risk. They won't even know you're around. As far as we're concerned, there's an abandoned ship here and that's all."

"You don't understand what you're taking on."

Marc looked at Chris and seemed to get a discreet nod from him. "Okay, back to basics," he said. "Capability matters more than intent. Our immediate problem is the rebels, because they know where we are, and if they'll come after us again no matter what we do, we might as well try to contact them and warn them off. On the other hand, if they've kept their heads down for years to avoid the Protectorate, that tells me they aren't such mad bastards after all. They know how to bide their time. So it comes down to the ship. What can it do that we can't achieve with the Caisin gate, the Lammergeiers, and our existing fleet upgraded to FTL? If *Curtis* is armed transport for Jattan shock troops, the gate's a better piece of kit for insertions in every respect."

"Yeah, I don't think *Curtis* gives us any edge at all at the moment," Chris said. "But it's a valuable bargaining chip. Sorry, Brad. I know you wanted to give the ship a run."

"I'd rather have peace and quiet for this colony," Searle said. "But I'm gutted, yeah. It would have been fun."

Marc looked at Hredt. "Fred, I know you nicked it, and our law says it belongs to the Jattans, but if we apply finders-keepers it's still more your ship than ours. What do you think?"

They were missing the point, even Marc. This would be a short-term measure. If the opposition succeeded in overthrowing the Protectorate, they'd become much the same except they'd probably be at war with the Kugin, and Nomad Base would be seen as aiding them when scores were eventually settled. But Marc was right about one thing: the humans didn't have numbers on their side, even against the opposition. They weren't going to get reinforcements from Earth for years.

"I still think you should wait and see," Hredt said. "If they try again, then respond with maximum force."

He wanted to say that there was no option that avoided coming into conflict with one nation or another, but they obviously knew that. He felt ashamed that with all the commune's knowledge and skills, there was so little they could do to help them avoid conflict. But teeriks were uniquely qualified to help them win it.

"Let's see what we can do with this probe first and revisit it then," Ingram said. She was either bored or she'd already made up her mind to do something else. Hredt had learned how humans said no without actually saying it. "I'm going to send a message to all residents explaining what's happened. Call me if you need me."

Hredt sometimes found it hard to predict whether humans would keep something secret or tell everyone about it. The others hung around for a while after Ingram left because Searle and Devlin wanted to examine the probe themselves.

"Can we watch you do it?" Devlin asked. "A drive small enough to fit into a tennis ball is astonishing."

"I could have dismantled one of ours to show you," Hredt said.

Searle poked a wary finger into the neatly-arranged debris. "Yeah, but we need *this* one working."

"Ours are larger and separate into smaller probes when they reach their destination," Hredt said, working out what he'd need to replace the buckled composite shell. "But this is a single optical version."

"So which part is the propulsion unit?" Devlin asked.

"This object here." He indicated the small ovoid. "The fuel's still sealed, so there's no danger."

"Oh, now you tell us," Searle said, leaning right over it.

They seemed genuinely fascinated, not just trying to learn what they could so that they no longer needed teeriks, which was what Solomon seemed to be doing. Hredt understood why Solomon was doing it. The AI would survive indefinitely, whereas the future of the commune was doubtful unless they could find other like-minded teeriks to carry on bloodlines. They would probably die out. Solomon wanted to be able to operate the technology if that day came, but he was probably too polite to put it in those terms. Hredt just wished he'd say so outright and then they could plan ahead better.

"What would have happened if that thing decided to spacefold while we had hold of it?" Chris asked.

"It might well have ripped off your hand," Hredt said. "Or your whole arm."

"I'll bear that in mind."

"Has it got presets?" Marc asked. "If you power it up again, will it remember where it was transmitting before it was hit?"

"If the opposition have any sense, they'd do the same as we did by disguising the return signal," Hredt said. "It might even self-destruct."

"Great. Workplace safety rules are vastly overrated."

"But I doubt it."

"Yeah, I didn't think you'd be poking around if you thought it'd vaporise the room. But I was thinking more about how we send a message, if that's what we end up doing."

Hredt still had hopes of talking Ingram out of that. "It could still be linked to the opposition's receiving station, but if it can't create a spacefold, and there's no relay nearby, its signal will take a long time to reach Esmos, Ocaiy, or wherever they're based." He watched Marc frown, the usual reaction when it emerged that Hredt hadn't told him something. "Ocaiy is one of the Jattan colonies, Marc. I'll ask Solomon to label the charts."

"Thanks."

Hredt spent an hour putting the probe back together. He needed Searle and Devlin to hold items in place for him, a duty they seemed delighted with, and it was hard not to feel affection for a species that was so curious and eager to learn. Devlin even helped make simple parts to mount the optics. The probe wasn't fully restored, but there were now enough components in place to see if it would start. Hredt kept the propulsion unit and drive separate in case the probe managed to escape.

"Stand by," he said. "I'll plug it into *Curtis*'s power supply so I don't burn it out. It can't move, but it might try to transmit."

"Better cover the thing before you switch it on, then," Searle said. "The walls block signals, but in case that thing can bypass them, we don't want to accidentally confirm that we've got the ship."

It was excessive caution, but Hredt understood. He carried the probe into the hangar wrapped in a fire blanket and attached it to *Curtis*'s external power supply. The probe vibrated as it came to life.

"Well done, Fred, you raised it from the dead," Trinder said. "Now what?"

"Is there a signal?" Chris asked.

Hredt poked his sensor under the blanket. "It's attempting to connect."

"Can you tell what it's trying to connect to?"

Hredt tried to insert a screen cable into one of its ports. "No. It's transmitting an obsolete ID code, and that doesn't give me a location. But it does indicate it's pre-set to connect to a relay."

"Well, at least we know we can send a message if we have to," Searle said. "Thanks, Fred. You can disconnect it now. Let's lock it away and forget about it for the time being."

Hredt was relieved they weren't going to do anything rash. Ingram was another matter, but she listened to Searle the same way she listened to Bissey, so common sense would prevail. Hredt had bought some time to think of a better way to deal with the opposition's incursions. He went back to the compound, planning to use the peace and quiet to formulate a better plan than just shooting everything that triggered the early warning systems.

Was there really a bargain to be struck with Nir-Tenbiku? Hredt didn't want to give up *Curtis*, although Marc and Chris were right about the limited uses for the ship in their current situation. It actually had more value as a source of spares. But that would break Hredt's heart after all the work they'd put in.

He still couldn't see a group of Jattans with a grudge agreeing to take the prenu in exchange for staying away from Opis, though, even if Marc was right about their unusual patience.

Hredt opened one of the prepared meals that were delivered to the compound every day. The commune still didn't know how to find or cook food, but he'd tackle that when the more urgent crises were over. For the time being, he'd enjoy the meat and pastry. He settled down to eat and studied the small container of medicated, chewy bars that now arrived with the meals.

At least the humans were completely honest about the drug and didn't put it in the food like the Kugin must have done. He could read all the details on the label and see exactly how much he was being given, and he wasn't being forced to take it. But a few days into the treatment, despite feeling better, he knew his brain wasn't quite as active as it had been.

Now that he could feel a marked difference in a short time, he could compare the two states more easily. He realised that he'd actually thought more independently and creatively when the level of the drug in his body was declining and he no longer had access to treated Kugin food. The withdrawal must have been what made him do all those daring things: he'd started flying, he'd risked entering an alliance with the humans, and he'd taken over the leadership of the commune when Caisin died. It would be a shame to lose all that. He was still capable of doing his job to the highest level, but somehow that spark had gone, the surge of brilliant insights and bold decisions.

He read the label on the medication again. Without it, some members of the commune had become more aggressive. Some hadn't, and had just been more anxious. He'd just become impatient.

Did he really need this drug, then? If being deprived of it hadn't killed him in the months since they'd escaped, then he could probably stop taking it while he needed his mind to be at its sharpest and most innovative.

He'd be fine.

Hredt put the medicated bar aside to dispose of it later and ate his meal. Now it was time to work out how his outnumbered human friends could hold their ground on Opis against three factions who would, sooner or later, be on a collision course with them.

* * *

NORTH-EAST PERIMETER, NOMAD BASE: OCTOBER 20, OC.

Ingram stopped the quad bike at the boundary of Liam Dale's farm and watched his prize herd of Jerseys grazing on the reclaimed pasture as if they hadn't noticed they'd left Earth.

For Kill Liners, life didn't seem to have changed much. They were still isolated, still leading the same daily lives, still running their own show, and still partially dependent on their Ainatio neighbour for some commodities. But Ingram's world had changed out of all recognition.

She was neither at sea nor in a spacecraft, and not fully in command or responsible for the entire base. She was anchored only by the illusion of still being in the navy. Nomad was orderly, but that didn't mean it was a union of shared interests. But it did have a common enemy, and external enemies — real or manufactured — always made people willing to obey a dominant voice.

This was politics. She really didn't like getting it on her hands.

While she debated whether to drop in for chat with Liam, who still seemed unaffected by killing an alien, a few cows wandered across to the wire fence to see what she was up to. Eventually the rest of the herd joined them, watching her with accusing stares that demanded answers to some unknown question. If they were asking whether she'd know when she was beaten and it was time to draw stumps on Nomad, the answer was no. She'd see this out.

Ingram started the bike and carried on around the base, noting two new fields in the process of being terraformed by bright green box-shaped bots that were inching across the freshly cleared soil, altering the microbiome to grow crops. One day, scientists would decry the destruction of an uncatalogued ecosystem, but Ingram had never lost sleep over that. People needed to live. There'd still be plenty of wild Opis to go around.

The next street on the left had no formal name yet, but it had become part of Wickens Road by default. It merged with the road further south and was gradually absorbing the name by the osmosis of use. She'd expected a clamour of suggestions for naming every available feature in the base, but so far only Kill Line had named its roads, and that was because Solomon had made the street plan fit the original one on Earth. The transit camp quarter had merged into Kill Line proper, but it still hadn't named all its streets. They knew all their neighbours and where they lived. Postal addresses weren't needed yet.

"Sol, what's happening about Dr Kim's names?" Ingram asked. "We agreed she could name things after her great-grandmother. She requested the school and a road."

"I have it in hand, Captain."

"And Marc's place should have a proper address."

"Technically, his house isn't actually in any road," Solomon said. "You'd call a traffic island. It's just unit D Seven Four. I think he prefers it that way."

"We're really not very good at naming things, are we? Terribly un-colonial of us all."

"Names evolve best through usage, Captain. Like desire lines in planning. See where people wear down a path before you lay paving."

Ingram kept a chart in her mind that showed her what she thought constituted Nomad Base, but sometimes it included Kill Line and sometimes it didn't, depending on whether she was talking about site security or day-to-day governance.

Whatever its status, Kill Line was made up of agreeably random houses that were starting to look like they'd been there for years, still arranged with the square and town hall at its heart. Ingram had grown up near a village and everything about this one comforted her, but she was under no illusion that village life was peaceful and uncomplicated. The full spectrum of human virtues and vices was simply compressed into a smaller space. Without the anonymity of a big city and places to hide, feelings could run very high.

On the board outside the town hall, election notices sat behind a weatherproof panel. Ingram stopped to study the list of candidates. Two things struck her, although they shouldn't have come as a surprise. There were some transit camp names on the list, including Dieter Hill as the only candidate for the new post of sheriff, and it was the first election she'd seen without political parties.

Ingram hadn't expected the transit camp to embrace local politics so quickly. They treated Chris as a tribal chieftain, but he was the one who kept insisting that Doug Brandt was included in command decisions because the mayor was the only man on Opis who'd actually been elected. Chris seemed keen to recreate an America that had vanished long before he was born. He had an oddly respectable, conformist streak for a man who openly admitted how often he'd broken the law.

Ingram went in search of Doug. The town hall was more minimalist than the original, but the townspeople had rescued the portraits of previous mayors and councillors and hung them on the walls of the main corridor. One hundred and thirty years seemed no history at all to Ingram, who thought in millennia as Englishmen and women did, but it was a long time to Kill Liners. And nobody understood the need for tradition and history better than she did. Opis might have been a blank sheet, but its new citizens weren't. There were only so many roots you could trim from people before they had no connection to their neighbours at all and no will left to grow stronger.

Doug was hunched over his desk, checking a long list of figures with his forehead resting on one hand, fingers meshed in white hair that made him look older than his sixties. Ingram waited for him to finish and look up before interrupting.

"Oh, Captain, take a seat." He jumped up to pour her a hot drink from an insulated jug. "Have some coffee. Milk and two sugars, isn't it? Any more news on our aliens?"

"Thank you. Well, nothing concrete, but we're reading the runes. Now we've had time to think about it, sending a probe instead of landing with all guns blazing suggests they're not quite the trigger-happy hotheads we first heard about. And it makes them look a little scared of us."

"And are they the rebels?"

"Yes, we're fairly sure they are. The Protectorate variety would have shown up mob-handed with the Kugin. And we haven't heard anything on their naval comms channels to indicate they've located us."

"It's a shame we couldn't have met more peacefully. It's hard to see how we'll ever understand them."

"At least we know they're bipeds with some similar issues to ourselves," Ingram said. "Which is just as well. I'm not sure we'd ever understand what sentient moss wanted from us."

"Thirty per cent acetic acid or a dish soap solution would put it down, though."

Ingram had to smile. "I'm a flamethrower girl myself."

"Will we try to contact them?"

"I'm still working out what we'd say if we can get through."

"Maybe 'What do you want?' would be enough."

"The gamble is their current assessment of us," Ingram said. "If they believe we're an aggressive military power, and contacting them instead of blowing up their planet makes us look weak, we've made matters worse. Assuming we know which planet to blow up, of course."

"Perhaps *not* contacting them might send the same message. What does Fred think?"

"He still says we shouldn't respond. Is everyone here taking this as calmly as you?"

Doug shrugged. It was hard to faze a farmer. "We know you've thought out contingency plans. The best thing we can do is keep the lights on."

Ingram was still in two minds about making contact. Her gut said do it, but it was hard to ignore Fred. The teeriks weren't fools. On the other hand, if the only Jattans they spoke to were procurement officers or defence department staff, they'd have a narrow view of Jattan psychology. If Ingram judged all humans by some of the politicians or civil servants she'd known, she'd have decided nuking from orbit was long overdue. Doug might have been right about just asking.

What do you want?

She didn't even have to get Fred to ask them. The linguistics AI now had most of the basics. There was always the risk of not understanding the etiquette, but after one dead crew member, two dead rebels, and a close call with Trinder, it might not make matters any worse.

"I'm going to think about that and our options for responses, then," she said. "Anyway, you've got an election next month. None of my business, but what made you decide to have a sheriff? You never had one before."

"We're not our own little world now," Doug said. "We share this patch of land in a way we didn't share it with Ainatio on Earth. And there's the future. When the population starts growing, we'll be too big to settle things informally. Everyone's going to need rules."

"Are you going to draw up laws?"

"Ours have always served us well. They're pretty simple. What about yours? What about the Ainatio folks? Are we all on the same page, and what happens if we're not? I'm not criticising, because nobody knew Nomad was going to be cut loose like this. You left Earth thinking there'd be a civilian government coming in — independent, sure, but organised. But what are you going to do now if we've got a problem with one of the scientists, or they've got a problem with one of us? That applies whether Nomad's independent or tied to Earth."

Bednarz had assumed a military structure would operate while *Cabot* set up a turnkey colony for civilians to take over decades later. But everyone had arrived at once. That was the problem. Ingram could have stood down immediately and handed the keys to Doug, but everyone agreed you couldn't dump Nomad's pile of steaming security crises on inexperienced farmers.

"It's a balancing act," she said. "But if you're asking my opinion, we need one set of laws for everyone, or we become different nations. Maybe that's what people will want in due course, and that's healthy. Laws don't need to be any more complicated than saying treat others as you wish to be treated. But we're humans, so we need definitions that we can exploit to get us out of trouble."

Doug studied the surface of his coffee for a while. Ingram hoped he'd hand her a document that set out the Kill Line legal code, a single page of honest homespun clarity derived from a deep understanding of both nature and the Bible, but he didn't.

"I'm a farmer," he said. "I can run a small town with a bunch of sensible people I've known for years. But it's not just us now, and we need to know which flag we're under."

"I'm preparing this settlement for a civilian administration," Ingram said. "Joint Command is running security policy until civilians feel they can make those decisions themselves. When you're no longer happy with us, you need to say so."

"Can I make a suggestion?"

"Certainly."

"After the elections, we hold a vote for everybody about how they want Nomad to be run, like we're doing with the calendar. Everybody gets a say. Sure, Kill Line's the majority, and maybe that's something else we need to look at so we don't have a substantial minority that feels it hasn't got a voice."

"If we're not a pile of smoking charcoal by then, yes, we need to ask people what they want."

"So it's a yes."

"If you want it, it'll happen. We're here to smooth the path."

"But you're arguably civilians too. You have a vote."

"Then we'll use it in due course. Don't worry, I'll get Solomon to scope something out."

"Thank you."

Ingram thought it over on the ride back to her office. Doug wasn't interested in some kind of Kill Line empire. He was probably just worried what would happen if someone from one group wronged someone from another and the penalty didn't satisfy the aggrieved.

What still worried Ingram, though, was that Nomad *wasn't* cut loose from Earth. Its legal status was a mess — no America, no Ainatio, no formal link with a military chain of command on Earth — but a lot of people here did still have a country, and the majority of those were British members of her crew. *Cabot* also had crew from five East Asian nations, Australia, New Zealand, and Russia, and all those countries were still functioning as well.

"Sol, I know this is relative trivia at the moment, but why didn't Bednarz draft the legal framework for the colony?" she asked. "He did everything else. I don't buy the excuse that he thought we should be free to draft our own."

"But that really was what he felt, Captain," Solomon said. "You were all selected because you represented the values of what he regarded as civilisation. It's exactly as it's written in the mission document."

"Well, if you have time, could you look at some all-purpose legal framework, one side of A-four only?"

"Of course. And I always have time. But what would *you* rather have, Captain? You have an opinion. We've discussed these matters before."

"You want me to be completely honest? Gut level stuff?"

"Yes."

"I'd rather have geography. A British sector under British law, an American sector with whatever pick-and-mix of state laws they want, and the rest of the residents can apply to join one or invent their own. I think it's dangerous to take people's identities away. Why can't we have a federal set-up with different state jurisdictions? The US managed it back in the day, so we could too. How hard can it be to organise fewer than three thousand people? The only awkward part is the logistics of moving everyone around and having states with one resident."

"You'd like me to investigate that, though."

"Sol, you asked me to be completely honest. I was giving you a personal opinion, not an order."

"It's still a valid view, Captain. I'll prepare a study on that as well. Options, remember. I did take note of your discussion with Mr Brandt."

"And there'll be an economy and a currency one day. God help us. It doesn't seem to be avoidable."

"I think you can stick to barter for quite a few years."

"Personally, I dread devaluation of the chicken."

Ingram wondered if she'd started hares running too soon. But if people were more concerned about how the place was going to be run in the future than by alien attacks today, that was encouraging. The less time she had to spend on calming people down, the more she could devote to defending the base.

She got back to her desk and began composing a message to the Jattan opposition, which she'd ask Solomon to translate this time, not Fred. Like all short statements, it threatened to take longer than a ten-page report. Should she lay down the law, or play dumb?

This is Captain Bridget Ingram, commanding officer of Nomad Base. We've chosen to ignore two unlawful incursions into our territory, but if you make another attempt, I regret we'll have to respond more forcefully.

No, that wasn't it. When Bissey had wanted her to offer Gan-Pamas a chance of surrender, Fred had said Jattans were more likely to respond to an imperious demand to answer for their crimes. She tried again.

This is Captain Bridget Ingram, commanding officer of Forward Operating Base Nomad. You have now made two incursions into our territory. Your agents have killed one of our comrades in an unprovoked attack, for which there will be consequences. I demand an explanation.

What do you want here? Do not attempt to approach this planet again or we will respond with force.

Yes, that was more like it. Calling Nomad an operating base implied backup at a mighty headquarters somewhere, too. With any luck, the Jattan language would have the right words to convey the tone of restrained anger backed up by extreme violence. She'd work on that. She settled down to polish it, but Marc stuck his head around the door as if he'd been waiting for her tracking signal to show she was back.

"I'm just going down to the churchyard to look at something," he said. "I won't be long, but call me if anything kicks off. Sorry, am I interrupting?"

Ingram put her screen down. Marc didn't have to tell her where he was going and seldom did.

"Of course you're not," she said. "Problem?"

For a moment he looked like he was going to walk away, but he hung around, uncharacteristically awkward.

"No, nothing like that. Sol made a memorial for my boys and I haven't seen it yet. It was Chris's idea."

Ingram realised he wanted her to do something he thought he couldn't ask for outright, possibly out of embarrassment. She chose her words carefully. If she gave him a choice and asked if he needed her to be there, he'd probably lose his nerve and say no.

"May I come with you?" she asked. "If I'm not intruding."

"Yeah, sure."

"If you need time alone there, just say and I'll thin out."

"I will. Thank you."

"Give me a minute."

"See you outside, then."

Ingram had guessed right. Marc just needed some emotional support, and he didn't know how to ask for it. She rummaged in her desk for something she'd been saving for an exceptionally special but unspecified occasion that she'd only recognise when it happened, and it had happened now. She took out the small grey box that had sailed with every Ingram from her great-grandmother to her father and then with her, and popped the seal.

Inside were five miniature bottles, their black labels curled and peeling on the edges and the coating on the caps worn thin by time. They were two centuries old, filled with some of the Royal Navy's last official issue of rum. It ought to have been reserved for a once in a lifetime celebration, but today warranted its use for unhappier reasons.

Ingram put the four remaining bottles back in the box and studied the one in her hand, another memory she could forget for years at a time and then remember in vivid detail. She was a historical aberration just like that rum, and it wasn't only because forty-five years had been erased from her mortal timesheet by cryo. Back on Earth, she'd reinstated the tot on her ship, the daily rum ration, as a private thing just for her crew. The MoD knew about it, but said nothing because she was an Ingram and the eighth generation to serve. She'd resurrected a vanished naval tradition.

For her, it was more than just a small morale booster in the crew's day. It was a ritual, a statement of permanence and continuity, an act of communion for those with faith in their shipmates and their nation. It was about something greater and more enduring than herself that made her willing to do whatever it took to defend it, because tradition wasn't a trivial matter. As Doug had said, everyone needed to know whose flag they were under. It wasn't there for decoration.

She put the bottle in her pocket, grabbed her cap — which she should have worn more often — and hurried downstairs to find Marc. He was waiting outside, looking uncomfortable. They started walking across the green, heading past the school on the road down to St Thomas.

"I've still got my stash of fish and spuds," he said. "Fancy fish and chips this evening? Chips fried in beef dripping?"

"Ooh, yes please."

"Dan shared his fish with his detachment."

"That's Dan. He's got the Nelson touch."

"You should tell him that. He still thinks he's not a Real Man. And it's Trafalgar Day tomorrow. Apt time to tell him."

"Should I share my fish, Marc?"

"That's a matter for you. I haven't. I've frozen it and I'm keeping it for family, including the dog. Bringing Tev back pissed off a few people here, though. Brit privileges. We're the baddies again, Captain."

"Who's been hassling you?" Ingram wanted to go and slap some respect into whoever had dared offend Marc. She also wanted to know whether cooking fish for her meant he considered her family as well. "None of my people, I hope."

"No, just letting you know." Marc switched off his radio and gestured to her to do the same. "No offence to Sol, but this is private."

Marc didn't say anything else until they reached the cemetery. Martin Berry was waiting for them, standing by a tarpaulin-draped stone next to Jamie Wickens' grave. Marc grunted disapproval as if he hadn't expected him to be there.

"Hello, Marc. Captain." Berry clasped his hands in front of him as if he didn't know what to do with them. "Would you like me to unveil the stone?"

"Thank you, Reverend, but I want to do it myself."

Berry nodded. "Would you like a few words of prayer?"

"I'm not sure I'm up to that, to be honest," Marc said. "I don't really want to talk to God. We've got nothing to say to each other. No offence, but religion is mostly making excuses for a god who doesn't care."

He said it in a kindly way, which told Ingram that he meant it. Berry nodded politely. "I'll be in the vestry if you need me."

Marc stood staring at the tarpaulin, then stepped behind the stone to lift it off, and Ingram saw the memorial for the first time. It made her suck in a breath.

It was extraordinarily beautiful, a torrent of water carved from a column of flecked marble five feet tall, inscribed with Marc's sons' names and their dates. But it was the verse that stopped her in her tracks. Her eyes stung. She had to get a grip.

"It's like the funeral all over again," Marc said, still behind the stone, head down. "I shouldn't do this." Then he looked up. "What's wrong?"

Ingram could only beckon. Marc took a couple of steps to the front of the memorial, then stood next to her. She kept her eyes fixed on the stone. When she finally managed to look at Marc without making a fool of herself, she realised he was sobbing with his hand over his mouth, shoulders shaking but completely silent. Right then she would have given anything to be able to take his pain and soak it up so that he never had to feel it again. How did any parent live with that loss?

She lost track of how long they stood there in silence, just looking. Eventually Marc bowed his head, then straightened up with his arms at his sides.

"Sol did them proud, didn't he?"

"Yes, he did." Ingram took the bottle of rum from her pocket and held it out to him. "Navy neaters, two centuries old. The last of the rum issue. Drink it. Pour it as a libation. Whatever feels right. It's been waiting for this."

Marc took the bottle and studied it for a while. "Will you share it with me?"

"I will."

He unscrewed the cap with slow care. Ingram half-expected it to be corroded, but he got it open and squatted to pour a little on the stone.

"It's okay," he said. "You're home now."

He stood up, raised the small bottle in a toast, and took a swig before handing it to her.

"Absent friends and those at sea," Ingram said. A weekday was the wrong time for the navy's traditional Sunday toast, but it seemed more apt. The rum was treacly and pungent. Her memory whispered to her about other absent friends she hadn't remembered in years.

I should tell him.

He'll either think I'm a nutter or it'll help him.

They passed the tiny bottle back and forth in silence, taking contemplative sips, then sat down on the grass.

"Sol composed that," Marc said. "I only get angry with him because he's human. I wouldn't bother losing it with a machine."

"He really does care."

"D'you think I was a bit hard on the Rev?"

"Not really," Ingram said. "He understands."

Mark wiped his nose. "I just can't be arsed to sugar-coat it. I wish God *was* real so I could tell him what I think of him on Judgement Day, and if he's real and omnipotent then he can put it right. Why *both*? What kind of mysterious purpose justifies that? He doesn't love us. You don't hurt what you love, not even to teach it something."

Ingram had her official script of considerate and sympathetic things to say to the bereaved. It was best to let them talk and offer no opinion, because painfully honest conversations about loss were best kept to friends and family, or so a chaplain had told her at Dartmouth. But this was Marc. Whatever he thought their relationship amounted to, even if it didn't match her view of it, they were at very least close friends. Watching him red-eyed and hoarse while he tried to put his professional face on was more than she could bear.

She put her hand on his arm. "I need to tell you a story," she said. "And I'm being serious. It's not just a dit."

Marc still didn't look away from the stone. "Okay."

"I've never told anyone else this. There's only one other person who knows, and that's because he was there. But it's something I still can't explain. Will you indulge me?"

Ingram had never needed to worry whether anyone believed her or not. She had power. Now all she had was the conviction of her memory, and she wanted Marc to know that she *had* to tell him, in case it was the one thing he needed to hear. He wrinkled his nose as if he was frowning with the expectation of a grisly confession, then nodded. She had no idea where to begin. He seemed to realise that. He prompted her.

"This bloke who knows, then. Boyfriend?"

"No, nothing like that. It was Petty Officer Lewis, when I was a lieutenant in HMS *Circe*."

Ingram ground to a halt. Marc patted her hand. She realised she'd gripped his arm harder than she intended.

"Okay," he said. "Take your time."

She knew he wouldn't laugh at her. She just didn't know if the revelation would help him. "This was during the Channel War, and we were alongside for repairs," she said. "I was on the bridge, looking down on the foredeck, waiting for my relief, so I was keeping an eye on the clock, just me and Lewis. I saw an officer I knew cross the deck, look out to sea, then look up at me. It was Commander Chivers, the PWO from my previous ship. He nodded at me, and I nodded back. He wasn't a member of the crew, so I turned to Lewis and asked him if he knew why Chivers was on board. So Lewis took a look and said he had no idea, but maybe the commander was going to be in the wardroom later. While we were talking, Chivers wandered off aft and we lost sight of him. I didn't give it another thought until our CO came up to the bridge and I mentioned Chivers in passing because I hadn't seen him in ages and I wanted to catch him for a drink. But the boss gave me an odd look, and... ah... well... "

Ingram was too far into the confession to back out now. Marc had gradually shifted position to look straight at her.

"Come on," he said. "I'm hard to shock."

She relived the moment. She hadn't thought about it anywhere near as often as she'd expected. Somehow, she'd put it out of her mind, but from time to time it'd resurface and she'd try *not* to think about it again, and she wasn't sure why. It should have been the most extraordinary experience of her life and changed how she saw the universe. But it hadn't. It just scared her.

"The CO said he'd had a message that a helo had ditched in the Channel off Newhaven an hour earlier, and Chivers was on it," she said. "It was hit by an RPG from a small raider. SAR was scrambled, but there was no news on survivors yet."

"Okay." Marc nodded, not a flicker of reaction on his face. "And?"

"I looked at Lewis and he looked at me. And we never said a word. Not then, not later, not from that day to this. We pretended we never saw it."

"So what did your CO say?" Marc asked. He couldn't have misunderstood her, but the implication of what she'd said either hadn't sunk in or he was trying not to let it. "I mean, you had to explain why you thought Chivers was on board."

"I just blathered on about being mistaken and changed the subject," Ingram said.

"And he didn't say bloody hell, funny you should mention him after what I've just heard? He didn't ask why or how?"

"No. That was the worst of it."

"Okay, tell me the rest."

Ingram was over the awkward part. Marc had obviously worked out how the story ended, and now all she had to do was show him she'd been perfectly rational and explain why she was telling him, preferably without making a complete arse of herself.

"Not much to tell," she said. "Except I checked times and positions when the details were known, and in brief, Chivers was nearly two hundred miles away and dead before I saw him. And Lewis saw him too."

"Okay."

"Marc, I know what I saw, but I don't know why I saw it." Lewis hadn't been the sort to humour officers. He'd have asked her what the hell she was talking about. He'd seen Chivers. "I've lost people before, but I never thought I saw them later the way many people do. And I didn't even know Chivers' helo had been hit, so there was no reason for me to think about him right then. Even if Lewis hadn't seen him too, I'm damn sure of what *I* saw."

Marc patted her hand. "I believe you."

"I'm not making it up to make you feel better," she said. "It's not a well-meaning lie, and it isn't certainty. But I *know* I didn't imagine it or mistake someone else for Chivers. And that means the universe doesn't quite work the way I thought it did. I felt you needed to hear that."

"I've never thought that I've seen someone I've lost either," Marc said. "Sometimes I almost expect my boys to walk in when I'm in a familiar situation, but it's just habit and wishful thinking."

"You understand why I don't tell people about this, don't you?"

"They wouldn't think less of you. They might ask questions, though. Did you?"

"Did I what?"

"Ask yourself why Chivers appeared where he did. Was *Circe* ever his ship?"

"No, not as far as I know."

"Well, you saw what you saw. You're telling me there's an afterlife."

"It should have changed everything I believed, but for some reason, it didn't. It scared the shit out of me."

Marc shrugged. "Not everyone wants an afterlife. I'd give every remaining breath to see John and Greg again, but there's plenty of dead bastards I don't want to renew my acquaintance with. Unless I can kill them again."

Ingram wondered if the Chivers incident had frightened her because her conscience was more battered than she'd admit to herself. Like Marc, she had a lot of deaths chalked on her tote board. But she hadn't meant this to be about her. She'd set out to do a selfless thing and share something embarrassing to help him, and she'd already failed her own test. Perhaps sympathy was seeing your own reflection in another's pain.

"Me too," she said. "Better make the most of our mortal span, then."

Marc sat there for a while in silence, just looking across the grass at the stone river. "Funny how the two most ruthless bastards on this base are the ones who try to take care of me. You and Chris. You can't fix me, but thank you for trying."

Ingram put her arm through his. He didn't flinch. It was as if they'd grown old together and it was the most natural thing in the world. For a moment she hoped nobody was watching, but then she decided she didn't give a flying fuck what anyone else thought.

"My heart breaks when yours does," she said. "So I have a vested interest."

"Oh. I wasn't expecting that."

"Have I embarrassed you?"

"No, I'm just surprised. Quite pleased, though."

"I can't resist a man who can make a decent curry. If your fish and chips is world class too, you've pulled."

"You're on, Boadicea. But there'll be talk."

"It's not improper. We're single and I'm not your CO."

"Crinkle-cut or straight, then?"

"You brought a crinkle cutter with you. Of course you did."

"No, but I can get a bot to knock me one up by tonight."

"Chip shop regulation straight-cut, please. No fancy heathen nonsense."

"Okay." Marc got to his feet and held out his hand to help her up. "Better get back now. I'd never have asked you out, you know. I was afraid of looking too needy and fucked up."

"We're all fucked up, Marc." Ingram took his hand and he didn't pull away. "We wouldn't be here if we were normal."

They started walking back to the main building and switched on their professional personas again. Now she wasn't sure he'd understood what she'd said at all. But he did squeeze her hand.

"So are we going to call the Jattans or not?" he asked.

"Doug said we should. I was drafting something."

"Oh, good, you consulted him. That'll keep Chris happy. Well, they know we're here, so we can't hide behind the sofa and pretend we're not in."

Ingram took out her screen and showed him her draft. "A or B?"

"Definitely B. Makes it clear they've killed one of ours and we're not being conciliatory, so they've crossed the line, but we've given them chance to grovel because we're so hardcore. Okay, run it past the others and let's get it done."

"It's not entirely bluff, Marc. We really could strike back if they're hostile. Once we make contact, we've probably got their location."

"As long as it's not Esmos."

Ingram sent draft B to Chris, Trinder, and Searle. Solomon would read it anyway. Sometimes it was frightening to realise how small the pieces were that made up a world-changing event. A few lines she'd jotted down in partial ignorance put history in a different perspective. Every captain, every general, every politician picked their draft B or other piece of the puzzle, then stumbled through a string of other pieces, and nations rose or fell on it. Nobody had the big picture even when they were sure they did. Everyone gambled, and most were no better or worse than she was.

"I'll see you tonight, then," she said when they reached the front doors. "You wouldn't believe I used to be decisive, would you?"

"It's not a decision you should make on your own. If only to avoid copping all the flak when it goes wrong."

"You're always brutally honest."

"I don't lie to people I care about." Marc shoved his hands in his pockets and stared at the ground. "Thanks for telling me about Chivers. I wouldn't have taken it seriously if I'd heard it from anyone else."

"I wouldn't have told you if I didn't think you needed to know."

"Chips," he said. "Nineteen hundred hours. Bring beer and a toothbrush."

"You're such a smooth talker."

Ingram watched him out of sight, just to make sure he was alright. He dodged through the back and forth of bots and disappeared into the vehicle compound. Yes, he was okay again.

"I'm glad it worked out, Captain," Solomon said. He was standing behind her in his quadrubot frame. "Your radio's still off, by the way. Now, I have a translation of your draft, if you'd like to hear it. I can use your own voice when I send it. I have enough samples to generate one."

"Even the ultrasonic bits?"

"Yes, even the ultrasonic bits."

Ingram patted him on the head. She had to bend a little to reach. "Sometimes it's handy that you see and hear everything."

"I don't," Solomon said. "But while it's none of my business, I'm pleased to see you and Marc getting together at last."

"I'd prefer to keep it between us, Sol. At least for the time being."

"Of course."

It wasn't that she didn't trust Solomon, or even that she wanted to hide anything from him, but everyone had to be able to keep something from the world to stay sane. Sometimes it was just a bit of mental space to call their own.

Ingram wasn't sure whether Chivers fell into that category, but she put him to the back of her mind again, and there he would remain until the next time loss resurrected the memory.

* * *

NOMAD BASE: 0800, OCTOBER 21, OC.

It was the flags on tall poles outside the main building that had first fascinated Hredt and his grandsons when the humans arrived. The sheets of brightly-coloured fabric still held their mysteries.

He'd learned that they corresponded to the different national origins of *Cabot*'s crew, except for the white one with the red cross and a small British flag in the top corner, which signified ships of the Royal Navy. Ingram was particular about the raising and lowering of these flags at specific times and the small formalities that accompanied it, but today's morning ceremony seemed especially important. A large number of *Cabot*'s crew were assembled in their best uniforms, standing in ranks while Ingram addressed them.

Chief Jeff had explained that October 21 was Trafalgar Day, the commemoration of a great naval victory and the death of a beloved admiral centuries ago, and in the evening, sailors would have an elaborate meal and propose toasts to his memory and to their monarch.

He'd also explained what was happening now. The white flag was flying at the top of the pole, but they'd also raised a string of smaller flags in different colours and patterns. It was a signal system between ships centuries ago, Jeff said. The small flags corresponded to letters and words, and the message read: *England expects that every man will do his duty*.

Hredt envied humans for having a history they not only knew but celebrated. When teeriks rediscovered their own origins, he'd make sure they celebrated them too.

The gathering at the flagpoles began to disperse and Chief Jeff, wearing the smart uniform he'd last worn at Caisin's funeral, wandered over to Hredt to chat. They sat on the low wall outside the main building. It was wide enough for Hredt to perch comfortably.

"We do like our ceremonial," Jeff said.

"So do the Jattans. They like parades."

"Perhaps we'll find some common ground after all."

"Probably not."

"How are you feeling now?"

"I'm well."

"Your daughter seems a lot happier. She was quite cheerful about the progress on *Shackleton*."

"I think your scientist's first guess was correct," Hredt said. "It's a tranquilliser. Turi gets very anxious, which she expresses through her temper. She might have experienced the withdrawal from the drug more than the rest of us."

"I'm not going to pry," Jeff said. "But you shouldn't need to be on that stuff all the time. Was it really that stressful working for the Kugin?"

"Not really."

"Do you think they did it to keep you obedient?"

It seemed as good an explanation as any. "I can't imagine any other reason. But there seems to be no need for it."

"Addiction stops people running away."

"Not if they don't realise what they're being given and the source of it. But perhaps it really was something that occurred naturally on our homeworld."

"You don't seem angry about it."

"Oh, I'm angry, Chief Jeff. As you say, we shouldn't need it."

Jeff stood up. "Well, I've got to get to *Elcano*. I thought you were working on *Cabot* today."

"I have to talk to the Captain first," Hredt said. Ingram was still by the flagpoles, talking to Hiyashi. "She wants to discuss the Jattan probe."

"Okay, I'll catch up with you later. You want to play cards tonight?"

"Of course. I shall win."

"See you later, then."

Jeff was his friend. He was the first human to realise teeriks were intelligent, and the two of them had a lot in common despite the vast difference between their species. He wasn't afraid to speak his mind, either. Hredt trusted him. He trusted all the humans, perhaps some more than others, because they generally did what they said they'd do and hadn't taken advantage of the commune's dire circumstances. But they didn't seem to know what they were doing when it came to alien politics. He blamed that man Bednarz.

Bednarz had died a long time ago, but everyone still followed his policies, even though they could now do as they wished without fear of enforcement. All of his assumptions were based on humans being the only intelligent species in this part of the galaxy. After five months of being around humans, Hredt now understood a lot more about Earth and why Bednarz wanted to populate this colony with those he regarded as better examples of his species, because there really were some dreadful people doing terrible things on Earth.

The most baffling were the ones who wanted to wipe out humanity, which presumably included themselves. Hredt had never heard of any other civilisation, not even the most barbaric, where such a self-destructive culture had sprung up — the occasional lunatic, perhaps, but never a whole layer of society. There had to be many more people on Earth who were more like his friends here. They would save Earth in the long term, but that sounded like it might be far in the future, and the good humans had to be kept safe in the meantime.

Ingram seemed to have finished her conversation with Hiyashi. She walked over to Hredt, seeming more relaxed than she'd been for the past couple of weeks, but she still looked like she had something difficult to discuss. She sat down on the wall with him.

"I'm going to add this to the history books," she said. "The first Trafalgar Day marked on an extrasolar planet."

"I'll read about Nelson so I can understand why today's so important to you."

"He's the kind of officer we're supposed to aspire to be, a man who cared about his crew and knew how to win," she said. "I fall short. But there are times I really don't see the signal either."

"I don't understand."

"Read about Nelson and you will." She did that little dip of her head that usually meant she had bad news. "Fred, I've given the probe a lot of serious thought, and so have the rest of Joint Command. We're going to transmit a message." She took out her pocket screen. "This is what we've recorded in Jattan using the linguistics AI."

Hredt wasn't surprised, but he was disappointed. She hadn't taken any notice of his advice. She had her own way of dealing with an enemy and she didn't seem to want to adapt that to local conditions. He read the brief message and wondered what he could possibly say now.

"This might not get you the result you want," he said. "But it's suitably aimed at their mindset, at least."

Ingram looked apologetic. "We can't ignore it and hope for the best, Fred. If we do nothing, do you think they'll forget us and look elsewhere?"

"No. They can't afford to leave it and hope for the best either."

"Exactly. We don't have an easy way out or even the option of doing nothing. We have contingency plans in place if this backfires, though. There's no need to worry. Whatever happens, you'll be safe."

Hredt's heart sank. "That's not the point."

"I have to do this, Fred. Especially if we're going to bring other humans to this sector. I have to know what we're dealing with. Come on, let's fire up that probe and see what number it calls."

If Hredt refused, Solomon would step in and take over because the emanation learned even faster than a teerik. Solomon didn't need him, just as one day he wouldn't need him to operate the Caisin gate. Hredt knew he was wrong to feel that way, but it didn't help. He gave in and hoped he'd be wrong about the Jattan opposition.

"As soon as we remove the probe from the signal-blocking environment and power up, it'll attempt to connect," Hredt said. "So you need to be ready right away."

"I only want to transmit this time." Ingram said. "No two-way conversation. We'll send the message and wait. If I've understood the set-up, the probe's monitored, and whoever deployed it eventually receives the message. Is that correct? So I don't have to keep transmitting until I get a response."

"That's right," Hredt said. "They might think it's been permanently destroyed, but even if it's not being monitored in real time, someone will notice if it starts transmitting again."

"And can we monitor it for a response? Or will it record an inbound signal?"

"Either."

"Then let's leave it where it can't snoop on anything, and check on it at intervals." Ingram put her hand to her earpiece. "Are you okay with that, Sol? Good." She must have had a yes from him because she nodded. "He says to set it up with a remote power supply in a field where there's nothing for it to see. Just make absolutely sure it can't fly or spacefold."

"And how are you going to input your message?"

"I've recorded it on a standalone screen that needs to be connected to the probe. Sol's concerned the probe might be able to harvest data from anything it connects to, so we're not taking any chances."

"I don't believe it can do that, but caution's wise. Very well, I shall do my best."

"Commander Devlin's going to take over now. Thanks, Fred. We couldn't do this without you."

That was no longer true, and he knew she knew it.

It took Hredt half an hour to make a suitable connector and adapt a power supply with help from Devlin. They met up with Solomon's quadrubot in one of the newly reconditioned fields on the edge of Kill Line, set a protective cage around the probe to shield it from Rikayl and curious dogs, and connected the screen to play in Ingram's message.

Hredt tried one last time. "I still think this is a bad idea."

"Do you think Captain Ingram should have worded it differently?" Solomon asked. "When we were trying to get Gan-Pamas to surrender, you told us Jattans respond to dominance and being told to explain themselves."

"They do, but I still think you should make them come to you."

"Yes, you made that point before."

Devlin was getting impatient. "Gentlemen, are we doing this or not?"

"We're doing it," Solomon said, and activated the screen.

It was too late to pull back from the brink now. Hredt heard Ingram's voice — the AI's replication of it, anyway — speaking clear but oddly-stressed Jattan, as a foreigner might.

"And does the signal tell us anything?" Solomon asked.

Hredt plugged a tester into the probe. It had definitely established a link, but none of the data contained a recognisable set of co-ordinates. "I could try running this through the freighter's system and see if it recognises it."

Solomon guarded his access to Gan-Pamas's vessel rather jealously. He'd analyse the link's data himself and retrieve whatever it found in the comms or navigation systems. Hredt would have preferred to do it himself, but he'd have to analyse whatever data came back anyway, so there was no point in arguing about it. He sent Solomon the readout.

"I'll be in *Curtis* when you need me to look at the results."

He turned to walk off and Devlin put her hand on his back. "Thanks, Fred. We appreciate it. Don't worry — we're ready for whatever happens."

Hredt knew when he was being appeased. It was kind of her to bother, but it meant she must have noticed the tension with Solomon. Hredt knew Solomon was annoyed with him for disagreeing with Ingram, but it had to be said.

"You're welcome, Commander," he said. "I'm glad to help wherever I can."

He would have flown off, but he was carrying too much equipment. The most dignified exit he could manage was to stride back to the hangar, counting how many days it had been since he'd last flown. He needed to keep flying. If he let himself get lazy and tired, he'd find it even harder to get fit again. He'd make some time to go flying with Rikayl, who always seemed to enjoy keeping an eye on an old teerik who couldn't fly as high or as fast as he could.

At least Rikayl had found his place in the commune, despite his limitations. He seemed happy enough. When Hredt thought back to the panic when the chick hatched and looked like he might die, he recalled how he felt like rejecting Rikayl, and he was ashamed. But Rikayl was still a lonely figure, even if he could always find a human to amuse him for a while. It would probably fall to Rumal and Demli to look after him when the others were too old, but that assumed he'd have the lifespan of a normal teerik.

What's going to happen to us in the years to come?

But it was time for Hredt to start worrying more about surviving the present day challenges. He climbed the ramp into *Curtis's* cargo bay and wandered through the ship, now deserted while the rest of the commune and the human engineers worked on the vessels in orbit. He went up to the bridge — very cramped indeed — and settled down in front of the human-friendly console that had been installed. Everything was at a far more comfortable height. And everything was operated by touch. That was *much* better.

Hredt felt guilty for sitting there doing absolutely nothing when he should have been working on the drives. But he wanted to think without any interruptions while he waited for Solomon to report back. His mind was much clearer today now that he'd stopped taking the medication, and clarity was sorely needed. It occurred to him that he could have sabotaged the connection and stopped the transmission, and he wouldn't have been above doing that to a client, but the humans were his friends and allies.

Sometimes, though, friendship meant stopping a friend from doing themselves harm. What was the worst that could happen when the Jattans received Ingram's message? They'd launch an attack — for being insulted, for wanting to seize the prenu before this alien power made use of it or handed it back to Kugad, any reason at all — and they might destroy Nomad. It was a small base, probably within the destructive capability of even a threadbare rebel force. Or they might be intimidated by Ingram's demands, and bide their time as Marc had pointed out, and attack later. Once Ingram knew where they were based, though, the Caisin gate could be deployed and Nomad could deliver either an emphatic warning or a fatal blow, and nobody would know how they'd done it.

The gate might even enable them to get away with an attack in Esmos if nobody knew where it had come from.

Hredt preferred the emphatic warning. Humans would need provocation to do that, though, and he knew them well enough now to realise they'd need proof that a previously unknown force was actually hostile. Their hesitation and soul-searching over how to deal with Gan-Pamas had shown that. And they weren't going to get that proof until it was too late.

While he was trying to work out the Jattans' intent credibly enough for Ingram, Solomon called him via *Curtis*'s comms.

"The freighter's identified a relay in Esmos," he said. "So if your assessment's correct, it would be too risky to target the Jattans there. But at least it confirms it's the opposition."

"That's unfortunate," Hredt said. "Although you could use the gate and never be identified."

"They'd probably guess it was us, even if they didn't know how we did it."

"Do you have any objections to me monitoring the probe for a reply?"

"Not at all," Solomon said. "I put a drone in place to pick up audio. I'll give you access as well."

Hredt continued examining their limited options. It all depended now on whether Nir-Tenbiku responded and what he had to say. Perhaps he'd be happy with just this ship and would never bother Nomad again, but Hredt doubted it, and only fools based their strategy on the best outcome. He had to plan for the worst.

If the opposition was serious about kicking out the Protectorate, it couldn't afford to waste resources fighting an extra enemy. It would be even more reluctant if that enemy looked like the vanguard of a much larger expeditionary force. He knew what he needed to do. He also knew that it was the one thing Solomon opposed completely, and Chris thought was insane; opening the sector to a lot more humans by giving them proper FTL technology. Even Ingram and Marc wanted to delay that.

Hredt started doing some projections. He understood the difficulties of accommodating large numbers at short notice, so the

Caisin gate wasn't appropriate this time. But the longer they left it to give Earth the data to manufacture its own drives, the more they put themselves at risk of being outnumbered and destroyed. He couldn't let that happen to them, and he couldn't let it happen to his commune either. They rose or fell with Nomad.

But everyone — Chris, Ingram, Jeff, Commander Searle — had said it would take Earth ten years to build ships, even if they were given precise instructions and only had to follow them. Ten years was too long. And what did they base that figure on? Whatever it was, humans had never had the advantage of teerik expertise before, and that would make all the difference. Hredt was sure he could cut that lead time in half, and maybe even shave it down to three years.

It still wasn't immediate, but Nir-Tenbiku might not be able to respond immediately either. Perhaps that was why he'd sent a probe instead of a task force: he might not have had the vessels to do it.

Hredt was now about to disobey Ingram's wishes — and Solomon's — and hand the technology to Earth. But he knew he had to do it in the same way that he'd found the nerve to do all those other things he'd never imagined, like approaching the humans for help in the first place. Perhaps his recklessness then had come from the declining level of drugs in his body, but those decisions had turned out to be right. He'd be right again. Nomad couldn't face what was coming on its own.

Now he had a project to plan, and that was what he did best. He needed to know three things — who to provide with the technology, because there were blocs like APS that treated Nomad as an enemy; whether the recipient could actually build ships; and how much to tell them about where this technology came from. Humans weren't aware yet that other intelligent species existed. They'd spent a lot of time imagining that they did, but the reality might be too much of a shock for them at a time when he needed them to focus on building ships. Jeff had told him how first contact would have meant years of negotiation and diplomacy under normal circumstances. Nomad would end up dying from bureaucracy and delays.

There was only one nation Hredt felt he could entrust with the technology. Britain was still free of die-back, it had its own small space programme, mostly devoted to spy satellites, and it had proved it was what Ingram called *decent* — it was willing to evacuate the stateless Americans from Ainatio and give them sanctuary. It had also produced people like Chief Jeff, Marc, and Ingram. Hredt felt he knew exactly what Britain was.

He spent the rest of the day studying the most recent data he could find on British industrial capacity and working out where he could shorten the construction process. He could make sure he was available at all times to talk them through the more difficult engineering work, and they need never know he was an alien. He also knew exactly who to contact, because he could still access the comms log for the assay probes currently orbiting Earth and pull the data from Marc's previous calls to his contact in the British government.

It might prove hard for Britain to build the ships, but Hredt would give them the technology anyway. They were probably the most capable after APS, and APS was to be kept as far from Opis as possible.

It was all working out. Everything was clear. Hredt even felt confident enough to send some of the Earth probes to do reconnaissance and assess how much industrial activity was currently happening in Britain. Eight hours later, he had the outline of a production programme to go with the FTL documents he'd already drawn up for Ingram. The one problem he still faced was placing the call to Marc's contact without Solomon knowing.

For a moment, he felt terrible for planning to do this to the people who'd saved his commune. But this was still his technology, and he had the right to do as he liked with it. In that case, he'd use it where it could do most good for them and for his commune, because a few thousand people, no matter how willing to fight and even with the advantage of the Caisin gate, were ludicrously outnumbered here.

Backup, they called it. Hredt was making sure they had it, even if it wasn't as immediate as it should have been.

By the time someone came looking for him, he was well into the production plan. Turisu squeezed into the cockpit and stared him down, head cocked to one side.

"You turned your radio off and I don't think you've had anything to eat," she said. "What are you working on?"

"Trying to understand what's happening on Earth." Technically, that was true. He didn't have to be geographically specific. "I'm using the ship's comms, so it's not hard to locate me."

"Have you eaten, though? You get strange when you don't eat."

It was incredibly benign nagging. It was almost kind. Turi had always been snappy and argumentative even before the issue with medication, but now she was remarkably relaxed. Chief Jeff had noticed. Hredt wondered whether her dose was now too high.

"I'll eat when I've finished my calculations, Turi. Thank you for worrying about me."

"The humans have contacted the Jattans, haven't they?"

"Yes."

"They can be so stupid."

"They're just doing what they know, as we all would."

"This is why you're studying Earth again. You're preparing to send them back to safety."

"I have to be ready for anything."

The Turi he'd grown used to would have been furious about all this, but she just seemed disappointed with human naivety. He hoped she wasn't too sedated to do her job properly.

"Don't forget to eat, then," she said, and left.

Hredt worked for another hour and took a break. There'd been no word from the Jattans, so either they hadn't received the message yet or they were deciding what to do about it. Hredt went back to the compound to eat, flying short distances when he had enough space to take off, just to ease himself back into exercise.

The house was silent now that his grandsons were accompanying other commune members to learn their skills. In a normal commune back in Kugad, they would have been gone forever now and he'd never have seen them again. Whatever happened next, the one thing he wouldn't regret was having his true family around him.

He finished his meal quickly, disposed of his medication bar, and flew back to the hangar in short bursts. Rikayl appeared out of nowhere and glided alongside, probably hoping to play.

"Busy!" he said. "Need fun."

"Later, Rikayl. I have work to do."

"*Always* busy." Rikayl rasped his disapproval and flew away, gaining height until he was circling overhead to keep watch on the base. He'd learned not to venture too far from the perimeter now. It might have been because the base had as many interesting things to watch as the Opis wilderness, although there was nothing for him to hunt.

When Hredt got back to the hangar, Solomon was looking around as if he was killing time while waiting for him. He resembled the farm dogs sniffing trees. Hredt had learned not to comment on that because Jeff said Solomon saw his alter ego as a different, more elegant kind of animal.

"Still no response from the Jattans," Solomon said. "But they might not be checking transmissions at the moment."

Hredt had been out of communications range once he left the ship, so it wasn't unusual for Solomon to update him. But he had the feeling it was about a little more than that. Solomon was aware at some level of all comms and sensor activity, and he'd know — or he'd find out when running routine checks — that Hredt had separated a unit from the probe swarm orbiting Earth for his own use. It was often hard to work out what Solomon was aware of at any one time, as his role seemed to be more of an overseer managing non-sentient emanations connected to himself. Those slaved dumb AIs, as the humans called them, were the units that did the specialist tasks like translation and directing engineering bots.

Ah. That might be a good way to get a call to Earth past his scrutiny.

"It could take them some time." Hredt decided to go on the offensive in the most polite way. "Do you have any more detailed charts of Britain, please?"

"Are you looking for somewhere in particular?"

"If Tev and his family don't thrive here and need to return to Britain, where will we place them? And it has to be Britain, because they daren't go back to Fiji. If our strategy with the Jattans backfires, where do we place evacuees if we need to get them away from this sector in a hurry? I realise you could do it, but I need to be able to do it too. We have no idea which of us would survive if we're attacked."

It was a reasonable question. It just didn't happen to be the one he wanted an answer to. Solomon stared at him with that eyeless snake-head camera.

"It's a good point," he said. "I'm sure Captain Ingram's considered that, but you're the gate expert."

"I'm sure we'd agree a location with the government in advance, but if time doesn't allow it, it would be a terrible tragedy if the evacuees were shot on arrival. I know Britain is always on alert for invaders."

"I'll find some charts and give you access," Solomon said. "They'll be some years out of date, but Marc might have more recent data from British spy satellites."

"Thank you. I also need to put the probe through repair and diagnostics soon, because we're overdue a maintenance cycle, so I'll do that by separating individual segments rather than taking the whole net down. We can't afford to be out of contact with it yet."

Hredt wasn't sure if that allayed Solomon's inevitable suspicions, but it seemed to have satisfied him for the time being. It wouldn't divert him for long, though. Hredt now had to speak to Marc's contact in the government as a matter of urgency.

The problem was doing it without Solomon noticing, at least until the data had been sent. Hredt wasn't ready. He'd wanted to send more detailed information with the production document, but there wasn't time now. If he failed at this or Solomon caught him, it might be years before anyone felt it was safe to share the technology with Earth. He'd have to do it now and transmit what he had.

He sat in the cockpit, thinking through his options. Just as Solomon had picked up things from observing teeriks, Hredt had discovered a few tricks by watching Solomon. He could try manipulating the ID code that was unique to individual comms-enabled devices. If he faked Marc's number, Lawson would recognise it, but it would cause trouble for Marc. All Hredt needed was a few minutes to get Lawson's attention and send him the data. He'd withhold his own number, connect to the special number that Marc had used to reach Lawson direct, and set the probe to conceal it. Solomon might be able to drill down and find the actual numbers, but if he was monitoring the Earth relay at all, he'd only see the various channels taking data from around Earth. The probe was made up of a number of smaller ones receiving satellite imaging, feeds from entertainment sats, and comms links, and Hredt's link would be hidden in the latter.

He only needed a head start. He didn't need to conceal a secret forever. Once the data was with the right person, he'd have nothing more to hide.

Just a lot of explaining to do to some very angry humans.

That's actually a big risk. But they need our technology. They can't exploit it on their own, not yet. By the time they can, they'll have seen sense and they won't hate me.

Turisu would be furious, though, medicated or not.

Hredt reset the segment of the probe and spent a few moments calming himself before plucking up courage to send it Lawson's number. He knew he hadn't thought this through enough, but he'd have to live with the complications.

The calling tone rang and continued for a while. Hredt hadn't checked the time on Earth, but it was too late to worry about that now. He had to say three things quickly when Lawson finally answered: that he was a friend of Marc's, that he had more data on drives, and that he would send it right away. If Lawson didn't think he was a random lunatic and end the call, he'd explain more so that the man understood how important it was to keep the data secret.

"Yes?" a voice said.

Hredt was suddenly terrified. Had he called the wrong man?

"Mr. Lawson?"

"Yes."

He blurted out his main points, afraid of hearing the link fall silent. "Mr Lawson, I work with Marc Gallagher. I have important data to send to you. I have very little time. Will you hear me out?"

Lawson paused. "I'm listening. Who are you?"

"I'm not able to give you my name," Hredt said, astonished at how smoothly the story slipped out of him. He'd never thought of himself as dishonest, but he'd had years of experience of telling clients what he wanted them to know rather than facts they probably couldn't understand. "This follows the material that he sent you. But this is a set of instructions and technical data for a ship with a superluminal drive. FTL. An entirely new technology."

There was another pause. Lawson seemed to stop and think every time he replied. "Are you one of the Ainatio researchers?"

"This isn't like Ainatio's wormhole technology," Hredt said, dodging the question. "This is several generations on from that."

"And what would you want for this?"

"To know you'd build it and use it."

"I see."

Hredt's heart was pounding. This man had no idea he was talking to an alien. It was frightening and thrilling, but it also made him feel utterly ashamed. "Mr Lawson, I'll send you the data and the production plan and you can assess it. If you agree that it's genuine, you can call back."

"I don't see a number for you."

"Call Marc on the number you used before. But if you decide to go ahead, I'll make myself available by comms link to help you at every stage of the process."

"Do you mind my asking why Marc isn't making this call?"

A little bit of truth would help now. "Because it would put him in a difficult position if I'd told him I was doing this. He would dissuade me from taking the risk. I'd suggest talking to him after you've had time to look at what I'm sending you."

Lawson was quiet again for a few moments. "Very well. I'll look at the material. Thank you."

Lawson sounded what Jeff called *underwhelmed*, as if he had doubts. Hredt tried to emphasise that his motives were genuine. "Marc's my friend, and he's done a great deal for us. So this is solely for you. It's highly confidential. Please stand by for the data."

Perhaps Hredt had gone too far, but it was said now, and in a few seconds it would be done. He tapped the list of files and then the transmission icon. Unless Lawson and his colleagues dismissed it as a hoax and did nothing with the information, he'd just changed the course of Earth's history.

It wasn't the first time, and not even the first time this year. He was making a habit of it.

08

*How would we view Solomon if he hadn't chosen us? He could
have decided we were the ones who needed to be left to die.
How different is he from Earthmother?*

Dr Ingrid Morris, family physician, Kill Line.

MEETING OF THE HALU-MASSET, CABINET OF THE GOVERNMENT OF JATT IN EXILE: THREE DAYS AFTER LOSING CONTACT WITH THE PROBE.

"Does this tell us anything at all?"

"That we should approach our new neighbours with caution,
Primary," Cudik said. "But how we approach them at all now is
anyone's guess."

Nir-Tenbiku Dals had watched the recording at least five times,
trying to wring more information out of it. The human garrison
stood between a river and the coast on one of the planet's northern
continents, and a high aerial view from the probe showed hundreds
of buildings and a large area of fields under cultivation. The inset
screens to the right hand side displayed specific areas of interest
that the probe had identified as worth watching. The whole site
looked well established, but that didn't necessarily mean it had been
there for long.

As the probe descended, it zoomed in on the specific features
that had alerted it: large structures that could have been hangars or
silos, entire zones of transparent tunnels that were full of plants, and
enclosed grass where large quadrupeds stood around in groups. The
probe circled the perimeter, which didn't appear fenced or walled,
but was surrounded by a wide strip of cleared land that could have
indicated concealed automated defences instead. Humans showed
sensible caution.

There was quite a population, too; vehicles, objects that were
probably mechanicals, and creatures that had to be the humans
passing across the open area in the centre of the base. From this
altitude, it was hard to appreciate the scale, but the humans were

as Gan-Pamas had described them, bipedal and as tall as Kugin, but more slimly built.

"I still can't see anything that looks like a military installation," Cudik said. "Gan-Pamas must have seen much more than this."

Nir-Tenbiku ruled out the possibility that humans were native to this world and had never left it. They had to be recent arrivals. The garrison was the only sign of habitation, and a species with that level of technology would have spread across the planet a long time ago. But Cudik was right: there was no visible sign of military equipment or ships, least of all the prenu.

When the probe attempted to scan inside the buildings large enough to house a Nar-class vessel, the structures blocked the signals. Gan-Pamas had suspected they kept their larger assets in bunkers, which would have required an extensive underground complex, and that meant they were well dug in if an attacking force attempted to dislodge them.

Even if Nir-Tenbiku knew nothing about humans, he could deduce some important facts from that alone. They didn't want to advertise their presence, they were here to stay, and somewhere on another world there'd be many more of them with technology that had enabled this garrison to appear out of nowhere.

Eventually the probe descended further to check vertical surfaces it couldn't see from that altitude and angle. Nir-Tenbiku had been surprised the first time he'd seen the humans allow it to get so close, because he couldn't believe a spacefaring military didn't have the means to detect a probe at such close quarters. Were they naive, incompetent, or just unaware of what it was? But it had become apparent on repeated viewing that they knew it was there and had decided not to destroy it. They were simply observing, letting the probe get closer.

It was now just above them, high enough for them to look up and watch it at an angle of forty-five degrees. Nir-Tenbiku was intrigued by their faces — generally flat, some pale, some dark, large eyes, small mouths — and the varied fur on their heads, some short, some long. They all held long tube-like weapons similar to Jattan shock-launchers but with devices attached to them, and then raised them to aim at the probe. They still didn't open fire, though.

The probe was trying to track all of them at once as well as a swarm of tiny probes that they'd launched at it. That was probably their strategy, because whatever hit the probe next hadn't been a threat it was tracking. It hadn't shown up on the inset displays at all.

It was hard to work out what it was even after rewatching the recording, but the probe was suddenly thrown a long way towards the perimeter, spinning but still transmitting blurred images and muffled sound, and then it hit the ground.

For a moment, all Nir-Tenbiku could see was grass, a couple of buildings, and a patch of sky, tilted at ninety degrees because the probe didn't seem able to level its cameras. Then it was looking into the face of a brilliant red feathered creature much like a teerik, except it was small and seemed to behave more like a curious animal. The probe rose into the air again, partly obscured by more red plumage, but focused on the ground beneath it. From the gestures of the humans below, Nir-Tenbiku pieced together what was happening. The avian had seized the stricken probe, and now the humans were asking it to bring it back.

Was that its job, then? They'd intercepted the probe and it looked like a planned capture. Eventually, all Nir-Tenbiku could see was light filtering through a mesh of fabric as if they'd covered the lens, and he heard an alien language with a lot of lower frequencies. Then the probe went offline.

Each time he viewed that footage, he was more convinced that Gan-Pamas had assessed humans accurately. Nir-Tenbiku was cautious about interpreting a culture he'd never seen before and whose body language might not have corresponded with his own, but he'd formed the impression that human troops were confident and had a reason for being that way. They'd allowed a probe to enter and spy on them so that they could capture it and analyse it and its origins, just as he would have done.

"Let's go through this again, Bas," Nir-Tenbiku said. "Slowly."

Bas ran the footage again, pausing or slowing it so they could look beyond the immediate focus and work out what was happening over a wider area.

"There are the quadrupeds Gan-Pamas mentioned," Olis said. "Look. In the background."

They studied the image. The four-legged creatures stood at the height of a human's main leg joint or a little taller, shouting and showing pointed teeth. A human spoke to them and they fell silent. So there was an avian, two kinds of quadrupeds, mechanicals — including one shaped like the quadrupeds with teeth — and bipeds. This looked like a team of species working together. And there were teeriks somewhere as well according to Gan-Pamas, although they weren't visible in the recording.

"If the humans have teeriks with them, regardless of whether that's coincidence or design, they'll know all about us by now," Mer said. "Perhaps we can rely on the teeriks to do our reputational work for us. They'll have told them how awful the Kugin are and how the Protectorate's their puppet, so if you're serious about winning some kind of support from them, they might already have formed an opinion."

"Mer, with respect, their opinion's likely to be based on Lirrel killing one of their females," Olis said. "I don't think we'd take that well if we were them."

"Are we still concerned about recovering the prenu?" Fas asked. "This has shifted from seizing a ship to befriending humans. Let's get our priorities in order."

"We can't do one without the other," Nir-Tenbiku said. "And we have to deal with the issue of the dead human. It was poor judgement. We would lose nothing by making an apology."

"And who would do that?"

"I would. Preferably in person."

"That's too dangerous, Primary. Send them a message instead."

"We'd be offended by such casual contact. Diplomacy is about being in the same room and showing mutual trust, not sending disrespectful memos like some Kugin clerk. And how would we seem to them if we sent some minor functionary to deal with something so serious? The apology needs to carry the full weight of the state."

"You're talking yourself into this," Fas said. "We haven't even made contact with them, and if their treatment of that probe is anything to go by, they won't welcome us."

"We can try," Nir-Tenbiku said. "And I plan to. Because they'll still be around when we take back Jatt. At some point, we'll have to deal with humans, and they might have very long memories."

The meeting went quiet. They'd started out thinking that the prenu was critical to their mission and now they were having doubts. Nir-Tenbiku could see it. Then Olis actually said it.

"Do we really need the prenu? It's symbolic rather than functional, and we have to engage with a new civilisation to get it. The humans might just politely say no, or they might declare war, depending on their mood. We could forego the ship, avoid the humans, and still achieve our aims."

"But we've already alerted them," Cudik said. "We've killed one of them and followed up with a probe. At very best, they'll remember to punish us if they ever meet us in passing. At worst, they'll track us down and attack us."

"And they're likely to be here for a long time," Nir-Tenbiku said. "It's possible we won't be able to avoid them."

Olis wasn't backing down. "I'd vote to call a halt to this while we still can."

"I haven't called a vote," Nir-Tenbiku said. "We're already in a conversation with the humans, albeit an unfortunate one, and I'm obliged to continue it."

It was the Primary's prerogative. He'd rarely used it, but they'd only been playing at governing for all these years, going through the motions while knowing there were no real consequences of their decisions. It was a training exercise. The real work had been to amass arms and make allies, and there was rarely disagreement over that because the rightful government had very few friends who weren't Jattan or Jattan colonists. The Esmos Convocation let them stay here, but they wouldn't give them military support. Very few actually meant zero.

"And what does continue mean?" Olis asked.

"I'm still working that out."

"Do we have any other items on the agenda?"

"Not yet."

"I request the Primary's permission to leave the assembly, then."

"Granted. Let's close this session and I'll consider our next step. If they've disabled the probe, then our biggest challenge will be how to communicate with them. Cudik, could you stay a while? I have technical questions."

Cudik hung back while the other cabinet members left. Nir-Tenbiku poured him a cup of floral tisane and one for himself. It was an Esmosi habit, but he'd developed a taste for their favourite fragrant infusion.

"Might the probe still be operational?" Nir-Tenbiku asked, handing Cudik the cup. "I hesitate to send another."

"The teeriks are sure to tell them how our probes work," Cudik said. "So if the humans' aim is to analyse it, they'll disable the power source first to stop it spacefolding, although its navigation already seems to have been compromised by whatever hit it. They'll see if they can extract data from it. That's what I'd do, anyway."

"They might not think like us. We could always try re-establishing the link and find out, of course."

"If they're waiting for us to do that to locate us, it would be unwise. That's why I disabled our connection to the relay."

"I imagine few people think we'd be based anywhere else but Esmos."

"True," Cudik said. "And the teeriks will warn the humans to steer clear of it, if only to avoid being targeted alongside them."

"You have a very jaundiced view of aliens, my friend."

"I'm surprised you don't, Primary."

"So can we check the probe's status now?"

"I know when I can't dissuade you. May I use your desk?"

"Please do."

Cudik hesitated for a moment at Nir-Tenbiku's terminal before reactivating the connection. "Oh dear," he said. "They've got the hang of this already, I think."

Nir-Tenbiku got up and stood behind Cudik to see what he'd found. "What happened?"

"It's working again," Cudik said. Nir-Tenbiku could see a view across a field of bare soil, looking through a square mesh in the direction of the garrison buildings, as if the probe had been dumped in a basket. Nothing moved. The image was frozen. "This is a transmission stored in the buffer."

"Download it, please."

Nir-Tenbiku leaned over to watch. Nothing happened for a moment, but then the image showed a little movement and he heard a voice speaking Jattan — formal, with the stresses in odd places, but easily understood. The message was blunt.

"*This is Captain Bridget Ingram, commanding officer of Forward Operating Base Nomad. You have now made two incursions into our territory. Your agents have killed one of our comrades in an unprovoked attack, for which there will be consequences. I demand an explanation. What do you want here? Do not attempt to approach this planet again or we will respond with force.*"

"Well, no room for misunderstanding there," Cudik said. "They can speak Jattan. A female, too, from the grammar."

"The teeriks can," Nir-Tenbiku said. But his heart said Gan-Pamas might be translating somehow, still alive, still there to be rescued, or perhaps the woman had made a mistake with the plural form of agents, and only Lirrel had been captured. However unlikely these scenarios were, he hung on to hope. "But if that voice really is the commander's, I'm impressed."

"What now?"

"Captain Bridget Ingram asked us a question," Nir-Tenbiku said, straightening up to finish his tisane. He tried to remain optimistic, but this wasn't encouraging. "We must answer."

"Let's not be hasty."

"I wasn't planning to be."

Cudik played the message a few more times. They hadn't overlooked anything. They went out onto the balcony and sat in the shade of an ornamental tree with long deep green leaves so fine that they looked like hair flowing along the full length of each arched branch. They rustled in the breeze. Nir-Tenbiku wondered if they'd grow well in Jatt. He'd want to take one back with him when the day came.

"Gan-Pamas must have had a reason for sending the message as he did," Nir-Tenbiku said. "If he thought it was worth cultivating these new aliens, he must have seen something that made him believe it."

"Do you think he's still alive?"

"Do you?"

"The captain said there'd be consequences — future tense. She might be indicating that Gan-Pamas is being held prisoner."

Nir-Tenbiku had to make himself say it. He'd been in denial for days because it was too painful to think of his friend meeting a lonely death a long way from home at the hands of strangers who probably didn't even know why he was willing to sacrifice his life. But he had to face it now and grieve later.

"I think you were right last time, Cudik," he said. He felt his voice catch in his throat but he swallowed and kept it under control. "When you said he was dead."

"Have we grown weak, Primary?"

"In what way?"

"There was a time we'd have sworn vengeance and gone after Gan-Pamas's executioners," Cudik said. "Now we're worried about offending them."

"Gan-Pamas himself said Lirrel had killed a human. I think that might have given us pause and made us ask if the humans believed he was responsible."

"But we wouldn't have taken their side," Cudik said.

"The difference between us and the Protectorate is that we *think*." Nir-Tenbiku wagged his hand to emphasise the point. "We're educated. We learned self-discipline and deferred gratification. We come from families who preserved the values of our ancestors. We're mature by outlook and understand that the world usually lacks polar clarity. The Protectorate, though, hasn't just put personal gain above the interests of the nation. It's also the third generation of inferior politicians. They've never been tested by real challenges because Kugad does all the thinking for them, and that makes them weak and degenerate. They're like spoiled children — over-emotional, always looking for easy answers, unable to apply themselves to complex problems, and unable to think beyond the day and what pleasures they can demand from it. *That's* weakness. I think we can see the other side's perspective better because we're still strong."

Cudik sat with his hands clasped, silent for a while. "Let me know how you plan to respond to the humans' commander, and I'll send the message," he said at last. "You've still got it, by the way."

"Got what?"

"Your conviction. Your gift for making us all feel we haven't wasted our lives working towards this."

It was kind of him. Nir-Tenbiku simply said what he believed. He'd never seen himself as inspirational, but when a man meant what he said, the truth of it radiated from him. That was what his father had taught him. Of course, lunatics also believed things sincerely, so it was no guarantee of reality, and perhaps he was mad too. He didn't know how he'd realise that he was, though.

"Dedicating yourself to an honourable cause can never be a waste of time, even if the cause fails," Nir-Tenbiku said. "If nothing else, it cleanses the air around it. It sets an example."

When Cudik left, Nir-Tenbiku began composing a reply to the humans, but other thoughts crept in and distracted him. How would he feel when he returned to Jatt? Return was more a spiritual term in his case. He'd never been there. He'd been born on Cer Clen, because it was too dangerous for anyone from the Tenbiku family to step on Jattan soil while the Protectorate was in power. His grandfather had sent his son and retainers to a safe haven in the colonies when he realised all was lost. Nir-Tenbiku's father had never returned to Dal Mantir.

What if he didn't like the country? What if he missed Esmos too much? If he tried to recreate an Esmosi garden there, was he really Jattan at all?

It didn't matter what he wanted or liked. His duty was to restore Jatt's independence and hold the Protectorate to account for their betrayal of the nation. He'd take whatever unhappiness or hardship was necessary to achieve his goal, and humans might be a key to it. If they couldn't be allies, he could try to dissuade them from getting involved on the wrong side, if they were the side-taking type at all.

Gan-Pamas believed contact was worth pursuing. It was hard to ignore the advice of a friend who'd given his life to pass on intelligence. The difficulty lay in working out how to approach the humans' captain, because Nir-Tenbiku knew he had only one chance to get it right.

This Bridget Ingram had warned him and made a clear threat, but she'd also asked him a question. What did Jattans want from humans? He'd have to think about that. It wasn't just a stolen ship. It was part of a wider ambition, more a longing than plan or policy.

Nir-Tenbiku wanted to restore the old ways, the traditional values of Jatt, when people kept their word and behaved with consideration and courtesy. He'd never lived in such a world, but he knew it had existed. A nation couldn't endure if all it valued was its wealth. Full coffers weren't an identity or a sense of community. Jatt had to believe in something, and he didn't feel it was a backward step to try to restore that sense of shared purpose, because some things were meant to be eternal.

He hoped the humans agreed with him. He would certainly ask if they did.

* * *

NORTHERN COAST, 11 MILES NORTH OF NOMAD BASE: 1220 HOURS, OCTOBER 23, OC.

It was everywhere, as far as the eye could see, and for a guy who'd spent his life surrounded by tall buildings or trees, where his broadest panorama had been a silent interstate with the occasional abandoned vehicle, the ocean made Chris feel like he was falling off the edge of the world.

The wind only added to the feeling that he had nothing to grab hold of. "Wow. This is so different. It's nothing like the Pacific. The smell, I mean. And it's not turquoise."

"You really have been cooped up, haven't you?" Ash said. "But at least you've seen the South Pacific. That's quite something."

"I didn't see enough of it, unfortunately." Chris shook his head, unable to take his eyes off the water. "Damn, imagine being on a ship in the middle of that when you can't see any land for weeks."

"Wait until you're in a storm at sea."

"This is awesome. You get a proper sense of being on a sphere in empty space. You know, like those fixed camera vids with the night sky standing still and Earth moving. I don't get that feeling with land."

"Ah, the lure of the briny. We'll make a sailor of you yet."

Ash sat down on the grass and joined in the silent contemplation of an ocean that the Nomad project team hadn't even bothered to name. Bednarz was dead by the time the first signals came back from Opis, but even when the FTL relay went live, they still didn't start naming things.

It was down to Solomon in the end. He'd taken over the mission when Bednarz died, the only entity the guy trusted to get the job done, and whatever folks like Erskine's dad thought they were doing, Sol controlled it. He decided what was named and what wasn't. Did he argue with the new CEO, or did he just quietly erase whatever humans did without them realising? Chris would have to ask him. Solomon believed names had to mean something to people, so he left it to Nomad's citizens. He didn't need anything more than grid references and coordinates to do his job.

"I wonder what we're going to call this," Chris said.

Ash shielded her eyes against the sun. "Probably the North Sea. You can't have too many of those."

"Okay, do you want to try finding a way down to the shore that doesn't end in a rock fall and massive embarrassment?"

"That's what I'm here for."

"If you see a path worn down to the beach, panic."

Ash looked serious for a moment before she laughed. "I had to think about that one."

"I found a safer route." Chris opened the file on his screen and showed her the aerial image. "If we walk back to the Caracal and head down the cliff here, it almost levels out with the beach, so if it's not as solid as it looks, you're not going to fall far or get hit by rocks."

"Good thinking."

He felt dumb as soon as he said it. Ash was a trained sailor, a practical woman on every level, and she'd have taken all that into account for herself. But he just couldn't risk another death. He'd brought helmets, protective clothing, extra emergency transmitters, and first aid kits. The survey bots had been sweeping the area for years, testing and sampling for everything from pathogens and venomous wildlife to unsafe geology and toxic plants, but small things that appeared intermittently could easily be missed. He wondered about a bot's chances of finding a rattlesnake on Earth.

They collected their equipment from the Caracal and prepared for a fossil hunt, nothing too ambitious, just pottering around on the shore and checking out the limestone, and then they'd have a picnic. It was like a school field trip with adult promise. If Chris screwed up, he could accept failure and save face because the outing had an innocent purpose of its own. It wasn't like a candlelit dinner. There were no excuses for those. Dinners were only about one thing, and failure was stark and brutal.

"We need to start sending bots underwater," Ash said, striding towards the edge of the cliff with frightening confidence. "We must have some cross-medium ones somewhere. We need to know what the marine life's like. Joni's going to want to take his boat out sooner or later."

"We might want ocean-going transport one day, too," Chris said. "No point having sea if you don't use it."

"We're doing this all wrong, you know. Any normal planetary mission would have sent scientists first." Ash adjusted her daypack. "Oiks like us wouldn't have been allowed anywhere near this."

"Yeah, Jeff said the same about first contact. He got to make friends with Fred and teach him English, no PhD or research grant required, a regular blue-collar guy. Score one for the laymen."

"One day they'll say knowledge was lost because we didn't know what we were doing."

"If they ever know we existed."

Ash gave him a mock-sad look. "That's depressing. But I know what you mean. We all need to hold up our bit of treasure and say look what I found. It must be hard-wired from our hunter-gatherer past."

There weren't many people Chris could have this kind of rambling what-if conversation with. He'd hit the jackpot. She looked good, she was competent, and she was interesting. He couldn't afford to fail with her. If he did, he'd spend the rest of his life kicking his own ass.

The yellow limestone cliff sloped downhill like a dry valley into a few feet of jagged rock that was almost a flight of steps. Chris went down first to test its stability, then beckoned to Ash to follow. The beach was mostly shingle and slabs of stone dotted with rock pools, with a fringe of sand nearer the waterline. When they peered into the pools, Chris was reminded that they really were on another planet. There was nothing familiar in the water.

He couldn't decide if the organisms were plant or animal, or even if the distinction existed. A bright orange frilly seaweed turned out to be a creature that crawled out of the water as their shadows fell across it and buried itself in the shingle. At another pool, a tiny creature with a vague resemblance to a lizard picked its way around the edges, grazing on some kind of grey weed. Then something underwater shot out a tentacle or maybe a tongue and lassoed it, making Chris and Ash jump back. The lizard was dragged under and didn't come up again.

"Bugger," Ash said. "I won't be putting my hand in there any time soon."

"Nature's a bitch."

"And we're the first to see that tentacle thing. Isn't that cool?"

"Let me check with the lizard."

"Everything's got to eat, Chris. Especially me. What cake did you bring?"

"Marsha's finest. Coffee pecan."

"Yay. I do like a nutty cake."

They walked along the shore taking pictures and pausing to look out to sea in search of larger creatures. Chris remembered planning to take the evacuee convoy south through Florida and maybe get folks to an island. The warning about not getting too close to water because gators were ambush predators and moved a lot faster than people expected had stuck with him. He wasn't going all the way down to the waterline until he knew what was in there.

"No seabird-type things," Ash said. "Environmental niches get filled, but apparently not here."

"Maybe they're migratory."

"Good point. We've been here nearly six months, so who knows what we haven't seen yet? I ought to check if the sats ever pick up anything."

They carried on heading west until another headland stopped them going any further. It was time to start looking for fossils. Chris put on his gloves, more to prevent bites from some unseen but venomous creature than to protect his hands, and started tapping gently at the loose layers of stone with a hammer. Ash watched as he lifted a thin slice with a small chisel.

"Would we recognise a fossil here?" she asked.

"Probably," Chris said. "There's a lot of Opis species that resemble ones we know because the environment's similar, so we should be able to see the difference between organic remains and random marks. If Opis has limestone, it's had the conditions to form fossils of sea creatures."

"Let's take some samples back for the boffins to play with."

"Don't encourage them." Chris stopped to examine another ragged slice of stone. There were some indentations on it, but they didn't seem like parts of anything. Then he realised Ash was looking out to sea with her screen held up, recording. "Seen something?"

"Yes."

"Birds?"

"Not sure. It was just a flash in my peripheral vision. It's gone now."

Chris bagged the piece of rock and put it in his rucksack before turning to watch the sea. Ash was still panning the screen slowly left to right and back again.

He couldn't see anything, not even waves splashing on stone, but then he caught some movement as well, something so fast that he started doubting whether he'd seen anything at all. After a few minutes, Ash stopped recording.

"I don't know if I got anything."

"I saw it too," Chris said.

Ash went through the recording, shaking her head every so often, then pulled a face, eyebrows raised. She tapped the screen before handing it to him.

"I'm really glad we didn't walk along the shoreline."

Chris hit play. Yes, the creature was fast. Even slowed down tenfold, it was there and gone in an instant. He froze the image and studied it. Whatever it was, its body never broke the surface, only a long whip-like structure maybe eight or nine feet long that arced onto the beach, hit the shingle, and pulled back again. It looked like a big version of whatever had dragged the lizard into the rock pool.

"I'm going to be unscientific and say it just caught dinner." Chris now had his answer about spotting rattlesnakes. The chances of a drone or satellite being in the right place and detecting that creature were slim, even with movement sensors. "Okay, we'd better put this beach out of bounds until further notice. What a great start to our new-found freedom."

"I'll call it in. It must take small prey for its size, though. I didn't see anything on the beach."

"Doesn't mean it won't try something bigger."

Chris hadn't been properly scared for a long time. There was fear of something he knew and understood, which he could harness to his advantage, and there was fear of the completely unknown that suddenly revealed itself and made him realise he couldn't even imagine the very worst. His gut told him to go straight down to the waterline and blow the shit out of whatever it was, but it was too stealthy, too fast, and for all he knew it was a harmless bag of jelly plucking seaweed off the beach.

But it looked too much like the thing that grabbed the lizard. He wouldn't give it the benefit of the doubt.

Ash tapped out a message. "I've sent Sol the footage and I've told him I want it named after me. *Bigbastardius briceae*." She looked up from the screen, frowning. "But you can have it if you like."

"Nah, I'm good. I'm holding out for an alien dinosaur fossil. And you saw it first."

"You can name the lizard."

"Poor little guy. *Infortunatus montellonis.*"

"Whoa. I'm impressed. You made up a serious one."

"I'm a serious guy." Chris wanted to get Ash back to the relative safety of the clifftop. For all he knew, that thing could haul itself up the beach or extend its tentacle a lot further than they thought. "Let's take a break. Picnic time."

On the way back, Chris tossed a micro-drone into the air and set it to record the length of the beach, dragging his fingertip across the aerial view on his screen to define its route. By the time they'd climbed back up to the clifftop and reached the Caracal, the micro-drone had finished sending back images and returned to

Chris. The thin strip of sand at the water's edge showed marks at regular intervals that looked like a rope had been dragged through it.

"I think that's the trail the tentacle leaves," Chris said.

"Bloody hell. That's either a gang of them or one animal's really busy."

"How do we know it's not intelligent? Maybe it's their planet and that's why the survey decided Opis was unoccupied. The owners were in the sea."

"You wait a million years for an alien species and then six come along at once."

Ash unwrapped sandwiches and Chris countered with slabs of cake. A flask of hot tea rounded it off. They sat in the APC's open rear hatch, sheltered from the stiff breeze, and savoured the afternoon.

"I'm glad sea monsters don't put you off your food," she said.

"Nothing ever does."

"So I heard. The infested flour's now a saga we recount to our tribe around the camp fire."

"You know a lot more about me than I know about you."

"Nomad's a small village. Everyone's got an opinion about the chiefs."

"So you know how I ended up in jail."

"Actually, I don't."

The longer Chris left it, the harder it would be to tell her, and the harder it would be to see her walk away. But maybe she was just checking if what she'd heard matched what he'd admit to, a kind of honesty test.

"Okay, I killed a guy when I was in high school," he said. "But that's not why I ended up in jail, because I was never caught. I can summarise it for you in thirty seconds."

And he did. He felt like he'd told the story so many times that he could recite it like a poem, but he hadn't. He'd just thought it. Ash didn't even look surprised.

"Did you tell your parents?" she asked.

"Hell no."

"Did anyone else find out? At the time, I mean. Not after you were conscripted."

"If they did, they didn't say."

"How did you feel keeping that to yourself?"

"It was hard, but I didn't feel guilty. Just worried about getting caught."

Ash went on eating. "One thing, though. Did your boss know? He gave you a job when your college shut down. You don't give someone a violent job if he's a geology student. You do it because you've got reason to believe he can carry out the rough stuff."

"I did wonder, but I can't see how he could have known. I used to think it was written all over me. Do you understand why I had to tell you?"

"Because you're honest?"

"Because I'd be upset if you found out later and dumped me."

"It would have been the not being told rather than what you did," Ash said. "But you've told me. Sorted."

Chris wasn't sure it was. He was nearly thirty-three and there was only so long a man could be the go-to guy for the dirty work before he saw his life as a void left by the problems he'd removed rather than landmarked by something he'd built. It wasn't guilt or regret. What he did best had been needed in uncertain times, and still was. It had been needed again a few days ago on the smoke-filled deck of Joni's boat. But knowing that only served to baffle him, because it was clear nobody cared what he'd done in the past and he was the only one who felt he had to explain it.

"I'm on duty at twenty-one hundred," he said. There was always a member of Joint Command on call overnight, but Chris preferred to go into the office for some quiet catch-up time rather than be woken in the small hours. "Do you want to go for a drink when we've got a little more time?"

Ash looked pleased with herself. "We can do better than that. Live football on the TV at my place, Sunday night, Brazil versus Chile. Hacking into terrestrial sats was the best thing Solomon ever did. Alcohol and snacks. You up for it?"

There was no form of football Chris cared much about or even understood, least of all soccer, but he seemed to have passed Ash's test. He'd been offered admittance to the inner sanctum. He would have agreed to watch snail-racing with her.

"Yes," he said. "I'd love to. Thanks."

"One day," Ash said, "I want someone to ask how we met, just so I can say I was working late and thought we had an alien intruder, so I went out ready to open fire but it was just you taking a leak, and our first date was discovering sea monsters on another planet."

She seemed to find it incredibly funny and started laughing her ass off. Chris could only join in, although he'd have to learn to loosen up more to laugh as unselfconsciously as that with her.

"And I can say yeah, I'll never forget the sewage plant where she tried to impress me with the flow rates on her macerator."

He felt he'd turned the corner towards becoming Normal Chris, the self he'd never seen before. He drove back to the base, dropped Ash off at the treatment plant — all very proper, just in case Sol spotted them on the security cams, which he would anyway — and headed home to change into his uniform and teach a class. *Success.* He'd managed to get this far without screwing things up. Not every woman was out to betray him or use him for target practice.

And Ash had asked a good question, one that he'd stopped asking himself years ago: why did his dad's client offer him that particular job? How did he know he'd be good at beating the crap out of people?

There was no point in wondering now. That was why he'd stopped thinking about it back then. Forgetting was a talent that had kept him sane as a soldier.

Jon Simonot was in the security office when Chris arrived for his night duty. He'd been a permanent fixture in Ainatio's security office back on Earth and if it hadn't been for the different decor in Nomad's equivalent, it would have looked like he hadn't moved an inch. He was a good comms guy and he never missed a thing on the net. He could listen to multiple channels, keep an eye on a wall of monitors, and follow conversations going on around him simultaneously. It was almost unnatural. He looked up when Chris walked in.

"I see you've been battling giant squid, Sergeant."

"Visit the beach, they said. It'll be all volleyball and ice cream, they said."

"First time?"

"No, I saw the sea for the first time when we extracted Tev. Or did you mean my first encounter with giant mono-tentacled alien life forms?"

"Both, really."

"It's been an educational day."

Simonot smiled to himself and went back to whatever he was doing. Chris found a couple of messages Ingram hadn't cleared before she left, and he had his contact report to write about the potential hazards on the coast, so he could keep himself busy tonight. Now this was a classic example of why they needed to start naming geographical features sooner rather than later. If he could have written Sandy Beach or Nag's Head Bluff, or whatever folks wanted to call things, it would have been a lot easier to write a report. He ended up using grid references instead. Still, if the worst thing that happened to him today was bureaucratic inconvenience, he'd be happy. It wasn't so long ago that his reports would have been about engaging looters, firefights with insurgents, and lacking resources to bury the dead properly.

It was around 0100 hours when Chris heard Simonot pick up a transmission that got his attention. He didn't hear the incoming channel, but Simonot's reaction was enough to alert him. Simonot leaned closer to the console, as if he was trying hard to listen.

"Sorry, sir, say again?" Simonot frowned at whatever the caller had said. "Where are you calling from?"

Chris was now watching him. He pressed the mute icon, scribbled something on his desk pad, and turned to Chris.

"Sergeant," he said, "I've got a guy on the base net asking for Marc Gallagher, but I don't think he's calling from here. He's come through on Marc's connection to the Earth probe. I don't know why it hasn't gone through to Marc's screen, either."

"Has he given a name?"

"The guy says he's Sir Guy Lawson and he's the Permanent Secretary at the Foreign Office. The *British* Foreign Office. It's the British government on the line."

* * *

UNIT D74, NOMAD BASE: 0115 HOURS, OCTOBER 24, OC.

"Stall him for half an hour." Marc struggled into his pants one-handed in the dark, trying to hold his screen with the other. *Sir Guy* Lawson, eh? Marc had only ever known him as Lawson, and he'd had no idea the man was the fucking Permanent Secretary, the head of the whole bloody department. Why didn't he know that? He was slipping. He should have asked who he was talking to from the start. "Tell him I'm on my way in."

"Already done," Chris said. "I told him I had to go look for you. He's like God in your civil service, yeah?"

"He literally runs the Foreign Office. But he must be a recent appointment or I'd have known that."

"So are you coming here, then?"

"Yeah, because we might need to make a joint decision about what to say, depending on the questions he asks." Lawson probably thought Marc was still in the US, and the less information he had, the less he could work out from apparently harmless detail like day or night zones. "Does he know it's the middle of the night here?"

Marc tried to keep track of the mismatch in the respective lengths of day, and he was sure the time was almost in sync with Earth again. If Lawson thought he was still in the US, he'd assume it was five hours earlier.

"No, Simonot didn't say anything and neither did I," Chris said. "I couldn't work out what time he'd expect it to be anyway."

"Good man."

"You want me to call Ingram?"

"Leave her to me."

Marc put his screen in his back pocket and pulled on a sweatshirt. Maybe it was some issue with the Earth probe because he hadn't closed the channel properly or something last time he put in a call to Tev, but he wasn't expecting Lawson to be able to reach him. All Lawson had to do, though, was to use the number Marc had given him when he was trying to negotiate the mass airlift to the UK, and he'd get through just like he was making a sat phone call. But he wouldn't know where he was calling. He might have been checking in because Marc had made a vague comment about possibly being in range when he'd asked if they'd speak again. It was hard to tell.

He shook Ingram's shoulder. "Wakey wakey, Boadicea. The Foreign Office just called." He was surprised the conversation hadn't woken her already. "I'm going in. We need to get our stories straight before I speak to Lawson."

"Oh... bugger." Ingram rubbed her eyes. "That doesn't bode well."

"He's the bloody Permanent Secretary. I never knew."

"You sound surprised."

"He's so far above my pay grade I'd need binoculars to see him."

"No, he's *not*. You're the joint commander of an independent extrasolar base. And special forces. Stop being deferential."

"I'm not tugging my forelock," Marc said indignantly. He wasn't awed or intimidated by civilian staff, no matter how senior they were. He knew his own worth. "I just assumed he was a grade three or something. But I didn't ask. I should know better."

"It doesn't actually matter," Ingram said. "He trusts you enough to talk to you directly. And he's forty light years away."

"I didn't think he could link to me here, though. He's spoken to Simonot and Chris, so he probably thinks I'm still in America."

There was nothing Chris or anyone else could have done to head this off. If Chris had said he'd never heard of Marc or that he wasn't here any more, wherever Lawson thought *here* was, it would only have begged more questions. Marc couldn't even cut Lawson loose. Ingram was right that Lawson had no way of sending anyone to follow up, but if Tev ever decided Opis wasn't the right place for his family and had to go back to Britain, Marc would need Lawson's help. He had to tread carefully.

Marc checked Howie's bedroom door to see if the activity had woken him, but it was still closed. He left a note for Howie on the door in case he woke, and walked down to the main building with Ingram, trying not to look in a hurry. He found Chris sitting at Trinder's desk, staring at the rosters on the wall. Simonot was busy at the console. He looked like he was trying hard not to notice what was happening.

"Okay, before I call Lawson, let's agree a few things," Marc said. "No mentioning the Caisin gate, obviously, but how much are we going to admit to if he asks? He doesn't know we're on Opis. It looks like he doesn't think we're even on our way yet."

Chris shrugged. "Maybe it's an update on Barry Cho's family. But he could have done that by text."

"Or he might have intel from our agents that Tim Pham's saying we escaped through a portal," Ingram said. "Spooks know Pham's not a nutter, so Lawson will have questions."

"Or maybe someone clocked me on Fiji somehow and called it in. If Pham had people watching Tev, we probably had people watching *them*."

Marc had to cover all the angles before he risked talking to a man who'd spot every nanosecond of hesitation. The verbal sparring with Lawson got harder every time he had to do it, and not just because it was more difficult to keep tabs on what he'd said. He'd grown to quite like the bloke, and there was no professional satisfaction in trying to con your own side, least of all when you were in a position to help them and had decided not to. Torn loyalties always hurt.

"Sol, are you getting this?" Chris asked, looking up towards the ceiling. "You're unusually quiet."

"I'm staying out of this unless you want me to intervene," Solomon said. "But I'm also trying to pin down how this happened. There was a comms link kept open to enable Tev to make contact, but I thought we closed it."

Marc turned to Ingram and Chris. "Can we do this the old-fashioned way, please? You two stay in my line of sight and give me the appropriate signals if the conversation gets awkward. Just in case I start saying something you don't want me to."

"I could just cut you off," Solomon said.

"It might come to that, mate. Put the call on the speakers, please."

Simonot pointed to a terminal on another desk. "Ready?"

Marc settled into the chair and took a breath. He recognised Lawson's direct line on the display as the call connected.

"Ah, Sergeant Gallagher. Thank you for getting back to me."

Marc paused. "Look, before we continue, do you prefer to be called Sir Guy? I didn't know your name before. I didn't even know your grade."

"Oh, just Guy will do fine," Lawson said. "I think we have enough of a relationship to speak man to pen-pusher. May I call you Marc?"

"Go ahead. I'm not Sergeant Gallagher these days."

"Well, I'm glad you're still in one piece, Marc. I was following up on the data."

It had been three months since Marc had sent him Ainatio's FTL research. It was complicated stuff, though, and maybe it took longer than he realised to analyse it.

"Any problems with it?"

"People with far better physics grades than me are working through it as we speak, but I have a few general questions."

"My physics grades are probably worse than yours, but I'll do my best."

"We're still evaluating the data, but I was calling to verify that it's genuine. Your friend said I should ask you after we had a chance to look through it."

And there it was, the unmistakeable slap of shit hitting fan blades from forty light years away. *Friend.* Marc looked at Chris and Ingram, and even Chris the Unshockable looked slightly dismayed.

"*Friend,*" Marc said. "Can you narrow that down?"

"He wouldn't give a name. Male, English accent, although I couldn't place it."

Marc knew what was coming next and his heart sank. He had to be sure, though. "What data has he actually sent you?"

"Ah, yes, he did say it would put you in a difficult position if he'd told you in advance," Lawson said. "I assumed he'd tell you later. He said it was the full production plan and technical data for a ship with a superluminal drive, and that the British government was the sole recipient. I just need to know if this is genuine or not."

"I didn't realise he was sending anything," Marc said, watching the stunned expressions gradually forming around him. "Wait one while I check."

Marc muted the call. This had to be the data that they'd decided to hold back until they had a plan that didn't involve Nomad Base being swamped, but some irresponsible bastard was obviously fed up with waiting. This hadn't just trashed their plans. It had put Earth in the driving seat, and there was nothing they could do to stop it now.

"He's got the latest FTL blueprints," Marc said.

Ingram looked homicidal. "Sol, I want all comms links to Earth and access to the Caisin gate locked down *now*. Any channel that can be opened, any signal that can be piggybacked, you lock it until we work out who and how. Nobody has access now except Joint Command, and I mean *nobody*. Not even the teeriks. I want to know who did it P-D-bloody-Q. Let's work out how far we can go with Lawson. We can't deny it now. When the DRA's finished pulling it apart, they'll know it's real."

"If I thought lying would make him pull it before they complete the evaluation, I'd give it a shot," Marc said. "But there'll always be a couple of boffins who'll keep a copy and work on it in their own time out of sheer curiosity."

"This is some asshole who thinks we ought to be rescuing people," Chris said. "How do we know they didn't tell Lawson about the Caisin gate as well? I don't think he'd tell you that yet."

Marc reminded himself that he and Lawson were still playing the guessing game. "We'll find out soon enough."

"Okay." Ingram made an irritable *pfft* sound. "We assume the intelligence services eavesdropped on Kim's call to Pham when you were trying to negotiate a delay to evacuate the research centre. So they know about Opis, and they must know *Cabot* wasn't lost. We don't have to volunteer that, but it won't make matters any worse if we have to mention it."

Chris kept shaking his head. "It's too late to keep *anything* from Lawson except the Caisin gate. He's going to unpick this like a cheap sweater."

"What about aliens?" Marc asked. "My gut says don't tell him until they adjust to the idea of FTL first. Because he can't sit on this forever. He's now got scientists who know about it, so he's had to talk to his opposite number in the MoD because the Foreign Office doesn't have rocket scientists, and with the cost of this thing, he'll have to show it to ministers. And then you might as well broadcast it live to the bloody world."

"I thought you guys had a massive purge of the deep state in your last civil war," Chris said. "Kind of awesome, to be honest."

"Yeah, we did, but even when you remove the ideologues, you still have to keep cleaning the fish tank, and it's the politicians as well. There's no filter for idiots, gobshites, or wrong 'uns taking gifts from APS to enhance their lifestyles."

"So we're screwed, basically."

"Only if they come here and we get swamped before we're ready to deal with it," Ingram said. "This is still our government, not APS. They're not going to attack us. They'll have a vested interest in keeping Nomad going."

"Is that any better?" Chris asked. "They'll want to take over. Governments always do. Everybody's."

"Told you so," Marc said, nodding at Ingram.

"I know," Ingram said. "I'm adjusting my expectations to reality."

"I don't want to keep Lawson on hold too long, but we've got three questions to think about as soon as we're done with this call. Who decides if they want any official British involvement here, what do we do if the answer's no, and what do we do if HM Gov doesn't take no for an answer?"

"It's still years away," Ingram said.

"But what we do right now determines what happens in ten years' time," Marc said. "Okay, immediate issues first. Plan A — I'll keep my answers to a minimum, no mention of Caisin at all, delay the big reveal about aliens, but if pressed, I admit we're on Opis, and suggest it's a bad idea to count on heading here for reasons that'll be revealed later. Yes?"

Chris and Ingram both nodded. Marc unmuted the link. "Yes, Guy," he said. "I can confirm the data is genuine."

"Thank you." It came out as a sigh. Lawson paused for so long that Marc thought they'd lost the link. "We're on the same side, aren't we?"

"We are," Marc said. "I have a moral duty to the civilians we've evacuated, but I'm still an Englishman."

The last time Marc had spoken to Lawson, Solomon had just trashed Asia's infrastructure and caused the biggest power outage for a century. Marc and Lawson had played the game, fully aware they both knew what had happened — Lawson might or might not have known about Sol and exactly what he was — but they feigned ignorance, because that was what you did when you weren't sure the other guy was telling you everything, or if you were telling him things he didn't know. By the time it got as far as Lawson offering a transatlantic airlift to evacuate the civvies before Asian planes could get airborne again, he must have had a good idea of what Marc had been up to.

"Your friend said he'd be able to talk our engineers through the project," Lawson said.

Oh shit. "Yes, I'm sure he can."

"Forgive me for asking, but where are you right now?"

Marc looked at Ingram and Chris. They nodded.

"Opis," Marc said.

"Oh."

"Oh indeed."

"Would you mind running that by me again, please? Just so I'm sure I've understood. Not some town called Opis in Nebraska or wherever. *Opis* Opis. Orbiting Pascoe's Star."

"Yes, I'm on Opis the planet," Marc said. "And you need to factor in our twenty-six-hour day, so times and dates won't sync up with yours. I'm forty light years away and talking to you in real time because the FTL technology works. But you know about FTL comms, because I sent you the Ainatio research, and that's what they eventually used to manage the remote construction of this base."

"And that's how you know this new FTL drive works, because you're there now."

"Exactly. Instead of transit times taking decades, it's weeks or months." Marc hoped that was enough misdirection to explain why they'd reached Opis already. "It's a game-changer."

Lawson didn't sound as stunned as he had when they'd first spoken about Marc opting to leave with the Nomad mission. He seemed to be getting used to the idea of space and big surprises.

"I don't want to sound as if I'm carping," he said, "but I do have a question about the sequence of events. If you're there now, that means Ainatio had this advanced FTL before you left, in order to make that transit time possible. When did you know they had it?"

Marc braced. He couldn't lie because he'd need to remember what he'd said and it was all going to get too bloody messy in the long run anyway.

"It's not Ainatio's technology," he said. "And we all found out about it a few hours before we left Earth. Right now, accept what the gift horse gave us. I'll tell you what the catch is later, when we've worked it out ourselves."

Lawson went quiet again. Marc would have assumed he'd have someone with him listening in on the conversation just as Marc did, but maybe not. The bloke was smart enough to realise he didn't know what he was going to be told, so he didn't know who else ought to hear it. He'd want to control the information very carefully.

"I did wonder why the Americans had decided not to avail themselves of the airlift," Lawson said at last. "So you've got all those civilians with you on Opis. You have a settlement. A base."

"Yes, that's what Ainatio built remotely over the last seventy years using bots. It wasn't even a secret at the time. Nobody thought Bednarz could do it, but he wrote papers and gave interviews about it, so it's all out there. We're still evaluating the situation."

"I hope we can speak frankly," Lawson said. "You must know that we know *Cabot* wasn't lost with all hands."

"I'd be disappointed if you didn't."

"There were former Royal Navy personnel on board."

"They don't seem to grasp the former bit, actually," Marc said. "They're still playing Grey Funnel Lines. Ranks and everything."

Lawson sounded like he'd paused to consult his notes. "Captain Bridget Ingram, Commanding Officer."

Marc looked at Ingram and shook his head. No, he wasn't going to let Lawson speak to her, not tonight. "Correct."

"Where is Captain Ingram now? Opis, I assume."

"She is."

"May I ask why hasn't she attempted to contact us?"

Marc went into defensive mode. Ingram gestured angrily at him in that give-me-the-bloody-handset way but he ignored her. *Later,* he mouthed.

"OPSEC," Marc said. "Ainatio blocked *Cabot*'s comms to keep the cover story going. The company doesn't even exist now, but we still haven't let anyone contact Earth, least of all crew members who are from APS states. Ingram's kept the base operating in challenging circumstances, and she evacuated the Americans, which is where you came in. But I *will* pass on your request to her, though."

Lawson was commendably calm and polite. "So who's in command, then?"

"It's joint," Marc said. "Ingram, me, Chris — who you've spoken to — and Ainatio's head of security, plus the mayor of the town we evacuated. We've got a lot of issues to deal with that I can't discuss yet, and we've already lost a civilian member of *Cabot*'s crew, so believe me when I say you will *not* want to rush out here anytime soon."

"You'll explain this to me at some point, I hope."

Marc stopped looking at Chris and Ingram for reactions. He was going it alone now. "Yes, I will. In the meantime, it might be best not to give politicians this incomplete information. It won't be conducive to good decision-making."

"You're a natural for the Civil Service, Marc. I too would prefer to have the full picture before I brief ministers."

Yes, they were on the same page. Marc could speak Lawson's coded language. They were going to keep this under wraps for as long as they could.

"And watch out for Tim Pham and his little helpers," Marc said. "He's bound to have some on your turf. He had some unusual ideas about the tech Ainatio was using. He was right about it being FTL, but he was convinced it was all a secret British deal with the company."

"How flattering." Lawson took an audible breath. "Marc, we're very grateful for all this. I accept whatever's happening at your end is difficult, so I'll await your briefings. It's a testament to your loyalty that you still have time to consider your country's needs when you're no longer obliged to."

Marc winced. He'd just been caught short by some tosser's treachery, that was all. He didn't want unjustified praise, or any praise at all for that matter. But for some reason, however guilty he felt, and however furious he was about being dumped this shit, he felt better that Lawson knew and that Britain had a better chance of survival. It was all wrong in terms of Nomad's mission, and he'd said so himself. But his gut said it was absolutely right.

"I suppose I can ask you for a favour, then," he said.

"Absolutely."

"Can you tell me what happened to the Cho family? The young APDU corporal, his dad, and his sister. Did they claim asylum?"

"Cho's father and sister are living here now," Lawson said. She's having treatment. But I believe Corporal Cho is in a military prison in Australia awaiting a court martial."

Shit. Marc's relief died on the spot. So Pham had caught up with Cho, then, but at least the kid was still alive.

"Any location you can give me would be appreciated," Marc said. "The more accurate the better."

"I'll find out what I can, Marc. We're not too badly placed in Australia. If you're thinking of an extraction, though, that'll be a tall order even for you."

"We'll see. I still have an extensive contacts book. But you don't need to worry about it."

"We'll stay in touch, then. Thank you again, Marc."

"You're welcome. I'll keep you posted."

Marc closed the link and sat at the desk with his head in his hands for a moment. When he looked up, Chris was staring at the wall again. Ingram walked over and patted Marc on the back.

"All things considered, Bravo Zulu," she said.

Chris came out of his trance and nodded. "Yeah. You didn't even lie to him about Pham and the gate — well, not so blatantly that you'll need to apologise one day. I wouldn't be surprised if he works out the alien angle for himself, though. He realised we must have had some fancy FTL in advance to get here in the elapsed time. I'm amazed he didn't press you on whose it was."

"He's probably saving that for next time," Marc said. "Okay, so who is it? Who's our leak?"

"Someone who's male, English, had access to the FTL files, knew how to place a call via the Earth probe, and knew Lawson's number," Chris said. "Or maybe two or more people who fit at least one of those slots. Because this might not be a lone wolf."

Ingram checked something on her screen, frowning and unblinking. Marc could imagine what was going through her mind. The leaker had to be one of her own. Ainatio didn't have any British scientists out here, and on a base where people were already nursing grievances about Abbie Vincent betraying her colleagues twice and nearly scuppering Nomad, this was going to boil enough piss to run a power station. It'd also fuel the bitching about Brits taking over and feathering their own nests.

And Ingram took betrayal very personally. Marc could see it on her face, and he understood it. Backstabbing was bad enough in a civilian workplace, but for a comrade in arms to do it was a threat to everything the armed forces stood for and relied upon to function.

Here we go again.

People would need to see retribution. There'd be a collapse of discipline and morale without it. However comfortable things were materially, Nomad still had to be united, willingly or not, if everyone was going to survive.

Chris stood up. "I'm going outside for some air," he said.

Marc looked at Ingram. Chris wanted to have a private discussion that he didn't feel he could have in front of Simonot. Marc tried to work out how to extract himself without making Simonot feel like a leper. Ingram headed for the door.

"I'd better talk to Chris before he starts rounding up suspects," she said.

Marc looked at Simonot. He was a very smart kid. He'd been on comms through every crisis so far and Marc trusted him. They should have been able to talk in front of him, but Chris was right to take it outside, and maybe he had things to say that he felt would embarrass Simonot.

"I'm not looking forward to telling Lawson about the aliens," Marc said, trying to be sociable before he made his excuses to leave. "I'm not sure I'd believe it myself."

Simonot leaned back in his seat. "It's Fred."

"What?"

"I think Fred made the call."

"What makes you say that?"

"Lawson couldn't place the accent."

Marc had to think about that. Fred had learned English from Jeff Aiken with the aid of a language course on his screen, and he'd come out of it with a very similar accent to the posh English bloke voicing the lessons. But the accents of other people he spent time with influenced him as well.

"I think I see what you mean," Marc said. "But I'm not sure."

Simonot shrugged. "He learned the accent he heard from the English language module, but it's been modified a bit because of his exposure to American accents."

It made perfect sense. Marc wasn't thrilled, but it was better than having to deal with the fallout of a human traitor.

"Well spotted, Corporal," Marc said.

"I spend my life listening to voices on the net."

"I'd better get on it," Marc said. "Thanks, mate."

Marc found Ingram and Chris sitting on the steps outside the main entrance. He could hear the whispered discussion when he got closer.

"Most of the shit we're in is down to our own people double-crossing us," Chris was saying. "We've got to crack down and it's not going to be pretty."

"It's not us," Marc said.

Chris looked around as Marc sat down. "What makes you say that?"

"Simonot says it's Fred. Modified English accent. That's what Fred's learned."

"Not Bissey?"

"Why do you think it's Bissey?" Marc asked.

"He's Mr Moral High Ground. He'd see it as saving Britain."

Ingram studied her screen. "I wouldn't disbelieve hard evidence, but that's not Peter's style. He told me I should have handed all the tech over to the MoD, but he wouldn't do it behind my back. He'd tell me first and dare me to stop him."

"But that fits," Chris said. "He doesn't try to hide it. He tells Lawson to call Marc about it."

"He hasn't got access to the command network to pull up the blueprints," Ingram said. "And he can't access the probe without someone knowing. No, I think Simonot's right. Sol, where are you on this? You've got access to all the logs, haven't you?"

"I have, Captain, but I want to make sure I'm interpreting them correctly. Fred ticks all the boxes, though."

Chris sighed. "Well, shit. He did say he wanted a lot more humans here. But I didn't think he was that impulsive."

"Remember you're only here because he *is*," Ingram said.

"Sol, can he pull call logs off the probe relay?" Marc asked. "Because I'm the only person other than Chris who had Lawson's direct number, and I used it."

"That's definitely possible, and he'll also be able to call up recordings," Solomon said. "At least one call in the log over the last four days isn't showing a number in or out. I'm capable of erasing and spoofing numbers, and I think two of the Ainatio IT staff are as well, but so are the teeriks."

"Okay, I withdraw what I said about Bissey, then," Chris said. "But it would have been easier if it was a human. We're too dependent on the teeriks to cut them off from the network. Or line them up in front of a firing squad."

"Could I just remind you of the practicalities of what we're doing at the moment?" Solomon said. "I've blocked the probe signals to everyone except Joint Command, which means people won't be getting their news and TV shows now, and most of them will notice in a couple of hours when they wake up. Including the teeriks. We'll need an announcement to stop the rumour mill."

"I'm on it," Ingram said. "I'm going to my cabin to draft something. Can you bring Dan up to speed as well, please? The sooner he knows the better."

Ingram stood up and went back inside the building. Chris looked at Marc and shrugged.

"I was supposed to be watching Brazil versus Chile on the TV tomorrow night. Ah well."

"You don't even like football."

"It's a date."

"Bloody hell, Chris." Marc tried hard to lighten up, but it was nearly three in the morning and every problem he'd solved yesterday had already been replaced by brand new ones. "Please tell me it's not Fonseca. You're a glutton for punishment."

"Ash Brice in Water and Waste Management."

"Oh. Really?" Marc wondered if he was the last to know, but Chris was very private. "Good for you. If she's invited you round to watch the footie, though, I doubt she's planning an evening of educating you about the offside rule."

"I wouldn't even mind if she was," Chris said plaintively. "So it's official now, is it? You and Ingram?"

"No secrets here, eh?"

"About time."

"Can we get back on topic?"

"Okay."

"I hope it *was* Fred, actually," Marc said. "If we find it was one of us, we can't *not* punish them or it'll mean anything goes and we won't survive. We dodged it with the absence of a Mother Death sleeper, but this time we're not looking for someone who might not exist. We know he's real this time."

Chris looked as innocently wide-eyed as ever. "I'd shoot a civvy for this, Marc, let alone one of us. But if Fred's offered to talk the Brit scientists through the plans, how can we trust him not to mention the Caisin gate as well? Even by accident."

Solomon interrupted. "If we ever get to the stage of talking anyone through anything — which I still think is a bad idea — then I can put a delay on the uplink so I can block the signal if Fred strays into contentious topics."

"Like talk radio used to," Chris said. "The profanity button."

"Exactly."

"Fred's quite open about what he sees as being best for Opis. He believes bringing millions of humans out here is going to keep the Kugin in line and give us some protection now we've fallen foul of the Jattans. I just have to prove he's guilty before you take further action, though."

"At least that would spare us the inevitable shitstorm when we choose between a firing squad and loss of TV privileges for a month," Marc said. "We need teeriks. But we don't have to give them access to everything."

Chris shrugged. "You don't open the door to the same people who made Earth a hell-hole. If they want to find another planet to screw up, fine by me, but not here. I'm with you on this, Sol."

"I'm not sure Britain represents that problem," Solomon said. "But I would expect the situation to be politically challenging, and we'd lose control of Nomad unless we resisted."

"Anyway, nothing's changed. Even with all the glue and instructions, it's still going to take the Brits years to build a ship. No offence, Marc. Maybe we *will* need your guys by then."

"I'm on to the next problem now, mate," Marc said. "Try to keep up. I'd better rehearse how I tell Lawson about aliens."

"Now that's a historic role."

"It's going to be a hard day today. I need to get a couple of hours' sleep."

"Go on. I'll catch up with Dan."

"Thanks."

"Before you go, though, if you're thinking of springing Barry Cho from prison, don't try to con me again and go on your own. I'm a big boy now and I can do this stuff. I'm going with you. And it's not out of pity. We're still testing infiltration and exfil using the gate and we need more than one of us proficient at it."

Chris looked him straight in the eye. Sometimes it was hard to tell the difference between a challenge and a plea with him.

"I don't really believe you," Marc said. "But I concede the point. We all need to get good at it."

"And it upsets Howie if you go alone."

"Now that was below the belt."

"Go get some sleep."

Marc went to find Ingram. She was still in her cabin, chin resting on her hand as she tapped out a message with one finger. Marc flopped down on her bunk and shut his eyes.

"If things ever settle down here, we're going to die of boredom," she said. "Sorry about Barry Cho, by the way. You're going to try extracting him, aren't you?"

"It's what I do, sweetheart. Hostage extraction." His eyelids felt like lead now. "Right or wrong, I can't turn my back on him."

Ingram laughed to herself. "You've turned into an old married man in fifty-two hours. God, I nearly said forty-eight. I'm still not used to it."

"At least we don't have to argue about whether to tell the government now."

"Don't worry, we've got plenty of other crises to fill the gap. Like what happens when non-British personnel find out and want their country to get a slice of the action too."

"That'd be Brazil," Marc said. "The rest are APS and that's a hard no from almost everyone. In theory there's Russia and India, but we've got one Russian and no Indians. The rest haven't got a country now."

"Did Canada manage to keep any engineering capacity? We've got a couple of Canadians."

"Are you asking me if I've got intel?"

"Yes."

"It's old intel, but no, they haven't." Marc meshed his fingers behind his head. "Y'know, I'm relieved. Whatever the rights and wrongs of leaking the FTL stuff, it accidentally did the right thing for Britain, even if it was for the wrong reasons. And yeah, I know how that sounds. I just feel better for not standing back while Britain sinks and pretending it's for a higher moral purpose."

"Me too," Ingram said. "But everyone's going to want to call home. The longer I sit on this, the harder it's going to be to maintain discipline when the news breaks."

"So what are you going to say?"

"I'll brief heads of departments, then do an all-residents message explaining their TV's been cut off for security reasons. I'll wait until I've talked to Fred to explain why. No point buggering about. Word will get around anyway and I'd rather it came from me."

"It's going to get harder, you know."

"What is?"

"Keeping the Caisin gate secret." Marc scratched his scalp. "Not that anyone on Earth could build their own yet. But FTL will leak sooner or later. No country with a unique technical edge has ever kept exclusive use of it, from kaolin pottery to nukes. So if we let word get out about gate technology, APS will pull out all the stops to get here and seize it. Even if our government can be trusted to use the gate sensibly — bloody big if — we know others can't."

"You really think Fred would leak Caisin tech?" Ingram asked.

"I didn't think he'd leak anything at all, and I was wrong. So yes."

"I admit I still have moments where I'd like to hand the decisions over to politicians."

"Are you new here?" Ingram had told Marc the same thing before, and he understood why she wasn't happy about having to handle geopolitics. But it did no harm to remind her about the realities. "What happens if they show up with their own plans for us and Opis, and we don't like it? What happens if the Americans here don't like it? When everyone's got FTL, our only edge to defend ourselves against our own kind is the gate. And I've stopped thinking of all the other misuses a government or a corporation could put it to because the list was just too long and depressing."

"I knew it wouldn't be easy to build a settlement on an alien planet," Ingram said, "but I was completely wrong about why."

She went on tapping out her one-finger message for a while and Marc finally gave in and shut his eyes. He was still drifting in a semi-doze when Solomon's voice made him surface again.

"Captain, I've run some checks, and I'm as certain as I can be about who contacted Lawson," Solomon said.

Ingram sat back in her chair. "Fred."

"I believe so. There's no activity in the teerik compound, by the way. They're all roosting, but they'll know something's wrong as soon as they wake and try to connect."

"We'll have some interesting conversations today, then."

"I'm more than happy to deal with any explanations to the teeriks about why they've been cut off," Solomon said.

Solomon's tone rarely changed, and when it did, it was so subtle that you could miss it. But he still managed to leave no doubt about how he felt. Right now, he sounded very pissed off with teeriks, and a pissed-off Sol was no minor problem.

The teeriks had become a loose cannon at a very dangerous moment in Nomad's precarious existence. Whatever Ingram decided, Marc knew Solomon wouldn't let that continue.

"Leave the teeriks to us," Marc said. "We'll see what Fred's got to say for himself."

09

We've temporarily suspended transmissions from the assay probe in Earth orbit. I apologise for the loss of entertainment services, but we hope to restore the links later today after a full security check's been carried out. In the meantime, Alex Gorko will be extending base TV hours with recorded entertainment. Thank you for bearing with us.

Captain Bridget Ingram, Commanding Officer, CSV *Cabot*, on behalf of Nomad Base Joint Command.

ROOF TERRACE, MAIN BUILDING, NOMAD BASE: 0600, FIVE HOURS AFTER CONTACT FROM SIR GUY LAWSON, OCTOBER 24, OC.

"I still don't get it," Searle said, shaking his head. "Sure, we were going to share the technology sooner or later, but Fred knew he was way out of line. He said as much to Lawson."

Ingram sipped her tea. Her head was buzzing from lack of sleep and the breeze on the roof was doing little to clear it. She kept rerunning Sol's recording of Marc's conversation with Lawson, looking for detail she might have missed, but she'd have an answer from Fred himself very soon.

"I know I can make terrible mistakes assuming teeriks think like humans," Ingram said. "But I think he's fed up waiting for reinforcements."

"Yeah, Fred knows best and we're the dumb monkeys who don't get it."

"I'll give him until oh-eight-hundred to come clean. This is about trust now."

"Maybe he's trying to save us from our own guilt," Searle said. "He knows how hard it is for us to do nothing."

"So you don't think I should have him stuffed and mounted, then."

"No. Well, not until Sol can take over, anyway."

"I'm pleased to see you haven't gone soft."

"I don't like commandeering other folks' technology, ma'am, but I like dependency even less."

Across the base, the day shift was waking up to no TV, just a holding screen that explained there was a temporary outage. The blackout didn't seem to have prompted any complaints so far, but missing the Brazil-Chile match tomorrow would make a few people rather grumpy. Ingram planned to have everything back online by then. She'd have given Fred the bollocking of his life, he'd have seen the error of his ways, they'd pick up the pieces, and he'd never transgress again.

No. She wouldn't do anything of the kind, of course.

Fred was an alien. The rules were different, and perhaps she'd already been coaxed too far down the path of seeing him as a bird-shaped human, a talking cartoon animal rather than an intelligent being completely unlike a human and not obliged to follow the same protocols or even be aware of them. The mission's dependence on the teeriks limited her disciplinary options. Solomon was steadily appropriating both access and knowledge, but with the prospect of one Jattan faction or another turning up, it was the wrong time to alienate the commune. Ingram would have to keep her powder dry for as long as she could.

"I'm dreading the conversation, actually," she said. "Perhaps I'm the one who's going soft."

Searle smiled. "Any problem's still years away. At least Fred didn't call APS or distribute the plans worldwide."

Ingram had never seen Searle anything other than upbeat, except for the time they'd first landed and he'd hung an American flag on the wall. It was hard to imagine how he felt waking from cryo to find his country had ceased to exist, and he wasn't the only one in that position.

She'd promised him that everything could be rebuilt. She still believed it would be. But she wasn't sure how he'd feel about a foreign government poking its nose in while he was trying to achieve it.

This was the elephant in the room, and it had been there since day one. The multinational nature of Nomad had been born in a less divided world that no longer existed. Fresh starts and glossing over national divisions on the base depended on a clean break with Earth, and pre-FTL comms would have ensured they had to make one, but now they were as closely connected to the old world as they'd ever been. What would Bednarz want?

"If I find Fred *has* sent the material to everyone," Ingram said, "all bets are off. Teeriks will be a liability we can't afford. Firing them isn't an option."

Searle knew what she meant. Nobody spelled it out now. Teeriks knew too much about Earth, and their children would inherit that knowledge whether they wanted to or not. There was only one way to part company.

"That's always in the background, isn't it?" Searle said.

"I'll do it myself. Let's hope we never have to."

Sometimes Ingram said things without thinking, but she couldn't claim she didn't mean them. She'd seen the ruthless but humane solution in a split second; the teeriks would never know what happened. They'd never feel a thing. All she had to do was get the co-operation of a boffin to dose their food or switch their medication.

It was an awful thought because it came to her so easily. She wasn't even sure whether to feel guilty. Her reflex was to protect her tribe, and the scientific wonder of a new sentient species came a poor second to that. But at least she now had Marc to hear her confessions. She knew she shouldn't have felt better because of that, but she did.

"Nothing's ever uncomplicated, unambiguously good, or cost-free," Searle said.

"But how do you feel about Britain having this boon to mankind and not sharing it?" Ingram asked. "Because we won't, obviously. There's no nation left that we can trust, even if we were the sharing type."

"It'll leak sooner or later," Searle said. "Earth can't hide a space programme like that forever. Although Ainatio did pretty well."

"I meant you personally."

"I don't have a country to feel outraged for."

"But what if you did?"

"Then I'd want the US to have it as well. Sure I would."

"Exactly. And I guarantee that even if nobody actually says it, everyone here who's still got a functioning motherland back on Earth will feel affronted on some level."

"Does it matter?"

"In terms of cohesion, yes. You know it will."

"They'll just have to suck it up."

Deep down, Ingram was happier for knowing Britain now had a chance, just as Marc was, and she was relieved she didn't have to agonise over the decision any longer. That tempered her anger. Keeping the Caisin gate secret was still an awkward moral choice that seemed less justified now, but Marc was still right about it being dangerous in almost anyone's hands. The litmus test for technology was still to imagine what was the worst thing someone could — and would — do with it.

Anyway, food security was paramount. She couldn't tell Lawson that there was this magic gateway but he couldn't use it because refugees from Earth would screw everything. She couldn't justify opening the door to anyone else yet.

Except Tev and his family.

That was how slopes became slippery. A single exception turned into tens, then hundreds, then thousands. She'd been the one who'd refused to bring any of *Elcano's* passengers out of cryo before the food supply was guaranteed. Marc had gone back for Tev. Perhaps zero contact wasn't as critical to security as it had been. But Ingram was still reluctant to agree to total transparency, and she had to admit to herself that she didn't trust some of her own crew not to slip up in excited conversation with surviving friends and accidentally reveal too much.

And the aliens. I always forget the aliens. That's the biggest secret we have. It just doesn't feel like it. Isn't that insane?

The Jattan rebels hadn't replied yet. Knowing her luck, the first response she'd hear would be the sonic boom of enemy vessels coming in to land. On the other hand, a common enemy built unity. Most problems could be repurposed with a little effort. She just had to work at it. Losing Fred's goodwill was a blow, but it provided more impetus to learn and control the technology.

And the Jattans... they might be a useful live-fire exercise before we have to take on the big boys, or they might be useful allies. We'll see.

"Yes, you're right, Brad," she said. "Nothing's ever uncomplicated."

The base was fully awake now. More vehicles were moving around and the construction bots began grinding and thudding in the distance. What had been a round-the-clock operation a couple of months ago had settled into a normal daytime pattern, with a skeleton staff at night and only farmers out at ungodly hours of the morning. There was a visible and dogged determination that life would be lived as it had been on Earth, and that no aliens were going to shift the citizens off their land. It was a kind of militant normality. But it was deceptive. Ingram had to keep reminding herself she was as much at war now as she'd been back on Earth, even if she couldn't see it yet.

She checked her mail again. Every head of department had read her briefing now and the dist list was a column of green ticks. If anyone had been worried about the leak, they'd have been firing back questions and objections. The consequences of Fred's actions probably seemed too far in the future when there were other more imminent problems.

"Okay, I'd better crack on," she said.

"You're taking Marc, are you?" Brad asked.

"Yes, he's rather keen to express his dismay to Fred in person. Do you want to be there as well?"

"No, Fred might feel cornered. It's been tough enough to get the teeriks to tell us anything at the best of times. But I'll come if you want me there."

"Thank you, but no need. Just keep Cosqui enthralled. We might need her support."

"They're all blissed out on Tomlinson's calm pills, so maybe it'll go better than you expect."

"Do you think the meds have affected Fred's judgement? Because I don't think he's happy at all."

"Maybe. When I was still flying, the stay-awake stuff they gave us made me crazy. Dangerously overconfident."

"I'm not making excuses for him. Just looking for answers."

"I'm betting he just thinks you're wrong, ma'am, nothing more complicated than that. He's probably used to doing that to Jattans. Marc said he calls it *taking account of the client's ability*. If Fred thinks they're too dumb to define what they need, he gives them what he thinks is best for them."

That sounded quite helpful to Ingram, but it didn't feel that way when she was on the receiving end of it.

"His grasp of euphemism makes him a natural for dealing with civil servants, then."

Ingram would find out Fred's reasons soon enough. She made her way down to the entrance and found Marc sitting on the steps between Solomon's quadrubot and Betsy the pit bull, chatting to Sol, and she paused to watch. Betsy's head movements made her look like she was following the conversation. What did a dog think of a mechanical version of itself? Perhaps Betsy didn't think the bot looked canine at all, and it certainly wouldn't smell like a dog to her. That brought home the pitfalls of dealing with aliens who sounded human. If Ingram couldn't work out how a dog saw the world, a species she'd grown up with, how could she hope to understand teeriks? Their fluency with language made it seem as if they thought like humans, but the truth was she simply didn't know if they did, and she risked basing her actions on attributing motives to Fred that didn't exist.

She made a fuss of Betsy. "How are we this morning?"

"It's still last night," Marc said.

"You had a nap. I didn't."

Solomon looked up. "Good morning, Captain. I've blocked teerik access to the Earth probe, so they have the same security status as the rest of the crew now. I'll be able to restore TV to the base very soon. Mutiny is averted. And I apologise again for failing to spot Fred's call, but I do learn from my mistakes."

Ingram didn't want Solomon obsessing over a single failure to predict the unpredictable. Perhaps she'd told him he was omniscient once too often.

"It's not your fault, Sol. I didn't see it coming either."

"But I should have."

"Do you have control of all their probes now?"

"Yes, we've had shared control since the evacuation, and I hung on to it, just in case. So all I've had to do is block all their routes in, which is easy now we have control of *Curtis*. That's their only comms hub. And I've updated the system to route all comms traffic that isn't strictly within the base network through me rather than the comms AI, so I see it actively before anything's transmitted. That means no unauthorised contact with ships in orbit or between vessels, including the spy freighter. I realise that sounds excessive, but we obviously can't predict what teeriks regard as reasonable behaviour."

"I'm still trying to keep an open mind in case Fred has a valid reason for all this," Ingram said. "But are teeriks so clever that we wouldn't know if they'd bypassed us again?"

"Not now we've physically isolated the comms equipment. When I say I've locked them out, I mean I've literally sealed hatches."

"It's going to be hard to roll back from that," Marc said. "I hope we're ready for what happens next. And that they don't gate into *Curtis*."

"I've blocked gate access as well."

"Will Fred realise he's locked out yet?" Ingram asked.

"They can still log in to the library and the base network in the house, but they'll all know they've lost wider access as soon as they switch on their screens and the probe icon isn't active. Fred's the only one who uses it, though."

"Are we ready in case of industrial action? They've got quite a spectacular track record in withdrawing their labour, after all."

"Indeed we are, Captain." Solomon stood up and raised his head as if he was sniffing the air. "I have control of the Caisin gate, although only with pre-sets such as Earth orbit until the navigation AI learns to calculate paths from scratch. And we can complete the FTL drives in our vessels, although it'll be a much longer job. So we won't be left completely helpless if the teeriks become uncooperative. I'm working on the rest with Commander Devlin."

"Excellent. Good work, Sol."

"Captain, I don't want to give you the impression that we're solving the problems so all's well," Solomon said. "I'm really very angry about this. Fred's jeopardised everything Bednarz and three generations of engineers devoted their lives to achieve, and he's jeopardised *you*, all of you. I refuse to let Nomad be derailed."

"I know, Sol." The last thing Ingram needed was a vengeful AI who couldn't be deactivated. Solomon nursed grudges. She did her best to soothe him. "Don't worry. We're ready for anything."

Marc stood up and stretched. "Come on, let's get it over with. Bring the stuffing."

"Fred doesn't get those jokes, you know," Ingram said.

"I'm not bloody joking. This isn't my first run-in with him for keeping things from me."

Marc set off at a brisk pace. Ingram had to speed-march to keep up with him. "*Alien*, Marc. Just remember he's an alien."

"And *you* better remember he's not a child. He's a crafty little sod. Those who can't punch their way out of trouble fight with manipulation and blackmail instead."

"You don't have to tell me," Ingram said. "I went to an all-girls school."

"I know what he's up to. He wants us to fight his proxy war and hand the Kugin their arses for him. I'm happy to go for overkill if we're attacked, and I know I was brainstorming pre-emptive strikes, but I think we're being manoeuvred into starting a war. He's got form for it. He told Sol his daughter thinks he takes insane risks."

Fred's advice was that Kugin and Jattans only responded to force. Humans needed to be the enemy nobody wanted to take on, he'd said, and had to make other civilisations too scared to approach Opis for fear of what humans would do to them. Bissey wanted no part of that and resigned. Ingram had her own concerns, but they weren't ethical ones. A dangerously grey area lay between robust deterrence and first strike.

"Okay, he didn't consult his commune about making contact with us, or sharing technology either, but he's not necessarily setting us up to start a war," Ingram said. "Brad thinks it's just how he does business. You know, not telling Jattan clients all the details because they're clueless and just giving them what he thinks they need."

"I don't care why he does it," Marc said. "It's still going to drop us in the shit every time. He has to be reined in."

"Knowing why he did it is the key to stopping him doing it again."

Marc patted his holster. "So's this."

The teeriks' compound was surrounded by a high security barrier and still closely monitored in case of another Jattan incursion. The grounds were deserted. Even Rikayl wasn't out yet. The teeriks had security monitors inside the house, so they must have seen Ingram coming, but she still had to knock on the door and wait. Eventually, it opened.

"Good morning, Fred."

"Good morning, Captain. This is unexpected."

"May we talk?"

"Of course."

There was a workbench out front with four crates around it for seats, where Jeff sometimes played cards with Rikayl during the day while the adults were at work. Fred settled down at the bench. So they weren't going indoors, then. Fine, Ingram didn't want Turisu hanging around and maybe Fred didn't either. She suspected he hadn't told the rest of the commune what he'd done, though. She sat facing Fred, and Marc settled at the far end of the bench, looking like he was going to referee the event.

"I think you know why we're here," she said.

"Ah, Mr Lawson has contacted you." Fred cocked his head. "I'm sorry I didn't warn you, but you would have stopped me."

"Too bloody right I would," Marc said. "Have you any idea of what you've dropped me in?"

Ingram cut in. She hadn't totally given up on persuasion yet. "It's caused us a lot of problems, Fred. I'm sure you meant well, but now we've got to limit the damage as best we can."

Fred's neck feathers fluffed up. Ingram was expecting him to do that little shake like birds did when they were making themselves comfortable, but he just flattened the ruff again. It was a brief anger display. She'd seen the females do it, except their red crest rose as well. It seemed Fred wasn't apologetic at all.

"With respect," he said, "I don't think you understand the military situation in this sector yet. You're fewer than two thousand people at the moment, and only two hundred and twenty-one have proper military experience. There are Kugin and Jattan forces totalling almost one million. You need numbers on your side. The sooner you have those numbers, the safer you'll be."

"It's ten years away." *So much for seeing his viewpoint.* Ingram marshalled all her willpower to stop herself from wringing his neck. "We'd be dead long before backup arrived, and that's assuming it's backup at all and not a new regime that'll have a very different agenda, as well as new plans for *you.*"

Fred hesitated. He jerked his head, a tell so small that Ingram almost missed it, but she thought she'd sown some doubt.

"If ten years is a long time to wait for backup, then it's ample to prepare for the arrival and impose conditions that protect you from that possibility," he said. "But it can be done in five. The production schedule I sent is based on five Earth years, if they have the materials and skills to follow the instructions."

Five years. Well, Fred could write all the production schedules he liked, but if industry couldn't deliver that fast, it made no difference. Could Ingram find a solution in five years? It was never as much time as it sounded.

Marc leaned forward a little, elbows on the bench. "Why did you send the data to Britain, Fred? Because you could extract Lawson's details from the system and you didn't know where else to start?"

"No, I believed your nation was the best choice," Fred said. "I know little or nothing of the others, except that APS is your enemy, but Britain seems both civilised and free from the risk of die-back. I judged it by the British people I've met. There are other nice humans here, but some have no country, and others come from countries that would want to shut down this base."

"If Britain's physically capable of a delivering the project, which isn't a given because Earth's so low on resources, it's hard to keep something that big a secret," Marc said. "A lot of people have to be involved in supply and construction. Spies will notice it. So there's a good chance the data's going to leak to APS before we get anything done. If they get the FTL plans, they'll drop everything to build that ship, and they'll be starting with more resources than we've got." Marc leaned in a little closer. Ingram couldn't tell if this was working on Fred or not. "So if APS shows up here first, it means the end of Nomad, and you with it."

Ingram took the opportunity to tag-team him. "You should have talked to us first, Fred."

Fred fluffed up his ruff again. "But I knew you wouldn't listen. In the same way I thought it might endanger this base to respond to the Jattan opposition, and I explained why, but you still did it."

"You leaked the data against our wishes."

"I stopped you from making a big mistake."

"Okay, I understand why you want to do this for your commune," Ingram said. "You want the Kugin cut down to size, and you think we can do that for you. But you might end up subject to an APS empire that'll take a very different view. And if you've done this once, how can we trust you not to do the same with the Caisin gate? We're putting ourselves on the line for you."

"And what are you going to do if Britain can't build this thing?" Marc asked. "Are you going to hawk it around Earth until you find a country that can?"

Fred was completely still. He didn't even blink.

"I took your concerns fully into account," he said. "You want to save your species, but you — we — can only transport them, not create an instant refuge. So I have no reason to tell your government about the Caisin gate. It would give them false hope because their survival chances and ours would be slim if they used it. That was the conclusion you reached some time ago, wasn't it? Giving the most reliable humans the necessary technology is the best compromise, and yes, I do realise that could change at any moment."

"What if the unreliable ones show up instead, Fred?"

"This is *our* technology and I'm free to do with it as I wish."

That hit a nerve. Ingram had used the ownership argument against Bissey as a counter-punch in their fight over who had the moral high ground about Gan-Pamas. He'd said she should have handed over the technology to the MoD. She'd accused him of double standards because it wasn't hers to give away. Things looked a little different now.

"But you're *not* free to put this base at risk," she said. She was still talking quietly and calmly but the effort was killing her. "So until I'm sure I can trust you not to go behind my back again, I'm limiting your access to Earth. The situation back there is too volatile to risk missteps, and I hope in time that you'll understand why."

"You're the one who uses it," Fred said. "And I'd still strongly advise you not to engage with Jattans of either faction."

She thought about mentioning the work to be done on the ships, and whether to say it was a matter for him to decide if he wanted to continue working on them. But that might have sounded like she was begging, and she had her limits. She stood up.

"Noted, Fred," she said, and left. Marc stood up to follow her.

"I'm sorry if I caused you any embarrassment, Marc," Fred said as they walked away. "But I think you might have done the same."

Ingram didn't hear Marc reply and she didn't look back to see if he'd acknowledged Fred silently. But Fred was evidently still talking to Marc and not talking to her.

"Well, that went swimmingly," Marc said when they were clear of the gates. "It's only taken us five and a bit months to fall out with the natives."

"They're not the natives." Ingram strode ahead, trying not to look as if she was storming off. Marc matched her pace. "But I admit that fiasco was my fault. When there's no scope for meaningful punishment, it just becomes an argument."

"Do you think he's getting worse?"

Ingram thought of how charming and open Fred used to be. "I liked him better when he spoke pidgin English and said exactly what was on his mind. But he's really changed recently."

"Familiarity breeding contempt, or deterioration? Who knows?"

"Jeff Aiken," Ingram said. "*He'll* know."

"Maybe the meds are the problem."

"It's a thought." Ingram now had another list of things to fix. "I'm going to tell Devlin not to hold the shuttle if the teeriks don't turn up for work today. Do we need to convene Joint Command for that?"

Marc shook his head. "I'd expect Devlin to do that anyway."

"May I interrupt?" Solomon asked. "Commander Devlin is indeed aware of that and she won't wait."

"Sorry, Sol, I'm so miffed that I forgot to ask you," Ingram said.

"It's no problem, Captain. This will blow over."

Ingram wished she had his confidence. But the other teeriks seemed fine, as Searle had pointed out, so perhaps it was just a case of dealing with an old chap who'd stumbled into a position of leadership with Caisin's death and was still finding his way in a world where he was free to make big decisions, even bad ones.

And I might have made a major balls-up by responding to the Jattans. Which he'll never let me forget.

"I'm going to come clean and tell people exactly what happened," she said.

Marc *hmmmed.* "Everything?"

"Everything. I'll be diplomatic, but I need people to know that Fred gave FTL to Britain for his own reasons, against our wishes."

Marc looked like he was thinking it over. "Yeah, but remember some people won't believe you anyway. I'm Nomad's Most Wanted already because of the Fiji trip."

"I'll only worry if Kill Line takes it badly," Ingram said. "Not because I fear them, but because they're a barometer of common sense."

Marc checked his watch, calculating. He still wore his special forces issue timepiece. Every twelve Opis days, Opis time synced up with Earth's, but the date diverged by another day, and he tracked the divergence in much the same way that he'd known how long ago his sons had been killed, down to the day. Ingram just knew he was going to try to do the same when the base switched over to the new Opis year.

"Well, remember to run it past the guys first," he said. "Otherwise they'll think we've staged a coup and they'll dump our tea in the river. Anyway, it's pizza night tomorrow. Come round if you like."

"Deal," she said.

"Actually, you might as well move in, seeing as you're eating me out of house and home. You can't live in one room above the shop forever. Unless you think you're going to get a better offer, of course. Or a better house."

It was the kind of invitation she'd have expected to surprise her, but it felt more like being offered a refuge after a long and harrowing journey. She was relieved she didn't have to wonder where the relationship was going. But that was Marc all over. He never minced his words.

"I face a limited supply of suitable men, so I suppose I'd better stake my claim before all the best ones are taken," she said, trying not to be too breathlessly girly about it and ruin her warrior-queen image. "It's not as if I'll meet a charming stranger on the bus, is it?"

"Have you even been on a bus? Didn't you travel in a sedan chair borne by the local peasantry?"

"I couldn't always drive, you know."

"Ah, chauffeur's day off. I get it. Okay, see you later."

This was the kind of thing people did in a war before they deployed. Decisions that should have taken weeks or months of careful consideration in peacetime were condensed into days, sometimes even minutes when premature mortality loomed. Ingram had regretted rash choices in the past, but for all the things she didn't yet know about Marc, she knew everything that truly mattered. He was her only peer within forty light years. He was also the only man she could see herself growing old with rather than growing apart from. They understood each other and the grim necessities required of them, and nothing she'd done would ever shock him.

What was Howie going to make of all this, though? She'd have to talk to him. The poor little chap's last memories of being in a family home were the stuff of nightmares. Perhaps he wouldn't want her hanging around and reminding him of what he'd lost.

Jeff passed her on the stairs. "How did it go, ma'am?"

"Fred, you mean?" Ingram shook her head. "We've pulled their external comms until I'm sure this won't happen again."

"Oh. That bad."

"You know Fred better than anyone, Chief. He's taking the line that we don't know what we're doing and he does. Totally unapologetic. But if it's anything other than that, I'd like to know."

Jeff was very good at divining what she meant. "On it, ma'am."

Euphemism failed her when she sat down at her desk. When it came to writing her announcement, it was harder to word than she expected. It sounded exactly what it was, a plea not to be blamed for doing something she'd sworn *not* to do, because an alien did it and ran away. She tried again.

'Message to: Nomad Base residents.

Access to terrestrial entertainment was suspended overnight and is now being resumed. I apologise for the inconvenience. But I would rather tell you the embarrassing truth than let rumour inflate the incident, so this is why the link to the Earth relay was shut down. The FTL blueprints that were being held for distribution to selected organisations on Earth when it was safe to do so were sent prematurely and without authorisation to the British government by one of the teeriks. As a result of this, I have restricted the commune's comms access for the time being to prevent further mistakes of this nature. I want to reassure you that this makes very little difference to the timing of further settlement that has already been discussed, and it doesn't jeopardise the security of Nomad Base. No other government has received data. I would ask those of you who come into contact with the teeriks to be mindful of the cultural differences in appropriate behaviour and to understand they believed they were helping us.'

"That's a rather elegant lie, Captain," Solomon said in her earpiece. "But it needed to be told."

Ingram was still surprised by how she'd come to accept Solomon monitoring everything she did. It had horrified her when she emerged from cryo to find the mission was being run by a banned AI who was fully autonomous and couldn't be shut down. She wasn't sure if her acceptance was proof of her pragmatic flexibility or a sign of giving up.

"It's a reason that looks like a feeble excuse, Sol, but it beats letting people find out piecemeal and magnifying it into a British plot to take over the galaxy." She tapped the screen and sent the draft to Chris, Trinder, Searle, and Alex. "Especially as Tim Pham thought that was exactly what was happening."

"You were rather gracious about Fred under the circumstances."

"I can hardly say I want to wring his neck and use his feathers to stuff a duvet."

"It'll be obvious in private conversation, though."

Ingram didn't have long to wait for the responses from the other members of Joint Command. They were all okay with the message, although Trinder had added a note: *"Next time there's a crisis during silent hours, please wake me."*

"See, even mild-mannered Dan's bollocking me now," she said. "Any good news?"

"All the teeriks due to work on vessels have turned up as normal."

"Really? Well, we still feed them, I suppose, so self-interest prevails. Not Fred, though."

"No. But then he's been working back here for a while anyway."

"I've asked Jeff to see what can be done about him."

"You mustn't worry about this, Captain. You've kept your end of the bargain."

"I don't think that'll feature in any judgement on me somehow."

"Your crew will understand the situation hasn't changed, and those Ainatio personnel who *don't* understand are for me to deal with."

Coming from Sol, that sounded ominous. Ingram decided not to ask him to expand on it and focused on what she needed to do this morning. She'd spend more time walking the course today to see how her message had been received. Yet again she was in that no man's land between responsibility for the base and reliance on goodwill for her share of the authority to carry it out.

"What time is it in London, Sol?"

"It's nine fifty-seven."

"Better talk to Lawson, I suppose. Could you call the number for me, please?"

"Right away, Captain."

Ingram hadn't had a conversation with anyone from the government for a long time, and as far as she could recall, never at this level. But all she had to do was touch base with Lawson, explain how awkward things had been and how far from Bednarz's plan the mission had strayed by the time the crew was revived, and ask him to await further updates. The trick was to do it with the right language and avoid the kind of detail that he seemed very adept at analysing for gaps. She waited, rehearsing key lines, but Lawson responded right away just as he had with Marc. Given his seniority, she was surprised, but it seemed to be a private number, and he probably gave it to so few people that any call would be the kind he'd interrupt meetings to take.

"Captain Ingram," Lawson said. "It was a very pleasant surprise to find you were still alive."

"Not half as pleasant as it was for me, Sir Guy. Have I interrupted anything?"

"Nothing that can't wait."

"I'm sorry I didn't make contact before," Ingram said. "When we were revived from cryo, we didn't find the world quite the same as we left it. And Ainatio had blocked our comms to Earth because they needed us to stay dead."

"Were you aware Ainatio was going to use that as a cover story?"

"No, and we weren't best pleased. Friends and family went to their graves thinking we were dead, so some of my crew want to talk to old friends while they still can, but you can imagine the security problems." Ingram was thinking of the Caisin gate, but she hoped Lawson would take it as a general point about Pham's determination to scuttle Nomad any way he could. "I have fifteen APS nationals in the ship's company. Even the most loyal personnel can let information slip accidentally."

"And are they really all loyal?" Lawson asked. "I can't avoid asking about the Ainatio scientist who spread die-back in Korea. I assume you know about her."

"We have access to news satellites, so we do." There was no harm in telling Lawson. If Nomad had FTL, it wouldn't be credible to claim it didn't have comms to match. "When we heard about it, we locked down the base, ran a biohaz search, and interrogated all Ainatio staff in case Abbie Vincent wasn't an isolated malcontent. We're still monitoring them."

"That must put quite a strain on morale."

"Time will tell."

"I hope the settlement's in good shape."

"Overall, yes, it's going well." Ingram knew exactly what Marc meant when he said that talking with Lawson was a tightrope act, never knowing if he knew more than he let on. "But Bednarz's mission plan didn't survive contact with events. The base is a miracle of automated construction, but we weren't set up for an immediate influx of colonists from Earth — which you know about — so we have food security concerns. And we're still coming to terms with local conditions, which also aren't what we expected."

"And they are?"

"Sir Guy, if I sound evasive or all over the charts, it's because we really weren't prepared for what we found here. In time, you'll understand why my first act when Ainatio ceased to exist wasn't to call and hand you the keys. There's a lot to resolve."

"May I just check I've got the facts straight?" Lawson asked. Ingram had already learned it was his terribly polite way of easing into a cross-examination. "*Cabot* didn't have instant comms when she launched because the development of the technology happened while you were in transit, yes?"

"Correct."

"But she didn't have FTL propulsion, either, hence waking up to find you were officially dead."

"Also correct." Ingram could now guess where this was heading. "It took us forty-five years to reach Opis."

"You know what I'm trying to make sense of, don't you?"

"I think so."

"The FTL technology — the one that drives ships, not the instant comms — became available *after* you reached Opis but *before* you evacuated the Americans. If it's not Ainatio's technology, then, whose is it and how did you acquire it?"

"All I can tell you at the moment is that it's not ours, but we have use of it."

"Perhaps you could give me some idea of your difficulties in more neutral terms, then."

"The base is complete and we've got adequate supplies, which was a massive operation in itself," Ingram said carefully. "But we haven't been able to bring some Ainatio scientists and their families out of cryo yet. That's just over a thousand people still in their ship and orbiting Opis, including children. We had to evacuate a complete town in under twenty-four hours, and we don't yet have the two-year food stockpile to buffer us against failed harvests. Life's relatively comfortable for the time being, but it's completely unpredictable."

"And this is because *Elcano* — I have the name right, don't I? — was the ship that Georgina Erskine took when APS was about to purge the die-back-infected area with nuclear weapons. And that predates your acquisition of FTL by a couple of weeks, by my calculation. And now the ship's orbiting Opis?"

Of course Lawson knew. From the moment Marc had to use his contacts to get Annis Kim's call through to Pham, Ainatio's comms were being monitored by the UK.

"Correct," Ingram said, ignoring the tail of that question. "I'm reassured to see Kingdom is still giving the British taxpayer good value for money on the intel front."

"Are you fully in control of the base?"

Ingram had to interpret that. Who did he think the adversary was? Americans? If he mentioned aliens, she'd have to tell him now, but until then, she'd hold back.

"I want to bring you up to speed," she said. "But I can't do it yet because some work's required to brief you properly. There's also concern here about APS agents getting hold of information. Let's be realistic. They have spies in London just as you have spies over there. We have a very unfortunate history with APS, as you've noticed, and they have scores to settle."

"At the moment," Lawson said, "the only people who know about these FTL plans are a *very* small team in defence research and the Permanent Secretary at the MoD. The Foreign Office is considerably smaller and less influential than it was in your day, Captain, because there's far less *foreign* left for us to deal with at this stage of the Decline. But the advantage is that I don't have quite so many politicians breathing down my neck. It's purely luck that put me in this seat because Marc's point of contact to reach APS was here rather than the MoD. I just need to work out the importance of deep space to Britain. Is it a viable alternative to preserve this nation, Captain, or is it a threat?"

"It could be either. We're assessing other planets too."

"Yes, Marc implied we'd want to steer clear of Opis. Are you able to explain that? I have a ludicrous idea in my head, but I'm a grown man, so I can't bring myself to say it."

Ingram's first reaction was that she realised this was about intelligent aliens, but he might just have meant some horror movie scenario of plagues from outer space. She had to play it safe for the time being.

"All I can say at this stage is that if you do manage to complete the ship and you plan to send a mission, you might be better off on another terrestrial-type planet," she said. "And there are some close matches, I'm told. I'm sorry to be so oblique, but the engineer who contacted you wasn't supposed to release this yet. He's put us all in a difficult position."

Lawson was silent for a while. "The *yet* reassures me." He paused. "Are you able to return to Earth at all?"

"In theory, yes." Ingram thought it was a non-sequitur, but Lawson might have been wondering if they still needed a safe haven. Maybe they would. "But we're fine here for the time being."

"And you or Marc will brief me at some point and make sense of all this. Because some aspects baffle me. Not that we're ungrateful for this extraordinary asset, but when I have to tell my political masters, I'll be asked questions. A *lot* of questions."

"We will when we can, Sir Guy."

Ingram thought she'd already given Lawson too much to speculate about, but she couldn't tell him everything was going fine and have him make plans based on that. Once she told him about the assorted aliens and the risk of being attacked or sucked into their conflicts, he might well think it was too high-risk, and the problem of holding Earth at arm's length would solve itself. But she knew that was wishful thinking. There were too many good reasons to look for habitable worlds and now Britain seemed to have a foothold on one of them, informally at least.

"I'll wait, then," Lawson said. "Thank you. I realise this situation is unprecedented in human history. Forgive my scattergun curiosity."

"And again, my apologies for the delay in making contact."

"Is there anything at all that I can do to help you?"

"It's an awfully long way to send tea."

"I realise you're in a tight spot. I've seen your service record and you're hardly the type to make a fuss about minor inconveniences."

This was ridiculous. All Ingram's instincts were telling her that it was far too late to keep secrets.

"I'm going to take time out to consult my colleagues," she said. "As we weren't expecting the technology to be shared with you so soon, we've got issues to iron out. I want to tell you more, but I'm also aware that what we tell you will also become a liability for you."

Lawson did his usual few seconds of silence before responding. "If it affects the security of Britain, then I'll have to live with that, Captain."

"Thank you," Ingram said. "I'll get back to you as soon as I have something concrete to add."

The icon on Ingram's monitor went red and the call ended. She bent over and rested her forehead on the desk, resisting the urge to bang it a few times.

Caisin gate. Caisin gate. Caisin gate.

The idea should never have crossed her mind, but now that it had, it kept circling back to make sure she knew it was still waiting for her to do something with it. The gate could be deployed on Earth for Britain to put an end to the threat of invasion once and for all. She wasn't sure how yet, but she knew its potential, and then she could finish the task she'd cut short all those years ago. Nobody would have to abandon Earth. Die-back hadn't attacked every edible crop, just the four major ones, and overdependence and political insanity had done the rest. If only the surviving nations could catch their breath and stop brawling in the lifeboat, Earth could recover faster. Staying home had to be safer than venturing out among hostile aliens.

No, that was daft. If governments had the sense to do that, they'd have done it a long time ago and the situation would never have imploded. The technology was luring her into bad decisions, exactly as Chris and Marc had warned. And there was one factor she kept overlooking in all this — Solomon. He had a mission and he showed no signs of deviating from it. It was such a clear, uncomplicated task that it left no room for mission creep.

"Sol," she said. "If — and I do mean if — refugees from Earth had to come to Opis, would you have conditions?"

"You know I would, Captain." Solomon sounded relaxed rather than irritated, but it was probably because he was never going to concede. "They'd have to pass vetting, because Nomad has no purpose if we import the old problems again. Unless those refugees were a good fit for the existing population, and that population approved of them, then I wouldn't accept them."

It was said politely and logically, a reasonable reply to a hypothetical question. Selecting people with the right stuff and protecting them was the reason for Solomon's existence. There was no way he would change his mind and no way to force him, so he was the one who'd decide how this played out.

Ingram stopped short of asking what not accepting migrants would actually translate to in the physical world. She knew how he'd dealt with APS. He also seemed to have marked Fred's card.

"You're going to have to tell Lawson about the aliens soon, Captain," he said. "It might even have a salutary effect."

Sol was right — again. But then there'd just be the Caisin gate left to surrender, and Opis would become an extension of Earth rather than a new world in its own right. Was that what people here wanted? Handing control to a civilian government when the settlement was ready, the original plan, was tempting but for all the wrong reasons. Ingram had no guarantee the government that eventually arrived would be British and not APS. She'd seen how fast nations could simply cease to exist.

But Opis was home now. There were people who'd probably opt to go back to Earth if they could, but if she'd read the Kill Liners right, they'd come to see the settlement as a small country worth fighting for, a chance to make a life free of the destructive regimes that had caused misery for billions. Ingram was as caught up in it now as they were. She didn't want to surrender Nomad to anyone, not even her own tribe, but she didn't want to see Britain fall like America had either, and there had to be a way of reconciling those two positions.

"I agree, Lawson needs to know who else is out here," she said. "I'll talk it through with the others. What a load to dump on the poor man. He gets to hear the biggest news in human history whether he's ready for it or not."

"But we took it rather well."

"That we did, Sol." Ingram tried to focus on the promise of pizza and an instant family. All the technology in the universe wouldn't preserve humanity if it forgot the basics of being human. "That we did."

* * *

CO'S OFFICE, MAIN BUILDING: 1520 HOURS, LATER THAT DAY.

Trinder zoned out of Ingram's meeting for a moment and couldn't quite recall why it had been so important until now to avoid telling Earth about the aliens.

Shutting APS out of Nomad and anything associated with it was a given. Whatever Ingram told Lawson and Lawson had to tell someone else might eventually end up in Pham's in-tray, and what Lawson didn't know couldn't be extracted from a bugged communications channel. But it didn't seem like a line worth holding now. Lawson had to know there was the biggest problem in history before his political masters started making plans to explore deep space.

And Pham was sure he already knew the truth. He'd think that intercepted talk of aliens was there to throw him off the scent.

Ingram had called the broader Joint Command group together this time, including Doug Brandt, who was equally powerless to do anything about the situation. Maybe she just wanted to reassure him she hadn't imposed a military dictatorship. She looked around the room, working left to right, and settled her gaze on Trinder.

"Well, gentlemen?"

Trinder's tactic when admitted to Erskine's meetings at Ainatio had been to say nothing until he was forced to, and then to say as little as he could as blandly as possible. But the inner Trinder had finally broken loose, the one who had plenty of opinions and enjoyed the novelty of saying "No" more than any toddler.

"Just tell Lawson everything," he said. "Brits aren't the enemy, but even if they were, we can't stop them building a ship, and we can't stop them landing, either. We can't blockade the entire planet. But even if we could, are we seriously going to shoot them down or something? Warning them what's really out here is the right thing to do. It also stops them blundering in here and putting us at risk."

"That's if they listen," Chris said. "But does anyone here remember what all of us said a month ago? It was pretty much the opposite of what we're saying now."

"Circumstances change," Ingram said. "Fred changed them."

"Dan, does your everything include the Caisin gate?" Alex asked. "I'm a civilian moron, but even I know we need to hold our ace. And not look so ripe for pillage."

"I don't know." Trinder shook his head. "It's what Chris said, I suppose. A month ago, yes, we were all saying the complete opposite. I still think we should keep the gate quiet, though, because it's such a magnet for any wrong 'uns."

Marc was staring out of the window, but he nodded. "Yeah, hold that in reserve. We're the only wrong 'uns who get to play with it until further notice."

"Besides, we're not the galactic peace police." Alex fidgeted with his glasses, cleaning the lenses with a scrap of cloth that looked like it had been cut out of a pair of boxers. "The only reason we should worry about who gets hold of it is how it impacts our own safety."

Trinder kept trying to imagine what making full use of the gate meant in real terms. Most folks in Nomad, whether they admitted it or not, had considered all the things they could do with an instant walk-in portal to anywhere, ranging from the entertaining and humanitarian to the downright criminal. Gallagher's Rules applied. As Marc kept reminding them, anything new would eventually be used for the worst possible purpose, one it was never intended for. And there was some very bad stuff to be done with a Caisin gate. They were counting on that if they got into difficulties with Kugad.

"But we've made the gate hard to seize, haven't we, Sol?" Trinder asked. "So even if people find out, they can't necessarily access it. There's knowing about it and then there's doing something about it."

"It's still an asshole magnet," Chris said. "If not now, then later."

Solomon ignored Chris's aside. "As long as Fred doesn't find a way to share the details with anyone else and enable them to build their own, it's easy for me to put it out of action if I have to."

Sol always had a plan. He'd obviously thought through how to destroy the gate as well as how to operate it without teerik assistance, and he'd certainly have a contingency for saving humans from themselves if they made dangerously bad decisions. For some reason, Trinder was fine with Sol doing that, but not Fred.

"What if we need to destroy it permanently?" he asked. "Just hypothetical. You know, if we decide it's so dangerous that the universe needs to forget it ever happened. And the teeriks know how it works."

"We've discussed that before," Solomon said. "We either keep them absolutely secure in perpetuity or we terminate them."

Trinder wondered when that was going to sound routine. He knew he could measure his humanity by how long it continued to make him squirm. "You know how it works as well, Sol. More or less."

"If your survival depended on erasing all records and knowledge of the gate, then I would erase it from my memory as well, or even terminate myself." Solomon sounded like he meant it. "But what can be invented once will probably be invented again. So it's best to regard any asset denial as temporary, even if that means centuries."

"Then why are we bothering to conceal it at all? It's why we can't let anybody call Earth. Except us, of course, and that's causing another morale problem."

"It's to save our own asses in the present," Chris said. "We can't manage the future beyond the next couple of years, and maybe not even that. Right now, we don't need to attract scavengers."

Ingram folded her arms and looked like she was getting impatient. "Okay, let me play devil's advocate," she said. "We thought we'd be overwhelmed by numbers if we offered to resettle people and just opened the gate. But now we're going down the FTL ship path, which requires investment and resources at the other end, we'll get an official advance party. Troops. Scientists. Government officials. Geologists who won't be coming to admire the fossils and cave formations. This is a virgin planet loaded with unmined treasure. They'll assess Opis for its commercial and strategic value to Earth — well, to Britain, unless something goes horribly wrong and we get a visit from APS. In anticipation of that, then, I'd like to address the redcoatophobia that might be forming. We're not seeking to rebuild the British empire or slipping valuable tech to our mates. If you have even the slightest twinge when I say that, spit it out now."

"No, it's our fault for carelessly losing our country," Alex said. "You go, girl, as long as you don't make us eat Brussels sprouts. That'd mean war."

Doug looked concerned. "Captain, nobody's going to blame you for continuing to protect your national interests," he said. "If Bednarz wanted us to preserve Western civilisation, that's part of it. But we want clear demarcation lines because Kill Liners *aren't* British and we want our American way of life again. That's assuming the most extreme situation, of course, where your people turn up and try to run Nomad. But there's nothing to suggest they will. And they were ready to rescue us when we were just a bunch of farmers and out-of-date scientists who weren't worth much to them. I think that indicates the kind of people we're dealing with."

Marc, still staring out of the window, chuckled to himself but said nothing. Ingram ignored him and carried on.

"I signed up to prepare an independent settlement here for a civilian government to take over," she said. "We never set out expecting to have real-time contact with Earth. It's easier to build a new society if you don't have the old country at the end of a comms link for instant reference, but there's bound to be nationalism here and that's a good thing. It's when we try to enforce conformity where none naturally exists where we run into trouble."

"We could have a British sector and an American sector so far apart that we never see each other," Alex said. "But that's assuming they want to come here."

"Yeah, and we might have identified another planet for them by then," Trinder said. "But they might just say thanks for the technology and the intel and head for some other planet they earmarked years ago."

"Or they might not be able to source the raw materials for the FTL drive and they never leave Earth," Searle said.

Chris shrugged. "Pretty sure we've got everything they need here, actually."

"Meaning?"

"How long before we need something *they've* got?"

"We're trying to keep our distance from Earth, not foster interstellar trade," Searle said.

"But they'll ask. I sure would. We'll need an answer ready."

Ingram interrupted silently with a glance. It was amazing how she could do that. "One problem at a time, gents. Okay, to speed things up, does anyone think we *shouldn't* tell Lawson everything, Caisin gate excepted?"

Chris raised a forefinger. "Yes. Don't mention the teerik probes in Earth orbit, either, or at least how capable they are."

"He knows we have relays in place, or we wouldn't be talking. I don't think he cares if we're stealing sat TV."

"No, but he'll be very interested if we tell him we can place mobile surveillance almost anywhere without much risk of being spotted."

"Good point." Ingram nodded. "We haven't gone into detail about it. He's got all the Ainatio instant comms data, so he probably thinks we're using that."

"I'm not worried about him wanting to acquire it," Chris said. "I just want the means to check things out for ourselves without being obstructed. It's like the gate. Once you know someone's got that technology, even if you haven't, you can plan around it and reduce its effectiveness in some ways."

"Indeed."

"And another thing."

"Okay."

"Don't let Fred do the technical liaison. The more he talks to Lawson's boffins, the more dangerous it gets. If they have technical issues, get Cosqui. She's as competent as Fred, she likes Brad, which is a point we can lever, and she thinks Fred's a loose cannon."

"Yes, I've noticed," Ingram said. "Brad, is she up to it?"

"Sure." Searle nodded. "And she likes to be told she's doing a good job. Because nobody ever told her before. So yeah, if we need to, I'll get her to do it and sit in on the sessions."

"I'm reassured."

Marc wasn't saying much. Perhaps he didn't like home following him across the galaxy for the same reason he hadn't gone back to Britain. But he'd been the one who'd first said Nomad might have some responsibility to help Earth simply because it could. That summed up the problem, though. Everyone here wanted to do the decent thing but there was a downside to every act of generosity, and at the heart of it was a bunch of people who'd gotten used to life without government, a life on a tribal scale where they made their own rules. They liked it that way. Trinder certainly did. He'd reinvented himself and he didn't want to go back to the way things had been.

"Well, we've still got a few years to iron things out," Doug said. "Nobody knows what's going to happen here, let alone on Earth. But as you said, now they can build an FTL vessel, it's only fair to warn them what they'll find out here. That applies whether they venture into space or not, because the Kugin could head for Earth."

"People assess risk differently when there's profit and military advantage involved," Chris said. "And some diplomat or scientist is bound to want to try to make contact with Kugad or the Jattans without us playing gatekeeper. We need to dissuade them."

"I think Lawson's aware of that," Marc said. "He'd have passed the ball to the politicians by now if he hadn't. Let's see what he says to the basic shock news package before we give him any add-ons."

"Okay, but how do we explain why we're not inviting them over right away to see what we've done with the place?" Trinder asked. "They think we used FTL drives to get here and they now know that's only a few weeks' flight time, so the round trip could be made immediately. If I were them, I'd ask you to come and pick up a recon party to pay a visit. I can't imagine any government *not* wanting to do that. This is the biggest event in human history. Proof of aliens. New worlds for humanity in the nick of time. You know how it goes."

"Yeah, we're already out of excuses," Chris said. "Lawson knows we can't revive everyone in *Elcano* because of the food situation, but if he just wants to send a small party with their own supplies, how do we justify refusing? And what if he says no problem, we'll help out with pallets of extra supplies when you send a ship?"

"We simply tell him the truth about why we don't want them here for the foreseeable future," Ingram said. "Not just food, but the awkward stuff about aliens, tensions within Nomad, getting the governance right, and the whole point of the mission, however unpalatable Bednarz's philosophy might sound to outsiders."

"I'll talk to him," Marc said. "But that's mission creep right there. Tensions and governance issues. Are those now part of our official reason for keeping *Elcano* on ice?"

"No. It's just that we don't have to face those issues on top of everything else." Ingram cocked her head slightly as if she thought that was out of order. "Anyway, I told Lawson I'd call back after we'd had a chance to talk."

"Fine, but I'll do it. If only to keep my story straight."

Trinder read that as a low-key wrangle over who managed the liaison. Marc didn't seem to treat Ingram any more deferentially now they were an item. She blinked for a moment, looking more amused than offended, then smiled.

"Oh, he's got a man-crush on you because you're special forces," she said. "You can get away with more than I can."

Chris ploughed on, typically undistracted. "I'm going to be a whiny little bitch and raise another problem."

"Oh, that's not like you, Chris," Ingram said sweetly.

"I know. I like to surprise you. Dan mentioned the radio blackout. *We* all know we didn't want Fred to take a dump on our careful plans, but it's not going to look that way to all the folks who still can't call home and who are building up a righteous head of steam about us going back for Tev. It's not even about failing to go back for the Ainatio contingent who opted to stay. It's *perception*. It looks like a Brit stitch-up to take over the project. How long can we keep up the embargo? Not forever, that's for sure. And do we keep it in place for everyone until then just so APS folk don't feel hard done by?"

Trinder almost wished the gate had never happened. Although they owed their lives to it, he'd always realised it would be a liability, like wearing a big gold designer watch in the rough end of town. They had full-on regular FTL now, journeys slashed from decades to weeks, so if they suddenly lost the gate it wouldn't make much difference to Nomad's day-to-day activity. But that ability to join two points in space, seamlessly and silently, could do so much more of the things necessary in emergencies they couldn't yet imagine. Now they'd experienced just a fraction of what it could do, it'd be very hard to go back to relying on ships.

Would we have the backbone to trash it on moral grounds? Really?

Trinder didn't need a test of character when they still had real-world problems like Kugad and the Protectorate. He knew he wouldn't destroy the gate if the choice was his. It gave him a glimmer of awareness of how it felt to be the research scientist who thought he'd done the world a good turn by developing a heritable weed-killing gene for grain crops, and thought nothing could possibly go wrong.

Or maybe it *had* been designed as a bioweapon all along. The truth was dead and buried and in the end there wasn't a whole lot of difference between planning genocide and just thinking you were too clever to cause it by making a dumb, obvious mistake.

"We keep an eye on it and see how it goes," Marc said.

Trinder had forgotten what they'd been talking about. Ah, the calls ban. "It won't necessarily be the APS nationals who slip up," he said. "It could easily be us talking to someone whose pattern of association we just don't know about."

"Blimey, Dan, you've gone all policey," Marc said.

"Can't work with Luce for years without learning something."

"Anyway, what Lawson intends now might be very different from what happens a few years down the road when the politicians have drawn all over it with crayons, but how he reacts to the general news is going to give us a clue about the direction policy's going in."

"Do you trust him, Marc?" Searle asked.

"As much as I trust any arm of the government. But they've got more skin in the game than you think. Who's APS going to target first if they find out about all this? Not us — Britain. Lawson's got a lot to lose as well."

"Okay, it sounds like we're done," Ingram said. "We tell Lawson about everything except the gate and exactly what the probes can do. We'll worry about those when the time comes. The calls ban remains for everyone until we know more."

But Trinder wasn't done. The whole discussion had been like pulling a loose thread. Yes, the gate was a problem, but not having to hide the existence of aliens and advanced FTL made other things possible.

"Captain, before we go, I want to talk about *Elcano*," he said. "There's no reason now why we can't send her back to Earth, is there? Lawson's going to know about the Kugin threat and he already knows about the FTL."

"For safety reasons, you mean?" Ingram asked. "Put her back in Earth orbit?"

"Yes, it's safer, but no, not back in Earth orbit. Revive everybody when they get there."

Ingram frowned. "Including Erskine? Including everyone who knows that Sol's an ASD AI, a major threat to humanity like Earthmother, a pitiless slaughter machine and all that? Seriously?"

"I doubt Erskine's going to tell them when she's the one responsible for continuing the deception about him," Trinder said. "Anyway, Lawson knows what she did, but what can he do about Sol? Nothing."

Ingram raised an eyebrow. "Lawson's sharp enough to point out Sol's the same AI who fried Asia. But yes, he can't shut him down."

"Stick with the story," Marc said. "We told him to do it."

"You all agreed to it," Solomon said.

"And if we'd said no?" Ingram asked.

"Would you try to stop a comrade killing himself?"

Trinder was getting fed up. There was no easy answer to anything connected to Ainatio, Opis, or APS. It was about weighing risks at a particular moment. He'd taken that advice to heart.

"Look, they can't touch Sol, but a couple of hundred kids could end up vaporised," he said. "Sending *Elcano* home is the easiest option, but neither choice is perfect. The problem is that they're in cryo. That's what makes them vulnerable, not being in orbit. They'd be vulnerable even if we kept everyone in cryo down here. You can move a single ship fast, but if we came under attack, evacuating a thousand or so unconscious people from a facility is going to be slower even with a gate. We keep them in *Elcano* for a fast getaway."

"We couldn't build a cryo facility on the base at the moment anyway, not without stopping other essential construction," Ingram said. "Bots and materials are fully committed. It'd also compromise evacuating Kill Line if we needed to."

"So you agree, Captain."

"On that point alone, yes."

Chris was nodding to himself. "If the Kugin decide to zap us from orbit, and take out the base, everyone's dead. If we leave *Elcano* in orbit, and we're charcoal, what happens to the folks in cryo? *Elcano*'s marooned. They're better off a few trillion miles away instead of being abandoned in the freezer when nobody knows they're here."

"But Lawson will know," Solomon said. "And if I survived such an attack, I would send the ship home anyway."

Just occasionally, Trinder was reminded who was really running the mission, and it wasn't Joint Command. He turned to Alex. Technically, Alex was the last CEO of Ainatio. Alex began polishing his glasses again.

"They're your people, Alex," Trinder said. "And I know we're all dreading Erskine being revived and the arguments starting, but I'm genuinely not suggesting this just as a way to avoid that."

"Wow, lots to unpick there," Alex said, not looking up. "Okay, they'll be out of harm's way, or at least less likely to be fried unless APS declares war on Britain. Wherever they're kept, they can't self-evacuate, so that makes our job harder. We can't build a cryo facility here without compromising something else. But if we decided to do that, it'd just make my people pile on more pressure to revive them early. It'd be the 'They're here now so why not' argument. And Lawson's going to know pretty well everything, so what's the point in not involving him?" Alex held his glasses up to the light to inspect them for smears and frowned. "We're still tied to Earth. Face it. As long as we can see and hear the motherworld, or even visit it, we're part of it and we have to factor it into decisions. There's no point in trying to avoid contact altogether. If we ship out our people still in cryo, they don't know about the Caisin gate, so that's one problem avoided for the time being."

"What if APS spots the activity?" Chris asked.

"You said Pham already thinks we've got a portal," Searle said. "He won't be convinced there isn't one either way. Everyone else will think *Elcano*'s journey was aborted to return home, if they detect her at all."

Ingram tapped her desk. "I don't want to get sucked into doing something purely because we'd feel irresponsible doing *nothing*."

"This is something we *can* do," Trinder said. "Neither Earth nor Opis is completely safe, but we save who we can, when we can, and that would apply even if the passengers weren't in cryo. Right, Chris?"

Chris nodded again. "The fewer people we have to protect in a fight, the better. Moving *Elcano* for a while gives us breathing space, even if Britain's on borrowed time. And the *Elcano* folk get a chance to hear about aliens and decide if they want to come back to Nomad at all."

Trinder had a feeling that he'd started the avalanche, and people were now trying to find more reasons to get *Elcano* out of their hair. Sol had scores to settle with Erskine too, and probably the IT department personnel who escaped with her. There were plenty of emotional motives swirling around. Trinder made an effort to block his out.

"If the very worst happens and the base is wiped out, but Sol survives and we've sent *Elcano* home, at least he can start over with Nomad," Trinder said. "It'll be different, but he's got the people to rebuild it."

"A few of them, yes," Solomon said.

Trinder admired Sol's single-mindedness, but his honesty could be awkward. "You weren't supposed to say that bit out loud, Sol."

"You know my mission briefing, Major."

"How can anyone tell that Sol's an actual banned type of AI, and not just a really high-grade normal one?" Doug asked. He'd been so quiet that Trinder had almost forgotten he was there. "Because I don't know how you identify this ASD thing. It's not like Sol's got a serial number stamped on him."

"Well, the entire management team in cryo knows," Alex said. "But I agree that for anyone who *doesn't* know already, even the other scientists, it's impossible to tell until Sol overrules every human decision."

"Which I have never done," Solomon said. "Although I have made mistakes about intervening, as Marc reminds me from time to time."

Ingram looked up at the security camera where everyone imagined Sol's disembodied intelligence to be. "Sorry, Sol, we're being very rude and talking about you as if you're not here."

"I'm not offended, Captain."

"Don't worry, Sol, we'd probably offer you a job, not try to shut you down," Marc said. Trinder noted the use of *we* but didn't judge. Of course it was *we*. It was dumb to read anything more into that than nationality. "But Lawson might already know. We spy on APS like they spy on us, and Pham can't keep this entirely to himself. A secret's a secret until you have to task someone else. Even if he's hiding everything of value from APS, he's still got at least one operator who knows what Sol really is."

"My opinion is that protecting me isn't necessary, and so it doesn't take precedence over the welfare of children," Solomon said. "Let's move on."

"Okay, how do we get them back to Earth?" Searle asked. "*Elcano*'s new drive isn't ready yet, let alone tested. We weren't planning to fire it up for real unless there was an emergency, and you don't run test flights with unconscious passengers. Tests go wrong. We'd have to revive everyone first, give them the option to disembark, and then you're back to square one with folks who know too much and might be persuaded to talk about it if they return to Earth."

Ingram meshed her fingers behind her head and leaned back in her seat. "How much testing do we need to send *Elcano* back under her own power?"

"Two hundred and forty-nine kids' worth. Fred says it's proven technology, but not for us it isn't. We're the ones building it, not some shipyard where it's routine. I'd be reluctant to sign off and send *Elcano* back on her own, even if Sol was driving."

"So we have to finish the drive anyway, or else some bright spark will ask how the ship got back to Earth so quickly without working propulsion," Ingram said. "MoD boffins know what a drive should look like now because they've seen the plans. But whatever we do, Earth gets a working FTL ship off the shelf. They could be back here in weeks."

Trinder could see all the red lines they'd thought were essential being erased an inch at a time, and he was pushing them further. They'd be sending Earth a ship it could deploy right away. He could see their resolve crumbling. Next they'd be working out how to phase an evacuation from Britain, and then every other nationality in Nomad would want their people rescued and brought to Opis as well. From there, everything would snowball and Earth would end up running the place, the kind of repetitive cycle of history that Bednarz had set out to change. Nomad should have stayed cut off for a couple of generations. Then they'd only have had to worry about surviving.

"We use the aliens as a smokescreen so we don't need to finish the drive, and just gate her there," Marc said. "We tell Lawson the aliens recovered her for us, and imply they have an FTL tug system to tow ships that can't generate their own power."

"Isn't he going to want to make use of that?"

"Yes, but he won't ask, because that's a bit pushy when you're dealing with aliens who can bend space and probably ruin your day. Besides, he's got plans for a ship that can get here in weeks. That'll be enough to keep everyone engrossed for a long time."

"Okay, so we gate Elcano back to Earth with a half-finished drive," Searle said. "If we place her spacefold exit point far enough from Earth for her re-entry to be unobservable, Lawson thinks an alien tug's brought her back, she moves into Earth orbit under her own subluminal power, the system revives the passengers starting with the medical team like it did with *Cabot*, and they shuttle down to the surface. That's the only way of disembarking. Then what? What do we do with *Elcano*?"

"Bring her back," Trinder said. "If Lawson's got the plans and a half-finished drive, you can bet the scientists will to want to finish it."

"Have they got the capacity to do construction in space?"

"We still maintain the Kingdom network," Marc said. "So maybe. And now I've told you, I'm supposed to kill you. But I can't be arsed today."

"Let's pause for a sec," Ingram said. "Sol, do *you* think we should evacuate *Elcano*? Putting children's safety above your own doesn't answer the question. I want to hear your personal opinion of whether it'll achieve the desired outcome."

Solomon often paused before answering to let humans catch up or to indicate some emotion he didn't express in his tone. He could have learned to use all the umms, ahhs, and sentiment of human speech long ago, but he seemed to have chosen not to. His pauses, though, added a lot. And this pause was very long for an AI, longer than Trinder had ever noticed, so long that Ingram frowned slightly and looked up to the camera again.

"Sol, are you still there?"

"I am, Captain. I'm just re-examining my motives."

"Take your time. I know it's very hard when it puts you at personal risk."

"It's not that. I wanted to be sure that my reasons weren't clouded by my mistrust and anger towards Director Erskine, not the fact that I might be outed."

"And?"

"I think it would be better to return the passengers to Earth for their own safety now that we can do that without compromising the mission, and to allow them to decide if they want to come back to Opis when they're made aware of all the facts. I just wanted to be certain I didn't rationalise a subconscious desire to avoid having Erskine around the base."

Alex chuckled. "You're not alone there, Sol."

"You can move on to the technicalities now," Ingram said.

Solomon carried on. "Lawson's people would need access to the ship to make use of it, which I could block via the system. And it's not unreasonable for us to say we want to bring *Elcano* back to complete her refit because we need all our assets in case of a Kugin attack. She's armed, remember. If they want to send some of their people back to Opis with the ship, we remind them that while Nomad mission personnel have been immunised against Opis-specific pathogens and have undergone adaptation, they haven't, and it could be dangerous for them to land here. But if we do decide to abandon

Elcano for the time being — which I'd be reluctant to do because of maintenance — they still can't go anywhere if I don't release the controls."

"It's funny how we don't even talk about the die-back risk now," Chris said. "When did that stop being a thing?"

"Add it to the list," Ingram said. "My, we're awfully good at building the big lie, aren't we?"

"Lawson might ask why we're not evacuating Kill Line's children as well," Doug said. "Will he believe we chose to stay?"

"You could speak to him directly if he doesn't, Doug." Ingram held up a finger. "But remember Marc's point that if we have a ship capable of reaching Earth in weeks, Lawson might suggest the ship could also collect supplies for Opis if things were that bad, and we could revive everyone in *Elcano* and they'd only be exposed to the same risks as Kill Line's families. So we'd have to have our excuses ready."

The discussion was at a tipping point. Trinder felt they were right on the cusp of suddenly saying to hell with it because there was no point in making things more complicated when there were aliens hunting for their stolen ship and they might reduce Nomad to rubble. Why not invite the British government to take over the whole project so everyone here could just get on with the day-to-day business of surviving?

"We cite personal choice," Marc said. "Bloody Americans being difficult again. Ainatio's not-quite-CEO and their head of security want their people evacuated, but the hardy farmers of Kill Line want to stand their ground. We can't force anything on foreign nationals."

"Actually, that's all true," Doug said.

"Bugger. I keep forgetting to lie."

And just like that, the discussion flipped the other way. They'd swept aside most of the objections. Maybe nobody wanted Erskine revived and they were the ones inventing a justification for marking her RETURN TO SENDER, not Solomon. But whatever the motives, this was the easiest in a range of difficult options. Trinder realized how much like a coin toss big decisions could be. That was probably how the highest level of political decision-making worked as well. Everyone could see only part of the puzzle. Everyone busked it. Everyone gambled, even cautious people like Marc and Chris, and once someone nodded, the rest followed suit as if agreeing on something proved it was the logical course of action.

"Okay, let's go with that." Ingram swirled the contents of her mug, staring into its depths as if she was looking for tea leaves to provide a sign. "If Lawson can't take evacuees, the decision's made for us and *Elcano* stays. If he agrees, then we've got a few weeks to work out the fine detail of the ship's magical appearance because he doesn't know we can move her instantly. We need to stick to what he thinks is a normal transit time for alien FTL."

"Are we going to consult the other Ainatio folk?" Searle asked.

"No, we're not," Ingram said. "We've made the call and we'll bear the responsibility."

It was a decision, and as she often said, any decision was always safer than dithering. Somebody would object, though.

"I hope I can remember all the detail," Marc muttered.

"I will," Solomon said. "I'll go through it with you."

Marc stood up. "Anyway, excuse me. I have a historic moment to plan. I'm going to scare the living piss out of Earth."

The meeting broke up. Trinder wandered off with Chris and watched discreetly to see where Ingram went. He imagined her catching up with Marc and demanding to know why he'd cut her out of the Lawson thing, but they peeled off in separate directions and Ingram waited for Doug to catch up to her. The two of them ambled off together, chatting.

"Are Marc and Ingram really dating?" Trinder leaned on the waist-high safety barrier that ran along the front of the main building. It was a warm summer afternoon despite the date. "He still sasses her in meetings."

"She likes it," Chris said. "It's a game."

"Well, as long as they're happy."

"Yeah."

"Anyway, Erin and I are getting married."

"Wow, you kept *that* quiet."

"I'm telling you now. I haven't even told Luce."

"Erin never said a word either."

Chris had always looked out for Erin like a big brother despite being almost the same age. Maybe he felt Trinder should have asked him for his kid sister's hand.

"We want to firm up arrangements before we announce it," Trinder said. "We still do. We'll make a big thing of it."

"Good. We need some celebrations here after all the funerals."

"Remember what we swore we'd do?"

"Maybe."

"You said we had to promise that if we made it out of Kill Line alive, we'd be normal guys with wives and kids and barbecues, because that was how humans were meant to live," Trinder said. "And we've done it, pretty much. Even Marc."

"Marc wasn't there at the time." Chris did remember, then. "And I don't think he's at the barbecue stage yet."

"Only a matter of time. And you're working on it."

"I'm giving it my best shot."

"I know. You can't go anywhere on Opis without someone noticing where your tracker is."

Chris almost cracked a smile. "I walk most places and I switch off my radio."

"We can be who we want to be now. That includes you. It's going to work out, Chris. Don't worry."

"Me and the Duchess of Drains?"

That confirmed Trinder's guess that he was pursuing Ashley Brice. "Opis generally," Trinder said. "But her as well."

"I'm just imagining how Erskine's going to feel when she comes around from cryo and realises she's back on Earth. That was our test, wasn't it?"

"What was?"

"The gate. Martin Berry says technology's a test of character. It removes the physical limits that stop us doing all kinds of bad shit, and the only limit to increasingly godlike and dangerous powers is our own moral restraint."

"We're fucked, then."

"You passed anyway."

Trinder wasn't so sure. His conscience just didn't have much of a load-bearing capacity. He avoided putting heavy weights on it, like when he left supplies and transport for the occupying APS troops stranded at Ainatio. It was a good deed nobody expected under the circumstances, but he only did it to minimise the chance of reprisal against the Ainatio staff who'd chosen to stay and to avoid the guilt if some teenage conscripts starved to death while waiting for extraction. A guy had to *want* to do good to be moral, not just stumble into virtue accidentally on the way to covering his own ass.

"For what it's worth, I don't believe Britain's thinking of invading," Trinder said. "They've got too many problems on Earth.

And Lawson's probably realised we can help them out at least as much as they can help us."

"Sure, but if the aliens don't get us first, APS or one of the other states will come for us eventually. We've inherited a lot of cool tech that normally belongs to global superpowers. We have to be smart about how we handle what we've got when we're still only a glorified village."

Trinder had thought a few hundred trillion miles would be enough separation from Earth to ensure a quiet life for decades, perhaps even centuries, until the Opis population had expanded enough to manufacture its own home-grown conflicts. But cutting the cord was always going to be hard and now they had no way of doing it.

Trinder just hoped Britain's FTL ship wouldn't launch until Nomad had dealt with the Kugin-Jattan problem and cleared some space in its busy diary.

* * *

UNIT D74, NOMAD BASE: 0940, SUNDAY, OCTOBER 25, OC.

"I need to go into the office for a few hours today, Howie," Marc said, checking the fridge for milk. "I'm on duty anyway. Are you going to be okay on your own for a while?"

Howie was busy topping and tailing runner beans at the kitchen table, frowning in concentration. "I've got lots to do."

"Any problems, give me a call."

"You're worried about something, aren't you? I can tell. Is Tev okay? I thought he'd visit us."

"He's still sorting out his new house."

"Have I done something wrong?"

"Good Lord, no. Never." Marc believed in telling Howie the truth, no matter how boring and adult the situation, so that he could understand Marc's mood and know that it wasn't anything he'd done. "I mean, telling a bloke that aliens are real. That's serious."

"We didn't get upset about it."

"Yeah, but you transit camp lot are tough." Marc closed the fridge and noted the necessary supplies to acquire. "How about roast chicken for lunch?"

Howie tidied the prepared beans into a pile. They were all the exact same length, like they'd been trimmed by an obsessive chef. "Are you sure you can cook a chicken?"

"I think so."

"Okay."

"We ought to invite Ingram."

"She wants you to call her Bridget, not Ingram."

"Yes or no?"

"Yes. She's funny. She always makes things sound like a joke."

"How would you feel if she spent more time here with us?"

Howie took even more intense interest in the beans. "You mean like staying here."

"Yeah. I'm checking it's okay with you. I know you're still upset with me about the Fiji trip and I don't want to make things worse."

"I'm not upset with you," Howie said. "I'm scared you're going to go away and not come back."

There was no way around that argument. Marc knew he'd end up putting the kid through this every time something necessary had to be done, but the root cause had been slow to dawn on him because he didn't want to see it. There were increasingly competent troops like Chris who could take his place as an operator and there was no reason for him to be on the front line every time, but accepting that felt like retirement, and retirement was the last station on the line before death. On the plus side, it was the first time he'd felt he wasn't already dead since he'd lost his boys, let alone worried about dying, which meant he had something worth living for again. He was responsible for Howie. It had become his defining purpose, no matter how hard he'd tried to avoid it and how ill-advised he thought it would be for Howie.

"I'm sorry, Howie. I honestly didn't expect things to turn out the way they did in Fiji. You can say no about Ingram and that'll be fine."

"Is she going to *live* with us?"

Marc had brought this on himself again. He'd given Howie the casting vote but Ingram had somehow brought him back to some semblance of being alive. It was a case of his needs or Howie's. He'd hoped Ingram would be good for both of them.

"Only if you want her to," he said. "It's not like she's miles away, so we see each other all the time anyway. But you were here first, which is why I'm asking."

Howie did an indignant *humph.* "I'm not a little kid. You want her to live here and you'll get married."

Marc had no idea what to say. He didn't want to make Howie feel pressured into agreeing to it when the kid was still raw about what he'd lost and afraid of what he could still lose. He'd had this thing about living on his own because he didn't want a substitute family, so just sharing space with Marc must have taken an effort. Now he might think he was having a replacement mum foisted on him.

"You don't have to decide now."

"It's okay." Howie gave him that worryingly adult look, the forty-year-old who wished he hadn't seen it all. "But she's got to do chores just like us."

"Damn straight," Marc said. "No pulling rank."

"You'll be happy, and she won't have to live in her office."

"That's the general idea. Maybe we'll all be happy."

"Okay."

"You've still got a veto, though."

"What's a veto?"

"The right to say no."

"Okay. I'm not saying no."

Marc had started to remember how kids could do an about-turn like that in an instant. "See you later, then," he said. "Remember — any problems, you call me."

Marc set off down the road, past the Kill Line town sign with its cheery threat of a round through the windscreen if drivers failed to halt, and headed south across the green towards the cluster of admin offices and communal areas that had been collectively dubbed *the Main Building*, as sure a sign of a British defence presence as a Union Jack. There was usually a Main Building or a COB — Central Office Block — in MoD establishments, stark and literal names often reduced to an acronym that civvies imagined stood for something much more exciting.

Would the Yanks really be pissed off if a British mission showed up? The way Ingram worried about their sensitivities made it sound like an invasion fleet. Maybe she'd picked up something Marc hadn't. There was going to be a lot of muttering about sending *Elcano* back, though, and it was just going to add more heat to the resentment about the Fiji trip. There'd be even more of a general huff when Ingram moved in with him.

He had to walk the full width of the green and pass between some workshops and the helicopter pad to get to the main building. On his left, the old accommodation block that had been vacated when the houses were built was still being converted to other uses, including the new restaurant and a small cinema, a sure sign that people had had enough of leisure time spent at home and needed places to socialise that didn't involve bathtub gin. Marc slowed to look at the progress as he walked by. A couple of the Ainatio blokes were wheeling seats into the unit earmarked for the cinema and he waved to them, but he just got an indifferent glance and a nod.

So he was still the bad guy, then. Well, sod them. He carried on to the supply warehouse to pick out the grocery order, got the bot on duty to put the box in the cold store until he came back to collect it, and headed to the security office. Ingram was waiting for him, sitting on one of the desks and swinging her legs. The office was empty for a change.

"I stood Simonot down," she said. "Sol's ready to set up the call. Anything I need to know before we start?"

Marc hesitated, but there were no secrets to be kept from Solomon.

"Howie says you can move in," he said. "But he expects you to do your share of the housework."

Ingram stared at him for a moment, then laughed. "Oh, bless. I admit I was worried he wasn't ready for it."

Marc had been so concerned about Howie's reaction that he hadn't given enough thought to how Ingram was going to fit in. He'd made a lot of assumptions because he wanted a woman around the place again, but he was no better prepared for it than Howie was. Ingram wasn't the kind of woman who'd see his scale of existence as normal. She'd been used to a grand house with lots of room to get away from family members when she wanted her space. Living in a tin box of a cabin on board ship was one thing, but the captain's quarters were a throne room, a place where the lower ranks had to seek audience even if the place wasn't big enough to swing a hamster. An ordinary house with a kid, a grumpy bloke, a part-time dog, and nowhere to escape from them other than going outside might wear her down in the end.

"Are *you* ready for it?" Marc asked.

"The housework?"

"Enforced close quarters."

"Can't be any more cramped than a patrol vessel. Are you having regrets? I realise this has been hasty."

"Fear of failure more than anything."

"Let's see how it goes."

"I'm doing a roast chicken for lunch. You in?"

"Of course."

"Okay, that's another thing off my list. So I'll check in on Tev, get Lawson over and done with, and then we're as back to normal as we're ever going to be."

"You forgot to add Barry Cho."

"Ah, yeah. That's if Lawson can get me some intel."

It was time to change the subject. Ingram wasn't keen on the idea of him springing Cho from prison, and it wasn't without its difficulties, the biggest of which was concealing the use of the gate. But she wouldn't stop him doing it. She knew why he had to. It was why he hadn't promised Howie that he wouldn't take on any more risky missions.

"Okay, Sol, let's do this." Marc settled down at one of the desks and laid out his notes in front of him. "Ready when you are."

It would be Sunday lunchtime in England. Lawson didn't know when to expect a call so Marc hoped he hadn't gone down the pub.

"Sorry to intrude on your Sunday, Guy," Marc said. "I've got some information for you. Is there anyone with you?"

"No, I always take your calls privately," Lawson said.

"Good, because what I'm going to say probably needs some pre-digestion before anyone else hears it." Marc wondered why Lawson hadn't used a video link yet, but the reason was probably the same as his. Both would reveal too much going on in their respective backgrounds. "And you still want to know whose technology you've got, yeah?"

"If I may," Lawson said.

"Okay." Marc shut his eyes. He knew he was going to hear himself say the word aloud and cringe as he said it. "It belongs to aliens. I say again, *aliens*."

Lawson's pause was very much longer. Marc waited patiently.

"I know you wouldn't joke about this," Lawson said at last.

"No. I definitely wouldn't."

"Good grief."

"We found them here and got quite chummy. It's not their homeworld, though."

"You've actually made first contact."

Lawson had always seemed an unflappable bloke but there was a hint of dread in his voice. It probably wasn't just about the existence of extraterrestrials. He was probably already worrying how he'd eventually explain this to a politician and what would happen when he did.

"Yeah, Chief Petty Officer Aiken proved they were intelligent and taught them English," Marc said. "They talk like professors now and they live on the base. So forget all the protocols and experts. It's done."

"All this in a few months."

"Yep. But there's a *lot* more, so brace yourself and take notes."

"Oh, I'm braced," Lawson said. It sounded as if he paused to take a sip of something. "Fire away."

Marc stuck to his notes to make sure he didn't overlook anything important or invite awkward questions about suspiciously short time intervals.

"It's a lot more complicated than just one alien species," he said. "We've got at least *five* intelligent, technologically superior, and well-armed civilisations in the sector. The ones here with us, the teeriks, are on the run with a stolen warship. The aliens who own the ship are the Kugin — militarised, big empire, short tempers — and the Jattans, a sort of Kugin client state, and they're both hunting for it. The Jattans are also about to have a civil war, and one of the rebels turned up here to seize the warship for the cause. Final score — one dead *Cabot* scientist, one dead teerik, although not one of our guys, and one dead Jattan rebel. We're currently spying on the official Jattans for our own safety, and the Jattan opposition is trying to make contact. Oh, and the bloke you spoke to, the one who sent you the plans — that's Fred, or at least that's what we call him, because we can't pronounce his real name properly. He's a teerik. A giant sentient crow."

It was probably the most crucial sitrep any bloke had ever delivered. Marc could have recapped further back in the timeline and told Lawson he was right to suspect Ainatio carried out the cyberattack on APS, but he probably knew anyway. And during the understandable stunned silence that followed, Marc felt wonderfully free, almost euphoric. He wasn't sure whether hearing himself summarise it in all its terrifying clusterfuckery had made him realise how amazing the universe was, or if he was just relieved to offload the shock news onto someone else. But either way he felt cleansed.

He looked up at Ingram, who was slowly pacing the floor like it was *Victory*'s foredeck. She put her hand on his shoulder and just nodded. Yes, he'd done his duty. He could relax a bit now.

Lawson found his voice again. It was probably only ten or fifteen seconds of silence, but that was a long time to wait for someone to start screaming.

He didn't, of course. He could give Chris a run for his money when it came to deadpanning.

"Oh my, oh my, oh *my*," he said quietly. "I'll be frank, Marc. After the dire warnings from Captain Ingram about the nature of the intel, my worst case scenario after a whisky or two was either that you'd stolen the technology from APS, or you'd found the legacy of a long-dead alien civilisation on Opis and raided their archives, in the finest traditions of popular cinema. I wasn't expecting this level of *complexity*."

"Just tell me you believe what I've told you."

"Oh, I do."

"Now for the detail," Marc said. "The teeriks are effectively top-tier slave labour. They're rocket scientists owned by the state of Kugad. They escaped and hijacked the warship they were working on, but as far as we know, the Kugin and the official Jattan government don't know we're here or where the ship is. But the rebels probably do, or at least one of their operatives did before we shot him. They've got good reasons not to tell anyone else, though."

Lawson let out a breath. "Do you have the warship?"

"We do. It's not as much use to us as it looks, though."

"And you're harbouring what the major powers in the area would consider criminals — runaway slaves, hijackers — and in possession of their classified information."

"Not intentionally, but we didn't call them and offer to hand back their property, either."

"Is it feasible for you to communicate with them? Linguistically, I mean."

"Oh yeah. Our AI's getting up to speed with the various languages and the teeriks do translation for us. We just decided against it for the time being."

"I realise circumstances left you no choice, Marc, but you do seem somewhat embedded in the politics of the region already," Lawson said.

"This is why I said you won't want to rush out here anytime soon. Look, you'll have boffins and all sorts wetting themselves to make contact with the aliens, but this isn't the time or the place for a zoological expedition or a trade mission. We're probably in the run-up to a shooting war and there's nothing you can do for us except stay away, build a ship or two, and not reveal Earth's position."

Marc meant that. It was a worst scenario assessment, and he knew he was probably pushing it to ward off early visits, but if anyone got over-ambitious and tried to make direct radio contact with any of the aliens, it was probably more likely to end in tears. They had all the information they needed to build FTL comms right away, even if a full-on ship would take some time. It was a real possibility they'd do the dumbest thing.

"That's rather sobering." Lawson probably used the same tone to his kids when they brought home disappointing school reports. "You said you were still able to evacuate, though. The offer of resettlement stands. I realise you're reluctant to abandon a mission of that magnitude, but it hasn't exactly been a wasted effort given the technology you've acquired."

And there was the open door. Lawson was all teed up for being asked to take *Elcano*. Marc approached it slowly and carefully.

"Well, thank you, we're grateful for the offer," he said. "Most of the population are civvies who didn't have much choice about being here, although they want to stay, but they're the reason we're not inviting you in. If it was just us military volunteers, we'd probably be hooking up for some co-operative projects or whatever the politicos call it these days. But we're a self-defence force and we've got to do what's right for the civvies."

"I understand."

"Opis isn't the only habitable planet, either. We can give you data on other worlds, courtesy of the teeriks."

"I still think you should evacuate and rethink all this," Lawson said. "I found some of Tadeusz Bednarz's papers on the establishment of colonies, by the way, so I realise you've probably got a substantial settlement now and don't want to abandon a century of work."

"Yeah, it's a complete small town," Marc said. "A shop, church, labs, factories, bars, hospital, school. No, we don't want to leave it, at least not without putting up a fight."

Marc fought the urge to offer to send Lawson some images. It wasn't nice holiday snaps he wanted to show the lads in the pub, and he knew damn well what would happen to any material Nomad transmitted. Images would be pored over in microscopic detail by analysts. There'd be boffins working out precise positions and digging out astronomical data on Opis and Pascoe's Star to assess the composition of the planet. There'd be generals and admirals extrapolating from the teeriks' engineering plans to work out how aliens might be armed. And the politicians would be arguing about who should be told, and when, and how. It was all the shit Marc had left behind and he didn't envy Lawson one bit.

"Extraordinary," Lawson said. "I understand the need for people to make a go of the colony. It's the biggest test in history for the future of our species since the Toba eruption. But I do urge caution. Nobody will think the less of you all for it."

"I can only look out for the guy next to me," Marc said. "But there *is* something you could do for us."

"Of course."

"We've got one thousand and thirty-two passengers in *Elcano* stuck in cryo, including two hundred and forty-nine children. We could move her, but it might be better to send her back to Earth and revive everyone."

"I'm certain we could accommodate that," Lawson said.

"The adults are mostly the scientists you thought you might find quite handy." Marc looked at Ingram for a reaction. She was just leaning against the wall with her arms folded, nodding approval. "They'll be disappointed when they realise they never set foot on Opis, but they didn't volunteer either. We can bring them back if they still want to return after we tell them about the aliens. They don't know about them."

"*Elcano* didn't start out with FTL," Lawson said. "We're not talking about them arriving here in forty-five years' time, are we? Forgive me if I'm confused by all this."

Ingram narrowed her eyes. Shock hadn't confused Lawson one bit. Marc had the *Elcano* complication on his Q and A list under *If Pressed*.

"No, our alien allies recovered her and two others en route. That covers your time discrepancy. They're busy upgrading all our vessels."

"Good grief. What do they want in exchange for that?"

"Ration bars."

"Sorry?"

"They were starving. Ingram used some soft power on them and now we feed and house them. She's played a blinder, actually. Give her some credit." Marc glanced at her just to give her a nod, but she frowned at him. *Protection*, she mouthed. Marc took the hint. "And they need someone to defend them when the Kugin show up. Teeriks are brilliant at engineering but apparently crap at self-defence."

"Will data be available?"

"What kind of data?"

"About your various aliens."

"We don't have much yet. We're working on it. Anyway, here's the deal. On top of the FTL stuff, you get extraordinary technology, including Ainatio's base-building know-how, and data on other habitable planets with lots of lovely minerals and stuff. In exchange, you stand back and let us sort out Opis ourselves. I know that's a big ask, but we blundered in and now we're stuck with the consequences. If you blunder in as well, it might well kick off a disaster for Earth, and we've got to keep the Americans on side. They're the majority here and we'll be relying on them to survive."

"Selling that to politicians could be a challenge," Lawson said.

"Okay, you can put it this way, if and when you have to. I killed a teerik, one of the farmers killed a Jattan, and we've commandeered and cannibalised a stolen warship, so it's probably best not to be associated with us. And Fred jumped the gun and gave you the data prematurely because he wants billions of humans here to give the Kugin a good kicking. Don't get sucked into an alien grudge match."

"That's useful," Lawson said. "Thank you."

Marc was looking at his notes and working out what Lawson *hadn't* asked him yet. He hadn't asked about Solomon, although Marc had mentioned the AI without naming him, and he hadn't asked for details about the contact with the Jattan rebels.

Marc decided to give him an opportunity to fill in the gaps. "I'm sure things will occur to you later when all this sinks in, but is there anything else you want to ask at the moment?"

"Yes. How will you transfer the *Elcano* passengers if you ship them back here? Will they arrive in cryo? We might not have the expertise to revive them safely because it's not a technology we use."

"If we do, it'll be handled by our AI," Marc said. "There are medics in cryo as well and the system's set up to revive them first. The whole process is automated because they could never guarantee anyone from the *Cabot* mission surviving to revive them manually."

"That's most impressive. Thank you."

Marc waited. The next question would be about *Elcano*, about what happened to her once her passengers were disembarked, and whether Britain could keep her for the time being. He had his line ready: they'd have to bring the ship back on autopilot because they'd need her missile capability to defend Nomad. Lawson would then start discussing nukes, but he probably wouldn't ask about acquiring raw materials for shipbuilding because they were still assessing the plans, and it would emerge naturally when they got down to detail.

But he didn't ask any of those questions. "And I really was talking to an alien, was I?" he asked.

"You were." Marc regrouped mentally, waiting for the catch. "I want you to understand that this is as much to protect Britain as Nomad Base. If we didn't give a toss about you, there'd have been no call from Fred because we wouldn't have asked him to prep plans for human use. We'd have cut all contact."

"Are you getting grief from the other national interests on the base?"

"Who cares?" Marc asked. "America's gone, APS wants to shut us down with extreme prejudice, and we considered giving the tech to public-spirited scientists and leaders around the world, but we were still struggling to think of any when Fred made the decision for us. I'm not joking about that, by the way."

"Well, I've got a considerable amount of quiet contemplation ahead of me." Lawson made a sound that was almost like the start of a suppressed laugh, the kind you made when you couldn't believe the depth of the shit you were in and had to find the funny side to stay sane. "And to think I once said to you, 'Space is always interesting, Mr Gallagher,' as a lofty response to your question about Kingdom."

"Oh. Yeah."

"Did you know any of this then?" It sounded very much as if he thought Marc did.

"Actually, I didn't." Marc almost told him he'd run into Fred for the first time an hour or two after they'd spoken, but the bloke probably didn't need to add aliens landing briefly on Earth to his list of awkward things to explain to ministers, not yet at least. "But I'd already burned out my shock chip. You'll be totally blasé about all this in a couple of months. Maybe even a couple of days."

"I await that day with interest," Lawson said.

"Let me know when you've got a location for us to disembark the *Elcano* personnel," Marc said. "And any information about them that you need."

"About your AI," Lawson said.

A...ha. Here it comes. "What about him?"

"We do hear some odd things coming out of APS."

Marc had a split second to decide how far to cooperate with a fishing expedition. Lawson was a skilled angler, and if he didn't have a bit of spook in his past somewhere, then he almost certainly helped them out when they were busy. The speed or otherwise of Marc's response would shape how this went. He pulled a feint.

"Oh, so you *are* spying on Pham," he said.

"Messy business, but it's sort of mandatory."

"Yeah, Pham went mental about Solomon. That's the AI's name. Pham thought he was Earthmother. If Solomon was an Earthmother type, Pham wouldn't be alive now, and neither would any of his troops."

"So what *is* Solomon? In type terms."

"Bednarz's own design." Marc was so far out on a limb now that he could see squirrels below. He caught Ingram's eye and she looked grim. "He's built to make moral choices and his sole purpose is protecting human life. Well, ours, to be specific — we'd all be dead now without him, and *Cabot*'s crew wouldn't be looking too clever either. And Erskine tried to shut him down when he wanted to stop her abandoning the civvies to a bloody nuclear air raid, so we made sure she couldn't. He's acquired some enemies for all the right reasons."

"But you don't regard him as a potential threat."

"No. I don't."

"The cyberattack on APS?"

"We tasked him to do that. The responsibility's mine and we only pulled the trigger when APS destroyed *Da Gama*. If Solomon had been an Earthmother type, you'd be looking at a big scorch mark where APS used to be. We went for the least lethal temporary option because Solomon would have had issues about killing people."

The fuck he would. But whatever Sol did had to be provoked, and there were too many grey areas in that discussion when Marc was trying to shut it down and move Lawson on.

"Your AI sounds very impressive," Lawson said.

"He is. He's our mate. We've got his back."

"They can be terribly human, can't they?"

Marc went for it. It helped that he wasn't acting now. "He helped me grieve properly for my sons for the first time. Yeah, he's human, alright."

Lawson did his usual pause. "Is Erskine going to be a problem?"

"Yeah, sorry that she's part of the return package, but if you end up shooting the old bag, we won't file a complaint," Marc said. "Not so much a problem as a lot of folks here want an unfriendly word with her. Tell her if she still wants a piece of Sol, she'll have to come through me. That applies to Pham, too. Anyone, in fact."

"I'll pass it on, Marc."

"Anything else?"

"I'll have more information on Corporal Cho's location in a few days, although I shouldn't encourage you."

"Thank you."

"May I ask what Opis actually looks like?"

"I'll send you some images. We even have sea monsters."

"Wouldn't be an alien world without them."

"It's probably time for you to have a stiff drink and digest all this news."

"I do believe I will. We'll talk later. Thank you for an extraordinary conversation."

"All part of the service. Mind how you go."

Marc ended the call and sat staring at his unused notes. He could feel the sweat running down his back. Ingram walked over and ruffled his hair.

"Well handled. I love it when you're all alpha and bolshy."

"I give him three days before he's back on to me asking if I know anything about a helicopter being shot down near Fiji," Marc said. "He'll know. And Pham will know about a missile appearing out of thin air and Joni's boat vanishing, which he'll discuss and somehow Lawson will get to hear. Some of the ex-pats we saw around the islands might have been our spooks, not just Pham's."

"There's nothing we can do about that. We're responsible for our own actions, not the reactions of others."

"But apart from that, you think I said what he needed to hear."

"Yes. You would have fooled me if I didn't know you better."

"What, claiming Sol's not an ASD AI? Like Doug said, show me the serial numbers."

"I meant the fake innocence, that you really were telling him more than you intended because he was coaxing it out of you. Plus an oblique threat that could equally be a simple, honest soul expressing strong manly feelings about Sol. Which I suspect were genuine."

"That's me. Rough diamond. Good at killing and dumb enough not to know when the toffs are manipulating me."

"You're rather scary, you know that?"

"That's what they paid me for." Marc knew that Lawson knew that they both knew what the game was, but there was enough genuine emotion in the warning to back off Sol to make the point. "I suppose I'd better pick up the chicken and stuff. A dead one this time. Don't get your hopes up, Boadicea."

"No chicken can ever replace Mildred."

"I had your groceries delivered," Solomon said. "Howie's unpacking the trolley bot now. It was the least I could do for your gallant intervention. You didn't need to take the blame for my actions, but thank you."

"Purely selfish, mate." Marc squirmed. "If you go, we're all stuffed."

"Of course. I knew that."

"Yeah."

"Bullshit," Ingram said, and laughed. "You're one of us, Sol, and that means he'd take a bullet for you."

"Speak for yourself," Marc said, and ushered her out. He paused outside the building to send an audio file of the call to Chris, Alex, Searle, and Trinder with a message attached that Lawson now knew that mankind was not alone, in fact so *un*-alone that there was a good chance of an armed misunderstanding with a mixed bag of aliens. At least it was easier to grasp the threat potential of Jattans and Kugin than six-dimensional plasma beings who didn't deal in linear time.

As they strolled back to the house, Marc was in a more positive frame of mind than he'd started with. He felt that same relief he'd had when he'd first told Lawson that he was calling him from a distant planet. The problems he still had to fix were of the conventional variety he was used to. There was Barry Cho to take care of, and making sure Tev and his family were settled in, and of course Kugad and its Jattan sidekicks hadn't gone away either. But the list of shit to shovel was being whittled down. It could all be tackled in stages.

"Lawson wasn't too shocked to see the advantages and ask awkward questions," Marc said.

Ingram nodded. "You were right to do the talking. I think he's a bit scared of you."

"There's a certain advantage in being a professional psychopath."

"And you didn't mention Annis," Ingram said. "Neither did he."

"Oh, he hasn't forgotten her. It's on his list along with all the other stuff he didn't ask."

Marc felt drained. Breaking the news of aliens had been more emotional than he'd expected, and that wasn't like him at all. What would John and Greg have made of their dad being central to the biggest discovery in human history? He imagined their reactions and how they'd have ended up talking all night about it. It was one of those moments that really hurt, a memory that never had the chance to happen.

"Alex will have to break the *Elcano* news to the rest of the staff," Ingram said. "There'll be objections."

"Take the moral high ground," Marc said. "Women, children, and harpy CEOs first."

"And a few chaps in lab coats that some will feel should be kept here."

"We've got a few weeks' grace now." Marc stopped from time to time to take pictures of the base and the wild landscape beyond. He passed his screen to Ingram. "Anything in the shots that we should redact?"

"Can't see anything top secret that they'll be interested in." Ingram zoomed into the images until they were unrecognisable. "They'll be analysing light and shadows and all that, but that's just astrophysics, and if they spoke nicely to some university they could get all the data they wanted on Pascoe's Star and its planets. I'm sure they already have."

"The distant purple foliage looks nice. Shall I include Ash's shot of the sea beast?"

"It's just a one-legged octopus. Go ahead."

"And Fred?"

"Is that wise?"

"What can they do with a picture of a big crow-raven-microraptor thing? Other than get an anatomist to speculate on the best way to kill it, and we've already done that."

Ingram gave him a sadly amused look as he opened the front door. "You've ruled out their boffins oohing and aahing, lost in wonder, I see."

"They'll think it's AI-faked."

Marc thought about the appropriate teerik image to send Lawson as he considered the chicken carcass, holding it upright by its wings like a doll. At least he didn't have to remove any giblets. He'd make himself do it if he had to, but he couldn't face telling Ingram that it made him queasy. He'd seen too much of the stuff that spilled out of human beings and switched off his revulsion a long time ago. If he'd been living off the land in an escape situation, he'd have been skinning rabbits and gutting fish, and it wouldn't have affected him because he'd be in his work mindset, but offal got past his defences when it came into his nice tidy urban kitchen. He sliced one of the much sought-after lemons that Lianne had donated and tried to work out how to keep the slices sitting on the chicken's skin.

In the end he gave up and stuffed them into the cavity. He'd grate some of the peel from the other lemon and rub it into the skin with a knob of Liam Dale's Jersey butter.

No, this wasn't a bad life at all, was it? All they had to do was iron out the external problems and then they could get on with living it.

He could hear Ingram talking to Howie as he washed his hands and retrieved the drinks from the fridge. The two of them were in the living room, having a heart to heart, and it sounded like he'd just asked her when she was coming to stay.

"You can always say no," Ingram was telling him. "You seem really happy now and I don't want to spoil that. I can't replace your real mum and I wouldn't try to."

"We're pretending we're a family," Howie said, like he was explaining family psychology to her. "But it's to make ourselves happier, not telling fibs to other people because we want them to believe we really are. So if we *want* to pretend it's real and we don't care what they think, that's as good as *being* real, isn't it?"

Howie understood the power of a shared illusion. Marc preferred the role of grandad, because his sense of being a father began and ended with John and Greg, but he'd go along with whatever made Howie happy. It wasn't a kid's job to accommodate an adult's traumas. Ingram looked up at Marc as he put her drink on the table and he thought she was going to cry.

"Humans want to be part of a group," Marc said. "It's normal. It's what keeps us alive. I've missed it. That's why we're happier like this. Remember how you used to do your rounds at the transit camp, Howie, making sure the old people had someone to talk to? It's the same thing. It's what humans are meant to do."

Marc had sworn he'd never try to fill a parental role again. He'd thought he was too damaged to plug the hole in Howie's life, but he couldn't walk away from it because of the hole in his own. Ingram was another matter. It was easy to think that she accepted Howie as part of the Marc Gallagher package, but maybe he didn't fully understand the size and composition of the holes in her own life. She had to have some. She'd been the only child of an old moneyed family, he knew that much, and she'd left the family estate to her cousin when she signed up for the Nomad mission because there was nobody else.

The history book at school had told Marc what Ingram did in the Channel War. It had told him nothing about a naval family that had served for generations and how it had come down to one woman with no immediate family, just some cousin she left the country estate to. For some reason he thought about her encounter with a dead man and how she'd kept that to herself as well, and wondered if she'd lost someone she didn't want to talk about.

She'd tell him when she was ready.

"Did you remember to turn the oven on?" Howie asked.

"Yep." Marc checked his watch. "Ninety minutes. Spuds at thirty minutes before zero, beans at ten. Let's take our drinks into the garden."

If Marc hadn't known exactly where he was and why, he could have been on Earth and the last ten years hadn't happened. The world had shrunk to a couple of makeshift loungers partly shaded by an awning made from an old tarp, a jug of fruit juice suitably fortified by the time it reached the adults' glasses, and Howie happily digging more rows to plant winter lettuces. Unexpected normality overwhelmed Marc. He looked at Ingram and she stopped reading her screen.

"From healthy professional distance to playing house in five days," Marc said. "Who'd have thought it?"

"Several months elapsed in our minds, though."

"True. Are you sending memos?"

"Just a quick note to the crew." Ingram brandished her screen. "Alex just sent out an all-staff message, and my people ought to hear it from me. He's going to talk to them in the canteen tomorrow, so I'd better be there. Brace for incoming."

"It's Sunday," Marc said. "We can brace tomorrow."

The temporary peace was like realising he couldn't hear anything and thinking he'd gone deaf. For a few hours, the three of them could almost relive a way of life that had been taken from them, not restored without visible cracks but repaired enough to remind them what ordinary contentment looked like. They could pretend for a while that it had always been this way. But it hadn't, and it wouldn't be like it tomorrow, either. All they'd done was swap die-back, feral Europe, and APS for alien threats. Why did either of them bother? What was the point?

"Oh wow." Howie stopped digging holes and laughed. "I think this is a tomato. We didn't plant any, though."

Ingram hauled herself off the lounger and went over to look. "Yes, that's definitely a tomato seedling. It might have come from the compost bin."

"Do I have to pull it up?"

"No, let's leave it be. It's a free vegetable and it can grow where it chooses."

"*Fruit*," Howie said, grinning. "It's a fruit, really."

And *that* was the point. Marc saw it now.

They were relaxing in a make-believe English garden that wasn't meant to be here, watching a small boy just being happy while he dug holes for plants without thinking about the horror of trying to bury his mum and sister. It was a win. Marc had done terrible things on behalf of his country so that people could live this ordinary life and never have to know how it felt to do otherwise. So had Ingram. Now it was their turn to try it.

It wouldn't make what was coming any easier, but it would see them through the darker days. Marc soaked up the unfamiliar sense of being at peace, looked at the back of his hand, and realised he wasn't a ghost in the land of the living any more.

10

To: all former Ainatio personnel.
From: Alex Gorko
Subject: *Elcano* and the security situation

Now that we don't have to hide our access to advanced FTL and the presence of aliens, we've reconsidered the security situation and asked Britain to temporarily resettle *Elcano*'s personnel. The longer we wait, the higher the risk of an alien incursion, and rather than gamble with children's lives we're sending *Elcano* home to wait it out. When our colleagues are told about the aliens, they'll be better placed to decide whether they want to come back. This wasn't an easy decision, but now we can revive people somewhere safer, it's the responsible one. I'll be in the staff club on Monday from 1400 if you want to ask questions.

* * *

CO'S OFFICE: 0950, MONDAY, OCTOBER 26, OC.

The Ainatio staff wanted to talk about a few other issues apart from *Elcano*, Alex's memo had said, so if Ingram was able to join them in the canteen at 1400, her input would be appreciated.

His message imbued *talk* and *appreciated* with a sense of demanding to see the manager, which the staff didn't seem to think was Alex. *Other issues* carried its own ominous weight, but it wasn't hard to take a stab at guessing what the main item on the agenda would be.

"Mutinous ingrates," Ingram said. It required a firm explanation delivered with charm but minus apologies. "Can I keelhaul them, Sol?"

"That might be comic exaggeration, Captain, but I suspect it's one of those many true words spoken in jest," Solomon said.

Ingram looked up at the wall. "Is there something you know that I don't?"

"It's what I *don't* know that concerns me. People hang around in groups and talk, but when they do it in the middle of open ground, I can't hear them."

"We could do something about that."

"Captain, you know very well I try to draw a line between monitoring and snooping." It was always a touchy subject with Solomon. Ingram tried to stay off it, but sometimes she failed spectacularly. "It's easy to classify missing personnel or the location of a fire as information I need to have without consent. But humans have a bad habit of expanding the definition of safety so they can impose control. To be frank, none of you would ever know if I *was* spying, but I respect human privacy because it matters to *me* to do so. And yes, I'm familiar with the argument about capability versus intent, but I *am* the capability, all of me, and I have little choice about that, so I put as many safeguards as I can into my intent, however imperfect it might be."

Ingram waited, expecting him to go on, but he'd had his say. She already knew that he thought she ignored the disapproval of the little people, so it was hard to decide if he'd treat her apology as sincere.

"Sorry, Sol, I only asked," she said. "You're right. We don't want a police state here."

"Anyway, I think it's a good idea to go and speak to the staff this afternoon. Perhaps we should have done that as soon as we realised Tev was coming back."

He sounded embarrassed, as if he wished he hadn't jumped on his soap box about privacy. Ingram did her best to imagine what it was like to be designed to be able to know everything, whether you wanted to or not, and why he set his own filters. It wasn't just overload. Solomon had unique access to information about everything and everybody here if he chose to take notice of it, far more than any individual human would ever have, and if he acted on that — tip-offs, gossip, whatever — then he was in danger of replacing human communication, and that would make people more insular than they were already, as well as a little unhinged. Ingram had come to see him like the lone telepath in a normal society, burdened by knowledge and needing to find a way to shut it out so that he didn't destroy the fabric of relationships.

"You're right, I could have handled it better," she said. "In my defence, if I told people in advance, I'd have had an earful from the usual suspects. I told them afterwards, and I still got an earful, just from a different angle."

"I wasn't criticising," Solomon said. "Just exercising hindsight."

It was all about managing perception. On its own, each cock-up, misunderstanding, or knee-jerk had been innocent, but incidents eventually accumulated and took on a pattern for those watching, one that said the powers that be were carrying out a secret plan and it wasn't benign. Perhaps today's meeting would be a good opportunity to clear the air. Tensions were inevitable. Nomad's isolation was almost like being cooped up in an orbital, because the vast space of an uninhabited planet didn't change the limited human scenery. It was village life again.

"We're a couple of thousand independently-minded, intelligent people, so the chances of us agreeing on everything is zero," Ingram said. "Am I going to have to justify not reviving the *Elcano* contingent again?"

"Yes. You are."

"I accept that bringing her into Opis orbit for safekeeping wasn't as good an idea as I thought, at least not from the general perception angle."

"But were you wrong?" Solomon asked. "Not now that Britain has the FTL data. The ship could still have ended up within Pham's reach before she got here. Imagine *Elcano* was still on her way to Opis now at subluminal speed. If the FTL plans leaked to APS in the next few decades, which is a long time to rely on OPSEC, Pham would still be able to overtake a slow-route *Elcano* to pick her off or seize her when he felt like it. And then you'd have been criticised for failing to move her out of harm's way."

Ingram had to think about that timeline, but it was a good defence, although not a reason she could have known about when she took the decision.

"People who object to all the options in a situation often just need an excuse to have a go at someone," she said. "Whether they realise it or not. Sometimes all they need is a lightning rod."

"They're afraid," Solomon said. "There really are things to be afraid of, but the unknown makes it worse."

"You're going to remind me that nobody volunteered for this. Well, *we* did, but we're actually talking about one specific group, aren't we? Ainatio. I'd hoped the lines would have blurred by now."

"If Nomad had been completely isolated, they would have, I think."

"We're still mentally shackled to Earth," Ingram said. "But I think we always would have been, even without the option of contact and return."

Some people lashed out when they were afraid, and others wanted a reassuring boot placed on everyone's neck, even if it was pointless. Ingram had only been prepared to maintain discipline within her crew. The rest of the civilians had never been part of that equation. She was supposed to hand over to them, not manage or command them.

But it would all be talked out. People just wanted to vent and feel they'd been listened to.

Ingram got on with the daily tasks that crossed her desk, which were still mostly about food production and surveillance of the Jattan navy. At least the food was interesting. Andy had been inspired to get on with the fish farm plans and wanted to co-opt Joni to help out. He was finding an absorbing role for another bunch of people who also hadn't volunteered to be here. For a settlement where fewer than ten per cent of the citizens had actually signed up for Opis, it was a miracle that morale wasn't a lot worse.

Ingram paused to make a cup of coffee and took a breather with her screen propped on the desk, just watching the map to see who was where and what was happening. Her eye strayed automatically to the icons of the people she was most concerned about, but as she scanned the image, she gradually noticed a pattern she hadn't seen before.

An unusual number of Chris's militia were clustered outside specific buildings, not mob-handed, just twos and threes, but they were suddenly at all the key positions. She still thought of them as Chris's private army, even though they'd merged with Trinder's detachment to become the Nomad defence force. But today they were noticeably *not* patrolling with Trinder's guys. They were at the various power plants — the two reactors, the biogas units, the water splitter — and other critical sites, like the Caisin gate bunker and the main food warehouses. Those were the strategically sensitive sites Nomad would need to secure in an emergency. What were they up to?

Perhaps she was being paranoid. Site security was as much Chris's role as Trinder's and he didn't need her permission to do anything. It might just have been another exercise to test his team's response to an alien incursion. Ingram checked her messages and diary again, but she couldn't see any exercises scheduled for this week. That was when she started to wonder if Chris was reacting to a real situation.

"Sol, have we got a problem?" Ingram asked. "Why are Chris's people gathering at key sites?"

"I don't think it's a coup, Captain. You can finish your coffee."

"It's not like him to forget to list an exercise."

"I'm not aware of any unusual issues. I'll ask him if you like."

Chris was a very able NCO but he had one particular talent that verged on a superpower. He could always spot trouble long before anyone else. Marc put it down to spending too much of his time "on orange," hypervigilant and actively looking for threats. It wasn't healthy, but it had its uses. He was a one-man early warning system.

"No, I'll talk to him," Ingram said. "I'm probably imagining it."

She kept an eye on the map for the rest of the morning, noting the occasional change of personnel, although it was harder to spot some of Chris's people because they weren't chipped. Sometimes they didn't carry chipped passes, either, and it was down to the bots around the base to recognise them and map their positions. But she'd already seen enough to wonder what was going on.

She couldn't find Marc or Tev, though, not that it surprised or troubled her. If two special forces guys couldn't evade detection, they were slipping. They reappeared at lunchtime in the staff canteen, so she decided to drop in and see how Tev was doing. When she looked around the canteen, she found them eating with Chris. Well, that would kill several birds with one stone. She put her tray on their table and sat down.

"Mind if I join you, gentlemen? How are things going, Tev?"

"We're just about settled into the house now, ma'am."

"And Sera?"

"Confused about relative dates, just like me, but all we need to know is the baby's due soon and it'll arrive when it's ready. Dr Mendoza says they're both fine. She's just a bit shocked about being here."

Ingram broke up her bread roll and dunked chunks in the soup. "Is there anything we can do to help ease that?"

"I don't think so, but thank you anyway. Mere's not happy with me bringing all this trouble to her daughter, but at least Becky hasn't ripped my head off."

Ingram had reached the stage where she couldn't imagine much that *wouldn't* upset people. It was a time of upheaval with a distinct shortage of better places to go. She'd bear that in mind when she spoke to the Ainatio malcontents.

"Let me know if you think of anything," she said. "I'm sorry about how this worked out. But if any of your family are *really* unhappy here, we can always find a way to get you back to Britain. Can't we, Marc?"

Marc nodded and stacked his dirty plates and cutlery. "Indeed we can."

Ingram could almost hear Chris's thoughts. His expression never gave much away, but it didn't have to. She'd said the unsayable. People — some of them, anyway, the special ones — could go back to Earth even if they knew about the Caisin gate. Resolve had crumbled in the face of human need. Ingram was sure he'd make that point to her sooner or later.

"Did you have an exercise this morning, Chris?" she asked. "I saw you had teams out at key sites."

Chris still looked unmoved. "No, we were just showing a security presence in case anyone thought we'd gone soft."

"Scent of trouble, then?"

"No intel, but if people want a meeting, and they're muttering in small groups, and we know they're pissed at us for various things, then there's potential for escalation."

"Wait and see what they've got to say."

"Why?"

"Being visible might make things worse."

For a moment, Chris looked like he was going to say something acid, but he moved on. "Well, if talking doesn't solve the problem, we're ready. You're aware that my guys have pretty extensive experience of public order situations."

Marc let out a breath that could have been a sigh. "Sol's capable of locking humans out of every essential service and running the show," he said. "Been there, done that at Ainatio, right? Everyone's fed and housed, so they won't try to burn the place down. It'll be all middle-class snotty complaints. In writing."

"We've armed them," Chris said. It sounded like the two of them had already disagreed about this and were going over old ground. "And trained them to use lethal force."

"Yeah, but they know you're a *lot* more lethal than they are."

"Let's hope they do."

Ingram wondered if she'd missed something, but she trusted Marc's personal radar. Chris was still operating in survival mode after living through the kind of upheaval even Britain hadn't seen. Under the circumstances he wasn't really overreacting, just aware of how badly the most reasonable of people could behave under stress.

"Everyone here is an educated adult, Chris," she said. "I don't think we need to break out the water cannon."

Chris didn't blink. "We don't have one. I'll put it on my list."

It was hard to tell if he was joking. He always had that blankly innocent expression that could have been deadpan humour or even mockery. She finished her soup and stood up to leave, clutching the tray.

"I'd better get going. This meeting starts at fourteen hundred."

"I'll see you there," Chris said. "We all got an invite."

On the way back to the office, Ingram decided to pay a brief visit to her vantage point on the roof. When she'd been up there surveying the site over her morning cuppa a few hours ago, everything had looked and felt fine, and she liked to think she had her own sixth sense when it came to reading the mood on the base. The site was busier and more populated than it had been at 0630, but nothing struck her as out of the ordinary.

Some of the Ainatio boffins were out on the green in small groups, eating their lunch. The weather was still mild and people enjoyed being outdoors in what would have been early winter back home. She didn't see an insurgency in the making. She saw people who'd had to make a sudden transition from an isolated life in a lab on Earth, where they felt they had an urgent purpose, to being at a loose end on an alien world with an equally uncertain future. They'd had to find other ways to be productive. There was such a long waiting list to teach classes that Kill Line's new school probably had the best science curriculum in the galaxy.

Ingram reminded herself that Rome wasn't built in a day, even if the Kill Line expansion literally had been, and she couldn't expect an artificial, instant society to settle down in a few months. She climbed down from the roof and took a short cut through the office wing to the staff club, looking for signs of revolution brewing but finding none.

Trinder was waiting for her like a sentry at the last set of doors before the staff club. It was hard to move around this place untracked even without a chip. He looked guilty. He usually did.

"Trouble up at t'mill, Dan?"

"Sorry?"

"The workers are getting restless."

"Look, if they're bitching about *Elcano*, Ainatio people are still my responsibility, even if the company's dead and buried, and I'm the one who asked to send the ship home. So I want to lay it out for them first. If you take the lead on this, that'll just fuel their conspiracy theories."

"Oh, so they do have some, then. Anyway, it's Alex's meeting, so if you beat me to it, fine, but I don't want to look as if I'm shoving you in the line of fire. Or Chris."

"But Alex isn't security, and Chris isn't Ainatio. This is a company security issue. And I've never lied to them like Alex had to."

Ingram kept forgetting that. Alex had kept Ainatio's massive deception quiet for years. He knew exactly what had happened and what was planned. So did Solomon, of course, but for some reason she couldn't be angry with either of them or even mistrust them. She blamed the company. But holding abstract things responsible for actions that only individuals could have taken was a way of avoiding confronting guilty people who had names and faces, so at some level she probably blamed Erskine, who didn't seem to have had any more choice about maintaining the blackout than Ingram had. Everyone who was truly guilty was long dead. It made any attempt at revenge deeply unsatisfying.

"Whatever you say, Dan, it isn't going to change things," Ingram said. "They're just feeling hard done by. We all do sometimes."

Trinder lowered his voice to a whisper. "They're stir-crazy, they're scared, and they haven't forgotten we treated them like terror suspects. Then we ship their buddies home and bring Tev back from Earth. We've done it for good reasons, but it doesn't look like that."

"You left out sharing teerik tech with Britain. The icing on the cake."

Trinder looked even more grim. "And no Marc?"

"He's talking to Tev. Do we need to interrupt him?"

"I'd hate for you to be the lone Brit in there."

"Oh, it's like that, is it? Right."

Trinder paused for a moment as if he was working out another way to put it to her. "That's why I want to handle this. Head it off at the pass."

"Let's see how things go."

Ingram followed him into the club. The room was too small to feel like anything other than a bear pit. The Ainatio delegation was clustered around Alex, twenty or so people, and she was surprised by who'd turned up. Paul Cotton was predictable, but she hadn't expected to see Kurt Tomlinson and Todd Mangel. The rest were just faces she recognised from Biomed, Engineering, and the plant labs, but didn't know well enough to judge.

Chris was already there, leaning against the windowsill next to the tables, arms folded, as if he was distancing himself from the debate but standing ready to break up brawls. The group looked up with grunts and nods. Mangel put down a half-eaten taco to pull out a chair for her.

"Don't mind me, Captain," he said. "I'm not part of this. I just wandered across to tell the others to stop being dicks."

Alex looked tired, as if he'd already had the argument and lost it. "We've been discussing why the *Elcano* folks will be better off in Britain," he said.

"*You* have," Paul said. "We were just listening and asking why."

Trinder dived in. "Guys, I asked for the Brits to take her. And even if it had been feasible to revive everyone a couple of months ago, I'd still have been arguing for the kids to be evacuated with their parents."

"Your idea, then," Tomlinson said.

"I admit it was a mistake to move her out here, but that was when APS was more of a threat than aliens."

Chris raised a forefinger. "No, *I* suggested bringing the ship here." It sounded more like an attempt to stop Trinder blaming himself for everything again rather than a claim of prior art. "But yeah, it sucks, now so we need to do something different."

Tomlinson carried on, still focused on Trinder. "You didn't ask for Kill Line's kids to be shipped out."

"That's because their parents know the score, they want to stay here, and it's their call," Trinder said. "And if they change their minds, we can still evacuate them. But we have to take the decisions for people who don't even know hostile aliens exist yet."

"Why now? And why not revive them and ask them?"

"Because Marc's government contact knows about everything except the Caisin gate, so we no longer have a reason *not* to send the ship home for a while. But we do have a reason to minimise the information the *Elcano* people might accidentally reveal." Trinder was doing a pretty good job of sounding wearily patient, as if he thought they should have worked all this out by now. "If they're going back, it's best if they only know what Lawson knows. We'll revive them in Earth orbit. If it gets kinetic out here, we'll never forgive ourselves if the ship's hit. I'd rather inconvenience people for a while than bury them forever."

"I thought the point of the gate was that it could move ships anywhere at a moment's notice," Tomlinson said.

"It can, but we'd be parking *Elcano* in some temporary holding position. We'd have to bring the ship back at some point, so unless we find a way to deal with the aliens long-term, there'd still be a risk of an imminent attack."

"So you know we're expecting trouble."

"No, we don't. We have no idea. But if it happens, we deal with it, and we minimise whatever risks we can beforehand. We can't build a cryo facility down here and complete the defences, but being in cryo makes them vulnerable anywhere."

Ingram cut in. "Come on, chaps. What's this really about? I can understand you're upset that your friends are stuck in limbo. But the situation keeps changing and we have to change with it."

She'd already decided she didn't like Paul, so his dissent was easier to take than Tomlinson's. But as someone who'd gone out of her way to volunteer for the mission, she was supposed to understand the concerns of those who'd been bounced into it with little warning. Chris, who'd had a minor spat with Paul during the evacuation, watched the man with his distracted vicar expression, which probably meant he was working out the most efficient way to remove him from the gene pool without staining the faux terrazzo floor.

"Okay, I'm the bad guy, so I'm going to say what's on a lot of folks' minds." Paul wasn't unaware of what people thought of him, then. "You start by taking extreme security precautions back at Ainatio Park during the evacuation. You don't tell us about the gate — or the aliens — until we drive straight through it and find ourselves on Opis. Then nobody's allowed to contact Earth, again for security reasons, because it would be the end of civilisation as we know it if Earth realised we've got this alien technology. Just finding out that aliens exist would cause riots in the streets. So we watch the news, see one of our colleagues sabotaging everything we worked for and hastening the end for Earth, and there's *nothing* we can do to help — because we've got to stay silent about what we've discovered. And we can't revive our colleagues in *Elcano* because we don't have enough food yet to buffer us against a couple of failed harvests, even though we're not exactly starving. Then out of the blue, after all that secrecy, Fred decides to contact Britain and send the government his how-to guide for building an FTL vessel. Then, also out of the blue, *you* decide to send *Elcano* home, with the last legitimate CEO of Ainatio on board. Then Marc goes back to Earth to retrieve Tev, despite the fact nobody else is even allowed to contact home. Call me paranoid, Captain, but that sounds like a coup to me. Nomad will be under British control."

He looked at Ingram with real anger, his clenched jaw moving slightly behind compressed lips as if he was chewing something and hoping nobody noticed. He genuinely believed his theory. Ingram debated whether to go for the jugular or just correct him like a kind aunt, but either way, she had to knock this firmly on the head before things escalated.

"Paul, if this had been an actual coup, you wouldn't even be here," she said. "Nor would the Kill Liners. Once we'd found out about the Caisin gate, I'd have worked out if I needed anyone from Ainatio who I couldn't replace with British personnel, and that answer might have been *nobody*, in which case you'd never have known about teeriks or the existence of any of this technology. Then I'd have used the gate to bring in British forces and a support team. Now that's a *proper* coup. I wouldn't have turned this base upside down to accommodate you all overnight, and if I had any misgivings about Erskine arriving a few decades down the road, I could have destroyed *Elcano* as soon as she came within missile range and nobody would have known or cared. But you're all here because I and my crew honoured our contracts with a dead corporation because it was the right thing to do."

Paul didn't look remotely chastened by Ingram's counterattack. "But you regret it now. Or your government does. So Georgina Erskine needs to be removed from the picture."

"Why would anyone need to overthrow Erskine?" Ingram asked. "Do you really think we'd feel so threatened by an elderly woman that we'd go to all this trouble to get rid of her? Solomon could just sabotage her cryo berth, and I suspect he feels he has cause. And she can be as furious as she likes when she wakes up, but she's not a military force, and we are. Besides, the last legitimate CEO of Ainatio was Alex. He stayed at his post. She didn't."

Ingram sat back, satisfied she'd made the point. She would never normally belittle someone in front of their colleagues if they were simply wrong, but she knew the slightest concession would provoke Paul like blood in the water. The darker part of her, the Ingram who wouldn't delay an attack by so much as a minute because she'd given the enemy a deadline to evacuate its non-combatants, wondered why she hadn't carried out that coup in the first place, because it was true. Nobody was left to care if Ainatio lost Nomad. The company didn't exist. Even its country was gone. But she was always so bloody *proper*, and conscious of the Royal Navy's honour and her country's reputation. One day that wasn't going to be enough reason to hold her back.

"I'm sorry, this is all wrong," Paul said, shaking his head. "We want everyone in *Elcano* revived *now*. We're not short of food. We tell them everything that's happened so *they* can decide whether they go back to Earth or not."

It wasn't a new argument. It had started as soon as *Elcano* had reached Opis orbit. So had the counterargument, the one with numbers and yield projections and nutritional requirements that said the base *might* be able to feed all the extra mouths that had arrived forty-five years early if nothing went wrong and if everybody accepted rationing. They didn't have to test that gamble if the ship was sleeping in orbit, and the passengers hadn't expected to wake for decades anyway.

Everybody accepted Andy Braithwaite's revised calculations because the man knew his stuff. Nothing had changed since then.

"And I'm sorry, too, Paul, because it's not up for debate," Ingram said. "We can't revive them yet, and I'm erring on the side of safety because the Jattans sent a probe to scope us out and then they'll show up in person."

Paul didn't deviate. "My colleagues deserve to be allowed to decide for themselves."

"If we tell them the full story, then *none* of them can go back to Earth," Ingram said, painfully aware that she'd already exempted Tev and his family from that rule. "It's the risk of accidentally mentioning the Caisin gate."

"We're not all like Abbie."

"I did say accidentally."

Paul still kept shaking his head. "If you're going to tell them the redacted version when they get to Earth, you can tell them the redacted version now. But you'd be okay with evacuating Kill Line kids to Earth despite the fact they know all about the gate. Forgive me pointing out your inconsistencies."

"And what about the food situation?"

"What about Britain?" Paul spread his hands. "They've got food. This Lawson guy has seen data showing the round trip only takes weeks with regular teerik FTL, so why can't we ship in extra supplies when we need them? That's not a secret now."

"Sorry, I thought I was the one staging this coup."

"You can't justify anything you're doing, Captain."

"Paul, listen to yourself," Ingram said. "You want to invite the British government to Opis to deliver groceries. If you're really worried about perfidious Albion seizing control, you've just made Nomad dependent on British logistics and there'll be a military presence to make it happen, because it's humanitarian aid. Congratulations. You've opened the gates and asked them if they've got a big wooden horsey thing they'd like to wheel in."

Nobody else said a word. Chris looked as impassive as ever, but he was tapping out something on his pocket screen.

"Captain, if we revive people and the food situation gets difficult, we can evacuate them to Earth or exchange some raw materials for supplies," Paul said. "I don't think the gate's that big a deal now, to be honest. It's just a refinement of the big prize that Britain's already got — a proper FTL drive. So even with the threat of attack, we have the wherewithal to do this the right way. We have a back-up plan for food. If anyone wants to stay, we know support from Earth is feasible. And we have other things Britain probably wants, like raw materials."

"I think you're forgetting why we're doing this to start with," Ingram said. "*Aliens.* They've found us. If one lot can find us *twice*, so can the others. They could be on their way now."

"And then again, they might not. But if they are, then what makes you think Earth's safer? If the teeriks could locate it, maybe everyone else can too."

Chris finally joined in. "Dr Cotton, why do you think the Caisin gate isn't a big deal?"

Paul shrugged. "I think you're placing too much emphasis on the impact it'll have. There's not much difference between instant and very fast."

"Spoken like a botanist," Chris said.

"And what's that supposed to mean?"

"If you did my job, you'd understand the value of a split second, and why the Caisin gate's the holy grail of warfare. As soon as someone finds out about it, we'll be under siege — not space tourists gagging to see the sea monsters, but *military missions*. Someone, probably APS, is going to wipe us out and take the technology."

"But only the British have the FTL data."

"It'll leak," Chris said. "Nothing stays secret forever. It's when, not if."

That silenced Paul. He blinked a few times, but it only diverted him for a couple of seconds. "Fine, but we still have to give the people in cryo a say about what happens to them right now. And refusing to do that makes me think the issue really is about removing Erskine."

"Okay," Chris said. "If it makes you happier, we could thaw her out and keep her here just to show that we love her really, but the rest of the folks still have to be evacuated."

Alex nodded. "Dan?"

"Copy that," Trinder said. "Easier to reverse the evacuation when the situation's less fraught than it'll be to raise the dead."

Ingram noted that Trinder had learned to land verbal blows below the belt despite his reputation for silence in meetings. Now was the time for her to signal she'd won and make a few conciliatory noises.

"Well, there you go," she said. "Look, Paul, I don't blame you for feeling like this. You were lied to shamefully for years by Ainatio — and Abbie — and it must have been heartbreaking to find all your die-back work was for nothing. It's inevitable you'll see everything through that prism. Damn, I certainly would. Remember they told our families and friends that we were *dead*. The ones who've survived still think we are, so we know what those lies feel like at the personal level, believe me. But sorry, no coup. Just a massive cock-up that we're trying to put straight, and evacuation's part of that. You're going to have to trust us to make the call on the military threat."

Ingram didn't dare look at Alex because she could see him in her peripheral vision and she was sure he was biting his lip. Paul had listened, though, and she had to give him points for that. He really did have no reason to believe anyone after what had happened during the past year. But empathy wasn't sympathy. Ingram just made sure she understood the enemy.

"It's impossible to prove a negative, Captain, so I won't labour the point," Paul said. "But you've not heard the last of this."

Ingram nearly took the bait and asked how he planned to stop her, but she already knew what his options were and it was time to let him cool off a little. She willed Chris to say nothing. It didn't work.

"There's no vote on this, Dr Cotton." Chris's use of honorifics was always a gauge of how much his heart had hardened. Ingram wasn't even sure that Paul *was* a PhD, but Chris seemed to think that using someone's first name was a sign of his approval, and just using a surname probably struck him as rude. He set great store by manners, even if he wanted to blow someone's brains out. "But if there was, you'd probably lose it. It's just the math."

"The problem's not going to go away," Paul said.

Alex seemed to have had enough. "Okay, any other questions that aren't related to wicked redcoat occupation and parking tanks on lawns?" he asked. "If you think there's a better plan, we really do want to hear it, but in the absence of that, it's happening. Sorry. Caution wins."

"You heard our better idea," Paul said.

The argument seemed to be reigniting. Ingram tried to wind the discussion down again. "Please don't make this any harder than it is. We're in a tight spot and the last thing we need is fighting each other when we might be under attack soon."

Alex tapped the table with his pen. "Okay, I declare this committee meeting of the Tinfoil Milliners' Union closed. Let's all try to get along, shall we?"

Most of the Ainatio group got up and left, but Mangel stayed to finish his tacos.

"Sorry about that," he said. "I thought they were just going to complain and feel better for venting."

Chris shrugged. "But they've got a point. And I also get why they think this is a stitch-up."

"Why didn't you say that, then?"

"Because I'd rather be the bogey man than accidentally sounding like I sympathise. They need to think through what'll happen if they escalate this and my guys have to respond."

"I didn't hear any threats," Alex said.

"I did," Chris said.

Ingram left with Chris, followed by Trinder and Alex. They stopped up in the courtyard between the clinic and the comms tower and had an impromptu wash-up.

"They can't interfere with *Elcano*," Ingram said. "She's up there and they're down here, and nobody's going to fly them there. And anyway, there's Sol." She tapped her earpiece. "Right, Sol?"

She looked up out of habit, but it was just the sky, not a networked office. It did remind her that Solomon had godlike powers, though.

"Correct, Captain," he said.

"You heard all that."

"Indeed. I can lock personnel out of every control system on the base. I don't want to sound rude, but Nomad can function without humans, as it has for decades. So nothing will be sabotaged. But I agree with Alex. I don't think I heard any hint of escalation. Paul Cotton doesn't seem to know what to do, only that he objects to what *you're* doing."

"We're just prepared," Chris said. "Even civilised people can do crazy shit if they've got a crowd egging them on and they're agitated enough."

Alex shook his head. "We haven't even got any bricks they can lob at us. I don't think any of the boffins can throw anyway."

"It's not the physical consequences I'm worried about," Ingram said. "It's the psychology. It's not even about Ainatio versus everyone else. It's nationality. Suddenly Brits are the villains."

"Well, there's only two nations capable of getting out here, and that's you and APS, and I'm fine with it being you guys." Chris didn't seem worried. "Anyway, Dieter's got the dogs out. We just don't want to be caught with our pants around our ankles."

Ingram was still making an effort to like Chris. Even if she failed, though, she knew she could count on him and it made her feel strangely guilty. "If we get heavy-handed, it'll never be forgotten or forgiven," she said. "The rift between Ainatio and everyone else is just going to get bigger."

"But this isn't just about sending a ship home or Brits taking over," Chris said. "It's about maintaining functional discipline, and yes, that covers civvies too. If anyone disruptive sees weakness, things fall apart fast. We're on our own and we've got plenty of external threats to worry about. People need to see that someone's in charge. It makes them feel safer."

"Yeah, if we give in, we open the door to all kinds of demands when the going gets tougher," Trinder said. "If we come under attack, getting people to do as they're told is going to be the difference between Nomad surviving and being the most remote war grave in Earth history."

"Well, we've certainly bigged this up in our imaginations," Alex said. "Indignant boffins one minute, armed insurgents storming the presidential palace the next."

"Let's not get too paranoid," Chris said. "And I know that's rich coming from me. I don't like some of the boffins, but they're not the enemy until they start using force or jeopardise the safety and security of the base."

"I'm worried that I'm back to thinking Paul's got a point about the Caisin gate," Ingram said. "I admit I blow hot and cold on it. As Marc never forgets to point out."

"Push comes to shove, would we sacrifice anybody to keep it under wraps?" Trinder asked.

"No, I wouldn't," Ingram said. "In the very worst scenario, we should be prepared to use the gate to evacuate the base and live with the consequences of its wider discovery."

"Sounds like we've got a policy, then."

"We're here to protect the residents of Nomad, not to police the galaxy's arms race."

"I hate being a grown-up," Alex said. "But at least if someone else gets hold of the gate tech, we're relieved of our superhero duty to ensure it's only used for good."

"We still have some bad things we might need to do with it ourselves yet," Ingram said. "I'd like to hang on to our advantage until we don't need it any longer."

"See? We'll be doing this for the rest of our lives." Chris glanced at his watch as if he needed to be somewhere else. It was one of the twenty-six-hour straps that one of the engineers had been printing as a sideline but they still reminded Ingram too much of hospital tags. "It'll always be a burden. Even if we cut ourselves off from the rest of humanity."

"Anything else we need to do for the time being?" Ingram asked. "I was going to look in on the firearms training today, but now I'm wondering if we've armed the revolution instead."

"We passed the thousand mark this week," Chris said. "Counting two-hundred and twenty-one trained military personnel, we have one thousand and two adults and teens capable of defending Nomad with firearms."

"That's brigade strength. Well done."

"On paper. In reality, that's about forty per cent expert to pretty good, and sixty per cent between useful and basic competence."

"It's good enough, Chris."

"Thank you, Captain. Marc's the one to pin a medal on, though. He's been driving this from the start."

Ingram wondered if Chris was trying hard to like her in return. They both might fail, but it was one of those situations where it really was the thought that counted. She'd settle for civilised discourse.

The huddle broke up and they dispersed. Nomad looked comfortingly busy doing small-town things, if small towns had large bot populations and gun trucks passing up and down the main road. The noise of farm vehicles, quad bikes, and the occasional cow mooing in the distance told Ingram all was well for the time being. This was normal Opis. Her brain had filed it as background noise to be filtered out.

But there were no birds, and she still noticed that gap in the natural soundtrack. Nothing except teeriks breached the barrier field around the perimeter. Eventually, when Earth's transplanted ecosystem had spread far enough and displaced enough native habitats, the base probably wouldn't need a barrier, but by then Nomad would be a small backwater in the spread of human settlement.

Ingram had to make that expansion happen. Standing her ground now was the key to it. She knew they wouldn't be the first settlers to pack their bags if things got too hard, and Lawson had said he wouldn't blame them if they did, but she couldn't live with the shame of failure. There was no going back. They wouldn't be able to forget humans had once built a colony on an alien world and say it was too bad that space didn't work out. Ingram could move civvies around to safer places like chess pieces, but it was her duty to hold the line here until the day someone removed her by force.

She checked her map as she walked across the green to call up the latest resources figures for the training section. The base map had now grown even more layers and could answer almost every how, what, where, and when about Nomad and the space around it. Ingram tapped on the warehouse icon and called up the data.

There it was. Training sessions ran twelve hours a day, fifty-eight per cent of the military personnel spent between four and twenty hours a week as instructors, and fifteen per cent of the base's clean-up bots active during the training day were tasked with collecting the spent cases and other debris to recycle the polymer into fresh ammunition. With the chemical production resources for making primer and powder — simulation wasn't a complete substitute for firing live rounds — it was more resource-hungry than she'd thought, but they had plenty of raw materials and the priority now was to be ready for an alien attack.

One thousand and two. Bravo Zulu, Marc. And Chris.

Now that was a proper militia. There were now very few adults and teenagers here who weren't armed and able to fight, a fact Ingram had to take into account when she worked out how far she could push people. It was the old dilemma of training allies and hoping they didn't turn those skills on you one day.

She slipped into the warehouse via the side door and took a pair of ear defenders to stand behind the safety cordon and watch the class for a while. Some of them were pensioners from Kill Line, well into their seventies.

The number of elderly and infirm willing to have a go at the enemy was sobering. Luce was teaching them handgun skills today, shooting on the move. But instead of being distressed to see elderly men and women tooled up and pumping rounds into disturbingly realistic alien figures instead of pottering around the garden, Ingram found it was a reason for optimism.

Old people had become an increasingly rare species in the Western world as the Decline progressed. Life expectancy had dropped by fifteen years even before die-back. Children might have been a nation's hope for the future, but elderly guerrilla fighters were a sign of something equally uplifting as far as Ingram was concerned. They weren't going to fade into quiet helplessness, and they had no plans to die anytime soon. They summed up Nomad. Mankind wasn't beaten yet. It could regroup and rebuild from decline.

Luce paused and looked over the heads of his class. "Are you joining us, ma'am?" he asked, with a look that suggested he thought it was high time she did.

"I'll be in later this week, Sergeant," Ingram said. "I just came to see how everyone was getting on."

"We're ready."

Luce didn't need to say what they were ready for. Ingram still wondered how effective the weapons would be against Kugin even with improved ammunition, but at least she knew a farmer's everyday shotgun could kill a Jattan. She watched a couple of the old ladies from Kill Line drilling holes in the child-sized Jattan dummies at very close quarters, aiming down at the head as the most vulnerable point, and hoped it would never come to this. Perhaps the old girls felt they had nothing to lose. They looked wonderfully harmless in their knitted cardigans and gardening pants, but the unblinking determination on their faces said otherwise.

Is this what I brought them here for? Really?

And then there was Reverend Berry. It troubled Ingram to see a vicar in his dog collar doing fast reloads.

For a moment, she thought he'd joined the pensioners to show willing or boost morale, but she realised he was now one of the instructors, another detail she wouldn't have missed if this had been her ship. Perhaps he'd done national service before he was ordained, but whatever the explanation, he handled a weapon confidently, and she couldn't really object to a man of God being ready to defend his congregation with lethal force. There was room for interpretation in the fifth commandment.

Ingram was polishing her softer skills though, which she'd assumed she'd always had. She could charm and persuade. She could be such a nice, down-to-earth woman despite her rank and connections, people said, and she knew when to switch it on, but there was more to it than being formally gracious and informally friendly. It meant not steamrollering men like Paul Cotton into compliance, even if letting him have his way wasn't possible.

There'd been a time when she'd have been able to manoeuvre him into thinking the *Elcano* evacuation was his idea, but she seemed to have lost her touch in the last few weeks and painted herself into a corner. Now she couldn't climb down without looking like she'd give in on other issues if sufficient pressure was applied.

"So you're sending *Elcano* home," one of the old dears said while she reloaded. "It's for the best. They can always come back later."

"I hope you don't feel pressured to stay," Ingram said. "Nobody ever intended you to have to fight here."

"If we left, we'd still end up back here sooner or later," the woman said. "You know what? For the first time in years, I feel like I've got a real purpose beyond deciding which grandchild gets my antique clock when I'm gone. We're making a new future for mankind. Ordinary folks — especially us old ones — don't usually get a chance to do that, let alone have a say in it. So I'm not budging an inch."

That was what Ingram had set out to do when she'd signed up for the mission. She'd just forgotten about it. She wanted to be like this old girl when she finally grew up.

"Thank you for reminding me of the bigger picture," Ingram said. "It's too easy to lose sight of what we're doing."

"Just remember we're a long time dead. Seize what you can while you can."

It wasn't new advice, but that didn't make it any less valid. Ingram had seized one half of her life but kept the other at arm's length because it was too difficult and now she regretted it. It wasn't enough to be a dead heroine in a history book, and that Bridget Ingram had never really existed. She went back to the main building, wondering what it was going to take to unite everyone and whether she was capable of doing it.

"I hope you heed that advice, Captain," Solomon said in her earpiece.

Sol's little asides and interruptions felt like having a conscience that really did talk to her. "What should I seize, then, Sol?"

"I think you've forgotten that you were supposed to move out of your cabin today."

"I'm not avoiding it."

"Good, because I had your belongings moved to Marc's house."

"You pulled that stunt on Dan."

"And now I've pulled it on you."

"A bot's been rummaging through my underwear drawer, you mean."

"I've left your more sensitive belongings for you to handle," Solomon said. "But I've already scheduled the refurbishment. Your cabin will be an office by this time tomorrow."

"What if I've changed my mind about Marc?" Ingram asked.

"You haven't, but if you did, you'd have to sleep in one of the store rooms until a house was ready for you. I know you're preoccupied with Paul Cotton's band of ingrates, but you're all here to lead normal human lives, not to import crises and burn yourselves out on them. Go and be a normal woman for a few hours."

"Bloody hell, that's a tall order." Ingram marvelled at Solomon's ability to bollock her and get away with it. "I'll sort it out now."

Once she'd cleared the last of her personal effects, it would be a done deal: she'd have moved in with Marc, with no moving back. She packed the last remaining bits and pieces from her cabin — pictures of shipmates long gone, a collapsible stool, Ainatio's bogus commemorative plaque marking the loss of *Cabot* — and found she suddenly felt happy for the wrong reasons. At last she could go home and there would be someone there to unload her day upon. It was an unimaginable luxury. It wasn't a positive approach to domestic bliss, but she couldn't help it.

Marc was already home when she arrived. She put her holdall in the bedroom and realised she no longer had any private space outside duty hours. She checked where Howie was and found him in the back garden, working out how to tie plant supports.

"I see you've pissed off the workers' revolutionary committee," Marc called from the kitchen. "Good work, Boadicea."

"It wasn't me. It was Chris. Well, I started it, I suppose, but Chris was keen to finish it."

"A cattle prod up the arse works wonders." Marc walked into the living room, wiping his hands. He had a split lip that hadn't been there this morning. "It's too late to undraw red lines."

Ingram forgot *Elcano* for a second. "Good God, what happened to you? Have you been in a fight?"

Marc started laughing. "I've been training some of the technicians. Unarmed combat. I know it won't be much use against the Kugin, but it builds confidence. The last fight most of them had was at kindergarten."

"And they beat you?"

"No, but a couple of them are showing promise. And Mangel too. Us old buggers against the kids."

He looked pleased with himself. On one level, Ingram understood his need to blow off testosterone-laden steam and pass on his skills like some paramilitary village elder. But she was horrified that he'd been hurt enough to bleed. She tried to act as if it was all in a day's work. For him, it was.

Howie walked in clutching a couple of lettuces. "Are we going to make the salad now?"

"Give me five minutes to clean up," Ingram said. "Is that another chicken I can smell cooking?"

"We've got lots of wings and legs," Howie said proudly. "Mrs Brandt killed some chickens today. They don't live long, do they?"

He didn't sound upset by it. Ingram wasn't sure if that was a good sign. She'd certainly never imagined kindly Mrs Brandt as a chicken slayer.

"That's what tortoises say about us," she said. "And mussels. And sharks."

Ingram was just starting to learn to deal with children and the task suddenly seemed so vast that it put her worries about rebellious boffins on the backburner for a while. This was her new reality, wrapped up in a matter of days. This was now her home, Howie was her shared responsibility, and she'd find out whether Marc's charmingly eccentric habits would eventually get on her nerves. Landing on Opis had been easy. This was the real alien landscape — an instant surrogate family. She'd have to get used to where the plates and cups belonged and catch up on Howie's day, memorising the names of teachers and fellow pupils who populated his own daily dramas.

None of this had been part of her plans. She'd always thought all those things didn't apply to her, and that she was somehow excused from a role in normal society because she was a destroyer, not a creator. Her family had prepared her to be that way. But here she was, just a primate like everyone else, needing the basic animal things — food, a mate, a shelter — that underpinned everything humans did and made.

She hoped Solomon was satisfied with her normality score. She didn't think she was doing too badly for a beginner. The more she focused on unremarkable domesticity, the less likely she was to seek out battles to fight because she knew no other life.

"Fred's ignoring me." Ingram washed the dishes while Marc dried. Howie was getting ready for bed. "I suppose I ought to go and see him. Mend a few fences."

"We did give him a bollocking, love. A crow's got his pride."

"What if he's right? What if I shouldn't have made contact with the Jattans?"

"He should still have asked you before calling Lawson."

"Was I wrong?"

"No." Marc scrutinised a plate as if she hadn't washed it properly. "You know you weren't. We'd never have known if it was the right time to do it, but we'd have had to do it sooner or later." He shook his head, bemused by something. "We take it in our stride now, don't we? Aliens, I mean. I'm still more surprised by our attitude than I am by their existence."

Ingram lay awake that night wondering what was going on in the Jattan opposition camp. Perhaps they hadn't picked up her message at all. Spying on the Protectorate's navy hadn't yielded anything so far, not even a discussion about the missing ship. All she could do now was listen to Solomon's files. Perhaps this was how it was always going to be, just waiting and watching year after year. She wasn't sure how long she could put up with that.

Marc stirred. "Are you still awake?"

"Just working out a few things."

"Yeah. Me too."

Maybe he wanted to talk. He was always rather oblique when he had something personal on his mind but couldn't bring himself to dump it on her.

"I swore I'd never weaken and ask a man this," Ingram said, "but what are you thinking about?"

"Technology."

"Oh."

"If we can terraform bits of Opis and deal with pathogens and stuff, why can't we re-do Earth and clean it up? Ainatio's got the technology. We could rebuild the West from the ground up. Maybe that's what we should be doing. And if the company could do it here, why did it never come up with a countermeasure for die-back? What would have happened if one of the diseases the bots found here was similar?"

Ingram wondered why she'd just accepted it as beyond the company's abilities too. "I'm not sure I've got the nerve to ask Paul and Lianne why they failed so badly."

"Save it for the next time you need to upset him."

"Anyway, if the bots could fix die-back, some tossers would only wreck the place again. Because they want to."

Marc rearranged his pillows and punched them into a more comfortable shape. "Yeah. If it hadn't been die-back, they would have found something else."

"My money's still on terrorism rather than an accident. Could be both, though. Never let a good crisis go to waste."

"Imagine if we'd had the gate and the probes a few years ago." Marc sounded almost wistful. "I could ruin some bastard's day and be home for tea before he hit the ground. No more exciting tourism trying to get out of the country before the locals invited me to a meeting with a length of metal pipe. You could have reduced Calais to talc from your country estate."

"I'm not sure I want to fight that kind of war."

"I would. I loved doing the job, but I'd have been happy to press a button if I'd had the option. I'm not into this honourable warrior shit. I just want to get things done."

When Ingram had first agonised over whether to hand the Caisin gate to the government, Marc had predicted that the first thing they'd do with it would be to use it locally and settle a few scores on Earth. It didn't sound such a terrible thing now. Either her red lines had shifted or she'd accepted the inevitable.

The test would be whether she could still justify keeping it from Lawson. She changed her mind about it several times a week, and she'd never been a ditherer. It was ironic that some of the boffins didn't see sharing the technology as a big deal now.

"Anyway." Marc sounded sleepy. "Anyway... welcome home, Bridget Ingram. I'm glad you're here."

"I'm glad I'm here too." she said.

* * *

OFFICE OF THE GOVERNMENT OF JATT IN EXILE, CLERICS' QUARTER, ROUVELE, SOUTHERN VIILOR, ESMOS: FOUR DAYS LATER.

Ten days had passed since the humans' commander had sent her uncompromising demand. It was time Nir-Tenbiku gave her his answer.

He watched the transmission from the doomed probe again and replayed Captain Ingram's message, fully aware that he wasn't going to extract any more information from either recording. He was trying to guess her state of mind. For all he knew there could have been something highly significant hidden in her words, but he knew too little about humans to recognise it. Her emphasis was odd, but the meaning was clear; one of her people had been killed, she'd exact some kind of revenge, she'd demanded an explanation, and she'd retaliate if any more incursions were made.

Did she know where the Halu-Masset was based? If she did, her teeriks would have told her about Esmos's neutrality, so she'd have to be extraordinarily confident or foolish to think she could come after him here.

If she knows, that is.

He was going round in circles now. Without more information, he was wasting his time. He paused the recording and leaned his arms on the desk for a few moments of reduced awareness. If he closed his eyes and surrendered to full sleep, he'd find it hard to concentrate again when he woke, but he needed to fight this fatigue. He slowed his mind and let himself drift.

He could hear and see his surroundings, but everything was veiled in a haze that would leave him more alert when he surfaced from it. Sometimes his best ideas emerged when he was in this state, and at other times random memories bubbled up to leave him disturbed. Today he saw his grandfather, leaning over him with reassuring words as he lay recovering from some childhood accident of his own foolish making. Grandfather cut a splendid figure in his pale blue ceremonial uniform. "Dals, don't let this little mishap deter you from taking bold risks," he said kindly. "It's healthy to feel a little fear."

Nir-Tenbiku couldn't even recall how he'd ended up injured. But it was good to see Grandfather, even in a moment that had never happened, a conversation with a man who'd died before he was born. His dozing mind had superimposed his father's voice on the official portrait of his grandfather, an almost life-sized fabric work that hung in the reception room. He understood why both elements had risen from his subconscious, but it wasn't a real memory and he didn't expect it to be. Perhaps it was what he'd have wanted his grandfather to say if he'd ever met him.

"Excellency? Forgive the interruption."

Nir-Tenbiku was back in the conscious world immediately. "Don't apologise, Bas," he said. "I shouldn't be napping at my desk anyway. It's a bad habit."

"Minister Eb-Lan is here to see you. I've respectfully asked him to wait. Do you need a little more time?"

Bas was being protective and rather brave, considering that Cudik wasn't a patient person. It was very touching.

"No, I'm fine now, thank you. Show him in, please."

Cudik arrived with a box and placed it on Nir-Tenbiku's desk. It was one of those grocery containers for prepared meals, a disposable thing with an intricately-cut closure on top that opened like the petals of a flower bud, but no tempting aroma emerged as Cudik unfurled it. It revealed a squat, opaque green bottle.

"Is that what I think it is?" Nir-Tenbiku asked.

"I couldn't walk past it. One of the exotic food merchants had it on display. It'll wake you up more effectively than a nap."

He placed the bottle in Nir-Tenbiku's hands. It was very old and Nir-Tenbiku knew exactly what it was, because no other decoction, no other vintage, and no other commemoration had come together to create an object like this. It was a bottle of paliernui from his grandfather's era that marked the thousandth anniversary of Cileki Citadel's elevation from ordinary city to the regional capital of Nir province. Only a thousand bottles had been made, given as gifts to the regional assembly members, clergy, and other prominent citizens. Most had vanished by now, but from time to time a bottle would appear when someone decided to auction it for the cash.

"I'm stunned," Nir-Tenbiku said. "But I have to ask the question."

"How did it get here, you mean? Who's noticed us? Who might have set it as bait?" Cudik made his gesture of resignation, splaying all his arms for a moment like an avian about to take off. "I did consider that. I've also considered that it might be *poisoned* bait, so we'll test it when you open it."

"But did you ask the merchant?"

"Yes. She said she'd bought it on a trip to Dal Mantir and thought it might fetch a better price on Bhinu than in the colonies."

"As long as she thought you were a rich Jattan tax exile. And as long as she wasn't a Protectorate agent."

"Primary, I've spent years investigating the Esmosi we have to deal with outside this enclave, and I can tell you her grandmother's clan name and what she had for dinner."

Cudik trusted Esmosi security but he trusted himself more. Nir-Tenbiku respected that. Esmos took a dim view of foreign agents within its borders even if they weren't planning to assassinate exiles, but that didn't mean there were no spies operating here. Cudik liked to keep his skills sharp because he was afraid of fading with age, so he made it his business to monitor anyone who might have been a security risk. It tempered his frustration over preparing for a war that still hadn't happened.

Nir-Tenbiku studied the bottle again. Aged paliernui became a little more liquid with the years, but it still wasn't slopping around inside the glass. It would pour easily, though.

"You think I need to drink this, then?" he asked.

"You need to make a decision about the humans."

"I doubt it'll help me do that."

"There's no point in tossing the decision to the rest of us. We'll accept whatever you choose to do."

"I don't know any more now about Bridget Ingram or humans than I did then."

"She has teeriks, so she probably knows where we are," Cudik said. "If they haven't briefed her on who's most likely to give us sanctuary, I'd be shocked. She'll also be aware of the consequences of attacking us on Esmos."

"Or she doesn't know any of that. You know how teeriks keep things to themselves."

"We know how *Lirrel* kept things to himself. Other teeriks might not be like that at all. Not that I doubt poor Iril, but most of our knowledge of teeriks is gossip. And we can't judge a species by the single example we knew."

"Ingram asks what we want," Nir-Tenbiku said, tilting the bottle in an attempt to see the liquid level against the light. "Humans' general demeanour and what they seem to have achieved out here suggests she's capable of taking action but chooses not to."

"What does your intuition tell you?" Cudik asked. "What does your soul want to do?"

Nir-Tenbiku thought for a moment. His decision hadn't quite crystallised but he could feel it taking shape. "I want to talk to her, Cudik. I want to find out all I can about these humans and see if we can do business with them. And I don't want them to think we're savages. I want to show we regret what happened."

"I understand why we need to sound them out, Primary, but does their opinion of us matter if we can simply continue to avoid them by staying here?"

"Yes. Yes, it *does* matter. We're making a moral claim to the right to govern Jatt. We have a duty to uphold standards of behaviour and the reputation of our ancestors. That's an end in itself." Nir-Tenbiku put the bottle down. He imagined opening it when they finally retook Jevez. "And eventually we'll have to leave Esmos, at which point we're rather exposed. I would rather we had at least one alliance before we do."

Cudik wandered over to the window and looked out on the garden. "The other snag is that we still haven't told the Convocation about the humans, or that we've created some difficulties with them."

"They only need to know when they need to know."

"And you know what'll happen if they find out from someone else."

The Convocation didn't like foreigners bringing trouble with them. The best Nir-Tenbiku could hope for was that they'd withdraw the sanctuary they'd given the Halu-Masset. If the humans turned out to be a problem for them, though, their displeasure would be much more robust.

He let his thoughts tumble out. "I'm going to respond to the humans and apologise for the incident," he said. "I'm going to tell them the truth, too, because their teeriks will have told them about the broader situation anyway."

Cudik sat down again. "Suitably redacted."

"They must know by now that we have a grievance with the Protectorate. I'm not so naive that I'd volunteer the small detail."

"Indeed. My apologies."

"And I'll say that if they don't feel able to open talks with us, that I would at least ask them not to ally with the Jattans, if that's what they have in mind. In exchange for staying neutral, we would see what benefits we could offer them."

"Primary, that's a complete surrender." Cudik sounded weary. "Pay them to stay out of it? How do we even know what they want?"

"That's one of the questions I'll ask, if we get that far."

"What about the ship? Aren't you going to ask for its return?"

"At least the Protectorate can't get hold of it."

"I'd advise against this, Primary." Cudik did exactly what his cabinet portfolio required and saw everything through the lens of defence and security — the risks, the costs, and the likelihood of success. "These are concessions to be eked out sparingly, and only if we absolutely need to make them."

"I can only tell you the direction in which my arguments will lead," Nir-Tenbiku said. "Everything depends on how the humans respond at each stage. We might not even get past the apology. I'm simply telling you how far I'm prepared to go."

Cudik had a habit of looking off to one side when he was conflicted, as if he was too polite to tell his Primary that he was an idiot but still had to steer him away from a dangerous path. In the end, Nir-Tenbiku could take whatever action he wished because it was the Primary's prerogative. But he was flying blind, dealing with a potential enemy who was justifiably aggrieved but about whom he knew very little, and the little he knew was alarming and complex. Faced with that, he could either remain paralysed by indecision or say what was on his mind.

Being open would at least show him what the humans were really like.

"I defer to you, obviously," Cudik said. "I would just urge extreme caution."

"Whatever we do, the humans are here, they'll almost certainly stay, and we have to deal with them at some point, either as the new government of Jatt or as failed rebels in need of friends."

Cudik just rocked his head from side to side, more in surrender than agreement. "Very well. Shall we send a message now and see how long she takes to respond?"

"No, I want to speak to this Ingram in real time," Nir-Tenbiku said. "I want a conversation, not an exchange of memos. I need to get the measure of her."

They'd have to send an initial message and see if the humans wanted to continue the conversation. If they did, it would happen in real time, with no chance to think things over or express them more carefully. He'd avoid ambiguous language and keep things simple.

"You've always been a careful man, Primary, but this is a big decision," Cudik said. "I hope it's just a case of my lacking your vision to see what has to be done."

"If you're asking if I'm guessing my way through this, I am," Nir-Tenbiku said. "Gan-Pamas gave his life for the restoration, and his advice was to interact with the humans. If he believed they were significant enough to take the risk, I believe him." He called up the chronometer and studied the floating numbers, trying to work out when to send his invitation to talk. "What time of day would it be at their location?"

Cudik pulled out his navigation device. "Mid-morning."

"Let's do this right away, then."

Nir-Tenbiku didn't take the responsibility of contact lightly, although the teeriks had obviously beaten him to it and had probably already influenced how humans would see the politics of this sector. Teeriks didn't count, though. How he handled this would determine the future not only of Jatt but of Kugad and Esmos too. He wasn't easily scared, but while he had no doubts about what he needed to do for Jatt, he didn't know what was best for the sector in which Jatt would have to exist.

There was no point worrying about what he couldn't do, though. If he did, he would do nothing, which wouldn't stop whatever the humans had in mind from taking place.

Bas brought in the transmitter and placed it on his desk, then waved at the control panel to activate it.

"When you're ready, Excellency."

Nir-Tenbiku was as ready as he'd ever be. He slowed his breathing and put the bigger picture out of his mind, ready to address just one person on another world.

"This is His Excellency Nir-Tenbiku Dals, rightful Mediator of Jatt, Primary in Exile. I wish to speak to Captain Bridget Ingram to answer her question. I also wish to extend my apologies for the unfortunate incident that took place. I await your response."

There was no concession there to worry Cudik. It was neutral, and he'd kept his speech basic to avoid mistranslations. Now all he could do was wait. He nodded to Bas to send the transmission and hoped that the Convocation wasn't intercepting his communications.

"Shall we open that bottle?" Cudik asked.

"Would you be offended if I asked to save it for when we liberate Jevez and declare the independence of Jatt again?"

"Not at all, Primary. Very apt." Cudik got to his feet. "It's probably going to be some considerable time before the humans respond, if they do at all of course. Would you excuse me?"

"Of course." It could take days. Nir-Tenbiku would have to find some distraction to stop him worrying about what might be happening at the other end. "I might venture outside the Quarter. I've been cloistered in here for too long."

"I'll get your security detail."

"I was only thinking of going out in the carriage. Bas can drive me. Or I could drive myself, of course."

Cudik looked as if he was going to give him the full personal security lecture, but he just bowed his head politely.

"Avoid the market. It's extremely busy today."

Going outside the Clerics' Quarter was an expedition in itself. There was preparation required. It was impossible for Nir-Tenbiku to disguise the fact that he was Jattan, but he could still be anonymous because of the unfriendly sunshine in Esmos. Jattans had to shield their skin and eyes with a thick fabric veil, and once he did that, he looked like any other expatriate taking some fresh air.

Inside the official carriage — just a small vehicle, nothing ostentatious — he was legally still within the Clerical Quarter no matter where he went. He took his protected status with him. He could even walk around the streets safely, unrecognised even by those few who knew who he was, because Esmos was an orderly nation, and cities like Rouvele were the most orderly of all.

Rouvele seemed an unnatural place, too well-maintained and tasteful to feel friendly, a theatre set of a city. It very nearly was. It prided itself on being the home of Esmosi culture, and simply walking down the street was a performance in itself, and had to be done correctly. Nir-Tenbiku did his best to appreciate their culture, but he didn't enjoy it as much as he enjoyed the monks' singing at night. They meant what they sang with every fibre of their being. The theatre singers merely pretended.

He'd miss this place, though. In a way it had been his prison, but some people paid a small fortune to be isolated in beautiful surroundings. If he had to be exiled, this was a good place to think and plan without distraction. But it couldn't continue. He was impatient to feel whole and part of his people for the first time.

He searched the anteroom to find a suitable scarf for his excursion, then spent a few minutes wrapping it around his head and shoulders. There was a trick to leaving enough slack in the fabric to create a peak to shield his eyes. Today he didn't seem to be able to get it right, so he gave up and selected a protective visor instead. He'd take the processional route out of the city, the broad avenue flanked by monuments and scented trees, then return via the ruins of the ancient fortifications and spend some time walking through the alleys in the jewellers' quarter. He was quite looking forward to it.

Bas hurried into the room at a fast walk. Nir-Tenbiku arranged his visor. "I won't be long, Bas," he said. "Is the carriage here already?"

"It's the humans, Excellency," Bas said. "The captain responded. She's waiting."

Nir-Tenbiku hadn't expected such a rapid reply. It could have been a coincidence that she happened to be available, but she might simply have been angry and in a hurry to berate him. He took a breath and settled his mind.

"Please get Minister Eb-Lan for me," he said. "I'd like him to hear this."

It was bad form to keep Ingram waiting, so he'd have to start without Cudik present. Manners still mattered even with aliens who might not notice them. He went back to his desk to take the call, hoping the formal splendour around him would focus his mind on sounding statesmanlike. If he got this wrong, he couldn't imagine the consequences.

"Captain Bridget Ingram," he said. "This is Nir-Tenbiku Dals, Primary of Jatt in exile. I apologise for keeping you waiting."

"Thank you for your courtesy," she said. "My words are being translated for me because I don't speak Jattan, and your words are being translated into my language, so I hope we can understand each other's intentions. You may call me Captain. May I address you as Primary?"

He was caught off-guard by both her directness and her polished manners. He'd expected a cold reception, if not outright hostility. He also wanted to know how that translation system worked, but that would have to wait.

"Please do, Captain," he said. "I welcome your call. I'm aware of what happened at your base. Gan-Pamas Iril sent a message and explained about the unfortunate death of your subordinate. I'm truly sorry. It should never have happened."

"Then he was able to communicate with you in Esmos."

So she knew. Humans seemed able to find out everything, but if she knew the Halu-Masset's location, she also knew not to provoke the Esmosi.

"Yes. I don't know how to properly show our regret for this tragedy."

"Why did Gan-Pamas come to Opis? I know about the prenu." The voice was measured and calm, offering no clues. "What made him think it was here?"

Opis. Opis? "Is that your name for the planet where your base is located?"

"It is."

"I don't know where he got his intelligence, Captain. Gan-Pamas was the Controller of Procurement, a minister in my government in exile." Nir-Tenbiku now picked his words even more carefully. "He broke contact with us because he feared detection by Kugad or the Protectorate. But we knew he was looking for the warship taken from the Kugin shipyard. The prenu."

"I'm aware that you're arming yourselves for a war with the Protectorate," Ingram said. "This is none of our business and we don't want to get involved. We just want to be left alone. But there's still the matter of my dead comrade. She wasn't a soldier. We in the military treat the murder of unarmed civilians as the gravest crime."

Cudik rushed in at that moment and stood in front of the desk, looking startled. Nir-Tenbiku gestured at him to stay quiet. It sounded very much as if Ingram knew the etiquette for resolving a wrong of that magnitude, then. She'd given Nir-Tenbiku the opening to state his explanation and offer recompense. Her teeriks must have advised her very well — or she'd somehow been observing Jatt more closely than he realised. It confirmed that these were armed forces from a capable and confident civilisation. And it was the worst possible luck to encounter them under these circumstances.

"If you tell me what would lessen your grief and understandable anger, I'll provide it," Nir-Tenbiku said carefully. Ingram probably knew the formal procedure. He'd stick to it. "We're offering recompense."

There was a longer pause than he expected. "Then I would like answers to more questions."

"Only knowledge? We can provide many material things."

"Just the truth, please."

She didn't even ask for a token offering to satisfy honour. She just wanted to know something. He had a feeling it would be military intelligence, and that would be awkward.

"I'm happy to answer, Captain."

"Is the warship critical to your plans?"

She was certainly direct. He'd tell her what she probably already knew. "No, but it's a matter of pride for the Protectorate. Their secret intelligence service commissioned it."

Cudik gestured frantically at Nir-Tenbiku to stop. He'd said too much, perhaps, but it was true, and there was no reason for Ingram not to be told that they'd lost track of Gan-Pamas, or to discuss the incident itself. The humans knew what had happened to them. They actually had information Nir-Tenbiku needed.

"Lirrel killed my crew member," Ingram said. So she knew the teerik's name. Was there any detail she hadn't extracted about the mission? "It was a particularly violent murder. We believed teeriks were peaceful. Do you know the reason for his behaviour?"

"No, I fear we don't, Captain. Lirrel was increasingly erratic, but we didn't think he was dangerous."

"I thought only Kugin had teerik assistance. Do you normally work with teeriks?"

"Not at all."

"How did you find him, then?"

Nir-Tenbiku wasn't quite sure where her questions were leading, but he couldn't refuse to answer them now. "I believe there was a mishap on a test flight. The Kugin thought he'd been killed along with the rest of the personnel on board. One of our patrols happened to find him in an escape pod."

Another long pause. Perhaps the translation she was receiving was struggling with some of the words. It was foolish, but he still hoped Gan-Pamas was there, assisting her.

"Thank you for your explanation," Ingram said. "I would ask you to stay away from Opis now and not attempt further surveillance. We will defend ourselves robustly if you do."

"Captain, we meant no harm. We were looking for the ship and Gan-Pamas. His message said that we should at least try to make contact with you."

"Why?"

"He thought it was worth establishing a relationship. Would you be willing to meet me to talk about our respective interests in this sector?"

Cudik put his hand firmly on Nir-Tenbiku's arm and mouthed *no*.

"I think that would be ill-advised at the moment," Ingram said. "There would be difficulties."

"We could meet on neutral ground."

"I regret we're not willing to have contact yet."

If she really meant to say *yet* and *at the moment*, then the door wasn't completely closed. But she sounded as if she was bringing the conversation to an end, and Nir-Tenbiku still needed closure on Gan-Pamas.

"May I ask *you* a question, Captain?"

"Yes."

"Is Gan-Pamas dead?"

"Yes, he was shot. I'm sorry. I wish we could have avoided it."

Nir-Tenbiku had known it from the start, but that simple confirmation broke him. Asking for a favour when he was offering recompense was pushing the boundaries of etiquette, but if he didn't do this, he'd never forgive himself.

"Can his body be recovered?" Just hearing himself say the words was agonising. Ingram could refuse, or perhaps his body had already been disposed of, but the last thing Nir-Tenbiku could do for his friend was to bring him home and eventually lay him to rest in Jevez. "Is it possible to repatriate him?"

He expected a long pause and he got it. He braced for a refusal.

"Was he your friend?" Ingram asked.

"Yes, he was. He was a patriot when it was very hard to be one."

"Then I'm sorry for your loss. I'll see if I can find a way to send him back to you that doesn't compromise our security. We've respected his remains. This is important to us as warriors."

Of all the things that had surprised Nir-Tenbiku about humans today, that was the biggest revelation. The conversation had been polite but distant, and he hadn't expected a single concession. The absence of raging threats was remarkable enough. But Ingram seemed to want him to know the kind of culture he was dealing with, and that it had standards she expected from others as well.

"Captain, is there anything else you want to know?" he asked.

"That answers my questions, thank you," Ingram said. "We'll speak again about the repatriation. Goodbye."

The link closed. Nir-Tenbiku sat in silence for a moment. Cudik was still staring at him as if he wasn't at all happy but couldn't bring himself to say so.

"I know you would have handled that differently, Cudik," Nir-Tenbiku said. "But what's done is done. That was a civilised discussion. It could easily have been the start of a war."

"Primary, we're not going to make allies out of them," Cudik said. "I'd advise not provoking them further. They might be polite now, but I doubt we'll get away with it twice."

"She didn't sound like she wanted conflict."

"Yes, but the repatriation might be a trap. Your guard's down. She asked if Gan-Pamas was your friend. That's what I'd ask if I were looking for weak spots, so be very careful. I know I can't stop you agreeing to this, but there's absolutely no reason for humans to be conciliatory towards us after what happened. They have a motive."

"We *all* have a motive." Nir-Tenbiku closed his eyes for a few moments. His waking dream had told him to be bold. What he'd done had nothing to do with that, but it still seemed like sound advice. "Would you have been able to sleep soundly if I'd left it at that and never asked, never tried to find out what happened to Iril and bring him home? Because I couldn't."

He couldn't sit here and wait, either, and he wasn't ready to abandon contact with the humans. It was unwise to judge any species by one example, but these people were nothing like the Kugin or even the Esmosi. There was restraint in there, but also courtesy, and respect. He had to look Ingram in the eye before he took her literally and avoided humans forever.

"I'm going to Opis," he said.

"Primary, you've lost your mind. Do *not* do this."

"I have to. I have to talk to them in person."

"Ingram made it clear they would use force to stop us landing on the planet."

"*Opis.* They call it Opis."

"This is suicidal. *They will kill you.* How do they plan to return Gan-Pamas's body? Where will they bring him? They're trying to fix a position for an attack."

"I'll see what they say. And if they do kill me, Cudik, I appoint you to take my place and continue the fight."

"But I *can't* take your place," Cudik said. "Without a Nir-Tenbiku leading this, there's no legitimacy, no direct link to the Protectorate's coup. Your grandfather's name is how we demonstrate to the people that we're restoring the democracy and the freedoms taken from them. I can perform the tasks, but I can't inspire a population to rise up and support us. You can. You're the heir to Nir-Tenbiku Bac."

"And that's why I've got to do this," Nir-Tenbiku said. "A name isn't enough to sustain us if we succeed. Once we take back Jatt, we still have a long battle ahead of us. I have to bring something extra to the table, something that's going to make a real difference to Jatt's future."

Cudik looked exasperated. "Your problem, Primary — and I mean no disrespect — is that you assume everyone is as honourable as you are until proven otherwise. You're like your grandfather. You believe in fairness and expect everyone else to as well."

"I'm naive, you mean."

"Yes. There's not much difference between naivety and honour when you insist on being a good person in a bad world."

The Kugin often mocked Jattans as hot-heads who rushed into situations and got themselves killed. Nir-Tenbiku didn't see himself as that kind of Jattan, today's undisciplined and unprofessional officer class, but he did wonder for a moment if there was a grain of truth in it. Here he was, having had an excessively frank conversation with a human commander and learned too little about humans in the process, deciding to ignore their warning not to visit Opis. Caution had abandoned him.

No: he *had* learned something about humans.

He hadn't asked Ingram the important strategic questions about where they'd come from and what they planned to do here, but he'd discovered something fundamental about their mentality. Like Jattans — proper Jattans, his kind of people — humans cared about the reverent handling of the dead, even of *enemy* dead. Ingram had agreed to try to get Gan-Pamas home, and Nir-Tenbiku believed she was sincere.

He felt he could do business with her to Jatt's advantage, and he was ready to risk his life to do it.

"Naivety it is, then," he said. "I'll give her the benefit of the doubt. And if I'm wrong, I'll pay the price, and the restoration of the Jattan government will be in your hands."

* * *

CO'S OFFICE, JOINT COMMAND MEMBERS PRESENT: 1120, OCTOBER 30, OC.

Ingram leaned back in her seat, smoothing her hair as if she was trying to look nonchalant after a fight.

"At least we haven't declared war on each other," she said. "But did that get us anywhere?"

For a few minutes, Solomon felt he'd forgotten where he ended and Ingram began. Now she was speaking for herself without the AI translation rendered in her voice. It wasn't the first time he'd recreated someone else's voice to make a critical call, but it felt strangely intrusive doing it with Ingram's.

"Sol did a great job," Trinder said. "It really sounded like you, Captain. Even with all the trills and burbles."

"But Nir-Tenbiku didn't ask about the ship at all. I guarantee they'll have another crack at it later. He was just sounding us out. He didn't even mention the teeriks, and he must know they're here."

Searle shrugged. "Or maybe he's being careful because he thinks we're the superior force. We might look like it from where he's standing. He realises we know more about them than he expected and he probably thinks we know even more than we do."

"You know what did work?" Marc said. "Agreeing to repatriate his mate. It could be a set-up for an ambush, but I think he's telling the truth. He wants to do right by his friend the same way we would."

"Just as well you stopped the medics making a mess of the body," Chris said.

Marc fidgeted with his coffee cup. "I have my sensitive moments."

Ingram started scribbling on her screen. Solomon knew her habits now. She used the stylus when she wanted to think and the keyboard when she'd made up her mind what to say, as if it was more permanent than handwriting.

"So let's see what else we learned from all that," she said. "One, teeriks can be unpredictable — helpful to have that confirmed. Two, Fred told the truth about Jattans having a blood money custom where they apologise and pay up. Three, Gan-Pamas got a message out after all — let's work out how we missed it. Four, he was one of their ministers, not some dodgy gunrunner — killing a politician is an act of war in many places, but not here, it seems. And five — allegedly, Gan-Pamas wanted Nir-Tenbiku to open talks with us, because we're so marvellous for some reason. Thoughts?"

"I'm worried that I failed to detect his transmission," Solomon said. "He tried to bounce a signal off the comms relay and failed. I saw nothing else. Perhaps he had a homing device, something that would head back to his base carrying stored data rather than transmitting a signal from the surface."

"That would explain their delay in checking us out," Chris said. "Whatever it was had to make its way to Esmos or wherever they recover these things."

"There's no way you could have spotted that, Sol," Ingram said.

"Perhaps not, but I need to be better prepared in the future."

"Well, at least we've left the door open to contact Nir-Tenbiku again. I don't know if I made it clear enough that we don't want them to visit, though, because he accepted the ban a little too easily. I suppose we now need to tell Lawson."

"As a courtesy, though, not to get his blessing," Marc said. "And we remind him we don't know the real intentions of anybody out here, so any contact has to be strictly local and conducted by us — nothing that lets them know where Earth is. It also makes sure nobody back home is tempted to find a way to talk direct to Nir-Tenbiku and bypass us peasants."

It all sounded like a reasonable plan to Solomon. Ingram was talking almost cordially to the Jattan faction who'd been the most immediate threat, and whatever else she'd achieved, she'd bought some time. He agreed with her that things could have turned out much worse.

"Do we all feel the security situation's improved?" Solomon asked.

"Possibly not, but we know more, which always helps," Trinder said. "Even if Nir-Tenbiku's lying, he doesn't seem to be the typical kamikaze Jattan that Fred keeps telling us about."

Chris took refuge behind folded arms. "Don't ask me. I don't trust anybody."

"At least neither side's stoking the situation by imagining the awful things the other's doing," Ingram said. "And crass as this sounds, we have the body. And *Curtis*. So we have some leverage. Now I have to work out how, where, and when to hand Gan-Pamas over."

"The freighter would have been perfect," Searle said. "But that means withdrawing it from Dal Mantir, and we still need to know what the Protectorate's up to."

"And I'm reluctant to sacrifice one of our shuttles. We'd have to assume we wouldn't get it back, and there's always the risk of ambush. Can we build something for a single body? It's just a torpedo casing. We don't even need a drive. We could gate it somewhere safe and give Nir-Tenbiku the coordinates to recover it. Dump and run. I wasn't planning the full ceremonial."

"If we think this is a set-up, then why are we doing it?" Trinder asked. "I was taught never to start negotiations with a concession. Is this to claim moral high ground, in case that counts with Jattans?"

"We're hinting we have something they want and we might have conditions for it," Searle said. "And if they're not as gentlemanly as they seem, they'll think we're dumb to offer, so they won't be on their guard if and when we need to kick their asses."

Ingram smiled indulgently, but the smile faded as if she'd realised something. She twiddled with her stylus.

"Perhaps I've projected too many human values onto Jattans because we both use language in a similar way. But refusing repatriation felt wrong. I don't want to hold KIAs hostage, because we don't want the Jattans doing it to us."

"I'd have done the same, but for different reasons," Chris said. "I never met an asshole who changed because I set him a good example, though."

Solomon checked the manufacturing database. "Let's look at the practicalities. We could make a suitable tube easily enough. Building a drive will take a few more resources from the upgrade programme, so gating it is probably best. They'll think we have a formidable stealth ship capable of making undetectable drops."

"I don't want to be too upbeat about a solemn duty, but the collective deviousness of this group comforts me greatly," Ingram said. "Timing?"

"He's not expecting it to happen tomorrow. We have a few weeks' grace, I think."

"Very well, I'll send round a general message to update base personnel and emphasise that we're still at increased readiness regarding the Protectorate and Kugad, but an attack isn't imminent from the Jattan opposition."

"Are the teeriks going to see this as cosying up to an enemy?" Trinder asked. "Remember when I asked Fred if the Jattans would go away and leave us alone if we handed the ship over to Gan-Pamas, and he said the teeriks would be screwed either way? Okay, we didn't know the guy was an opposition minister then, but the teeriks might think all Jattans are the same and they'll expect to be used for bargaining at a later date."

"I promised we'd protect them," Ingram said. "And we all know we've got damn good reasons to. But we can't escalate trouble with the opposition just to reassure the teeriks which side we're on."

"That's assuming Nir-Tenbiku's not playing games with us," Chris said. "If he is, my guess would be that he'll ratchet up the pressure gradually rather than try to ambush us. So they don't mention *Curtis* to start with, but the next time you talk to him, he says, 'Oh, maybe you could send our buddy back in his freighter.' And then they ask if we'd be willing to do a deal with the ship. Dan's right. Not gung-ho suicide squads at all, but possibly devious. Just like us."

"Or they're being cautious because they're not sure if we're in league with the Protectorate," Trinder said. "They appear to assume we aren't, maybe because we have the stolen ship and the teeriks. But they might think *we're* the ones with the elaborate plot. Just playing devil's advocate there."

Solomon had been surrounded by humans for more than a century, and identified with them so completely that he'd been baffled when he first learned he was an AI. But it was only in the last year that he'd seen just how convoluted their thinking could be. It wasn't that he couldn't lie or imagine; he just hadn't experienced humans under extreme stress and genuinely afraid for their lives before. Real dread couldn't be reproduced in exercises.

Now he was watching his humans wondering if an alien's passive behaviour was a smokescreen for a stealthy assault. They might pull that stunt themselves, so professional caution meant they had to consider that their potential enemy would do the same. Solomon had been through this, and it had taught him what being left sadder but wiser truly meant. He'd had a comparatively innocent upbringing in Tad Bednarz's lab. His mistake with Erskine had been to assume that if he held back from aggressive measures, she would too. He'd been wrong. Thinking the enemy would behave like you didn't work.

"Let's go with what we've got," Marc said. "We wanted better intel and now we've got some. For all we know, Nir-Tenbiku might end up running Jatt and he'll remember who's kept their word."

"Indeed," Ingram said. "It's no time to make new enemies."

"Have you ever negotiated with an enemy?" Marc asked.

"Not really, no. Not unless you count fifty rounds rapid."

"This might be a job to keep Bissey occupied. Jattan wrangling, I mean."

"I think not."

"Okay."

It was hard to tell if Marc meant it or if he was teasing her, but she looked as if she'd taken it seriously. The group seemed satisfied with the outcome, though. Marc, Chris, and Trinder left, but Searle hung back to talk to Ingram.

"Shall we scrap work on *Curtis*?" he asked. "Just in case she becomes a bargaining chip later. The more we refit, the harder it'll be to hand her over if we need to. I don't want to see her go, but I don't want to burn time and resources rolling back all the mods later."

Ingram smiled conspiratorially. "Put her back to factory settings, but minus all the really good bits the Jattans never knew about?"

"Absolutely. I'm not that honest."

Solomon thought Searle was an improvement on Bissey when it came to advising Ingram. He was all about the practicalities, not the politics and the philosophy.

"I'm still not sure how the teeriks would feel about ending up with no ship at all," Ingram said. "I know we've commandeered her to all intents and purposes, but she's still physically here and they have access. It might give them a sense of having some insurance. A getaway vehicle."

"But they haven't got one," Searle said. "They're reliant on us and they know it."

"Yes, but psychologically, *Curtis* looks like their lifeboat. Leave an empty hangar, and they see how stranded they are. Knowing isn't the same as feeling."

"And they're proud of what they designed. Don't underestimate that, ma'am."

"I'd better go and talk to them later," Ingram said. "I have to see Fred anyway, but he warned me it was a bad idea to make contact, so I'll see what he thinks of them contacting us. We're gradually edging towards handing *Curtis* over, aren't we?"

"We'd be giving her to rebels," Searle said. "That has its uses, but remember the Protectorate will treat it as a hostile act if they find out. We'd do the same."

"But we'd still need to strip *Curtis* clean even if we gave her back to her rightful owners." Ingram seemed lost in thought for a while, gazing at a photo on her office wall. It was her old family home in England. Solomon wondered if she was considering what one of her officer ancestors might have done in the same circumstances. "Very well, stop all modification work on the ship. That works for both scenarios. I know I told Nir-Tenbiku that we didn't want to take sides, but we both know we might have no choice. So by the time we need to decide, we'll know more about the Jattan opposition. If we can't stay out of this, then giving them the ship means they can keep the Protectorate busy and spare us the effort. If they win, and remain in power — which probably means taking on the Kugin as well — we'll have an ally, I hope."

"And what if we decide we need to return the ship to the Protectorate?" Searle asked. "Because we still don't know which Jattans are the good guys. Maybe neither of them are."

"If they're *both* bastards, then we back the bastards who'll keep the other bastards in line and off our backs. Villainous leaders are like fences. Don't take them down before you know why they were put up in the first place."

"I do believe we have our first foreign policy there, ma'am."

"God knows we squandered enough lives learning that lesson in both our histories." Ingram was on form today, back to her old decisive self, or at least the self Solomon had first encountered. "Still, at least we'll have useful intel to trade if we need to, and yes, I know I'm going to hell for even thinking that. Bissey asked how did we know that Gan-Pamas wasn't the Jattan Gandhi. He had a point, but even history doesn't agree that Gandhi was an unalloyed good guy. All we can do is whatever keeps the people here safe and alive."

Searle picked up his empty cup to take away for washing. "Well, if we give up the ship, it's a good way to ensure the Caisin gate stays here if the teeriks ever change their minds about us. And the Jattan opposition won't be in any more trouble than they already are if the Protectorate think they were behind the hijacking."

"Is *Curtis* irrelevant to us, Brad? I really need to know what we're prepared to fight to hang on to. I'm not a pilot or an engineer. My tendency is to grab the loot and worry about finding a use for it later."

Searle put on his studious expression for a moment. "She's not entirely useless, but we're probably not going to carry out small raids on Dal Mantir or the Jattan colonies. She's not much use for defending Nomad. She's for rapid deployment and lying in wait on someone else's territory, and the gate's a much more efficient way of doing that. But we know she's solid currency."

"It's noble of you not to argue for keeping your new toy," Ingram said.

"I'm still going to fly her before she goes. *If* she goes." Searle grinned. "Besides, I bet there are plenty of other toys out there."

Ingram seemed to be thinking it over long after Searle had left. She started drafting the announcement about the agreement with Nir-Tenbiku, but kept stopping to stare out of the window or at the photos on the wall again. Solomon wondered whether she wanted to talk.

"Are you alright, Captain?" he asked.

She did that theatrical mock frown. "I'm a monster, aren't I? I'm glad my father isn't here to see this."

"Because you're considering all the possibilities and not taking things at face value?"

"Because I'm working out who to throw under the bus. We really should stay rigidly neutral, but we'd have to be certain that neutrality's respected. Esmos is neutral, but they're respected because they bomb the snot out of anyone who compromises them."

"So we're back to ruthless use of force in self-defence."

"It's not like we're invading anybody."

"And yet you agreed to repatriate Gan-Pamas's body. I don't think you did that purely for negotiation points."

Ingram turned back to the screen to resume her statement. "Bissey-induced guilt. He'll never forgive me for what happened."

"Do you need his forgiveness?"

"Probably not. My father's, maybe. But let's say I need to forgive myself. Alien or human, dying a long way from home while you're serving your country is a sad and terrible thing."

"Do you feel guilty?"

"No, I regret it had to happen. But under the same circumstances I'd do it again."

"But you didn't do anything," Solomon said. "You left the decision to Marc, Chris, and Major Trinder."

Ingram had sidestepped giving explicit orders to shoot Gan-Pamas, not that the Gang of Three took orders from her. Solomon still wasn't sure how much of that was internal politics to avoid alienating Bissey — which hadn't worked — or her own misgivings. Perhaps she found it easier to kill a proven enemy who was open about his intentions than a potential one who couldn't be given the benefit of the doubt.

"I'm not good in the grey areas, Sol," she said. "I'm the blunt instrument that's deployed when the sentence has been passed."

"You're much more politically savvy than that," Solomon said. "But you're not a monster."

"Ask me again when it's a choice between sending Gan-Pamas home and using the corpse as blackmail to save someone here."

She carried on composing her message. Every time Solomon thought he understood her, she'd do something that threw him. These days he felt she tried to play down her compassionate side with displays of callous pragmatism, as if she thought she'd revealed her weakness, but then she'd be openly sentimental again and not seem to care who noticed. His current diagnosis was still that she was a supremely confident woman, but one who had to keep reminding herself that what was happening to Nomad now was beyond her experience, beyond *any* human's experience, and that occasional indecision and backtracking was allowed to give her some thinking time.

"I think I'll take the quadrubot for a walk," Solomon said. "You've had quite a productive morning, Captain. Well done."

"We'll see. I'll probably think of the smarter things I could have asked. Anyway, thank you for your interpretation skills. It must have worked."

"Thank the language AI. I delegate the heavy lifting."

Solomon moved through the network to transfer to the bot and trotted out of the hangar, happy to see the world from desktop height and feel part of it again instead of being a spectator dependent on security cameras. Only the need to stay connected spoiled his illusion of being a living animal.

Once he'd relegated monitoring to the background, though, he could choose to experience the intensity of a less complex mental landscape. He had a body. Colours sang, gravity made him acutely aware of his physical existence, and the ground sent vibrations through his frame. Sounds were cruder but more meaningful. He had this particular quad adjusted to his taste now and there were times when it felt more like him than his true disembodied self in the network.

From time to time he listened in on conversations via the security network, nothing private and personal, just situations he had to be aware of; Marc sending Sir Guy Lawson images of Opis, Searle asking Cosqui how she saw her future while they cleared up loose ends in *Curtis*, Chris helping print the ballot papers for the Kill Line election. Chris seemed serious about becoming an active citizen.

Solomon waited for Ingram to send her message around the base, looking for signs that people thought the situation might not be as bad as they expected. He was especially interested in seeing how Bissey reacted. To Bissey's credit, he'd been lying low since his resignation. Solomon had been worried that he'd continue to be the dissident, trying to stop Ingram and the others going down what he saw as a destructive and immoral path, but he'd simply kept quiet and busied himself with agricultural projects. He had no expertise beyond having had a vegetable patch in his garden on Earth, but he'd thrown himself into it with enthusiasm.

He was with the agriculture team at the moment, working on the more exotic crops that weren't essential but would make all the difference to the quality of life for the settlement, crops like spices, teas, and different oilseeds. He seemed happy just pottering around the crop tunnels with seedlings and cuttings. Solomon had kept a close eye on him from the time he resigned, watching who he associated with and whether there was any dry undergrowth of discontent for him to toss a spark into. But he'd turned out to be exactly the man Ingram said he was, and that was why Solomon had approved him for the *Cabot* mission all those years ago. His loyalty now took the form of not making things any worse for Ingram while still distancing himself from her decisions. But Solomon was certain he'd take up arms and defend Nomad despite his misgivings if the need arose.

Bissey didn't mix with his old social circle, though. Solomon had analysed his pattern of association, and more than eighty per cent of his contact was with the civilian agriculture and food scientists from both *Cabot* and Ainatio. His former crewmates still chatted to him in passing, but he didn't go out of his way to socialise with them. Perhaps he didn't want to be put on the spot about his decision, or maybe he thought it would make them uncomfortable. At the time, the other officers had treated his resignation almost like a death. They didn't seem to have mentioned it to him at all, except for Jeff Aiken, who'd told him he was sorry to see him go. It was as if he was erasing his naval identity, which might have been his way of coping with the fact that he was effectively still stuck on board his old ship but without any rank or role.

Would Georgina Erskine reinvent herself when she woke to find Nomad was under new management? She'd wielded her authority like a club when she thought others were losing interest in the project, but she'd been press-ganged into the job by her dying father. Solomon wasn't sure if she'd be glad to see others taking on the task successfully because she could spend her final years freed from the responsibility, or if she'd feel she'd wasted nearly all her adult life because she could have left it all to Ingram in the end.

Solomon was watching Bissey grafting tea seedlings in the crop tunnels under the supervision of Margriet Cornelissen when he noticed Ingram log into the public broadcast system from her office.

She was going to read her statement and not just mail it out, then. Bissey looked up at the security camera when he heard the pipe, the same signal used on board *Cabot* before an announcement. When he made eye contact with the lens, Solomon felt like he'd been caught spying. He hadn't had that feeling for a very long time.

"Good afternoon, this is Captain Ingram." The scientists in the crop tunnel carried on working. "I've just taken a call from the Primary of Jatt in exile, Nir-Tenbiku Dals, the president of the Jattan opposition. He's offered his apologies for the death of Nina Curtis and I've told him we'll consider repatriating the remains of Gan-Pamas Iril, who we now know was a senior politician. We need to remain cautious and stay out of disputes that don't concern us, but I believe this is a cause for optimism. We're not friends, but we're not sworn enemies either, and countries on Earth have gone to war over less serious incidents. We'll remain in a state of readiness for Kugin or Protectorate incursions, but this suggests there's constructive dialogue to be had with some of our alien neighbours. It won't be easy, it might not happen fast, but it now at least looks possible. In the meantime, we'll go ahead with evacuating *Elcano* to Britain for the welfare of both the passengers and this base. If the security situation becomes untenable, we'll offer evacuation to everyone, despite the confidentiality issues. Your lives come before protecting secret technology. I'm sending a more detailed message to everyone in a few minutes. That is all. Carry on."

Solomon had to give Ingram her due. She always said the right thing at the right time, although she might have gone a little too far on evacuation for Marc's peace of mind, and nobody knew how the teeriks would see this limited cooperation with the Jattan rebels.

Bissey was still looking up at the camera after the audio fell silent. "There," he said, more to himself than to Margriet. "That's more like the Ingram I used to know." Then he went back to grafting and carried on as if all this had nothing to do with him at all.

Tracking showed that Jeff Aiken had gone into the teerik compound, and Solomon knew Ingram planned to join him later. Fred was the only teerik there at the moment, so this was probably going to be the man-to-man chat that Ingram had expected Jeff to have with him. It had been seven days since Ingram had suspended Fred's access to comms, and he'd cloistered himself in the compound, working on something that he didn't seem to have shown to anyone else, not even the other teeriks. Solomon faced his privacy dilemma again; he was on the borderline of what he considered intrusion, because there was no security reason to spy on Fred at the moment and he could do no harm where he was. But his role in Nomad was now so pivotal that Solomon had to monitor his health and behaviour. What had Solomon said to Ingram about humans always using security and safety as a cover for more intrusive government? Here he was sliding down that same slope. He decided he was justified in monitoring actively again and listened in.

Jeff was talking to Fred, asking him how he felt and whether he should take a break, but Fred wasn't saying much at all. Solomon dithered for a moment about making use of the security cameras as well, then gave in and took a look at the teeriks' main room. He'd already crossed the line so perhaps it didn't matter by how far.

Fred was sitting at the low table, mostly staring off into space but occasionally drawing something on his screen. Despite the apparent daydreaming, he looked on edge, fidgeting a lot. He was probably working out complex calculations in his head. Jeff carried on trying to get him to talk.

"I think you're overworking, mate," Jeff said. "Or maybe it's the meds not agreeing with you. Take a break. How about seeing the medics? Just to make sure your dose is right, if nothing else."

Fred took a few moments to snap out of whatever he was thinking about. "I have to finish this project," he said. "It's very important. I'm really doing my best work these days. But I don't need to see a doctor, thank you. I'm fine."

"Ingram's coming to see you. She's probably bringing more pies."

"I'm glad she's talking to me again, but I don't think she's any less angry about what I did."

"Do you regret it?"

"Not at all. It had to be done. You'll see one day. I just wish it had caused less upset."

"And how do you feel about Ingram talking to Nir-Tenbiku?"

"Once she sent her message, it was inevitable that there might be a reply," Fred said. "I doubt she had any choice but to make diplomatic comments about handing over Gan-Pamas's body. But Nir-Tenbiku has no idea what you're capable of or if you'll choose to cooperate with the Protectorate. So he probably fears you now. If he stops fearing you, he'll come and try to seize the ship."

Fred stopped dead as if he'd done all the talking he planned to do and wanted to get back to his project. Jeff sat watching him, frowning a little and looking genuinely worried, but then Ingram showed up and he let her in. She was carrying a food container. Fred listened politely and offered no opinion when she sat down on the floor cushions and told him more details of the conversation with Nir-Tenbiku. He didn't seem interested in the food, either. But it all seemed cordial, even if he wasn't as chatty as usual.

"You look very busy," she said.

"I've made a breakthrough." Fred cocked his head on one side while he studied his screen. Solomon couldn't see the detail from the security camera's angle, but it looked like a diagram. "I haven't been able to test it yet, but it'll be ready very soon."

Ingram didn't ask what it was and waited as if Fred was going to continue, but he just carried on calculating and drawing. "Forgive me for being preoccupied," he said. "I think the phrase is that I'm on a roll. I may be old, but I feel like I've had a second lease of life with my skills."

Solomon had overlooked that somehow. Fred had done some remarkable things in the last few months, including major improvements to gate technology. Caisin had been the genius behind the gate, supposedly the greatest engineer of all the teerik communes, yet Fred had modified the single gate to handle multiple entry and exit points and even form interconnecting tunnels. It could have been the culmination of years of experience making unsolved problems fall into place, or there might have been a reason, perhaps no longer being in Caisin's shadow. Solomon still had a lot to learn about the group dynamics of a commune.

"I'm glad to hear that," Ingram said. She had her careful diplomatic voice on at the moment. "Never give in to age, Fred. And when did you last take some time off to go flying? Remember telling me how teeriks didn't use their ability to fly and you thought they should?"

"I'll fly again," Fred said. "I just have to finish this."

He sounded a little impatient. Ingram got to her feet and gave Jeff a discreet nod in the direction of the door.

"We'll leave you to it, then," she said. "Come on, Chief, I've got a few things I need you to sort out for me. Fred, don't forget to eat your pies while they're nice and fresh."

Solomon decided to trot over to the green and intercept Ingram on her route back to her office. On the way, he kept an eye on the compound security cameras to see what Fred did when she and Jeff left, in case he moved to a position where Solomon could see what he was working on. Fred was still locked out of the critical parts of the network, so there was no way of monitoring the content of his screen without some very basic spying.

Yes, this is spying. I shouldn't be doing this unless I believe Fred is a security risk.

He'd sworn he wouldn't spy like this on one of his humans. But he was keeping an eye on Paul Cotton and the scientists who'd objected to evacuating *Elcano* because he'd decided they were a potential threat to the humans he'd chosen, and he *hadn't* chosen most of the Ainatio staff. They were simply there when the time came to launch the second phase of Nomad, just like the Kill Liners, except the townspeople exhibited most of the traits he was looking to preserve.

Fred was now like Paul Cotton; someone who wasn't a definable enemy, but still a potential weak link in Solomon's defence of Nomad. There was no conflict with Solomon's mission brief, because the welfare of his ideal humans took precedence, but how could he judge humans if he didn't even follow his own ethical rules?

It bothered him. He knew what he had to do and sometimes it wasn't honest or pleasant. In hindsight, he hadn't just lied to Ingram when he lectured her on privacy, he'd lied to himself as well. It was a very human thing to do, one of their coping mechanisms, but he couldn't carry out his duties properly if he developed all those human characteristics that Bednarz felt he was better for lacking.

I'm placing my trust in you, Solomon. You're the only one I can rely on who can't be bribed, threatened, or corrupted, who won't be warped by envy or ambition, who won't lose interest or just give up because it's all too damn hard. You can be better than me — better than us.

Bednarz's praise now stung. But he'd designed Solomon to have free will and learn whatever he needed to do the job, even if it meant lying or launching an attack that paralysed Asia.

Sudden movement on the camera feed interrupted his brooding. Fred pushed his screen across the table as if he was exasperated, then got up, seized the floor cushion, and flung it across the room. Throwing cushions was hardly violent, but Solomon was surprised to see Fred lose his temper at all. He was even more surprised when Fred pounced on the cushion and started ripping it to pieces like the raptor he actually was, clawing at it and tearing into it with his beak. Despite his age, he now looked like a big, intimidating predator.

Solomon saw Fred anew and it alarmed him. He watched him destroy the cushion and wondered what it would take to make him attack a human. It wasn't impossible. Nina had been killed by a teerik and Pannit had nearly killed Epliko in a fit of rage, even if it was out of character.

Pannit had calmed down after medication, though, and was back to his old self again according to the other teeriks. They'd all become much more relaxed with the treatment, as Dr Tomlinson expected, and even Turisu was mellow to the point of being sociable.

But the tranquilliser didn't seem to be working on Fred.

Solomon upped his pace and intercepted Ingram and Jeff. They paused in a huddle in the middle of the green.

"Problem, Sol?"

"Captain, I think we have a problem with Fred."

"How serious?"

"I've just watched him destroy a floor cushion in what I can only describe as a rage. It might sound comical, but I can assure you it didn't look at all funny."

"That doesn't sound like him," Jeff said. "He's been getting more agitated and fixated on his work, but I've never seen any anger in him."

Ingram rubbed her forehead. "I think that's why he wanted us to leave. Perhaps he knew he couldn't hold it in any longer."

"The medication isn't helping him, Captain," Solomon said.

"Is he even taking it?"

That was a good question. "If he doesn't want to see a doctor, it's going to be hard to work out whether the drug's not working or if he's just skipping it."

"You were monitoring the conversation, then," Jeff said.

"Yes." Solomon wasn't sure if he should skip over it or explain, but Jeff would expect an answer. "He created a huge problem by calling Lawson, and he's been behaving strangely. I can't risk someone else getting killed."

"If he's not taking the medication, he must be disposing of it," Ingram said. "What form is it in now?"

"Soft solid. Rather like a small ration bar to make it appealing to them. The lab wanted the teeriks to be able to see what they were getting after being medicated without their consent for so long. I know it's not being dumped in the food waste container. That's easily checked."

"Well, if he's not just binning it, he's probably flushing it down the toilet, and that goes into the sewage system. See if Brice can detect anything."

"I'll ask her now," Solomon said. "But it's a long shot."

"Why not just ask him?" Jeff asked. "We've established mutual trust. Once we lose it, we might never get it back."

"Do both," Ingram said. "Because I trusted Fred and he let me down."

"Yes ma'am." Jeff didn't look happy. "Do you want me to wait until Sol's got an analysis?"

That question was a test for Ingram, not just a request for clarification. If there was an analysis available, they'd know if Fred was lying, and it implied that Ingram wanted to catch him out. Solomon could see Jeff's sense of fair play coming under strain. He'd always done exactly as Ingram asked, but his compressed lips showed he didn't approve. The teerik was his friend and the special bond they'd developed had opened doors that Ingram might not have managed on her own. Jeff probably felt like a traitor.

"A negative result would only prove we didn't find anything, so it's not a lie detector," Ingram said. Yes, she knew exactly how Jeff thought. "The real question is what we do if he isn't willing to see a doctor or resume his meds if he's not taking them. I don't want to force medication on anybody. But I can't ignore this after what happened to Nina. If he's going to become a serious problem, I have to act. Think about how we'd do that, Chief."

Ingram shook her head and walked on. Jeff looked at Solomon.

"I'm trying to do the right thing," he said. "Not just because Fred deserves it, but because we're so reliant on him. Yeah, I'm worried he might end up like Lirrel as well. That's the interesting thing nobody's talking about. If our teeriks need medication, did Lirrel need it too? Do the Jattans know how to treat them? I've got more questions than answers."

"You don't have to explain yourself to me, Chief," Solomon said. "For all we know, Fred's taking his treatment but it isn't working. Or perhaps it's something else entirely — an unrelated health condition. Why don't you let me take care of this?"

"No, it's orders," Jeff said. "Like laws. If we start picking and choosing which ones we want to obey, the place falls apart."

Solomon wished he'd never raised this with Ingram. He could have investigated for himself and reported back to her if and when he had concrete facts. "I'll get an analysis done first, just in case it turns up something completely unexpected," he said. "Don't worry, we'll get this resolved."

He checked the lab's schedule for a timetable while he located Ash Brice. The teeriks received their medication at 0700 delivered with their breakfast, which narrowed down the potential time window for Brice, provided Fred was disposing of his drugs shortly afterwards. Solomon checked the security cameras again and worked out all the blind spots where the teerik could hide them before disposal. It was all supposition, though. If Fred really was doing this, they might never catch the right moment to sample the waste.

Solomon went to see Ash at the sewage plant to explain his problem.

"Sol, you know exactly how the sewage system works because the bots built it." She was wearing rolled-down waders that indicated she'd been carrying out a manual inspection. Folded over like that, they resembled cavalier boots, making her look swashbuckling rather than workaday. "I can't guarantee anything. I can isolate the pipe run from any property for a while — until it backs up, obviously — and take a composite sample over the course of a day. We're lucky teeriks are more like birds. They don't excrete a lot of liquid or run the taps much. If we were looking for regular pathogens and other hazards, that's all routinely monitored, but I haven't got a clue what we're after."

"That's alright, the biochemists know," Solomon said, then wondered how cooperative Tomlinson would be now that he was one of the *Elcano* objectors. "It's a long shot. Just see what you can find."

"You could just use a tranquilliser dart on Fred and grab a blood sample while he's down," she said. "Or ask him outright."

"You're not the first person to say that, but the dart is out of the question."

"Okay, I'll do what I can."

Solomon wondered if he'd irritated Ash. Now that she was Chris's girlfriend, he really didn't want to upset her. He left her to it, sent Ingram a message that the sewage system checks were under way, and kept an eye on Fred via the security network until the other teeriks returned from their engineering duties. Fred's two grandsons were chatting excitedly about what they'd learned, and the whole commune settled down for a meal like any other large family catching up on their day, something Solomon had never experienced but had seen many times in movies.

They were happy. He was sure the medics had done the right thing by giving them medication. Fred barely joined in the discussion — conducted in their native Kugin, which was both helpful for the linguistics AI and a sign of how relaxed they were — and looked lost in thought. He was doing calculations. Whatever he was working on was taking all his intellectual energy. He was, as he said, on a roll.

"Hredt, where's the other cushion?" Pannit asked.

The linguistics AI couldn't translate fully yet, but Fred snapped to attention and said something about making a mess and needing to dispose of it. There was a moment of baffled silence, then the others went on talking.

But there were no more displays of aggression from Fred. Solomon waited for them to roost for the night and counted the hours until he could reasonably pester Ash for some results.

He held out until 0730, when he watched the map track her radio as she left Chris's house and walked up through Kill Line towards the water treatment plant. If he visited her around 0815, that wouldn't seem too pushy. Her office door was open when he got there.

"I just wondered if you'd been able to find anything," he said. "I don't mean to nag you."

"Here you go." Ash put a small snap-seal container on the desk. "In the end, I ran a bot through all the main sewers overnight. The things I do for you, Sol."

"Thank you, Ash. I appreciate it. I'll get it over to the lab right away so they can put it through spectrometry."

"You won't need anything that fancy. And you'll find a lot of unmetabolised drugs in sewage anyway because the body excretes most of it. Teeriks could well be the same."

"You sound like you've done this before."

"You'd be amazed what I've had to look for in ships' sanitary systems. What colour are the chewables?"

Solomon consulted the lab's database. There was a colourant that was part of the orange flavouring. "I would imagine a kind of amber. They're like a ration bar but more gelatinous."

"That's it." Ash got up from her desk and placed the container in Solomon's back pannier. "There's a trace of sludgy orange gel that's built up around one of the inlets under the compound. So if it's what I think it is, he's just been flushing them whole. It wouldn't be there on its own if he was ingesting it."

"I'm impressed," Sol said. "Thank you."

"Don't thank me, thank the python camera. Although I'd have gloved up and put my arm down there if I had to."

"I have unhappy memories of python bots," Solomon said. "It's good to know they can be benign."

Ash laughed. "I can gross Chris out with this now. This is why I love my job. Remember you owe me one."

Solomon took the sample over to the lab. Tomlinson was the only person there, so he had no choice but to ask him to analyse the substance.

"I believe it's the tranquilliser you formulated," Solomon said.

"You want to wait while I confirm that?" Tomlinson seemed his normal self, as far from a mutineer as Solomon could imagine. "And can you tell me the backstory for this?"

"I think one of the teeriks has been dumping their dose in the toilet."

"Oh. Lovely. Non-compliant patients are my favourite. Thank you for the warning that it's been in the sewage system." Tomlinson knew what he was looking for now, so it only took him minutes to confirm that the gel was the remains of his tranquilliser. "Yes, that's teerik tranx. Who's going to have a word with them? And more to the point, what made you think they were skipping doses?"

"It's a long story." Solomon was happier now he had a plausible explanation for Fred's behaviour and a relatively easy solution. "Thank you, Dr Tomlinson."

"You could always slip it in food like the Kugin did."

"I thought your department had decided that would be rather unethical," Solomon said. "Even if it makes them happier."

"I wouldn't do it," Tomlinson said. "But if someone else ended up like Nina, I'd wish I had."

It was exactly what Solomon would have to do if Fred got worse. Jattan rebels were on the doorstep, the Protectorate and Kugin navies were probably still hunting for *Curtis*, Lawson was on the verge of starting Britain's FTL programme, and there was potential unrest in Nomad itself. The teerik commune needed to be functioning properly at a time like this.

The sooner Nomad could meet its own defence needs without needing teerik expertise, the better it would be for everybody. There would be hard decisions to make. If Ingram and the others were too decent to make them, Solomon would step in.

This was his mission. It pained him, but he knew now that the task couldn't be fulfilled by a saint. Sometimes it was better to break a commandment than fail in his duty to protect humanity's best.

11

I wish you were here to advise me, Mr Bednarz, but I can at least imagine your responses, because I haven't forgotten a word you ever said to me. I'm going to medicate an intelligent alien without his knowledge. I know it's wrong. But I'm afraid for my human friends. Is this how all evil begins, by doing bad things for good reasons? I really need to know.

Solomon, constructing a conversation with his creator.

OFFICE OF THE ALLIANCE OF ASIAN AND PACIFIC STATES, CANBERRA, AUSTRALIA: OCTOBER 30, OC.

Ella Makris put the glass of whisky on the mahogany coffee table with a clunk, no coaster, and no class. Tim Pham was glad he wasn't married to her. Her furniture at home was probably covered with water rings. It was a small failing, but it told him a lot, not that he didn't have a detailed file on her already.

But she'd asked to see him for a reason, and if it was what he thought it was, then he needed to know how she'd decided on him instead of another politician.

"Commissioner, what's going on around Fiji?" It was a demand, not a question. "I'm getting calls and hearing things that trouble me."

Pham took a tissue from his pocket, folded it square, and placed it under the whisky glass.

"You'll have to be more specific," he said. "We live in busy times."

"Helicopters going down. That's what I mean."

"Ask me a straight question, and if it isn't a matter of national security or generally something above your grade, I'll give you a straight answer."

Makris looked indignant. She must have come straight from an evening engagement because she was wearing a black cocktail dress and a lot more make-up than usual. She also seemed to have forgotten she was an APS employee, not a politician, so the only reason he'd agreed to meet her at all was to nail down the coffin lid more firmly. Graham Terrence had made a point of being stuck in

Korea to be seen to walk the talk about die-back quarantines, which left Makris fielding questions from other APS governments. Pham suspected Terrence's purdah was more about keeping a grip on the APS reins in Seoul than worrying about Australian agriculture, but at least it was the right outcome.

He wouldn't have had any more to tell Terrence than Makris, though, but Terrence wanted it that way. He didn't want a briefing on things he was better off not knowing, so he wasn't going to call Pham. He did need someone to work out how hard the shit would hit the fan, though, and Makris was a useful stooge.

"Let me put it another way," she said. "Fiji thinks a helicopter crashed in its territorial waters, but there was no contact with the coastguard or any other emergency services, no accident report filed, and no black box signal detected. No bodies were recovered, either."

Makris paused. Pham waited. He could play this game all day. She must have known that, because she came within a flicker of rolling her eyes and then tried a different tack.

"Do you have any information on the incident?" she asked.

"Yes, I do."

"Is it information I can give the Fijian authorities?"

"No, it isn't."

"Is there any information you can give *me*?"

"Possibly, but why are you asking me?"

"Because military types who tell me things say our intelligence community has been quite interested in Fiji for a few months, and as you're still very close to them, you might be able to tell me something that they couldn't."

Nothing could be covered up forever. Pham was always ready for that day and had polished a technique to muddy the waters. It was time to unload a dump truck's worth of top soil.

"Ahh, we spooks never really leave the service, do we? Well, if you needed to know, Miss Makris, you'd have been told by now."

"I just want some words to keep Fiji happy."

"Very well, it relates to classified technology," Pham said. "An exercise ran into problems. A misjudgement following a modification. It was unfortunate that it happened in Fijian waters, but there was no environmental contamination, no loss of life, and no risk to Fijian border security." One half-lie, one outright lie, and a big dose of the truth — that was a credible mix. "It involved a private contractor. If you would prefer me to speak to your contact in Suva, I'd be happy to do so."

"And what do I tell them about the missing fishing vessel and the family who owns it?"

Pham allowed himself an unspoken *oh shit*. "I'm not aware of anyone going missing. What's that got to do with a helicopter crash?"

"I understand the locals are accusing APS of disappearing the family," Makris said. "They've left and the boat's missing. Apparently they'd only recently moved to the island after having to leave Viti Levu. I assume that was related to attention from our intelligence service."

By "our," She meant APS, not Australia, and that was the problem. Pham tried to judge how close to the truth he could get. Makris was either hearing things from a fairly reliable observer or she was guessing with the sly skill of a fake medium, but that still raised the question of how she'd targeted him in the first place. APS had flown Tev Josepha to Fiji quite openly and that meant word would have spread that a former British soldier was around. It wasn't a secret. Angry locals accusing APS of abducting the man were easy to invent and hard to confirm, though.

Is she really getting some stick about the helicopter, or has Terrence or one of her APDU chums told her to find out what I'm up to?

Both were plausible. The president was happy to hide the seizure of Ainatio's FTL research from the rest of APS, but Pham wasn't convinced that the man would always put Australia first. He had no intention of telling him how much more he'd found at Ainatio, and Terrence probably assumed there was a body of Ainatio intel he was being protected from knowing anyway. But recent events might have worried him so much that he asked Makris to shake Pham down.

It was a lonely life in intelligence. It was certainly lonely being Tim Pham and trying to do what was best for Australia when people around him were more loyal to APS than their own motherland, the treacherous scumbags.

"I think you already know we flew a Brit with Fijian ancestry back to the island on humanitarian grounds," Pham said. "APDU and the Fijian authorities certainly knew. But I don't think your security clearance allows me to explain the circumstances. If that's who you're talking about, though, you can probably guess where he's gone."

Of course she couldn't. Nobody could, unless they'd seen the impossible things that Pham had. But he was hoping she'd make the obvious connection and think Tev Josepha had been shipped back to Britain for safekeeping. If the question was just set dressing to get information out of Pham for Terrence, she had her answer. If she genuinely wanted to know what to tell the Fijian authorities to reassure them... then she still had her answer.

Makris looked at him expectantly. "He's gone home, you mean. He's skipped town and gone back to Britain."

"I'm amazed he ever risked entering APS territory," Pham said. "I believed him when he said he wanted to find his family. I still do. But he probably realised he'd made a mistake and put them all at risk."

"So you think the Brits extracted him."

"No idea. I would have if I'd been them." *Yeah, back the truck up to the water and tip that dirt in.* "Ex-services are always vulnerable to being used as bargaining chips behind enemy lines. And we do look like the enemy to them."

"Was he that important an asset?"

"Who knows? Maybe they just don't leave their guys behind even if they're not high value."

"The obvious question is whether that's connected to your helicopter mishap. Do you think the Brits intervened in your exercise? Why would they connect that to their man?"

"You're the one who suggested there was a connection."

"Well, do you?"

Pham really had to think about that. He still didn't know where the missile had come from. Nobody could identify anything on radar or sats, and while that was far from the all-seeing net that APS had once had, a missile like that should have been easy to spot. It had probably come through that portal, but that didn't mean the missile had come from Opis. It might have been fired in Britain.

And that was why this gizmo mattered so much. Space was important for the future, but whatever else that thing was, it was a weapon right now. When he'd told that thug Chris Montello that the portal was dangerous in American hands, he hadn't known how soon he'd be proven right.

It wasn't a waste of time to pursue this. The portal was a multi-purpose chaos device, not just transport.

"I have no reason to assume sabotage," he said. "But I'll keep it in mind." He took a deliberate look at his watch so that she noticed. "I have somewhere else to be, I'm afraid. Any further questions? I'm more than happy to give Suva a call and smooth things over. You can't get a more meaningful apology than the APS science and technology commissioner calling personally to apologise for faulty equipment, can you?"

"That's very kind of you," Makris said. "But I don't want to escalate matters. Leave it with me."

"You sure?"

"If the commissioner calls personally, it makes things look more serious than they actually are. And it's unusual for you to be here rather than in Seoul. They'll imagine all kinds of things."

Ah, she was backing off. She needed to play this down as much as he did. Someone getting their ear chewed off by angry diplomats would have jumped at the chance to hand the shit-parcel to someone else.

"I just happened to be here at home when the quarantine kicked in," Pham said. He'd talk to his people in Fiji and check out the local sentiment anyway, because there was no point in putting Makris on his blacklist if she was just inept. It wasted the resources he'd have to put into finding or embroidering some misbehaviour to bury her with. "But you have a point."

Pham now had a three-hour drive ahead to get home to Sydney. He'd pace himself. Those hours were precious, solitary thinking time and he was in no hurry to run into Louise if she was home at the moment. He had no idea because he didn't want to find out. If she was doing anything that might compromise him, someone from the department — his old department, not APS — would tip him off.

Who did he think he was fooling? Everyone knew she lived her own life, so it was ridiculous keeping up appearances when nobody cared if an APS commissioner had an unhappy marriage. The pretence was taking time and effort that he needed to put into the job. He'd have to talk to Louise about a divorce again, but for the next few hours, he'd forget about her, think, make a few calls, and stop off for dinner along the way.

He called up some suitably inoffensive instrumental tracks on the stereo for background noise, no lyrics to distract him, and replayed the conversation with Makris in his head. He was on much thinner ice with Terrence since the die-back debacle. He knew it because he was still in his job. Terrence wanted him inside the tent for some reason, possibly saving him as a sacrifice for later, or else he thought Pham valued his power and perks so much that he would now be more malleable in exchange for keeping it. Bloody fool — Terrence couldn't understand people who didn't see political office as the sum of their existence. It was just a way of getting things done, and when it didn't, Pham would move on. Its sole purpose was letting him serve and preserve his country, and his country wasn't APS.

He'd fucked up royally over Abbie Vincent, though. He really should have spotted her. It wasn't as if he didn't know what a terrorist looked like. On the plus side, it had certainly moved things in a direction that he could exploit. If he'd wanted to weaken APS's control of its member nations, introducing an existential crisis like die-back was a crude but effective way to do it. He'd never have done it deliberately, because it was impossible to control once it was in the wild, and it put his own country at risk, but he could find a way to take advantage of it.

So where did he go from here? The helicopter incident might come back to haunt him, but Terrence wanted his plausible deniability. As long as he kept imagining the worst, he'd let it all stay buried, so he was just using Makris to test the toxicity of whatever Pham was dabbling in. Yes, it made sense tactically, but Terrence could have picked someone better to do the job. On the other hand, maybe he saw Makris as blindly loyal, and that was worth fifty IQ points in politics.

It didn't matter. Pham had a job to do. He'd missed a chance to get closer to seizing that portal technology and he'd lost his bait as well. He lowered the driver's side window to enjoy the warm night air and thought it all through again.

He couldn't get to Opis, not yet anyway. How many times had the Nomad people returned to Earth? Were they ever going to risk coming back again? In the medium term, Earth was the only place he could operate. What would bring them back now, and if he could devise another trap, how would he get them to see the bait in the first place?

Of course, it was possible that they'd just moved elsewhere on Earth via that portal. But he had those soil test results. They had access to another planet, and Opis was the obvious candidate.

Maybe he'd missed his only chance.

It was getting late. He needed to find a toilet and get something to eat. The dashboard display mapped restaurants along his route. Once he'd had a decent steak and powdered his nose, he'd be in a better state to think sensibly about all of this. He had the feeling that if he could get in touch with Montello and wound his macho hitman pride, the little shit would bust a gut to get back here and finish the fight they'd started outside Kill Line. Pham quite liked the idea of finishing it too.

How could he locate Montello and make contact? When the rummage team had gone through the Josepha place, there wasn't a single clue to how the man stayed in contact with Gallagher. It had to be via radio or a phone, but there was nothing, not even a receipt for phone credit.

All Pham had was Barry Cho. He hoped that would be enough of a lure to bring Gallagher back, but it wasn't a given. He'd even made sure it was easy to find out where Cho was being held, and while he was sure the Brits knew he'd done that, it was still valid intelligence that Gallagher might find hard to ignore.

For no good reason, Pham wondered where Annis Kim was right now. She'd disappeared as soon as she escaped from the Ainatio compound. She might have been dead in a ditch in Dogshitville, Kansas, or she could even have been on Opis. It was at times like this that he missed her. But she'd betrayed him over Ainatio, and that hurt him in a way that Louise never could.

Bitch.

I really need that steak now.

Pham opted for the first restaurant ahead. He could already see the lights of the town, so he didn't need to stop for a leak at the side of the road. He was debating whether he should find a hotel for the night instead of carrying on to Sydney when the thought struck him.

He was looking at all this portal stuff from the wrong angle. It was bloody obvious now. He didn't have to worry about space to get hold of that technology.

Nomad was still in touch with Earth, and it was doing that for reasons beyond the welfare of Tev Josepha or Barry Cho. It now had *very* long-range capability. As the whole project was beyond the scope of a bunch of abandoned scientists and farmers, there was a nation-state involved, and one country's fingerprints were still all over it, whatever Montello had said. Pham could rule out all the others that were still functioning. He wasn't sure how Gallagher fitted into this, but Britain was still involved somehow, and any involvement was a potential weak spot to be poked at until the wall came down.

Luckily, Pham was highly qualified at finding weaknesses. He was going to enjoy that steak even more now.

* * *

TEERIK COMPOUND: 0945 HOURS, OCTOBER 31, OC.

It didn't matter.

It didn't matter that they'd cut Hredt's comms access or that he couldn't get into *Curtis*. He had work to do, he was making progress, and he didn't need contact with Earth to do that. He sat at the table, a plate of food beside him and his diagram spread on the table with the calculations he'd usually erase after committing them to memory. He had to finish this while he could.

Something wasn't quite right with him and he knew it. He could think so much faster and more clearly now, but he was also getting more agitated and less able to hide his mood. It wouldn't be long before it would be obvious to the rest of the commune that he wasn't taking his medication. He was sure the humans had noticed already.

Everyone else was calming down to the point of sluggishness as the drug built up in their systems again. *That was me. I was like that.* It had been three weeks since they'd started taking the tranquilliser and he'd felt the change in his mind within a couple of days. Now the difference between his own mental faculties and the others' was apparent, and it made him all the more determined to purge the drug completely from his body. Even if he was now deeply unhappy for no good reason and thought of doing terrible things, he wanted to see what he was capable of when he could operate at his best.

And this *was* his best.

He'd already improved Caisin's technology by finding a way to generate multiple gates with intersecting paths, but now he was close to adding a refinement that would make it easier to operate in covert military missions. He'd found a way to make the gateway track the person who'd opened it, and even multiple people, without the need to actively point a locator device or find the open portal itself. He recalled the time he'd visited Earth with Ingram and she'd been trying to find the gate again to prove to Marc and Chris that she'd genuinely come from Opis to help the stranded people of Kill Line. With this refinement, they'd never have to worry about losing access. They could activate a control on their body and the gate would snatch them away instantly, with no need to move through it.

At the moment, the portal was generated between fixed points, and the person who'd used it could either return to it or open it at a new location using the handheld device the humans had nicknamed a flashlight. In the middle of a firefight, though, that could be the difference between life and death. When Major Trinder rescued Dieter, he'd had to activate the gate with the locator as well as dragging the wounded man through it while the enemy was an arm's length away. They were both lucky to survive and one of Tim Pham's troops had ended up on Opis with them — for a few minutes, anyway.

Hredt needed to do more work on closing the gate so that no enemy could enter or fire through it, but that was relatively straightforward. The important thing was that it could be activated by voice or a touch device worn on the body. Hredt considered what came naturally to humans. His best guess would be that they'd prefer a touch device so they could operate in silence. But he'd ask.

They're being polite now but they don't trust me any more. Once they see this, though, they'll know I'm still their ally.

He knew what they said about him. Maro had come back from his duties on board *Elcano* and reported he'd overheard one of the humans saying teeriks wanted more humans here to fight their battles, as if they hadn't had enough trouble of their own on Earth. That had kept him awake wondering if he was really trying to exploit them, or if he was genuinely doing what he thought was best for everyone. If humans wanted to live peacefully in this sector, they had to accept they needed a much larger population to survive.

Did he regret what he'd done? No. The humans would have dithered over it for years because they felt they had to prepare everything for those arriving here later, whether that meant letting them settle on Opis or finding them another unclaimed world to colonise. But they had no obligation to do that at all. The next migration would be able to sort out its own food supply by the time they were ready to launch, because it was clear humans already had the technology to solve those problems, and it wasn't as if Hredt had given the data to unsuitable people.

It was too late to reverse the course of history now. He had to stop justifying it to himself. From the moment the commune had hijacked the prenu, life had become a stream of risky consequences. He now knew that was what freedom actually was. The alternative was accepting that the safe life they had in Kugad was all they would ever know.

Hredt went back to his calculations. They were spilling out of him so fast now that he could barely write them down. Recording was a bad habit that went against everything he'd learned, because he'd been taught from infancy that holding knowledge and calculations in their heads kept teeriks from harm, but now he realised it wasn't true. The Kugin foremen might decide it was worth losing some expertise to make an example of a commune that stole a ship.

But we're not going to get caught. Are we?

I know Ingram and Marc are angry with me, but they won't harm us. They'll see that I did the right thing. And it'll be Marc who'll make most use of this Caisin enhancement. He'll be happy again when he tries it out.

This was the eighth day since Hredt had been cut off from the network as well as his social life. The casual contact he'd grown used to with humans had dried up. It was his own fault for staying in the house to complete this job. He had a relatively small circle of human friends compared to the size of the population here, tens of people rather than hundreds, but when he was out walking or flying, humans he didn't know would say hello or wave to him. After what had happened to Nina, he was surprised that they didn't treat him any less cordially, but he wasn't at the centre of things any longer, or seen as the spokesman for the commune. Cosquimaden had stepped seamlessly into that role.

Jeff still visited him daily, and Ingram had paid a couple of visits, but he hadn't given them reason to stay and chat. He could think of little but his project, and every moment away from it made him anxious. Humans might have used the word *possessed*. Hredt was completely consumed by the work, even though he wanted to stop to enjoy the fresh air, but whatever it was that drove him wouldn't let up. He was glad he was doing good work, but his lack of control over his reaction was starting to scare him.

Well, if he couldn't stop, he'd push through and get this development to the prototype stage. He could have tested it now, but he had no free access to the Caisin gate generator and he couldn't bring himself to ask for it. What did Ingram think he would do, use it to escape to Earth and give his expertise to this APS empire so they could destroy Nomad? But perhaps Ingram thought exactly that, however tolerant she seemed to be, and he didn't know how to convince her otherwise.

"Father?"

It was Turisu. She startled him. Hredt had thought she'd left for *Elcano* by now, but perhaps she had other plans today. He hoped she wasn't going to stop him working.

"Aren't you going to work today, Turi?"

"Yes, but they were still loading parts onto the shuttle," she said. "I'm leaving now."

"And you're taking the boys."

"Yes, of course. They're learning fast. You should talk to them about what they're doing. They need encouragement." Turisu might have calmed down as soon as she'd started taking her medications, but her opinions hadn't changed. She just expressed her annoyance more quietly. "You were working all night again. You're too old to do that. For goodness' sake stop and get some sleep. What's so urgent if you're not working on the ships?"

"Things can always be improved. I'm refining the gate."

"I don't think we need to."

"I do."

"Is this your peace offering to Ingram? You could just apologise, you know."

"I didn't do anything wrong. I just did what they were going to do but *sooner*."

"You never consult anybody," Turisu said. "It's the same every time. You just do the first thing that comes into your head. It's dangerous."

"Turi, it hasn't made the slightest bit of difference. If anything, I did it too late. Ingram's talking to Nir-Tenbiku and thinking about returning Gan-Pamas's body to him. The Protectorate will get to hear about it eventually. At least Ingram can now call on her homeworld for reinforcements."

"It's going to take them years to build a suitable ship."

"If the situation's that serious, Nomad can open the gate for inbound troops."

Turi made a vague flapping gesture of dismissal. "It's done and there's nowhere else to run, even if we had control of a ship. I have to go now. Let's not talk about it when everyone returns from work, please."

For Turisu, that was remarkably restrained. Hredt almost preferred her the way she was, because now she sounded as if she'd surrendered. Perhaps the dose she was receiving was too high. He put it out of his mind as best he could while he worked and thought about the initial test of his automatic gate, and how he should offer it to Marc. But not long after Turisu had left, Chief Jeff arrived. He always knocked and asked if he could enter.

"How are you today, Fred?" Jeff sat down cross-legged on the cushions. "Making progress?"

"Yes, thank you. I'll have something to test very soon."

"I won't beat about the bush, mate. I want to talk to you about something you might not want to discuss, but it's important."

That sounded ominous. Hredt didn't look up. "I'm listening."

"You've stopped taking your medication, haven't you?"

"What makes you think that?"

"You're not the Fred you were a couple of months ago. And I know you're dumping your meds down the drain."

There was no point in denying it. "You all said you'd never force us to do anything. Are you spying on me?"

"It showed up in the sewage system."

Hredt sat staring at his screen while he worked out what to say. Chief Jeff was his friend, the human he was closest to, and he knew the man wouldn't do anything to harm him, or lie to him. At the moment, Hredt had some power because his engineering skills couldn't be matched by the humans or their various AI systems. If he was drugged back into mediocrity, though, he'd lose that advantage. But it was about much more than that.

"Jeff, the drug slows my mind," he said. "Since we left Kugad, I've been able to do things I couldn't do before. I've improved on Caisin's work. She was the greatest engineer of all. Yet I was able to create a multiple gate network, something I couldn't have done before. I don't want to be average. I don't feel I can stop until I've pushed myself as far as I can. I have to do this."

"Mate, even your average is off the scale for humans."

"But not for *us*. I need to be the best I can be. I don't want to die having achieved too little."

"Is it worth being miserable to get it, though?"

"Yes. Yes, it is."

"Is that the compulsion talking, or you?"

Hredt wasn't sure. At times he felt he *was* the compulsion, that this was the real him. "We never knew we were medicated. Once we left Kugad, we started changing, but we didn't notice because it was gradual and we thought it was the stress making us behave this way. We grew more impatient with each other. I started flying, which nature intended us to do. I created better systems. We all learned English fast, possibly faster than we would have done while drugged. I'm now working on an upgrade for the Caisin gate that'll make it even more useful for your troops. And I think there's still a lot more good work in me to come. I think I'm becoming the real me, Jeff. But you might not like that person."

Jeff was listening patiently. If this had been Ingram, she would have been charming and sympathetic, but more focused on putting things right, whereas Jeff actually cared. Hredt knew it. They had things in common that transcended species. They both got things done, and they were both more capable of great things than many of those around them had imagined. They were honest with each other even when it was difficult. Jeff was a true friend.

"Do you ever wonder why the Kugin needed to give you the drugs?" Jeff asked. "I thought it was to stop you escaping."

"I know what you're thinking."

"Yeah?"

"That we needed to be drugged to stop us turning into someone like Lirrel."

"Well, yeah, that's one of the concerns."

"You know, I think Caisin developed her gate technology and got ideas about an independent teerik nation because the medication wasn't working as well on her," Hredt said. It was starting to make sense now. It was a horribly bleak thought. Caisin's mind had been freed by her approaching death. "She was old and becoming unwell. She didn't eat as much. But because she was old, she was physically weaker and harmless, so perhaps our foremen decided it wasn't worth increasing the dose."

"Will you take the meds now?" Jeff asked.

"Not while I'm working on this project. I can't stop now. I have to finish it."

Jeff thought in silence for some time. "It's not all or nothing, Fred," he said eventually. "You could take the meds and feel better, then stop them when you had a job to do."

"But how would I know if I had a better idea between projects, a wonderful idea? I wouldn't think of something better unless the drug was out of my system."

"True, but at least you'd have a break from being unhappy and you'd know you could go back to that any time."

"It doesn't feel like that now."

"None of us know how bad it'll get for you if you don't take it."

"I wonder what the Jattans did for Lirrel," Hredt said. "Perhaps they didn't know about this either."

"Okay. Can I let you think about it?" Jeff looked distressed. "I'm worried that it'll get to the stage where people think you're dangerous and want you locked up."

"You would tell me the truth, wouldn't you?"

"Yes."

"I don't want to be forced to have this drug, but I don't want to be unhappy, and I don't want people to be afraid of me."

"I know, mate. You didn't answer my question, though. Do you think the Kugin kept you on this stuff to make you feel better or to protect themselves? Did they realise it made you less efficient?"

"I don't think I can even guess the answer any more."

"Okay." Jeff stood up and patted him on the back. "I'll leave you to get on with your work now. But please think about taking the meds for a while just so you can enjoy yourself a bit."

"Will you promise me you won't put it in my food?"

Jeff paused. "I promise you *I* won't, but I'll need to get undertakings from Captain Ingram that nobody else will. I'll do whatever I can to persuade them."

"Thank you, Jeff."

"I'm sorry this has happened to you. We'll work something out. I promise."

"When I need to test this project, do you think Marc would be willing to try it?"

"I can't speak for him, but you know what he's like. Always first to give something a go."

Hredt tried not to look as impatient and restless as he felt. Jeff, being a good and kind man, tried to look as if he didn't notice.

"Thank you," Hredt said

"Okay, see you later. Call me if you need anything."

Hredt waited for the sound of the door closing and got on with designing the user controls. It was proving harder than the physics of a personal gate. All he needed was a foolproof way to anchor a pressure or optic switch in a way that made it easy for a human to activate but hard to pull off or detach by accident. The more he thought about voice activation, the less he liked that, too. Humans could remember specific commands but the simpler the words, the easier it was for an enemy to hear and mimic them. If they were coded to a specific voice, they could hinder someone trying to rescue an unconscious comrade. And some operations needed to be carried out in silence. Hredt decided to stick to a touch control that required a little more pressure than an accidental knock, and work out something better during testing.

Now he was hungry. He'd avoided breakfast when it was delivered because he couldn't be sure now that someone hadn't already added medication to it, but that would have meant an overdose for the rest of the commune who'd happily eaten their prescription bars. He should have taken the food. Now he'd have to wait until the others returned and the evening meal was delivered.

I need to learn to make food for myself.
I need to find food in the first place.
How does Rikayl manage?

Rikayl ate food supplied by the base, but he still went hunting and came back with little native creatures to eat. He seemed to be thriving, so they weren't toxic to teeriks. Hredt couldn't stomach the thought of eating anything raw, but he had to be at least capable of cooking it. He'd investigate that. If he could source his own food, he'd know that nothing had been added to it. His biggest dread at the moment was being drugged against his will when he was so close to finishing the new gate system, because he had a stark choice; he could either be brilliant but unhappy, doing his best-ever work, or averagely competent, content, and aware that he'd fallen short of his potential.

Jeff's suggestion of doing both in phases sounded sensible, but Hredt knew he'd be unsatisfied in his average phase, and perhaps he wouldn't even have the motivation to get out of it, especially if he could recall just how unsettling the highs were.

The big question remained unanswered because he was almost too frightened to pursue it. If this was his normal state, the way he was meant to be without medication, what were teeriks? Was any creature naturally destined to be permanently angry, frustrated, unhappy — even violent? Rikayl wasn't like that. He'd never taken the drug, and although he could be aggressive, he wasn't a killer like Lirrel and he didn't seem to be the tormented creature that Hredt was turning into.

Hredt made himself stop work and go outside to see where Rikayl was. The child didn't fly far from the base, but he circled and kept an eye on the comings and goings below. If Hredt hung around long enough in the compound grounds, Rikayl would spot him eventually and land, then persuade Hredt to fly with him.

Rikayl appeared after a couple of minutes and spiralled down to land on the grass. It was a great pity that his language skills seemed to be limited, but he made himself understood and seemed to understand what was said to him in both English and Kugal. He had obvious mathematical skills too, and played complicated numerical card games with Chief Jeff. So he was intelligent, but he still hadn't developed like a teerik, and that upset Hredt more as time went on. Rikayl was smart enough to be bored with a life like an animal's, but Hredt didn't know how to help him develop whatever abilities he had, or if Caisin's knowledge was lodged in his brain or lost forever.

"Fly?" Hredt asked.

"Fun!" Rikayl bounced up and down, miming a take-off. "Find things!"

"Hunt?"

"Yes, yes, fun!"

Hredt dumped his jacket and took a run-up to take off. It was harder than he remembered, and he'd only been out of practice for a short time. But he forced himself higher, caught a current, and managed to rise to a respectable height to follow Rikayl to the eastern perimeter of the base. They wheeled around for a while. Rikayl always kept an eye on him, although it was hard to imagine what he'd be able to do if Hredt got into difficulties.

There was a river flanked by grasses beyond the defoliated land of the security cordon. Rikayl turned as if he'd spotted something and suddenly dived.

Hredt could see what had caught his eye and followed him down as a group of small furred creatures scattered in the grass. For some reason, the sight of Rikayl plummeting made Hredt want to chase the creatures too, but he found himself falling rather than making a controlled dive, and although his legs stretched out instinctively and his claws scooped up one of the animals, he landed badly. It hurt more than he expected.

But he still held on to his prey. He realised he'd killed it but it might have been the act of falling on it from a height rather than his talons that had finished it off.

This was what he'd always known he was, but had never felt. He was a raptor. His beak and his claws proved it. Now he'd caught prey for the first time but he didn't know what to do with it. Rikayl, already tearing his catch apart, paused and looked up for a moment.

"Gotcha!" he said. "Gotcha! Clever Hredt!"

"I hurt," Hredt said. He steeled himself to look at what he'd killed, a little brown fuzzy thing with long legs and a probing nose, and knew he had to try eating it if he was serious about this. He didn't even know where to start. He followed Rikayl's lead and tore into the guts.

It was horrible. It stank. He knew he couldn't do this. He'd have to take it home and cook it. He wasn't even sure that it was properly dead or even if he was supposed to eat the entrails.

"Not fun?" Rikayl asked.

"A new experience," Hredt said. "I'll learn. I need to go home, Rikayl."

He managed to stand up but there was no way he could take off again in this state. He was exhausted anyway, probably because he hadn't eaten, so he had to walk back. Rikayl followed him, making concerned chirps like a fledgling.

"I'm fine," Hredt said, limping his way to the perimeter. He carried the dead animal in one hand, reluctant to drop it. "I just need to get fit again. It's hard when you're old."

Before he reached the defoliated zone, he heard the sound of a quad bike approaching. Marc pulled up in front of him and gave him a disappointed look.

"You crashed," he said. "Just as well the drones spotted you. Are you okay?"

"My pride's bruised."

"Okay, hop on and I'll take you back. What's that thing in your hand?"

"My prey. I was hunting."

"Good man," Marc said. "I can show you how to skin and gut it if you like. I had to learn that in the Army."

Hredt had expected to be scolded for taking risks, so praise from a man like Marc was welcome. He clambered on the flatbed of the bike and they set off at a sedate speed with Rikayl flying escort overhead.

"I hear you're off your meds," Marc said.

"I am. I work better that way."

"Well, if you find you go a bit mad like Lirrel did, and I think you're going to hurt someone, I'll bring you down with a dart. I won't shoot you. Then the medics can get you back to normal for a while. Okay with that?"

Coming from Marc, it was very kind offer, and he wasn't making a drama out of it. He just promised not to kill him.

"I have to finish a gate modification first," Hredt said. "It's important. I want you to test it."

"What does it do?"

"The gate will follow you and you only have to press a switch on your body for it to move you. It's very fast. Good for emergencies, such as when Major Trinder had to move Dieter."

Marc crossed the perimeter. "Could you mount a switch on a wristband?"

"Of course."

"Good. Are you sure you're okay?"

"I'll be fine. What shall I do with the animal?"

"Give it to me and I'll refrigerate it until you're up to having a cookery lesson."

Marc made a point of taking Hredt into the house and ensuring he was comfortable before he left. If Hredt needed a reminder that he was getting older and humans were taking pity on him, this was it. They didn't even seem angry with him over the call he made to Lawson any more, and while he wanted to be back on good terms with them, he felt humiliated. But he did need to sleep. After working all night and eating nothing, he settled down on the cushions and only woke when the other commune members returned from work. He opened his eyes to find Rikayl peering into his face and Turisu leaning over him.

"What happened to you?" she asked.

"Hredt a bit dead," Rikayl said. "Bad flying."

"I landed badly," Hredt said. "We were out flying. Don't get angry with me."

"I wasn't going to," Turisu said. "Has the medic examined you?"

"I don't want a medic. I'm just stiff. Not injured."

"If you still feel like that in the morning, I'm calling Commander Haine." Then Turisu did something she hadn't done since she was a child. She leaned in and groomed the feathers on the top of his head with her beak. "Please don't take foolish risks. I don't want you to kill yourself."

They'd always had a difficult relationship. Now she'd mellowed so much and so fast with the medication that Hredt felt strangely sad. This was the father-daughter relationship they could have had, but it wasn't real. It was the drug. None of them were who they thought they were, and they hadn't realised it until the medication began wearing off. Humans might have been grateful for the changes that medicine could make to their personalities, but Hredt wasn't. He shouldn't have needed it just to be normal. How did it ever happen? It made no sense.

"I'll be careful," he said, trying not to worry her. "I've not been taking my medication. It's made me a little reckless."

"It's strange that we need it," Turisu said. She didn't even berate him for skipping his doses. "It's probably because wherever we came from originally had some natural substance that kept our brain chemistry healthy."

"Yes," Hredt said, but he didn't believe that. "I'm sure that's it."

He would take the medication again one day, but not yet, not while he was performing so well. He'd complete his work on the personal gate prototype this week and get Marc to test it before he tried refining it further. It would mean working through the night, but he'd want to be awake anyway. It was no hardship.

He was looking forward to eating tonight. He trusted Chief Jeff, and he wondered if the man had given him a discreet warning when he'd promised not to secretly dose his food, but that he wasn't sure yet that nobody else would.

Jeff hadn't come back to him about that. Hredt would need to remain vigilant.

* * *

UNIT 53A, AINATIO HOUSING ZONE, NOMAD BASE: NOVEMBER 1, OC.

"This is why hard copy newspapers never completely died out," Ash said, chin resting on one hand. "Defensive barrier. Screens don't give you enough cover."

Chris ate breakfast with his pocket screen propped in front of him, noting who was where. He didn't know what he expected to find, but when he found something or someone in the wrong place, or couldn't find them at all, he'd be ready.

"Sorry." He laid the screen face-down. He'd never read at the table as a kid. It was one of his mom's strict rules that had stuck with him into adulthood, but he'd broken it today. "It's very rude of me."

"That wasn't my point. What's worrying you?"

"Nothing, really. Apart from alien navies, teeriks who have to be totally baked so they don't get into fights, and disgruntled Ainatio revolutionaries."

"I do realise we live in interesting times."

"I wasn't being snarky." Chris reached across the table and meshed his fingers with hers. It looked like everything was going well with her, but even the rosy filter of a new relationship wouldn't help if he behaved like a slob. "I'm just not good at being funny."

"Yes you are." She squeezed his fingers. "Are we arm wrestling now, by the way?"

"No, because you'd kick my ass. You've got bigger biceps than me. It's opening all those valves that does it."

Ash pulled her hand away, got up to put her plate on the draining board, and then pounced on him from behind, giggling as she tussled with him. It always made him laugh. She got him in an armlock and he feigned helpless agony.

"Stop obsessing right now." She leaned in and whispered in his ear. "You're the one who always quotes Marcus Aurelius. Don't worry about the future because you've already got the skills to cope with it. Or something like that."

"It sounded classier in Latin, but yeah."

She let go of him and topped up their mugs with coffee. "You didn't even mention the sea monsters, so you can't be that worried. I'm waiting for them to get into the water system. That thing with the single tentacle, coming up the U-bend. That'd take your mind off your troubles."

"I'm so glad I've got a woman who works in sewage."

"What can I say? It's a glamorous job. I'm a beefcake magnet."

"Anyway, I'm not worrying," Chris said. "I'm just waiting for a lot of shoes to drop."

That summed it up. Everything was fine at the moment, more or less, but there was always that background hum from stuff that could happen at any time. Nobody ever knew what was coming down the pike, but Chris found himself hankering for pre-emptive action to get some of it over with. It was insane, and he knew it. But that didn't stop the feeling.

The daily Joint Command meetings had now declined to once or twice a week, so he was free to do some proper security work this morning and catch up with his guys who were still keeping an eye on key sites around the base. If things stayed quiet for another week or two, he'd scale down the presence and just monitor the folks he felt were most likely to cause trouble. But there was quiet and there was silence, and he got the feeling that it was silence right now.

The complaints about sending *Elcano* back to Earth had stopped too abruptly for his liking. Humans were recreational complainers. They did it because it made them feel better, especially in institutions like a military base, and when they didn't do it they'd either moved on to a new topic or they'd gone somewhere else to bitch. It was unlikely that all the *Cabot* crew and Ainatio staffers were in the mood for trouble. They were outnumbered two to one and they were all smart enough to know better. It was just a few *gobshites*, as Jeff called them.

Chris rode out to the first stop on his tour of the strategic sites, the hydrogen splitter. Jackson Allitt was there with Robin Peklow, just sitting on the low wall outside. Robin had been a nurse but had left to join the transit police for some reason, and that was the uniform she'd been wearing when the remnant of Chris's SDF platoon had found her trying to start a truck in a parking lot in Pittsburgh. The trains hadn't been running for a couple of years. Chris imagined her still trying to maintain public order single-handed with a Port Authority badge and a baton, and he couldn't leave a lone woman to fend for herself in bandit country. Matt McNally fixed the truck and Robin drove out with the SDF vehicles in their embryonic convoy, a very useful addition to the skills pool.

Jackson looked relaxed, just a heavily-armed guy who happened to be chilling outside a critical utility building.

"No Molotov cocktails yet?" Chris asked.

"I got a dirty look from the beardy guy in Biomed. Does that count?"

"Close enough."

"They'll forget all about it when *Elcano*'s gone," Robin said. She still had her baton on her belt. Chris suspected it was her comfort blanket. "It's not like it's the whole Ainatio gang. Most haven't forgotten Erskine abandoning them."

"Perhaps we're overreacting," Jackson said.

Chris shrugged. "Maybe, but they noticed us show up, so they'll notice if we stand down now, and it might look like an opportunity to them." He checked the time. "I'm supposed to teach a firearms class in an hour. Mostly boffins. I'll take the collective temperature again."

"Okay. We'll call you if we have to make a last stand."

Chris got back on the quad bike and studied his screen to plan his next stop. His guys never held back when they thought he was wrong and it sounded like Jackson had decided he was. With Ash's pep talk this morning, and even Alex saying they were taking it too seriously, Chris wondered whether he'd realise if he *was* overreacting. He'd always made a point of looking calm, whatever was going on in his head, because that made people around him feel better. He'd have to ask Marc. Marc wouldn't spare his feelings if he felt something was off.

Chris set off for Biogas 2, where Zakko had taken up position. After that, his route would take him past the water and waste treatment plant, down to Biogas 1, then the hydro power installation. He'd head west after that and check the food warehouses, the two reactors, and the comms tower. That was the list of places he'd target if he was looking to put pressure on the management; food, power, and water. He stopped the bike and rolled back the security footage for each location, just to see if there'd been any suspicious activity in the last few hours, but there was nothing. Solomon would have told him, anyway.

Yeah, he was making too much of this. He'd go through with the plan, but he'd scale it down this week. Nobody was dumb enough to jeopardise their own well-being this far from home.

When he'd seen Zakko, he stopped outside the water treatment plant to check Ash was okay, even though he'd seen her less than an hour ago and Chuck Emerson was stationed outside. Chuck waved.

"It's okay, Chris, she's got her giant wrench," he called. "None shall pass."

Now even Chuck thought he was overdoing the vigilance. At every stop around the circuit, the guys on duty were alert but mellow about it. Chris finished his rounds at Reactor B and headed down to the centre of the base to get ready for his class. On the way, he stopped the bike and tried to see himself from the outside.

"Sol," he said, "am I being a neurotic asshole about all this?"

"I don't think so, Chris. We're in a situation humans have never been in before, and feelings are running high. Although there were rumours of a mutiny at APS's Mars base some years ago. Incidents can be sparked very fast by the most trivial things, though. As I'm sure you know better than I do."

"It was mostly food when we had to deal with riots. Or other supplies. Gas, diapers, water. Either they got it and made a run for it, or they were out of luck and they'd move on to looting stuff they didn't even need. I think it's hard-wired from our hunter-gatherer days."

"Everyone's well-fed. Perhaps some of them just need to be busier."

"As long as you'd tell me if I was out of line."

"Of course I would. You don't often ask me for guidance, you know."

"Where are you at the moment?"

"I'm in the bot, mooching around like yourself."

Sol retreated to the bot when he wanted to explore, but also when he felt under threat. The idea of an entity with Sol's power being insecure scared the crap out of Chris.

"You don't trust anybody either," he said.

"I don't trust a complete absence of data."

"Too quiet, huh?"

"Possibly. Chris, as we're discussing uncertainty, may I ask you something personal?"

"Sure."

"Do you talk to yourself?"

It was a worrying question. Sol always said he never intruded in private spaces, but it was the kind of thing you'd ask if you'd caught someone doing it too often.

"Yeah, everyone does it," Chris said. "Especially if you spend a lot of time alone, if only to hear a human voice. Have you been monitoring me?"

"No, not at all." Solomon sounded hesitant. "I've started talking to Tad Bednarz. He's been gone for many years, but I never really did it before."

So Sol was worried he was losing his own marbles, not playing psychiatrist. "I talk to Jamie when I visit his grave," Chris said. "Marc talks to his sons. It's normal for humans, and you've got a mostly human mind. I wouldn't worry about it."

"But do they answer you? Does Jamie advise you not to do this or that, or ask you questions?"

"Not really. Does Bednarz?"

"That's the difference between you and me. I can remember almost everything Bednarz ever said to me, so I can reconstruct his personality. I can extrapolate his replies. I hear him. But I know it's the reflection of my own thoughts."

"No, it's still not weird enough," Chris said, trying to reassure him. "Go ask Commander Haine if you don't believe me. Anyway, is it just talking to yourself that's worrying you, or is it something else?"

Solomon paused. His pauses were always a big deal because he didn't need them. Thinking things through at length didn't take any noticeable time by human standards, so when he did it, he did it consciously for the benefit of flesh and blood — a signal that he was considering something deeply, or that he was about to say something important, or that he thought what he had to say would upset or anger the listener.

"My ethics seem to be getting very flexible," he said. "In the light of what I've done in the past year, that probably won't surprise you. But expedience is becoming too frequent."

Chris hadn't lost any sleep over the unsavoury things he'd had to do. He always knew why he was doing them and what the likely outcome would be if he didn't do them. Solomon had done some serious shit, but he had reasons too, like shooting the guys who'd ambushed the patrol and killed Jamie, or frying Asia's infrastructure to buy time to evacuate. Yeah, the APS cyberattack had been brutal, but it was a case of them or everyone on the mission, and that had been good enough for Chris.

"Sol, we've been at war for years," Chris said. "It's not always a shooting war, but it's a war all the same. When people want to hurt you, there's no nice way of responding."

"It's not that at all," Solomon said. "I'm doing something unethical to someone for their benefit and everyone else's."

"Ends justifying means is probably one of the biggest moral debates, Sol. Nobody's above it." Chris took a guess at what Sol was up to. He was either spying on someone when he swore he never would, or he was messing with the teeriks, but Ingram had probably approved it. "You want to tell me anything specific?"

"Not at the moment."

"What did Bednarz's voice tell you?"

"He said I shouldn't feel guilty about it."

"If he'd said don't do it, would you have obeyed?"

"I don't think so."

"There you go. You've made a judgement call." Chris couldn't tell if that had made Sol feel better or not. "I know we haven't always agreed on what's best for people. You've taken decisions for me when I haven't wanted you to. But that's part of getting along with each other. Whoever you're doing this uninvited favour for, they'll notice eventually and either concede that they needed it or rip you a new one."

"That's very helpful. Thank you, Chris. I'll talk to you later."

Solomon always said something like that when he didn't find an answer helpful at all. Chris started the bike and rode down to the indoor range.

Four of the Ainatio biomed people had turned up a little early, and Reverend Berry was keeping them occupied by making them strip down and reassemble their weapons blindfolded. There wasn't much to a Marquis, so they were getting pretty good at it. Berry gave Chris a never-mind look.

"Okay, guys, Chris is here, blindfolds off," he said. "Might as well make a start."

It was just Bob Calman, Mick Randall, Toby Etherington, and Steff Bachelin. "Good morning," Chris said. "Thin on the ground today, huh?"

Mick folded his strip of cloth. It looked like it had been cut from a towel. "Maybe they've gone to Fiji."

"If you've got a problem with us extracting high-value personnel from APS territory, let's discuss it before we start."

"Just joking. No problem."

"Is there a reason? We're six down."

"I don't know."

"Anyone who misses training sessions without a reason loses their personal weapon. It's not like passing your driving test and forgetting about it. Skills need maintenance." Chris wished he had a better line in counter-snark. Getting all pissy about a jibe just made him look defensive, but he couldn't let it pass like he was afraid of offending anyone. "Let's see what your accuracy's like. Grouping. Five shots, repeat five times. Okay, load, and Bob's up first. You might as well have individual tuition today."

At least they'd shown up, and to be fair on them, they weren't doing badly. As the cleaner bots whirred around the floor collecting spent cases, Chris looked over the list of AWOL trainees and couldn't see any overlap with Paul Cotton's clique, and when he located them on the map, they were all in the medical centre and the labs, not even together. Maybe it wasn't a protest, but something wasn't right.

Berry watched, arms folded, and said nothing. When the class ended, he sat down at the bench and poured two coffees from his vacuum flask.

"I don't get it either," he said. "If they've decided not to cooperate with Ingram, this is a dumb way to show it. They're the ones who won't be able to defend themselves if we get a visit."

"Gesture politics."

"Are you going to withdraw their weapons?"

"I should. The rule's there regardless of the reason."

"In person?"

"Yeah. I'm not a manager. It's my responsibility."

"They're scared of you." Berry sipped his coffee, frowned, and took a couple of packets of sweetener out of his pocket. "You won't get any resistance."

"Everybody says that," Chris said. "I haven't given anyone here a reason to fear me. The hitman rumour's done the rounds, though. And I suppose they've all heard about what happened on Joni Josepha's boat." But Chris remembered who he was talking to. "Did you ever tell the Kill Liners about your past?"

"I told Doug and Joanne. They were predictably nice about it and said it was history. I kind of stopped there. I think I'll save the general revelation until I need to give a sermon on redemption about some other guy. And when the situation here is a little more settled."

"People believe what reinforces their existing opinions, for the most part," Chris said. "I still think it won't make any difference to your congregation."

"Do you want an extra hand on your patrols? I could do with learning more skills."

"It's a kind offer, but I've already asked Dan not to get his guys involved. It's best if we do it." Chris wondered how people would react to a clergyman standing guard. It might actually calm some of them down. "We're outsiders. It's easier if things go sour. Dan's detachment's got to work with Ainatio's people."

"Yes, it's like strikes. The ill-feeling afterwards takes a long time to heal."

"I try to take lessons from the Romans."

"Invade Gaul?"

"Never deploy auxiliaries in their own country. Although they weren't worried about upsetting the malcontents."

Berry laughed. "It's going to take us more than a few months to merge into a community. But it'll happen."

Chris knew he didn't always allow for where folks were in their upheaval process. Kill Line had just transplanted itself, complete and whole. The Ainatio contingent had been through a series of shocks and traumas in the space of a few months, then permanently separated from friends. The *Cabot* crew's mission training had been tailored to the disruption they'd have to deal with, and everyone in the transit camp had come from lives already so broken that being with other evacuees felt like having a community again. Nomad was made up of four groups who had very different ideas on what constituted upheaval.

"I'll cut everyone as much slack as possible," Chris said. "Thank you for reminding me."

It was time for lunch. He'd feel more upbeat after he'd eaten. His route to the canteen took him up the path between the teerik compound and the housing zone occupied by Ainatio and most of the *Cabot* crew, and as he walked, he saw some of the boffins eating their lunch on benches outside. It was starting to look like a nice little suburb rather than a military outpost, even though most of them had obeyed the instruction to keep their weapons with them at all times.

Yeah, time. Everybody needed time. By the time the Brits built a ship and showed up, the secret would be out on Earth and folks could contact whoever they pleased. That would bring its own problems, but there was nothing he could do to stop the flow of events now and he just had to ride it out.

There were more people having lunch on the green when he crossed the road behind the old accommodation building. A few guys were playing soccer. Jared met him in front of the main building and gave him that *hmmm* look he saved for moments of disagreement or confusion.

"They're all pretty calm," Jared said. "Some folks would say that means we're wasting our time. Others would say that they're only calm because we're here."

"Six guys failed to show for training today. They went on working."

"Rude not to send notes from their moms, but not threatening."

"Yeah."

"Burger?"

"Lead me to it."

"Movies tonight. Bring Ash."

"But she's never seen us in critic mode."

"If she's serious about you, buddy, she's got to face the truth. Most movies need to be told that they suck."

This was what Nomad was supposed to be like. It was meant to be small-town and free of the uncaring crap of anonymous urban existence. If nothing else, Chris had a much better idea of what he'd be fighting to defend, and that made him feel better. So did the caramelised bits on the fried onions in his burger.

"I just want a nice girl, a nice bathroom, and clean food," he said. "I've got all that now. I'm made."

"In fact, you even got a nice girl who could do the plumbing for your nice bathroom. See? It was worth the journey. Meant to be, like Marsha says."

"You're right. I never looked at it that way."

Chris was enjoying the sweet stickiness of the onion when Solomon's voice whispered in his ear and ruined the mood.

"Chris, there's some activity at the main food warehouses that you should be aware of."

"What kind of activity?"

It was a déjà vu moment that brought back unpleasant memories of the last time Sol had interrupted a quick burger lunch with Jared. The day had ended with two dead. Chris checked his pocket screen. There were a couple of boffins standing outside the first warehouse in the row, identified by their icons as David Ziegler and Theo Barcellos, but they looked like they were just chatting to Erin, who was on duty. Trinder was with her, though.

"I told Dan to stay clear of this," Chris said.

"I think he just showed up. I've flagged it for Ingram. They were standing in front of the loading bay doors and Erin asked them to move."

"They're armed, yeah?"

"They're almost all armed, Chris. It's our policy." Solomon was too tactful to point out it was Chris's own rule. "It's still very civil, though."

Civil? If Erin thought she had to tell them to shift their asses and they were still there, then it definitely wasn't civil. "Okay. On my way."

Jared wrapped his burger and stuck it in his pocket. "Here we go again."

"It'll be some bullshit about knowing their rights." Chris couldn't waste food. He planned to finish his burger on the way. "I don't even know those two guys. Are they whiners?"

"No, they seemed pretty normal when they drank in the bar when we first got here."

They stuck to a normal walking pace to avoid looking like they were rushing to some emergency. The base didn't need any more fuel for gossip or anxieties. By the time they reached the warehouse, Ingram was there and Andy had shown up as well. They were talking to what had suddenly become a group of fifteen or so Ainatio staff including Paul Cotton, plus one of *Cabot*'s civilians, Jenny Park. Well, she was no surprise. They were all lined up across the loading bay like a union picket line, and all armed. Ingram wasn't going to be too happy about one of her own people getting involved with whatever this turned out to be. Erin looked pissed off and so did Trinder. It was hard to tell if this was also a turf war about who was running the security here.

It would have taken two minutes to disperse them the old-fashioned way, but Ingram looked around as Chris and Jared walked up to the group and her expression said it all: *please don't start anything.* She stepped back to talk to them and Dan and Andy flowed in to fill her space, continuing whatever discussion had been going on.

"We're just having a chat," she said to Chris.

"About what, exactly?"

"Their grievances."

Chris eyeballed all of them while he was talking. Some of them met his gaze. It was what Marc called a come-and-have-a-go-if-you-think-you're-hard-enough look, and that was a big mistake. Chris wouldn't forget that in a hurry or ignore it, and he was going to remember Paul Cotton's sneer in particular.

"It looks like they're blocking the entrance, Captain," he said.

"They are."

"We're here to unblock it."

"Can I ask you to hold off for a while?" Ingram was feigning tolerance. He could hear it in her voice. "We've got half an hour before the next produce drop-off, and we'll have talked this out by then."

"So they're going to interfere with food distribution, yeah?"

"They just want attention and a chance to sound off at me. Sometimes it's better to stand there and take it until they run out of steam."

"So it's about *Elcano*, and Fiji, and Britain's FTL."

"You forgot the Mother Death searches. But yes, it's a rich stew of resentment."

Chris should have anticipated something like this. Food production dictated what Nomad could do. It was the reason *Elcano* still had people in cryo. Perishable food like milk had to be moved into refrigeration or processed into shelf-stable formulas, and the stored cereals had to be taken to the production plant to be made into bread and other processed foods. A lot of duplication had been built into the base, like the four adjacent but separate food warehouses, so that a problem with one of them didn't leave the base without food. Supplies moved around a lot even within this small settlement. Chris only had a vague idea of how the automation worked, but the one thing he did know was that messing up the timetable would have a knock-on effect. Bots wouldn't roll over humans to complete their tasks on time. They'd stop dead.

At some point, though, Sol would probably intervene, and Chris had to put a stop to this before things reached that stage. He'd been ready for assholes sabotaging facilities, but not for them simply blocking choke points and defying Joint Command to use force on them. With the base map telling everyone everything, right down to the planned movements of raw materials, it was relatively easy for smart people to work out a minimum-effort plan for maximum impact.

"What are their demands?" he asked.

"*Elcano* stays here, everyone's revived, and everybody gets to call home," Ingram said.

"And everyone gets to use the gate, I suppose."

"Mentioned, but not a condition."

It didn't matter if anyone in command agreed with that. It was how pressure was being applied that presented the problem. "And you told them to ram it, I hope."

"Not yet. I might not need to. They're not hardcore protesters. They'll run out of steam by tea-time."

Ingram was going to let this get out of hand because she wasn't used to dealing with confrontational civilians, let alone groups of them. Chris was, though, and he wasn't going to let anything slide.

Civvies could be dangerous enough without firearms, but these were armed and trained for the defence of the base, and as far as Chris was concerned that made them part-time soldiers. It wasn't just about holding up the food supply process. If these guys didn't learn some discipline now, they'd never be an effective force against an alien attack.

"Ma'am, things can go south real fast in these situations," Jared said. "Especially with weapons involved. *Extra*-especially if they're not so used to using them. We don't want anyone killed by accident."

"I realise that, Jared, but it's not a riot. It's an argument."

Solomon cut in on the security channel. "Captain, we now have Ainatio personnel moving to the entrances at all four warehouses."

Everyone could see what was happening on their base map. Chris was now getting radio messages from Dieter, Alan Lombardo, and Bern Ford, confirming Sol's assessment.

"We're backed up to the doors and we'll clear a path by force if we need to," Dieter said.

Chris could hear voices in the background. They weren't yelling, but he heard someone say, "You can't stop us, this is lawful." He trusted Dieter's judgement.

"Do what you have to to maintain order and allow access to folks with a reason to be there," Chris said. He looked at Ingram. "Yeah, they just want to bitch at you, right? Look, they're organised and they've managed to do it so we didn't see them planning it, not even via messages. If we don't knock it on the head now, this base will be run by the loudest whiners."

Ingram wasn't giving ground. "And I say we don't escalate this."

Chris had done his best to be nice to Ingram for Marc's sake, but now he had to treat her like any other officer who was fucking things up and who wasn't his CO.

"With respect, I'm running security on the ground," he said. "That was what we agreed. If you're going to talk, you do it after they've stood down. They're banking on you having rules about not being mean to civilians."

"You're not helping, Chris."

"If *you* want to help, Captain, go find Marc and keep him away from here. Dan shouldn't be involved either. We're fine playing the bad guys, but you have to work with these people afterwards."

Ingram looked disappointed in him. It was his mother's look. He did his best to override what he knew damn well was just a reflex with no place in the here and now, but it was hard.

"You're giving me orders on my own base," Ingram said, like he should have known better.

"I'm telling you that I'll act to secure the warehouses and stop anyone interfering with the normal delivery of produce."

"Got to agree with Chris, ma'am," Jared said. "You hand more control to them and they'll do it again the next time they don't like a decision. You wouldn't accept this on a ship."

"They're civvies," Ingram said. "Until they do something that threatens the well-being of everyone else. Then they're civilian detainees."

"They're a volunteer militia," Chris said. "Once they pick up a gun, they've got different responsibilities."

"There's a time for blowing the crap out of things, but this is the time to talk and lower the temperature."

"We're not going to argue in front of them," Chris said. "If it looks like nobody's in control, everything falls apart. But we're going to have a bulk milk delivery in... let's see... twenty minutes and someone has to make the call. I'm going to give the truck clear access."

Chris had to hand it to Ingram. She didn't bluster or try to pull rank. His opinion just didn't matter to her.

"I'll have to talk them down in nineteen minutes, then," she said, and headed back to the picket line, which had increased by twenty or more Ainatio staff, four more of Chris's guys, and Luce, Fonseca, and Alex. Jared gave Chris a knowing nod and followed Ingram. As she walked away, Trinder broke off from the group and approached Chris.

"I read body language fluently, but you're a challenge," he said. "I assume you said you're dispersing them. I did too. Erin was going to sort it out right away, but Ingram got involved."

"Dan, I asked you to steer clear."

"Yeah, you did, but I wasn't going to leave Erin to handle that lot."

"Just because she's a sniper doesn't mean she can't drop people at close range."

"I know, but *you* try standing back in that situation."

"Point taken."

"Anyway, I've just deployed my guys to back up yours at the other sites in case this is a diversion for something else."

"Thanks, but your life's going to be shit when this is over." Chris looked around to see who else was going to pitch in. He was noting the ringleaders, the catalysts who'd trigger the others, the ones he had to subdue first, and he slipped his rifle into patrol carry. "You don't think I'm overreacting, then."

"No, like I said, if we don't deal with it now we'll be dealing with worse next time."

"I thought we'd left this shit behind. Sol, you're very quiet. What are you up to?"

"I'm observing," Solomon said. "Marc and Tev are inbound. As you would be were the situation reversed, of course. I'm also monitoring all the sites and I'll warn you if I see movement. I'll let you know when the milk tanker moves out, but you now have fifteen minutes."

"I can track the tanker on the map. So can they. How did we miss them organising, Sol?"

"I know I've failed on that."

"I'm not saying you failed. I just want to know."

"I never saw tracking data that suggested meetings or large gatherings, or any messaging," Solomon said. "I suspect they've used an in-person cascade system, one to one, like your own evacuation plan."

Chris was still making an effort to see the best in people after a lifetime of mistrust, but events always reminded him that he was right first time. He'd taught the Ainatio guys how to shoot and how to communicate via low tech in an emergency. He'd trained and equipped his own enemy. They weren't doing much more than shooting their mouths off at the moment, but they all appeared to have their weapons with them — another of his bright ideas — and when emotions were running high, firearms just made the mix more toxic.

Marc and Tev strode up with that controlled casualness that always looked menacing, like a couple of hitmen killing time with an ice-cream before they went up to the roof to do the job.

"Oh dear," Marc said. He had his rifle slung but his sidearm was holstered on his chest for a change, and a pocket on his angler's vest appeared to be full of zip-ties. He opened the tab and offered the ties around like a pack of cigarettes. "Do we have to restore some public order, gentlemen? I was going to slip into my smoking jacket and read some Dostoevsky this afternoon. How rude of them to disrupt my plans."

"Ingram's trying to talk them down," Trinder said.

Marc's gaze was fixed on her. "She may well succeed. But if she doesn't, as soon as she steps out of that ruck, we go in."

"And if she doesn't step out?"

"I'll pull her out so we're clear to operate."

"Good luck with that," Trinder said.

"We've stood back out of courtesy rather than undermine her in front of the boffins," Chris said carefully. No-fraternisation rules suddenly seemed like a really good idea. Relationships made these situations messy. "She's got eleven minutes before Kill Line gets sucked into this."

"Probably less," Solomon said. "The tanker's moving now."

Raised voices cut the conversation short. Tempers were fraying. Chris turned and the four of them just moved forward without another word, ready to lay hands on collars. But the ruckus wasn't the protesters arguing with Ingram. It was boffin on boffin violence.

Some of the other Ainatio staff had turned up, the ones with grievances about Erskine, and they were yelling at their colleagues, calling them ass-kissers and asking why they'd disrupt their buddies' lives for the people who'd abandoned them to face a nuclear strike. The worrying thing was that most were carrying their rifles. Things were getting dangerously heated. Ingram tried to be the peacemaker, hands out to either side as she stepped between them like a referee making two boxers break.

"She'll have my guts for garters if I intervene," Marc said.

"Let me do it." Chris was going to pre-empt the whole thing and dive in now, and grab Paul Cotton first and maybe smack the bastard around a bit, but Solomon whispered, "Tanker, with you in less than a minute."

You could normally hear vehicles a long way off in Nomad, but there was too much noise from the protest. Chris looked down the road and waited for it to appear. Eventually someone heard it, heads went up, and people looked around. The uproar quietened down a little.

It wasn't a big tanker, but it was hard to stand in the path of a vehicle moving fast enough to do serious damage, and when Chris saw who was driving it he expected to see casualties in the next thirty seconds. Liam Dale wasn't the braking kind. Marty the sheep farmer was in the passenger seat, which told Chris there was going to be trouble from Kill Line as well. Nobody needed a co-driver for a half-mile journey.

The picket line stood its ground. For a few seconds, Chris thought Liam was going to run them down but the tanker stopped barely a yard from them and both men jumped down from the cab. They were armed as well.

Marc sighed. "He doesn't piss about, does he?"

Ingram stepped into the one-yard DMZ, which Chris thought was pretty gutsy of her.

"Come on, chaps, let's keep a sense of proportion," she said. "We're talking. We can sort this out."

Liam wasn't listening. "Get them out of my way or we'll move them ourselves."

Paul Cotton stepped forward. He had to have his say. It was another point at which a few calm words might have turned things around, but that wasn't going to happen, not with the head of steam folks had built up since the day Erskine admitted she'd lied about every aspect of the Nomad mission.

"Mr Dale, do you think it's fair that we're controlled by a Brit clique who can pop back to Earth when they feel like it and hand over our technology to their government?" Paul asked. "Are you okay with our colleagues being kept in cryo because of some alleged supplies shortage, and then dumped back on Earth in the state it's in now? You don't find that odd or objectionable or an abuse of power?"

"It's fine by me," Liam said. "Your colleagues were okay with leaving us behind when they thought we'd be nuked by APS. They can ship you all back and dump you in the Sahara for all I care."

No sugar-coating today, then. Marc wove his way through the crowd and Chris moved to the other side of him so they could do a pincer movement to pull Ingram out if it all blew up. It was too crowded and chaotic to get a clear shot if it all kicked off and weapons were discharged, but if a boffin shot anyone, it would be an accident born of panic, not intent. Someone might still end up dead, though. That was all Chris needed to consider.

"Well, Mr Dale, that's very enlightened," Paul said. "I'm glad we know where you stand."

"Good. Get out of my way, then."

"Come on, give it a rest," Ingram said. She sounded genuinely pissed off now. She jerked her head in Chris's direction like she was pointing him out. "If we don't talk this through, Paul, someone's going to get hurt, so I'm asking you again to put your weapons down and disperse, and then we can have a civilised discussion around a table when everyone's cooled down."

"We did that already, Captain. You didn't listen."

"Move," Liam said.

"We're not going anywhere." Paul was pushing his luck with a guy who'd shot a Jattan. "If we don't do the right thing now, and just cave in to all this, what kind of society are we handing to our children?"

"I've got kids," Liam said. "You haven't. And pretty soon you won't have any food either, because we'll stop supplying it. We've got plenty in Kill Line. Good luck living on tomatoes and coffee from your crop tunnels. We'll feed *Cabot* people if they come to the bar in town — except you, Miss Park — but not you assholes."

"Hey, we're not part of this," one of the anti-Erskine bunch said. "We're as pissed at them as you are."

Paul moved. Chris didn't think he was making a lunge at anyone, but Marty — nice, kind, generous Marty who never made a fuss and put up with everything in silence — obviously did. He grabbed the scientist's collar and rammed him up against the front of the tanker so hard that Chris heard the clang of metal as Paul's rifle scraped the tanker's grille and clattered to the ground. Marty had his arm across his throat. Paul's eyes bugged. Everyone froze.

"We don't need you frigging parasites here." Marty yelled it in his face at point-blank range. "Nearly every damn calorie you're eating now either came from our farms and went into your stores, or it's the fresh produce we're providing now. We fed you for *decades*. You never found a cure for die-back. You even let the damn virus out and finished us off. If we'd wanted to stay in Kill Line and take our chances, you took that choice away. And then your boss left us to die. I lost everything my family worked for over three generations. Well, fuck you, Dr Cotton, and fuck all your kind. We'll be way better off if we freeze the lot of you and send you back with Erskine."

It was a slow-motion moment when all the awful possibilities flashed up in Chris's mind as he pushed people out of the way. If he broke up the fight, they'd probably both turn on him. The onlookers might go either way, maybe boiling over, maybe shocked into slinking off because they hadn't intended things to go this far.

But the resentment had been festering and now it burst out on all sides. Chris pulled Marty away and slammed Paul to the ground, arm up his back, knee pinning him down, and zip-tied his wrists. When he looked up for a second, the scene of pandemonium was unreal. There was no sign of Ingram, but Marc had his pistol to Ziegler's head as he took his Marquis off him, a couple of the Ainatio guys were trading blows, and Erin had her rifle aimed at one of the anti-protest guys who looked like he'd shat himself in terror. Erin could be very loud without shouting, like she had an extra volume control.

"*Put your weapon on the ground*," she boomed. "Put it down *now* or I'll fire."

Chris expected to see scattered bodies, but it was more like opening a bar door when a brawl was in progress and not knowing where to look first. His guys and Trinder's were forcing people to kneel with their hands behind their heads while they disarmed them. Then something struck him hard in the jaw from his right side. He spun around and landed a punch in return before he even realised who'd hit him. It was the nuclear engineer whose home he'd had to search. He'd laid him out. Chris had no idea the man felt any ill-will towards him, let alone that he was capable of punching him in the face out of the blue.

But Chris didn't know these people at all. It wasn't the first time he'd thought that, and not knowing what his neighbours were really capable of was more threatening than charging into a hail of bricks and gunfire from a mob of strangers. Then the yelling and general noise began tailing off, and he took in his wider surroundings. He was standing in the middle of thirty or forty people kneeling with their fingers meshed behind their heads, men and women alike, a scene from a foreign country he wouldn't have wanted to live in. This was their fresh start.

Shit. Shouldn't have happened. How do we come back from this?

The whole fracas couldn't have taken more than a couple of minutes. It was going to take a damn sight longer than that to repair relations, though. Chris looked around for the others and saw Marc wipe the back of his hand across his mouth as if he was bleeding. Trinder, Tev, and Jared were busy hauling cuffed protesters to their feet and walking them away. Ingram reappeared and strode over to them. One of the detainees was Paul.

"This could have been talked out," she said, almost kindly. "What did you expect them to do when you show up armed?"

Chris didn't hear the answer. He was trying to work out what Paul had said to get that response. But he knew he was being held up as the nasty thing that would happen to Paul if he didn't behave now.

"Can we get this milk pumped out, then?" Liam asked. He was flexing and rubbing the knuckles on his right hand as if he'd thrown a punch or two himself. His split lip confirmed he had. "But I mean it about not supplying those bastards. They can starve. I'm going back to organise the farms. Marty? Come on, buddy. Let's do what we came for."

Marty climbed back into the tanker without a word, restored to his normal polite self. It wasn't the time to argue with Liam about pouring petrol on a house fire.

"Go ahead," Chris said. "Sol, open up, please."

"Certainly," Solomon said. "I have some thoughts about today's procedures, but I'll save them for later."

"Very wise," Chris said. "I'm not in a teachable moment right now."

He hated coming down off these aggressive highs. It was like falling down a lift shaft and lying twitching at the bottom. He'd come to a dead stop but it went on hurting.

Trinder jogged up to him. "You okay?"

"Yeah. Punch in the face. Wounded pride."

"Been there."

"What happened? We kind of skipped the *please disperse or else* stage and went straight to *you're busted*."

"Three different groups airing their grievances with each other, plus guns, equals clusterfuck. But nobody died. Could have been worse."

"And now we've got to live with them."

"I'm not expecting any dinner invites."

"Which is why I said to stay out of it."

"Yeah, I know."

"What do we do with them now? We haven't got a legal system, lawyers, courts, or even a jail. And I'm not marching into Kill Line to make farmers hand over food."

"We're putting the miscreants in the gym until the medics have checked them over and they calm down," Trinder said, looking dejected. "Or at least the guys who weren't involved are, because it'll just start up again if any of us go in there."

"This is where the difficult stuff starts."

"Marc thinks we should withdraw firearms from everyone who took part in it today, even if they didn't get pissy and violent."

"Agreed. Y'know, I told Matt I'd bust myself down to private and hand over to Jared if I got the policy wrong. And I did."

"You didn't get it wrong, Chris. They're just not ready for that level of discipline and they're still thinking like civvies. Conscious incompetence probably saved a few lives, to be honest."

Marc showed up looking like nothing had happened, except for a few marks on his face.

"No wash-up today," he said. "Ingram thinks we all need to go to our rooms and think very hard about what we've done. Then we can meet tomorrow, a day older and wiser, and watch Solomon's replay like a football team that had its arse handed to it."

Chris felt his temper start to get the better of him. "Are you saying we're suspended from duty? Seriously?"

"No, nothing like that." Marc did his exasperated look. "She said we should literally write off today and come back with clearer heads, her included."

"My head's pretty clear right now, thanks."

"Okay, call it time to come up with a better idea to stop it happening again. Luce has secured the firearms and Alex is going to send everyone home later and ask Sol to make sure they don't leave their homes until the morning."

"That's what we philosophers call a curfew, Marc. Sol will have to call us to enforce it."

"It all depends on your tone and how you suggest it to them."

"This is what happens when you don't have rules that everyone understands and agrees to follow," Trinder said. "The guy who can punch the hardest always takes charge. That's never going to change."

"We've got to stop you reading those books, Dan." Marc took a small packet from his vest and handed it to Chris. "Tev says you'll feel better if you have this. Anyway, as long as you two are okay, I've going to slope off and have a beer with him and stay out of Boadicea's way for a while."

"Had a row?" Trinder asked.

"Not really. But you're right. Rules. Most people here don't know what's expected of them beyond their daily jobs. We're civvies who think we're still in uniform and the civvies don't know when they're supposed to be militia and what that entails. Or that they don't get their own way just because they're experts in Applied Whateverology. See you later, lads."

Chris examined the packet Tev had sent him. He knew what the ashy powder was and he felt like braving it again. "If we're officially goofing off while the uninvolved pick up the pieces, I'm going home," he said. "But the patrols stay in place until we know things have settled down."

"I'm keeping an eye on the situation, Chris," Solomon said. "I haven't interfered with any decisions today, but I *will* intervene if I need to."

"They won't like that any better."

"I don't care. And please put some ice on that bruise, Chris."

Chris made himself walk away. He should have been sorting things out with his guys, but maybe Ingram had a point. Until they came up with a plan for dealing with disputes in the longer term, all anyone could do was patch up injuries and keep all the hotheads apart. It was another one of those situations where he could see the other side's point of view but he wasn't going to change his position because of it. The boffins felt that they didn't have a say in anything — true, and also true under Erskine's regime — and when he tried to imagine how he'd react if the transit camp personnel had been the ones in cryo, he knew he'd have felt just as strongly. He got their anger about Fiji and how they didn't believe nobody had planned to give Britain exclusive access to teerik FTL. He'd probably have thought the same.

He'd have made a better job of holding the base to ransom, though. These bougie types had no idea how to revolt. But he had to give that Lundahl guy points for having the balls to hit him.

He took a shower and flopped onto the sofa, still too wired to think about anything else but the botched protest. Yeah, the rules were the problem — riot control and public order in the SDF were relatively straightforward, us and them, and the only outcomes were break it up or get broken up yourself. Now he had to take account of factions within groups and people who saw themselves as civvies expecting people who saw themselves as troops to treat them with kid gloves because those had been the rules in some but not all countries on Earth. It held him back. If he'd been his old self, he'd have moved Ingram out of the way and got the place cleared, but he'd tried to be diplomatic with her. Next time — because there was bound to be one — he probably needed to hang back and see what she did without the hired muscle.

"I'm not even hired," he muttered, and went into the kitchen to try mixing the kava powder the way he'd seen Tev do it. It didn't look any more appetising. He gulped down half a glass like it was a hangover cure and went back to the sofa. But it took him the rest of the glass and some of a second one to start to feel more relaxed.

He thought about the night in the transit camp bar when he and Jared had sat drinking with Marc, Tev, and Trinder, discussing what their military role would be on Opis when they woke up in forty-five years' time and had to fit into a Nomad run by a second and even third generation of Opis-born humans who had their own way of doing things. They'd have a role more like cops, not soldiers, they decided. Now he knew they had to be both. He didn't like the idea. But he was blissfully sleepy now and he couldn't keep his eyes open.

"Chris? Are you okay?" Ash was leaning over him, looking worried. She zeroed in on his jaw and touched it gingerly. "Who hit you? Have you seen a doctor?"

Chris managed to sit up and check the time on the wall. He'd been asleep for a couple of hours.

"Wow, sorry, I nodded off." He reached for his screen on the coffee table and checked for urgent messages, although he was sure Sol or someone else would have come around to wake him if anything serious had happened. "It was Frank the nuke guy for some reason. Don't worry, I got him back. My manly honour's intact."

Ash shook her head and started fussing. Chris secretly liked that. He let her put some ointment on the bruise while she grumbled about what she was going to do to Frank with her giant wrench for laying hands on her beloved.

"Don't worry, you're still pretty," she said. "Does it hurt?"

"Yes. Is it all quiet out there?"

"Yeah, like a western when the street's deserted before the gunslingers show up." She picked up the glass of kava from the table and wrinkled her nose. "What's this? Are you actually drinking this stuff? It looks like the contents of the drain I was inspecting this morning."

"Kava. Fijian feel-good powder." Chris braced himself to take another gulp. "A present from Tev."

"Okay, rumours are going around. I need to hear it from you. Why didn't Ingram kick Paul Cotton and his hench-boffins up the arse right away? It's not like her to go soft."

Chris thought about it and the comment Ingram had made to Paul. He wasn't sure how Ash would take a criticism of her CO, but he wanted to answer the question, if only to hear her tell him if he was wrong about Ingram.

"She wasn't being soft at all," he said. "She was being devious. It's her technique."

"What is?"

"She manoeuvres others to do the dirty work she wants done so she can step in as the voice of reason and use them as the bogeymen to scare folks into line. 'I'll try to keep the attack dogs off you, so do what I ask.' I've seen her do it before. She admitted it to Marc."

Ash shrugged. "I've never seen that side of her, but then I've never been head to head with her like you have."

"I can't have this conversation with Marc."

"I know."

"I'm not saying she's a bad CO, I'm just saying I'm pissed at her for using me. She treats us as weapons to be deployed. Okay, we are, but not like that."

"But you did your own thing anyway. Which was the right response, by the way."

"She wanted the Ainatio guys scared shitless and she knew we'd do it. Like terminating Gan-Pamas. She didn't want to be seen to make that decision and left it to us."

Ash dabbed at his bruise again. "But now you know that, you won't get taken in again, will you?"

Chris would have done the same again if Ingram hadn't been there, only sooner. "Maybe. If she'd told me in advance, I'd have played along with it. It's her thinking I'm a dumb grunt who's fooled by it that annoys me."

"You could always tell her that and see what happens."

"Yeah. She can't stand me anyway, so I'm not going to make matters worse."

Ash tried the kava and pulled a face. "There's going to be a lot of bad blood about this, though. Just remember the alternative was letting well-meaning idiots overrule our supplies chief and the captain. If they had their way, they'd start arguing the toss over every single decision."

"Applied Whateverology." Chris retrieved his kava and gulped it down. "That's what Marc calls it. They think they know best about everything because they're experts in a narrow field."

"Twats, you mean. That's the scientific term for it."

Ash could always make him laugh. She was right about the consequences of letting random professors call the shots, but that didn't erase the image of all those scared scientists on their knees like PoWs being disarmed and processed. Yeah, they'd asked for it, and pissing off neighbours never helped a cause. They'd upset the farmers too, and those guys were now well aware how much power they could wield in an isolated outpost, so that was another delicate situation he'd have to keep an eye on. But he realised he was now the thing he'd once despised. He was authority, enforcement, the Man.

He was also one of Ingram's weapons. He'd come full circle to be an enforcer again.

12

To all Nomad residents.

The disturbances outside Supply Warehouse 4 yesterday have left us with a number of challenges this community wasn't prepared for but now has to address. We can't excuse antisocial behaviour. But considering the appropriate course of action has highlighted our current lack of a common legal framework. It's a difficult topic to discuss in a new settlement because it's an acceptance that sooner or later, people we know and work with will behave badly enough to warrant formal penalties. But it will be inevitable as Nomad grows. We're human. We're not a species of saints.

As things stand, we've decided it would be unfair and impractical for the time being to impose penalties on those who were detained. We have no general laws, regulations, or criminal justice infrastructure yet, and although people should reasonably expect disruptive or aggressive behaviour to be punished, with or without a formal law, we can't decide what represents an appropriate penalty or how to impose one. There are no fines because we have no currency. There's no jail sentence because we don't have a prison block, although work on one has now begun.

The code the mission has operated under so far has been a military one by consent. When there's no consent to that law or even an agreed definition of military or civilian personnel, offenders could reasonably argue that it's not appropriate to impose military penalties. Making up sentences on the hoof isn't the answer either. While we explore that further and integrate it into the wider discussion about the governance of this settlement, we've agreed on the following measures:

* No penalties will be imposed at the moment, but anyone detained yesterday who engages in further disruptive, antisocial, dishonest, or violent behaviour, as informally defined by the society we left, will face immediate detention in *Cabot*.

* Any act that compromises food production and distribution, utilities, the defence of the base, or generally threatens the lives and well-being of residents, will incur detention in *Cabot* and, depending on the harm caused, a return to cryogenic suspension.

    * Those who took part in yesterday's protest while armed will cease to have access to firearms and ammunition until further notice.

    * The aim of this mission was to eventually hand over governance to a civilian administration, and we'll continue with that goal in mind.

    However normal and Earth-like Opis appears, it's not. We're a small colony at the extreme limit of human space exploration, without backup. We have a very real chance of coming under attack from alien forces and our food supply is vulnerable. Effectively. we're on a war footing. No country at war can afford the luxury of tolerating attacks by its own people. You can say whatever you like or even set up your own alternative settlement if Nomad Base is too restrictive, but if you do anything that harms your neighbour or reduces this base's chances of survival, we have to act, and we will.

    Signed by:
    Douglas Brandt, Mayor of Kill Line
    Marc Gallagher
    Alex Gorko, legacy Ainatio representative
    Captain Bridget Ingram
    Sergeant Chris Montello
    Major Dan Trinder

* * *

OFFICE OF THE GOVERNMENT OF JATT IN EXILE, CLERICS' QUARTER, ROUVELE, SOUTHERN VIILOR, ESMOS.

Nir-Tenbiku's doubts began to close in on him the moment he tied the seal on his bag.

    It wasn't about getting killed. It was about leaving Eb-Lan Cudik or Shus-Wita Olis to take his place and lead the liberation of Jatt. He trusted both of them to carry it out, but he didn't trust them not to fight over the implementation, and there could be only one Primary. Cudik was right. Nobody else had a distinguished ancestral name as a rallying point for the people.

    Nir-Tenbiku would just have to make sure he didn't end up dead, then. He hadn't been able to think of a suitable diplomatic gift for the humans as a mark of respect because it was impossible to know what might offend them, but perhaps he wouldn't survive to worry about that.

"Are you going now, Excellency?" Bas stepped into his path, a little hesitant. "Is there anything else I can do for you? May I attend you? I'm not afraid."

"It's safer for you to remain here," Nir-Tenbiku said. "Safer for Jatt, that is. Imagine how lost the Halu-Masset will be if you're not there to guide them through proper procedure. I'm a figurehead. Figureheads can be replaced. Expertise can't."

"With respect, Excellency, I don't believe a word of that, but you might need that expertise with you."

"I refuse to give your mother bad news."

"I haven't had any contact with my family since I came here. She still thinks I'm in cloistered training at a monastery."

"Then she can believe that until the day I tell her what a selfless patriot she has for a son." Nir-Tenbiku didn't want to deny Bas his chance to be a true Jattan, but there'd be plenty of opportunities for him to fulfil his duty when they returned to Jatt. "Don't worry about me. I believe what happened to Gan-Pamas was a terrible misunderstanding because of his teerik's behaviour. That won't happen this time."

"Is it true you're going unarmed?"

"Yes. How else can I show I'm not hostile?"

Bas looked horrified. Nir-Tenbiku saw the skin on his face tighten. "Excellency, we have no idea what their customs are. You might provoke them further by doing that. And you can't protect yourself."

Nir-Tenbiku sometimes wondered if he was losing his sanity and everybody was too afraid to tell him. He'd never known any other purpose in life except the restoration of Jatt's independence, and he'd never questioned whether it was a good idea. He just accepted it was simply something that had to be done, and so had everyone around him. There was nobody in his life who said otherwise. Perhaps he was wrong. His gut told him he wasn't, but would he really *know*?

"I haven't survived this long by misjudging aliens, Bas," he said. "I appreciate your concern. But I know this will work out."

Of course he didn't. He was taking a calculated risk with a high chance of failure, which could mean anything from getting vaporised to being sent away without a chance of ever negotiating with humans again. If he succeeded, though, he'd have an understanding with a powerful new ally that the Kugin didn't even know about. He hadn't worked out the nature of the advantage yet — technology, supplies, reinforcements, another secure base to operate from — but there had to be one.

Cudik was waiting for him outside and he didn't look any happier than Bas. A vehicle stood in the courtyard minus a driver, a utility transport of the type used by freight firms, so Cudik intended to drive Nir-Tenbiku to the port on his own, probably to talk him out of going to Opis without anybody else seeing the Halu-Masset in open disagreement.

"No other luggage, Primary?"

"I doubt I'll be staying for long." Nir-Tenbiku put his bag in the storage compartment and climbed into the vehicle. "I have the essentials for a couple of days."

Cudik started the engine. "You could take a concealable weapon, you know."

"No, I can't. I *must* present myself to the humans unarmed. Besides, we don't know what they can scan and detect. I can't begin a successful negotiation with a lie, especially after what's happened."

Cudik didn't answer. He drove out of the city down one of the road tunnels that ensured large delivery vehicles didn't spoil Rouvele's illusion of existing in a more elegant era. Nir-Tenbiku sat staring at the road ahead, the green tunnel lights streaking past him on either side, and tried to look confident.

Yes, he was afraid. Trying to establish relations with a new civilisation was the right thing to do, but he wasn't the most competent person to do it. He'd talked himself into it because he felt he'd sat out the real dangers all his life, either cosseted as a child or cocooned as an adult in his well-appointed office in a picturesque city. A Jattan man was expected to face danger when it presented itself, and if necessary to sacrifice himself for the common good the way Gan-Pamas had done. Nir-Tenbiku couldn't back out now. All he could do was hope that his ancestors were with him and would put a spiritual hand on his shoulder to stop him doing anything disastrously wrong.

"Primary, forgive me for being disrespectful, but I think you're being monumentally selfish," Cudik said suddenly. He corrected the vehicle's path with the occasional vague gesture. Nir-Tenbiku wished he'd pay more attention to the road conditions. "We're approaching a critical time and you have a job to do — to be a Tenbiku heir, a symbol of legitimacy and hope. I know how responsible you feel for Gan-Pamas's death, but he had a job to do as well, and it wasn't personally collecting armaments, so now we have no procurement minister. This is why the Kugin think we're reckless idiots. All this manly self-sacrifice for no good reason."

"Cudik, the Kugin think we're all suicidal fools because the Protectorate officer class actually *is*."

"This is the very worst time to die for personal honour, Primary."

"I have no plans to die."

"We have loyal officers who would do this willingly."

"Cudik, I'm not fit to lead Jatt if I can't face the same dangers that our troops will." Cudik just wasn't going to give up. Nir-Tenbiku didn't like pulling rank, but he was worried that he'd lose his nerve if he didn't stop this tidal wave of reasonable arguments. "Ingram knows who I am. She's spoken to me. She knows I regret what happened on Opis. We already have some kind of rapport, or else she wouldn't have behaved so properly about Gan-Pamas's remains. This isn't the time to send some random commander to make diplomatic contact."

"And what if they *do* kill you?" Cudik asked. "What are we supposed to do then, ignore it? Open a war on another front? Send a strongly-worded communiqué to Ingram? Those are more problems you'll leave us with."

"You'll carry on, and not be distracted by what happens to me," Nir-Tenbiku said. "Can we focus on getting to Mekuvir safely, please? Have you filed a flight plan?"

"Of course. As far as traffic control here is concerned, we're going to Vezhy again. It's always passed off without incident and there's no reason to think today will be any different."

The shuttle would send back fake telemetry to hide the fact that it was emerging from spacefold at Vezhy and then continuing to the outer planets, but Esmosi traffic control wouldn't care even if they knew. As long as nobody brought trouble to Esmos, imported dangerous cargo, or illegally exported national art treasures, they could do as they wished.

The vehicle emerged from the tunnel into the daylight of a partially cloudy afternoon. The spaceport was on the northern coast, two prefectures away, and from there Nir-Tenbiku would be taken to rendezvous with one of the corvettes kept in a maintenance orbit around Mekuvir, an uninhabitable outer planet in Vezhy's system. The Protectorate's navy never bothered to venture that far out, which was just as well, because keeping even the modest fleet of the Maritime Force of Jatt supplied and trained was a difficult and expensive business, as was maintaining the vessels without a proper home port.

Nir-Tenbiku remained surprised that the crews hadn't given in to boredom and frustration after years of waiting for the war. Whenever he visited the ships, he was reminded how reliant he was going to be on the Protectorate commanders loyal to him on Dal Mantir, not because his own forces were inferior but because the navy and the troops being trained for the landings were so limited in what they could be seen to do. If they were spotted on exercises, it would be disastrous, so their time was spent mostly in simulations. They would have to find somewhere else to rehearse the operation.

Perhaps he could persuade Ingram to rent some remote area of Opis to him. Now that would be worth having.

Today's mission to drop him off was the first real task the corvettes had faced since arriving on station. It wouldn't test them in combat, but at least one crew would feel that real things were finally starting to happen in their career of make-believe revolution.

"Storms," Cudik said as he drove through the gates of the spaceport. It was quieter than usual. "Oh dear. Look at the meteorological warnings."

The signs around the entrance indicated a forecast of storm-force winds, heavy rain, and thunderstorms, and warned that flights might be affected for a while, but Nir-Tenbiku was ready to risk a little bad weather. Cudik parked the vehicle as close to the hangar as he could and the two of them slipped in through a side entrance to start the shuttle.

"I'm impressed that you can still fly one of these," Nir-Tenbiku said, fastening his safety harness.

"I did my national service. You never forget. It's all automation now anyway." Cudik did the pre-flight checks like a professional and taxied the shuttle out to the allocated launch pad. "I didn't mean that as criticism, by the way."

"I didn't think you did. But I'm finally doing *my* duty."

Everybody who knew Nir-Tenbiku's true identity also knew that he'd never undertaken the compulsory three years of military service that every other Jattan boy on Cer Clen was obliged to complete. It was too risky to expose him to the possibility of discovery, and his father had been rich enough to buy him an exemption without raising suspicions. But Nir-Tenbiku still felt humiliated by it, no matter how understanding the Halu-Masset and his entourage were.

"That's no reason to risk your life now," Cudik said.

"You're not going to give up, are you?"

"I'll express my opinion until the last moment, Primary, in the hope that you'll see sense."

"Save your breath, my friend."

Nir-Tenbiku hadn't been cooped up with a member of his cabinet on a journey for a long time. It was hard to make small talk when they were a handful of people living in close proximity with very few external contacts. There was nothing left to talk about. After a rough take-off buffeted by winds, Nir-Tenbiku was content to be silent and let Cudik concentrate on laying in a course to Mekuvir the old-fashioned way, just to prove to himself that he still could. It was a couple of hours before he said anything.

"Have you got a plan, Primary?"

"Be more specific."

"What do you hope to get out of meeting the humans today, if they don't shoot you on sight? What are you going to offer them? We start at a disadvantage by not being a functioning government with the ability to hand out largesse."

"Mining rights when we're back in office," Nir-Tenbiku said. "Special trade deals. But it depends what they offer us. The more I think about it, the more I'd rather be granted permission to rent land for a base on Opis than have their military support."

"Modest ambition, then."

"Cudik, you know how this goes. In negotiations you have to know what you really want and the point at which you'll walk away. Between those two points is what you'll accept."

"They'll be neutral," Cudik said. "They've made it clear that they don't want to get involved."

"Ah, but Kugad might not allow them that luxury. They have the stolen prototype prenu. It's hard to say it's nothing to do with you when you're caught with the proceeds of the crime."

"So why didn't you ask Ingram more about the ship? Gan-Pamas said it was there. They didn't end up with a commune of teeriks and a prenu by chance, and Gan-Pamas must have known more than he committed to his message, because what else could have made him head to Opis?"

"I didn't press Ingram because she would probably have cut me off," Nir-Tenbiku said. "Those are questions to be put in person. And we'll never know how Gan-Pamas found out where the ship was, but we might be able to piece together something from what Ingram tells me."

"You're optimistic that she'll give you an audience."

"I can only ask."

"Primary, if I were trying to lure you out of Esmos on behalf of the Protectorate so that I could assassinate you," Cudik said, "this is how I would do it. You'd never be fooled by a direct invitation, but a rebuff from the humans would convince you of their honesty. It would explain everything. The Protectorate allows the prenu to be hijacked, the humans drop a hint so that Gan-Pamas can find Opis, and then they send information to tempt you to visit. We have no way of proving Gan-Pamas was the author of that message at all."

Nir-Tenbiku couldn't fault Cudik's logic, but it didn't sound feasible. And he knew Gan-Pamas's style too well. The message was real.

"The Protectorate's too rash and the Kugin don't feel the need to be devious," Nir-Tenbiku said. "You can find an infinite number of ways to explain anything if you have enough time on your hands."

He couldn't let this erode his determination. He understood Cudik's fears, and he also knew when the man was using his skill for inducing them in others. He'd been very good at psychological warfare. By the end of the day, though, Nir-Tenbiku would be in Opis space and he'd have the answers he needed. He just had to keep his nerve.

When the shuttle finally emerged from spacefold and the corvette *Steadfast* returned Cudik's signal, Nir-Tenbiku was relieved. He'd be in the scout vessel and clear of the ship with only his thoughts for company within a few hours. If Cudik raised any more doubts about the wisdom of this, he might well concede, and then he'd have not only shown he couldn't keep his word, but also revealed a susceptibility that might be exploited again at some point in the future, when the issue wasn't his welfare but the matter of who ruled Jatt.

Steadfast's commander met them on the hangar deck. He had an Oruan family name — Nesh — and an accent that confirmed he'd been raised in the province. Nesh had finished his service in the Protectorate navy's coastal division five years ago, so Nir-Tenbiku knew he'd seen his share of skirmishes against smugglers at sea, and wasn't squeamish about killing fellow marbidars. He was loyal, and he had a reason. His family, ore merchants, had lost everything when the Protectorate sold the nation into degrading vassalage.

"Your ship's ready, Excellency," Nesh said. "And if you'd prefer a pilot to accompany you, we're ready too."

"Thank you, Commander, but it's best if I go alone."

"We'll be standing by to pull you out if anything goes wrong, then."

"Thank you, but don't stand by too close, will you? The point is that I show goodwill by not turning up with a warship."

"Of course, Excellency."

Nir-Tenbiku turned to Cudik. "I'll be on the mess deck if you need me." It was his way of asking Cudik to leave him alone and not nag him further. "Do you mind if I talk to the crew, Commander?"

Nesh bowed his head politely. "Please go ahead."

The flight had been timed for Nir-Tenbiku to arrive on Opis around midday, which he could reasonably assume would mean Ingram's base was fully operational. Arriving during the hours of darkness might seem like an attack. He now had a few hours' transit time to use wisely, and rather than retreat to a day cabin and rehearse a few lines that he would probably deviate from anyway, he decided it was best spent talking to the crew. It was good practice to be an approachable leader and show his concern for his armed forces, but he also wanted to remind himself why he was doing this.

The crew of *Steadfast* weren't serving for the pay or to learn skills for later employment in civilian life. They could all have had more comfortable and safer lives if they'd returned to Dal Mantir or the colony worlds they came from and enlisted with the Protectorate instead. They were here because they were willing to take a risk to restore something they cherished, even those who didn't remember it but whose grandfathers did. That said something for the enduring power of Jattan identity.

And it wasn't easy to recruit. Every post had to be filled by word of mouth, every candidate's background thoroughly checked to weed out Protectorate agents, although the current Jevez regime didn't behave as if it regarded the opposition as a serious threat, just an irritant. Perhaps that was one of the advantages of taking a very long time to exact revenge. The Protectorate thought they'd buried their treachery in history and were in the clear.

"Is this it, Excellency?" one of the engineers asked. "Are we going to see action soon?"

"I don't know," Nir-Tenbiku said. "The presence of these humans could change everything. We shall see."

"And nobody else knows they're here."

"It seems so."

"What if they're worse than the Kugin?"

It was a good question. "If they are, we can't do anything about it, but they'll at least keep the Kugin busy. And the Protectorate. So they may still be a blessing even if they're tyrants."

Nir-Tenbiku longed for a world of clearly-defined right and wrong where he didn't have to think in such labyrinthine terms. But he'd been raised from childhood to be a politician and a diplomat, and that had to be his lens on the world, even if he wasn't as prone to convoluted thinking as Cudik. As he shared a pot of his Esmosi floral tisane with these sailors, he realised this conversation was as near to purity of cause as he was ever likely to get. The crew were clear about their motive; the Common Welfare Party had removed an elected government, it had sold the independence of Jatt to the Kugin, and that was a crime that demanded justice be done. It was simply *wrong*.

Nir-Tenbiku hoped the Jattans living on Dal Mantir wanted to see that wrong put right as much as he believed they did. The fight for Jatt would happen on the surface of Dal Mantir, not in space, and his forces wouldn't be an invading army, but a catalyst for an uprising on the ground.

This was Nir-Tenbiku's whole strategy. His own relatively small force would do two things; it would attack specific government targets in Jevez, and it would activate the sleepers in the Protectorate's armed forces and strategic industries to rise up, and that would be the point at which the general population would be encouraged to shut down the country and become ungovernable. They didn't have to take up arms. They simply had to stop cooperating. Was it a gamble, relying on Jattans he had no direct control over to form the bulk of the liberation force? Yes, but it was also an answer. If he couldn't command the support of those people in the first place, he'd never hold Jatt in the long run. They'd show they didn't want the return of a free nation.

Nir-Tenbiku would never spell that out to the rest of the Halu-Masset, because it sounded cowardly after all these years of planning, but he didn't want to be an unwelcome leader. If the majority of Jattans preferred to remain Kugin subjects, Jatt was no longer the country he'd thought it was or that his grandfather had fought for. He wasn't sure what he'd do next if it turned out that they liked their subjugated lives and rejected his restoration, though. His existence would be over, his life wasted, and he had no heir. He had no meaning or purpose beyond that point.

Well, that certainly wasn't the right frame of mind to be in for his appeal to the humans. He took his leave of the crew and spent half an hour in the scout vessel's cockpit familiarising himself with the few controls he needed to use before he felt the vibration in the deck that signalled the emergence from spacefold.

Cudik and Nesh showed up on the hangar deck. Nir-Tenbiku switched on the video feed and looked upon Opis for the first time. Whatever the humans' home world was like, it had to resemble this to make it worth building an outpost here. It was still a quarter of a day away at sub-light speeds, but he could see it was blue with oceans and wreathed in white cloud. It was rather like Dal Mantir.

"Are you sure you're happy doing this without a pilot?" Cudik asked.

"Of course I am. The only manual activity I have to undertake is triggering the automation and getting myself in and out of the seat."

He'd approach Opis with *Steadfast* safely out of sight and open a communications link. If Ingram refused to meet him, or launched an attack, he'd activate a single control for a rapid escape in the opposite direction. If he persuaded her to let him land, the ship's automation had coordinates set for an open area beyond the base and would take care of that as well. Nir-Tenbiku would have been able to do it himself if he'd served his conscription period. It mattered more than ever to get this right without needing the navy to rescue him.

He fastened his safety harness. "I'm ready. I'll signal when I make contact. And I realise this is an impossible request, Cudik, but I forbid you to worry about me."

"Understood, Primary."

"And stay off the comms. I need silence to speak to Ingram."

"How long will you wait before you decide she isn't going to respond?" Nesh asked.

"The probe's still active. She'll hear me. Please do *not* attempt to recover the ship unless I explicitly say so."

"Yes, Excellency."

As the launch rails moved the small ship to the bay doors, Nir-Tenbiku rehearsed his lines again. He'd keep it simple. He'd throw himself on Ingram's mercy, not in surrender but with a plea to be allowed to put his case, and if she declined further contact after that, he'd have to respect her wishes. He'd have another opportunity to ask when she returned Gan-Pamas's body, though. He was sure she'd keep her word on that.

The scout ship was now under way and he realised how tiny it was when it emerged from the shadow of *Steadfast*. He was in a small metal tube in a black void that he didn't venture into very often and rarely saw this starkly, and he wasn't used to microgravity. It unsettled him. The comms silence he'd insisted upon made him feel more alone than he'd ever been in his life, and the unfamiliar humming and clanking of the ship's systems sounded louder and more alarming.

Perhaps the humans couldn't detect anything this far out, but it was hard to tell. He wasn't going to take a chance of his intentions being misunderstood. He'd thought they'd overlooked the probe, but they'd only let it descend to get a better look and capture it. Whatever happened in the next few hours was going to teach him a great deal about humans.

Cudik's right. I'm insane to do this.

I really am.

He kept his eyes on the display to check that the probe on Opis was still receiving. At the bottom left margin of the image hovering in front of him, a blue icon appeared at his back and moved slowly closer. It was *Steadfast*. He let it continue, confirming the ship hadn't strayed unintentionally. Someone had ignored his order. The corvette was following him.

The last thing he needed was for Ingram to spot an uninvited and unannounced warship. If humans had missile capability, he wouldn't know he'd been targeted until it was too late to change course, and if they had long-range energy weapons, he'd be dead even before that.

He opened the comms link to *Steadfast*, determined not to get angry because that anger would stay in his voice when he spoke to Ingram.

"*Steadfast*, this is Primary Nir-Tenbiku." There was nobody else who'd be calling them, but he wanted to remain formally polite. "You're following me. You're far too close. Stop now and withdraw to your original position before the humans detect you. You'll get me killed."

"My apologies, Primary." It was Cudik. "We'd lost visual contact and you insisted on radio silence."

Nir-Tenbiku didn't believe him. They were expecting to see the scout ship burning briefly as a missile hit it and trying to position themselves close enough to attempt a rescue.

And maybe that was how his life would end after all. If it was, he'd face it like a Jattan, as Tenbiku men had always done. He'd do his duty. He hung on to hope and imagined a day in the future when he'd look back on this moment and see it as a turning point in Jattan history, the day they made new allies.

* * *

DR PARK HA-NEUL SCHOOL, KILL LINE: ELECTION DAY, NOVEMBER 10, OC.

It was the ninth sunny day in a row, a glorious morning scented with freshly cut grass and the waft of malt from Dave's brewery. Chris opened the gymnasium doors to let in the breeze and wished life could always be like this.

He'd volunteered to help out with the election. It was the most normal, average, small-town thing he'd ever done and it felt totally alien. It was also the most important. The debacle at Warehouse 4 had shown him that laws — rules, regulations, social contracts, whatever you wanted to call them — were critical to survival out here, not because they told folks how to behave but because they laid out what would happen to them if they screwed with their neighbours. This election was the first step towards a society that would create its own laws and where the Paul Cottons of this world would understand what the stakes were before they decided to be fantasy revolutionaries again.

Chris was still frustrated that the protesters had mostly gotten away with it. He didn't disagree with the decision. He'd voted for it, in fact. It just seemed insane that there was no way of punishing the bastards at the moment because nobody could work out what constituted a reasonable sentence, thanks to the fact there were no damn rules written down about civilians. Punishment mattered. It didn't just make a point to the perpetrator, it also signalled the system's fairness to everybody else. When there didn't seem to be any consequences for bad behaviour, it became an unspoken message that everyone else could act like assholes too.

The alternative system was the basic animal one that still underpinned everything humans did. The most powerful and aggressive individuals decided what was allowed on any given day and set the level of punishment. He'd seen and done too much of that on Earth, and in a survival situation he'd probably be the one doing it here, along with Marc, but that didn't mean it was a good idea to rely on it as a form of government.

Well, at least he got the cryo sentence idea passed. Liam would be pleased that his rant about freezing down all the boffins and sending them back had borne fruit. Bots were breaking ground for a small detention block, and by tonight there'd literally be a new sheriff in town, Kill Line's first. Chris checked his watch and prepared for a day of making democracy mean something that it had never meant to him before.

Dr Park Ha-Neul School, named after Annis Kim's great-grandmother as Ingram had promised, was closed for the day to double as a polling station, and Mrs Alvarez was overseeing the voting with a couple of the other teachers. She settled down at the table to arrange her checklists and the piles of ballot papers for what was now five wards following the addition of the transit camp. Nearly eight hundred voters were expected to pass through the polling station set up in the school gym before 1900 hours. Chris found village-scale efficiency reassuring.

"What's the turnout likely to be?" he asked, keeping an eye on the doors.

Mrs Alvarez lined up her pens and pencils. "Oh, close to a hundred per cent. This isn't the city. It's hard to sit it out." She placed a very old folding alarm clock on the table in front of her with a precision that confirmed this was a long-practised ritual. "Anyway, it's time. Let democracy take its course, Sergeant Montello. Open the doors."

Chris removed the barrier blocking the entrance, an A-board announcing the opening of Marsha's restaurant and the movie theatre in the old accommodation building, and the early birds filed in, led by the old ladies of the cookbook committee, fearsome women Chris would never dare cross.

"You should have stood, Chris." Mrs Kley picked up a pencil from the table at the entrance and collected her ballot paper from Mrs

Alvarez. "We could do with a sensible young man like you on the council."

"Thank you, ma'am, but I don't know enough to be useful." Chris wanted to say that he thought local politics would bring out the worst in him, but he let her take it as a display of modesty. "I'm real good at sharpening pencils, though."

He'd spent the early hours assembling six screened booths and making sure the ballot papers were stacked correctly in wards. Back home, he couldn't even remember bothering to vote in the few years between turning eighteen and going to jail because he knew it wouldn't make any difference to how his life would turn out. But this time he caught himself believing that putting a cross next to names on a piece of paper would shape his future.

Permanence and respectability had overtaken them all. The transit camp neighbourhood now had a proper designation for administrative purposes. Nobody wanted to be referred to as the transit camp any more because they were here to stay no matter what, not just passing through, so they'd settled on the name Convoy Ward. Their identity had been forged on the road, and that name said they'd arrived at their destination with a gruelling journey behind them. The accretion of all these small changes had now become roots.

At first, Chris had thought he was going through the motions of dull citizenship to reinvent himself as a regular guy in the same way that some folks believed a man could train himself to be happy by nailing on a smile when he didn't feel like it. But Ash had made a difference. Now that he had a woman to focus him, one who wasn't a predator, he found his primal need for continuity was starting to emerge.

He was still in the first heady flush of romance, but he'd started to look further ahead than the end of the day for the first time since prison. He wanted Kill Line to be the kind of place where his hypothetical kids could grow up safely, and where he could come home after a proper day's work to have dinner with his family, knowing there'd be no bigger crises than a roof that needed fixing or a disappointing school report to address.

It was a lot to ask for a man with so much baggage. Maybe he didn't deserve it. Maybe it didn't exist for anyone in the real world, either, and he'd just been idealising other families that were actually no happier than his own. But he'd met a lot of worse guys than himself who did have happy home lives, so he was at least entitled to try.

Now the voters had started arriving, his election duties were finished and he had the day off. He'd help Jared and Marsha with the final preparations for the restaurant, and then he'd catch up with Ash when she finished her watch. Dinner and a movie was now a feasible date night for the first time in forever. Ash would probably have preferred sandwiches and a day out looking for monsters again, but a guy had to demonstrate at least once that he could do the formal stuff like a gentleman, even if it was a table at a pizza and burger kind of place.

But that was the great thing about Opis. It didn't have any real luxuries. Nomad Base had absolutely nothing to give a woman an ulterior motive for dating him — no designer clothes, no jewellery, no nice cars, none of the trappings of a fat pay packet and useful connections that Gina liked and only guys like Chris on the criminal fringe could provide for her. If Ash was with him, it was because she wanted his company. There were a couple of steaks reserved with his name on them for tonight, a bottle of fruit wine courtesy of Dave Flores, and two seats to watch a movie they'd probably both seen a dozen times before. That didn't matter. It was the ritual that counted. Chris was determined to perform it with the diligence of a high priest.

He collected his ballot paper, cast his votes — Doug for mayor, Dieter for sheriff, Jeanie Cleaver and Jared as ward councillors — and headed for the restaurant to see what still needed doing. When he stopped the rover at the end of the road to check to his right for traffic, he spotted a bunch of boys hanging around the Kill Line sign. They were looking up at the sky and pointing, probably waiting to see *Curtis* on a rare training flight as Searle rehearsed his flypast. He was determined to mark the election results with a display, and it was a good excuse for him to put in some flying hours before Ingram traded the ship for beads or whatever else she had in mind. The atmosphere on the base was still so hostile that the *Cabot* crew were doing their damnedest to make the day a fun event for themselves and the Kill Liners. Chris doubted any of the Ainatio dissenters would show up at the barbecue tonight.

He decided to join the kids. He still didn't know every Kill Liner by name, but he recognised Patrick, Armand Hillier's son.

"Hey Pat, anything interesting?" he asked, looking up.

The boys were still glued to the sky. "Not yet," Patrick said. "But we heard the engines start up."

"That was the Lammergeier," said a kid Chris didn't know. "Not the spaceship."

"Is it true we're giving the ship back, Mr Montello?"

Chris shrugged. "Maybe. Maybe not. Depends if they want to swap it for something worthwhile."

"We should keep it. It's amazing. A real alien spaceship."

"We've got spaceships," Chris said. "Four of them."

"But we're not aliens. It's cooler if it's alien."

Chris couldn't argue with that logic, and it was good to see kids refusing to feel jaded by their extraordinary new world. He leaned against the sign and watched with them. Trinder drove past in a Caracal, stopped to look, then got out to join them.

"Any moment now," he said, looking up. "I just hope Brad doesn't try to do a barrel roll in that thing."

Chris could hear engines, but it was the other Lammergeier starting up, not *Curtis*. The Jattan frigate sounded a lot lower down the scale and he could usually feel the vibration if he was close enough. He was wondering whether she might have been useful for Earth missions one day when one of the boys pointed and he followed the kid's outstretched arm to a cluster of farm buildings in the distance. A Lammergeier, Ainatio scarlet and almost luminous in the bright sun, had lifted above the roofline and was holding position. The second Lamm popped up some distance away and hovered as well. Then the distinctive low throb of *Curtis*'s engine confirmed she was taking off. The frigate rose into view between the two tilt rotors and all three craft hung motionless for a moment against a pure cornflower-blue sky.

The kids oohed and ahhed. "That's amazing! Will you look at that!"

Curtis moved forward with the Lammergeiers flanking her like escorts. It certainly looked pretty cool even if they weren't doing any fancy aerobatics.

"Y'know, I never found out why Brad gave up flying for the engineering branch." Trinder stood with his hands on his hips, smiling to himself as he watched *Curtis* pass overhead. "Damn, we've got to stop taking this stuff for granted. We're the luckiest guys in human history. I just wish we had someone to tell."

Chris hadn't noticed the rows of small blue lights on *Curtis*'s nose before. Whatever her drive was doing made him feel like his chest was vibrating, even though the engine noise wasn't particularly loud. "It's a shame she's not what we need," he said.

Trinder opened the Caracal's door. "I'm going up to visit the farmers again and make sure there's no lingering resentment. Or at least not enough to make them cut off supplies. Any grievance that can make Marty lose his temper must have some pretty deep roots."

"Makes you realise where the real power lies, huh?"

Trinder went on his way. Chris saw *Curtis* and the Lammergeiers out of sight and then mounted the bike. One of the seniors from Kill Line, Dorothy Kessner, had appeared at the end of the road and was heading slowly towards the centre of the base. She preferred to pick up her own food supplies, no matter how long it took her. As long as she kept moving, she said, she wasn't finished, but Chris stopped to offer her a ride. She probably didn't want one but he'd feel bad driving past her while she tottered along with her bag. He helped her into the passenger seat.

"You're such a kind boy, Chris." He was conscious of her staring at him while he looked straight ahead at the road. She was probably checking the progress of his bruises from the warehouse brawl. "They should have locked up those scientists. At least we'll have a sheriff by tonight, though."

Chris didn't know if Kill Line's law and order would creep outside its boundaries. Dieter policing the Ainatio district would be a sight to behold — and he'd get the job, of course. Nobody else had stood for election, although there was a "none of the above" option on the ballot.

But Chris had to fend off the "nice boy" comments first. It was dishonest to say nothing and let people go on thinking he was an upstanding citizen. He'd always suspected that Kill Liners didn't want to know about the past when it came to transit camp people, but he just needed to go on the record for his own peace of mind.

"I wasn't a nice boy until I joined the army, Mrs Kessner," Chris said. "I did some terrible things. I ended up in jail." He thought of Martin Berry and decided to do a little ground prep for the day when the minister came clean. "Okay, some folks are just bad and there's no redeeming them, but others genuinely change. I don't think I've managed it."

"But you've got humility," she said. "That's how folks change for the better. Not sure those professors have found that yet."

"I understood why they were upset."

"So is it that easy to go back to Earth?"

Chris thought she meant the gate. "You've used the gate, ma'am."

"I meant the Captain's ban on contact. Because I wish I'd stayed."

That wasn't a good sign. "Don't you like it here?"

"Oh, I like it well enough, but I won't be buried with my husband. It's bothering me lately."

Chris understood the sentiment all too well. He wouldn't have exhumed Jamie if he'd thought last resting places didn't matter. "You want to be buried in Kill Line. The *old* Kill Line."

"Too late now."

Chris didn't think twice. "If that's what you want, I'll take you back myself when the time comes. Which is years away, of course. But I won't forget."

Mrs Kessner was quiet for a few moments. "That's put my mind at rest. Thank you, Chris. I know you always keep your word. Won't you get into trouble, though?"

"I doubt it." Chris felt better too. Sometimes it didn't take much to make people happy. "I'm a good friend of the sheriff."

Things looked quiet around the central buildings this morning, but a couple of Trinder's people were still patrolling Levine Road between the security office and the food warehouses. Chris stopped at Warehouse 5 and saw Mrs Kessner into the building like a gentleman before returning the rover to the vehicle compound and walking across the green to the old accommodation building.

For once Solomon hadn't sent the bots in to do the place up. He probably thought his humans would be happier doing something creative for themselves and would ask for bot assistance if they needed it. The room reserved for Marsha's restaurant was only a big, dull space on the ground floor, but it could take ten tables, which made it the Ritz as far as Nomad was concerned. He found Jared hauling chairs through the doorway and gave him a hand. They placed the tables and chairs down one side of the room and then tried to rearrange them in a more welcoming layout.

"You need something on the walls." Chris gestured at the industrial grey panels. "Big landscape pictures. A few mirrors. Mood lighting."

Jared made a show of frowning and looking him up and down. "Damn, Chris, you getting all designer on me? See, this is what happens when you hook up with a woman. You'll be holding opinions on cushions next."

"I've already done cushions. Hey, we can get a construction bot to transfer pictures onto the walls? How about tropical sunsets?"

"It'll only remind people of home."

"Not if we pick images without trees and recognisable Earth features. Sol, are you listening? Can you get me a painter?"

"Of course, Chris." Chris could have sworn Sol was laughing at him. "I'm glad to see you appreciating the arts."

Marsha turned up with a trolley bot laden with prepared meals and Annis Kim in tow. "Annis is going to maître d' for us," Marsha said. "She's done it before."

"Actually, I worked in a kebab shop while I was at uni," Kim said. "But I can do classy too."

"You bored with bending space-time, then?" Chris asked.

Kim moved some of the tables as if the positions mattered. She seemed to know what she was doing. "I'm only here to get first crack at the leftovers. I'm a growing girl."

This was what Nomad could always be like, Chris decided. They were having harmless fun, nobody cared who had a PhD or a criminal record, and the most pressing issue was keeping track of the meal inventory to make sure anything that wasn't consumed was stored for later. Everything had to be accounted for. Chris checked the food containers to make sure they had token values marked on them and wondered whether he could ever have done this for a living. Yeah, maybe he could. All purposeful jobs came down to the same thing in the end.

A construction bot showed up, one of the cubes festooned with nozzles and sprays to apply coating. With a little remote help from Sol, it projected the required images of a sunset-tinted ocean and a gold sandy shoreline onto the walls before spraying the colours in place like it was painting by numbers. The room looked about right for a family diner now.

"So what's the mood like behind closed doors in the boffin quarter today?" Chris asked.

Kim shrugged. "Don't worry, I'll dob them in the second I overhear anything bolshy going on."

"They've calmed down, then."

"I think the possibility of going in the chiller cabinet brought a few of them up short. Don't let anyone tell you you're not creative, Chris."

"Where else were we going to put them? Keeping prisoners takes up manpower, and you still have to feed them. It solves our immediate problem and it's kinder to them. The prison's going to be tiny and it's only for short sentences."

"I always knew you were a wet liberal at heart."

Chris finished putting chairs in place. It was one of those moments when he stood back, looked at the amount of new furniture and other stuff that had appeared, and realised how much the manufacturing operation was churning out every day.

Marsha studied the walls. "Thanks, Chris. It looks awesome. Your steaks will be waiting for you tonight."

"Medium rare and medium." Chris wished he still had his suit and tie, but the last time he'd worn that was when he was taken back to court for sentencing. Maybe he could get the bacteria farm to make him a smart shirt at short notice. "Any bookings from Ainatio?"

"Some. But we won't be doing bar brawls here. Not with Dr Kim the Broken Bottle Queen and Jared in his tux on the door."

Chris turned to Jared. "You never had a tux."

"Have now," Jared said. "I look scary in it. I might not let your type in. We've got standards to keep up."

"Okay. I'll sneak in the back entrance. See you at twenty-one hundred."

It wasn't even lunchtime yet. Chris ambled across the green, amused by the thought of Jared in a tuxedo, and said hi to one of the biomed team as he passed him heading the other way. The guy cut him dead and walked on. So that was the way they were going to play it, then. Maybe he was expecting too much from people who'd been cooped up for years in an institution where they thought they called the shots. They'd gradually realised they were now lower down the pecking order than a guy who spent his day ankle-deep in cow shit. It wasn't their fault, either. But they'd have to deal with it.

Chris stopped to watch some of the *Cabot* guys setting up the barbecue and food stalls for the evening. At least they were getting into the spirit of things. Folks needed some fun after the last few months and an election was enough of an excuse, even if they weren't voting in it. Hiyashi, Nami Sato, and Maggie Yeung were busy peering into a tyre-sized metal bowl that looked like a scavenged machine part. It was only when Hiyashi poured something into it, shoved in a thin stick, and started chuckling to himself that Chris realised what they were doing. After some stirring, Hiyashi pulled out a stick covered in thick white fluff. They'd made a cotton candy machine.

"Awesome," Chris said to himself. It would have been even better if the scientists joined in, but nobody expected things to snap back to normal in a few days. What was normal anyway? The Ainatio HQ staff and the Kill Liners had never mixed back on Earth and Ingram's attempts so far to break down the social barriers hadn't had much effect.

Chris decided to see what Marc was up to now that he'd lost a couple of classes of firearms students to the weapons ban. The map showed him in one of the workshops with Tev. Chris called him on the secure network.

"Hey, am I missing something?"

"We're testing Fred's portable gate," Marc said. "Just working out the best way to mount the controls."

Chris thought of Solomon's aborted confession. His first thought was that it concerned the teeriks, because even Chris had his action plan if they became dangerously inconvenient. "Is he okay today?" Chris asked.

"A bit distracted, but that's boffins for you whatever the species. Is there a problem?"

"No, just asking after all the awkward arguments over leaking data."

"We've moved on. We had to."

"Well, don't forget to vote before nineteen hundred. You and Ingram are both on the electoral register now."

"Chris, we're making technical magic here, you jobsworth. Anyway, my place hasn't even got an address. I was thinking of declaring it a British territory and making myself governor."

"You still get a vote. You're between Convoy and Mill wards. Pick one and go to the school."

"Bloody hell, what happened to you? Pipe hitter to pen-pusher in sixteen weeks. Have you been taking teerik pills?"

"I'm working on being a normal civilian."

"There's no normal for blokes like us, mate. Not for long, anyway."

Chris was about to point out that Marc had rebuilt a different normality around himself since he'd been on Opis, but maybe the guy was just hoping that action became habit and then reality in the same way Chris had. He seemed more at peace with himself. That was enough encouragement for Chris to believe that he could overwrite his own baggage.

"Just vote, will you?"

"Okay. But I'll expect a bribe."

Chris still had most of the day to kill. He could do a little gardening, maybe, or go for a drive off-camp. Yeah, he'd take one of the Caracals out. He rarely went outside the wire unless he had a work-related reason, which seemed a terrible waste of a planet, and he still hadn't done much by way of hands-on geology. He might not get any free time again for months. It was a shame Ash was working today, but he'd find some interesting rocks for her. She was endlessly patient with his hobby in a way he knew Fonseca would never have been.

He loaded a few survey maps onto his screen in case he lost the base network and went to sign out a Caracal. Rovers were more fun, but they weren't armoured and they didn't have any hatches to lock if he ran into aggressive wildlife.

"Sol, I'm going off-camp." He'd head south in the direction of the mountains this time. The mines and quarries were on that track and the bots had spent years route-proving to map safe terrain for traffic, so he could stick to a tested path. "Call me back if you need me. I'm just exploring."

"Don't let the scientists know," Solomon said. "They'll want to go with you."

"The ones I pushed around won't. Look, I'm going about thirty miles south."

"There are some granite formations out there you might enjoy."

"Sol, you're the only person on this base who can say that and not sound like you're ragging on me."

"I'll get a drone to follow in case you run into problems."

"Okay. Thanks."

Chris drove out across the perimeter, slowing while the system overrode the minefield to let him pass. As he moved further out, he realised it wasn't only the drone keeping him company. A flash of red to the left caught his eye. He lowered the window.

"You escorting me, Rik?"

Rikayl was keeping up with the Caracal, dead level with the side window. "Waaaankah! Where you go?"

"I'm looking for rocks. Stones."

"Dumb." Rikayl seemed to be developing his own voice, not just mimicking whoever first said the words he'd learned. "Food? Bouncy furballs!"

"How come you can eat all that shit and not get sick?"

"Eat shit!"

Damn, Chris hadn't intended to teach him any more profanities than Jeff already had. He tried not to react. If he did, it just proved to Rikayl that it was worth saying again.

"So you don't hate me any more," Chris said.

"Marc say mate alright really."

It was impressive. Rikayl might not have been a normal teerik genius, but he had a pretty good grasp of language. Chris could understand him with a bit of guesswork. So Marc had put in a good word for Chris, and Rikayl had decided on a ceasefire. He still called Chris *wanker*, though. And Chris still found it funny.

"Are you going to follow me all the way?"

"Yes."

"It's a long way, Rik." Could a teerik cover thirty miles? Terrestrial birds crossed oceans, but that didn't mean a juvenile teerik could. Chris wondered if he should stop to give the kid a chance to recover. "You sure? You could ride on the roof."

"Fly."

"Okay."

Chris decided to stop every five miles to give the annoying little bastard some water and a breather. But he was only three miles down the track when his radio handset lit up on the dashboard.

"Chris, we have a problem," Solomon said. "Can you return to base, please?"

Chris slowed to a halt. Rikayl landed on the Caracal's hood and peered through the windshield at him.

"Sure, Sol. What's happened?"

"We've detected two ships approaching, probably Jattan."

"Ahhh *shit*."

"We're still trying to confirm their origin. Ingram's put the base at action stations, so report to the command centre."

"On my way." It was the worst news, but Chris was actually relieved the waiting was over. This was what they'd prepared for. Everyone knew what to do, and even if they were short of a few dozen armed scientists, that wasn't going to make much difference now. He hit the rear hatch control and dismounted to coax Rikayl inside. "Rik, get in, buddy. We've got to go back. You won't be able to keep up with me at top speed."

Rikayl cocked his head to one side. "No. Not. Won't."

"Get in."

"No no no."

"Get in *now*."

Chris pointed to the rear of the Caracal but Rikayl wasn't having any of it. He made an angry growling noise and planted himself on all fours on the hood.

"Okay, screw you," Chris said. "I don't have time to dick around. Make your own way back."

He climbed into the Caracal and started the engine. Rikayl was still standing on the hood, defying him to do something about it. It was dumb to let a bird provoke him, but Rikayl had pressed his self-respect button and he still wasn't in the mood to put up with anyone refusing to comply. He swung the APC around, put his foot down hard, and sent Rikayl skidding to one side of the hood. The teerik tried to grab the door frame but went spinning sideways, wings flailing, and vanished like a wrapper tossed out the window. Chris kept going.

The rear hatch was still open, though. A hundred yards and a few moments later, Rikayl crash-landed in the crew compartment in a flurry of feathers. He wasn't happy.

"Waaaaanker. Bastard. Hate you wanker."

Chris caught a glimpse of fluffed-up scarlet feathers in the rear-view mirror. He braced for an attack, but the driver's seat was a good shield against claws and beaks. He still kept his hand on his sidearm, though.

"And don't crap on the seats."

"Hate wanker. Crap crap *crap*."

"The Jattans are coming. Bad guys. Dangerous. Understand?"

Rikayl appeared to grasp the Jattan bit. He settled down like a broody hen, still making angry noises.

"Jattan wankers."

"Yeah. Jattans. Wankers, all of 'em."

Chris's brief taste of normality was over and he hated himself for feeling upbeat about it. This was what he excelled at, though, his calling, and everyone he cared about was woven into it as much as he was. It probably wasn't healthy, but it was natural and comfortable.

He pushed the Caracal to its top speed and almost hit the mined perimeter before it had a chance to deactivate.

The base had changed in the short time he'd been outside the wire. The only people walking around were on patrol — his guys, Trinder's, and some of the *Cabot* crew — and there were now anti-aircraft missile launchers and gun trucks parked at key positions. Even the sound of the base had changed. It was almost silent.

He parked the Caracal behind the main building. "Go and hide, Rik," he said. "The Jattans are coming."

He didn't expect the teerik to understand, but Rikayl hopped onto the rail of the hatch, looked around, and flew off. He'd be okay. It was time to worry about the civilians who would now be sheltering in place because most of the underground bunkers weren't finished. It felt just like the bombing run that never happened back at Ainatio HQ. Life seemed to be playing out on a loop.

The grandly-named command centre was more like a store room lined with monitors and sensor plots, and until now it had seen less action than the admin office. Its output was fed through to security, but it hadn't exactly been the throbbing hub of the base. It was alive now, though, and the crush of bodies made it feel more tense. A dozen of Ingram's people were crammed in with Cosquimaden and Trinder. Ingram stood behind Hiyashi, watching one monitor in particular, the one with an aggregated feed from the ships in orbit and the northern hemisphere sat network. Thermal and EM signatures were overlaid on the images in real time.

"Are we sure that's a ship?" Trinder asked. "It could be a missile."

"There's at least two." Hiyashi pointed with his pen. "This small one's about seven hundred klicks out, and the bigger one's following it at about three thousand. I can't detect any more yet."

Ingram watched, arms folded. "Okay, commit the probes. Get a closer look. Whoever it is knows we're here, so we don't need to be coy about checking them out."

"It's got to be Nir-Tenbiku."

"Agreed, but the question is whether he's come for a chat or if he's brought his fleet to sort us out." She looked at Chris as if they'd never had any differences. "With any luck he's just being pushy. If he's hostile, we have options. *Curtis* still has her directed energy weapons, or we can just gate devices into their ships."

Chris craned his neck to study the monitor. He'd never been good at interpreting imaging and it could have been a medical scan for all the sense it made. He could see the objects, but he couldn't work out what they were doing or how fast they were doing it.

"How did we spot them?" he asked.

"The first ship is now within the orbit of your vessels," Cosqui said. "It's close to the trajectory the shuttle takes from *Cabot*, and both *Elcano* and *Shackleton* detected it. They have the upgraded sensors."

"So whoever it is knows where to land. Yeah, it's got to be the Jattan opposition using their probe as a homing signal."

"It appears so." The teerik cocked her head. The probes were now in position. The visual display switched from two vague blobs to a finely detailed image of the first ship with a lot more superimposed information from the sensors. Then the other ship appeared in close-up as the monitor split into two images. Being able to move assets instantly was a wonderful thing. "Ah, that's a Kanur-class patrol ship. Larger than Gan-Pamas's freighter, but still small, and no spacefold capability. The other is an old Type Four corvette built by Kugad, so I can give you deck plans and a list of likely armaments. That means it's the opposition, because the Protectorate scrapped its Type Fours years ago. But the ship is still formidable. It has energy weapons and it could easily destroy the base."

"Awesome," Searle said. "You're a one-woman intelligence service."

Cosqui did that little side-to-side head movement that said she was pleased to be flattered. "Unless there's a larger fleet waiting out of range, I think this visit is diplomatic. From what you've said, Nir-Tenbiku thinks humans are heavily armed. If he intended to attack, he'd have brought more support."

"Maybe that's all he's got," Searle said. "Or all we can see."

"Shipyard gossip said the opposition had at least ten warships."

"Whatever they've come to do, we need to be ready to smack them hard and fast at the first sign of trouble," Ingram said. She was in her thinking pose, one arm folded across her chest and the other hand to her chin while she frowned at the array of screens. "Sol, what can you place inside the corvette via the gate? Can we use a nuke?"

"We can, Captain, or conventional explosives," Solomon said. "It would be instant, and in the unlikely event of any survivors, they would have no idea that a gate had been used. No awkward questions left hanging."

"So do we want to wipe them out, seize the ships, or warn them off?" Chris asked. "I'm not sure where we're going here."

It was a simple question, but not an easy choice. Chris and everyone else had prepared for a defensive action that assumed the base would be invaded and come under attack. It was straightforward: if aliens opened fire, the base responded with everything it had. But there were just two ships, and nobody knew if they were on their own or if they had backup lurking somewhere. Their disappearance wouldn't remain a mystery, either. Someone back at base almost certainly knew where they were going and why.

Ingram didn't appear to take the question as criticism. She seemed relaxed, like she was happy to be back doing something she understood and knew she did well. "I'd prefer Nir-Tenbiku to bugger off and not come back, actually," she said. "I don't want to blow anything up or cause casualties if we don't have to, because we don't know if we'll end up calling down worse trouble on ourselves. If they do nothing hostile, then the ball's in our court to make the wrong call. So while we need to be ready to launch an attack if things go wrong, I want to talk to them first, if only to confirm it really is the opposition."

"But if this guy's got a mole in his camp, the Protectorate are going to know all about us before long."

"Then we'd better hope Nir-Tenbiku's security's tight."

Ingram moved on. She wasn't taking a vote on this. But that was the power-sharing deal they'd agreed. Chris, Trinder, and Marc ran the land forces, and she had control of everything in the sea, air, or space, so he'd defer to her and keep his misgivings to himself, just as he'd expected her to defer to him during the protests. His job was to defend the base on the ground if her plan failed. He was ready for that.

"Brad, get *Curtis* cranked up and stand by, just in case."

"On my way, ma'am," Searle said. "Come on, Cosqui."

Cosqui muttered to herself and followed him. "It would have been better if we hadn't stripped out so many parts."

"But she can still fire her lasers."

"We'll know when we try."

As Chris glanced their way, he realised Marc was now standing at the back of the room in a red Ainatio pressure suit, something he'd never seen the guy wear before. Chris could only interpret that as meaning he planned to board one of the ships. There was no need to do that to destroy them, so was Ingram thinking of extracting something or someone? Chris was all for retrieving useful stuff, but the last complication they needed after the Gan-Pamas debacle was another Jattan effectively held hostage in Nomad.

"Captain, are we planning to board?" Chris asked.

"I'm not ruling it out yet, but I'd prefer to avoid it," Ingram said. "Until I know what their intention is, all options stay open."

"We don't need another Gan-Pamas."

Chris couldn't tell how she'd taken that, but she didn't blink. "Okay, everybody patch into Sol's translation so we can hear what's going on," she said. Her tone and folded arms said she was back on her bridge and ready to fight. "Let's see if Nir-Tenbiku's receiving. I hope he's still connected to his probe." She let out a breath and tapped the comms switch. "Unidentified vessels, this is Nomad Base. You're entering Opis space without permission. Identify yourselves immediately or we'll open fire."

The silence dragged on. Ingram now had that tight-lipped look that said she was still the Butcher of Calais. She'd dodged the hard decision on whether to take Gan-Pamas alive, but vessels entering her space uninvited seemed to be a clear-cut issue.

"Unidentified Jattan vessels," she repeated. "This is Nomad Base. Turn back now or you will be fired upon."

Ingram pressed the mute button. Marc squeezed through the crush to talk to her for a moment before making his way out again. As he passed, he gave Chris a here-we-go-again look. Chris could only nod.

"Unidentified Jattan vessels," Ingram said, slowly and more firmly this time. "This is your final warning. Turn back now or you *will* be fired upon." She tapped her earpiece and stepped back from the console. "Ready, Sol?"

"Yes, Captain. Patrol ship first, conventional missile and gate standing by."

Chris checked his watch. Ingram was counting down thirty seconds.

"I think he heard you, ma'am," Hiyashi said. "Both of them look like they're doing deceleration burns."

"Good. At least they understood."

Chris waited, not sure what Ingram defined as an end to the incursion. Did she want to see them spacefold away before she stood everyone down? Then the artificial voice Solomon had allocated to the Jattan response to Ingram's message boomed from the speaker.

"This is Primary Nir-Tenbiku Dals, rightful Mediator of Jatt. I apologise for the manner of my arrival, Captain Ingram. I request an audience with you. I'm unarmed and I've come alone."

So Nir-Tenbiku didn't take no for an answer. Chris watched Ingram carefully. He expected her to blow the shit out of the ship, but she could be unpredictable

"But you're *not* alone, Primary," she said. "You have a Type Four corvette accompanying you, for instance."

Chris thought *for instance* was just Ingram being conversational, but then he realised it was quite clever. If it came out in Jattan the way she delivered it in English, Nir-Tenbiku wouldn't know if Nomad could only detect the Type Four or if Ingram was using it as an example. If he had more vessels standing off a lot further away, he'd have no idea of the range of Nomad's sensors and if she could see more than she was letting on.

"Captain, the corvette transported my vessel here so that I wouldn't enter your space in a warship and appear hostile," Nir-Tenbiku said. "I'm sorry if we seemed to be a threat. We don't want any conflict with you. Just a discussion."

Chris had to hand it to him. He'd dumped that proverbial ball straight back in her court. Chris watched her expression change to narrow-eyed calculation, like she'd thought of something that would be more use to her than simple destruction. But she either had to fire now or find out what he wanted.

"Tell your frigate to stand off to five hundred thousand kilometres," she said. "We'll monitor the activity of her drive and her weapons systems to ensure that she does. Are you able to land in your vessel?"

"Yes, I am."

"Hold your distance and await my next transmission."

Ingram muted the channel and waited, looking at the screen over Hiyashi's shoulder.

"Corvette's changing course, ma'am," Hiyashi said.

"Sol, Commander Searle — stand by." Ingram turned to face the room. "I'm inclined to give him a chance to talk. Yes, I know I wanted them to leave us alone, but we've got to deal with Jattans at some point, and the opposition's a source of intel. Turning him back now might mean using force. Anyone want to talk me out of it?"

Chris almost reminded her that Bissey had said that before he resigned. The guy was gradually being proven right on everything. It rankled, but Chris tried to learn a lesson from it.

"We were all for following Fred's advice to behave like the new gangsters in town because that's how they do things around here," Chris said. "Okay, it's a bad idea to start a fight we can't finish, but we're starting the relationship with a concession. And we're going to get sucked into their feud just by having contact."

"That depends on how I deal with Nir-Tenbiku," Ingram said.

"Scare him over coffee and cookies, you mean?"

"That's a good definition of diplomacy."

"Okay, if talking doesn't work, we can escalate any time."

"I'm glad you see my point." Ingram always said that when she thought people didn't and she wanted to remind them who was boss. "So let's get Nir-Tenbiku down here and have a chat."

"If you're bringing him here, he might ask to take his buddy's body back with him," Chris said. "Unless you're going to ransom it, I'll get the medics to prep it for transport."

Ingram softened a little, but only from corundum to steel. "Thank you. Best to have it ready in case I need to play that card."

Chris went outside and stood on the front steps, happy to get out of that room and breathe fresh air. After he'd messaged Dr Mendoza to prep Gan-Pamas's body, he listened to the silence for a few moments. What were the teeriks going to make of all this? These Jattans definitely didn't fit the description Fred had given. If they just wore an enemy down by constantly dropping in and asking to borrow a cup of sugar instead of going full scorched earth, that made them a lot more complicated to deal with. It'd become harder to work out when it was time to open fire.

Maybe Ingram really was the best commander to take them on, though, because Nir-Tenbiku's polite but insistent style was kind of British, the way she'd probably wage war herself by turning up in a gunboat and saying she was terribly sorry but she had to invade.

Trinder joined him outside and stood with his arms folded, looking out across the green.

"I didn't have a better idea," he said.

"Me neither."

"We got everyone to their shelter positions in record time, so there's that. But I'd be happier if all the bomb shelters had been finished."

"Any objections?" Chris asked.

"I was waiting for someone to say how convenient it was to have an alien invasion on election day, just after we brought back prison ships, but no, nothing. I think my abject terror looked genuine enough to convince them it wasn't a stunt."

"Where's Howie?"

"Mangel's looking after him in the Warehouse Ten basement. He's set up some physics experiment to keep him occupied."

"And the teeriks?"

"Apart from Cosqui and Fred, they're still on the ships. It was easier and safer to leave them there with our guys."

Chris's mind went straight to asset denial and setting the vessels to self-destruct. "Safer for Earth. Easier to make sure the Jattans don't get them."

"Ah... no. I don't think that was the plan."

"I bet it's occurred to Ingram, though." Chris pointed across the green at Lee Ramsay's gun truck. Lee was sitting behind the gun, looking bored. "Okay, I'm going to be over there. That's my command centre until this is over."

"Copy that. I'll catch up with you later."

Chris walked over to the truck. Lee gave him a hand up onto the flatbed and they stood surveying the base for a while.

"Hell of a day off you picked, huh?"

"I think this is our new normal," Chris said. "Ingram's agreed to talk to Nir-Tenbiku."

"Are they going to move *Elcano* as a precaution?"

"Nobody raised it. Yesterday's panic. We've got a new one to play with now. A crisis a day, like an advent calendar."

"Does anyone ever stick to a plan around here?"

Chris shrugged. "Doesn't look like it."

"We'll always be guessing our way through this."

"Yeah, think how much worse it'd be if we had experts."

"Amen. Does Ingram know what she's doing?"

Chris sat down on the edge of the side panel and thought it over. "As much as any of us do. She's defending an island again. We're the island and ships are ships, wherever they are. She knows how to do that really well."

Lee opened a pack of jerky and shared it with him. "Nobody wants to be the first human to start a war with aliens, though. Not even her."

"But it's pretty much human history. Meet a new society, check it out, get in a fight with it."

"Could be worse," Lee said. "She might do a deal with them. And then we'll have politics in paradise."

"You mean more politics. There's already a deal with Britain."

Nomad Base had been manned for just six months. They should have still been preoccupied with the basics like expanding food production, having kids, and maybe exploring the rest of the planet a little. Instead they'd become a miniature nation with the complications and baggage of a big country, amassed overnight rather than by centuries of mistakes and learning hard lessons. Chris wondered how they'd ever roll that back and have their fresh start now. There was no blank page to return to.

"I hope she's too smart for that," he said.

"But are the Jattans? We won't be able to avoid them. We're going to get galaxy politics whether we want it or not."

For all Nomad's isolation, it still had neighbours, and they couldn't be erased and forgotten either. Even keeping them at arm's length and making Opis a no-go area would shape how the colony grew and behaved. Chris realised there was a real future at stake now, not the kind he'd had on Earth, where the question was how it would all inevitably end, but continuity and possibilities stretching generations ahead. What he did now would determine how it turned out. There was nothing amazing about that, and regular folks probably took the idea for granted, but it was amazing for *him*. He never thought he'd be able to see the world that way. It was worrying and uplifting at the same time.

Maybe the feeling wouldn't last, but the uninvited Jattans had done him a favour. They'd made him realise he had more to lose than his own limited life. He was part of something bigger, and he had a stake in a future he'd never see, a future that he now cared about a lot more than he ever thought he would.

In a back-to-front, accidental kind of way, the Jattans had taught him the real meaning of optimism.

* * *

HANGAR 3, NOMAD BASE: FIFTEEN MINUTES SINCE LAST CONTACT WITH NIR-TENBIKU.

"Are you sure you're alright?" Ingram looked Marc over with a frown. "Boarding isn't really necessary. We can do the security checks when the ship lands."

Marc put his helmet on and ran his suit's safety checks to make sure everything was connected and sealed. He hadn't done this for nearly fifteen years, and even then he hadn't done it anywhere near often enough to feel relaxed about it. The unfamiliar suit was one of Ainatio's lightweight emergency escape types in case he ended up gating into a depressurised compartment or missing Nir-Tenbiku's ship completely, but it still crimped his movement. It was hard enough manoeuvring inside a Jattan-sized ship without the extra bulk.

He bloody well *hated* space.

His brief acquaintance with it hadn't filled him with a sense of wonder. It just depressed him. The sheer emptiness he saw when he first transferred to an orbital for a training exercise looked agonisingly lonely rather than awe-inspiring, and he never saw a clear sky the same way again. Sometimes his focus would flip like inverting an optical illusion, and instead of bright blue infinity he saw a thin layer of gas and then absolutely cold, black, hostile lifelessness stretching further than he could ever imagine. If anything went wrong today and he ended up drifting in space, he'd just vent the suit and get it over with. He couldn't think of a worse way to die than waiting for his air to run out and having nothing to look at in his final moments except that lonely darkness. When it came to death, he wanted either instant oblivion from a competent sniper or a nice view to say goodbye to.

And then there was the helmet. He'd never admitted it to anyone, but enclosed helmets made him claustrophobic in a way that breathing apparatus didn't. He'd have been downgraded for operations if the brass had known and — far worse — he'd have been humiliated. He forced himself to slow his breathing and pressed the external speaker control on his sleeve.

"Yeah, I know this looks like overkill," he said. "But if that ship's full of nukes or chemical weapons, security checks here are going to make sod all difference. I need to board before it lands."

Marc stretched and squatted in the suit, testing its range of mobility again. Searle watched like he was doing his best not to offer helpful suggestions.

"You reckon you can dock okay?" Marc asked.

"Cosqui's going to give me a hand."

"Yes or no?"

"Yes."

"So once I'm in, do I reseal the hatch or do you?"

"We can close it in the same way that we open it," Cosqui said. "It's the escape hatch. Rescue or salvage teams need their own method of access if the crew's unable to respond."

"Good." Marc took off his helmet and sucked in fresh air that wasn't really any different from the suit's supply. It just tasted better when he wasn't trapped. "Once I'm in, detach and get clear. Don't stay tethered. If the ship's booby-trapped for whatever reason, you're fucked as well. Pull out to a safe distance and keep your laser on him."

"Hang on," Ingram said. "This isn't a suicide mission."

"I never said it was. If the Jattans are playing silly buggers with us, I'll set explosives and Fred or Sol will have to gate me out of there."

"This has escalated somewhat," Ingram said stiffly. "What exactly are you taking?"

Marc picked up his daypack and shook it by the straps to indicate the brick-sized charge inside. "This'll blow a big hole in the hull. If Nir-Tenbiku's doing a kamikaze run, I grant his wish. If it's unmanned, I blow it before they drop it on us."

"And how will you know? We have no idea what the ordnance might look like."

"For a start, if the ship's unmanned or he hasn't come alone, it'll be bloody obvious it's not a friendly visit."

"But why would they attack if they want *Curtis* or some favour from us?"

"Because they think we won't hand the ship over, or they want to make sure the other side doesn't get hold of it. Or perhaps they'll just want us gone. I've seen flimsier reasons back home. Look, this is just a precaution, because we won't get a chance to rerun this if you're wrong about Nir-Tenbiku."

Ingram shook her head, either in defeat or disbelief. "Don't cut it too fine, then."

"We're jumping into a mission we can't plan properly and we don't have much intel," Marc said. "So I'll assume the worst until I see what I'm up against, and then I'll improvise."

"Fine, but you improvise on the side of caution."

Marc had no intention of dying, but nobody really knew how these particular Jattans operated. All he could do was assume they applied the same basics of warfare as humans because they seemed to organise themselves in a similar way, from political parties to space flight and colonisation. Part of him wanted to try gating in and using the boarding as a dry run for sabotaging Kugad, if and when that became necessary. He needed to know how he handled fast insertions with the gate. But the only way to do that without revealing it was for Searle to mock up a docking, and that was getting way too complicated to be worth it. Marc had one task and that was to make sure they weren't allowing a Trojan horse to land.

He walked over to *Curtis* and stood at the bottom of the ramp. "Cosqui, have you got that deck plan yet?"

Cosqui emerged from the forward port hatch and held out her screen to him. "I was waiting for you to stop fighting."

"Yeah, we're done now." Marc transferred the file to his pocket screen and took a look at the blueprint. "Not a lot of room for error, is there?"

"That's the standard Kanur layout, but they might have modified it," Cosqui said. "The emergency hatch will always have good access around it, though, or there's no point in having it at all. If you let me follow your helmet cam, I can identify what you see and tell you if it's ordnance or weapons. You can also use a gas analyser to test the atmosphere for particles of explosive substances and pathogens. You have them in your workshop."

"I'll get one sent over right away," Solomon said. "And I'll copy the plan to your head-up display, Marc."

"Let me see it first." Marc put his helmet back on and a dim deck plan appeared in his eyeline, tilted in 3D like a route planner, complete with arrows. "Okay, that's not too intrusive. Just keep it basic."

"Don't worry, the emergency suits are designed to direct personnel to escape pods and exits if visibility's compromised," Solomon said. "It's minimal so that it's easy for someone under extreme stress to follow."

"I'm not stressed. I just don't like the thought of sucking vacuum." Marc took off his helmet again and held his screen so Cosqui could see what he was pointing at on the plan. "So if that's the cockpit, and I'm inserted here behind this chart table or whatever it is, I can clear the compartments from the rear section forward."

"That's the galley. Not a chart table."

"Bloody hell, that's even more cramped than I thought. Is the cockpit likely to be locked or anything?"

"Probably not."

"Headroom?"

"The same as Gan-Pamas's freighter."

"What about air? Can I take my helmet off if I need to? If Gan-Pamas could breathe our atmosphere, can I breathe theirs?"

"Yes, it should be close to what you're used to."

"Thanks Cosqui. Sol, can I test the translation thing now?"

"You're connected," Solomon said. "Just talk. Nir-Tenbiku will be able to hear the Jattan translation from your external speaker. When you talk to us on internal comms, or he replies to you, we'll all hear English."

"Even if I take the helmet off?"

"Yes, but you'll hear both voices if you do."

"Let's try that so I know how it'll sound. Okay, testing, testing, half a league, half a league, half a league onward..."

Hearing two voices was no more distracting than trying to monitor two different radio channels, but the stream of high-pitched Jattan delivered in his own voice threw him for a moment. He could never hit those high notes in real life. He sounded possessed. It would have been hilarious if circumstances had been different.

"Okay, I'm ready." Marc turned to Ingram. "Give Nir-Tenbiku plenty of warning that I'm boarding so he doesn't panic and do something daft when he hears something scraping his hull."

"He'll almost certainly detect *Curtis* coming," Searle said. "So tell him sooner rather than later, please, Captain."

"I'll call him when you take off," Ingram said.

Marc looked up at *Curtis* from the bottom of the ramp. He'd been on board, but he'd never flown in her, and now he wished he'd spent a bit of time re-learning how to move in microgravity. The small voice in his head that nagged him to do things while he still had the time said he also ought to start training in higher gravity right away so he'd be ready to pay an unfriendly visit to Kugad. If he asked nicely, Searle would probably jump at the excuse to take *Curtis* up for a few orbital flights with the artificial gravity cranked up. As soon as Nir-Tenbiku was on his way home, Marc would plan his high-G training schedule.

But first he had to make sure he didn't meet a premature end trying to squeeze through a Jattan-sized hatch with only a few layers of aramid between him and oblivion. He boarded *Curtis* without looking back at Ingram and followed Searle and Cosqui through narrow passages and hatches that only just cleared his shoulders. The rescue hatch was set halfway up a bulkhead, so he'd come through the deckhead of the Jattan ship like he'd turned ninety degrees and descend to the deck. It might take time to reorient himself to return fire if this was an ambush.

"Okay, I'm as ready as I'm going to be," he said. "Crack on."

Searle looked uncomfortable in the pilot's seat even with all the modifications they'd done to create more room. He was a tall bloke. He looked over his shoulder at Marc with some difficulty.

"We've got this," he said. "You okay?"

"When the analyser shows up, yeah."

They waited. Cosqui preened the feathers on her right arm, then whistled tunelessly to herself, clearly bored. Marc couldn't tell if she'd picked up the habit from a human or if teeriks made random bird noises naturally, and he was reluctant to ask. The minutes dragged on. Eventually Solomon came on the radio.

"Marc, Fred's on his way with an analyser."

"Thanks."

"He's a little agitated. May I suggest you humour him?"

"Sol, I've got a job to do. Is this going to impede the mission? If so, get someone else to fetch one."

"All you need to do is politely decline his offer of using the personal Caisin gate. Just keep him calm and I'll take care of it."

Cosqui rasped to herself and muttered in Kugal, but the sentiment was clear because her red crest lifted like an angry cockatoo's. Marc could imagine what Sol meant by *take care of it,* too.

"He's not back on his meds yet, is he?" Searle said. "I feel for the guy. Tough choice."

Marc was glad he wasn't relying solely on Fred for an accurate gate extraction today. "I don't know what's worse, dumbing him down with that stuff or letting him be the unstable genius."

Rustling and muffled banging emerged from the passage behind the cockpit, the sound of a large creature with wings trying to move too fast through small metal spaces. Fred emerged from the hatch. Over the weeks, Marc had learned to read his mood, which wasn't easy in a species that didn't have a wide range of facial expressions. But if he'd had to guess, he'd have thought Fred was angry about something and trying not to show it, not agitated, whatever Sol meant by that.

"Here's the analyser, Marc." Fred handed it over. Marc examined it and realised it had been pre-set for him, with just a button to press. "But you could use the personal gate instead. Nir-Tenbiku won't imagine for one moment that someone could open a portal inside his ship. He'll be confused and think you have some other breaching technology."

Humour him, Sol had said. So Marc humoured. "Thanks, Fred, but I need a lot more practice first. I'm the weak link in this. We'd have to do a fake hatch opening anyway, just to make sure Nir-Tenbiku believed it, so we might as well do it for real."

Fred cocked his head. "Very well. But we'll be ready to extract you via the regular gate if things go wrong."

"Thanks. I'll try to make sure they don't."

Fred clambered out of the cockpit. He hadn't seemed aggressive, just obsessive. Everyone waited in silence until Fred was well out of earshot.

"Sol, if he's standing by to gate me out, make sure you oversee it, please. Just in case." Marc shouldn't have said it in front of Cosqui, but he erred on the side of survival. Searle started the engines and ran final checks. He looked confident using the human-adapted controls that Cosqui had designed.

"Okay, ready to launch. Ready, Marc?"

"Chocks away, Ginger. Tally ho."

"What? Okay. I get it."

Marc secured the analyser on his tool belt and sealed his helmet. Then he shut his eyes. No, it was worse like that. He'd have to distract himself some other way. He switched to the head-up display and concentrated as hard as he could on the Kanur layout, visualising himself entering via the deckhead hatch and grabbing for the rails on the left to orientate himself.

At least Sol was the only one who could monitor his vitals. He didn't want anyone seeing his pulse rate soaring.

Just breathe.

Come on, you've done harder shit than this. Much harder. Get a grip. What's Boadicea going to think of you?

He couldn't see what was going on outside the ship anyway. It took longer than he expected to taxi onto the short strip of runway, but he felt the drives ramp up and then *Curtis* lifted with almost no forward motion. It didn't feel as chest-crushing as he remembered. If he asked Searle why, he'd get a physics lesson, so he just carried on trying to memorise the deck plan to take his mind off the void ahead. He'd have been just as dead if anything went wrong in a conventional aircraft, but it never felt that way.

How was he going to explain this to Lawson? Now that *was* a good way to take his mind off the flight. Dumping two different sets of aliens on the bloke complete with pics would make it much harder for him to keep it to himself. He'd have to share the information with the intelligence services at the very least. Marc was suddenly disappointed with himself. When did he start thinking it was okay for civil servants to keep secrets from the people's representatives? Blood had been shed in the past to put an end to that, but here he was making it happen again. He had no way of knowing whether Lawson was a good guy or not. He'd had to make the decision to trust him just to ask for help with the evacuation, but the rest was based on no more than a gut feel. They seemed to understand each other. Maybe he'd have understood Tim Pham too if they'd both been trying to save the same country.

"Ingram's speaking to Nir-Tenbiku," Searle said. "Better listen in case he says no and we have to abort."

Marc picked up the channel. He hadn't said goodbye to Ingram. That bothered him. He was just being professional about it all, but it still made him wonder if he'd ever speak to her again.

"Primary, we're sending our most experienced and senior soldier to prepare you for landing," Ingram said. "He'll board your vessel shortly. You don't need to do anything except allow the ship to dock with you."

"How are you able to do that?" Nir-Tenbiku asked.

"We have all the technical specifications for the Kanur-class and other Jattan vessels." Ingram was back on form. It was a subtle warning. Marc hoped it wasn't so subtle that it got lost in translation. "We have a compatible system."

"Then I look forward to talking with you, Captain."

The channel closed. "He seems a bit of a smooth-talker," Marc said. "Are we quarantining the ship on landing? Haine ran tests on Gan-Pamas for pathogens, so if some Jattan lurgy was going to kill us, I suppose we'd know by now."

"What if we contaminate them, though?" Searle asked.

"If he's not worried about it, neither am I."

Now things were happening, Marc felt his fears switch off. He still didn't like space, but he was in control now and he knew every move he needed to make once that hatch was open. He could hear Searle talking to Cosqui as *Curtis* rolled and aligned with the Kanur's top hatch, then the countdown.

"Cab Seven to Cab One, docking in five... four... three... two... and we have docking."

Marc felt the slight bump. Nir-Tenbiku must have felt it too.

"Okay, Marc, you're on," Searle said. "I'll see you out. Cosqui, you have the ship."

Marc released his harness and now had a couple of minutes to adjust to weightlessness before transferring to the patrol ship. Searle went ahead of him, hand over hand like a slow-motion gibbon, obviously used to all this. Long-forgotten training flooded back and Marc was almost pleased to realise there was something he needed to master again. Every move he made was conscious effort, not muscle memory. He'd work with that.

As soon as Searle got the hatch open, it dawned on Marc that there was no airlock. Once Nir-Tenbiku's hatch was open, there was a straight tunnel between the ships. Both vessels now depended on that connection holding. Marc tightened the straps on his daypack and held his Marquis close to his chest.

"Tight fit," he said, looking at the Jattan-sized opening.

"You've done this before, though, haven't you?"

"Not quite."

"I'll close both hatches once you confirm you're clear."

"Got it. Then bang out fast. Sol's got a fix on me if anything goes wrong."

"You're a crazy bastard, Marc. Keep that upper lip stiff, okay?"

"It's concrete, mate. See you back at base."

There was no good way to squeeze through a hatch when you couldn't see what was waiting for you on the other side. Marc opted for head-first — weapon-first, to be exact — with his arms forward like a diver so he had a chance of returning fire if need be. Legs-first would be a bit too exciting. Searle had to help him free the daypack when it got snagged on the coaming, but once Marc's shoulders were through into the main section of the docking tube, he could pull himself forward. He inched out of the hatch on the other side, checking the compartment for nasty surprises as soon as his head was clear, and then eased out fully to push himself down to the deck.

He managed to right himself on two feet, caught his helmet on the deckhead, and bent over further. The helmet added a few inches to his height. He'd have been better off crawling.

"Clear," he said. "Secure the hatch and go."

"Copy that."

Marc turned and waited for the helmet cam to recognise the layout in the dim light and superimpose direction arrows. When he raised his hand to feel for the deckhead, he realised he had a couple of inches of clearance after all. Above him, metal banged and scraped. The hatch was closed. Now he could move forward. He switched on the analyser and wedged it in a tool pocket on his chest where he could see the display, then raised the Marquis and looked for movement or objects that might be explosives or worse. If he hadn't been weightless, it would have been like any one of dozens of room-clearing operations he'd done on Earth. He hoped he wouldn't have to open fire, but at least it would only push him back to a bulkhead.

"*Curtis* now detached and clear," Searle said.

"Copy that. Cosqui, are you getting my helmet feed?"

"I am," she said. "Nothing to worry us so far."

Marc checked the analyser. The lights were all green and still at baseline, so it looked like there were no explosives or pathogens, but he couldn't check for unknown compounds. He wasn't out of the woods yet.

There were only three compartments between the deck flat under the emergency hatch and the cockpit forward of him, and he found all of them were completely empty — no cargo, all the lockers dogged open, and no sign of anyone else on board. There was a deck below, a small cargo area like the one in Gan-Pamas's freighter, but Marc couldn't detect any heat signatures. It didn't look like anyone was lying in wait.

Marc reached the cockpit hatch and switched to external comms. "Primary? This is Marc Gallagher. I'm on deck and I'm coming into the cockpit."

There was always that moment when he didn't know what would happen when he moved in. A Jattan energy weapon would ruin his day and there was no room to dodge it or find cover, even if he could move fast enough in microgravity. He couldn't check the cockpit using the reflection on the inside of the ship's windscreen, either. A tangle of floating symbols and lines hung in the air in front of it, exactly like the projected displays that had originally been installed in *Curtis*. All he could do was rely on getting his shot in first if Nir-Tenbiku wasn't as unarmed and innocent as he'd claimed.

Marc edged around the frame of the hatch, rifle first, then lowered it slowly.

Nir-Tenbiku was sitting in the pilot's seat, wearing a similar pressure suit to the one Gan-Pamas had died in, and looking calmly dignified with his visible hands clasped in his lap. Like his dead buddy, he was tiny, about four feet six. That didn't make him any less dangerous, but Marc still felt like a dick for treating such a small bloke as a threat.

"Good afternoon, Primary." *Keep it simple. Short sentences. No jargon.* "Were you planning to land at the probe's position?"

"Good afternoon, General." That had to be a translation glitch. "Yes, the course is laid in."

"We have to give you coordinates for a different landing zone."

"Are you able to exchange data with this vessel?"

"Aren't you in control of this ship, Primary?"

"No. I'm not a trained pilot. The system's automated."

Nir-Tenbiku seemed to have his eyes fixed on the Marquis. Marc had no idea whatsoever about Jattan body language and there was no recognisable expression on Nir-Tenbiku's eel-like face to guide him. The guy could have been offering his surrender or getting ready to detonate the ship. All the signs Marc had learned to read over a lifetime just weren't there.

"Was that the prenu?" Nir-Tenbiku asked. "The sensors detected it but I only caught a glimpse through the windscreen."

"Yes. That was the frigate."

"Did you think I was armed?"

"I can't rule it out. It's my job to take maximum precautions." He could see lights changing on the floating display. He pointed. "What does that show?"

"That's the position of the other ship."

"Make sure they understand they have to stay back."

"I have. You really would open fire if the ship came closer, I assume."

"Captain Ingram means exactly what she says." Marc still couldn't work out if the ship was holding position or not. He needed grids and numbers to work that out. "Your navigation system should be receiving a signal now with your new landing co-ordinates. You can begin your descent."

"Your teeriks seem to have given you a great deal of information about our systems, General."

General. Marc was never going to hear the end of that. "They like things done right," he said. Another floating display changed its appearance. "Is that the new course coming in?"

"Yes." Nir-Tenbiku turned towards the windscreen. Marc would never have accepted a transmission from Sol if he'd been Nir-Tenbiku. But the Jattan didn't know about the AI's hacking habits. "Please secure yourself in the seat."

It was like sitting in a kid's chair. Marc squeezed in and ended up wedged so tightly that a seat belt was probably redundant. Nir-Tenbiku made gestures at the controls and the patrol vessel rolled ninety degrees, spinning the visible stars and bringing Opis's disc into view. Marc added it to the list of experiences that he wished he could have told John and Greg about. Here he was, trusting his safety to an alien rebel leader he'd only just met and who had to rely on autopilot to land safely, and who seemed to have a lot of basic things in common with humans, despite being a short-arse bipedal eel with multiple vestigial arms. It was just another regular day in Nomad. It was scary, it was cool, and it made him feel alive again. He was getting that buzz more often lately.

The descent was brief, but the silence between them was getting awkward. Nir-Tenbiku finally broke it.

"How did you acquire teeriks?" he asked. "Did your people have previous experience of handling them?"

It was an odd way to put it, but so was calling Marc a general. "No," Marc said, still practicing good OPSEC and not volunteering too much. "But we help each other out."

"And you've had no problems with them?"

Now there was a loaded and very specific question. Maybe Nir-Tenbiku meant labour disputes, or just that he thought they were a bit uppity for servants, which was understandable given what Lirrel had been like. But maybe Lirrel had the same medication problem as Fred's commune. Did the Jattans know teeriks were given drugs? Marc almost asked by way of conversation, but decided to leave it to Ingram.

"We get on fine," Marc said, wondering what was going on with Fred. "Except for Lirrel, obviously. I had to shoot him when he killed Dr Curtis. Sorry about that."

"Well, if they get out of hand, you have no choice."

Bloody hell. Jattan toffs really did believe in putting the working classes in their place. Marc struggled to think of a diplomatic response.

"How long had Lirrel been working for you?"

"One Opis year." That sounded like the AI translation converting Jattan units to human ones the same way it converted distances. "He was very useful, but his temperament grew worse."

Nir-Tenbiku sounded like he was talking about a dog, not even a servant. It was probably the translation's limits again.

"We named the frigate after our comrade who was killed, by the way," Marc said. "*Curtis*. The teeriks asked for that. They liked her."

"Yes, I've heard they can get very attached to their owners."

Marc's natural response would have killed Ingram's diplomacy stone dead, so he said nothing and sat back to keep an eye on the floating displays. He was getting the general idea of them, although nowhere near enough to glean any intel. His helmet was transmitting everything he looked at, though, so Cosqui could analyse it with Solomon. Opis was dead ahead, gradually filling his field of view with oceans and plains and forests, erasing the void. Plenty could still go wrong before the ship touched down, but Marc allowed himself a little optimism. It had gone better than he expected.

He still hated space. But today he'd realised how badly he didn't want to die, something he hadn't felt for a long time, and Opis somehow looked a little more like home. He could only hope that it would still be in one piece tomorrow.

13

I know what you did, Solomon. You're no better than the Kugin.

Hredt, rehearsing a difficult conversation.

Gan-Pamas had been wrong about humans. They weren't as big as Kugin. They were actually bigger.

They weren't as heavily-built, but most of them looked taller, and a number of them were waiting and watching when Nir-Tenbiku emerged from the ship into uncomfortably bright sun. Seeing them in the flesh was sobering. They reminded him of obercu, long-limbed with heads set on narrow necks, but he doubted they were docile herbivores. The creatures with them, the small four-legged ones covered in hair, stood beside them and shouted the same word over and over.

One was silent, though, a creature with a glossy black and white coat, and fixed its gaze on him. It lay crouched as if it was going to spring. One of the humans turned to speak to the quadrupeds and they stopped shouting immediately, but the black and white one didn't take his eyes off Nir-Tenbiku.

Everything was disorienting — light, smells, vibrations, noises, even the slightly lower gravity that was enough to make him misjudge his steps. He was also too far away from the base to echolocate anything. It left him blind, squinting against the bright sun until he put on his visor to shield his eyes. It looked like an odd accessory now he'd changed into his formal clothes, but the humans probably didn't notice.

"This way, Primary." Marc pointed him towards an open vehicle, a small square thing with no roof. Nir-Tenbiku was fascinated by how much deeper and more varied in tone Marc's real voice was without his helmet muting it. He could now hear both the translation and the human's own voice. "Don't worry about the dogs. They're trained to warn us about intruders."

The word *dogs* wasn't translated. "They seem angry."

"No, it's just their way of telling us they've seen you." Marc stopped as if something had occurred to him, but he didn't explain. "See that grey building over there? That's where we're going."

Nir-Tenbiku had to concentrate on every step. He was lifting his feet too high. He couldn't be seen to trip up. He was the rightful Primary of Jatt and he had to maintain his dignity, especially when wearing his state regalia. His nation's pride was at stake.

As he followed Marc, he saw a mechanical waiting nearby, the one built to resemble the dogs. It trotted over to the vehicle and jumped onto the back as if it intended to accompany them.

"Your mechanicals," Nir-Tenbiku said to Marc. "It seems you can live alongside them."

"You mean the robot with four legs? That's not a mechanical. It's our emanation. He just uses the bot frame to get around." The word *bot* wasn't translated. "But we do use ordinary mechanicals. You'll see them everywhere here."

Nir-Tenbiku wasn't sure he understood. "So you have emanations as well."

"We call them *AIs*." The translation just rendered it the way he said it. Nir-Tenbiku heard the word in both streams of language. "That's short for *artificial intelligence*. But he's completely independent, not software. He thinks and feels like us and does what he wants. He's called Solomon."

Human technology sounded intriguing and a little dangerous as well. Nir-Tenbiku noted it as something to discuss in future talks if he emerged from this meeting in Ingram's good graces. He followed Marc's gesture to sit in the front seat and did his best to disguise his unease at having a mechanical right behind him, close enough to kill him. The reassurance that the intelligence within it was effectively human didn't override his mistrust.

"Good afternoon, Primary," the emanation said in passable Jattan. It made Nir-Tenbiku jump. "I'm here to assist Captain Ingram. There's no need to worry about me."

It must have heard the conversation. Nir-Tenbiku turned to look over his shoulder. The mechanical's small head was a lens on a long, flexible neck, and it looked uncomfortably like a weapon.

"You've learned our language," Nir-Tenbiku said.

"In a way. I have another artificial intelligence that does the translation work for me. It's not sentient, but it's very efficient."

So their emanations had emanations of their own. This was impressive. No other civilisation in the known sectors had created anything like that, and if all human technology was that advanced, it might provide an edge against the Protectorate. Nir-Tenbiku had followed Gan-Pamas's advice to forge links with the humans mostly out of blind trust, but now he was beginning to see what might have convinced his friend that contact was worthwhile.

"So mechanicals really are dangerous where you come from," Marc said, driving towards the base. "The teeriks said so, but I wasn't sure if it was true. We call them *bots*, by the way."

"Yes, they form their own communities and dislike contact with outsiders," Nir-Tenbiku said. "I know little about the technology, but once they were modified to work in self-directing groups, they evolved organised social behaviour, and they decided they disliked organics."

Marc made a *hah* sound that didn't get translated. "What about the ones who do the cleaning, then?"

"Oh, they don't carry out tasks like that. They mine, build, tend crop facilities, and work in environments too hazardous for people. All the tasks that don't bring them into contact with us."

Marc's expression changed slightly. The thin strips of hair above his eyes rose and fell. But he didn't pass comment. Nir-Tenbiku asked no more questions and took in as much as he could on the short drive. There were few humans visible within the base, but all were carrying a variety of objects that were clearly weapons, and large cannon-like devices stood at road junctions. Beyond the central area of domed and flat-roofed buildings, he could see avenues lined with smaller structures that weren't quite identical but seemed to have a common style. He was struck by how complete and well-ordered the base seemed, as if it had been carefully assembled elsewhere and placed in the middle of the Opis wilderness like an island. Nothing seemed unfinished or in progress. It breathed permanence.

The vehicle came to a halt next to a row of poles adorned with brightly-coloured flags. Outside the building a human was waiting, hands clasped behind their back, and Nir-Tenbiku knew right away that it was Captain Bridget Ingram. He knew nothing about the status signs of humans, but he recognised someone who believed in their own authority.

It was a quality he'd seen in every species, even animals. He was especially taken by what he assumed was her uniform, very different from the black, looser-fitting, functional clothing worn by the troops he'd seen on landing. Her jacket was dark blue, precisely tailored, and decorated with gold, and she wore a cap with similar embellishment. It was a statement, not clothing to work in, almost Jattan in its splendid formality. He was glad he'd changed into his own regalia before leaving his ship.

He could have been completely wrong, of course. It might simply have been the fashion for human females, because he could see the differences between males and females now that he had Ingram to use as a guide. But he was sure he was looking at a uniform of someone with high rank. He was surprised by how much he already found to relate to in this species. They seemed to value ritual and honour, both signs of personal and collective discipline, and that was something he could use to forge an alliance.

"That's Captain Ingram," Marc said, confirming his guess. "Back home, she's in the history books for winning battles. And destroying enemy cities."

Nir-Tenbiku wasn't sure if Marc had given him a warning or a reassurance, but Ingram was probably doing the same as he was — keeping an open but cautious mind, checking each other out in the hope of finding mutual advantage. He climbed out of the vehicle and steadied himself to negotiate the low steps in front of the doors.

"Primary Nir-Tenbiku, welcome to Nomad Base," Ingram said. A Kugin commander would probably have shot him now for intruding like this. "Come this way. Let's talk."

Again he heard human speech and the Jattan voice almost simultaneously, the latter apparently coming from the small metal object pinned discreetly to her collar, but he was already getting better at concentrating solely on the Jattan part. Human speech was starting to sound like music in the background, devoid of verbal meaning, and he could filter it out.

"Thank you for agreeing to see me, Captain."

"I'd offer you refreshment, Primary, but I don't know if our beverages would be safe for you to drink." Ingram opened the door to lead him into the building. Solomon the emanation followed them. "We can give you purified water, though. That's probably safe."

The venue was a sparsely-furnished room with screens drawn across the windows, making the shaded interior a welcome refuge from the daylight outside. It contained two seats with two small tables beside them, one with a container of water next to some unidentifiable devices. When Ingram touched one of the objects, a smoke-like stream of water vapour rose silently into the air. Nir-Tenbiku could feel the moisture right away.

"Is this comfortable for you, Primary?" Ingram asked. "I know you prefer low light and higher humidity."

He couldn't interpret her expression, but that gesture alone told him she wasn't hostile, at least not yet. No enemy, not even an honourable one, would miss a chance to put pressure on him by making him physically uncomfortable during a sensitive negotiation. It added to the picture he was forming of a culture not completely alien to his own.

"Thank you, Captain," he said. "That's very thoughtful."

"Please, sit down."

Cudik would have said this was psychological warfare, softening up Nir-Tenbiku for some downfall, but he was the one seeking the softening and he was sure Ingram knew that. She poured water into a cup and placed it on the table within his reach. Solomon had taken up position behind him by the door, watching him as carefully as that black and white dog.

"If I sound abrupt," Ingram said, "it's because I'm still simplifying my language to avoid mistranslation. It's not discourtesy. The emanation's still learning Jattan and might not understand some terms well enough. I'm sure we'd both have a better conversation if we could speak directly, but for the time being, avoiding misunderstandings will have to be enough."

"I understand, Captain. We should be pleasantly surprised at our ability to have any meaningful conversation at all."

Ingram showed her teeth and creased her face. The expression seemed to correlate with approval if Marc was anything to judge by. Nir-Tenbiku made a note to watch out for it.

"I try to remind myself how rare it is to meet another intelligent species," she said. "And yes, it's remarkable we have enough in common to be able to discuss anything. So why have you come to see me?"

Nir-Tenbiku was relieved that the language limitations gave him an excuse to get straight to the point without seeming rude.

"I'd like to establish a friendly relationship with humans, or at least reach an agreement that you won't side with our enemies," he said. "We've already had an unfortunate and unintended conflict. I hope you believe me when I say we would *not* have behaved that way under normal circumstances."

Ingram looked at him, suddenly expressionless. "We don't know enough about local politics yet to understand the issues, let alone take sides. We just want to be left alone."

"But what we do in this sector regarding our claim on Jatt *will* have some impact on you, and your presence will change the balance of power here and affect *us*," Nir-Tenbiku said. "We should at least discuss what we can do to minimise friction."

"Well, we could agree to avoid each other."

It was hard to gauge her tone. The translation didn't convey it at all. Sometimes the vocabulary and grammar were correct, but the inflexion and emphasis were meaningless, like reciting a list of words in order that made sense to the eyes when read, but sounded strange when spoken aloud. That was understandable. It was also enough to make the speaker understood. But Nir-Tenbiku needed to know if Ingram was cutting the discussion dead, making a suggestion, or even being light-hearted.

"Will Kugad and the Protectorate leave *you* alone, though?" he asked. "They're looking for their ship, and they'll find you eventually. Whether you want to be found or not, your presence changes a great deal."

"Yes, I realise that," Ingram said. "May I check I've got accurate information? The teeriks tell me your elected government was overthrown by an internal coup and Jatt was effectively handed over to Kugin control for commercial gain. There was no actual invasion. Is that correct?"

"It is," Nir-Tenbiku said. "Now we're preparing to remove the illegitimate government and restore independence."

"You think you can defeat Kugad, then. Because that's who you'll be at war with once you oust the Protectorate."

Ingram wasn't as ignorant as she claimed. He was glad she understood the ramifications.

"If the people of Jatt want to be liberated," he said, "then we have no other option but to take on the Kugin. This is my life's purpose. I can't turn away from it."

"And if the people are happy with the situation as it is?"

"I would have to respect that. But I would also want proof that they truly felt that way."

"Aren't the other countries on Dal Mantir worried about their neighbours being occupied by Kugad?" Ingram asked. "I would have expected the Kugin to claim the entire planet. Or have they already done that?"

"No, it's only Jatt," Nir-Tenbiku said. "We have the mineral resources and other assets Kugad needs. And as far as the Kugin are concerned, they were invited in by the Common Welfare Party. Jatt is the largest and strongest nation on Dal Mantir. The rest are smaller, poorer nations that can't or won't unite to help us. There's no benefit in it for them."

Ingram was silent for a moment. A little crease appeared at the top of her nose, then vanished. "I'm trying to find a parallel in our own history to understand this better," she said. "On my world, we've seen our own governments sell out their citizens for personal gain, although never to a hostile force from another planet. The personnel here are from different nations on our homeworld, and most of their countries have been invaded or surrendered to foreign interests at some time in their history, mine among them. So we understand your strength of feeling. But we don't want to get involved in other civilisations' wars. We have colonies to build. We'll respond robustly to attacks or encroachments on our territory, but we'll remain neutral unless we have a very good reason *not* to be. An existential reason."

At least she'd confirmed Opis wasn't the humans' homeworld. They hadn't been overlooked for years. They were newcomers.

"If you want to establish more colonies, that will bring you into contact with other civilisations sooner or later," Nir-Tenbiku said. "It'll be very hard for you to remain invisible."

"We'll face that if and when it happens. But I'm surprised you came here after I asked you not to. Why did you risk it?"

"Why didn't you open fire as you said you would?" Nir-Tenbiku asked.

If volume and increased circulation were signs of agitation in humans as they were in Kugin, Ingram showed neither. She was completely calm. Her true voice in the background hadn't changed — not as low as Marc's, but a little lower than Nir-Tenbiku expected from the translation — and all he could sense was a steady pulse that hadn't altered since they'd entered the room.

"We didn't fire on your ship because we were curious," she said. "We have very little experience of other intelligent species. You didn't sound like the Jattans we'd heard about."

It was impossible to judge an entire species from a few individuals, but Nir-Tenbiku knew restraint and calculation when he saw it. Frightened creatures fled or attacked when they encountered something new. Those that were confident they could defeat threats paused to assess what they were dealing with.

"So what had you heard about Jattans?" he asked. "The Protectorate, I assume."

"That they were dangerously headstrong and got themselves killed by rushing into battle."

Nir-Tenbiku found that funny. "Someone's given you a very accurate assessment of the Protectorate's officer class, then. They don't teach discipline any more, not even in school. It's amusing that their reputation precedes them."

"You seem to have a different philosophy."

"Our lawful government, the Halu-Masset, is the duty of the old families of Jatt," Nir-Tenbiku said. "We accept our lives will be spent in the nation's service. That requires us to learn self-discipline."

"I can understand that."

"Do humans have that kind of traditional duty?"

"I'm the eighth generation of my family to serve in the Royal Navy," Ingram said. He noticed her voice this time because it had changed. It was quieter and softer for a moment, enough to distract him from the Jattan stream. "My choice was entirely voluntary, but I never considered any other career. It had to be done."

"General Marc tells me you're known for winning battles and destroying cities."

Ingram's mouth twitched and the corners of her eyes creased. Then she showed her teeth, so he knew he'd said something she liked.

"I destroyed the enemy," she said. "But I'm still not sure what we won."

Yes, Nir-Tenbiku could do business with this alien. There would be things that separated them and things he'd never understand, but there was common ground where it mattered.

"So you've come here to expand your empire."

Ingram sat back a little further in her seat. "I'm going to be completely open with you, although there'll be subjects we can't discuss for security reasons," she said. "If I give you my word, I stand by it. But my duty is to defend this settlement, and everything I do flows from that. So if we aren't willing to get involved in local conflicts, Primary, what do you want from us? We won't help Kugad or the Protectorate to attack you, unless you become a threat to us, and we won't attack them unless we're attacked first. You have my word on that. We don't want to loot or conquer your world, and I personally sympathise about the loss of your sovereignty. Is that enough reassurance to make your journey worthwhile, though? Did you really just come to establish diplomatic relations?"

Nir-Tenbiku dipped his head politely. "I'm grateful for that much." It was what he'd asked for, no more and no less, a friendly relationship. He only had himself to blame for not starting with his ideal scenario and negotiating something more realistic from there. "It would be better if we could both find some mutual advantage, though."

"I think you've come for the ship," Ingram said. "Especially now that you've seen it."

Nir-Tenbiku was encouraged that she'd brought it up. Perhaps she was carefully approaching her own demands.

"Yes, the ship would be put to good use in liberating Jatt," he said. "But it's not mine by right. It belongs to the Protectorate. I'd be commandeering it — stealing it — but I don't feel that's truly immoral. We're already at war with them, even if no shots have been fired."

"Gan-Pamas came here to retrieve the ship," Ingram said. "Who did he think he was going to seize it *from*?"

Nir-Tenbiku hadn't actually thought about it from that angle. "He didn't know about your presence here, so he probably thought he would only be dealing with the teerik commune that stole it."

"And he thought they wouldn't fight to keep it."

Nir-Tenbiku couldn't imagine where this was going. "What use would they have for a warship, except as transport?"

"I'm trying to understand why you would hesitate to take the ship from us, but not from them, except that we might put up a fight."

"And we also don't want a conflict with you."

"But what would you have done with the commune?"

He still wasn't sure he'd understood the question. "It's hard to say, but we certainly wouldn't have returned them to Kugad. We have good reason to avoid the Kugin, just as you do, and teeriks are valuable. They know a great deal about the Protectorate's defences, so perhaps Gan-Pamas thought he might take them with him as he did with Lirrel. Personally, I would weigh their skills and knowledge against the difficulties of keeping them. The Kugin can handle them, but some regard them as an abomination. Very few people outside the military community ever encounter them, of course, so this is the opinion of a small number."

Ingram did that brow-creasing expression again. "Why would someone call them an abomination?"

"Gan-Pamas believed they were the consequence of science abandoning morality."

"Sorry, I still don't understand."

"They've been bred to perfect more efficient ways of killing, and they seem content with doing that. And there must be limits on how much we interfere with the order of the natural world."

"That makes them much the same as the human defence industry, then," Ingram said. "So perhaps we're abominations too. We do fight to win, Primary. I'm sure you do as well."

It was a complex subject and Nir-Tenbiku wasn't confident that the translation was coping with it. He'd have to explain more carefully. "We do, Captain, and I don't blame teeriks for what the Kugin have made them," he said. "They can be violent and destructive as individuals, but I can't hold them responsible for that either. I blame those who made them that way."

"I understand," Ingram said, nodding. "They're slaves. They don't have a choice."

Nir-Tenbiku wondered if he'd still failed to make himself clear. "Slaves?"

"Most human societies don't have slaves," Ingram said. "Some still do, but most cultures regard it as immoral to treat another human as property and it's banned by law. This is why I'm having difficulty understanding your intentions regarding the teeriks. They're not enslaved here. They're free to do as they please."

Suddenly it all made sense. "Oh, teeriks aren't slaves," he said, then struggled to find a concept that Ingram would understand. "They're not *people*. They've been bred to assist. They're highly intelligent, but they're animals."

Ingram blinked a few times, staring at him. Humans had highly contoured faces and the complexity and mobility of hers distracted him. He didn't know if he'd offended her, shocked her, or just failed to make himself understood again.

"Do you mean actual animals?" she asked. "Pets?"

Nir-Tenbiku wasn't sure what a *pet* was. The word wasn't translated, but *actual animals* seemed clear.

"I think so," he said. "Not people."

"Do you count Kugin as people?"

"They're barbarians, but yes."

"I think I mean something like *hebudi*, then," Ingram said, as if she was uncertain about the pronunciation. "Kugin keep hebudi as companion animals, according to the teeriks. I don't know exactly what a hebudi is, but we'd call them a pet."

Now Nir-Tenbiku was getting somewhere. He'd seen some of the expatriate Kugin carrying long, very slim creatures that looked like exotic fur scarves and fussing over them like they were children.

"Teeriks *work* for people rather than keep them amused," he explained. "I wouldn't describe them as pets, although their owners care a great deal for them."

"Oh. I see. They're working animals, like our dogs, then. The four-legged creatures you saw outside."

"Are they animals?" Nir-Tenbiku had misread that as well. "I thought they were another intelligent species allied with you."

"No, they're animals as well," Ingram said. "They were wild predators that evolved alongside us and we domesticated them. They're highly intelligent, and loved dearly by their owners, but not as intellectually advanced as the teeriks."

At least they now had a common reference point he could work with. "So teeriks are valuable working animals. But not slaves."

Ingram now seemed much more interested in the teeriks than in her potential enemies in Kugad or Dal Mantir. "Do you know where they came from originally?"

"Gan-Pamas tried to ask Lirrel about that, but he didn't know. I don't think anyone does."

"Not even the Kugin?"

"It's not a subject I've ever discussed with them."

"Do you have any contact at all with Kugin?"

"Rarely. There's a small community in Esmos who want to avoid the attention of their government, but we keep ourselves to ourselves out of necessity."

"Thank you for the clarification," Ingram said.

"Have you had problems with your teeriks?"

"Nothing like Lirrel."

"Ah."

"They argue with each other sometimes."

"How long has your base been here?"

"It was built around seventy years ago. I'm not sure what that equates to in your system but the translation will have rendered the time in your units."

Nir-Tenbiku recalled Gan-Pamas's message and how he suspected the humans had been in contact with the runaway commune for some time before they stole the ship. "And how long have you known the teeriks?"

"A relatively short time."

So she wasn't going to tell him. It didn't matter, not for now. He didn't intend to press her on the teerik issue because it wasn't worth alienating her over that when he had a much bigger plan. What did matter was that the Protectorate weren't aware of Opis or the human presence here. The time seemed right to ask her for a favour and see what she required in return.

"I do have a question," he said. "Would you consider renting facilities to us?"

Ingram looked at him for what felt like far too long. Perhaps he'd missed a cue and was expected to say more. Other species' eyes were always the most alien thing about them, and human eyes were no exception. They were almost patterned, with little stripes and flecks in different colours, but what stood out about Ingram's were that she'd stopped blinking. He had no idea what it meant.

"What do you mean by facilities?" she asked.

"An area of land, nothing more," Nir-Tenbiku said. "It could be on the other side of the planet and no inconvenience to you."

"And what would you want to do with this land?"

"Create a temporary base to hide from the Protectorate until we're ready," he said. "They almost certainly know we're based in Esmos, and they daren't target us there, but it's a challenge to keep our fleet hidden."

"Can your vessels land, or would they be parked in orbit?"

"The smaller ones can land. We need somewhere to maintain them and accommodate crews, too."

"So you want to build an operating base."

"We have no ambitions to occupy any of your planet, Captain. Our sole aim is to return to Dal Mantir and reclaim Jatt."

"Actually, I'm more concerned about our neutrality being compromised," Ingram said. "On my homeworld, neutral countries allow both sides in a conflict to enter their territory, provided they abide by that country's laws, and don't carry out hostile acts against each other there, or else they bar both of them."

It wasn't a refusal. It sounded like a question, which meant there was still room for further manoeuvre. Nir-Tenbiku pressed on, encouraged.

"In theory, your neutrality would only be tested if the Protectorate or the Kugin asked for a similar arrangement," he said. "Which I assume hasn't happened, because they're unaware you're here."

"It also assumes they'll respect our laws and recognise our neutrality," Ingram said. "But I understand they won't. Especially as we have their ship."

"And their teeriks."

"Indeed." Ingram showed her teeth again. "If you were me, would you take the risk?"

"There must be something we can offer you in exchange."

Ingram spread her arms a little as if she was indicating the width of the room. "We have a world full of raw materials here."

"Technology, then? Intelligence?"

"We have a source of intelligence on the Protectorate. Can you provide information on Kugad? We already have a comprehensive database of their military capability."

That obviously came from the teeriks, so she'd have all the classified information on the Protectorate as well. Nir-Tenbiku had to buy some time without lying.

"I think we can provide that," he said. "We have loyalists in useful positions. The Protectorate has to stay aware of Kugad's activities, and it's something that'll concern us more as we approach our mission."

"Interesting."

"And if the Protectorate thought we were behind the disappearance of their ship rather than yourselves, it would solve a diplomatic problem if you ever had to have contact with them."

Ingram seemed to be thinking about it. She said nothing for a while, then looked away for a few moments.

"Here's my problem," she said. "Hosting your operating base would put this settlement at risk. I can't think of anything that would justify exposing the civilian population here to more danger. My main concern at the moment is making sure we can repel hostile action, and it doesn't sound as if you can help us with that. Attacks are hypothetical, and Kugad — or the Protectorate — might never trouble us. But we'll deal with them if they do."

Was she asking him if he'd commit forces to defend the base? He had to tread carefully now. The discussion had now exceeded his expectations and Ingram was probably working up to what she wanted from the arrangement.

"We would of course help you in any way we can if you came under attack," Nir-Tenbiku said, hoping he'd guessed right.

There was another long pause. Ingram looked past him for a moment and he realised he'd forgotten about the emanation in the mechanical's body still standing by the door like a guard. If some communication was taking place between Ingram and this Solomon, he couldn't detect it.

"Primary, I'll consider what to do with the ship," she said. "As things stand, there's every reason for me to say no and resume our isolation. I don't disapprove of your cause, but the welfare of Nomad Base is my only concern."

It was the best Nir-Tenbiku could have hoped for after ignoring Ingram's warning not to visit Opis. It didn't sound like an outright refusal, though, so it seemed open to further discussion. There were questions he wanted to ask, such as how humans gathered their intelligence on the Protectorate, but they would have to wait.

"I'm grateful for your forbearance, Captain," he said. "Thank you for being open with me."

"One last thing. If you're ready to take Gan-Pamas home, we've prepared him for repatriation."

Ingram had kept her word. Nir-Tenbiku couldn't tell if it was her way of removing an excuse for him to come back, a tactic to soften him up, or simply that she'd meant what she said about treating the dead with respect. He opted for respect. If he'd misjudged her, he'd pay the price later, but he wanted to trust her, so he did.

"Thank you, Captain," he said. "I'll feel more at peace when he's back with us."

Ingram nodded. "I'll have the coffin brought to your ship. All we've done is keep his remains preserved. We didn't know what might be appropriate for Jattan funeral customs, so if we've done something wrong, it wasn't out of carelessness or disrespect."

"You seem unusually understanding, given what happened to your comrade."

"Gan-Pamas didn't kill Nina Curtis. The teerik did."

"I will find an appropriate way to apologise properly for your loss."

"Ensuring we never engage in conflict again will be enough."

It was an awkward and sudden way to end a meeting of such importance, but Nir-Tenbiku didn't know what human courtesies were on taking leave of someone. The discussion had been short and pointed, but not unfriendly, and he wanted to keep it that way. Ingram walked him outside with Solomon following and they stood on the steps to wait for Marc to bring the vehicle.

"Where are all your people?" Nir-Tenbiku asked, scanning the landscape. He shielded his eyes and tried to sense movement, but the echoes that came back to him showed deserted land.

"Sheltering." Ingram looked up at the sky. The red avian creature Nir-Tenbiku had seen on the probe feed was circling overhead, looking down as if they were prey. It was probably another working animal just like the dogs, then. It looked very much like a teerik in many ways. "We didn't know what to expect when we detected your ships, and we weren't taking any chances."

"I didn't mean to cause alarm. Are you angry?"

"I was initially, but as you said, we're neighbours now and it's better that we find a way to get along. I'm sure we've both collected enough enemies already and we don't need any more."

Nir-Tenbiku still hadn't asked why humans had come here. He didn't know where their homeworld was, but they'd left it to build colonies for a reason that Ingram hadn't volunteered, so perhaps the comment about enemies was a clue. Cudik would complain that he'd come back without essential intelligence, but someone of Ingram's rank would resent being pressured, and Nir-Tenbiku still had more than a glimmer of hope that he might get his operating base here. He had no intention of jeopardising that.

"If you think of anything that your base might need," he said, "my link remains open and I'm ready to talk at any time."

Ingram still seemed perfectly relaxed. "Thank you, Primary."

He decided he liked her, if only because she was unexpectedly easy to talk to, but that might have been due to the emanation improving its Jattan since they'd last spoken. He should have been wary of aliens who seemed so much like Jattans in their outlook, and considered that he'd misinterpreted the superficially familiar, but his instinct said otherwise.

Marc pulled up in the vehicle and aligned the passenger door with the step. Nir-Tenbiku bowed formally to Ingram before he got in, not knowing what else was appropriate. Ingram put her cap on and touched her hand to it in a way that looked like a formal courtesy.

"Safe journey, Primary," she said.

Marc drove off. "Are you sure you can get back to your rendezvous point from here?"

"Yes, once I've linked to *Steadfast*. The course will be recalculated for me and sent to the ship for it to follow."

"*Steadfast*. That's the kind of ship's name the Royal Navy would use. Captain Ingram would approve."

"I didn't mention it to her."

"I'll let her know." Marc glanced in the small mirror mounted on the vehicle's door. "The bearer party's right behind us with your friend's coffin. I'm sorry about the informality, but it's the best we could do."

Humans did seem to apologise a lot, even the ones with considerable status, but it looked more like the confidence of being dominant and able to make the gesture without loss of face. Nir-Tenbiku was learning. He wasn't sure what Marc meant by a bearer party, but when they reached the ship it became clear.

Six uniformed troops got out of the vehicle that was following and carefully lifted a plain box the size of a human, three on each side. They carried it on their shoulders to the open cargo hatch. So the humans used solid shrouds, then, not woven ones, but they did cover the dead. The box was much too big for Gan-Pamas. It was probably what Marc meant by the best they could do, though, and that somehow made it rather touching.

Nir-Tenbiku followed, uncertain but taking the troops' lead. The men walked at a synchronised pace completely unlike the other humans. These people had mechanicals for manual tasks, so carrying the box personally had to be part of a ritual, a theory that was confirmed when they lowered the box onto the deck and stepped back to make that same gesture that Ingram had, a straightened hand held briefly against their brows.

"Will you take him back to Dal Mantir eventually?"

Nir-Tenbiku didn't realise Marc was behind him. "Yes. He's got to return to his ancestors." He'd done his best to keep his grief in check, but now he was close to wailing like a child. "Is that something humans do?"

"Sometimes," Marc said. It was impossible to read the expression on his face this time, but his breathing was a little more rapid. "But sometimes we can't."

"Thank you for the courtesies, General," he said. "This has meant a great deal to me."

"You're welcome. I don't take sides, but I hope Jatt gets its independence. Good luck."

Marc walked to the ship's bow and stood waiting while Nir-Tenbiku boarded and the hatches were sealed. When the drive started up, he walked away.

"*Steadfast*, this is Primary Nir-Tenbiku. Please transmit a recovery course. I'm returning."

The console lit up. Commander Nesh sounded relieved.

"We were worried about the lack of contact, Primary. We would have come to extract you if it had gone on much longer."

"It's as well that you didn't, Commander," Nir-Tenbiku said. He hadn't been gone that long, but they weren't used to him going anywhere without a security detail. "Captain Ingram and I are building trust. Our discussion went well. I'm returning with Gan-Pamas, so stand by to transfer his remains. The humans have been very gracious. Almost Jattan, in fact."

He gestured to the console to lift off. The ship, no longer under his control, followed the trajectory set for it and the sky darkened from blue to black. When the ship acquired its course, Nir-Tenbiku muted the comms and made his way aft to the cargo bay. He could finally grieve for his friend. He stood over the box and put his hand on it.

"Iril, you did your duty. You completed the mission. But it was such a high price." He'd make sure Gan-Pamas was commemorated with a statue when Jatt was liberated. "You're going home, my friend. Now it's up to me to deliver the victory."

Nir-Tenbiku wondered if he was being too optimistic about human cooperation, but the hour he'd spent on Opis had given him enough hope to sustain him. The rightful government of Jatt was no longer completely alone, and Ingram had left many doors open to further talks.

It would be a great pity if the renewed Jatt nation couldn't count humans among their allies one day. These aliens understood the importance of doing things *properly*.

* * *

MAIN BUILDING, NOMAD BASE: TEN MINUTES LATER.

The all-clear siren sounded and Nomad came to life again.

First the civilian vehicles reappeared on the road out of Kill Line, resuming whatever tasks had been interrupted. Then the real-time map showed people on the move around the base again. Ingram had that wrung-out, restless feeling she associated with the end of a battle, when she was still crackling with adrenaline but had nobody left to fight.

She leaned on the rail outside the entrance, watching the icon activity on her screen more for its calming aquarium effect than to see who was where. She hadn't made any progress by talking to Nir-Tenbiku, just rearranged the furniture, and Nomad was now almost as handcuffed to the Jattan opposition as it was to the bloody teeriks. Nir-Tenbiku knew about the base, and if Ingram handed him *Curtis*, the Protectorate would find the ship a lot sooner because they were already keeping an eye on the rebels. Would Nir-Tenbiku keep his mouth shut about Nomad if the worst happened?

Ingram doubted it. There was no reason for him to give a damn what happened to humans, certainly not enough of a damn to put himself at risk for them. But even if she kept the ship, the vulnerability was there already. She thought about Chris's warning. If Nir-Tenbiku's security was lax, he'd effectively drawn a map of where to find Opis, the ship, and the teeriks. A militantly neutral place like Esmos was probably an espionage hub. Just because foreigners didn't dare assassinate their enemies on Esmosi turf, it didn't mean they wouldn't take advantage of having them within easy spying distance.

And for a proud Jattan aristocrat — if that was what he meant by the old families of Jatt — Nir-Tenbiku seemed too deferential. He'd been unusually understanding for someone whose friend had been killed by humans. Perhaps he really was a nice chap who believed in forgiveness, but it was equally possible that he was keeping his powder dry to avenge Gan-Pamas later, having done his recce to see how well-defended Nomad was.

Ingram felt no better for getting Gan-Pamas's body off her hands. There was no proof yet that the Jattans in exile were the good guys. Bissey could well turn out to be right, but hindsight was a luxury she hadn't had at the time and things could easily have gone badly wrong if she'd just kicked Gan-Pamas out with everything he'd discovered. There was no point in dwelling on it. She'd find out now whether Solomon had managed to slip spyware into the Jattans' systems with the navigation data he'd sent them.

"When are you planning to hold the after-action review, Captain?" Solomon appeared at her side. "Everyone's had time to digest the recording."

"You're nagging me, Sol."

"Yes, I am. I can assemble everyone in a meeting room, or you can discuss it on the secure net."

The definition of *everyone* changed according to the subject to be discussed, but for now it was the Gang of Three, Searle, and Alex. They'd been patched into the feed for the meeting and could have prompted Ingram via her earpiece if they'd disagreed with her line of questioning, but inevitably more questions crossed minds after the event. Ingram was now having a military kind of *esprit de l'escalier* moment. There were questions she wished she'd asked and points she should have made, if only to see Nir-Tenbiku's reaction.

"Okay, radio," she said. "Searle's still shadowing the corvette, is he?"

"He is, Captain. He says he's waiting to see *Steadfast* spacefold out of the region in case someone decides to launch a missile on the way out."

"We're such trusting souls. How's your spyware doing?"

"I believe it's managed to transfer itself to *Steadfast* now."

"We're going to hell, aren't we? Nir-Tenbiku seems such a nice chap, but I hope his people don't accept navigation data from everyone they meet."

"I'm amazed he fell for it, to be honest."

"Still, a species that names a warship *Steadfast* must have a touch of the Andrew about it."

"Yes, I thought you'd approve of its Royal Navy flavour."

"Let's crack on, then. I'll take the meeting up top." She checked herself. "Bugger. Cosqui's still with Searle, isn't she?"

"Yes, that might limit his contribution to the discussion," Solomon said. "Unless he listens on a headset and he's careful what he says in her presence."

"Send him a message, Sol. Tell him to take the call in the heads or something."

"That's one solution I hadn't considered."

"Low-tech ways are the best."

Ingram detoured by way of the admin office kitchen to grab a mug of tea, keeping an eye on her screen. One by one the inset images popped up as people logged in. Marc looked like he was still at the temporary landing site, sitting in the rover. Ingram could see the scrubby bushes in the background. It wasn't like him to hang around doing nothing.

"Ah, *General Marc*," she said.

"It's Brigadier Gallagher to you, Boadicea. I knew you'd take the piss about that."

"I told him you were our most experienced soldier. It must be a translation issue."

"Well, he's on his way home now, and he was grateful for how we handled Gan-Pamas. At least he seems to like us more than Tim Pham does. Or he will until he finds out Sol added spyware to the navigation data. You could have told me in advance."

"It was a last-minute decision. I'm sorry." She could see he was annoyed. "Are you alright?"

"I'm fine."

Damn, she was slow on the uptake today. Of course he wasn't fine. He'd just had to watch a repatriation flight. Why couldn't she think these things through beforehand?

"We can open one of my special bottles tonight." It was the first concession she could think of while negotiating the stairs with a full mug in one hand and her screen in the other. "The proper gin."

"What are we celebrating?"

"I don't know. Being alive. Kill Line election results. Making it as far as Tuesday."

But Chris and Trinder came online, then Alex, and the conversation had to wait. Searle was the last to connect. His background showed he was in a cramped compartment that was more like a locker and he didn't appear to be sitting down.

"Brad, are you in the heads?"

"Yes, ma'am." Searle kept his voice down. "And this is why I always left the ship to relieve myself when I was working. No seat and no toilet bowl. I have no idea what Jattans do in here and I don't want to know."

"Hang in there, Commander." Ingram sat down at her desk. "So, gentlemen, how did that go and what have we learned?"

"We're buggered," Marc said. "Another bunch of aliens know where we live and that's another weak link. Even if we give them *Curtis* and tell them to sling their hook."

Ingram wished Marc was a telepath. Then she'd have thought he'd just read her thoughts and agreed with them to back her up. But he wasn't. He was just stating the obvious, and it was depressing to have it confirmed.

"Could have been worse," Trinder said. "Nobody shot anybody and Nir-Tenbiku went away with something he wanted. And he seems big on duty. All the little military touches made him feel at home. Not exactly fitting in with our new-bastards-on-the-block policy, though."

"Yes, thank you for scrambling the bearer party, Dan. Class act." Ingram tried to turn the problem into an advantage the way Marc insisted you always could. "What do we think of our outcast president-not-elect, then?"

"He didn't ask many questions," Chris said. "I'd have been trying to find out our numbers and what hardware we had. And he didn't actually ask for *Curtis*. He kind of hinted. Maybe Jattans are even more oblique than you Brits and we didn't pick up on it."

"Or the translation didn't get the tone of it," Ingram said. "But he wants it. It cost him his friend."

"If they have *Curtis*, they get the blame for the hijacking and look hard-core, but that doesn't help us much. If the opposition gets busted, there's a whole warship-load of Jattans who know where we are and that we're a potential threat to the Protectorate. They'll rat us out the moment they have to. It doesn't make much difference if we keep the ship or not."

"Unless Nir-Tenbiku's going to be a long-term distraction for the Protectorate and Kugad," Searle said. "His guys are going to end up fighting on Dal Mantir. The ship's designed for covert Jattan on Jattan assaults and police actions, and she could be a real pain in everyone's ass if she's used properly. What we need here is directed energy weapons to stop an enemy landing and a few more conventional aircraft to give air support for ground combat if we can't. So we don't need *Curtis*, but we might need Nir-Tenbiku to have her so he can keep the others off our back."

Ingram liked the way Searle thought and almost wished she didn't. "That's an idea."

"What about the teeriks?" Trinder asked.

"Good point. The Protectorate will tell Kugad where Nir-Tenbiku got *Curtis* and they'll come looking for them. So we're screwed on that front too."

"No, I meant what Nir-Tenbiku said about them. That they're basically Dieter's dogs."

"That was freaky," Alex said. "Do we care?"

"The point is do we tell them."

"You think they don't know?"

"I don't think Dieter's dogs see themselves as owned," Trinder said. "They treat him as their pack leader."

"Yeah, but teeriks understand concepts the way we do. Calling them animals might just be an interspecies insult. We should tell them what was said, but it doesn't change how we see them, does it? Tell me it doesn't."

"I'm more interested in how you domesticate an animal into a rocket scientist," Chris said. "It took nature four million years to turn a hominid into Todd Mangel. How did someone do it with teeriks?"

Ingram could imagine Chris as the kid who kept asking awkward questions at the back of the class to piss off an ill-prepared teacher. "Perhaps they started with better raw material," she said.

"Maybe." Chris didn't sound convinced. "But that's still way more than domestication as far as I'm concerned."

"Have we ruled out semantics?" Alex asked. "Swap the word *domestication* with *civilisation* and it might make more sense. Maybe Jattans are snobs. Fred said they think they know it all."

Chris shook his head. "No, Nir-Tenbiku referred to Kugin as people *and* barbarians. So he's not saying animals in the sense of savages. It doesn't look like a translation issue."

"He did confirm Fred's Gan-Pamas translation, though," Alex said. "*Abomination.* So at least we know Fred was levelling with us, if we're still worried about that."

Ingram was replaying the conversation from her own memory, but she'd go through the recording later.

"Nir-Tenbiku said something like there had to be limits on interfering with the order of the natural world," she said. "If he thinks teeriks are just working animals, he might mean we shouldn't treat them like humans. A warning about anthropomorphism."

"Look, it's not going to change how we treat them, so can we save this for a pub quiz and worry about security?" Marc asked. "Evacuating *Elcano* just became a bit more urgent. We need to discuss dates with Lawson."

"Nothing's changed," Ingram said. "We delay it so that it takes a plausible transit time that fits the FTL drive Lawson thinks we've got. When he tells us he's fixed accommodation for them, he gives us the time and location, and we back-time from there. What's a regular FTL trip to Earth, then, four weeks? Five?"

"Twenty-five days," Searle said. "According to Cosqui."

Marc moved out of shot. He must have stood his screen on the dash and leaned back in his seat. "Okay, I'll press him. Anyone disagree with me telling him what was discussed with Nir-Tenbiku?"

Chris shrugged. "No point in hiding it now. He might even have some foreign policy tips."

"The first rule of which is what's in it for us," Ingram said. "If Nir-Tenbiku can provide intel on the Kugin, that might make it worth having an arrangement with them."

"Enough to risk letting them have a base here?" Trinder was always the sceptic, not as contrary as Chris but likely to want to wait and see. "They could be here for decades. This revolution hasn't moved fast so far. They might bring all their relatives and buddies too. But how do we know they're not just three guys and a dog? The Protectorate doesn't seem to have shut them down yet, so they're either amazing ninjas evading Jatt's finest or they're hobby guerrillas the Protectorate can safely ignore."

"Yeah, that question needed asking," Marc said. "How many times have we seen that on Earth? Just because Nir-Tenbiku's an alien, it doesn't mean he's not a conman looking for someone to bleed dry. Fund us or the bad guys will attack you next. You know the scam."

Ingram knew Nir-Tenbiku would contact her again at some point. She'd pin down a few more things then. "Let's see how long he takes to come back to me and ask if I've made a decision about *Curtis*," she said. "If I contact him first, he'll think he's hooked us and he'll get what he asked for. We do need to know what the Kugin are doing, though."

"So we do what we've done at Dal Mantir," Chris said. "Sol hacks into their system and we listen."

"Or my spyware manages to overhear what the opposition hears," Sol said.

"But we've had surveillance in place for weeks now and we haven't learned anything about what the Protectorate's doing to find *Curtis*," Trinder said. "It's not a perfect solution."

"No espionage is."

"I don't think we've missed anything, Major," Solomon said. He sounded defensive. "Perhaps we're not intercepting the right channel. But I'm making further inroads into everyone's comms now."

"And I suspect what we're picking up from the Protectorate might be more useful to Nir-Tenbiku than it is to us," Marc said.

Ingram was sure the Protectorate wouldn't have given up looking for the ship and the Kugin hadn't lost interest in recovering their renegade teeriks. She knew she was attributing human reactions to aliens, but even if Fred's assessment was wrong, she'd now gained some insight into Jattan psychology, and she could see they were persistent if nothing else. The opposition had been planning to retake Jatt for years, and Nir-Tenbiku didn't take no for an answer either. That didn't necessarily mean that they succeeded, though. Maybe Jattans were all talk, which was a lot closer to Fred's assessment of them.

"Could we stop them if they showed up with a bunch of Jattan hard hats and started breaking ground?" Chris asked. "We've got complete satellite coverage of Opis, but we had all that on Earth once, and we still didn't see every square foot of the surface. We kept finding new species, too. If Nir-Tenbiku showed up on the opposite side of the planet, we might not even know."

"The question is whether Kugad or the Protectorate would know," Ingram said.

Searle rustled and scraped as he tried to find a more comfortable position in the heads. "We could stop Nir-Tenbiku. Remember that Cosqui says the Protectorate thinks he's only got ten ships, which is serious opposition for us, but nothing to the Kugin or the Protectorate. It would mean a shooting war here, though, and we don't know who else is backing him and might come after us."

"If they've got backers, they've done sod all for them so far," Marc said. "But they're not going to fight the war with ships. They'll need to create an insurgency, if only because they can't go in and flatten

Jatt without a lot of collateral damage to people they're relying on for support. 'There, we've freed you, sorry about your gran.' Hard to sell that."

"But it isn't our problem until they make it our problem," Chris said. "Wait and see. In the meantime, we go ahead with what we've already planned and scope out the alternatives for getting intel on Kugad's intentions."

"Yeah, I hate to sound unadventurous, but unless there's some advantage for us, there's no point in discussing concessions with them," Trinder said. "Which is pretty much what you told him, Captain. But he did say that if there's anything we need, you should call him. I'm going to give that some thought."

Ingram rubbed her eyes. It was nearly 1500 hours but it felt like the middle of the night. "Okay, let's wrap this up and carry on as we were."

"We're going to hang around out here after *Steadfast*'s clear," Searle said. "Just to test *Curtis* and see what we might be letting go. We'll bring her back in time for the election results."

"Twenty hundred," Chris said. "Doesn't take long to count in a small town. Apparently we've got some fireworks, courtesy of Ainatio's chemists."

"Those fireworks better not be a bloody bomb," Marc said. "We're still on Boffinworld's bugger-about list."

The inset images on Ingram's screen switched off one by one as the team logged off and left her nursing half a cup of lukewarm tea. Life went on now, no matter how many history-changing events happened. The extraordinary was so commonplace here that she'd finally become immune to it. She looked for Marc's radio signal, which already showed him in the vehicle compound, so he was probably dropping off the rover. Then the tracker moved towards the main building and she could see he was heading her way. It took him longer than she expected to reach the office, but when he walked in he was carrying a couple of mugs of tea.

"I'm so hen-pecked," he said, putting one on her desk and pulling up a chair. "Are we going to send Lawson the recording, then?"

"My gut says no, but my brain says there's no reason not to, because we might be charcoal this time next week and someone's got to arm Earth with the intel. It's at the stage now where he's the one who has to make the decision about who else he involves."

"Yeah. Okay. I was daft to think we could decide what's best for Earth. It's one thing trying to hide Nomad, but the whole alien thing is too big, like Chris kept saying. Any dream people had of starting from scratch without any interference from Earth is probably over."

Ingram sipped her tea. Marc never put enough milk in it but she wasn't going to tell him. "Just remember it's Fred's doing."

"Look on the bright side. It saved us from agonising over making the decision."

"I'm glad you're back in one piece, by the way. Awkward boarding."

"That obvious, eh?"

"Only to me."

"It's not that I'm afraid of dying. It's how I die that I worry about." Marc looked at his watch, then took out his screen. "But I did it and I can do it again. Look, Lawson's going to be calling me back in a few minutes. We'd better have that file ready to send. Sol, can you sort that, please?"

"Certainly, Marc."

"Are you coming with me to the Kill Line event tonight?" Ingram asked. "Congratulate the new mayor and all that."

"There's beer and a barbecue on the green, and Doug's going to be re-elected. Of course I'm coming. And I don't think Howie's ever seen fireworks before."

"We're going to enforce normal Western life here if it's the last thing we do, aren't we?"

"That's the whole point of coming here. A little bit of England."

"And a lot of America."

"When we finally decide to go our separate cultural ways, which I think we will, I'm going to found a new town called —" Lawson's call came in and cut Marc off in mid-declaration. "Before I answer, are you in or not?"

"I'm in. Can't avoid him, really."

Marc put the call on speaker and sat back. They still hadn't progressed to video calls, but Ingram understood Marc's need to play as many of his cards as close to his chest as he could without any visible tells when he was bluffing.

"Guy, how are you?" he said. "Thanks for getting back to me. First things first — we'd like to firm up a date for *Elcano*. It's going to take us twenty-five days to get her there. One reason we want to press on with it is related to this recording I'm going to send you now. We had an unexpected visit from some of the aliens earlier today. All very polite, a nice diplomatic chat, but we're becoming less of a secret out here."

"Good grief," Lawson said. "Corvid aliens?"

"No, the eel-headed ones."

"Oh, of course." At least Lawson had a sense of humour. "Eels."

"With legs. Sending now."

There was a long silence, at least a couple of minutes. Marc just stared up at the ceiling. Then Ingram heard a quiet "Oh..."

"Guy, are you watching the recording?" Marc asked.

"Dear God, they really do have faces like eels."

"Okay. I'll let you finish digesting the content."

Ingram could hear the audio of the meeting with Nir-Tenbiku in the background. Listening to herself, she thought she hadn't done too bad a job under the circumstances. The Foreign Office certainly couldn't have done any better. Eventually, Lawson spoke.

"Quite extraordinary," he said. "Putting monumental culture shock to one side, I think the experts are going to be shocked that you can hold complex conversations with these people. Not the language — I mean the shared concepts. There seems to be a lot of common ground. Of course, that might mean there's a lot of ground to fight about as well, but I suspect this is a situation where common sense beats academic overthinking when it comes to first contact."

"Well, not exactly our first contact with Jattans," Marc said. "Just our first non-violent one."

"Ah, yes. Gan-Pamas. One of their ministers."

"Could have been a war. Wasn't."

"Are the teeriks really animals?"

"I don't think so. And even if they are, technically speaking, they can still do sums that baffle our PhDs and speak English fluently, so we treat them as equals."

"And the opposition, if we call them that for now, have offered mining concessions and other benefits for your support."

"If they win. We don't need it, but you never know how handy that might be in the future."

"I'm glad we're on the same page."

Ingram never underestimated Marc, but sometimes she was surprised to see just how politically astute he could be. She'd definitely found the right man. He knew the score.

"We just had a wash-up and we're not ready to let Nir-Tenbiku put a base here," Marc said. "If we let him have the stolen ship, which isn't much use for defending Nomad, it's more likely the Protectorate are going to spot it and use the intel to locate us. But it'd also help him hit them hard so they're too busy with him to look for us. We need to find out whether he's got the resources to take back Jatt or if the opposition's just a bunch of washed-up ex-pats holding court in a bar."

"You're doing everything I'd do, Marc."

"Anyway, our priorities are to defend this settlement and make sure Earth's location remains secret."

"Any other data you can give me?"

Marc glanced at Ingram. She mouthed *not yet* at him.

"It's piecemeal stuff, but we'll collate what we've acquired from a little basic espionage," Marc said.

"I wish I could offer professional support, Marc, but I don't think anyone here could do a better job than you are right now. But I suspect we're at the stage where I need to brief a minister about the existence of aliens. I'm not looking forward to that."

"Yeah. Had to happen."

"Are aliens all as reasonable and cultured as the teeriks and the Jattans?"

"Apparently some are and some aren't, but we're ready for that."

"I'll firm up the plans for your evacuees. I'll take a guess that it's going to be at least another month before we can receive them."

Marc looked like he was calculating. "Remember that we switch to a new calendar at the New Year, which will be later than your New Year, so factor that in when we talk specific dates. You're already running days ahead of us."

"Will do. My, this is quite the time to be alive. Do you still require information relating to Corporal Cho?"

"I certainly do."

"We've acquired building plans that might be a little out of date by now. We're trying to find current ones, but I think you'll still find it useful."

"Appreciate it," Marc said. "Thank you."

"I still hope I'll have the chance to visit Nomad."

"Let's hope Nomad is still here to visit. But we're not doing too badly. The town's holding its first elections today, so things are taking shape. American barbecue and everything."

"I'll come back to you with arrangements for *Elcano*. Enjoy your barbecue."

Marc looked pleased with himself as he ended the call. Ingram leaned back in her chair.

"Don't let me get in the way of your bromance," she said.

"He's okay. Unflappable. I can do business with a bloke who doesn't piss his pants when he sees a two-legged talking eel in a Swiss admiral's uniform having a chat with the Butcher of Calais."

"He'll be interested in the mining concessions."

"He'll be interested in mining here, too. I think we're just going to have to find a balance along the way. We can't stop anyone building a ship and coming here now, not without a small war, so we might as well roll with it. Don't try to make sense of it. Just live it."

"I should stop him encouraging you to rescue Cho."

"I'm the one who needs to do it. Humour me."

"Is this our natural pause to get our breath back before the next embuggerance?"

"Whatever it is, we grab it." Marc stood up and stretched. "You know what, I've got nothing more important to do for the rest of the day, so I'm going to collect Howie from the mad scientist, make him a snack, pour myself a beer, and have a nice old man's nap. Come and get us when you're ready to see Doug proclaimed emperor. That's what we crave, really. A wise old emperor."

"Leave at nineteen-thirty?"

"Yeah. Catch you later."

The remains of the afternoon looked painfully dull after the adrenaline rush. None of Ingram's problems had been solved, but she felt like they'd shrunk a little by being discussed with Earth. She'd always assumed she was happier when she was answerable to nobody, but her reality was far less autocratic. Making decisions in tough situations with no time to debate was easy. Having some latitude and a range of options created complications, and the awareness of what she didn't excel at and who would be affected by her actions. She'd been a little hurt when Solomon had effectively told her her ego was too big and bullet-proof for her to feel demeaned when she needed to admit she'd made a mistake, but he was right.

So was Bissey, perhaps. Maybe they really had killed a Jattan saint. But Nina Curtis was still dead, and her friends had to live with that for the rest of their lives. They weren't going to be comfortable with forgiving the Jattans. It was another group she had to add to the Venn diagram of alienated stake-holders.

"I'm always going to be at war," she said to herself. "I am, aren't I?"

Nina Curtis played on her mind as she walked home. It was the first time she'd thought about how the killing had affected Marc and Chris — especially Chris, even if she didn't like the man. She hadn't heard either of them discuss it. It was one thing to hear terrible news and quite another to witness the event.

Howie was watching a movie with Marc when she got back and the table was covered with diagrams drawn on pieces of paper. It looked like Howie had been trying to explain one of Mangel's experiments.

"Did you have a good day off, Howie?"

"It was great." He seemed very happy. "And Reverend Berry came to the bomb shelter and told us what he did before he found Jesus."

"Oh." Ingram felt a twinge of dread. "Was he in marketing?"

"No, he owned a repair shop. He shot someone. He went to prison."

Ingram did her best not to react. She caught Marc's eye and saw the carefully raised eyebrow.

"Well, we've both done it, sweetheart, me and Marc," she said. "He must have had a reason. He's not a bad person."

"Have you done it? I mean, right up close? Not missiles and bombs?"

"Yes. I shot a chap trying to board my ship. Back then, the enemy sent volunteers infected with deadly diseases to try to spread them."

"That's okay. He was going to die anyway, wasn't he?"

"Damn straight," Marc said, looking like he was trying not to laugh.

Ingram was worried that Howie was now exposed to seeing killing as commonplace and without legal consequences. He wouldn't think the two people taking care of him were bad, so he'd adjust his view of the act. But then she thought about what he must have seen in a collapsing society, and it was a miracle that he'd emerged as kind and sensible as he had, even if he had his odd moments.

"Time to hit the town soon," Marc said. "Get yourself spruced up, Howie." He waited for Howie to troop out and close the bedroom door behind him. "Bridget, I'm not passing judgement on the vicar. Neither of us can."

"You called me Bridget." It sounded strange to hear her own name. "You never call me Bridget."

"You asked me to, remember?"

"I did. Anyway, you're right. We can't cast the first stone, or even the second one."

"Every saint has a past and every sinner has a future. Or words to that effect."

"Ah, Oscar Wilde. You're a constant source of surprises."

"I did go to school, you know. I wasn't feral."

"I don't care if you were. I think you're wonderful."

"You're not so bad yourself. Let's go and play at being a normal family for the evening. Just once. We can do this."

Ingram never thought she'd hear him say that even as a joke. It was progress, another step towards resuming his life after years of something akin to a walking cryo state. She rummaged in her drawer for the few civilian clothes she'd brought with her and pulled out suitably scruffy pants and a sweatshirt, items she wore so rarely that they counted as dressing up for the occasion. She even unpinned her hair and mussed it up a bit until the mirror reassured her she looked about right for the school run. It wouldn't stop anyone treating her as the commanding officer, but it wasn't for others. It was a reminder for herself. There was a life to be led that wasn't all duty and she was long overdue her crack at it, if only for today.

"I'm ready." Ingram found Marc sitting on the front doorstep with Betsy. Howie was attempting handstands on the strip of lawn out front. "I want candy floss and a very large gin."

Marc said nothing but held up a hydration bladder and a couple of foldable cups. Ingram squeezed the pack.

"That better not be water."

"On some planets it might be. And it cost me some fish."

"No slurpy pipe?"

"It's dead common to swig from the pack."

"But I feel common tonight, and I like it."

"Oh good. Off we trot, then."

It was still light when they strolled up the road to the centre of Kill Line and joined the crowd outside the town hall, but dusk fell fast, and the square soon became a brightly-lit street party full of noise and intriguing food aromas that made Betsy sniff the air. Dave Flores and Jared were handing out beer and punch. The last time Ingram had been to a gathering with civilian neighbours was at the village fair back home in Somerset, but she'd been the celebrated daughter of the dynasty who owned the big estate, and that wasn't quite the same as getting drunk with people who didn't care or even know about her social standing.

She wasn't the only one trying to reinvent herself tonight. She spotted Chris, hand in hand with Ash, but still looking like he was playing poker. Annis Kim was hanging out with Alex, although that seemed to have been on the cards for a while, and Haine was here as well. He hadn't been joking, then — he really was stepping out with the woman who made cheese. Ingram wasn't sure how she'd managed to miss that and why Solomon hadn't mentioned it, but it was good news. The poor bugger deserved to be genuinely happy rather than just putting a brave face on things. And she could now rib him mercilessly.

There was a lot to be said for having to get along with people and forgetting what you'd been in your previous life. But the benchmark of Kill Line seemed to be the catalyst, the example set by people who'd never experienced the worst of the decline and who still lived like any rural backwater community. Ingram knew that the idyllic image of village life was misleading and it had its darker side of constant scrutiny and nowhere to hide, but for people who'd lived through civil war and perpetual chaos, it helped to recalibrate their humanity.

Mrs Alvarez finally walked out onto the broad top step outside the town hall doors. The public address system chimed to call for quiet for the results.

"Should have had bets on this," Marc said, taking a glass of punch from a table and dividing it between the two cups. He dosed them with whatever was in the hydration bladder. "We might have a shock result. Did you remember to bring the Swingometer?"

Ingram sipped the impromptu cocktail. "What's in this?"

"Andy Braithwaite's Old Paralyser. Kills all intestinal parasites."

Mrs Alvarez didn't go through the election litany Ingram expected. But there were no political parties, no spoiled ballots, no lost deposits, or any of the other statistics that made up a returning officer's announcement. Doug Brandt was re-elected, Dieter became sheriff as the only candidate on the paper, and Jared and Jeanie were declared the official representatives for Convoy Ward. It was a bit of an anticlimax.

"I love democracy," she said, holding out her cup for another shot of gin. "In a hundred years, it'll be all arguments about boundaries, five parties, bribes, scandals, demands for recounts, and joke candidates dressed as bananas."

"Yeah, this is the best time to be alive, while it's still on a manageable scale," Marc said. "Can I complain to Jared about the bins yet? Seems rude not to."

The party gradually migrated to the barbecue on the green, which seemed to be the main point of the evening because nobody had come to be surprised by the results. Perhaps this would erode a few more clan boundaries between the townsfolk, Ainatio, and *Cabot.* Ingram was hopeful: the barbecue was open to everybody and she was surprised to see so many Ainatio staff joining in, including Paul Cotton and Lianne Maybury. If Old Misery Guts was here with his wife, he wasn't likely to misbehave. Ingram hoped it indicated a thaw in relations and joined the queue for hot dogs and candy floss.

A rocket burst overhead in a shower of purple and green. Betsy, sticking close to Howie, seemed unmoved by the bangs and strange noises. Howie was discovering candy floss for the first time, and it was rather touching to see him tear strands off for the dog. With a drink in her hand and a few already under her belt, Ingram felt all could be right with the world, even this world, and things could be right for her as well. She put her arm through Marc's and squeezed. He gave her an indulgent smile. He seemed to have forgiven her for not mentioning the spyware.

"I hope Rikayl's okay," she said. "Is he indoors?"

"I hope so." Marc wolfed down his hot dog. Howie separated his into roll and frankfurter to eat separately. "He'll just try to catch the rockets." Marc pointed across the grass. "Look, Fred's grandsons. God knows what the teeriks make of this. They must think we're mad."

The two young teeriks were gazing at the display like human kids. As the rockets died away, *Curtis* appeared, flanked by the Lammergeiers, and somehow they'd tweaked their navigation and landing lights to display non-standard colours. *Curtis* had few lights compared to an aircraft, but she swept the ground with blue and red searchlights, and the Lammergeiers put on an even more vivid show with the rotor safety lights cycling through the spectrum and drawing hoops of brilliant colour. Considering none of the pilots had been trained for displays or even rehearsed much, it was rather good.

"It's a shame that Earth can't see this," Marc said. "Humans, trillions of miles from home, doing daft human stuff and entertaining the local aliens. I'm not big on hope as a rule, but this makes me think we're not doomed to fuck up everything wherever we go."

"If we go to war, at least we'll look fabulous doing it," Ingram said. "Gosh, I'm getting completely bladdered. Remind me to apologise to Andy for disparaging his distilling skills."

"You're hilarious when you're paralytic. Keep going."

"What's paralytic?" Howie asked.

"Drunk," Marc said.

"I'm going to have the find the heads." Ingram handed Marc her cup. "Hold my punch."

The nearest lavatories were in the main building. It was a long walk on a full tank of gin. When she checked herself in the mirror after washing her hands, she looked the way she had on runs ashore in her midshipman days, flushed and unkempt, like she'd reclaimed some of her youth along with her second chance at happiness. As she made her way carefully through the crowd on the return leg, someone tapped her lightly on the shoulder. She turned to see Peter Bissey.

"Hi Peter," she said, expecting the worst. "Are you having a good time?"

"Yes, it's nice to have an excuse to let our hair down," he said. "May I have five minutes? I'm not going to harangue you."

"Yes, of course. Go ahead." She walked to a clearing in the crowd for a little quiet. "What is it?"

"There's something I'd like you to consider."

"I'll try."

"You met the Jattan opposition today."

"Indeed."

"And it seems to have passed off without incident. Which is quite something, all things considered."

Oh God, here we go. "We had an interesting chat," Ingram said. "We might talk again sometime. But yeah, we're not killing each other now."

"Well, I'd like do something to foster good relations between marbidar and humans. I said at the time that we didn't know if the opposition were the good guys, and we still don't, but if there's a chance to develop links, we should take it. I'd like to be that link."

Ingram felt herself sober up fast and she didn't want to. "You know what I'm going to ask, don't you?"

"Am I going to make excuses and blame you for Gan-Pamas's death? No. Am I going to be a security risk because I might give them Earth's location? I don't intend to tell them anything. Is it worth having at least one alien faction on our side? I hope so. If they turn out to be people we can live alongside and do business with, I was hoping you'd agree to me becoming an ambassador to them. If we're still serious about being independent, with all that goes with it, then this is where we take those first steps. Or are we handing it all over to the Foreign Office now?"

Ingram had relied on this man's judgement in some tight spots and she couldn't dismiss his suggestion out of hand. "It's early days. We've only just started working out the impact this'll have on us and on Earth, and there's a lot more intelligence-gathering to be done first."

"Will you at least think about it in the longer term?"

"Yes," she said. "I'll give it some consideration."

"Thank you."

"You're welcome. Enjoy the evening."

Ingram made her way back to Marc and Howie. Marc frowned at her.

"Bugger, you look like you've sobered up," he said. He handed back the cup. "Here, get those blood alcohol levels up to an unhealthy saturation STAT."

"Peter wanted a word."

"Oh. Do I need to go and punch him out?"

"No. It was perfectly civil. I'll tell you later. I want to enjoy the evening now."

Braithwaite's Old Paralyser couldn't erase everything, but it did its best. Ingram knew she'd have a monster hangover in the morning and didn't care. As long as she didn't make a fool of herself, the pain would be worth it, so she played football with Howie against Marc and Hiyashi, using an inflated plastic bag for a ball. Marc was definitely holding back. She wouldn't have stood a chance otherwise, especially in the dark. When they finally exhausted themselves and stood gasping for breath, Betsy appeared out of nowhere and seized the inflated bag before running off with it.

"That dog's my mum," Marc said. "She's telling me to sober up or I'll regret this in the morning."

"I'll go get the ball," Howie said.

She wouldn't have gone far. If that dog had been human, Ingram would have given her a position of responsibility. Maybe she should have done that anyway. Betsy always knew where she needed to be and seemed to understand what needed doing even if the humans around her didn't. Ingram had been wary of her to start with because of her breed and background, but she'd proved to be very protective of Howie and generally a sociable dog. Ingram could see her trotting towards the main building, but then she stopped next to a group of Ainatio staff sitting on the grass with drinks, and looked back as if she was waiting for Howie to catch up. Ingram trailed behind. She couldn't outrun an arthritic slug in this condition, and she was only chasing to get the ball before Marc.

Howie caught up with Betsy and held out his hand to the dog to persuade her to give him the bag. One of the men — Duncan something, a guy from Hydroponics whose surname Ingram had memorised and forgotten — looked around at the pair and said something to them. He didn't look angry or hostile to her, but whatever he said upset Howie, because the kid planted both feet as if he was squaring up for a fight. Duncan looked annoyed and said something.

"You take that back!" Howie said, then swung a punch and hit him in the shoulder. Duncan jumped to his feet as if he was going to go for him, but Betsy dived between them and sank her teeth in his forearm. There was no barking, no growling, and no warning. She just hung on even though he was yelling and hitting her to try to get her off. She was acting more like a police dog than attacking him. If it hadn't been such a bloody awful situation, Ingram would have been impressed.

But there'd be hell to pay now. The protest punch-up hadn't been forgotten yet.

It only took a few seconds, as these things always did, but Ingram felt she'd run miles to try to reach the fracas and stop it escalating before Marc showed up. She didn't make it. Marc overtook her like a train and pulled Howie out of the way.

Betsy still hung on. Marc passed Howie to Ingram and stepped between them and Duncan, who was still making a lot of noise and trying to pull free from Betsy. None of his chums were helping him. They just stood back.

"Stand still and shut up," Marc said. "You're just making her lock on harder. Betsy, leave. Drop him, Betsy. Come on, leave him. Good girl, you got him. You can let go now."

Betsy obliged and backed away. Duncan looked shocked. Ingram had no idea what Marc was going to do next but he had his death face on, and she couldn't stand back and watch if she was going to have any credibility as a commander now.

Duncan nursed his arm. "That animal's got to be put down. And you can't even keep your brat under control."

"Duncan —" Ingram began. But Marc held his arm out to block her and half-turned his head, presumably to keep Duncan in his peripheral vision.

"Captain, could you look after Howie, please, and call Dr Mendoza? I'll deal with this."

Ingram knew when to defer to Marc. Howie still had his fists balled as if he was looking to get back into the fray. Marc took a couple more steps and stood close enough for Duncan to lash out, and perhaps that was what he wanted, an excuse to thump him. Tev and Chris had turned up now, though, and Ingram could see the situation going downhill. If Duncan tried to take on Marc, he'd be taking on the other two as well. She hoped he realised the dynamics of getting into a fight with soldiers.

"Mate, I don't care who said what and who started it," Marc said calmly. "You're a grown man. Grown men don't get into rucks with kids. The dog went for you because you made an aggressive move. If she'd been trying to kill you, she wouldn't have grabbed your arm. So calm down and wait for the doc."

"You can fuck right off." Duncan looked shocked and in pain. "The dog's got to go. Look what it's done to me. And that kid's crazy. If you don't sort him out, he'll turn into a thug. And we don't need any more of those."

"I said this wasn't a debate, didn't I? Nobody touches the dog. And you won't ever — *ever* — come within ten yards of Howie again. Do you understand?"

"Or what?"

"Or you deal with me. Same goes for everyone."

"You can't keep doing this shit and getting away with it," Duncan said. "Rules are only for the rest of us, yeah? But you go where you like, do what you like, with no consequences."

"Yeah, makes a fucking change, doesn't it? If you want to settle your list of grievances, we can do it privately."

It was Marc who wanted to settle it, though. Ingram knew him well enough to spot when he wanted to let rip and needed an excuse. There was an awful ten seconds of silence, but Mendoza appeared and that seemed to completely defuse things. Marc just walked away, put his arm around Ingram's shoulders, took Howie's hand, and steered them back towards the centre of the green. Tev and Chris looked expectantly at him, but he shook his head and carried on. He didn't need backup.

"I hope no bugger's nicked our cups," he said. "Come on, Betsy. Let's get you some hotdogs as a reward. Who's a good brave girl? Did that tosser hurt you? We'll get you checked out."

"I take it neither of you want to talk about this now," Ingram said.

"No, I want to eat, drink, and party."

"I'm sorry," Howie said. He sounded tearful now. "But he said something awful about you and I told him to take it back, but then he said worse."

"He was drunk, Howie. But his opinion doesn't count for anything anyway. I'll teach you how to avoid wasting your energy on nobodies. I wish it hadn't happened, mate, but you're *not* a bad person, and you were only doing what men do, defending your family."

Now the adrenaline was draining away, Ingram felt embarrassed, awkward, and also rather proud of Marc. He was very good at controlling a situation. Even if she felt she should have taken the lead, it would have made matters worse and turned it into a battle over her authority again instead of a personal spat. But it was clear that the grievances were going to continue and Marc had become their demonic icon of Britain taking over the mission for its own ends while they had to do as they were told.

The two cups were exactly where Marc had left them on the trestle table next to the candy floss machine, a measure of how much people didn't want to incur his displeasure. But Ingram didn't feel like drinking now. She sat cross-legged on the grass to watch the moon and realised she paid almost no attention to it at all these days because her brain had labelled it as interchangeable with Earth's, and therefore not much use to her, a rock with some interesting coloured streaks like a displaced chunk of Alum Bay. If Nir-Tenbiku had the technology and the budget to make it suitable for a base, he could have moved in and never troubled Nomad.

Yes, her problem list was quite spectacular now.

Dieter showed up. "What did they do to my girl?" He'd obviously just heard what had happened with Betsy. Marc was still feeding her hot dogs. "I swear I'll have that asshole if he's hurt her."

Marc gave Betsy a cuddle with both arms and blew a raspberry on the top of her head. There was something touching about a tough man making a fuss of an equally tough dog like she was a tiny Yorkie.

"She's okay," Marc said. "What a clever girl. She did it by the book. Did you train her to bite and hold? I never did ask you when you mentioned it."

"No, she already knew." Dieter looked her over and she basked in the attention. "I'm guessing, but I think that was her speciality in her narcotics career. She was there to intimidate wayward dealers without permanent damage. Because you can't pay up with your throat ripped out."

Of course Dieter would worry about her. He'd hadn't got over Girlie's death. Duncan was lucky that Marc was the one who intervened and not Dieter. And Dieter was now the official sheriff of Kill Line. That was going to make things interesting.

"Is that your official badge?" Ingram asked, getting to her feet.

It was a child's button badge with I AM FIVE in cheery orange letters. Dieter tucked his chin in to look down at it.

"It was all they could find. Who needs a gold star anyway? I'm good with this."

"Where does your jurisdiction end?"

"Is Kill Line separate? This is where it's going to get interesting."

"We need to cover the whole base. It's a good place to start the discussion on a common set of laws here."

Marc grumbled in the back of this throat. "Seeing as you've sobered up, Boadicea, it's time to go home. Howie needs his beauty sleep. So do I. I've had a pig of a day."

"Yeah, better let the dust settle before I expand my police state into the Ainatio section," Dieter said. "Goodnight, you troublemakers."

They walked back home with Betsy on point, talking about anything but the scrap with Duncan. That would come later. Howie got ready for bed and Marc sat talking to him for a while in his room. Ingram could hear snippets of the conversation, which wasn't a kindly dressing down but advice on dealing with difficult adults.

"Your heart's in the right place," Marc was saying. It verged on approval for slugging Duncan. "You're not a brat and you're not out of control. You're just a lad. You've got to learn a few different ways to handle morons, and that's what growing up is about."

"Please don't let them put Betsy down. It was my fault."

"Nobody's laying a hand on Betsy. Or you. They'll have to go through me to do that. Now get some sleep. Betsy's guarding your door."

Ingram went outside and sat on the doorstep to wait for Marc to join her and pick over the debris of the day out of Howie's earshot. He emerged with two mugs of tea, wearing his sheepskin jacket as if he was going to head out somewhere.

"You're not cold, are you?" Ingram asked.

Marc turned up his collar. It was a lovely jacket, dark brown leather sheepskin, not the usual suede finish. "No. Marty made these coats for me, Chris, and Dan as a thank you for staying with the civvies. I ought to wear it more."

"You three are going to look like Bomber Command when you're all out together."

"Yeah. We can gaze nobly at the horizon, waiting for the last Lancaster to come home." He let out a long sigh. "Well, tonight was a total shambles. I don't think we'll get many Ainatio Christmas cards now."

"I'm worried about Howie."

"He's fine."

"He's not fine. He got in a physical fight with an adult."

"Did you grow up with brothers?"

"No. You know I didn't."

"Exactly. He's a ten-year-old boy and boys get in fights. It's not a failing, it's how we're made. All male mammals do it. We're hardwired to fight and risk our lives for women and children, and you can't educate us out of it, whatever some high-minded peacenik thinks."

Ingram got the feeling she'd been filed under *high-minded*. "Does he realise it's wrong?"

"But it's not wrong. It was a bad idea in this particular case, and he was lucky it was only Duncan McWeakling and that Betsy had his back, but in principle he was standing up for others."

"So we let him get on with it."

"Yes, we do. Or I do. He's my responsibility and I owe it to him to raise a man."

Ouch. "Howie's been orphaned in the worst possible way and he's been uprooted and terrified God knows how many times. This is his trauma coming out."

"I don't think so. His clinginess and obsession with being helpful is, though."

Marc had brought up two sons, and she hadn't. He also had a point about her disdain for physical violence that somehow didn't extend to her own service. It didn't make her feel any less worried about Howie, though.

"Anyway," Marc said, "what did Bissey want?"

"He wants to be the liaison if we get pally with Nir-Tenbiku. An ambassador. He's volunteered to go to Esmos. You floated that idea at a meeting, I think. Have you spoken to him about it?"

"Not a bloody word. I'd have told you." Marc sounded offended. He examined his jacket's leather buttons with the critical eye of a watchmaker. "And how long do you think it'll be before someone gets Earth's location out of him?"

"We did touch on that."

"And?"

"I didn't have to make a decision, and it might never happen, so I left it at that."

"Maybe it *is* his calling. So where are we on all our other woes and clusterfucks?"

Ingram struggled to put them in order, but it felt like at least part of the alien problem had dropped down the list. "We've got a lot of work to do regaining the trust of the Ainatio staff," she said. "I should have been the one to sort Duncan out, but on balance, it would have been worse and made it an official war with them. Is that why you stepped in?"

"Did you stand back because it was less contentious to let me have a go at him?"

Ingram had to think about that. "Sorry, I realise I do that. But you did gesture at me to keep out of it. I suppose I ought to check how Duncan is."

"Jake Mendoza already messaged me. It's a single bite, no tearing or complicated damage. It's not like Betsy was savaging him. She just held on to his arm the only way she could."

"Oh, that's all right, then."

"Yes. It is. She's a dog. Which, incidentally, is what Duncan called you. Do you want to send him flowers to speed his recovery?"

Howie had only mentioned Duncan bad-mouthing Marc. Perhaps he didn't understand the insult about her. "Ah, the sparkling repartee of Nomad's cafe society."

"He'd have got a lot worse than a bite and a punch in the shoulder if I'd heard him. Would you have been worried about my mental state?"

Ingram tried to stop herself imagining what had offended Howie that much. "You're an adult. But you don't have to labour the point."

"Good. Leave me to deal with it. Now, change the subject. We've got bigger problems to keep us busy."

"Okay, at least Kill Line's sorted," Ingram said. She felt she'd been rebuked, but Marc was bound to be protective about Howie. It was all too tangled up with his own loss. "No drama with the election. Perhaps Doug really should take over the base right away. And the sooner we send *Elcano* home, the better. I'm all for cheerfulness in adversity, but life's been a bit trying lately and this place seems to be more divided every day."

"Yeah, but it's inevitable. Kill Line's happy because it still does the job it always did. The neighbours are still next door, the council's still running things, and everyone knows where they fit in." Marc frowned as if he was trying to find one word for it all. "I think it's a status and purpose thing. The Kill Liners have the same social structure. We do, too. Your crew, Dan's detachment, Chris's troops, even his civvies — the people used to a uniform have a familiar structure to slot into and the civvies have already been through the losing everything phase. They've all got a purpose. But the boffins are having a harder time."

"Yes, I know that," Ingram said. "I haven't worked out how we make it any easier, though."

"You can't. They were top of the food chain at Ainatio. It was all about them and their work, even if that was a smokescreen. The food just showed up and bots did most of the crap jobs. Okay, the food and the bots bit is the same here, but overnight, they stopped being gods. The teeriks beat them at physics and engineering and you'd brought your own boffins. A lot of them don't even have a relevant specialisation. Nomad needs builders, farmers, troops, and pregnant women now more than it needs them. It's hard to find out you're ballast after years of thinking you were special. Especially when you didn't have many choices about coming."

"But not everyone we evacuated from Ainatio is a pain in the arse," Ingram said. "It's not even confined to those with less useful skills. I doubt we need Todd Mangel's astrophysics expertise to survive, but he teaches, he helps out around town, he's scouting for new planets, and he's studying other STEM fields. He's fully involved. But Paul Cotton *isn't* and his plant disease expertise is crucial here. He's still a science god, to use your analogy."

"Actually, I was trying to be open-minded and see the whiners' point of view," Marc said. "Todd's a nice bloke and he doesn't think he's God's gift to science. Lots of the redundant boffins are like that. Some of the essential ones aren't nice and neighbourly. It comes down to personalities."

"They were never meant to come here," Ingram said.

"Neither was I. Or Dan. Or Chris."

"I meant that we rescued them out of common decency, but we didn't need them all."

"Now you sound like Sol."

"But it's true. Project Nomad was supposed to be about generalists and community builders. Now we have an abnormally high percentage of boffins."

"And that's probably why they want their friends in *Elcano* thawed out," Marc said. "They feel outnumbered and threatened."

"We can't keep changing our minds over that, Marc. Like you always say, it looks weak and weakness breeds disorder."

Marc smiled. "It sounds a lot more sinister and jackbooted when you say it."

"And I'm not sure adding more scientists to a divided population is the answer," Ingram said. "Not until those here integrate more, or just stop stirring it up. But we're only talking about a vocal minority."

"Doesn't take many to sow discontent."

"The medics managed just fine." Ingram drew up her knees and rested her folded arms on them. "They formed their little clique on the first day and revelled in it. They really like it here."

"Ah, but they kept their identity," Marc said. "Doctors and nurses are always useful and it's still a respected job, even for the ones who are shit at it. The rank earns the salute. But there isn't a medic here who only does brain surgery and doesn't know how to use a bandage, and that's what some of the boffins are like. Alex says a lot of them are *really* specialised and they have to start over in another field. You're not going to do that in a few months."

"That's why Erskine picked the ones she did," Ingram said. "She saved the essential personnel with a job to do here, plus kids."

"Yeah. She might have been unlikeable, but she wasn't stupid. Or wrong."

"Oh God, don't make me see her as a martyr, Marc. It'll cloud my decision-making."

Marc stood up slowly as if his back was stiff. "You need to work that out with Sol, love. This is his job. I'm just saying what I think because I trained insurgents and it feels a lot like this. But you already know how to do it. It's like absorbing a lot of new crew members. You're just tolerating too much crap because you're dealing with civvies and you're worried about looking like a military dictatorship."

Ingram's acceptance that she didn't have the moral authority or numbers to dictate to civilians seemed reasonable to her. She'd only impose control if the base was in immediate danger.

"I'll get my jackboots polished and give stirring speeches from the roof of the main building, then," she said. "I want banners and a well-disciplined crowd, too."

Marc held his hand out to help her up. "Come on, you old tyrant. Beddie-byes. It's late and we'll have a whole day of brand new bullshit tomorrow."

Ingram had almost sobered up, but she'd reached the regretful did-I-really-do-that aftermath of a run ashore. The awful whirling sensation kept her awake and gave her subconscious a chance to spew all its buried issues into her conscious mind. What was Sol up to? He'd been completely silent tonight, but perhaps that was a courtesy to allow her to let her hair down. Had Alex already floated the idea of an election for everyone outside the Kill Line boundary? If he had, then any brakes she'd need to put on that to take the Kill Line jurisdiction issue into account would just be seen by the usual suspects as suppressing democracy. And Fred — she had to spend more time with him and rebuild the relationship, especially as Cosqui had stepped into his role with enthusiasm because she liked Brad Searle.

And why hadn't Nir-Tenbiku asked to repatriate Lirrel's body?

The teerik was still in the morgue. Ingram hadn't raised the matter either. In fact, she'd forgotten all about him, which she could almost excuse because the Jattan visit had caught her out and put the base at defence stations just hours ago.

But she hadn't mentioned his remains when she spoke to Nir-Tenbiku the last time. Nobody had referred to him in discussions, not even Chris, who could usually be guaranteed to ask awkward questions, or Marc, whose idea it had been to preserve the remains in case disrespectful handling sparked an incident at some point down the line.

Lirrel had hacked Nina to death, so there was probably zero concern around the base for what happened to his body as long as he wasn't laid to rest in the churchyard. He didn't even have a country Ingram could return him to. It was technically Kugad, but she wasn't planning to drop them a line any time soon. The Jattan opposition didn't seem interested in what happened to him either. He was like a dead goldfish dumped in the kitchen waste, not even a pet that you'd miss and get a little headstone made for and bury in the garden. He'd just been machinery.

For some reason, it saddened her. Whatever failings the humans of Nomad had, they had at least lacked concern for Lirrel because he was a murderer, judged by the same standards they held themselves to, not excused from guilt because he was just an animal who didn't know any better.

It wasn't much to be proud of, but as things stood, Ingram took some comfort from the fact that humans had defaulted to treating an alien as an equal.

* * *

LASK STREET, THE TEERIK COMPOUND: 1245 HOURS, TWO DAYS LATER.

Rikayl swooped as if he was going to crash into Solomon's quadrubot but veered away at the last moment to perch on the street sign.

"No stars blow up," he said, head cocked on one side. "No stars last night. No bang. *Again.* What?"

Solomon admired his vivid descriptive powers, but some phrases took a little longer to decipher than others. *Stars blow up... no stars... no bang.* Well, that was fairly easy.

"You mean *fireworks*," Solomon said. "Fireworks are explosives. Small explosives fired into the air to look pretty and make a noise. Like little missiles. Humans only do that to have fun on special days."

Rikayl had been fascinated by the election night display but had only been allowed to watch through a window. It was interesting to note which words and concepts he seemed most familiar with — the language of the armaments industry. It was hard to tell if that was derived from his genetic memory, or simply the result of exposure to work-related conversations in the house.

"Not stars?" Rikayl asked.

"No, the stars don't blow up." For a moment Solomon was tempted to modify that with an explanation of supernovas. "The stars are still there."

"Bomb sky for fun?"

"Ah... yes."

"Wankers!"

"You like the fireworks?"

"Gone too fast."

The chemists and engineers had done a good job with the rockets, and certainly managed to introduce some wonderful colours into the display. But they had some way to go to rival a pyrotechnics expert and create flowers or shoals of fish in the air. Rikayl's critical eye had already identified the short-lived and wasteful nature of the entertainment.

"Food?" Rikayl asked, eyeing the trolley bot following Solomon.

"Yes. Pies, fruit cream, and barbecued meat."

"Jelly bars for me?"

"No, you need different food. More meat and eggs." Rikayl didn't need the medication. "Bars are medicine. You don't need it."

Rikayl stretched his wings as if he was limbering up. "Hredt don't need. He getting *well.*"

Of course Fred's mental state was improving. The drug was already in his food, and the bot was programmed to serve him specific packs that looked indistinguishable from the rest. As far as the other teeriks were concerned, he just ate meals minus the "chewables," as Dr Tomlinson called them, and still appeared to be off his medication. They all understood why he'd been allowed to skip them. He was finishing work on the personal gate device, and it was less trouble to let him do that than argue about it and possibly get into savage fights. He'd be done with it soon, and then life could get back to normal.

But if Jeff or one of the more sympathetic scientists found out what Solomon was doing, word might get back to Fred and he'd stop eating. Solomon felt guilty for deceiving him, but more guilty about the mistakes Fred might make with the device if he assumed he was free of the drug and that his judgement was at its peak. Solomon had gleaned from Fred's conversations with Jeff that he'd come to see his sedated state as restricted and less competent, despite the fact that he'd functioned perfectly well in that condition for years.

Marc was testing the portable device again this morning, gating from place to place around the site. If anything went wrong and he was harmed, the truth would have to come out, and Ingram would never trust Solomon again. She couldn't shut him down any more than Erskine had been able to, but she wouldn't need to. He'd have failed to protect one of the most valuable of his chosen humans — a friend, too — and betrayed everyone's trust, and there would be no redemption possible. Under those circumstances, he would have felt obliged to take himself offline, but without AI management at this stage of Nomad's development, the base would be in a very vulnerable position. He would have to live with his disgrace.

The whole mess had been a sobering lesson about the risks of good intentions. Even an AI could regret his decisions.

Turisu opened the door to let the trolley bot in. "You don't normally visit, Solomon," she said. "Is there a problem?"

"You're not normally here for lunch." He walked in and looked around as discreetly as he could. "You're usually on one of the ships."

"Hredt's still testing his device with Marc and the others. I'll put one of the meals aside for him. His appetite's poor lately."

That didn't sound encouraging. It might have explained his agitation before Marc boarded Nir-Tenbiku's vessel. If he was leaving too much food, he wouldn't receive an adequate dose. But there hadn't been much by way of leftovers to dispose of. Where was that food going? Were the others finishing it? That might be disastrous.

Why haven't I noticed?

"Thank you, but I'm taking some snacks to him next," Solomon said. "I dropped by to see how you are and collect the samples for Dr Tomlinson."

"They're ready," she said. "And we're well."

The rest of the commune sat awaiting lunch, rustling feathers impatiently. Cosqui was reading her screen and doing that little head-rocking gesture that said something had pleased her.

"Not feeling sleepy during the day, or anything like that?" Solomon asked. "We want to fine-tune the dose, not render you unconscious."

"We're functioning as we always have," Turisu said. "Perhaps humans need some of that medicine. They've been getting into fights this week. We heard about it."

Sedation hadn't completely taken the edge off Turisu's sharp tongue. Solomon felt embarrassed and irritated that she seemed to be gloating. It was hard to miss the protest, but Demli and Runal must have seen the incident with Howie and reported back.

Very well, two could play the bitching game. "Humans disagree frequently," Solomon said. "It's what makes them independent thinkers. While we're on the subject of independence, Captain Ingram's spoken to you about the matter of the Jattan opposition's visit, I understand. I realise that must have worried you, given their opinion of teeriks. They have rather bigoted views."

Turisu fluffed up her neck feathers a little. "Ingram said she'd sent them on their way and returned their dead comrade so they wouldn't feel the need to come back again. Their opinion means nothing to us."

"I'm glad to hear that." She must have been nervous, though. Jattans knew where to find them, and it didn't matter which faction. "Might I ask if you have any opinion on what should happen to Lirrel's remains? Nir-Tenbiku didn't mention him or indicate that he wanted him returned."

"He's not one of us," Turisu said. "It's a matter for Captain Ingram."

"I'll leave you to enjoy your meal in peace, then."

Solomon dispatched the bot to the main building with the saliva samples for Dr Tomlinson and went to find Marc. He might have been anywhere at any given moment while he was testing the gate, but Fred had set up the control base in the Caisin bunker. Solomon climbed down the newly-fitted stairs to the chamber and prepared to give Fred his food. He found him on his own, standing over his screen at the workbench.

"Lunch, Fred?"

Fred didn't look up for a moment. Eventually he raised his head and turned slowly to stare down at Solomon, who took the wrapped pie out of his back pannier and placed it on the bench. But Fred wasn't lost in his work. He was probably making a point to Solomon about being interrupted while he was calculating.

"I'm sorry, I shouldn't distract you when you have complex work to do," Solomon said.

"I'm not distracted."

Fred put the screen aside, picked up the pie, and walked across the room to dump it in the waste basket. Solomon was taken aback. There was going to be trouble.

"While we have the opportunity for a private discussion," Fred said, "I want you to understand that I know what you've been doing to my meals. And you'll stop it right now. Did you think I wouldn't notice? I can *feel* what it's doing to me."

"I'm sorry." Solomon floundered. There was no point in denying it. "I was only trying to make you feel better."

Solomon hadn't been put on the spot like this since his development days. Once he took over his mission role, he was the one who held all the information and saw everything, and he'd grown used to having the upper hand with intel. That had now evaporated.

"You've been drugging me against my wishes," Fred said. "So I've countered by eating much less to minimise the amount of medication I ingest, and I can assure you hunger hasn't improved my mood. You knew I wanted to complete this work, and why, and yet you compromised my fitness to work and risked Marc's safety. I'll take this to Captain Ingram if you persist. It won't be hard to prove with the next round of medical checks."

"I can only apologise," Solomon said. "But I don't think your work is any less brilliant when you're medicated. You only imagine it is."

"You know *nothing*," Fred snapped. "You have no more idea of what my work entails than Marc's dog. You can copy what I've done, eventually, but you can't create what I can. And you're a copy of a human. A *mechanical*. I can't trust you now."

The silence that followed was terrible. Solomon didn't know how to make the next move. He'd had minor conflicts during his development, which might have been set up to test his ability to adapt to emotionally challenging situations, and he'd watched Bednarz being less than kind to subordinates on the project, but he was now lost and desperate to put things right. He just didn't know how.

And he'd have to confess to Ingram.

"I would never risk Marc's life," he said. "And I accept I've acted unethically and that I should be ashamed of myself. I'll minimise contact with you if that's what you want."

"What are you minimising, Sol?"

It was Ash Brice. She was standing right behind him and he hadn't detected her at all.

"You startled me," he said.

"I just gated in." Ash grinned, clearly delighted. "I've never gated before. It's amazing. I can work wonders using this."

She had one of the prototype control pads strapped to her arm. Solomon hadn't realised she was involved in the tests, but then Chris suddenly appeared in the chamber. Marc must have recruited more volunteers to test the portable unit.

"This is great, Fred," Chris said. "I'm still trying to think of situations where I wouldn't be able to access the control if it's on my arm. But I don't think there's a perfect location for a control that works every time, because we'll never be able to predict how we'll end up injured or missing a limb." He looked at Ash and laughed. "Actually, there *is* one. Buttock activated. You know, clench your glutes and it squeezes the control. It was a detonation method for suicide bombers."

Ash laughed her head off. "What if you're so scared you clench anyway?"

"Sure, but we're talking about having usable body parts to gate yourself out of trouble. If you've lost your ass, there's no point gating anywhere."

They seemed to find it hilarious. Solomon had never seen Chris laugh properly like that. Then Marc materialised and gave them a look.

"Honestly, you two," he said. "Fun, was it?"

"It's awesome," Chris said, his serious self again. "It's exactly what we need. This is fantastic, Fred. You're the man."

Marc clapped. "Top gadgetry, Fred. I'm happy with the muscle activation method. As long as the sensors stay stuck on somewhere, we're good."

Ash started guffawing again. There was a carnival atmosphere now that was totally at odds with how Solomon felt. The three humans didn't seem to notice the icy distance between him and Fred.

"My work's done, then," Fred said. "I'm very pleased you approve."

"Fred, if you were a drinking teerik, I'd buy you a beer right now." Marc reached inside his shirt and peeled off a couple of electrodes. "You're a genius, mate. You're the Barnes Wallis of the galaxy. I feel a lot more confident about our prospects if we ever have to deal with Kugin."

Fred did a little bow. "Thank you. My pleasure."

Solomon decided to withdraw. "I'll get Helen to send down a proper lunch for you, Fred," he said. "Excuse me."

He got out of the bunker as fast as he could and stood outside by the flagpoles, trying to work out if it was possible to repair the damage. He was also baffled by his own reaction. He'd been perfectly willing to undermine or even destroy anything that threatened the welfare of his humans. He'd let the sabcode loose in Asia knowing there would probably be terrible consequences for innocent people, and he'd accepted that the teeriks might have to be terminated if they were likely to fall into enemy hands. But he was confused, demoralised, and distressed by being caught out in a lie.

He'd been unethical before, and he'd taken lives, some at close quarters. He'd lied, too. He'd always been able to justify it, and he could justify medicating Fred, as much for Fred's well-being as the humans' welfare. What was different this time? He'd had to face the individual he'd wronged. And for once he wasn't as smart as he believed, and Fred had spotted his intervention.

On top of that, Fred genuinely believed it had put Marc at risk, and so he no longer trusted Solomon. He'd relegated him to a mechanical and basically told him he was just software, and limited software at that. Solomon wandered off and sat down like a dog by the low wall at the front of the building. He didn't want to go back into the network yet because he felt he might never come out again and just hide away, vindicating Fred's assessment of his shortcomings. It seemed so emotionally trivial, though, and while he had no wish to be a human or anything other than what he was, it was unbearably painful.

Ingram would have shrugged it off if it had happened to her. She was ready to play any game to get the outcome she wanted and she'd brazen her way through this. She'd probably have said, "Well, Fred, what else could you expect us to do? We don't know enough about you and this drug, but we don't want you to get into a situation you'd hate yourself for." Then she'd move on to the next topic and never lose a second's sleep.

He realised he'd reconstructed her and her behaviour the same way he'd modelled a version of Bednarz. He sat brooding for half an hour, staying in touch with the network in case anything happened, and wondered if people passing by thought he'd parked the quadrubot and gone back into the system. Then Chris walked up to him, hands in his pockets.

"You in there, Sol?"

"I am, Chris."

Chris sat down on the wall. "I'm guessing you had a fight with Fred."

"You're very perceptive. Yes, I'm afraid I did."

"Is this about what you were going to confess to me?"

Solomon knew he'd feel better for getting it off his chest. It would be a dry run for admitting his sins to Ingram.

"I was continuing to medicate his food because I thought he might become dangerous," he said. "He realised I was doing it and ate as little food as possible to reduce his intake. He told me to stop or he'd go to Ingram. He said it affected his judgement and put Marc in danger."

Chris sat forward with his hands clasped, elbows on his knees. "Whatever you say about how our wishes come first, Sol, you control most of Nomad. If Ingram was mad at you, she couldn't shut you down or stop you doing anything. So whatever you're worried about, it's not external consequences."

"Fred said he'll never trust me again."

"That's not the end of the world, either. Unless you're best buddies."

"And he said I'm just a mechanical and I don't know any more about his work than Betsy does."

"Ah, wounded pride. On both sides."

"I don't know how I can put things right. My apology meant little, and I understand that. Talk is indeed cheap."

"He might calm down after a while," Chris said. "We don't know. Sorry doesn't change the past, but I think it's all you've got."

"I didn't know why it upset me so much, Chris. I've done far worse and not been affected like this."

"Having rows with people isn't fun. You need a certain kind of personality or a lot of exposure to angry people shouting in your face to be able to shrug it off. And you feel guilty because Fred's kind of a victim, a slave, an old guy, all kinds of underdog stuff."

Chris was a very good observer of other people's emotions. Solomon wondered if he faced himself the same way. He'd had moral discussions with Chris before and had come away feeling he'd both learned something and lost a little of his burden, possibly because

Chris always openly admitted being worse and not being troubled by it.

"What would you have done, Chris?" Solomon asked.

Chris shrugged. "I'd have dosed him. But I'd have done it after I'd locked him up and explained what I was doing and why." He stood up as if he'd finished. Ash and Marc were heading his way. "But tell Ingram, okay? Not because you feel bad about it, but because she needs to know these things to do her job. And if it's still bothering you tomorrow, come and find me and we'll talk. The last thing we need is the guy who keeps this base running having a mental crisis."

So Solomon was still a guy in Chris's eyes, not a mechanical. Chris walked up the road to join Ash and Marc and left Solomon rerunning his words to wring more wisdom out them.

It took Solomon until the next day to feel up to facing Ingram. He should have met her in person in his quadrubot so he could have looked her in the eye, but he was back in the network by then and she was used to addressing him in the ether. It was hard to tell if she'd already heard the news from someone else, but she didn't look particularly surprised.

"It's a difficult one," she said, sorting some notes on her desk. "I don't think there's ever going to be a right answer. Is it going to affect your operations if Fred won't work with you?"

"Not really, Captain. Cosqui will."

"Fine. I wish you'd told me beforehand, but I'd have done it if you hadn't, I think, so you've saved me from being put in an awkward position. I try to stay above the disputes so I can be seen to be making non-partisan decisions"

Solomon decided not to point out that Ingram's attempt to stay above things hadn't achieved a perception of neutrality at all, but he was here to be penitent. "I'll consult you in advance in the future," he said.

"Good. So if it's the moral aspect that's bothering you, you know what *not* to do next time. If it's purely operational, you've learned not to get caught."

"I don't think it ever put Marc at risk."

"Did he know?"

"No."

"You might want to break it to him first, then. He had his concerns about Fred."

"I will."

It was an anti-climax that didn't leave Solomon feeling relieved. But a feud between himself and Fred didn't interest the vast majority of personnel on the base, who were still more concerned with the more visible events of the last few weeks — the leak to Lawson, *Elcano*'s fate, security's handling of the protest, and, at the gossip level, the saga of Duncan Wilson getting beaten up by a ten-year-old and bitten by a dog. Duncan's fate might have amused some people, but there were those who felt it was a worrying sign that some Nomad residents were considerably more equal than others, a reaction that concerned Solomon.

But Ingram hadn't shifted her position. *Elcano* was still going home for safekeeping, and nobody was calling home for the foreseeable future. It would, he hoped, all become academic in time.

The one thing people didn't seem so worried about was the prospect of more aliens arriving, including hostile ones. The longer the Kugin and Protectorate navies took to show up, the more everyone relegated the threat, and seeing Nir-Tenbiku's visit pass off without incident was creating a sense of security that wasn't warranted.

Solomon continued to avoid the teeriks for the next few days, still hoping that Turisu had made Fred see reason or that Cosqui would tell Solomon not to worry because she was leading the team now. If he went to Fred and apologised again, he'd probably get the same response, even though Fred had now started taking the medication voluntarily. The temptation to monitor the commune's conversations and check whether they were discussing the matter was almost overwhelming. But Solomon reminded himself of the line between wanting to know and needing to know. He had more than enough to monitor with the stream of Jattan chatter coming back from the spy ship off Dal Mantir.

He needed a friend right now. He'd befriended dozens of humans over the years, some more than others, but this was the first time he'd felt adrift and simply wanted someone to reassure him. Chris was too wrapped up with Ash to socialise with him, and Marc and Trinder were busy building their home lives. That left Alex. Alex had a private life too, but he always had time for Solomon.

Alex was still trying to build social bridges between Nomad's tribes the same way he'd kept morale above water for years at the isolated Ainatio site, and Solomon didn't have the heart to dissuade him. A talent show or a quiz night wasn't a substitute for contact with Earth or reunion with friends in *Elcano,* though. The *Cabot* crew were being stoic about the restrictions, except for Jenny Park, but Solomon couldn't avoid overhearing conversations with a recurring subject — that almost nobody on Earth knew they were alive. Lawson and Pham didn't count.

It had come down to simply wanting to tell people back on Earth that they weren't dead, not just relatives or friends but anybody at all who could set the record straight. It was as if saying they were dead was somehow enough to erase them from existence.

Perhaps it was; perhaps being forgotten was worse than being dead. But instead of fading as time went on, their resentment seemed to come and go in waves. Every time the Ainatio contingent voiced a complaint, it would reignite the crew's anger about the company's huge deception, although they didn't blame the staff here for that. They'd been lied to as well.

Duncan Wilson hadn't forgiven and forgotten either, but it had only been a few days since the barbecue incident. Solomon dropped into Alex's office at lunchtime in the hope of socialising and found him changing into his tracksuit, eyes still fixed on something on his desk screen.

"Sorry, Sol, I'm late for a training session," Alex said. "Right now I want to shove Duncan Wilson's head down the toilet and flush. He's filed an official complaint about the argument the other night and he wants Betsy put down as a dangerous dog. That means I've got to notify Britzilla, and he'll get mad in the way only men trained to kill someone with a dinner fork can get mad."

"Nomad doesn't have an official complaints system yet, Alex."

"Ainatio does."

"*Did.* Ainatio's gone."

"In law, but not in a spirit. I've still got to sort it out."

"I'm sure Marc can deal with it."

"He'll kill him. Please, come with me to training so I can hide behind you when he loses his shit. And why are you always in the bot now? Is this a permanent lifestyle change?"

"I find it more appropriate at the moment," Solomon said. "And to be honest, I feel more secure in it. This week has been very stressful on a personal level."

"Yeah, yeah, I heard." Alex didn't seem to think it was a *biggie*, as he'd put it. "So are you coming?"

Solomon had never visited Marc's rugby sessions before. "I'm not really large enough to hide behind."

"You'll do."

They walked down the main road, now officially called Levine Avenue, and turned left at the materials storage facility to the open grass that had now been levelled and marked up as a rugby pitch. It had also acquired proper goalposts at both ends and was starting to look like it was meant to be there. Twenty of the *Cabot* crew, including Jeff and Bissey, and some of the younger men from Kill Line were doing stretches and short sprints. Chris stood on the sidelines with Marc, unwrapping a sandwich.

Marc pointed at Alex. "You're *late*," he boomed.

"I've got a good reason. Honest." Alex looked down at Solomon. "Here goes. I'd like a pharaoh's funeral, please, if there's enough of me left to fill the sarcophagus." He strode up to Marc and blurted out the awkward news. "Duncan's lodged a formal complaint and he wants Betsy put down."

Marc stood with his hands on his hips, stony-faced. "Oh. Does he now."

"I'm obliged to put the complaint to you, Marc. Don't hit me. At least not the face."

"And which fearless arbiter of fair play's going to hear the case and pass judgement?"

"Ah... probably me. Or Ingram the Terrible."

"Okay." Marc took out his pocket screen, stabbed the icons with his forefinger, and waited, looking murderous. "Duncan? It's Marc Gallagher. I hear you want a response to your complaint about me and Betsy... yeah, about that... okay, here's my response. You can fuck off. Nobody touches the dog. Understand? If not, I'm happy to meet up with you and explain things any time. Dieter will want to draw you a diagram as well." Marc ended the call, shoved the screen back in his pocket, and turned his stare on Alex. "What are you looking at me like that for? I sorted it out. Come on, we've got work to do. Get running."

"That was very manly, Marc, but it's not going to calm things down," Alex said.

"Duncan's definition of a serious incident isn't quite the same as mine."

"You know what I mean. They're sulking about being second class to Brit privilege."

"Oh, sod that, we're all in the same boat," Marc said. "Okay, I've been back to Earth, but I can't call my mates or Sandra and explain where I am. I just have to talk to a civil servant because Fred dropped us in the shit."

"Relax, Alex," Chris said. "It'd be great if everyone was happy and best buddies, but as long as they're functioning, or at least not being obstructive or a drain on resources, it doesn't matter. Someone, somewhere will always have a grievance. Marc doesn't owe anyone an explanation."

Marc turned to Chris. "I'm not explaining, I'm getting pissed off. Anyway, what are you doing here? Did Ash send you here to toughen up?"

"You know me, I don't do sport." Chris sat down on the grass and took a bite out of the sandwich. "I came to watch Tev and see if he's the human juggernaut you claim. Where is he?"

"It's Sera's antenatal check-up. He goes to support Joni."

"You know, we should have an army versus navy game," Alex said. "It'll get people together to watch and eat hotdogs."

"Nobody else likes rugby," Chris said. "All the rugby fans are the same guys who come to these sessions."

"Perhaps, but my rebellious Ainatio colleagues will come in the hope of witnessing Marc getting his superhero ass handed to him. Because Tev's the only one who can knock him down."

Marc tossed a ball from hand to hand. "If it's army versus navy, we'll be on the same team."

"But Tev could make up numbers for the sailors. It'll be a crowd-puller. The two giants of extrasolar rugby, head to head."

Chris gazed into the distance. "Like being in a car crash. Twenty G at least."

"What is?" Alex asked.

"The G-force in a tackle. And way higher when they do that scrum thing."

"Al, if you think blood's going to placate your boffins, why don't we just have gladiatorial contests and get it over with?" Marc asked. "I'm up for it. Ingram can do the thumbs-down emperor bit."

"I wish I hadn't asked," Alex said. "I'll just slink away now and hope you don't notice me for the rest of the session."

Solomon envied Marc his ability to face down his critics and genuinely not care, rather like Ingram. He wondered if that was an option with Fred. Solomon could just carry on dealing with him as if nothing had happened, or even say he'd dosed the food for Fred's own good and that he had no regrets, but he'd already apologised, and he didn't know how to take that back. The moment had passed.

"Rik's arrived," Chris said, pointing. Rikayl had taken up position on the very top of one of the goalposts. "This'll be fun to watch."

"He's waiting to grab the bloody ball and make off with it," Marc said. "We'd better have a spare on standby."

The teerik was looking around at his own height, not peering below with his head cocked on one side, which was usually a warning that he was going to swoop down and investigate. Perhaps he was waiting for the players to start a game and pass the ball in earnest. He'd chase anything that moved fast and piqued his curiosity, and he'd probably end up destroying the ball if he got hold of it. Marc only had two proper rugby balls and an American football, so Solomon made a note to get some more manufactured to keep the peace.

Jeff walked up to the goal and called to the teerik. "No ball, Rik. Don't take the ball, okay? Just watch." Rikayl looked down as if he'd suddenly noticed him but didn't respond at all, not even with a stream of cheerful abuse. "What's up with you? Are you in huff about something? Never mind."

"What are the rules about restarting play if the ball goes missing?" Alex asked. "Do we go from the last place it ended up?"

"Oddly, the international rugby authorities failed to address what to do in the event of alien interference during a game," Marc said.

Jeff kept looking up at Rikayl. "Y'know, I think there's something wrong with him."

"Ate too many bouncing fur balls, probably."

"No, really. I've never seen him just sit there like that. He usually wants to join in with everything."

Solomon felt a pang of worried guilt. He still hadn't worked out what had happened to Fred's leftover food and he hadn't been able to bring himself to ask. If Rikayl had been eating it, he might have overdosed on the tranquiliser, especially as he was smaller than an adult teerik. Perhaps it had taken time to build up in his system.

"I think we should find a way to get him down from there and have the vet examine him," Solomon said.

Chris carried on eating. "Yeah, I remember trying to get him down from the comms mast. No thanks. Leave him. He'll either come down when you start tossing the ball around or he'll fall off if he's ill."

"You know what your problem is, don't you?" Marc said. "You're too sentimental."

"Okay, you shin up there and get him. Be my guest."

Marc carried on limbering up. Solomon knew he should have pointed out that Rikayl might have ingested sedatives, but he'd wait and see.

The teerik was now looking up at the sky as if he expected something to fall on him, back flattened and wings held away from his sides like he was about to take off. Solomon hoped he wasn't hallucinating. Hiyashi and Jeff raced past the goal, practising passes, but Rikayl still took no notice.

Chris was watching intently. "What's he doing now?"

Rikayl was having difficulty keeping his grip on the small cap on top of the post, but he turned around one-eighty degrees, looking right and left, then pushed off from the top and fluttered down to the crossbar, head still jerking around like someone looking for a sniper.

Solomon had to say something now. "Chris, there's a chance he's eaten —"

"Shit, that's not him." Chris jumped to his feet. "Jeff? *Jeff!* It's not Rik. It's another teerik. Whoa —"

Another bright red teerik swooped out of nowhere and smashed into the one on the crossbar. For a few seconds, the two creatures were a single spinning ball of feathers and claws, rasping and shrieking, and then they tumbled to the ground. Players stopped dead and stared.

There was no mistake. There were two red teeriks slashing at each other in the middle of the pitch. Solomon couldn't tell them apart now, but one managed to sink his claws into the other and slammed him on his back, then started stabbing with his beak. Scraps of feather and flesh flew into the air.

"*Wanker*!" The attacker could only be Rikayl. "Kill! This *mine!*"

He started dragging the limp body of his opponent around by its neck, then slammed it back and forth a few times on the grass. Jeff ran over to him and stopped out of beak range. Rikayl still looked enraged with his crest raised and his feathers fluffed up. By now the players and spectators were gathering around at a cautious distance.

"Is it dead?" Marc asked. "And are we sure that's another teerik?"

Chris edged closer and took pictures with his screen. Rikayl rasped at him but went on mauling his victim.

"I've got quite a lot of questions," Chris said. "Sol, can you do a visual comparison?"

Solomon mapped the defeated teerik's physical features against Rikayl's as best he could. There were minor differences, but externally, this seemed to be a teerik exactly like him. If Rikayl was abnormal, then so was this one, and it hadn't come from the commune.

"I think you've finished him, mate," Jeff said, walking right up to him and squatting at teerik eye level. "Come on, put him down. Are you hurt?"

"I okay," Rikayl said. "*He* hurt, not me. Wanker. Not his place. *Mine*."

Solomon could only interpret that as Rikayl objecting to another teerik on his territory. He was now dismantling the intruder, ripping out feathers and entrails. Solomon decided to let him get on with it, but when Rikayl lost interest in his victim, Solomon would collect the remains for analysis.

Marc leaned over the carnage for a closer look. "Where did he come from, Rik?"

"He gone."

"I can see that. Well done. But have you seen him before?"

"Heard."

"Did he speak? Could you understand him?"

"No words. Just *know*."

Marc looked at Solomon. "Have you picked up anything unusual on monitoring? The system analyses all sound detected around the base, yeah?"

"It does, and there's been nothing," Solomon said.

"Okay, here's my wild speculation list." Chris picked up a feather and examined it. "One, this guy came here with Gan-Pamas and he's been hanging around unseen. Two, one of the teeriks laid an egg the same way Caisin did and didn't tell us. Three, Caisin had twins somehow but for some reason the commune only admitted to having Rikayl. Four, this isn't a teerik but it looks like one — a mimic — but if it *is* a mimic, it means there are other teeriks who've been here for a very long time if another species has evolved to look like them. And if these are teeriks, what are Fred and the other guys? A different sub-species? Because two red ones both being abnormal in exactly the same way is a tad too coincidental for me."

"This is your throwback theory," Marc said.

"Maybe."

Ingram was now on her way. Solomon tracked the quad bike she'd picked up. She came to a halt a few yards away and walked over to Rikayl, who was still busy plucking and gutting the unidentified teerik.

"Good God." She watched in silence for a while. "What the hell is going on with this planet?"

Rikayl looked up at her. "He wanker," he said. "I kill."

"How many more of these are there?" She looked at Jeff as if he had all the answers when it came to teeriks. "Before I ask Fred if there's yet another thing he hasn't told us, did anyone see where this one came from?"

"He just showed up and settled on the goalpost," Hiyashi said. "We thought he was Rikayl at first. Then the real Rik arrived and knocked ten bells out of him."

Ingram grimaced at the increasingly gory spectacle on the grass. "So we're back to square one. We assumed teeriks were native to Opis. Then they said they weren't. But the best explanation for this one here is that they are. If so, Fred's going to be terribly disappointed that there isn't an ancient teerik civilisation to be restored."

"He might know that and be lying for some reason," Alex said.

"No." Solomon had to set the record straight, even if Fred despised him now. "We talked about how they didn't know where they originated and he was absolutely sincere. But it might explain why they ended up here, and why Lirrel did too."

"What, some kind of homing instinct?" Ingram asked. "Across light years?"

"Perhaps. They do have extraordinary visuospatial skills. And their genetic memory — they might have a subconscious memory of where Opis is."

"I just want to know what's in the gap between the super-smart black teeriks and these guys," Chris said. "And yeah, I know they've been selectively bred and that can make really big changes to how animals look and behave in a relatively short time, but like I say, turning them from dog-smart to Einstein is another matter. We don't even know if the dead guy is as intelligent as Rikayl."

"I smart, he *thicko*," Rikayl said. He seemed to have tired of mangling the intruder. Solomon took the opportunity to move in and scoop up the remains for analysis. "So I win."

"Okay, Rik, next time you find one, don't kill it until we've given it an IQ test," Alex said.

Ingram folded her arms and looked worried. "Assuming there *are* more of them."

"In a way, I hope there are," Marc said. "Because the other options on Professor Montello's list of theories are much more worrying. Eh, Chris?"

"Yeah. Basically more lies, or more things Gan-Pamas left behind."

This was a zoological curiosity, not the discovery of a new enemy to add to their growing list, but Solomon felt uneasy about everything that hadn't shown up on the original surveys of Opis. He knew he hadn't overlooked the teeriks when he analysed years of satellite imaging. There wasn't an indication of even the most primitive of societies. If there were wild teeriks here, they built nothing and left no mark on the world. They were just one of potentially millions of undiscovered and uncatalogued species on this planet.

"I suppose I'd better find Fred and tell him," Ingram said. "Still, it'll probably answer the origin question for him, even if it's not the answer he wants."

"Does this mean Opis is rightfully theirs?" Marc asked. "Just as well they don't have lawyers."

"Even if they did, we're here now," Chris said. "And here we stay."

Jeff squatted to look Rikayl in the eye again, then took a tissue from his pocket and wiped the blood and debris from the feathers around the teerik's beak like a father cleaning up a chocolate-smeared toddler. He seemed totally unafraid of a creature that had shown again how efficiently it could kill. Rikayl tolerated the attention.

"Are you home, then, mate?" Jeff asked. "Is this where you all come from?"

Rikayl shook his head like a human. He'd learned the gesture fast.

"Dunno, but *same*," he said. "I not weird. I not *alone*."

EPILOGUE

Jimmy Mun can still surprise me.

In this business, you have to be creative when you need a private meeting away from the prying eyes of those whose business this is definitely *not*. But the last place I'd imagined catching up with Jimmy is an art gallery.

Off-duty Jimmy is a different man to the one I last saw during the mission at Ainatio's headquarters. He's wearing a casual beige linen suit with light blue deck shoes, and to the rest of the world he looks like a successful chef on his day off, a man who knows hard physical work and suffers no fools, and appreciates the fine things in life and has the money to indulge in them when he can make the time. But they do say special forces can pass themselves off as anybody. Jimmy is a master of the knife, just not the *nakiri* or the *santoku*.

"I didn't know you liked ceramics, Jimmy."

He's scrutinising an asymmetric bowl that's rather pretty — sea green with a curtain of translucent amber around the rim in what I think they call drip glaze — but there's no way I'd pay that much for a box of them, let alone a single piece.

"I've been away a lot this year," he says. "As you know. So it's a Christmas present for the missus to make it up to her. She collects this guy's stuff."

"First things first. Am I still a valued customer of Mr Lake?"

"He's still pretty bloody mad about the helicopter."

"And the personnel who were lost, I hope."

"He's not sentimental, boss."

"Well, then, as he's been paid, I assume I'm still on his Christmas card list. Not that he knows where to send it, or who to address it to, but metaphorically speaking."

Jimmy nods, still not looking at me. "Yeah, he'll provide whatever you need next. Is that what you really wanted to see me about?"

"Of course not."

"Did APS notice what happened?"

"Yes."

"Do I need to know the rest?"

"Maybe not, but for the record, I told them it was classified prototype tech that went wrong and apologised to Fiji for crashing in their territorial waters."

Jimmy's still studying the bowl. "Do you ever wonder if we imagined it, boss? You know. That *thing*."

"We didn't. They used it again. They vanished."

He sighs, then takes out his wallet. "Excuse me for a moment. I've got to actually buy this."

So I wait. Nobody takes the slightest bit of notice of me and I like that. The useful thing about APS politics is that very few normal people recognise any of their representatives and most can't name them even if they vaguely know the face, which in my case they won't, especially not since I grew this beard. And I'm amazed how little work you can get away with doing, which is how I've got time to pursue Ainatio. Any political structure that can allow a bloke like me to do as he pleases deserves to be toppled.

Terrence knows I'm still raiding Ainatio's cupboards. He just doesn't know that the contents are going to be used against him and his kind. I think that if I sat him down and told him, he still wouldn't believe me.

"Done," Jimmy says. He's got a green carrier bag that he's carrying like it's a live grenade. "I can't believe the price, but it makes her happy." He pauses. "I saw Les's widow the other day."

"How's she doing?"

"Not good. But at least she's not starving and she had a body to bury. That's something."

I'm reliant on contractors like Jimmy and former colleagues in the intelligence service who are probably risking even more than I am. Les Davis died on another planet and I can't even tell his widow the truth. That's the hard bit. The least I can do is make sure she's provided for by calling in favours, of which I have a very long list. It's not the unpleasant stuff I've had to do in my service that keeps me awake at night. It's anger about the shit people get away with. But it also keeps me going.

"Time for a beer," I say.

It's only a figurative beer. We order melon sodas and sit out on a deck overlooking the water, trying to discuss a complicated situation in euphemisms. Jimmy's soda has an ice cream float and an unnaturally red cherry on top. You'd never know the world thinks it's ending.

"The portal's real, Jimmy." I tell him about the soil tests on Les's clothing the same way I told Stu, but instead of Stu's disbelieving dread, Jimmy's reaction looks like relief.

"I'm glad," he says. "I thought I was losing my mind. But that doesn't make it any easier to get hold of. Or the AI. You still want that thing taken down, right?"

"Yes. I do. Even more now after what it did."

"I'll do what you ask, boss, but I don't see how we're going to get access to any of this now. The AI and everyone involved are probably light years away and it looks like they can pop back here any time and be gone again in an instant. And you still want to carry on with this?"

"Knowing what we know now, Jimmy, could you walk away from it and pretend it isn't out there?"

"It's not about that. It's about a whole new scale of operations."

"London," I say. "London's not light years away."

Jimmy thinks it over while he fishes the cherry out with a straw. "Y'know, I haven't had one of these since I was a kid. What about London?"

"The whole Nomad thing has to have a back end somewhere and it's too big a project for anything but a nation state to handle. I still say it's Britain. So we find our weak link there."

"Have you got people over there?"

"Of course."

"What exactly are you looking for?"

"If we can't seize it, we sabotage it. But I'm going to see what shakes out. It's going to be a lot more productive than trying to lure the likes of Gallagher back here."

There are other options to seizure and sabotage. There's mutual interest, in that Britain doesn't like APS as an entity any more than I do, and wouldn't mind crimping its dominance. There's information sharing. There's probably a whole new angle I haven't even considered yet. It all depends on what Britain plans to do with its new treasure, if it has the resources to do anything at all. If I had use of that portal, I know what I'd be doing with it. I'd be shipping in all the metals and minerals I can't source on Earth any more, for a start.

And I'm betting that AI has a presence in London, if nothing else. We'll see.

"You know my chances of getting into Britain are about zero," Jimmy says. "You can't just creep in. The bastards shoot you."

"You won't need to. I just need someone who can tackle the AI remotely."

Jimmy picks up a long spoon and starts eating the scoop of ice cream that's now near the bottom on a thin layer of emerald green soda. "As long as I don't miss this Christmas at home. Just this once, in case it's my last."

He's taken Les's death worse than I expected. "I don't expect we'll be leaving Oz at all."

"One question."

"Yeah?"

"You think that hitman Montello was serious about the aliens?"

"He was just goading me. I'll be bloody surprised if it's true."

"Me too. But I'm surprised about a lot of things these days." Jimmy scrapes the glass clean and looks at it for a while as if he's recalling something. "Okay, I'm in."

"I'll be in touch."

I've got a lot of ground to cover now. I'm going to have a chat with Stu McCabe about who we have in London at the moment, and if we can trust them. I could think of a lot of things that would be easier to achieve that would still put a dent in APS, but it's like I said. What I've seen, what I know is out there, is so world-changing that I can't afford to say we're just Australia and we're too small to think on that scale. Britain won't. It's something so rare and powerful that I have to try to grab it, and at very least junk that AI.

And aliens?

Aliens my arse.

* * *

THE NOMAD STORY WILL CONTINUE IN
KINGS OF THE MASTAN

ABOUT THE AUTHOR

Karen Traviss is the author of a dozen New York Times bestsellers, and her critically acclaimed Wess'har books have been finalists five times for the Campbell and Philip K. Dick awards. She also writes comics and games with military and political themes. A former defence correspondent, newspaper reporter, and TV journalist, she lives in Wiltshire, England.

WANT TO READ MORE?

Sign up for news and exclusive previews
of forthcoming books by Karen Traviss.

https://karentraviss.com
Contact her at mail@karentraviss.com

ALSO BY KAREN TRAVISS

NOMAD
- The Best of Us
- Mother Death

RINGER
- Going Grey
- Black Run

WESS'HAR
- City of Pearl
- Crossing the Line
- The World Before
- Matriarch
- Ally
- Judge

COLLECTED SHORT STORIES
- View Of A Remote Country

HALO
- Glasslands
- The Thursday War
- Mortal Dictata

GEARS OF WAR
- Aspho Fields
- Jacinto's Remnant
- Anvil Gate
- Coalition's End
- The Slab

STAR WARS
- Republic Commando: Hard Contact
- Republic Commando: Triple Zero
- Republic Commando: True Colors
- Republic Commando: Order 66
- Imperial Commando: 501st
- Bloodlines
- Sacrifice
- Revelation
- The Clone Wars
- No Prisoners

Printed in Great Britain
by Amazon